# 涉外經濟
# 法律英語

陳慶柏 編著 ◆ 方元沂 校訂

五南圖書出版公司 印行

# The Englisth Language of International Business Law

★ ★ ★

為提高中國涉外經濟法律英語水平，陳慶柏教授經過多年的艱辛努力，根據他在美國史丹福大學法學院、英國倫敦大學倫敦經濟學院、艾克斯特大學法律系研修期間所使用的一些國際經濟法資料編寫了此書。

該書與其他國內流行的有關國際經濟法教材相比有以下三個明顯的特徵：

其一，它以經過整理的原著形式出現。這樣做，不僅能幫助讀者更直接更準確地掌握有關國家的經濟立法，而且還能使讀者學到與此相對應的、道地的、純正的、規範的涉外經濟法律英語。

其二，它所介紹的國際經濟法內容比較全面系統：既有大陸法系的經濟立法，也有英美法系國家的經濟立法；既包括了中國外貿工作者必須掌握的基本法律，如契約法、買賣法、產品責任法、商業組織、智慧財產權、海上貨物運輸、關貿總協定和歐盟競爭規則，也包括從事國際金融活動所應瞭解的一些重要法律，如票據法、證券法、銀行法、保險法、信用狀法、投資法等。

其三，該書收入了很多當代流行的現代法律英語辭彙和習語，使文章更具新穎性和實用性。

我相信，《涉外經濟法律英語》一書的出版發行一定會在推動中國對涉外經濟法律英語的學習、研究與運用，提高中國涉外經濟法律服務質量方面發揮積極作用。

最後，在向涉外經濟法律工作者、司法工作者、律師以及外貿、金融、政法院校國際經濟法專業師生推薦該書的同時，我也希望此書在今後的實際使用中不斷提高和日臻完善。

對外經濟貿易大學法學院教授
博士研究生導師
1994年7月

# The Englisth Language of International Business Law

★ ★ ★

　　既能用來作為經貿學院本科生高年級學生和研究生選修課和必修課還能用來作為這類院校雙語教學或主要課外閱讀材料的《涉外經濟法律英語》的第三版在法律出版社和廣大讀者的關愛下即將問世，它與前兩版相比有以下五點不同：

　　其一，填補了一個空白。在前兩版中由於擔心書太厚未收入案例分析，在第三版中我加進了六十多個從英美商法教科書中精選出的可供教學用的經典濃縮案例（over 60 classical condensed cases for teaching International Business Law）。

　　其二，增加了三個方面的法律。它們是：(1)美國侵權法；(2)英國財產法；(3)英國繼承法。

　　其三，調整了課文安排與組合。新版共分上中下三篇。上篇為國際貿易，中篇為國際金融方面的法律，下篇為供教學用的經典案例閱讀與分析。最後為附錄。

　　其四，刪除了過時的原第二十課（關於「歐共體競爭規則」）。

　　其五，調整了英文書名，將"English Language of the Foreign Economic Law"改為"The English Language of International Business Law"。

　　希望新出的第三版在幫助提高我國整體法律英語水準和促進中國高校雙語教學方面繼續發揮它應有的作用。

陳慶柏

2000年10月於北京

長期以來,在中國高等院校教學中存在著知識傳授與英語教學相脫離的「兩張皮分家」現象。在國際經濟法專業教學領域似乎也不例外。這與當前中國經濟與世界經濟接軌,涉外經濟活動日趨活躍、涉外法律事務日趨增多的形勢很不適應,為此,迫切需要提高涉外經濟法律英語水準,迫切需要有一本將涉外經濟法律學習與相應英語教學融為一體的涉外經濟法律英語教材。編者正是從這一目標出發,經過數年的努力編寫了此書。

本書共編31課,主要內容有:

第一部分導論。介紹法的一般知識,包括世界主要兩大法系,英美法律制度,美國民事程序以及中國讀者關心的美國商業訴訟的幾個問題。

第二部分美國契約。

第三部分英國和德國商業組織。

第四部分國際貿易法,包括代理、關貿總協定、國際貨物買賣、國際貿易融資、海上保險和歐洲經濟共同體競爭規則和仲裁。

第五部分智慧財產權,包括貿易秘密、專利和商標、著作權以及與此有關的權利。

第六部分美國產品責任法。

第七部分國際金融法,包括匯票、支票、本票,德國銀行法、美國證券法、國際投資法、信用狀法。

第八部分如何提高法律英語寫作水準和附錄。附錄中收有一篇本書編者所寫的論法律英語特點的文章,供讀者學習法律英語參考。

本書每課課文由以下幾部分構成:1.課文正文。收入正文的每篇文章均選自1990年代美英有代表性的經濟法教科書或法學雜誌。2.辭彙表和課文注釋。為幫助讀者容易理解原文,便於自學,在每課課文之後,附有英漢對照的辭彙表和法律英語中的習語表,並對課文中的必要背景知識、法律概念、語言難點進行了注釋。3.練習。它由課文問答、句子段落翻譯(側重漢譯英)和判斷題組成。透過做練習可以鞏固學習成果,進一步消化課文中的法律知識以及提高學生對法律英語實際運用能力的作用。

本書可供具有大學三年級英語水平的對外經濟貿易、國際金融,特別是國際經濟法專業師生選用，也可供有較好英語基礎的有關政府部門的涉外法律工作者、司法工作者、律師和其他涉外法律工作人員以及準備到國外攻讀國際經濟法的人員學習與參考。

在編寫此書過程中得到了對外經濟貿易大學博士研究生導師沈達明教授的指導與鼓勵，和該校國際貿易研究所王景仙先生的幫助，在此一併致以衷心的感謝。

由於編者才疏學淺，書中紕漏之處在所難免，懇請讀者批評指正。

陳慶柏
1994年10月於北京

# 目錄 CONTENTS

# CONTENTS 目錄

## 目錄 CONTENTS

目録 CONTENTS

# 目録 CONTENTS

# 上　篇
## 國際貿易法

# 法律的一般性介紹
## Law in General

## Law

Laws are the rules people need to agree upon if they are to live in peace together. From the earliest times, and in the most savage tribes, laws have been made to say what men may do and what they may not. People cannot obey the law, however, unless they know what it is. So one of the first marks of a civilized people is to have its laws clearly written down and known by everyone.

Nearly four thousand years ago, King Hammurabi gave a code of laws to the BABYLONIANS. Another important set of laws was the Ten Commandments, given by Moses to the Israelites. The ANCIENT ROMANS had a fine legal system, on which much modern law is based. Today, not all countries have the same laws.

## Courts of law

Courts are where cases are tried. A case may be about a criminal offence, such as stealing. Or it may be a civil offence, like a dispute between two business firms.

A court has a high seat for the JUDGE, or magistrate, tables and seats for LAWYERS and newspaper men, and seats for the public. If there is a prisoner, he stands inside a little enclosure called the dock. People who are connected with the case may be called to give evidence. They have to swear to tell the truth, and can be punished for not doing so.

## Crime

Crime usually means breaking the law in a serious way. Murder (killing someone), assault (injuring someone), and stealing are crimes. A person who has committed a number of crimes is called a criminal. Parking a car in the wrong place is not a crime. It is an offence, however, and the motorist can be punished for it.

When a crime has been committed, the POLICE are mainly responsible for catching the criminal. They must catch the right person. It would be wrong to punish an innocent man who has done nothing. So the police must take the man they catch to COURT, and a magistrate or a JUDGE and JURY must decide whether he is innocent or guilty.

If he is guilty, a criminal can be sent to PRISON for a serious crime. If the crime is not serious, he can be fined (made to pay a sum of money). A criminal can also be put on probation. He will not be punished unless he commits another crime. A probation officer is put in charge of him.

# Judge

A judge is a LAWYER who has worked for most of his life in the COURTS and knows the law thoroughly. He needs a very keen brain and must be fair to both sides.

In some countries, such as Britain and the United States, there is a JURY to help him, and he does not have to decide whether the prisoner is guilty or not. The jury settle guilt or innocence, but the judge helps them by explaining the law. He also sees that the trial is properly run, and sums up the main points before the jury decide. The judge fixes any punishment or sentence.

In civil cases (disputes that are not crimes) judges often decide the matter themselves without a jury.

# Jury

A jury is a group of men and women, usually twelve, who listen to a law case. They take a solemn oath to give an honest verdict or decision about what they think is the truth. They do not need to be experts in the law. The JUDGE helps them on legal points. They only have to decide what happened.

The first juries in England were in NORMAN times. Many countries have copied this system. In Britain, until recently, all twelve jurors had to agree before a verdict was reached, but now only ten have to agree. In the United States, all twelve have to reach the same decision. Otherwise there has to be a new trial, with different jurors.

In AUSTRALIA, in civil cases, there are sometimes only four people in a jury. In Scotland there may be as many as 15.

# Lawyer

People who wish to become lawyers have to study the law for several years. Lawyers earn their living by advising people and speaking for them in the COURTS. The law is too complicated for most people to understand without help. In Britain there are two kinds of lawyers: a solicitor works mainly in his office and may speak only in the Magistrate's Court; a barrister's job is to speak in all kinds of courts. At present only a barrister may become a JUDGE.

In the United States the words are attorney and counsellor, but the same lawyer may do the work of both barrister and solicitor.

# Justice of the Peace

A Justice of the Peace is also known in Britain as a magistrate. Magistrates are men and women who give up part of their time, without pay, to try cases in the local COURTS and to carry out certain other duties. Usually there are two present in the court. They may deal only with smaller CRIMES. More serious cases must go before a JUDGE. Magistrates are not usually LAWYERS, but they have one (the clerk) to help them. They also take short training courses in their duties. A few magistrates are full-time, paid lawyers.

In the United States, Justices of the Peace are local officials. In some states they are appointed by the governor. In other states they are elected. Their powers are similar to those of a British magistrate. In large cities the same job is done by POLICE magistrates.

# Police

The first duty of a police force is to see that people obey the law. But the police are not only concerned with catching criminals. They have to do such jobs as direct traffic, control crowds, find lost children, rescue people in danger, and give first aid in accidents. In many countries people often go to a policeman for help when they are in trouble.

Most policemen and policewomen wear UNIFORMS. Those doing detective work often wear "plain" clothes, so that criminals will not know what they are. If a policeman sees a person actually committing a CRIME, he can arrest him on the spot. To make an arrest at other times he must get a court order called a warrant.

The police cannot try to punish people themselves — they must take them to the COURTS. But in some countries, especially those ruled by a DICTATOR, there are secret police who arrest people who protest against the government.

# Prisons

When a person has been tried and is found guilty of a CRIME, he may be sent to prison for a certain time. He may, however, be let out early if he behaves well. Sometimes people are put in prison while they are waiting for their trial.

Prisons used to be very harsh places where people were cruelly treated. In some countries they still are. But most civilized countries are trying to make prison a better place, where criminals can learn how to fit into an ordinary working life and live honestly when they come out. Today, there are many "open" prisons, where certain prisoners are not kept locked up in cells, but have some freedom.

## New Words

| | | |
|---|---|---|
| 1. | savage tribes | 野蠻民族 |
| 2. | marks *n.* | 特徵 |
| 3. | code of laws | 法典 |
| 4. | King Hammurabi | 漢摩拉比國王（西元前1792年至西元前1750年） |
| 5. | Babylonians *n.* | 巴比倫人 |
| 6. | the Ten Comandments | 基督教十誡 |
| 7. | Moses *n.* | 摩西（猶太教、基督教《聖經》故事中猶太人的古代領袖） |
| 8. | legal system | 法律制度；法律系統 |
| 9. | case *n.* | 案件；判例 |
| 10. | try *v.* | 審判 |
| 11. | civil offence | 民法上的犯法行為；民事過錯 |
| 12. | criminal offence | 刑法上的犯法行為；刑事犯罪 |
| 13. | business firm | 商行；商號；貿易公司 |
| 14. | prisoner *n.* | 犯人；囚犯 |
| 15. | evidence *n.* | 證據 |
| 16. | swear *v.* | 發誓 |
| 17. | murder *n. & v.* | 殺人罪；謀殺罪；殺人；謀殺 |
| 18. | assault *n.* | 傷害罪 |
| 19. | innocent *a.* | 無罪的 |
| 20. | guilty *a.* | 有罪的 |
| 21. | probation officer | 監督緩刑犯的官員 |
| 22. | civil cases | 民事案件 |
| 23. | criminal cases | 刑事案件 |

**24.** oath *n.*            宣誓

**25.** verdict *n.*            （陪審團）正式裁決；判決

**26.** Norman Times            諾曼時代

**27.** Justice(s) of the Peace            治安法官（有時縮寫成JP，在英國英語中有時也用 magistrate表示同樣的意思）

**28.** first aid            急救

**29.** detective work            偵探工作；偵查工作

**30.** plain clothes            便衣

**31.** plain clothes policemen            便衣員警

**32.** warrant *n.*            逮捕令；逮捕證

**33.** prison *n.*            監獄；牢獄（類似的詞還有goal、jail和penitentiary）

**34.** civilized countries            文明國家

**35.** civilized people            文明民族

**36.** cell *n.*            牢房（尤指小牢房和單人牢房）

**37.** dock *n.*            （刑事法庭上的）被告席

## 🍀 New Phrases and Idiomatic Expressions

**1.** to agree upon (on)            一致同意

**2.** to have sth. done            做某事；使某件事完成

**3.** to be connected with            與……相聯繫

**4.** to give evidence            給予或提供證據

**5.** to be punished for doing or not doing sth.            因做某事或因不做某事而被懲罰

**6.** in a serious way            嚴重地

**7.** to commit a crime            犯罪

**8.** to be responsible for (doing) sth.            負責做某事

**9.** to be sent to prison for a crime            因犯罪被監禁

**10.** to be put (or placed) on probation            被處以緩刑

**11.** to be put in charge of sb. or sth.            被指定負責某人或某事

**12.** to be fair to sb.            對……人公正

**13.** to sum up sth.            總結某事

**14.** to take a solemn oath            莊嚴宣誓

**15.** to reach a verdict or a decision            （陪審團）正式裁定或裁決

**16.** to go before a judge            出庭

| | |
|---|---|
| **17.** on the spot | 當場 |
| **18.** to be found guilty of a crime | 被判決犯了某一種罪 |
| **19.** to be let out | 使……釋放出獄 |
| **20.** to be kept locked up in cells | 被關入牢房 |
| The jailer locked the convicts up in the cells. | 監獄管理員將犯人關入牢房 |
| **21.** to earn one's living | 謀生 |

 **Notes**

**1.** Law are the rules people need to agree upon if they are to live in peace together.

法律是人民爲在一起平安生活需要一致同意的規則。

If they are to live in peace together.

如果他們想在一起平安地生活。

**2.** legal system

法律制度或法律系統，包括法的淵源、法院系統和律師界（sources of law, court system and legal profession）。

**3.** The jury settle guilt or innocence.

陪審團認定有罪或無罪。

**4.** He also sees that the trial is properly run...

此句中的「to see that」是「to see it that」的簡要表達形式，意思是「注意」，「必須保證」。

**5.** Lawyers earn their living by advising people and speaking for them in courts.

「律師」一詞在英美語中的表達方法是不同的。lawyer是英國英語，attorney or attorney at law（律師）是美語。

 **Exercises**

## I. Answer the following questions in English:

**1.** What is law?

**2.** What is court?

**3.** What is crime?

**4.** Is there any difference between a crime and an offence?

**5.** Do the judge and the jury do the same job in court?

**6.** How do lawyers earn their living in the West?

**7.** Is justice of the peace the same as magistrate in U.K.?

**8**. Can a police arrest people as he likes?

**9**. What are 'open' prisons?

**10**.When will a person be sent to prison?

## II. Translate the following sentences into Chinese:

**1**. Laws are the rules that define people's rights and responsibilities towards society.

**2**. Courts are where cases are tried. A case may be about a criminal offence, such as stealing. Or it may be a civil offence, like a dispute between two business firms.

**3**. Crime usually means breaking the law in a serious way. When a crime has been committed, the police are mainly responsible for catching the criminal.

**4**. The jury settle guilt or innocence, but the judge helps them by explaining the law.

## III. Translate the following Chinese passages into English:

**1**. 對「法」一詞下一個令人滿意的定義是非常困難的事。一般來說，在西方人們將「法」說成是：人們想要共同平安生活而需一致同意的規則。

**2**. 法院是審判民事案件和刑事案件的地方。審判民事案件的法院叫民事法院；審判刑事案件的法院叫刑事法院。

**3**. 一個犯了罪的人稱之為罪犯或犯人。一旦法院裁定他有罪，他有可能被收監。

**4**. 在審理刑事案中，陪審團的任務是裁定有罪或無罪。法官的主要任務是幫助陪審團解釋有關法律。

**5**. 西方律師以向人們提供法律諮詢和在法庭上為人們辯護謀生。

**6**. 員警只能在犯人正在犯罪時對他逮捕。一般情況下，他必須有法院簽發的逮捕令才能進行逮捕。

## IV. Translate the following English passage into Chinese:

Law is the ordering of activity; it spells out the rules of game. In different countries not only are the "rules" for business different, but the ways they are applied vary. Newton Minow, former ECC chairman, commented that in Germany, under law everything is prohibited except that which is permitted. In France, under the law everything is permitted except that which is prohibited. In the Soviet Union, everything is prohibited, including that which is permitted. And in Italy under the law everything is permitted, especially that which is prohibited.

# 世界主要兩大法系
# The Two Major Legal Systems in the World

Two major structures have guided the development of legal systems in most countries of the world. Common law is the basis of law in countries that have been at some time under British influence. Common law countries do not attempt to anticipate all areas in the application of a law by writing it to cover every foreseeable situation. Instead, cases in common law countries are decided upon the basis of tradition, common practice, and interpretation of statutes. Civil or code law countries have as their premise the writing of codes of conduct that are inclusive of all foreseeable applications of law. Codes of law are then developed for commercial, civil, and criminal applications. Precedents are important in understanding common law as it is or has been interpreted. The laws themselves are the important factor in understanding the legal environment in civil or code law countries.

Even in common law countries there are often codes of law. The Uniform Commercial Code in the United States is a good example of a code of law governing business activity. However, common law does not differentiate among civil, criminal, and commercial activities, and thus a business may be liable under any of these laws. Code law countries separate the three types of activities, but there are always areas where codes are not sufficiently specific and must be interpreted by courts. Most countries use either common or code law as the basis for their legal system, but they rely on a combination of the two in applying the legal system to actual disputes.

Perhaps the best example of how common and code law differ is in the recognition of industrial property rights. Industrial property rights include trademarks, logos, brand names, production processes, patents, even managerial know-how. In common law countries, ownership of industrial property rights comes from use; in code or civil law countries, ownership comes from registering the name or process. The implications of this difference are obvious: a company may find itself in litigation in a code law country to gain the rights to use its own names or logos, and it may not win!

There are many other ways in which code and common law systems affect the legal environment of those managers who are involved in international economic activities. Some of these are liability of the business firm for product damages, requirements for an effective contract, defenses for noncompliance with a contract, and liability of business owners. Suffice it to say here that good legal counsel is an essential component of effective international business.

## New Words

| | | |
|---|---|---|
| 1. | civil or code law countries | 大陸法或成文法國家 |
| 2. | common law countries | 普通法國家 |
| 3. | precedent *n.* | 先例；判例；慣例 |
| 4. | differentiate *v.* | 區別 |
| 5. | industrial property rights | 智慧財產權 |
| 6. | logos *n.* | 商標（智慧財產權的一種） |
| 7. | patent *n.* | 專利 |
| 8. | litigation *n.* | 訴訟 |
| 9. | managerial know-how | 管理訣竅 |
| 10. | defense (defence) *n.* | 辯護；答辯；抗辯 |
| | an defence attorney | 辯護律師 |
| | The accused man made no defence. | 被告未作答辯 |
| 11. | legal counsel | 法律顧問 |
| 12. | code *n.* | 準則 |
| | codes of conduct | 行為準則或規範 |

## New Phrases and Idiomatic Expressions

| | | |
|---|---|---|
| 1. | at some time | 有段時期 |
| 2. | to decide upon | 決定 |
| 3. | to have sth. as one's premise | 以某事作為某人的根據或前提 |
| 4. | to use sth. as the basis for sth. | 將某事作為某事的根據 |
| 5. | to be involved in sth. | 捲入某事 |
| 6. | Suffice it to say that... | 只要說……就夠了 |

## Notes

1. Common law countries do not attempt to anticipate all areas in the application of a law by writing it to cover every foreseeable situation.

   普通法國家不打算預先考慮法律運用的所有領域，以書面形式將所有可預見的情況包括進去。

2. Civil or code law countries have as their premise the writing of codes of conduct that are inclusive of all foreseeable application.

大陸法或成文法國家以包括一切可預見的法律運用行為規範的書面形式為前提。

3. Uniform Commercial Code：統一商法典

美國統一商法典於1952年問世，共分九篇：總則、買賣、商業票據、銀行存款和收款、信用狀等法規。該法典已被除美國路易斯安那州以外的所有州所採用。

4. defense for noncompliance with a contract.

對與不依契約履行所進行的抗辯。

5. Suffice it to say here that good legal counsel is an essential component of effective international business.

無需多說，法律顧問是有效國際貿易必不可少的組成部分。

 **Exercises**

## I. Answer the following questions:

1. What law is the basis of law in English-speaking countries?

2. How are cases decided in common law countries?

3. What is the important factor in understanding the legal environment in civil or code law countries?

4. In what ways do common and code laws differ?

5. What are the two principal legal systems in the western world?

## II. Translate the following Chinese passages into English:

1. 美國、英國是普通法國家的代表。這兩個國家的法律有很多相同的地方。

2. 世界上主要有兩大法系，一個是以美、英為代表的普通法系；另一個是以法、德為代表的大陸法系。

3. 現在大陸法系與普通法系的差別正在縮小。

   例如：美國的統一商法典就是一種成文法（a code of law or written law）。

4. 在英國、美國等普通法國家，案件的裁決是以傳統、習慣做法和對成文法的解釋為依據。

## III. Translate the following English passage into Chinese:

In the western world there are two principal legal systems: the civil law system and the common law system. The civil law system is largely derived from Roman law and is found throughout western continental Europe and other parts of the world, especially those areas colonized by continental European countries. For example, in the United States the law of Louisiana is based primarily on the civil law system of France, while in the rest of the United States, settled principally by English colonists, the common law system prevails.

# 英國法律制度
# English Legal System

## Types of Law

The law in England, falls under two main divisions. Firstly, there is the criminal law and secondly there is the civil law, Criminal law imposes a standard of behaviour so as to protect the community. It provides that where a criminal wrong is perpetrated, the offender will be punished. If an offender should kill or injure or steal, the criminal law provides that he should be punished either by being imprisoned or fined or perhaps do community service. Until about twenty years ago the death penalty could be imposed where a murder was committed but nowadays the death penalty can only be imposed in cases of treason and, for some reason, blowing up one of the State's dockyards. The civil law includes administrative law. There are the common law and several codes such as the Sale of Goods Act which specifies rules for effecting sales of goods, the Arbitration Act which contains rules for arbitration and the Companies Act which contains provisions concerning the setting up and running of companies. Administrative law consists mainly in government regulations.

## Bodies of Law

We have in England what is known as a "Common Law" system as compared with a codified system. Where there is a codified system you look at the Code and you find what the law is on any particular topic. In England, initially, the law was judge-made and there was a system of precedents. The judges' decisions were recorded and became the law and their decisions were followed in comparable cases. Nowadays the judge-made law is supplemented by legislation i. e. Acts of Parliament and these contain the law on various topics, such as, the Sale of Goods Act, the Arbitration Act and the Companies Act. Similarly, in criminal cases the law was initially judge-made but murder, stealing, forgery and the like are now defined in statutes. Some of the law is still not to be found in statutes. There is for example no statute relating to the duty of care. There is a tort of negligence which in effect is that if someone fails in their duty of care to another who suffers loss, the defaulter must pay damages. There is a duty not to be negligent. The modern law of negligence was created in a famous court case concerning a snail in a lemonade bottle. The purchaser of this bottle poured out a drink for his girl friend and she saw the remnants of a snail in her drink and this upset her. She had not bought the bottle from the distributor and it was the manufacturer who had been negligent. The courts decided that in such cases the manufacturer owed a duty to the ultimate consumer even though, they were not in a contractual relationship. This is an instance of the common law in operation. There are many regulations which are made by Government Departments. For such regulations to be enforceable they must have force of statute and the statute has to give the relevant Ministry authority to issue orders.

## Legislative Process

The legislative process in England has three parts i.e. House of Commons, House of Lords and Sovereign. We have in England the House of Commons, where members are elected by universal suffrage. There are about 650 constituencies and the person who receives the most votes in the constituency is elected. There are four main political parties and the party whose members form the majority in the House of Commons is asked by the Queen to form the Government. The leader of that party becomes prime minister and appoints ministers, some of whom form the cabinet. Mrs. Thatcher is now prime minister, our first lady to hold this office and about twenty of her ministers form her cabinet. The House of Lords is the second chamber. Some Lords are members by reason of inheritance whereas others who have distinguished themselves in life are made Life Peers i.e. peers until they die. One of my partners is a peer, having inherited his title from his father. For a statute to be enforceable in England it must pass through both the House of Commons and the House of Lords and must be signed by the Sovereign, an inherited position. The Queen in England is a constitutional monarch and the constitution requires her to sign Bills which have passed through the two Houses of Parliament. She is obliged to act always on the advice of her ministers. Prince Charles, her eldest son, is the new apparent. In England we have no written constitution and the duties of the Sovereign have therefore evolved by custom, a notion similar to common law. Some of the rights of individuals are to be found in Magna Carta, an agreement negotiated in the thirteenth century. Some of the constitutions of other counrites, i.e. the United States, have their origins in Magna Carta.

## Criminal Courts

There are, in England, criminal, civil and administrative courts. The bulk of the criminal cases are resolved in Magistrates' Courts and basically these are of two types. There are the

Justices of the Peace who are appointed with local jurisdiction because they are worthy citizens and a minimum of three sit to form a bench. All court hearings in England are in public, save when juveniles are involved. In the big cities there are stipendiary Magistrates i.e. junior judges who sit on their own. The more important criminal cases are determined by the Crown Courts. Where a serious offence is alleged there is a right of trial by jury, usually by twelve people. Juries should be unanimous but on occasions majority verdicts are accepted. In such cases the Judge advises the jury of the law, explains the evidence and the jury's decision is final. They decide whether the accused is guilty or not guilty. An accused is assumed to be innocent unless proved guilty and any doubt is resolved in his favour. The Old Bailey in London is perhaps the most famous criminal court in the world. There can be appeals to the Court of Criminal Appeal generally on questions of law and thence to the House of Lords. Theoretically appeals to the House of Lords are to the whole chamber but in fact there are about twelve Law Lords, i.e. peers appointed for life due to their legal expertise and these Law Lords decide appeals. The Lord Chancellor of England holds an interesting position as he presides in the House of Lords, when sitting as a legislative body — he physically sits on the woolsack, he is the senior law lord and he is a politician usually with a seat in the cabinet. He thus has combined executive, legislative and legal functions.

# Civil Courts

The majority of civil cases are determined in the county courts in England — local courts with limited jurisdiction. The more important cases are heard however in the High Court which is divided into three divisions; the Queen's Bench Division, the Chancery Division, and the Family Division. The jurisdiction of the Queen's Bench Division extends to most types of civil action, for example claims in contract and tort. The Chancery Division is mainly concerned with business disputes, tax matters and dealing with the property of deceased persons. The Family Division is concerned with problems concerning marriage, family property and children.

In the Queen's Bench Division are the specialised Admiralty and Commercial Courts. The Admiralty Court is concerned with shipping disputes, involving collisions, salvage, mortgage priorities and cargo claims. The Commercial Court is concerned with cases of a commercial nature, for example insurance claims, or charter party disputes and appeals from commercial arbitrations. In the Commercial Court the strict procedural rules are often waived to expedite trials. Disputes are usually between non British people as foreign entities often elect to have their claims litigated, or arbitrated, in London.

In the Chancery Division, there is the Companies Court. This court mainly deals with the problems caused when a company goes out of business, or when it fails to regulate its business in accordance with various statutes.

# Appeal Courts

Appeals proceed from the Divisional Courts to the Court of Appeal usually out of right and thence to the House of Lords with leave either of the Court of Appeal or the House of Lords itself. From the House of Lords there is no appeal. The House does however hear appeals from abroad; when acting in this capacity, the House is called the Privy Council.

# European Courts of Justice and Human Rights

Since England joined the EU (i.e. the European Union), its system of law has been subject to the European Court of Justice and the European Court of Human Rights. The European Court of Justice has responsibility for insuring that EU law is observed with regard to the interpretation and implementation of the treaty of Rome and other treaties signed by the member states. The court's decisions must be accepted by the courts of member states and there is no right of appeal. The European Court of Human Rights was set up by the Convention for the Protection of Human Rights and Fundamental Freedoms to ensure that the contracting states under the convention observed the engagements undertaken. The United Kingdom has accepted the court's jurisdiction, which extends to all cases concerning interpretation and application of the convention.

# Other Courts and Tribunals

A review of the English legal system would not be complete without mention of special courts outside the ordinary system. These can broadly be called administrative tribunals. Their purpose is to regulate the great mass of social legislation and to provide a forum for hearing disputes between the individual and the state. For example, the English social welfare system provides that qualifying applicants may receive pensions and payments when they are out of work. Naturally, there may arise disputes as to whether or not a particular person is qualified, and increasingly, use has been made of special tribunals with statutory powers specifically tailored for such cases. The tribunals however, are not given a completely free hand to make decisions. The ordinary courts do have the power to review tribunals decisions and indeed in many cases there is appeal from tribunals to the ordinary court system.

# The legal profession

The legal profession in England has two branches of practitioners; barristers and solicitors. The judiciary are selected from practitioners, usually barristers. Each profession has developed independently, and each has its own controlling body. No one may practice in both jobs at the same time, although a barrister may become a solicitor and vice versa. It is possible that in the future the two branches will combine, people doubt whether this occurs within the next five years. Applying the analogy of medicine and doctors, barristers are specialist advocates and solicitors general practitioners.

# Barristers

Barristers usually present i.e. argue cases in court. They usually prepare the formal pleadings which summarise the claim and the defence to the court. They also give opinions, or second opinions, on difficult legal questions. Although barristers have the exclusive right to be heard in the higher courts, both barristers and solicitors may appear in a High Court action on the hearing of interlocutory matters which proceed a trial, in the country court and in the magistrates' court. Those wishing to become barristers must apply to become a student at one of the Inns of Court. There are four Inns of Court; Lincoln's Inn, Gray's Inn, the Inner Temple and the Middle Temple. The Inns of Court are unincorporated societies governed by judges or senior barristers. Having become a student at one of the Inns prospective barristers must satisfy various requirements, which include taking examinations. It is also a requirement that before being called to the bar, or qualifying, a student has "kept service" by dining in the hall of his Inn a certain number of times. Having passed the examination and kept terms, a student must become the pupil of a senior barrister for a period of six months before being allowed to practice on his own. A barrister will not normally deal directly with a client but must be instructed or briefed by solicitor. Barristers are under an obligatory duty to conduct cases in a proper manner. They must for example inform the court of all relevant legal authorities relating to the case even though the law may not support their client's case.

# Solicitors

A Solicitor advises his client on legal, financial and other matters. Not all the solicitor's work is of a purely legal nature but most of it requires some degree of legal training. When a matter comes to litigation, the solicitor's function is to prepare the case for trial and arrange for the availability of any necessary witnesses and any documents which may be required. Solicitors are also concerned with the costs of the case. A successful litigant can usually recover about three quarters of his costs from the unsuccessful litigant. We have already seen that a solicitor's right of audience is limited and if the case is before the High Court, he will have to instruct a barrister to present the case. In order to qualify as a solicitor it is necessary to complete an examination set by the Law Society. The Law Society is responsible for enrolling solicitors, the prescribing of qualifications, setting the examinations, issuing practicing certificates and preserving minimum standards of behaviour. Having completed the examination, it is necessary for a student to serve a period under articles with a solicitor. This involves spending two years with a firm of solicitors gaining experience in a number of areas of the law. After this two year period, application must be made to the Law Society for admission as a solicitor.

 **New Words**

| | | |
|---|---|---|
| 1. | criminal wrong | 刑事上的不法行為；刑事犯罪 |
| 2. | civil wrong | 民事上的不法行為；民事過錯行為；民事不法行為 |
| 3. | perpetrate *v.* | 犯罪 |
| 4. | offender *n.* | 犯罪者；罪犯 |
| 5. | imprison *v.* | 收押；監禁 |
| 6. | fine *n. v.* | 罰款；罰金 |
| 7. | community service | 為社會服務 |
| 8. | death penalty | 死刑（在美國也被稱為capital punishment） |
| 9. | **treason** *n.* | 叛國罪 |
| 10. | administrative law | 行政法 |
| 11. | arbitration *n.* | 仲裁 |
| 12. | codified system | 法典化制度 |
| 13. | precedent *n.* | 先例；判例 |
| | law of precedents | 先例法 |
| 14. | statute *n.* | 法令；法規；成文法 |
| 15. | tort *n.* | 侵權行為 |
| 16. | defaulter *n.* | 違約者；拖欠債務者 |
| 17. | damages *n.* | 賠償金；損害賠償 |
| 18. | contractual relationship | 契約關係 |
| 19. | enforceable *a.* | 可強制執行的；有強制性的 |
| | This contract is not enforceable. | 該契約不能強制執行 |
| 20. | House of Commons | （英）下議院 |

| | | |
|---|---|---|
| **21.** House of Lords | （英）上議院；貴族院 |
| **22.** sovereign *n.* | 君主 |
| **23.** suffrage *n.* | 投票同意 |
| universal suffrage | 普選；全民參政權 |
| **24.** constituency *n.* | 選區；全體選民 |
| **25.** chamber *n.* | 議院（國會兩院中的一個） |
| **26.** constitutional *a.* | 憲法的；符合憲法的 |
| **27.** bill *n.* | 法案 |
| **28.** the new apparent | 新的合法繼承人 |
| **29.** peer *n.* | 貴族 |
| **30.** Magna Carta | 英國大憲章 |
| **31.** Magistrates' Courts | （英）治安法庭（刑事審判系統的最低審級） |
| **32.** Justice of the peace | 治安法官 |
| **33.** jurisdiction *n.* | 對案子的審判權；司法管轄權 |
| **34.** bench *n.* | （總稱）法官；法庭 |
| **35.** save *prep.* | 除……外 |
| all save sb. | 除某人以外所有人 |
| **36.** juvenile *n.* | 青少年 |
| juvenile delinquency | 青少年犯罪 |
| **37.** stipendiary Magistrates | （比一般裁判官權力大的）受薪裁判官 |
| **38.** the Crown Courts | 王室法院；王冠法院 |
| **39.** offence *n.* | 犯法；犯罪 |
| **40.** jury *n.* | 陪審團 |
| **41.** evidence *n.* | 證據 |
| **42.** the accused | （尤指刑事案中的）被告；在民事案中常用「the defendant」 |
| **43.** the Old Bailey | 倫敦中央刑事法院的總稱 |
| **44.** appeal *n. v.* | 上訴 |
| **45.** thence *ad.* | 所以；因此 |
| **46.** Law Lords | （英）上議院受理上訴的法官 |
| **47.** Lord Chancellor | （英）上議院中受理上訴的高等法官 |
| **48.** county court | 郡法院 |
| **49.** High Court (of Justice) | 高等法院 |
| **50.** civil action | 民事訴訟 |

| | | |
|---|---|---|
| **51.** | Admiralty and Commercial Courts | 海事商務庭 |
| **52.** | waive *v.* | 放棄 |
| **53.** | leave *n.* | 允許 |
| **54.** | Privy Council | （英）（大寫）樞密院；顧問團 |
| **55.** | the Convention | 公約；協約；協定 |
| **56.** | tribunal *n.* | 法院；裁判庭 |
| **57.** | forum *n.* | 訴訟地；法庭 |
| **58.** | statutory power | 法定權力；成文法所給予的權力 |
| **59.** | practitioner *n.* | 執業者（尤指律師、醫生等） |
| **60.** | barrister *n.* | （英）大律師；出庭律師 |
| **61.** | solicitor *n.* | （英）律師；訴狀律師 |
| **62.** | advocate *n.* | 辯護人（大律師的首要工作） |
| **63.** | pleadings *n.* | 原告的訴狀；被告的答辯狀 |
| **64.** | interlocutory *a.* | 法院發出的臨時性命令的；中間裁決的 |
| **65.** | Inns of Court | （英）四大律師學院（內殿、中殿、林肯、格雷，均為自願組織起來的未取得公司法人資格的社團） |
| **66.** | bar *n.* | 律師界 |
| **67.** | client *n.* | 客戶；當事人 |
| **68.** | witness *n.* | 證人 |
| **69.** | litigant *n.* | 訴訟當事人 |
| **70.** | right of audience | 出庭權；發表意見的權利 |
| **71.** | admission *n.* | 進入 |
| | admission to the bar | 進入律師界 |

## 🍀 New Phrases and Idiomatic Expressions

| | | |
|---|---|---|
| **1.** | in cases of | 在發生…… |
| **2.** | to consist in | 存在於 |
| **3.** | and the like | 等等 |
| **4.** | to owe a duty to | 對……負有義務 |
| **5.** | by universal suffrage | 用普選的方法 |
| **6.** | to hold one's office | 擔任職務 |
| **7.** | by reason of | 由於；因為 |
| **8.** | to pass through | 通過 |
| **9.** | on the advice of | 按……勸告 |

**10.** to have origins in        起源於……

**11.** the bulk of        絕大部分

**12.** to sit on one's own        自己開審

**13.** to be divided into        被分成

**14.** for life        終身

**15.** to act in one's capacity of        以……身分

**16.** to have responsibility for        負責

**17.** to provide a forum for        為……提供（訴訟的）地方

**18.** out of work        失業

**19.** out of right        無權

**20.** to be given a complete hand to do sth.        被放手做某事

**21.** to second opinions        支持……意見

**22.** to satisfy various requirements        符合各種不同的要求

**23.** to be called to the bar        取得律師資格

**24.** under a duty to do sth.        有做某事的義務

**25.** to advise sb. on sth.        向某人提出有關做某事的意見

**26.** to arrange for        為……作安排

**27.** to be concerned with        關心……；對……感興趣

**28.** to qualify as        取得……資格

**29.** to set examinations        出考題或考卷

**30.** to serve a period under articles        按學徒合約完成一段實習期，有時也可用to be articled to a solicitor for a period of time來表示同樣的意思。

 **Notes**

**1.** The jury's decision is final.
陪審團的裁決為最終裁決。

**2.** EU, European Union.
歐洲聯盟，簡稱歐盟。Now it has a total of 27 member nations.

**3.** the Treaty of Rome：羅馬條約。

It was drawn up in 1957 in a single document in German, French, Italian and Dutch languages, all four texts being equally authentic.

1957年簽訂，有四種文本，德語、法語、義大利語和荷蘭語。這四種文本具有同等的法律效力。

4. Applying the analogy of medicine and doctors, barristers are specialist advocates and solicitors general practitioners.

用醫學和醫生的比喻，大律師是具有專門知識的出庭辯護人，（小）律師是一般的執業者。在此英語句子中，在general practitioners前的are被省略。

5. Law Society

（英）（小）律師的團體 —— 律師協會；大律師的團體叫the Bar Council（大律師協會）。

6. a firm of solicitors

律師事務所，有時也稱law firm，美國稱law office。

7. High Court of Justice

（英）高等法院。1880年前分五個庭，1880年後分三個庭，分別是：衡平庭（Chancery Division）；王座庭（Queen's Bench Division）；家事庭（Family Division）。

8. under articles with a solicitor

根據與律師簽訂的實習契約。此處articles表示articles of apprenticeship（實習契約）

9. legal profession：律師界

10. The Magna Carta：英國大憲章

為英國貴族從國王手中爭得自由權利的重要法律文獻。1215年6月15日，英王約翰在貴族的脅迫下簽署了這個大憲章，共63條，其主要精神是限制王權，保障封建領主和教會（英國國教）的特權及騎士、市民的利益。例如，規定任何自由人非依合法判決不得任意逮捕、監禁、沒收財產，非經議會同意不得向封建領主徵收額外稅金，承認教會自由等。

## Exercises

## I. Answer the following questions:

1. what is criminal law?

2. What is civil law?

3. How many kinds of courts does England have?

   What are their main duties?

4. What is the most important feature of English legal profession?

5. Is it necessary to have death penalty?

6. What is arbitration? What the advantages and disadvantages of arbitration?

## II. Translate the following English passages into Chinese:

**1**. Arbitration Act in UK contains rules for arbitration and the Companies Act contains provisions concerning the setting up and running of companies. Administrative law consists mainly in government regulations.

**2**. Appeals proceed from the Divisional Courts to the Court of Appeal usually out of right and thence to the House of Lords with leave either of the Court of Appeal or the House of Lords itself.

**3**. Statutes are Acts of Parliament and English law is found in the appropriate Act. For example, the law relating to theft is to be found in the latest appropriate Theft Act, which will include many related offences such as burglary, robbery and blackmail.

**4**. Barristers, frequently called Counsel, are generally specialists, advocates and advisers to solicitors; they are governed by the Bar Council and are on qualifying "called to the Bar". They are either selfemployed or "employed" in the same manner as solicitors.

## III. Translate the following Chinese passages into English:

**1**. 民法和刑法的不同取決於法律所追求的兩種各自目的的差異 —— 賠償或懲罰。

**2**. 大多數民事不法行爲（或民事違法行爲）並非犯罪，例如無故意損害意圖侵入他人的土地或住宅就不構成犯罪。

**3**. 國會是英國歷史上最早的普通法法院，其司法權現由上議院，即貴族院行使。

**4**. 王座庭的管轄權比衡平庭和家事庭的範圍更廣，它同時有第一審管轄權和上訴審管轄權，民事管轄權和刑事管轄權。

## IV. Indicate whether each of the following statements is true or false by writing "T" or "F" in the space provided:

    **1**. The British people have what is known as a "common law".

    **2**. The English Company Act contains provisions concerning the setting up and running of companies.

    **3**. In U.K. the bulk of the criminal cases are resolved in the Old Bailey in London, the most famous criminal court in the world.

    **4**. The legal profession in England only has one branch.

While the primary purpose of this programmed learning aid is to acquaint the student with the major principles in those areas of the law which affect businessmen, it is also useful to have some elementary understanding of the nature and source of law, legal history, and the legal system and procedure used in this country. This lesson will deal briefly with each of these topics.

*Nature of law.* No single definition of the word "law" can satisfactorily reflect the many aspects and changing character of the law. Over the centuries philosophers have discussed the nature of law and the related concept of "justice". While there are almost as many concepts of the term "law" as there are people who have pondered the question, at least four basic concepts can be identified which may be of assistance to those who seek to understand our legal system. These basic concepts are:

1. Law as what is right. Under this concept there is some great and all pervasive code of what is right and wrong. This moral sense of what is right or wrong may be derived either from some divine source or from the nature of man himself.

2. Law as custom. Under this concept law is the accumulated customs and traditions of a society which reflects that society's interaction with its environment.

3. Law as command. Under this concept law is a body of rules which is issued by the political authority and enforced through various sanctions.

4. Law as social engineering. Under this concept law is regarded as a means of social control which seeks to balance various competing and conflicting interests and values within a society.

Different schools of jurisprudential thought place differing degrees of emphasis on each of these concepts. Those who place primary emphasis on the concept of law as what is right are known as the natural law school. The historical school of thought emphasizes the aspect of custom and tradition whereas legal positivists stress the concept of law as command. Those who look at law primarily in terms of its use for social engineering are known as the sociological school of jurisprudence. Another group-known as the legal realists —— reject the idea that any theory or group of theories can adequately define law and focus on law as a dynamic, changing process.

*The functions of law.* Law of some variety has been a part of society since the time of the most primitive societies. Initially the primary purpose of the law was to keep the peace, but as society became more complex and developed, the law took on additional functions. Today, at least eight major functions of law can be identified: (1)to keep the peace, (2)to influence and enforce standards of conduct, (3)to maintain the status quo in certain aspects of society, (4)to facilitate orderly change, (5)to allow for maximum self-assertion by the individual, (6)to facilitate planning and the realization of reasonable expectations, (7)to promote social justice, and (8)to provide a mechanism for compromise solutions between polar principles and positions.

There are limits on the use of the law in certain contexts. For example, the Constitution of the United States and the constitutions of the various states typically place limits on the application of law; the courts themselves have traditionally refused to concern themselves with insignificant or moot matters and hypothetical questions.

*Anglo-Saxon legal background.* The law and legal system in the United States have been heavily influenced by the Anglo-Saxon legal tradition which dates back to the year 1066 and William the Conqueror. Certain aspects of our legal procedure such as juries and witnesses sworn under threat of perjury have their roots deep in this tradition. One of the most significant features of the Anglo-Saxon legal tradition, which distinguishes it from the civil code system prevalent on continental Europe, is its heavy reliance on "common" or judge made law as opposed to statutory or codified law. Thus the Anglo-Saxon and now the Anglo-American legal tradition is characterized by its reliance on prior judicial decisions or precedents as a guide to the law that should be applied to essentially new but analogous situations arising today.

*Sources of law in the United States.* The law in this country is a product of a number of different sources. Foremost, of course, is the Constitution of the United States which separates the government into the three coordinate branches, grants certain enumerated powers to each of these branches, reserves certain powers to the states, and sets limits on the power of the federal and state governments to enact certain kinds of legislation or to engage in certain kinds of activities relating to their citizens. Each state has also adopted a constitution which sets out both the form and operation of government in that state and also places certain limits on its power. A third source of law is the enactments of the legislative bodies —— that is, acts of Congress, statutes of state legislatures, and ordinances of local governing bodies acting within the powers conferred on them by state legislatures. The common law —— that is, the judge-made law —— is also a very important source of law in this country. In addition, a great deal of law is what is known as private law, where two parities voluntarily assume a set of obligations with reference to each other under such circumstances and conditions that a court will enforce their private agreement. The "contract" is a common example of such private lawmaking.

*Legal systems in the United States.* There are 51 separate court systems in this country —— the federal system and the court systems of each of the 50 states. Each of these systems functions independently of the others and each is composed of courts having general jurisdiction and other courts which perform only specialized functions. The courts of this country are unique in that they have the power to declare legislation unconstitutional. This gives the courts a place of special importance in our government. In addition to the court systems, the federal government and virtually every state government contain administrative tribunals which are not formally courts but which do exercise many quasi-judicial powers.

1.*The federal court system.* The Constitution of the United States establishes the Supreme Court and vests certain original and appellate jurisdiction in it. The Constitution also empowers Congress to create a system of subordinate courts. In general, these federal courts have jurisdiction over cases directly affecting the federal government, over matters of interstate character, and over cases between citizens of different states or of a state and a foreign country where the amount in controversy exceeds $10,000.

The courts in the federal court system (along with a brief summary of their jurisdiction) are:

2.*Supreme court.* The Supreme Court has original jurisdiction in those cases affecting ambassadors, ministers and consuls and those cases to which a state is a party. The Supreme Court is the appellate court of last resort for cases arising in the lower federal courts and for cases appealed from state courts which involve interpretation of the federal constitution and federal statutes. As a general rule, appeal to the Supreme Court is a matter of privilege and not a matter of right and the Court will decide whether or not it wishes to hear a particular case.

3. *Court of appeals.* Judges of the Court of Appeals generally sit in panels of three and hear appeals taken as a matter of right from the district courts or from various administrative tribunals. The Court of Appeals does not have any original jurisdiction; that is, it does not sit as a trial court to hear any cases.

4. *District courts.* The district courts are the general courts of original or trial jurisdiction in the federal system. The district courts also hear certain types of suits against the United States where the amount in controversy is less than $10,000. In cases seeking to enjoin the operation of a federal statute on constitutional grounds, a three-judge court is required. The bankruptcy court, master in chancery, and U.S. commissioners are attached to and are a part of the district court and carry out certain specialized functions for the district courts.

5. *Court of claims.* The Court of Claims is a court of original jurisdiction established to hear certain contract claims against the United States. If the amount in controversy is less than $10,000, the suit may be brought in either the Court of Claims or in a district court. Appeals

from the Court of Claims are taken directly to the Supreme Court.

6. *Court of customs and patent appeals.* The Court of Customs and Patent Appeals is primarily an appellate court which hears appeals from the Customs Court and from various patent administrative boards and commissioners. Appeals are taken directly to the Supreme Court from this court.

7. *Customs court.* The Customs Court is located in the port of New York and has jurisdiction to hear various claims and decisions made concerning import duties.

8. *Tax court and court of military appeals.* The Tax Court and the Court of Military Appeals are actually quasi-judicial agencies with some judicial powers.

***Federal administrative agencies.*** Administrative agencies are outside the regular court system but in most cases they exercise rather broad judicial type of powers. Most agencies have investigative, prosecutorial, and adjudicating functions in their statutorily designated areas of operation. Theoretically, administrative agencies have specialized expertise and are capable of dealing rapidly and flexibly with problems in their area of expertise. Among the federal administrative agencies are the Federal Trade Commission, Securities and Exchange Commission, Nuclear Regulatory Commission, Interstate Commerce Commission, National Labor Relations Board, and the Federal Communications Commission.

***State court systems.*** While each state has its own court system which is unique in certain details from those of the other states, there are a number of fundamental features which tend to be the same. All of the states have a system of inferior courts — for example, justice of the peace, police, municipal or traffic courts, and small claims courts — which have limited jurisdiction and are not courts of record. There is also a system of courts of general or specialized trial jurisdiction — for example, criminal, circuit, civil, juvenile and probate courts — which are courts of record. All states have some appellate court or courts. The more populous states usually have intermediate appellate courts and all states have an appellate court of last resort. Appeals are more likely to be available as a matter of right than as a matter of privilege.

***Legal procedure.*** In order to undertake a meaningful study of business law, particularly where that study includes the reading of actual case decisions, it is necessary to have a basic understanding of legal procedure. The Anglo-American legal system operates under what is known as the adversary system. The system is presided over by a theoretically unbiased and essentially passive judge. In a civil law action — as opposed to a criminal action — one party, known as the plaintiff, claims to have been injured by the other party, known as the defendant, and seeks to prove both factual and legal entitlement to relief. At the same time, the defendant seeks to prove that the plaintiff is mistaken as to what happened factually and/or as to the defendant's legal liability. Both parties normally employ lawyers to represent their case to the judge (or to the jury if one is used) and to convince the judge or jury of the soundness of their case and the weakness of the other party's case. Thus, the development of facts and legal issues is essentially within the control of the adversary parties. However, the judge is responsible for guiding the proceeding according to certain procedural rules and for making decisions on questions of law that arise. Moreover, in certain kinds of specialized cases like domestic relations, the judges may take a rather active role in guiding the proceeding.

A civil action is normally initiated by the filing in the court clerk's office of a "complaint" which sets out the basis for the court's jurisdiction over the matter, sets forth the essential claims the plaintiff has against the defendant, and demands that the court grant the plaintiff certain specified legal relief. The "complaint" along with a "summons" is then served by a legal officer upon the defendant named in the lawsuit. The summons notifies the defendant that a lawsuit has been initiated and that there is a certain, specified time in which to defend the suit. Service of the summons is normally accomplished by personally serving the defendant with the summons, although in certain situations it may be done by mail or by publication in a newspaper.

If the defendant wishes to defend himself or herself, an "answer" to the complaint must be filed within the stated time. In the answer the defendant either admits, denies, or alleges insufficient information to admit or deny each of the allegations in the plaintiff's complaint. The defendant may also raise certain affirmative defenses which are normally legal reasons for denying the plaintiff the desired relief even if the facts are essentially as the plaintiff alleges them to be. The defendant, within certain limits, may present related claims that s/he has against the plaintiff. Under certain circumstances, the plaintiff must then file a responsive pleading known as a "reply" that admits, denies, or claims lack of information as to the facts alleged by the defendant and upon which the plaintiff bases affirmative defenses or counterclaims. If the defendant believes that the complaint does not state facts which would entitle the plaintiff to a judgment even if they are true, the defendant may challenge the sufficiency of the complaint by filing a motion to dismiss or a demurrer. If the judge agrees that the motion to dismiss or demurrer is well taken, the case will be dismissed without ever going to a formal trial.

A recent addition to legal procedure is the pretrial conference. This is a meeting between the opposing counsel and the judge in an effort to narrow the issues for trial or, if possible, to dispose of the case without the necessity of a trial. If a trial is held, the first item of business is to choose and swear in the jury if it is to be a jury trial. This is followed by opening statements by attorneys for both sides in which they outline the claims and contentions they will be making in the course of the trial. The plaintiff's attorney then presents the plaintiff's case through the presentation of documentary evidence and the questioning of witnesses. Then the defendant's attorney presents the defendant's case through the use of documentary evidence and/or witnesses. At several points in the course of the trial each party may make a motion to the court that s/he is entitled to judgment as a matter of law because of weaknesses in the opposing party's case and the judge will rule on the motions. Following the presentation of the defendant's case, both attorneys will sum up the case and make their final arguments. If the trial is before a jury, the judge will then instruct the jury and they will retire to render a decision. If no jury is involved, then the judge will either decide the case immediately or take it under advisement.

Following the court's decision, either or both parties may attempt to appeal the case on the grounds that some material error of law was made in the course of the trial or in the final decision.

## New Words

| | | |
|---|---|---|
| 1. | programmed *a.* | 按程序教學法編排的；有計畫的 |
| 2. | source of law | 法源 |
| 3. | ponder *v.* | 考慮；思索 |
| 4. | pervasive *a.* | 普遍的 |
| 5. | divine *a.* | 神聖的 |
| 6. | accumulated *a.* | 積累起來的 |
| 7. | interaction *n.* | 相互作用；相互影響 |
| 8. | a body of rules | 規則的總和 |
| 9. | social engineering | 社會工程 |
| 10. | jurisprudential *a.* | 法學上的；法理學上的 |
| 11. | natural law school | 自然法學派 |
| 12. | historical school of thought | 歷史推理派 |
| 13. | sociological school of jurisprudence | 社會法學派 |
| 14. | legal positivists | 法律實證主義者 |
| 15. | legal realists | 法律現實主義者 |
| 16. | a dynamic, changing process | 動態變化過程 |
| 17. | primitive societies | 原始社會 |
| 18. | standards of conduct | 行為準則；行為標準 |

| | | |
|---|---|---|
| **19.** the status quo | 現狀 | |
| **20.** self-assertion | 自我維護 | |
| **21.** social justice | 社會正義 | |
| **22.** polar principles | 截然對立的原則 | |
| **23.** foremost *adv.* | 首要地，最重要地 | |
| **24.** enumerated *a.* | 列舉的 | |
| **25.** enact *v.* | 制定（法律） | |
| **26.** enactment *n.* | 制定（法律） | |
| **27.** legislative bodies | 立法機關 | |
| **28.** legislature *n.* | 立法機構；立法機關 | |
| **29.** ordinance *n.* | 命令；法令 | |
| **30.** private law | 私法 | |
| **31.** public law | 公法 | |
| **32.** court system | 法院系統 | |
| **33.** administrative tribunals | 行政法庭 | |
| **34.** quasi-judicial power | 準司法權 | |
| uasi-contract | 準契約 | |
| quasi-judicial agencies | 準司法代理機構 | |
| **35.** empower *v.* | 授權；准許 | |
| **36.** subordinate courts | 下級法院 | |
| **37.** controversy *n.* | 爭論；爭議；爭辯 | |
| **38.** the appellate court of last resort | 終審上訴法院 | |
| **39.** district courts | （美）（聯邦系統的）地區法院 | |
| **40.** original jurisdiction | 初始管轄權；原管轄權 | |
| **41.** suits *n.* | 訴訟；起訴；控告；訟案 | |
| **42.** bankruptcy court | 破產法院 | |
| **43.** master in chancery | 衡平法院的助理法官或主事官 | |
| **44.** court of claims | 索賠法院；行政法院 | |
| **45.** investigative function | 調查職能 | |
| **46.** prosecutorial function | 起訴職能 | |
| **47.** adjudicating function | 裁決職能 | |
| **48.** expertise *n.* | 專門知識；專家鑑定 | |
| **49.** Federal Trade Commission | （美）聯邦貿易委員會 | |
| **50.** Securities Exchange Commission (SEC) | （美）證券交易委員會 | |

| | | |
|---|---|---|
| **51.** | courts of record | 記錄法院 |
| **52.** | circuit courts | 巡迴法院；巡迴法庭 |
| **53.** | probate courts | 遺囑檢驗法庭 |
| **54.** | adversary system | 對抗制；辯論式的訴訟制度 |
| **55.** | unbiased *a.* | 無偏見的；公平的 |
| **56.** | legal entitlement to relief | 獲得救濟的法律權利 |
| **57.** | the soundness of the case | 案子的有效和合法性 |
| **58.** | an "answer" to the complaint | 對（原告）起訴書的答辯書 |
| **59.** | allegation *n.* | （訴訟一方對提不出證明的事項所作的）聲明；陳述；聲稱 |
| **60.** | counterclaim *n.* | 反請求；反訴 |
| **61.** | motion *n.* | （訴訟人向法院提出的）請求；申請 |
| **62.** | demurrer *n.* | 異議；抗訴 |
| **63.** | pre-trial conference | 審前會議 |
| **64.** | jury trial | 有陪審團參加的審判 |
| **65.** | opening statements | （審訊開始時）辯護人所作的概述 |
| **66.** | contentions *n.* | 爭點 |
| **67.** | documentary evidence | 文件證據 |
| **68.** | material error | 重大錯誤 |
| **69.** | legal relief | 法律上的救濟 |
| **70.** | moot *a.* | 爭論未決的；不切實際的；可討論的 |

## ♣ New Phrases and Idiomatic Expressions

| | | |
|---|---|---|
| **1.** | to acquaint sb. with sth. | 使某人瞭解某事 |
| **2.** | as a means of | 作為一種手段 |
| **3.** | in terms of | 按照；根據；以……的措辭 |
| **4.** | to focus on | 集中於……；著重於…… |
| **5.** | to place limits on sth. | 對……進行限制 |
| **6.** | to allow for sth. | 將某事考慮在內；將……估計在內 |
| **7.** | to concern oneself with sth. | 關心某事 |
| **8.** | to date back to | 追溯到…… |
| **9.** | to distinguish sth. from sth. else | 將某事與其他事區分開 |
| **10.** | as opposed to | 與……相對而言 |
| **11.** | to be characterized by | 以……為特徵 |

| | |
|---|---|
| **12.** to separate into | 分成 |
| **13.** to set limits on | 對……進行限制 |
| **14.** to engage in | 從事；參加 |
| **15.** to set out | 陳述；闡明 |
| **16.** to be composed of | 由……組成 |
| **17.** to vest...in... | 給予；授予 |
| **18.** to appeal to | 上訴 |
| **19.** to hear a case (appeals, claims...) | 審理案件（上訴，申訴……） |
| **20.** to sit in panels of three | 三人一組進行開庭 |
| **21.** to sit as a trial court | 作為審判法庭進行開庭 |
| **22.** on constitutional grounds | 以憲法為理由（或根據） |
| **23.** to be attached to | 附屬……；附加於…… |
| **24.** to be taken to the supreme court | 求助於最高法院 |
| **25.** in most cases | 在大多數情況下 |
| **26.** to be presided over by | 由……主持 |
| **27.** to take a rather active role in doing sth. | 在做某事方面發揮積極作用 |
| **28.** by filing of a "complaint" | 提交一份控告狀 |
| **29.** to serve a summons | 發傳票 |
| **30.** to dismiss a case | 了結一個案子；駁回一個案子；不受理一個案子 |
| **31.** to render a decision | 作出裁決 |
| **32.** to take sth. under advisement | 對某事進行周密考慮 |
| **33.** in the course of | 在……過程中；在……期間 |

 **Notes**

**1.** One of the most significant features of the Anglo-Saxon legal tradition, which distinguishs it from the civil code system prevalent on continental Europe, is its heavy reliance on "common" or judge-made law as opposed to statutory or codified law.

與在歐洲大陸盛行的大陸法不同的是，盎格魯撒克遜法律傳統很大程度上依賴普通法或者法官制定法，這與制定法或成文法相對。

the Anglo-Saxon legal tradition在此句中以early English legal system表示；大陸法系可說成civil code system或code law system，也可用continental law system來表達。

**2.** Those who look at law primarily in terms of its use for social engineering are known as the sociological school of jurisprudence.

那些主要從社會工程眼光看待法律的人，就是人所共知的法學上的社會學派。

**3.** The law in this country is a product of a number of different sources. Foremost, of course, is the Constitution of the United States...

The Constitution of the United States is one of the oldest written constitutions in world, which was drawn up at Philadelphia in 1787. This Constitution established the fundamental structure and principles of U.S. government.

**4.** There are 51 separate court systems in this country它指the federal system and the court systems of each of the 50 states.

聯邦法律系統加上50個州中的每個州的法律系統共51個法律系統。

 **Exercises**

## I. Answer the following questions:

**1.** What is your definition of law?

**2.** What are the differences between the natural law school and the sociological school of jurisprudence?

**3.** What functions does law perform in the United States? What functions does law perform in socialist China?

**4.** Can you tell the main sources of law in the United States?

**5.** How much do you know about the Constitution of the United States?

**6.** Why are there 51 separate court systems in the United States?

**7.** What is meant by adversary system?

**8.** What legal procedures should be followed if you want to sue somebody?

## II. Translate the following phrases into English:

1. 受理上訴的法院
2. 自然法學派
3. 行為準則
4. 終審上訴法院
5. 法院判決
6. 民事程序
7. 上訴程序
8. 原告
9. 被告
10. 發傳票
11. 美國憲法
12. 立法機關
13. 美國聯邦地區法院
14. 美國最高法院

## III. Indicate whether each of the following statements is true or false by writing "T" or "F" in the space provided:

_____ **1**. Most legal scholars agree that there is a single definition of the word "Law".

_____ **2**. The "natural law school" places primary emphasis on the concept of law as what is right.

_____ **3**. From its origin until today, the sole purpose of the law is maintaining the peace.

_____ **4**. The Anglo-Saxon legal tradition is characterized by its heavy reliance on the "common law".

_____ **5**. The foremost source of law in the United States is the Constitution.

_____ **6**. U.S. courts have the power to declare legislation unconstitutional.

_____ **7**. Appeal to the U.S. Supreme Court is a matter of right.

_____ **8**. All state court systems in the United States are identical.

_____ **9**. The Anglo-American legal system operates under the adversary system.

_____ **10**. A civil action is usually initiated by the plaintiff's filing of a summons against the defendant.

_____ **11**. If a demurrer is granted, a case will not go through a formal trial procedure.

_____ **12**. Either party may appeal the decision of a civil court.

## IV. Translate the following Chinese passages into English:

1. 19世紀初期，美國民事訴訟法受傳統的英國法的約束，即受訴訟格式（form of action）與嚴格的訴訟狀（pleadings）制度的約束。

2. 美國最高法院由8名助理大法官（associate justices）合稱爲美國首席大法官（chief Justice of the United States）的院長組成。

3. 美國法律界認爲，州法院雖沒有聯邦法院那樣聞名，但事實上它們比後者更爲重要，因爲有關契約、準契約、親屬關係、繼承等涉及日常生活的爭議案都由州法院審理。

4. 由於美國每一個州都有權制定自己的司法制度，因此各州的法院組織有很大的差異。

# 美國民事訴訟程序
# American Civil Procedures

## Complaint

A lawsuit is begun by the filing of a document known as a "Complaint" with the court. The person or company which files the complaint is known as the "plaintiff" or "complainant". The complaint is normally prepared by the plaintiff's attorney and sets forth the facts of the matter being complained about and the nature of the damages being claimed by the plaintiff. Thus, for example, if the plaintiff believes that the other party has breached a contract, the complaint will describe the contract and the reasons why the plaintiff believes the other party has breached the contract and the amount of damages which the plaintiff contends were caused by the breach. The party against whom the complaint is directed is known as the "defendant". A plaintiff may name several defendants to a lawsuit if he chooses.

The only requirement for the filing of a complaint is that the plaintiff pays the filing fee required by the court in which the complaint is filed. This fee is a relatively small sum (normally not in excess of $60) and is not based upon the amount of money involved in the dispute. In other words, the court filing fee is the same whether the plaintiff claims damages of $10,000 or $10,000,000. Thus, the American system is different than the system in some other countries. In some countries, the amount of the filing fee is determined according to the amount of money which is involved in the dispute.

There is no requirement that the matters asserted in the complaint be reviewed or approved by a judge or other court personnel before the complaint is filed.

## Jurisdiction

A preliminary observation is necessary about the legal concept of "jurisdiction". In the United States, each state has its own court system which handles disputes which can be resolved according to state law. Furthermore, each state enacts its own laws which are not necessarily the same as the other states. In addition, there is a Federal court system which handles disputes which are governed by laws enacted by the United States Congress. There are some situations wherein state laws are applied in Federal court and vice versa.

The court system in each state and the Federal court system have laws and court rules which describe the circumstances under which a defendant can be made the subject of court proceedings in their particular court. These laws and rules define what is known as the "jurisdiction" of the court. If a court does not have jurisdiction over a defendant, then that defendant must be dismissed from the lawsuit and does not have to participate any further in the proceedings.

Generally speaking, the principle of jurisdiction is concerned with the relationship of the defendant to the state or district in which the complaint has been filed. The general principle of the jurisdictional laws and rules is that a defendant should not be required to be present and defend a lawsuit in a state or district with which he has had no contact or relationship. Challenges of jurisdiction of the court are frequently made by defendants in situations where a foreign based company has been sued in a state or district where it does not maintain a branch office, warehouse or other business activity. The laws and rules regarding jurisdiction are very complicated in their application, however, and it is very difficult to make general statements about the scope of a court, jurisdiction without a thorough analysis of the facts of each case.

Although there are some differences in the court systems of the various states and federal court systems, the discussion in this lesson has been written so as to describe the features of the litigation system which are generally common to both the Federal and the various state court systems.

# Summons

When the complaint is filed in the court, the clerk of the court issues a "summons". This is normally a printed document upon which the court stamps its seal. In modern practice, the seal in many courts consists of an ink-imprinted rubber stamp. The words printed in the summons advise the defendant that a complaint has been filed against him and that he should file a response to the complaint with the court.

Until the summons has been "served" on the defendant the defendant has no duty to respond to the lawsuit. In other words, if a plaintiff files a lawsuit but never makes "service" on the defendant, then the lawsuit is eventually dismissed by the court and the defendant need not worry about it.

"Service" (or "service of process") is normally accomplished by handing a copy of summons and complaint to the defendant (if an individual) or to an officer or managing level executive of a corporation if it is a defendant. It is important to know, however, that the laws concerning the Federal Courts and the laws in most states also allow service to be made on a defendant by mail. Therefore, it is very important, that a foreign company receiving a summons either in the mail, or in person, (either in or outside the U.S.), immediately seek advice from an American lawyer for the protection of its interests. A failure to promptly do so within 30 days after receipt of the summons may result in a judgment being entered against the company, and its U.S. located assets being seized a short time later.

# Answer or Motion

In most courts, the law allows the defendant 30 days after the receipt of the summons within which to file an "answer" or other document with the court denying the allegations contained in the complaint and denying any obligation or indebtedness ("liability") to the plaintiff.

Sometimes, a more appropriate response of the defendant will be to file a "motion" with the court challenging the jurisdiction of the court, or challenging some technical legal deficiency which is contained in the complaint filed by the plaintiff. A motion is a document which the defendant's lawyer prepares and files with the court, and which asks for an appointment on the court's calendar (called a "hearing" or "hearing date") at which time the lawyer will explain the nature of the challenge to the judge. At the court hearing, the lawyer will typically ask the judge to issue an order either "dismissing"(terminating) the litigation or compelling the plaintiff to file a different complaint which does not contain legal deficiencies. Motions are usually accompanied by lengthy written arguments prepared by the defendant's lawyer explaining the legal basis for the challenge. The legal reasoning by which these arguments are prepared is discussed in lesson 6 (see topic "Legal Principles").

As noted above, some response (either an answer or a motion) must be filed in the court by the defendant (normally within 30 days), or a judgment will be filed against him. The obtaining of this type of judgment is known as entering the "default" of the defendant. As indicated, once the plaintiff obtains such a judgment against the defendant, he can then seize his assets. Such a seizure of assets may in most states be allowed within only a few days after the judgment has been obtained.

# Trial Date Request

If the complaint is not dismissed by motion at this stage (or if the plaintiff is able to file another complaint which cures the defects in the prior complaint), and the defendant files an answer, the matter is then "at issue".

The plaintiff at this time normally asks for an appointment on the court's calendar to conduct a trial of the matter. This is commonly known as asking for a trial date. Typically, there is a delay from the time of this request until the trial date, of somewhere between one and four years, depending on the congestion present in the court system of the particular area of the country where the matter is pending.

# Discovery

### 1. General Philosophy of Discovery

During the period of time after the defendant has filed an answer and before the trial takes place, the parties normally engage in "discovery". This is a process by which each side learns or "discovers" information which the other side contends are the true facts. The process is basically simple in its objectives and purposes and the laws of the Federal government and of the various states specify the procedures by which discovery may be accomplished. These procedures are designed to allow each side the opportunity to question the other side and learn about all of the evidence which the one party has, or claims to have against the other. Therefore, in discovery, the defendant will usually ask the plaintiff such questions as: "Why did you sue me? What are you contending I did wrong? What facts do you rely upon to support your complaint against me?" On the other side, the plaintiff will usually ask the defendant such questions as: "Do you deny that you did the things I alleged in my complaints? If so, what do you contend are the true facts?" The questions asked in practice will be much more extensive and detailed than these examples, but these examples illustrate the general nature of the inquiry in discovery.

The purpose of the discovery procedure is to attempt to eliminate any shocks or surprises at the time of trial. In other words, the purpose of the discovery laws is to allow both sides the opportunity to learn in detail exactly what facts the other side is contending against him. Before present day detailed discovery laws were enacted (about 40 years ago, and in some places, much more recently), it was often the case that one party could conceal an important fact or contention and then present it during the trial of the dispute. At that time, his opponent was often put to an unfair disadvantage because he then did not have an opportunity to investigate the new facts, or adequately prepare his opposition and contentions opposing the new facts. The hope of the discovery laws is to promote fairness and justice by giving each party advance knowledge of all of the contentions of his opponent, and in that way providing him with an opportunity to adequately prepare his response to those contentions.

As a matter of practice, the discovery process in America has become much more complicated than is suggested by the simple principles just discussed. The statutes in each state and in the Federal government, define in great detail the procedures by which the discovery process shall be conducted and there have been many disputes and court decisions with regard to the proper interpretation of those rules. Furthermore, as practiced, the discovery process has become a very time-consuming, costly procedure.

At the present time, the various statutes and the court decisions interpreting those statutes typically allow each side to conduct lengthy questioning of their opponents and other witnesses and to conduct inspection of documents possessed by the other party. Some of these procedures are discussed below.

## 2. Deposition

The legal procedure for the questioning in person of witnesses who have knowledge about the subject matter of the dispute is called a "deposition". At the deposition, the person being questioned (being "deposed") has the right to have his lawyer present with him, and normally does. The lawyer for the other side, then asks him questions. Typically, the questioning lawyer will ask about the circumstances of the dispute and what the person being questioned (the "deponent") knows about the dispute, or matters which are relevant to the dispute. If the questions are improper, the lawyer for the deponent can object to the questions being asked and have his client refuse to answer them. The deposition is normally conducted in the office conference room of one of the attorneys' offices, and a stenographic reporter is normally present to record the questions and answers. After the deposition has been completed, the reporter will have the stenographic recording transcribed into a written form and bound in a booklet. This written transcript of the deposition can then be used as evidence at the trial of the lawsuit.

Depositions are commonly used in litigation because they give the opposing attorneys a chance to not only ask questions of company executives or employees or other witnesses, but also to immediately ask additional questions about the answers those persons give and through this process obtain a very complete understanding of what the opposing party believes the true facts to be.

Even though the deposition is conducted privately by the parties outside the court, it is nevertheless a very important matter because of the fact that the transcribed testimony may be used as evidence during the trial. Therefore, things said at a deposition may strongly influence the way in which the issues of the dispute will be decided at the trial or may be important in determining whether an amicable settlement of the dispute will be made before trial, and if so, for how much money. For example, if a defendant company's employee testifies at his deposition (in a products liability lawsuit) that the company had not carefully tested the product, or had ignored complaints of purchasers about dangerous qualities of the product, then it will be much more difficult to make a favorable settlement, or make a successful defense at the trial.

### 3. Interrogatories

Interrogatories are written questions which the attorney for one side prepares and sends to the attorney for the other side. The side receiving the interrogatories is then required to supply the requesting party with written answers to the interrogatories. The written answers are prepared by employees of the party with the assistance of the party's attorney and are normally due within 30 days after receipt of the interrogatories (although oftentimes, the parties will agree to allow a longer time for answer).

Typically, the interrogatories will ask the party to describe his factual contentions regarding the dispute, the names of the persons who are expected to give testimony about the subject matter of the dispute, and to identify documents in the possession of the party which pertain to the dispute. The work involved in answering interrogatories can be quite burdensome and time-consuming in lawsuits involving complicated factual situations.

Written interrogatories are often used in addition to depositions and other forms of discovery because interrogatories require the responding party to research its company files to give detailed written answers. Thus, a witness at a deposition may truthfully testify that he cannot remember certain things, or has no knowledge about some aspect of the problem. On the other hand, if the company defendant is asked the same question by written interrogatory, it must search its files and records, and if the answer is available from those records, it must provide the asked for information. For example, although a local company representative being deposed may not know which company written documents refer to a particular problem, or which persons in the home office participated in a particular decision, a written interrogatory about the same subject would require the defendant company to review and research its files, inquire among its employees and reveal the information if it is contained in the files or is known by others within the company.

Interrogatory answers, just like deposition testimony, can be introduced as evidence at the trial and so great care must be used in making the answers to interrogatories.

### 4. Production and Inspection of Documents

In most states and in Federal Court, the parties may also inspect documents in the possession of the other which pertain to the facts concerning the dispute which is the subject of the lawsuit. Normally, the party possessing the documents is requested to produce the documents at the office of the opponent's lawyer. There typically, the opponent's lawyer will make reproduction copies of the documents for further study and possible use at trial. Oftentimes, the inspection is done before or at the same time as a deposition and the deponent is then questioned about the documents. For example, if a company has been sued by a terminated distributor, the defendant company will be required to produce all documents which relate to the reasons for terminating the distributor, such as correspondence between branch and home offices, reports generated within the company regarding the distributor's performance, any documents submitted to the board of directors for approval of the termination decision, etc.

Like depositions and interrogatories, the production and inspection of documents is normally done by the parties without court supervision (unless there is a dispute between the parties about some aspect of the document inspection being conducted). The documents produced may be used in court as evidence, however, so great care must also be exercised in connection with the production of documents.

# Observations About The Discovery Process

### 1. Initiation of Discovery

In most courts, the various discovery procedures do not require court approval before they are begun. Thus, requests for production of documents, depositions and interrogatories can all be done in most courts without any participation by the judge of the court. If one party feels the other is making improper discovery requests, or is not reasonably responding to discovery requests, he may make a motion to the court and ask that the violating party be ordered to obey the discovery rules. The court may impose money fines and more severe penalties on parties who violate discovery rules.

Moreover, it is not unusual for the court to impose such penalties in cases where parties have willfully refused to properly cooperate with regard to discovery procedures. It is not uncommon for judges to impose fines of several hundred dollars (or more) on offending parties. Furthermore, the courts on occasion will order that a judgment be entered against the refusing party if he continues to disobey the discovery rules. This of course is a most serious penalty because in the case of a defendant, he is prevented from showing facts in his defense and once a judgment has been entered, he must either pay the amount of the judgment or have his assets seized. Therefore, a company which becomes involved in litigation must take its obligations to respond to discovery very seriously.

### 2. Cost and Burden

The amount of time and expense which must be devoted to discovery by a party to a lawsuit often comes as a surprise to companies which have never been parties to a lawsuit before. Thus, in some lawsuits, a party may be required to assign employees to many hours (or days) of work, sorting documents and investigating company records to locate and categorize information and documents requested by the other side. Still additional time must be devoted to conferences with the company's attorneys about compliance with the requested production of documents and preparation of answers to interrogatories. So also, depositions and preparation for depositions can require the expenditure of a substantial amount of time.

The fact that compliance with the discovery requests is time consuming and burdensome is not a basis for objection, however, so long as the discovery request is reasonably related to the controversy which is in dispute in the lawsuit. Moreover, the courts define what may be discovered in a very broad manner and generally allow the parties to make detailed discovery inquiries.

# Pre-Trial Conference

In the Federal courts, and in some state courts, there is a "pre-trial conference" before the trial begins. At this conference, which usually takes place from two to four months before the trial begins, the parties each submit written documents summarizing their contentions of fact and law and listing the names of the persons whom they will use at the trial as witnesses as well as a list of all documentary or other evidence which they plan to use at the trial. The parties then confer (perhaps several times) and combine their two pre-trial documents into a pre-trial order which, after it has been approved by the judge, is signed by the judge.

The purpose of the pre-trial conference is to make each party prepare in advance for the trial and to confer and carefully define the issues of the lawsuit, and discuss the evidence which will be presented, so that the trial of the matter will proceed in an efficient and orderly manner.

# Trial

The trial is the time when the parties present their evidence to the court for its decision. Typically, this evidence consists of both documentary evidence (such as contracts, letters, etc.) and the testimony of witnesses (including by means of deposition transcripts).

## 1. Practical Considerations

Countless books have been written and popular movies made about the drama of the trial, strategies and tactics to be employed at trial, the clash and impact of the various type of personalities of the parties and witnesses, etc. The practical businessman would be interested to learn, however, that the great majority of commercial and business lawsuits are compromised and settled between the parties before a trial takes place. Such a compromise before trial is known as an "amicable settlement" or "settlement".

This fact emphasizes the value and importance of the discovery process. Thus, during the discovery process as each side learns about the contentions of the other, and sees what type of documentary evidence and witness testimony the other side has, there is a tendency for each side to re-evaluate his position and back off rigid or doctrinaire positions. In other words, as the discovery process progresses, the lawyers for each side are better able to predict how the evidence will be received by a judge or jury, and oftentimes make recommendations of settlement based on this evaluation. This is not to imply that each side changes its position at this stage, for sometimes it is simply the party who has been unreasonable from the beginning who finally realizes that his position has no factual or legal support —— and becomes more conciliatory and reasonable.

A party's responses to discovery, along with an attitude of firmness during the preliminary proceedings, are thus often very important to the possible achievement of an amicable settlement of a lawsuit.

## 2. Judge or Jury Trial

In most types of civil litigation, the parties may choose to have the factual areas of dispute decided by a judge or a jury. Either party to the lawsuit may request that the dispute be decided by a jury.

Jurors are selected for service to the courts as jurors by the staff of the office of the court administrator at random from the roll of registered voters. Typically, they are required to serve for a period of several weeks. For this service, they are paid a nominal amount (for example, approximately $8.00 per day in Los Angeles, California). It is the policy of most major corporations to continue to pay their employees' regular salaries during the time they perform jury service as a matter of public duty.

There is no requirement that the jurors have reached any specific educational level. However, after their names have been selected, they are required to pass a very basic, and not very demanding intelligence/comprehension test. Jurors are drawn from all walks of life, economic and educational classes, both sexes, all adult ages, and varying racial and cultural backgrounds.

The theory of the system is that a jury of 12 persons (the typical size of the jury that actually decides the case), because of their diverse backgrounds and experience, is as well or better qualified to decide factual issues as a single judge. On the other hand, some lawyers criticize the jury system by saying that because of their lack of legal education and experience, jurors do not always understand evidence presented about complex business disputes or disputes involving scientific or technical issues. These critics say that jurors are too often guided by sympathy, prejudice or other misconceptions rather than by an understanding of the factual testimony and evidence presented.

At the time of trial, the jurors are brought into the courtroom in large groups (50-100 at a time) and twelve of them are then picked by lot by the court clerk to potentially be the jurors who will decide the dispute. The lawyers for each side then have an opportunity to question the jurors about their background and experience and to reject some of them (who are then replaced by others, also drawn by lot). When the final jury selection has been made, the trial begins and the parties present their evidence.

### 3. Conduct of a Trial

The first step in the beginning of a trial is the selection of a jury, as described above, if a jury has been requested by one of the parties.

The next event in the conducting of a trial is for the lawyers for each side to make an "opening statement" to the judge or jury (if a jury has been selected). The plaintiff's lawyer is the first to make an opening statement and he explains the nature of the parties' dispute and what facts and evidence the plaintiff will present to support his side of the case. The defendant's lawyer then has the opportunity to speak and he describes the defendant's version of the dispute and the nature of the evidence which he will present.

The plaintiff's witnesses are then presented to give their testimony about the facts of the dispute. First they are questioned by the plaintiff's lawyer. This is called "direct examination". At this time, the plaintiff's attorney asks each witness to testify about facts which will help prove the plaintiff's version of the dispute. After the witness has answered the questions from the plaintiff's attorney, the witness is then questioned by the defendant's lawyer. This is called "cross-examination". By cross-examination, the opposing lawyer seeks to cast doubt on the witness's story. He will ask the witness questions designed to show such things as a poor memory of the events, inconsistencies or inaccuracies in his testimony, doubts on the part of the witness about his testimony, etc.

The defendant then presents his witnesses and they are then subject to cross-examination by the plaintiff's attorney.

As a part of the testimony process, the witnesses frequently present other "evidence" in the form of written documents, such as correspondence between the parties before the dispute occurred, contract documents or invoices, and public/governmental records, and also such things as photographs, maps, scale models, or anything else that will help to explain the matter being testified about.

After all the testimony and evidence has been presented, the attorneys for the parties are given an opportunity to speak and make "closing arguments." At that time, each summarizes the testimony and evidence in a manner most favorable to his side and argues why the judge or jury should decide in favor of his client. In cases where no jury has been selected, the attorneys for the parties at this time often also present a written summary of their version of the facts and the relevant principles of law to the judge for the purpose of persuading him to decide in favor of their respective clients. These written papers are sometimes called "briefs" or "closing briefs".

### 4. Decision

After the testimony and evidence has all been presented and the lawyers have made their closing arguments, and any briefs have been filed, (as discussed above) the judge or jury then makes a decision.

In a case decided by a jury, the judge first instructs the jury with regard to the applicable principles of law before they are allowed to make a decision. When they start making their decision, the jury will normally first have to decide what are the true facts of the controversy. In most cases there is typically a controversy between the parties as to which party's version of the facts of the dispute is correct and at trial, there is usually conflicting evidence with regard to the true facts of the matter. The jury must first decide in such cases of conflicting factual evidence, whether one side may be lying or exaggerating, or giving evidence based upon faulty memory or poor observation of events, etc. After the jury has decided what it considers to be the true facts of the dispute, it then applies the applicable principles of law (as explained to them by the judge) to those facts. For example, the members of the jury must then decide whether the defendant had breached his contract or a product was "defective", in light of the applicable principles of law which have been explained to them by the judge.

For the purpose of making their decision, the jurors go to a conference room in the courtroom and confer privately together. During the time they are conferring, no one is allowed to talk to them. If they do not make their decision in one day, they are allowed to return to their homes at night after promising that they will not discuss the lawsuit with anyone. They then return the next day to confer together some more, and this procedure is followed until a decision is reached. In a complicated case, the jury may confer for several days before reaching a decision. After they reach a decision, they advise the judge who then in the courtroom, in the presence of the parties, their lawyers and the jury, announces the decision.

For a decision of the jury to be valid, the twelve jurors must agree upon a decision by a majority of nine to three. In other words, if they agree that the defendant is not liable to the plaintiff (that is, has not committed any violation of law or caused any damage to the plaintiff) they must make this decision by a vote of nine to three. In the same way, if they find that the defendant should be liable to the plaintiff they must make this decision and also decide the amount of damages which will be awarded to the plaintiff, also by a vote of nine to three. In some cases, juries are not able to agree by the necessary nine to three vote on which way to decide the case and in those cases, the judge declares a "mistrial" and the parties must then start all over again and have another trial to decide their dispute.

# Judgment

After the judge or jury, if a jury was requested, makes its decision, that decision is then written into a document known as a "judgment". The judgment states whether the decision was for the defendant or the plaintiff. If the decision was for the plaintiff the judgment states the dollar amount of the damages or other relief awarded to the plaintiff.

When a plaintiff has obtained a judgment, he can have an officer of the court seize and pay over to the plaintiff the money or other property of the defendant if the defendant refuses to voluntarily pay the plaintiff.

A judgment may normally be enforced by a plaintiff for a period of many years (for example, a period of ten years in California). Thus, even if a defendant company does not have assets in the United States at the time a judgment is entered against it, if it later does own assets in the country, (even several years later) it is possible that the judgment could be used to seize the assets of the defendant at that time.

# Appeal

If after the trial, one of the parties is dissatisfied with the result, he may appeal to a higher court. This court may have different names in the various states, but its common designation is "appellate court". Usually the appellate court consists of three judges who review the proceedings in the trial court and then issue their decision either "affirming" (agreeing with) the trial court judgment, or "reversing" (disagreeing with) it. If the trial court's judgment is reversed, the appellate court may either order that a new (another) trial be conducted in the trial court or it may under some circumstances order that judgment be entered for the party who lost in the trial court.

Normally, the appellate court will not re-examine the decisions of the trial court (judge or jury) with regard to which side's contentions of facts are correct. The philosophy of this rule is that the trial court is best able to decide factual matters because it actually sees the witnesses' faces, hears their voices, etc., and thus can better judge whether they are lying, exaggerating, uncertain, etc. The appellate court makes its decisions on the basis of written transcripts of the trial court proceedings. It does not receive testimony from witnesses or other evidence.

The appellate court thus usually only decides whether the trial court has applied the wrong law or has misinterpreted principles of law in making its decision.

A party dissatisfied with the appellate court's decision may in some cases have the right to appeal that decision to the State Supreme Court or the United States Supreme Court, which has the final say in the matter. Such appeals are only very rarely made (to the U.S. Supreme Court, for example, only in unusual cases involving interpretations of the U.S. Constitution or unusual issues relating to Federal statutes or procedures) and it is unlikely that the average company would ever have any experience with such appeals.

## New Words

| | | |
|---|---|---|
| 1. | lawsuit *n.* | 訴訟；訴訟案件（又譯：官司） |
| 2. | complaint *n.* | （原告的）起訴書；訴狀 |
| 3. | contend *v.* | 爭論；為……鬥爭 |
| 4. | plaintiff *n.* | 原告 |
| 5. | defendant *n.* | 被告 |
| 6. | jurisdiction *n.* | 管轄權 |
| 7. | wherein *ad.* | 在那裡 |
| 8. | vice versa | 〔拉〕反過來也是一樣 |
| 9. | preliminary *a.* | 初步的；開端的 |
| 10. | challenge *n. v.* | 挑戰；正式提出反對 |
| 11. | answer *n.* | （被告的）答辯狀 |
| 12. | motion *n.* | 申請；請求 |
| 13. | summons *n.* | 傳票 |
| 14. | asset *n.* | 資產 |
| 15. | compel *v.* | 迫使 |
| 16. | default *n.* | 不應訴；不應訴（或缺席）判決；一造判決 |
| 17. | cure *n. v.* | 糾正 |
| | to cure the defects | 糾正缺陷 |
| 18. | congestion *n.* | 積案情況；擁擠 |
| 19. | pending *a.* | 懸而未決的 |
| | a pending case | 未決案件 |
| 20. | discovery *n.* | 發現（程序）；要求告知 |
| 21. | specify *v.* | 具體說明 |
| 22. | accomplish *v.* | 完成 |

**23.** evidence *n.* 　　　　　　　證據

　　Law of evidence 　　　　　　證據法

**24.** opponent *n.* 　　　　　　　反對者；抗辯人；對造；敵手

**25.** time-consuming *a.* 　　　　費時間的

　　energy consuming 　　　　　消耗精力的

**26.** deposition *n.* 　　　　　　筆錄證言；非公開出庭的作證

**27.** depose *v.* 　　　　　　　　在非公開出庭的作證中被發問；被宣誓作證

**28.** deponent *n.* 　　　　　　　在非公開出庭的作證中被發問的人；宣誓證人

**29.** stenographic *a.* 　　　　　用速記文字寫成的；用速記文字報導的

**30.** testify *v.* 　　　　　　　　證明；作證

**31.** interrogatory *n.* 　　　　　書面質問；書面質詢

**32.** oftentimes *adv.* 　　　　　常常，等於「often」

**33.** terminate *v.* 　　　　　　　終止僱傭（某人）；了結

**34.** generate *v.* 　　　　　　　產生；發生

**35.** supervision *n.* 　　　　　　監督；監察

**36.** controversy *n.* 　　　　　　論戰；爭論；辯論

**37.** pre-trial *a.* 　　　　　　　審前

**38.** impact *n.* 　　　　　　　　影響；效力

**39.** personality *n.* 　　　　　　人格；品格；個性

**40.** compromise *v.* 　　　　　　妥協；互讓解決

**41.** rigid *a.* 　　　　　　　　　僵硬的

**42.** doctrinaire *a.* 　　　　　　教條主義的

**43.** jury *n.* 　　　　　　　　　陪審團

**44.** juror *n.* 　　　　　　　　　陪審員

**45.** conciliatory *a.* 　　　　　　和好的；調和的

**46.** nominal *a.* 　　　　　　　　名義上的

**47.** intelligence *n.* 　　　　　　智力

**48.** comprehension *n.* 　　　　理解

**49.** demanding *a.* 　　　　　　苛求的；要求高的

**50.** adult ages 　　　　　　　　成年人年齡，在法律上還常用「majority ages」表示同樣的意思

**51.** diverse *a.* 　　　　　　　　不同的；多種多樣的

**52.** critic *n.* 　　　　　　　　　批評家；愛挑剔的人

**53.** prejudice *n.* 　　　　　　　偏見；成見

**54.** misconception *n.* 　　　　誤解；看法上的錯誤

| | |
|---|---|
| **55.** opening statement | （審理開始時）辯護人（律師）對法官或陪審團所作的有關案情概述 |
| **56.** version *n.* | 對個人觀點的描述或看法 |
| **57.** direct examination | 原告律師對原告證人的訊問；直接詰問 |
| **58.** cross examination | 被告律師對原告證人的訊問；反詰問 |
| **59.** inconsistency *n.* | 不一致；前後矛盾 |
| **60.** invoice *n.* | 發票 |
| **61.** closing arguments | 律師對證言和證據的總結；辯論終結 |
| **62.** decision *n.* | 裁定；判決 |
| **63.** damages *n.* | 損害賠償金 |
| **64.** judgment *n.* | 判決 |
| **65.** enforce *v.* | 強制執行 |
| **66.** appellate court | 上訴法院（庭） |
| **67.** affirm *v.* | 表示同意；肯定；維持（下級法院的判決） |
| **68.** reverse *v.* | 表示不同意；推翻；撤銷（下級法院的判決） |
| **69.** contention *n.* | 爭點 |
| **70.** categorize *v.* | 分類 |
| **71.** confer *v.* | 商量；商議 |
| **72.** briefs | 律師向法官所作的對案子所涉及的事實、法律原則的總結 |
| **73.** closing briefs | 律師向法官所作的對案子所涉及的事實、法律原則的要點歸納或總結 |

## ♣ New Phrases and Idiomatic Expressions

| | |
|---|---|
| **1.** to file a document | 提交某一文件 |
| **2.** to set forth | 陳述；闡明 |
| **3.** in excess of | 超過 |
| **4.** to make "service" on the defendant | 向被告發傳票 |
| **5.** at issue | 在爭論中 |
| **6.** in practice | 實際上 |
| **7.** to have sb. present with him | 使某人與他一同出席 |
| **8.** to give testimony about sth. | 就……作證 |
| **9.** in the possession of | 占有…… |
| **10.** to relate to sth. | 與……有關 |
| **11.** to exercise great care | 做到十分小心謹慎 |

**12.** in connection with　　　　　　　　與……有關

**13.** in the case of　　　　　　　　　　就……來說；至於……

**14.** to devote sth. to something else　　把……獻於；將……用於……

**15.** in advance　　　　　　　　　　　提前

**16.** to be interested to do sth.　　　　　有興趣做某事

**17.** at random　　　　　　　　　　　　任意地；隨意地

**18.** all walks of life　　　　　　　　　各行各業

**19.** to be picked by lot or to be drawn by lot　　　　　　　　　　　　用抽籤方式選擇

**20.** to cast doubt on sth.　　　　　　　引起對……的懷疑

**21.** to be liable to sb.　　　　　　　　對……承擔責任

**22.** to have experience with sth. or sb.　　　　　　　　　　　　　　　有和某事或某人打交道的經歷

## ♣ Notes

**1.** A preliminary observation is necessary about the legal concept of "jurisdiction".
對「管轄權」作些初步的評論是必要的。
在美國法中，管轄權分爲對事物的管轄 jurisdiction over subject matter (or subject matter jurisdiction) 和對人的管轄jurisdiction over person。

**2.** The obtaining of this type of judgment is known as entering the default of the defendant.
獲得的這種判決就是人所熟知的對被告的不應訴判決。
default-judgment for the defendant對被告所作的不應訴判決或缺席判決。
default 經常用來表示default judgment。
在契約法中，default 常表示「不履約」或「拖欠債款」。

**3.** ...before the trial takes place the parties normally engage in "discovery".
在審理發生前雙方當事人常會採用發現程序。
根據美國律師界的看法，該程序有以下幾種作用：1.保全審理時不能出庭證人的證言；2.暴露事實；3.明確當事人雙方的爭點；4.將證言凍結，防止僞造；5.當雙方當事人發現他們之間唯一爭點爲法律爭點時，便於援用簡易判決程序；6.有助於雙方的和解；7.有助於審理的順利進行（如果無法和解必須進行審理的話）。

**4.** In some cases, juries are not able to agree by the necessary nine to three vote on which way to decide the case...
在有些情況下，陪審員不能以9票對3票的方法判案……
agree的用法主要有以下五種：
(1)He agreed to sue him.　他同意對他進行起訴。
(2)The appellate court agrees with the trial court judgment.　上訴法院同意審理法院的判決。

(3)The judge agreed with him.　法官同意他的意見。

(4)The defendant agreed to his proposal.　被告同意他的建議。

(5)Both agreed on these terms.　雙方都同意這些條件。

 **Exercises**

## I. Answer the following questions:

**1**. How do you begin a lawsuit?

**2**. What should be the most important content of complaint?

**3**. How do American courts charge filing fee?

**4**. What is jurisdiction? How many kinds of jurisdiction do you know? What is the general principle of it?

**5**. Can you tell the exact meaning of summons? How is it served?

**6**. What is the default of the defendant? In what case will a defendant obtain such judgment?

**7**. What is discovery? What is the purpose of discovery law?

**8**. How do you define the word of "deposition"?

**9**. What is usually done at the pre-trial conference? Why is it necessary?

**10**.In what way can an amicable settlement be achieved?

**11**.What is your comment on jury system?

**12**.What does judgment state?

**13**.What is the duty of an appellate court?

**14**.When can one appeal to the United States Supreme Court?

## II. Translate the following Chinese passages into English:

**1**. 美國民事訴訟程序主要包括：(1)選擇合適的法院；(2)原告向法院提起訴訟；(3)法院對被告進行傳喚；(4)被告進行答辯；(5)發現或調查；(6)召開審前會議；(7)審理；(8)判決；(9)上訴；(10)判決的強制執行。

**2**. 審前會議一般在發現程序結束後，審理開始前的2-4個月裡舉行。在會上，雙方律師與法官作正式交談，目的是為了對事實和法律爭點達成協定。

**3**. 美國法院的管轄權有對物的管轄權和對人的管轄權兩種。

**4**. 在某些情況下，對受理上訴法院判決不服的一方有權向有最終決定權的州最高法院或美國最高法院提出上訴。

## III. Indicate whether each of the following statements is true or false by writing "T" or "F" in the space provided:

____ **1**. "Complainant"or "plaintiff" refers to a person or a company which files the complaint.

____ **2**. In the United States, the filing fee required by the court is a very huge sum of money.

____ **3**. If a court does not have jurisdiction over a defendant, then that defendant must not be dismissed from the lawsuit.

____ **4**. In most courts, the law allows the defendant 30 days after the receipt of the summons within which to file an "answer" or other documents with the court denying the allegations in the complaint.

____ **5**. The purpose of the pretrial conference is to eliminate matters that are not in dispute and to determine what issues remain for litigation.

____ **6**. Normally, the first important job of the jury is to decide what are the true facts of the controversy.

____ **7**. The judgment is actually a written document which states whether the decision was for the defendant or the plaintiff.

____ **8**. After a judgment has been entered the party which is aggrieved thereby or dissatisfied with the result, may not appeal in the United States.

# 幾個可能使中國商人感興趣的訴訟問題
# Particular Aspects of the Litigation Process Which May Be Interest to Chinese Businessman

## Frequently Litigated Matters

Particular areas in which foreign companies have become increasingly involved in litigation in recent years are as follows:

### 1. Products Liability

In most states, a manufacturer of a product will be held "liable" (ordered to compensate a plaintiff for damages suffered)if the product is "defective" and the plaintiff is injured because of the "defect". There would not appear to be any limit as to the type of products which can be the subject of such lawsuits. For example, there have been products liability lawsuits involving all types of industrial machines, tools and equipment ,all types of cars , airplanes, motorcycles and other vehicles, foodstuffs, medicines, toys — in fact, every type of product imaginable. The various states each have somewhat different definitions of what constitutes a "defective" product.

In California, the California Supreme Court has provided one definition ,which states that a product is "defective", if the product has failed to perform safely as an ordinary consumer would expect when used in an intended or reasonably foreseeable manner. Furthermore, the court decided that it was not necessary for the plaintiff to prove that the manufacturer acted unreasonably or negligently in order for the plaintiff to be successful in the lawsuit if the judge or jury decides that the product is "defective".

The subject of "products liability" is a complicated one, but the above discussion should alert any company importing products into the U.S. to investigate means to protect itself against the possibility of liability. Such protection may be available through insurance, or in some rare cases, through contractual arrangements with American based businesses. It is suggested, however, that no Chinese exporter should feel that he can forego insurance or other protection just because he carefully produces a high quality, safe product which has never injured anyone before. This is because American courts and juries may have a different opinion about the safety of the product, and judgments against defendants in cases of serious injuries can be in an amount of hundreds of thousands of dollars (or, in a recent case against Ford Motor Company, where the "Pinto" automobile was found to have a defective gas tank, the judgment was in the amount of several million dollars). Furthermore, even if successful, a defendant can spend many thousands of dollars in legal fees defending such actions.

### 2. Illegal Trade Practices

As a general matter, there are extensive Federal and State laws which seek to encourage free business competition by preventing substantial restraints thereon. These laws are usually summarized as "antitrust laws" or laws against "restraint of trade". The legal principles involved in this subject are so extensive and complicated, however, that only the briefest summary can be made in this short article.

Some areas which the businessman should be particularly careful of, are:

(1)"Price fixing": agreements (whether among competitors or between a producer and its distributors or retailers) or other practices designed to fix prices are illegal.

It is illegal for a manufacturer or a distributor, for example, to agree on the resale prices which their customers shall charge at the time of resale. Thus, a manufacturer cannot sell its product to a distributor with the agreement that the distributor will in turn sell the product at an agreed upon specified price. The theory of the law is that such an agreement restrains free competition and that the purchaser should be free to charge whatever price upon resale as he may think is appropriate or competitive.

It is the policy of the United States Government (which is enforced by the Department of Justice) to vigorously enforce the rule against price fixing and in some cases charge violators with criminal violations and ask the courts to impose large fines and even prison sentences on the violators. A famous case of a few years ago involved several competing American electrical equipment manufacturers who met periodically to agree upon the prices which they would all charge their customers. When this agreement to fix prices was proved in court, both the executives and the companies received heavy fines and some of the executives also were required to serve time in jail. A more recent case involved price fixing agreements and agreements not to compete for the business of certain customers among competitors selling paper and cardboard products. The companies (over twenty of the major U.S. producers) have had to pay criminal fines, and settlements and judgments in lawsuits, totalling more than $500,000,000 and several executives have had to spend time in jail.

(2)"boycott": a concerted refusal by a group of businessmen to deal with another businessman is generally illegal. An example was when a large department store agreed with a number of suppliers of its competitor that the department store would only do business with the suppliers if they refused to sell to the competitor or sold to him only on unfavorable terms. The court decided that this conduct was unlawful and the large department store was ordered to pay money damages to its competitor.

(3)Agreements between competing companies to not compete against each other in specified territories or for the business of certain customers are illegal.

(4)"Tying agreements" or "tie-ins": These are said to exist when a seller refuses to sell a product unless the buyer also a grees to buy another product from the seller as well. For example, a manufacturer of computers will not be allowed to require its customers to buy computer cards from it as a condition of buying a computer.

(5)"Exclusive dealing agreements": Agreements by which a seller obtains his customer's agreement not to buy another company's competing products should be closely examined as to their legality. Under some circumstances such agreements violate the antitrust laws.

(6)Different prices charged to different customers having the effect or potential to destroy competition are, as a general matter, illegal. The Federal prohibition of this practice is embodied in the Robinson-Patman Act. A seller may sometimes be able to justify different prices based on cost considerations or because a lower price was required to meet the competition. Nevertheless, if a company is planning to sell the same product at widely differing prices in the U.S., it should have its proposed selling arrangements carefully examined by counsel.

(7)"Dumping": The practice of selling goods in the U.S. at a price below the price at which the same or similar goods are sold in the home market is known as "dumping". If the International Trade Commission of the U.S. government finds that such "dumping" has caused an injury to a U.S. industry, then the importer of the goods will be subject to costly and troublesome penalties. If a foreign company is found by the U.S. government to have been engaged in "dumping" its ability to successfully market its goods in the U.S. market will be seriously hindered.

Penalties for violation of the laws discussed above can be quite severe, (including criminal penalties in some cases) and it is suggested that any agreements (written or simply oral understandings) with other with regard to the distribution and sale of products in the U.S. be carefully scrutinized by American counsel to avoid any violations of U.S. anti-trust or anti-dumping laws.

# Arbitration

Because of the cost and delays associated with litigation, many companies participating in international transactions place clauses in their contracts which state that any disputes between the parties shall be settled by "arbitration" rather than litigation in the courts. By such clauses in their contracts, parties may specify in which city and country the arbitration shall take place, and what rules or law shall govern the arbitrators in making their decisions.

Arbitration is a procedure whereby one person (or three persons) appointed by the parties, listens to the evidence of the parties to the dispute and then makes an award of money damages to one party or the other, These persons ("arbitrators") are normally not judges and the arbitrations usually do not take place in a courtroom. Technical rules of evidence are many times not followed in arbitration proceedings and in the U.S., there is normally very little basis allowed for appeal to the official court system. That is, a party dissatisfied with the decision of the arbitrators normally has no recourse to the courts.

Unfortunately, there has also been a great deal of litigation conducted with regard to the meaning of contract clauses calling for arbitration, and their enforceability. Furthermore, some arbitrations have also been criticized for delays and the process has also been criticized by some on the ground that it is more risky than litigation because of the lack of the technical legal rules and procedures which have been developed for the courts over the years for the purpose of achieving fair and just trials.

It is therefore very important that (1) the advisability of including an arbitration clause in a contract and (2) the precise wording of the arbitration clause be discussed with American counsel before a contract with an American company is signed.

# Legal Principles

Both the Federal government and the state governments enact laws ("statutes") which govern and apply to the conduct of business. Therefore, when business disputes occur questions often arise with regard to the meaning of particular words in the statute which applies to the dispute.

When the appellate and supreme courts decide such disputes, they write a decision (sometimes called an "opinion") explaining the reasons for their decision and explaining the proper interpretation of the words of the statute which applies. These decisions are then printed in books and thus provide a source of guidance for those who may have similar disputes in the future. Legal principles stated in printed court decisions are sometimes called "precedents".

There is also a body of law known as the "common law". This is because with regard to some disputes the appellate and supreme courts make decisions which establish legal principles even when there is not a statute which relates to the subject .These decisions are also printed in books.

When a client consults an American lawyer and describes a set of facts to him (whether it is a dispute or simply a desired course of action, such as entering a contract, or marketing a product) the lawyer will then consult the relevant statutes and printed court decisions (sometimes simply referred to as "cases") and on that basis advise the client accordingly. This process is generally called "legal research".

The general purpose of legal research is to find and examine statutes and printed court decisions which relate to or most closely resemble the facts of the dispute in question or the business project or transaction being proposed so that the attorney can then predict what a court would say the legal rights, duties or liabilities of a client are with regard to that particular dispute or proposed business project.

As an example, some fire insurance policies in the U.S. provide that if damage to the property is caused by "explosion" then there will be no insurance coverage for such explosion caused damage. Thereafter, as buildings became subjected to fires and other disasters, disputes arose as to what was meant by the word "explosion" as used in such fire insurance policies. For example, sometimes a fire would take place in a building for a period of time after which the heat of the fire caused some of the contents in the building to "explode" causing even greater damage. Sometimes, on the other hand, an explosion of some substance located in a building would occur after which a fire would occur and the major damage would not be caused by the explosion but by the subsequent fire. In some cases, there would be a dispute as to whether the combustion that occurred was properly defined as a "fire" or as an "explosion". In these cases, disputes arose as to what constituted a "explosion" and also to what extent there was insurance coverage when both a "fire" and an "explosion" occurred. In such cases, it was necessary for the lawyers to look at other printed court decisions which discussed these various definitions, and then prepare an argument based upon an analogy to the earlier decisions, explaining why the insurance policy either provided insurance coverage or did not provide insurance coverage.

This example about a fire insurance policy is mentioned only to illustrate the basic nature of the process of legal research. With regard to such legal concepts as "doing business" as those words are used in jurisdiction statutes (for example, statutes saying that a court has jurisdiction with regard to companies "doing business" within their state), or with regard to commercial trade practices which are "in restraint of trade" (as those words are used in statutes defining illegal trade practices) the legal research work of the attorneys may be considerably more complicated. This is because there are literally hundreds of statutes enacted by each of the states and also enacted by the United States Congress and in turn there are thousands of court decisions interpreting these various statutes, as well as stating principles of "common law" (discussed above). It is the task of the American lawyer to find the statutes and the printed court decisions which most closely discuss the dispute or business project or transaction which he has been asked to give an opinion about or represent a client with regard to.

In the preventative law context, the lawyer must analyze these statutes and court decisions and give his client an opinion as to the meanings of various words in a contract or an opinion with regard to the client's legal rights and duties if he embarks upon a proposed course of conduct or contractual arrangement (or with regard to the legality or illegality of such an arrangement). In the dispute context, the lawyer must give his client an opinion based upon the statutes and printed court decisions explaining the client's rights or liabilities with regard to the dispute. In the litigation context, the lawyer will not only give his client a legal opinion but will also typically prepare a legal argument for use in court which explains his client's legal position in a way which is most favorable to the client.

Opinions of lawyers given to clients will therefore frequently make reference to statutes or printed court decisions to explain the lawyers' opinions as to their client's rights and duties, or chances of success in prevailing in a dispute or litigation context. Foreign clients are sometimes surprised by the large amount of hours of legal research preparation which are necessary for American lawyers to spend in order to give opinions about certain types of business transactions and disputes or litigation. The reason as explained above, however, is that the American lawyer in some situations must consult many statutes and a hundred or more legal decisions (and analyze those decisions and try to resolve inconsistencies which sometimes exist between those decisions) in order to give careful and well reasoned advice to his client.

## Negotiation and Settlement of Disputes

Negotiation techniques and strategies have been the subject of countless books and articles, in many countries and in many languages.

For the Chinese businessman negotiating a dispute with his American counterpart, however, he enters an area in which the difference in cultural and business customs of the two countries are perhaps the most pronounced.

For the sake of brevity in this lesson, we shall reluctantly have to pass over the many interesting cultural aspects of this situation. Rather, we would point out only one aspect of this situation — one which was alluded to at the beginning of this lesson. That is, the American acceptance of litigation as an aspect of their business culture (albeit an unpleasant and disliked one). Therefore, a foreign businessman faced with a dispute may be surprised at how quickly the subject of litigation is mentioned or discussed.

Furthermore, he may become surprised in some disputes at how litigation or the threat of litigation is used as a bargaining tactic of his opponent (who in many cases was in a close business relationship with him before the dispute). In this regard, it should also be noted that American businessmen have become increasingly aware in recent years of the great reluctance of Chinese businessmen to engage in litigation and some have used this as an advantage in their negotiations.

The threat of litigation is consistent with the general American approach to the dispute bargaining process in which bluff plays an important role. Thus it is not uncommon for the American businessman in the dispute situation to make a settlement demand that greatly exceeds the amount he is actually desirous of settling the dispute for (or offering an amount which is much lower than the amount he is actually willing to pay to settle a dispute). In this way, he leaves room for bargaining with the hope that through bluff or other shrewd bargaining tactics he will be able to make a settlement which is more favorable than would otherwise be obtained if this settlement figure were frankly stated at outset.

It is therefore suggested that the Chinese businessman faced with an American commercial dispute frankly recognize the cultural differences (which he may be more aware of in other contexts). In this way, and with the aid of a lawyer who is attuned to and familiar with the cultural differences of the two countries, a more favorable and less unpleasant outcome can probably be achieved.

One warning is also appropriate here. Under the American law ,some statements of apology or sympathy written after a dispute has arisen, can be construed as evidence against the sender. This evidence is sometimes called an "admission". Therefore, once a dispute has become apparent, the Chinese businessman should be very careful not to make any statement or write any letter which could later be construed as an admission that the sender was admitting that his company made a mistake, was responsible for damage to the other side, etc. Therefore, statements such as "we are sorry to have caused you this problem" or "your complaint is well taken", etc. should be avoided. Furthermore, if a Chinese company receives a letter accusing it of breach of contract (or asserting the breach of some other legal duty), it should promptly consult American counsel about this. Under some circumstances, a failure to deny liability by a responding letter will also be construed by courts to be an admission of liability.

# Negotiation to Enter Contracts

The Chinese businessman entering into a new business relationship with his American counterpart, and preparing to negotiate a contract, must also keep in mind the American business and litigation environment discussed above. Thus, the American businessman will seek as much as possible to mention and define every contingency that may arise in the performance of the contract of the parties. In this way, he seeks to avoid possible misunderstandings with regard to the expected performance of the parties, and at the same time have his own contractual rights clearly defined should a dispute or litigation on the subject arise.

To the American businessman, in the event of a disagreement or problem with regard to a performance under a contract, his first move will probably be to look to the words of the contract for guidance. He will have a tendency to rely on a strict and literal interpretation of the words of the contract in deciding what position to take with regard to the problem. And, although a good relationship between the parties will be helpful in resolving a disagreement, it will normally have less importance than it does in the East. Therefore, a Chinese businessman entering into a contract with an American company must also carefully define in detail the performance he is expecting from that company, covering as many contingencies as possible. He should not too strongly rely on their relationship to resolve future differences. Disagreements over matters not expressed in writing could become very difficult to resolve later on.

It is because of this American tendency of strict interpretation of contracts that phrases often appearing in Chinese contracts, pledging "cooperation", "good faith", or the "mutual respect for the rights of the others", are not common in American contracts. For one thing, the American businessman tends to regard such things as being understood and unnecessary to express in writing. For another, and importantly, such phrases have little relevance in a litigation context. Since such phrases only state general expressions of intent, rather than specifically defined performance, the American courts will normally take the position that such phrases do not afford any basis to decide the right or wrong of disputes between the parties.

The above discussion is not to suggest that good faith and mutual respect are not essential ingredients in the American business relationship. Thus, in dealing with the various cultural differences, the businessman should not lose sight of this factor and be certain that he makes a thorough inquiry into the background and past relationships of his potential business partner. On the other hand, the Chinese businessman will also be well advised to follow the American custom of having his contract and business transaction thoroughly reviewed by American counsel before signing.

# Conclusion

It is hoped that this lesson will contribute to a little better understanding of the litigation process and American negotiation and preventative law practices which are closely related to and influenced by the litigation process. Litigation is even for American businessmen, an unpleasant and distasteful matter. On the other hand, it must be faced as a reality in the American business environment, and the greater the understanding which the Chinese businessman has about it, then the better able he will be to make decisions of business planning and strategies, including those of a preventative law nature, which are in the best interest of his company.

## New Words

| | | |
|---|---|---|
| **1.** | litigation *n.* | 訴訟 |
| **2.** | process *n.* | 程序；（法律）手續 |
| **3.** | litigated *a.* | 被訴訟的 |
| **4.** | product liability | 產品責任 |
| **5.** | plaintiff *n.* | 原告 |
| **6.** | defective *a.* | 有缺陷的 |
| **7.** | California *n.* | （美）加利福尼亞州 |
| **8.** | complicated *a.* | 複雜的 |
| **9.** | alert *v.* | 使……認識到 |
| **10.** | forego *v.* | 忽略；放棄 |
| **11.** | defendant *n.* | 被告 |
| **12.** | illegal *a.* | 非法的 |
| **13.** | price fixing | 定價；價格壟斷 |
| **14.** | distributor *n.* | 批發商；銷售者 |
| **15.** | retailer *n.* | 零售商 |
| **16.** | restrain *v.* | 限制 |
| **17.** | appropriate *a.* | 合適的 |
| **18.** | Department of Justice | （美）司法部 |
| **19.** | vigorously *adv.* | 用力地 |
| **20.** | fines *n.* | 罰款；罰金 |
| **21.** | anti-trust law | 反托拉斯法 |
| **22.** | periodically *adv.* | 定期地 |
| **23.** | executive *n.* | 主管業務的人；經理 |

| | | |
|---|---|---|
| **24.** cardboard products | 薄紙板產品 | |
| **25.** settlement *n.* | 和解（有時也用amicable settlement） | |
| **26.** judgment *n.* | 判決 | |
| **27.** boycott *v.* | 抵制；聯合起來拒絕與……做交易 | |
| **28.** a large department store | 大百貨公司 | |
| **29.** unlawful *a.* | 非法的 | |
| **30.** money damages | 損害賠償金 | |
| **31.** tying agreements or tie-ins | 搭賣協議或搭配銷售 | |
| **32.** exclusive dealing agreements | 獨家交易協定 | |
| **33.** legality *n.* | 合法性 | |
| **34.** potential *n.* | 潛力 | |
| **35.** counsel *n.* | 律師 | |
| **36.** dumping *g.* | 傾銷 | |
| **37.** home market | 國內市場 | |
| **38.** penalties *n.* | 懲罰；處罰 | |
| **39.** hinder *v.* | 阻礙；阻止 | |
| **40.** scrutinize *v.* | 仔細檢查 | |
| **41.** arbitration *n.* | 仲裁 | |
| **42.** clause *n.* | 條款 | |
| **43.** govern *v.* | 支配；指導 | |
| **44.** procedure *n.* | 程序 | |
| **45.** whereby *adv.* | 靠那個；憑藉那個；藉以 | |
| **46.** arbitrator *n.* | 仲裁人 | |
| **47.** arbitration proceeding | 仲裁程序 | |
| **48.** enforceability *n.* | 強制法；強制性 | |
| **49.** furthermore *adv.* | 而且；此外 | |
| **50.** enact *v.* | 立法 | |
| **51.** legal principles | 法律準則；法律原則；法理 | |
| **52.** cause of action | 案由；訴訟理由；訴訟原因；訴因 | |
| **53.** legal research | 法律研究 | |
| **54.** resemble *v.* | 與……相似 | |
| **55.** predict *v.* | 預言 | |
| **56.** fire insurance policies | 火災保險單（或契約） | |
| **57.** provide *v.* | 規定 | |

| | | |
|---|---|---|
| **58.** insurance coverage | | 保險範圍 |
| **59.** thereafter *adv.* | | 之後；以後 |
| **60.** combustion *n.* | | 燃燒 |
| **61.** constitute *v.* | | 構成 |
| **62.** analogy *n.* | | 類似 |
| **63.** illustrate *v.* | | 表明 |
| **64.** literally *adv.* | | 如實地；不誇張地 |
| **65.** preventative law | | 預防法 |
| **66.** course of conduct | | 行為過程 |
| **67.** legal argument | | 法律論據 |
| **68.** resolve *v.* | | 解決 |
| **69.** inconsistency *n.* | | 不一致 |
| **70.** counterpart *n.* | | 對手方；副本；複本 |
| **71.** pronounced *a.* | | 顯著的；明顯的 |
| **72.** brevity *n.* | | 簡潔 |
| **73.** reluctantly *adv.* | | 不情願地 |
| **74.** albeit conj | | 儘管；即使 |
| **75.** bluff *n.* | | 虛張聲勢；嚇唬 |
| **76.** shrewd *a.* | | 精明的 |
| **77.** apology *n.* | | 道歉；認錯 |
| **78.** construe *v.* | | 解釋 |
| **79.** admission *a.* | | 承認 |
| **80.** contingency *n.* | | 意外事故 |
| **81.** performance of the contract | | 契約的履行 |
| **82.** distrustful *a.* | | 不信任的 |
| **83.** ingredient *n.* | | 組成部分 |

## ♣ New Phrases and Idiomatic Expressions

| | | |
|---|---|---|
| **1.** to become (be) involved in sth. | | 使陷入；使捲入；參與 |
| **2.** to be held liable to do sth. | | 使負有做某事的責任或義務 |
| **3.** to be successful in sth. | | 在做某事方面獲得成功 |
| **4.** to protect oneself (itself) against sth. | | 保護自己免受某種東西的侵害 |

| | | |
|---|---|---|
| 5. | to have a different opinion about sth. | 對某事持不同意見 |
| 6. | to enforce the rule against sth. | 對某事強制執行規章 |
| 7. | to impose sth. on sb. | 將……強加於某人 |
| 8. | to charge sb. with sth. | 控告某人做了某事 |
| 9. | to serve time in jail (to spend time in jail) | 被監禁；坐牢 |
| 10. | on unfavorable terms | 以不利的條件 |
| 11. | to compete against each other | 互相競爭 |
| 12. | to be embodied in sth. | 收進……之中；包括在…… |
| 13. | to become subjected to sth. | 使遭受……帶來的災難 |
| | to be subjected to intense air attack | 遭受猛烈的空襲 |
| 14. | to cause an injury to sb. | 給某人帶來損害 |
| 15. | to be subject to | 隸屬於……；受……支配 |
| 16. | to be engaged in doing sth. | 從事某事 |
| 17. | with regard to | 關於 |
| 18. | to be associated with | 與……有聯繫 |
| 19. | to participate in | 參加；參與 |
| 20. | to have (no) recourse to the court | 能（不能）訴諸於或求助於法院 |
| 21. | a set of facts | 一系列的事實 |
| 22. | to enter a contract | 訂立契約 |
| 23. | to look at | 研究；查看 |
| 24. | in restraint of | 對……限制 |
| 25. | to make a reference to | 查看……；查閱……；查詢…… |
| 26. | for the sake of | 由於；為了；為了……利益 |
| 27. | to be desirous of | 渴望……；十分希望…… |
| 28. | to leave room for | 給……留有餘地 |
| 29. | at outset | 開始；開端；開始 |
| 30. | to be alluded to | 被提及 |
| 31. | to accuse sb. for sth. | 因……控告或指控某人 |
| 32. | in the event of | 如果發生；萬一 |
| 33. | to be attuned to | 使與……協調或合拍 |
| 34. | to have little relevance | 有極少的實用性；沒什麼意義 |
| 35. | to lose sight of | 忽略…… |

**36.** to make a thorough inquiry into sth.　　　　對……進行徹底調查

 **Notes**

**1.** ...every type of product imaginable: every type of product which you can imagine.

**2.** The various states each have somewhat different definitions...: Each of the 50 states in the U.S. has slightly different definitions...

**3.** ...if the product has failed to perform safely: if the product has not functioned properly...

**4.** ...no Chinese exporter should feel that he can forego insurance:...no Chinese exporter should think that he can go without insurance...

**5.** Ford Motor Company：福特汽車製造公司。

美國還有兩家大的汽車製造廠商，它們是：General Motor和Chrysler。

**6.** ...a defendant can spend many thousands of dollars in legal fees defending such action...

這裡的「action」指訴訟action at law（法律訴訟）

**7.** the United States Government: the Government of the United States.

在現代英語中，名詞或名詞短語可用來當形容詞用，如：study plan (plan for study) 和foreign affairs minister (minister of foreign affairs) 等。

**8.** the Robinson-Patman Act：羅賓遜－派得曼法案

This is one part of American anti-trust legislation, which was passed in 1936 by Congress when amending the Clayton Act. According to American legal scholars it is this statute which most directly affects the pricing of products today in the United States.

其他的反托拉斯法還有「Sherman Act」（舒曼法案）和上面所提到的「Clayton Act」（克萊頓法案）。

 **Exercises**

## I. Answer the following questions:

**1.** What is meant by product liability?

**2.** How has the Californian Supreme court defined "a defective product"?

**3.** Why can't a Chinese exporter forego insurance or other protection just because he carefully produces a high quality, safe product which has never injured anyone before?

**4.** What is price fixing? Is it legal in the States?

**5.** What is "boycott"? Can you illustrate it by giving an example?

**6.** What are "tying agreements or tie-ins"? What law are they subject to?

7. What is dumping? What will the U.S. government do if finding such dumping has caused an injury to a U.S. industry?

8. What is arbitration? What are the advantages and disadvantages of arbitration?

9. Why is legal research necessary?

10. What should the Chinese businessman do once a dispute has become apparent?

11. Why are phrases like "cooperation" "good faith" or "the mutual respect for the rights of the others" not common in American contracts?

12. Is it a good suggestion for the Chinese businessmen to follow the American custom of having their contracts and business transactions thoroughly reviewed by American counsel before signing?

## II. Translate the following English passages into Chinese:

1. In most states, a manufacturer of a product will be held "liable" if the product is "defective" and the plaintiff is injured because of the defect.

2. As a general matter, there are extensive Federal and State laws which seek to encourage free business competition by preventing substantial restraints thereon.

3. If a foreign company is found by the U.S. government to have been engaged in "dumping" its ability to successfully market its goods in the U.S. market will be seriously hindered.

4. Because of the cost and delays associated with litigation, many companies participating in international transactions place clauses in their contracts which state that any disputes between the parties shall be settled by "arbitration" rather than litigation in the courts.

## III. Indicate whether each of the following statements is true or false by writing "T" or "F" in the space provided:

_____ 1. The subject of "product liability" is a simple one.

_____ 2. It is legal for a manufacturer or a distributor to agree on the resale prices which their customers shall charge at the time of resale.

_____ 3. A party dissatisfied with the decision of the arbitration normally has recourse to the courts.

_____ 4. The antitrust law of the United States can be found only in the Robinson-Patman Act.

## IV. Translate the following Chinese phrases into English:

1. 產品責任法
2. 保險單
3. 非法貿易行徑
4. 搭賣協議
5. 不能求助於法院
6. 有缺陷的產品
7. 在美國傾銷產品
8. 監禁
9. 國際貿易委員會
10. 訴因
11. 商業爭議
12. 訴訟
13. 預防法
14. 反托拉斯法
15. 重金罰款
16. 強制執行
17. 對此持不同意見
18. 受理上訴的法院
19. 聯邦法院系統

## 美國契約法
## American Contract Law

**第七課 Lesson 7** | **對契約和要約的介紹 Introduction to Contracts and Offer**

# Introduction

Contracts are essentially promises, or groups of promises, to do something in the future. If the promises have certain characteristics defined by law, then the promises give rise to rights which will be protected by society and the breach of the promises will give rise to enforced remedies. The general contract law which will be discussed in this and the following five lessons is based largely on statutes and the common law. The Uniform Commercial Code (U.C.C.), which is now law in all of the 50 states, includes a statutory enactment of the law of contracts for the sale of goods which differs in some respects from the general contract law. The discussion of contracts will on the whole be based on general contract law; where the law of the sale of goods based on the U.C.C. differs from the general principles, those differences will be pointed out.

*1. Classifications of contracts.* Contracts are divided into various classes based on their characteristics; these classifications are not all-inclusive or all-exclusive and the same contract may fall into various different classifications depending on the characteristics which are determinative of the class in question. Contracts may be unilateral or bilateral. A unilateral contract is one in which only one of the parties makes a promise, whereas in a bilateral contract each of the contracting parties makes a promise. An example of a unilateral contract is where A gives B a radio in return for B's promise to give A $15 next week. An example of a bilateral contract would be C promising to give D $10 next week in return for D's promise to make a dress for C.

Contracts may be valid, unenforceable, voidable, or void. A valid contract is one which meets all of the legal requirements for a contract and which will be enforced by the courts. An unenforceable contract is one which generally meets the basic requirements for valid contracts, but which the courts are forbidden by a statute or rule of law to enforce; for example, under the U.C.C., contracts for the sale of goods with a value of more than $500 must be in writing to be enforceable. A voidable contract is one which binds one of the parties to the transaction but gives the other party the option of either withdrawing from the contract or of insisting on compliance with the contract. A void contract is a contract which is of no legal force or effect and therefore is really not a contract. For example, in some states a contract to pay a wager or gambling debt is null and void and courts will not aid in its enforcement.

A contract is said to be executory until all of the parties have fully performed their responsibilities under the contract; at that point it becomes an executed contract. A contract may be either express or implied. An express contract has its terms, conditions, and promises specifically set forth in words; whereas an implied contract is one where the essential elements are not set forth in words but must be determined from the circumstances, general language, or conduct of the parties.

*2. Quasi contract.*  There are some situations where one person confers benefits on another person under such circumstances that it is clear they were not intended to be a gift and where the other person accepts the benefits even though s/he has not promised to pay for the benefits. Such a situation does not fall within the usual concept of a contract where a return promise would normally be made; yet the courts often imply a return promise in order to avoid the injustice that would result from allowing the person to retain the benefits without paying for them. In such a case the recovery allowed the conferer of benefits is the amount of the unjust enrichment that would otherwise occur. There can be no recovery in quasi contract if there is an express contract actually covering the situation nor can there be recovery if under the circumstances the beneficiary is justified in believing that the benefits are a gift or if the benefits are conferred without the beneficiary's knowledge or consent.

# Offer

In order to have a contract there must be a mutual understanding as to what each party will give and receive in return. Prior to the existence of a contract, the parties normally engage in negotiations in an effort to arrive at that mutual understanding. What usually occurs is that A will set forth a proposition — the offer — which, if accepted by B will result in the making of a contract. An offer to contract has two aspects: (1) the offeror indicates what s/he will do or not do, and (2) he indicates what s/he demands in return. The offer must be communicated to the offeree and the communication may be written, oral, by some acts, or by any combination of these means of communication. From all of the circumstances it must appear to the ordinary, reasonable person that the offeror did in fact intend to make an offer. The offeror's actual state of mind is irrelevant; what is important is whether the offeree is justified in believing that an offer was made. The offeror must state the terms of the offer with reasonable certainty, or at least provide a basis for determining them with such certainty. If the terms are not reasonably certain then the offer will be void and the courts will not make a contract for the parties where they did not make a valid one themselves. The omission of a minor or immaterial term will not affect the validity of the offer or contract but the omission of a material term or an agreement to agree later on a material term will preclude the making of a valid contract. Usage of trade is occasionally used to fill in minor omitted terms or to clarify terms.

The actual making of an offer must be distinguished from what is described as "preliminary negotiations" — a period during which the parties seek to determine the bargain the other is willing to make but where no definite statement of what is offered and what is demanded in return is made. Advertisements pose a special problem as to whether they constitute an offer. Normally they are considered only invitations to negotiate or to make an offer; however, an advertisement will be held to constitute an offer if it contains a positive promise and a positive statement of what the advertiser demands in return. The offer to pay a reward is an example of an advertisement which is usually held to constitute a binding offer that can be accepted by performing the requested act. Bids normally are considered invitations to make offers unless the bid advertisement states that the job will be let to the lowest bidder without reservation, in which case it is an offer to let the job to the lowest bidder, likewise auctions, unless they are stated to be without reserve, are merely invitations to make offers which may be either accepted or rejected by the auctioneer.

*1. Terms included in offers.* A common problem is determining whether a particular term is included in the offer or in the contract between the parties. As was already indicated, the offer must be communicated to the offeree in order to be valid and is not effective until it has been so communicated. Sometimes the offeror prints certain of the terms of an offer on a tag or ticket attached to merchandise or given to the offeree (for example, when a person receives a ticket when parking a car/or checking a coat or is sent a tag in the mail along with some other material). Have such terms been communicated so as to form part of the offer, particularly if they are in small type or included among many other terms? In such a case, a determination must be made as to whether such terms were likely to be noticed so that it is reasonable to conclude that they were communicated.

*2. Termination of offers.* Once made, an offer gives the offeree the power to convert it into a binding contract by accepting it. However, offers are not open-ended and binding for an infinite period of time; they may be terminated in a number of ways: (1) by a provision in the offer itself, (2) by the expiration of a reasonable time, (3) by revocation, (4) by rejection, (5) by death or insanity of the offeror or offeree, (6) by destruction of the subject matter of the proposed contract, or (7) by the performance of the proposed contract becoming illegal.

If the offer specifies that it must be accepted within a certain period of time, then it must be accepted within that time period; a late acceptance does not bind the offeror unless s/he chooses to be bound. If no time is specified, then the offer will remain open for a reasonable time; the determination of what is a reasonable time will depend on all the facts and circumstances of the particular case. Such factors as rapidly changing market prices will result in only a very short time period being considered reasonable.

Normally, the offeror has the right to revoke the offer at any time before it is accepted by the offeree; however, if the offeror contracts to keep it open for a certain specified time (an option), then it is irrevocable for that period. Also, if the offeror knows or has reason to know that the offeree will change his position in reliance on the offer, then the offer may be held to be irrevocable under the doctrine of promissory estoppel (to be discussed in more detail later) if the offeree does indeed change his or her position in reliance on the offer. If the offeror wishes to revoke the offer, s/he must communicate the revocation to the offeree and in most states the revocation is not effective until actually received by the offeree. Offers made to the public — as in the case of rewards or advertisements may be revoked if done in essentially the same manner as the offer was originally made. If the offer was for a unilateral contract where acceptance would come by doing the requested act, then an attempted revocation would normally not be effective if the offeree had already begun performance at the time of the revocation and completed his performance within a reasonable time thereafter.

If the offeree rejects an offer it is terminated and any later attempt to accept it will not be effective. Both a counteroffer and a conditional acceptance are considered to be rejections since, by implication, both amount to a rejection of the original offer. However, an inquiry regarding the terms is not to be considered a counteroffer and does not terminate the offer. Death or some legal incapacity, such as insanity, of the offeror or offeree automatically terminates an offer as does destruction of the proposed subject matter of the contract without the fault of either party. In addition, if prior to the acceptance of the offer, a statute is enacted which would make performance of the completed contract illegal, the offer is terminated.

**3. Offers under the Uniform Commercial Code.** Under the U.C.C. an offer does not fail for lack of definiteness because certain terms have been omitted if the court has a basis for supplying them and granting an appropriate remedy. As will be discussed later in more detail, the U.C.C. contains provisions for determining price, time for performance, and other similar terms in cases where the parties intended to conclude a contract but left these provisions open. Under the U.C.C., a written promise by the offeror to leave an offer open for a stated period of time is valid and binding for a period of up to three months even though the offeree has not actually purchased an option by giving consideration to the offeror.

## 🍀 New Words

| | | |
|---|---|---|
| **1.** | remedy *n.* | 救濟；補救 |
| **2.** | all-inclusive *a.* | 包羅萬象的 |
| **3.** | unilateral *a.* | 單邊的；單務的 |
| **4.** | bilateral *a.* | 雙邊的；雙務的 |
| **5.** | all-exclusive *a.* | 排斥一切的 |
| **6.** | valid *a.* | 有效的 |
| **7.** | unenforceable *a.* | 不能強制執行的 |
| **8.** | voidable *a.* | 可使無效的；得撤銷的 |
| **9.** | void *a.* | 無效的 |
| **10.** | legal requirement | 法律要求；法律要件 |
| **11.** | transaction *n.* | 交易 |
| **12.** | option *n.* | 選擇權 |
| **13.** | legal force or legal effect | 法律威力；法律效力 |
| **14.** | wager *n.* | 賭注 |
| **15.** | null *a.* | 無效的 |
| **16.** | executory *a.* | 待履行的 |
| **17.** | executed *a.* | 已履行的 |
| **18.** | express *a.* | 明示的 |
| **19.** | implied *a.* | 默示的 |
| **20.** | whereas *conj.* | 而…… |
| **21.** | essential elements | 要件 |
| **22.** | quasi contract | 準契約 |
| **23.** | injustice *n.* | 不公正 |
| **24.** | enrichment *n.* | 致富 |
| **25.** | beneficiary *a.* | 受益人 |
| **26.** | consent *n.* | 同意；答應 |
| **27.** | offer *n.* | 要約；升價 |
| **28.** | proposition *n.* | 提議；建議 |
| **29.** | means of communication | 通訊手段；送達方式 |
| **30.** | offeror *n.* | 要約人 |
| **31.** | reasonable *a.* | 合理的 |

| | | |
|---|---|---|
| **32.** state of mind | | 思想狀態；精神狀態 |
| **33.** offeree *n.* | | 受要約人 |
| **34.** irrelevant *a.* | | 無關的 |
| **35.** irrevocable *a.* | | 不可撤銷的 |
| **36.** terms of the offer | | 要約條件 |
| **37.** minor *a.* | | 次要的；較不重要的 |
| **38.** immaterial *a.* | | 不重要的 |
| **39.** omission *n.* | | 遺漏 |
| **40.** invitation to make an offer | | 要約邀請 |
| **41.** preclude *v.* | | 排除；阻止 |
| **42.** usage of trade | | 商業慣例；貿易慣例 |
| **43.** preliminary negotiations | | 起初的談判 |
| **44.** clarify *v.* | | 澄清 |
| **45.** bargain *n.* | | 買賣契約或協議 |
| **46.** advertisement *n.* | | 廣告 |
| **47.** pose *v.* | | 提出；造成；形成 |
| **48.** bid *n.* | | 出價；買方遞盤或者投標 |
| **49.** bidder | | 出價人；買方；投標人 |
| **50.** auction *n.* | | 拍賣 |
| **51.** auctioneer *n.* | | 拍賣人 |
| **52.** tag *n.* | | 價格標籤 |
| **53.** merchandise *n.* | | 商品 |
| **54.** open-ended *a.* | | 無限制的 |
| **55.** binding *a.* | | 有約束力的；有拘束力的 |
| **56.** provision *n.* | | 規定；條款 |
| **57.** infinite *a.* | | 無限的 |
| **58.** revocation *n.* | | 撤銷；撤回 |
| **59.** insanity *n.* | | 神智失常；精神錯亂；精神病 |
| **60.** expiration *n.* | | 期滿 |
| **61.** rejection *n.* | | 拒絕；否決 |
| **62.** subject matter | | 標的物 |
| **63.** fault *n.* | | 過錯 |
| **64.** thereafter *adv.* | | 之後；以後 |
| **65.** revoke *v.* | | 撤銷 |

| | | |
|---|---|---|
| **66.** the doctrine of promissory estoppel | 禁反言原則 | |
| **67.** terminate *v.* | 終止；結束 | |
| **68.** counteroffer *n.* | 反要約 | |
| **69.** performance *n.* | 履行 | |
| **70.** statute *n.* | 成文法 | |

## 🍀 New Phrases and Idiomatic Expressions

| | | |
|---|---|---|
| **1.** to give rise to | 引起 |
| **2.** on the whole | 總的看來 |
| **3.** to be divided into | 被分成 |
| **4.** to fall into | 屬於 |
| **5.** to confer sth. on sb. | 授予；賜給 |
| **6.** prior to | 在……前 |
| **7.** to result from | 由於……產生；從……發生 |
| **8.** to result in | 結果是；結果造成 |
| **9.** to engage in | 從事；參加 |
| **10.** to be communicated to sb. | 將……送達給某人 |
| **11.** to convert into | 轉換成；兌換成 |
| **12.** without fault of | 沒有……的疏忽或錯誤 |
| **13.** for lack of | 因缺少…… |
| **14.** to have a basis for doing sth. | 有做某事的根據 |
| **15.** to conclude a contract | 成交訂約；訂立契約；簽訂契約 |
| **16.** to leave sth. open | 使……保持有效 |
| **17.** in cases | 在碰到……情況下 |
| **18.** to give consideration to sb. | 給某人對價 |

## 🍀 Notes

**1.** Such factors as rapidly changing market prices will result in only a very short time period being considered reasonable.

"being considered reasonable": which is considered reasonable.

**2.** s/he: she or he.

**3.** quasi contract: quasi 是拉丁文，表示「好像」、「仿佛」（as if）。

Quasi contract means an obligation which law creates in absence of agreement. 法律界將這樣的契約譯成「準契約」。

**4.** to leave these provisions open: without these provisions being written down or mentioned.

 **Exercises**

## I. Answer the following questions:

**1.** What is a contract? How many kinds of contracts do you know?

**2.** How do you define "offer"?

**3.** What are the two aspects of an offer to contract?

**4.** Can you tell the difference between an offer and an invitation to make an offer?

**5.** In what ways can an offer be terminated?

**6.** Does UCC have different requirements for an offer?

## II. Translate the following Chinese passages into English:

**1.** 契約從本質上講是指未來做某事的允諾或一組允諾，有人還認為契約是法律上能強制執行的協議。

**2.** 一項有效的要約必須具備以下幾個條件：(1)必須包含訂約意圖；(2)其內容必須明確肯定，且應包括簽訂契約的主要條件；(3)要約必須傳達到受要約人。

**3.** 無論是反要約還是有條件的承諾都被視為對要約的否決，只有原要約人承諾或接受後，才能形成契約。

**4.** 根據美國統一商法典的規定，如果法院認為有提供漏掉條件的基礎，一項要約不會因為缺少明確肯定就變得無效。

## III. Translate the following English phrases into Chinese:

**1.** an unenforceable contract

**2.** an express contract

**3.** quasi contract

**4.** void and voidable contract

**5.** offer and acceptance of offer

**6.** terminations of an offer

**7.** under UCC

**8**. granting an appropriate remedy

**9**. insanity of the offeror

**10.**invitations to negotiate or to make an offer

## IV. Indicate whether each of the following statements is true or false by writing "T" or "F" in the space provided.

_____**1**. The provisions of general contract law and those of the Uniform Commercial Code are identical in every respect.

_____**2**. A contract may be either unilateral or bilateral.

_____**3**. An offer must always be communicated in writing to be effective.

_____**4**. The omission of a minor term invalidates an offer or a contract.

_____**5**. When the offeree accepts the offer, a binding contract results.

_____**6**. A counteroffer is considered to be a rejection of the original offer.

_____**7**. Once made, an offer gives the offeree the power to convert it into a binding contract by accepting it.

_____**8**. Bids are normally considered as offers.

_____**9**. Under the UCC an offer does not fail for lack of definiteness because certain terms have been omitted if the court has a basis for supplying them and granting an appropriate remedy.

第八課
Lesson 8

承諾和同意的真實
**Acceptance and Reality of Consent**

# Acceptance

Since contracts rest on the mutual agreement of the parties, it is a prerequisite for a completed contract that the offeree indicate a willingness to be bound on the terms contained in the offer — this is known as acceptance. Under the common law, the acceptance must correspond in all respects with the offer if it is to be effective; a purported acceptance which does not so correspond is nothing more than a counteroffer or conditional acceptance which then requires acceptance by the other party in order for a completed contract to result. Where the offer requests an act in return for a promise, as in the case of a unilateral contract, acceptance is not complete until the act, as requested, is completed. Under some circumstances, however, where the offeree begins performance, the offer is irrevocable until s/he has had a reasonable time to complete the performance. Where a promise is requested in return for a promise, as in the case of a bilateral contract, the offer is accepted by making the requested promise. Where the parties reach an agreement and also agree to later reduce it to writing, a contract has been formed and even a later disagreement on the terms of the writing will not affect this fact; however, where only negotiations were conducted and the parties understood there would be no contract until a written contract was agreed to by both parties, then no contract exists until the form of the written contract is agreed to.

A party cannot be bound to a contract without his or her express or implied consent. Thus, silence in response to an offer that provides such silence will be construed as consent, is normally not effective as consent unless (1) there is some evidence that the silence was intended as acceptance, or (2) prior dealings or other circumstances impose on the offeree a duty to reply. Such circumstances might well include a situation where benefits are conferred on the offeree under such conditions that it was clear they were not intended as a gift and the offeree was aware of this when accepting them. It is also necessary to the formation of a valid contract that the offeree intends to accept the offer; for example, in a unilateral contract the requested act must be done with the intent of accepting the offer. Occasionally courts make an exception to this rule in reward cases and allow a person to collect a reward for doing a requested act even though s/he did not know of the reward offer at the time s/he performed the act.

*1. **Communication of acceptance**.*   In order to be effective, an acceptance must be communicated to the offeror. If the offer spells out the time, place, or method of communication, then these terms must be complied with and any attempt to accept at a time, place, or manner other than that specified is a counteroffer. If no such time, place, or manner are specified, then communication may be in any reasonable manner as long as it is received prior to termination of the offer. When the acceptance is made orally to the offeror, the contract comes into existence at that time. However, where the acceptance is by the mails or telegraph, problems sometimes arise because of the delay between dispatch and receipt or the nonreceipt of the acceptance. If the mode of communication used to convey the acceptance was authorized by the offeror, then the carrier is considered to be the agent of the offeror and the acceptance is effective to create a contract when it is put in the hands of that agent; for example, if acceptance by mail was authorized, then it is effective when a letter of acceptance is deposited in a mail box. Where the acceptance is sent by an agency that was not specifically authorized by the offeror or by trade usage, then it is not effective until received and only then if it is received within the time it would have been received if it had been sent by the authorized method of communication.

*2. **Acceptance under the U.C.C.***   The U.C.C. focuses more on the intentions of the parties and less on the technical requirements of form that prevail under the common law. Thus a contract can be made under the U.C.C. in any manner sufficient to show agreement even though some terms may be left open and even though the moment of the making of the contract is uncertain. Acceptance may be by any reasonable means, and where orders for immediate shipment are made acceptance may be by either promptly shipping the goods or by giving notice of acceptance. If nonconforming goods are shipped and no notice is given that they are being shipped only for the buyer's convenience, then there is a breach of contract at the same time there is acceptance. Under the U.C.C., contracts can be made through the exchange of printed forms even though those forms contain conflicting terms. So long as the parties act as if they have a contract, then a contract exists with its terms consisting of those terms on which they agree, or which were added by one party's form without objection by the other party. Conflicting terms or those on which they disagree are disregarded. Supplementary terms supplied by the U.C.C. or by trade usage are used to fill in terms discarded as conflicting. Where no means of communication of the acceptance is specified, then acceptance may be by any reasonable means. If additional or different terms must be agreed to under the terms of the acceptance of offer, then such agreement must exist or the purported acceptance is a rejection or a counteroffer.

# Reality of consent

**1. Misrepresentation.** In order for a contract to be enforceable it must have been entered into voluntarily, fairly and honestly; an offer or acceptance that was induced by innocent misrepresentations or by fraud is not binding on the person so induced to make the offer or acceptance. Misrepresentation is the creation of an impression in the mind of another person which is not in accord with the actual facts of the situation. Misrepresentation of a material fact which is justifiably relied on by the person to whom the misrepresentation is made is grounds for avoiding a contractual promise. Whether or not the person making the misrepresentation knew it was false does not affect the voidability of the contract. The misrepresentation must be of a material fact, that is, the fact must have been a relevant or contributing factor in the decision to contract, and the circumstances must be such that it can be assumed that the contract would not have been made if the person had known the true facts. The misrepresentation must be of an existing or past fact; a prediction as to a future fact does not fall within the misrepresentation rule. In addition, in order to be entitled to a remedy for misrepresentation, the party seeking the remedy must have been justified in relying on the misrepresentations. S/he must neither know they were false nor be in a position that in view of his or her knowledge and experience and in view of facts and circumstances s/he should have discovered the falsity. The remedy open to the person to whom the misrepresentation is made is rescission —— that is, s/he may return what s/he has received and recover what s/he has given, or its value. In order to be entitled to this remedy, s/he must act to rescind within a reasonable time after learning of the misrepresentation.

**2. Fraud.** Fraud is an intentional misrepresentation of a material fact made with the intent to induce another to rely on it and to surrender a legal right or piece of property; thus fraud essentially is an intentional misrepresentation. Where actual fraud is shown, the injured party who justifiably relied on the fraudulent statement has a choice of remedies. S/he may rescind the contract as s/he can in the case of a misrepresentation, or may affirm the contract and bring a tort action for deceit, which would allow him or her to recover damages for the injury sustained. Again, a person who has been defrauded must act within a reasonable time after discovery of the fraud so as to preserve his or her rights.

**3. Duress and undue influence.** Contracts made under duress or undue influence are voidable. Duress is the exercise of some unlawful constraint on a person whereby one is forced to do an act that one would not otherwise have done. In contract law, duress means the use of threats of bodily or other harm which are used to overcome a person's free will and induce the person to enter a contract through fear or force. As presently interpreted, duress includes threats of physical harm, threats to bring a criminal action which are used to gain an advantage to which the maker of the threat is not legally entitled, and the unjustified withholding of a person's goods for the purpose of forcing that person to pay an unreasonable charge. A threat to initiate a civil suit is not considered to be duress unless it amounts to an abuse of civil process or unless it is based on an unfounded claim and the maker of the threat knows that because of the financial position of the other person the suit would likely bring financial ruin to that person.

Undue influence is the use of a confidential relationship, in which one person owes another a duty to look out for the latter person's interests, and where the duty-bound person uses this position for personal benefit at the expense of the person to whom the duty is owed. By allowing such contracts to be voided, the courts protect against unfair contracts which are shocking to the conscience and are obtained through breach of a confidential position.

*4. Mistake.*  Under some circumstances, a party will be relieved of his or her contractual obligations on the grounds of mistake. Mistake in this context does not mean ignorance, inability, or bad judgment; nor is a party entitled to relief merely on the grounds that s/he made a bad bargain. The types of situations where relief may be available are where the mistake results from an ambiguity in the negotiation of the contract or where there was a mistake as to a material fact which induced the making of the contract.

If in negotiating a contract, the parties used language which is susceptible to more than one interpretation, and one party honestly draws one interpretation while the other party draws another, then the courts will usually hold that no contract resulted since there was no meeting of the minds or mutual agreement. Where a mistake is made as to the existence or nonexistence of a present or past material fact, a court may or may not grant relief from contractual obligations, depending on the facts of the particular situation. If both parties were under a misunderstanding as to the existence or nonexistence of the material fact, this is known as a mutual mistake and it is grounds for recision of the contract. Where the mistake is unilateral in that it is made by only one of the parties, the contract may or may not be enforced. If one of the parties realizes that the other person is operating under a mistaken belief and seeks to take advantage of the error, relief will be granted. While negligence on the part of the party making the mistake usually will not justify the granting of relief, it will be granted where the negligence was slight, where enforcement would impose an unwarranted hardship on the person who made the mistake, and where relief would not impose a material loss on the other party. Relief will also be granted to reform a written document which contains a mistake and which does not correctly set out the actual agreement of the parties. A mistake as to one's legal rights under a contract is usually not sufficient grounds for granting relief, as ignorance of the law is not considered to be excusable.

**New Words**

| | | |
|---|---|---|
| 1. | prerequisite *n.* | 先決條件 |
| 2. | acceptance *n.* | 承諾；接受 |
| 3. | purported *a.* | 聲稱的 |
| 4. | correspond *v.* | 一致；符合 |
| 5. | form *v.* | 形成；訂立 |
| 6. | reward *n.* | 獎賞；報償 |
| 7. | convey *v.* | 傳達 |
| 8. | authorize *v.* | 授權 |
| 9. | non-conforming *a.* | 與（契約）不符的 |
| 10. | conflicting *a.* | 牴觸的；衝突的 |
| 11. | supplementary *a.* | 補充的 |
| 12. | misrepresentation *n.* | 不正確說明；虛偽陳述 |
| 13. | avoid *v.* | 撤銷；廢止；使無效 |
| 14. | voidability *n.* | 可使變得無效 |
| 15. | contributing *a.* | 起作用的 |
| 16. | prediction *n.* | 預言 |
| 17. | falsity *n.* | 虛偽；不真實性 |
| 18. | rescission *n.* | 取消；廢除；撤銷；解約 |
| 19. | rescind *v.* | 取消；廢除；撤回；撤銷 |
| 20. | fraud *n.* | 欺詐；詐欺 |
| 21. | innocent *a.* | 無罪的；清白的 |
| 22. | affirm *v.* | 肯定；批准；確認 |
| 23. | tort *n.* | 侵權行為 |
| 24. | sustain *v.* | 蒙受；遭受 |
| 25. | defraud *v.* | 騙取；詐取 |
| 26. | preserve *v.* | 保護；維持；維護 |
| 27. | prevail *v.* | 勝過 |
| 28. | duress *n.* | 脅迫 |
| 29. | undue influence | 非正當影響；不正當影響 |
| 30. | unwarranted *a.* | 未經擔保的；無正當理由的 |
| 31. | surrender *v.* | 交出（文件） |
| 32. | deceit *n.* | 欺騙行為 |
| 33. | negligence *n.* | 忽略；過失 |
| 34. | relief *n.* | 救濟；補救 |

| | | |
|---|---|---|
| **35.** | excusable *a.* | 可被原諒的 |
| **36.** | construe *v.* | 解釋 |
| **37.** | susceptible *a.* | 易受影響的 |

 **New Phrases and Idiomatic Expressions**

| | | |
|---|---|---|
| **1.** | to rest on | 依據；依賴 |
| **2.** | to reach an agreement | 達成一項協定 |
| **3.** | to be aware of | 知道；意識到 |
| **4.** | to make an exception to this rule | 對該規則表示反對；將此規則作為例外 |
| **5.** | to spell out | 講清楚 |
| **6.** | to comply with | 遵守；與……一致 |
| **7.** | to come into existence (being) | 使……產生；使成立 |
| **8.** | mode of communica-tion | 傳遞方式 |
| **9.** | to be put in the hands of | 使……變為某人所有 |
| **10.** | to focus on | 集中 |
| **11.** | so long as or as long as | 只要 |
| **12.** | in accord with | 與……相符；與……一致 |
| **13.** | the grounds for doing sth. | 做某事的理由 |
| **14.** | to be justified in doing sth. | 有做某事的理由 |
| **15.** | in view of | 鑒於；考慮到；由於 |
| **16.** | to be relieved of | 被解除…… |
| **17.** | to correspond with | 與……一致 |
| **18.** | to initiate a civil suit | 提起民事訴訟 |

 **Notes**

**1.** Under the common law, the acceptance must correspond in all respects with the offer if it is to be effective.

按普通法，承諾必須在所有方面與要約保持一致才有效。

In contract law, this rule is known as "mirror image rule." （「鏡子形象規則」）

**2.** If acceptance by mail was authorized, then it is effective when a letter of acceptance is deposited in a mail box.

若被授權以郵寄方式承諾，當它被投入郵箱時，承諾生效。

In English as well as in American law this rule is called "the doctrine of mail-box rule" or "deposited Acceptance Rule"（「發信主義」），大陸法實行「到達主義」（Receipt of the Letter of Acceptance）。

**3.** ...it can be assumed that the contract <u>would not have been made</u> if the person had known the true facts...

按傳統語法，此句子的動詞形式是「虛擬語態」（the subjunctive mood），但在現代語法中，將此種句型稱爲「unreal conditionals」，即非眞實條件句。

**4.** A party cannot be bound to a contract...: a contract is not binding on or to a party
一方當事人不能受契約的拘束或對一方當事人來說契約不具有約束力。

## Exercises

### I. Answer the following questions:

**1.** What is acceptance?

**2.** What are the essential elements of a valid acceptance?

**3.** How do you understand the word of "misrepresentation"?

**4.** Can you tell the difference between fraud and misrepresentation?

**5.** What is meant by undue influence and duress?

**6.** In what case will a mistake entitle a party to relief?

**7.** What is mutual mistake?

**8.** What is relief?

### II. Translate the following Chinese passages into English:

**1.** 根據普通法的規定，要使一項承諾有效，它必須與要約完全一致。這就是英美法中常提到的所謂「鏡子形象」規則。

**2.** 《美國統一商法典》對承諾的規定有很大的靈活性。只要有足夠事實證明有協議存在，即便缺少某些條款，也能訂立契約。

**3.** 要使契約得以強制執行，契約的訂立必須是自願的、公平的和誠實的。

**4.** 錯誤說明是對某一事實的虛假陳述。如果這個事實是一個重要事實，只要另一方對這重要事實的非眞實說明產生依賴，他就有理由撤銷契約。

III. Indicate whether each of the following statement is true or false by writing "T" or "F" in the space provided:

    **1.** An acceptance must correspond with the offer in all respects in order to have a binding contract under common law.

    **2.** A unilateral contract is the exchange of a promise for a promise.

    **3.** If an acceptance by mail was authorized, it becomes affective when it is deposited in the mails.

    **4.** Silence in response to an offer is usually construed to be an acceptance.

    **5.** Fraud is unintentional.

    **6.** Under the U.C.C., contracts can be made as long as the parties concerned act as if they have a contract.

    **7.** An offer or acceptance that was induced by innocent misrepresentations is usually binding.

    **8.** Contracts made under duress are void.

    **9.** Mutual mistake is grounds for rescission of a contract.

    **10.** A party cannot be bound to a contract without his or her express or implied consent.

# 第九課
## Lesson 9

# 對價
# Consideration

With a few exceptions, a promise is not enforceable by way of court action unless it is supported by consideration. Consideration is usually defined as either a detriment to the promisee or a benefit to the promisor, which was bargained for and given in exchange for the promise. The detriment must be a special kind of detriment — a legal detriment — which means the surrendering of a legal right or the assuming of a legal burden. It does not have to have any economic value. Such a detriment to the promisee usually produces a benefit for the promisor, although a detriment without any corresponding benefit is considered to constitute consideration. However, mere benefit to the promisor without corresponding detriment to the promisee does not constitute consideration.

*Pre-existing obligations.* A promise to do something that one is already obligated to do or a promise to refrain from doing something that one is already bound not to do is known as a pre-existing obligation. A promise to perform such a pre-existing obligation does not constitute consideration. There are four main types of situations in which pre-existing obligations may exist: (1)criminal or tortious acts, (2)acts which the holder of an office is obligated to perform, (3)acts which the promisee is under a contractual duty to the promisor to perform, and (4) acts which the promisee has already obligated himself by contract to perform but which through some unforeseen factors are more burdensome than either of the contracting parties contemplated when they entered into the contract.

Since individuals in society owe an obligation to the rest of society not to engage in criminal or tortious activity, a promise to refrain or to actually refrain from such activity does not constitute sufficient consideration to support a contract. Likewise, a promise to engage in such activity is against public policy and void. A person who holds an office, particularly a public office, is obligated to perform those acts which are incidental to that office. If an officeholder promises to perform what s/he is already obligated to do that promise will not constitute sufficient consideration to support a contract. If this were not true, such officeholders would have an incentive to withhold the performance of their duties until they received additional compensation. At the same time, a distinction must be made between (1) those acts which are part of the official duties, and (2) acts which are similar to those performed as an official but are actually performed outside of the official duty; a promise to perform the latter will constitute legal consideration.

If a person owes a contractual duty to perform a certain act, a promise made by the person to whom the duty is owed to pay additional compensation for that same act is usually not enforceable because there was no legal detriment to the person already obligated to perform. An exception to this rule is sometimes made in cases where unforeseen difficulties arise which make performance more expensive or difficult than was anticipated by the parties when they entered into the contract. In this case, a new promise to pay additional compensation will generally be enforced. Where the parties to a contract desire to leave the obligations of one party the same but to increase the obligations of the other party, they should clearly and convincingly terminate the old contract by mutual agreement and enter into a new one. The courts will enforce the new arrangement only if it is clear that it was entered into in good faith and free from any fraud, duress, or undue influence.

***Debt, compromise, and composition.*** If a person promises to discharge a liquidated debt on payment of part of the debt at the place where the debt is payable and at or after the time the debt is due, such a promise does not constitute legal consideration and a contract based on such a promise will not be enforceable in the courts. However, for this rule to be applicable the debt must be liquidated — that is, the parties must be in complete agreement as to the amount — payment must be made at or after the due date, payment must be made at the place called for, and payment must be made in the same medium of exchange called for. A creditor may make a gift of a balance following a partial payment or the debtor may offer some additional consideration in the form of something s/he was not obligated to do and then the contract will be enforced.

An accord and satisfaction is the compromise of a disputed claim that exists between two parties; if there was an honest dispute as to the amount or existence of a claim, such a compromise will be held to constitute consideration and will be enforceable. A composition is an agreement between a debtor and two or more of his or her creditors whereby the debtor agrees to pay each creditor a pro rata share of his or her claim and each creditor agrees to accept that amount in full satisfaction of his or her claim. Such agreements are considered to be exceptions to the usual rule requiring consideration in order to be enforceable and are generally enforced, as long as they are free from misrepresentation, fraud, duress, or undue influence, on the grounds that sound business practice requires enforcement.

Forbearance to sue. Because a person has a right to seek court enforcement of claims s/he may have against others, a promise not to bring suit on a claim, which a person reasonably believes s/he has, is consideration and will support a simple contract. The promisor need not be the party threatened with suit, and a promise made by a third person may be supported by the promisee's forbearance to sue.

*Bargain and exchange.* In order to constitute consideration, the detriment to the promisee or benefit to the promisor must be bargained for and given in exchange for the promise. If it was intended as a gratuity it will not constitute legal consideration. Normally, the courts will not look into the sufficiency of the consideration as long as some legal consideration has been given. However, if the exchange is marked by gross inequality of considerations and there is evidence of unfair dealing such as fraud, duress, misrepresentation, or undue influence, the courts may refuse to enforce the contract. If a sufficient or nominal consideration is stated in the contract to have been given, but in fact has not been given, then the contract or promise will not be enforced.

*Past consideration.* Consideration in the form of a benefit conferred in the past — known as past consideration — is not sufficient consideration to support a contract because at the time the promise is made, the promisee is under no obligation to the promisor and suffers no legal detriment in exchange for the promise. At the same time, past consideration should not be confused with situations where a promise is made to discharge an existing, but unliquidated, debt.

*Consideration in bilateral contracts.* If a bilateral contract is to be valid, both of the contracting parties must make legally binding promises. If one of the promises is illusory — that is, worded so that fulfillment of the promise is left to the option or election of the promisor — then neither party is bound by the contract .Similarly, if either or both of the parties reserve the right to cancel the contract at will, it is not a binding contract. However, if the contract provides that it will be in force for a stated period after the cancellation or if the cancellation can come only at the occurrence of a stated event not within the control of one of the parties, then the contract is supported by consideration and is enforceable.

*Situations not requiring consideration.* In order to avoid injustices, certain promises are enforceable even though they are not supported by consideration. The most common situation not requiring consideration is where a person makes a promise which s/he reasonably can expect will induce the promisee to rely on the promise and to take some definite and substantial action or forbear from some substantial course of action which is detrimental to the promisor. In such a situation the promise will be enforced on the grounds of promissory estoppel — since the promise led the promisee to justifiably rely on the promise and to change the position to his or her detriment, the promisor is estopped from setting up the lack of consideration as a defense to enforcement of the promise. A common example of a situation where promissory estoppel may be applied is the charitable subscription — the promise to make a gift to some religious, educational, or charitable organization. If the organization changes its position in reliance on the promised gift, then the promise to make a gift will be enforced.

In general, a promise to pay a debt which is barred by the statute of limitations will be enforceable although in some states it must be in writing. Likewise, a promise to pay a debt that was discharged in bankruptcy will usually be enforced. However, a promise to pay a debt discharged in a composition agreement will not be enforceable unless supported by a new consideration.

***Consideration under the U.C.C.*** Under the Uniform Commercial Code, a promise in writing to hold open an offer made between merchants is enforceable for up to 90 days even though it is not supported by consideration. Also, under the U.C.C., an agreement modifying a contract for the sale of goods needs no consideration in order to be binding.

## ♣ New Words

| | | |
|---|---|---|
| **1.** | consideration *n.* | 對價 |
| **2.** | court action | 法院訴訟 |
| **3.** | detriment *n.* | 壞處;損害 |
| **4.** | promisor *n.* | 允諾人 |
| **5.** | promisee *n.* | 受允諾人 |
| **6.** | assume *v.* | 承擔 |
| **7.** | preexisting *a.* | 先存在的;事先存在的 |
| **8.** | tortious *a.* | 侵權的 |
| **9.** | unforeseen *a.* | 預期不到的;未預期的 |
| **10.** | contemplate *v.* | 期待;期望 |
| **11.** | public policy | 公共政策 |
| **12.** | officeholder *n.* | 公務員;官員 |
| **13.** | incentive *n.* | 刺激;鼓勵 |
| **14.** | compensation *n.* | 補償 |
| **15.** | distinction *n.* | 區別;區分 |
| **16.** | convincingly *adv.* | 有說服力地;令人信服地 |
| **17.** | compromise *n.* | 妥協 |
| **18.** | an accord and satisfaction | 有約因的和解;和解與清償 |
| **19.** | composition *n.* | 和解協議 |
| **20.** | pro rata share | 按比例計算的份額 |
| **21.** | forbearance *n.* | 克制;忍耐 |
| **22.** | gratuity *n.* | 賞錢;小費 |
| **23.** | liquidated debt | 已清算確定的債務額 |
| **24.** | unliquidated debt | 未被清償的債務;未清算確定的債務額 |

**25.** gross inequality                 嚴重的不公平

**26.** unfair dealing                  不公平的交易

**27.** illusory *a.*                    虛幻的

**28.** occurrence *n.*                 發生

**29.** defense *n.*                   辯護；抗辯

**30.** promissory estoppel        允諾後不得反悔（原則）；禁反言原則

**31.** charitible subscription      慈善捐款

**32.** bar *v.*                      阻止

**33.** statute of limitations       時效法

**34.** modify *v.*                   修改

## 🍀 New Phrases and Idiomatic Expressions

**1.** to bargain for                為……簽訂協議

**2.** to refrain from               忍住；抑制；制止；戒除

**3.** under a contractual duty    有契約義務

**4.** to owe sth. to               欠……什麼

**5.** to hold an office             擔任公務

**6.** to enter into a contract     訂立契約

**7.** to make a distinction between        將……區分開

**8.** to be similar to              與……相似

**9.** to be free from              不受……影響的；沒有……的

**10.** in good faith                善意地；出於誠意地；誠實地

**11.** to be marked by            以……為特徵的

**12.** in force                    生效

**13.** to be estopped from doing sth.    被阻止做某事

**14.** to forebear from            克制不做某事

**15.** on the grounds of           根據；以……為理由

**16.** under no obligation        沒有義務

## Notes

1. Consideration is usually defined as either a detriment to the promisee or a benefit to the promisor, which was bargained for and given in exchange for the promise.

   對價通常被解釋成對受允諾人的壞處，或對允諾人的好處。相互達成協定的目的是爲了對價，給予對價是爲了換取允諾。

2. An accord and satisfaction is the compromise of a disputed claim that exists between two parties.

   有約因的和解是一種對存在於雙方之間有爭議債權的妥協。

   「accord」指解除原來的債；「satisfaction」指存在使和解契約生效的約因。

3. In general, a promise to pay a debt which is barred by the statute of limitations will be enforceable although in some states it must be in writing.

   一般說來，償還被時效法所阻止的債務的允諾是可以強制執行的。儘管在一些州，這種允諾必須是書面的。

   In all states of the United States there are statutes that specify the length of time within which a legal action may be brought on a contract. These statutes are called statutes of limitations（時效法）。

   The length of time varies from state to state, but a commonly specified time in states is six years. Under the U.C.C., the statute of limitations for breach of contracts for sale of goods has been reduced to four years.

## Exercises

## I. Answer the following questions:

1. How do you define consideration?

2. Can a preexisting obligation constitute consideration if and when it has been performed?

3. What is the exact meaning of accord and satisfaction?

4. Is past consideration a sufficient consideration to support a contract?

5. In what cases are promises enforceable even though they are not supported by consideration?

6. What are the essential elements of a valid consideration?

7. What is meant by promissory estoppel?

8. What is the U.C.C. rule regarding consideration requirements?

## II. Translate the following Chinese passages into English:

1. 對價是為了獲取他人允諾而付出的代價。買賣契約中的價格，保險契約中的保險金都是對價的例子。

2. 按照英美法的解釋，一項有效的對價必須具備下列幾個條件：

   (1)對價必須合法；

   (2)對價必須是待履行的對價或者已履行的對價，而不能是過去的對價，過去的對價不是對價；

   (3)對價必須具有某種價值，但無需充分；

   (4)已存在的義務或法律義務不能作為對價。

## III. Indicate whether each of the following statements is true or false by writing "T" or "F" in the space provided:

_____ 1. Consideration may take the form of the surrendering of a legal right or the assuming of a legal burden.

_____ 2. The performance of a pre-existing obligation constitutes consideration.

_____ 3. A composition is the compromise of a disputed claim.

_____ 4. A promise not to bring suit may be valid consideration.

_____ 5. Past consideration is a good consideration.

_____ 6. One of the basic elements of an enforceable contract is that an agreement must be supported by consideration.

_____ 7. Valid consideration may consist of money or other property, services, a promise, or a sacrifice or the giving up of some right.

_____ 8. Consideration is what a promisor demands and receives as the price for his promise.

_____ 9. A common example of a situation where promissory estoppel may be applied is the charitable subscription.

_____ 10. Ordinarily the courts do consider the adequacy of the consideration given for a promise.

# 當事人訂約能力和不合法
# Capacity of Parties and Illegality

## Capacity of parties

*1. Capacity.* Capacity is the ability to perform legally valid acts; that is, the ability to incur legal liability or to acquire legal rights. To have a legally binding contract there must be two parties to the contract — a promisor and a promisee. The same person can not act in both capacities. Of course, there can be more than one promisor and more than one promisee as there is no legal limit to the number of persons who can be parties to a contract. Everyone is presumed to have the capacity to contract, and if a person wishes to defend an action based on an alleged contract on the grounds that s/he did not have the capacity to contract, s/he must affirmatively set out the defense in the answer to the complaint.

*2. Minors' contracts.* The law accords special protection to minors who are generally defined by statute as persons under 21 years of age in some states and under 18 years of age in others. This protection is given by allowing the minor to disaffirm his or her contracts. A minor's contract binds both the minor and the adult unless the minor exercises his or her right to disaffirm the contract; thus the minor's contracts are not void but rather only voidable at his option. If the minor chooses to be bound by the contract, then the relation between the parties is the same as it is between two parties who both have the same capacity to contract. In general, minors may disaffirm their business contracts even though the business is operated as a means of self-support. The common-law rules relating to minors' contracts have to some extent been altered by statute and there are some differences between the states in the coverage and terms of these statutes.

Minors may become members of partnerships and they may subsequently disaffirm the partnership agreement without incurring liability to the other partners for breach of the agreement. A minor partner may disaffirm his or her personal liability to creditors of the partnership, but s/he may not withdraw his or her partnership capital to the injury of such creditors.

Minors are liable for the reasonable value of necessaries furnished to them; this liability is based on quasi contract and not on any express promise to pay. Necessaries are those things which are essential to the minor's continued existence and general welfare and generally include food, clothing, shelter, medical care, a basic education or vocational training, and the tools of the trade. The class of society that the minor was born into affects what will be considered to be necessaries for the minor. The minor is liable only for the reasonable value of necessaries actually furnished to him or her, and is not liable even for necessaries if s/he is already adequately supplied with them by a parent or guardian.

A minor has the absolute right to disaffirm his or her executed contracts — except contracts affecting title to real estate. This right may be exercised at any time from the time the contract is entered into until a reasonable time after the minor reaches majority age; contracts affecting the title to real estate can not be disaffirmed during minority but only during a reasonable time after reaching majority age. The minor is bound until s/he does disaffirm, and failure to do so within a reasonable time after reaching majority amounts to a waiver of the right to disaffirm. The right to disaffirm is not conditioned upon the minor's ability to return any consideration received, but the minor normally must return any consideration still in his or her possession so as to prevent the right of disaffirmance from being used as a device to defraud adults. The minor will be entitled to recover any consideration given the adult after disaffirming a contract. If the minor misrepresented his or her age to the adult, this does not prevent the minor from disaffirming in most states; however, on disaffirmance of the contract the minor must return the consideration received and account for its use and depreciation in value.

A minor may not ratify his or her contract until s/he reaches majority age. Ratification consists of words or acts which signify an intent to be bound by the contract. In the case of an executed contract, failure to act within a reasonable time after reaching majority age amounts to ratification regardless of whether the minor realizes s/he has the right to disaffirm. Some courts do not hold mere inaction sufficient to ratify an executory contract. Ratification makes the contract valid from its inception and once accomplished, it can not be undone.

*3. Insane and drunken persons.* The contract of an insane person is voidable if it was made while s/he was under that incapacity; however, if the person had been declared insane by a court then most states hold contracts made by the insane person to be void and of no effect. The usual test of insanity is whether or not the contracting person at the time the contract was entered into had sufficient capacity to comprehend the nature of the business being transacted. Like minors, insane persons are liable for the reasonable value of necessaries furnished to them. If the contract is fair and the other person had no reason to know of the insanity, then upon disaffirmance the insane person must return the other party to the status quo. Alternatively, if the other party had reason to know of the insanity, then upon disaffirmance the insane person need only return any consideration or proceeds of the consideration still remaining in his or her possession. An insane person may ratify the contract once the disability is removed or it may be ratified by his or her legal guardian. Any person who at the time of contracting is too intoxicated to comprehend the business being transacted is generally treated in the same manner as if s/he were insane.

*4. Aliens, corporations, fiduciaries and government entities.* In general, there are no restrictions on the right of an alien in the United States to make contracts. Corporations are allowed to enter into such contracts as are permitted by their charter of incorporation. Trustees, receivers, administrators, guardians, and executors may enter into contracts in their official capacity within the scope of their authority as set out in the statute, agreement, or order from which they draw their authority. Governments and governmental units generally have the capacity to contract and may sue on their contracts. However, governments and governmental units may not be sued without their consent; such consent is set out in a statute where it is given.

# Illegality

A contract is illegal if either its formation or its performance is contrary to the public interest and to public policy. In general, illegal contracts are void. While there is a wide variety of situations which may produce illegal contracts, the discussion in this lesson will focus on three broad categories of such contracts: (1)contracts in violation of positive law, (2)contracts expressly made void by statute, and (3) contracts contrary to public policy.

*1. Contracts in violation of positive law.* A contract which provides for the commission of a crime or whose nature tends to induce the commission of a crime is illegal. Similarly, a contract which cannot be performed without the commission of a tort is illegal; however, the fact that a tort is committed during the performance of a contract does not in itself make the contract illegal.

*2. Contracts made illegal by statutes.* Statutes which expressly deal with the legality of certain types of contracts may be divided into three groups: (1) criminal statutes, (2) statutes expressly declaring contracts void, and (3) regulatory statutes. States commonly have statutes which either prohibit or regulate wagering. Generally, wagering contracts are illegal and will not be enforced. Wagering contracts should be distinguished from contracts to shift a risk. In a wagering contract, a risk is created for the purpose of bearing it — such as a bet on a football game. A risk-shifting contract — such as an insurance contract — is legal so long as the person purporting to shift the risk actually had the risk. Stock and commodity market transactions entered into in good faith are speculative contracts and not illegal as wagers.

Some common examples of statutes declaring certain types of contracts illegal are usury laws and Sunday closing or blue laws. These statutes often make the contracts void and may subject the parties involved to various penalties and forfeitures.

In order to protect the public, states have enacted a wide variety of statutes regulating the conduct of various types of businesses and professions. The most common type of regulation provides for the obtaining of a license before a person, partnership, or corporation engages in a regulated activity such as the practice of law or medicine or the carrying on of a trade such as barbering or plumbing. If a person contracts to perform such a service or engages in a regulated business without first having obtained the required license, any contracts s/he makes are illegal. Again, however, a distinction must be made between regulatory statutes which require proof of skill and character before the issuance of a license, and those statutes designed to raise revenue and which permit the issuance of a license to anyone who pays a certain, often substantial, fee. The failure to obtain a license required by a revenue-raising statute does not affect the legality of a contract made by the unlicensed person.

*3. Public policy.* Public policy is a rather nebulous concept which accords courts flexibility to require that contracts be consistent with current mores and concepts of fair dealing and the general welfare. Of course such mores and standards vary over time and also vary between different areas of the country. Public policy is applied on a case-by-case basis and there is no simple standard or rule to guide its application.

A contract is illegal if it purports or tends to induce a public official to deviate from the duty s/he owes to the public or if it purports to grant the official additional or less compensation than s/he is allowed by law. Likewise, a contract which tends to induce a breach of duty on the part of a fiduciary such as a trustee, administrator, or guardian is illegal. A contract which purports to relieve a person of liability for his or her willful negligence or from the consequences of a duty owed to the public is illegal. However, reasonable limitations on damages not attributable to willful negligence may be agreed to legally, and where there is no duty owed to the public and the parties are on an equal bargaining basis, an agreement relieving one of the parties of his or her liability for nonwillful negligence is legal and can be enforced.

A contract that is in direct restraint of trade is illegal; thus an agreement not to compete with someone else in a particular trade or business is illegal. However, contracts which operate only as reasonable restraints on trade and which protect valid interests of the parties are legally permissible. Such a restraint must be ancillary to another contract between the parties such as a contract of employment or a contract of sale of a business, the restraint must be for the purpose of protecting interests created by that contract, and the restraint must be no greater than is reasonably required to protect those interests. Thus, such a restraint is normally limited in space and may also have to be limited in time. A restraint which is not so limited may not be enforced at all or it may be enforced only to the degree it is reasonable.

There are, of course, a great many other diverse types of contracts which may be considered illegal as in contravention of public policy. For example, a contract which tends to interfere with marital relations might be illegal on grounds of public policy. A detailed listing of these situations is not possible here but the reader should be aware that a contract whose terms or effect runs contrary to generally accepted societal norms runs the risk of being declared illegal on the grounds it contravenes public policy.

*4. Effect of illegality.* As a general rule, a court will not enforce an illegal contract and will leave the parties in the same position in which it finds them. One party can not recover damages for breach of an illegal contract, and there is normally no recovery in quasi contract for benefits conferred. However, if the interests of the public, as opposed to the interests of one of the parties, are served by allowing a recovery of some sorts, the courts will allow such a recovery. A party who is justifiably ignorant of the facts or special regulation which make the bargain illegal may recover the consideration conferred on the other party. And a person protected by a regulatory statute may recover for breach of contract entered into with a person who has not complied with the statute. A contract made for the purpose of aiding the commission of a crime is illegal. However, mere knowledge that the article sold will be used illegally does not make the sale illegal unless the intended use is the commission of a serious crime.

A party may rescind an executory illegal contract before the performance of the illegal act and recover any consideration s/he has given to the other party. If a contract contains a legal portion and an illegal portion and the illegal portion is divisible, then the legal portion may be enforced and the rest disregarded unless the illegal parts go to the principal objective of the contract. However, if such a contract can not be so divided, the entire contract is illegal and void.

*5. Unconscionable contracts under the Uniform Commercial Code.* Under the U.C.C., a court may refuse to enforce a contract or a contract clause if it finds the contract or clause to be unconscionable. To be unconscionable, it must be commercially unreasonable and unfair at the time the contract was made. This provision is commonly used to refuse enforcement of contracts where one of the parties used a position of economic or strategic superiority to drive an unreasonable and unfair bargain.

### 🍀 New Words

| | | |
|---|---|---|
| **1.** | capacity *n.* | 行為能力 |
| **2.** | incur *v.* | 引起 |
| **3.** | acquire *v.* | 獲得 |
| **4.** | presume *v.* | 推定；假設 |
| **5.** | alleged *a.* | 聲稱的 |
| **6.** | affirmatively *adv.* | 肯定地 |
| **7.** | minor *n.* | 未成年人；未達法定年齡的人 |
| **8.** | disaffirm *v.* | 撤銷；取消 |
| **9.** | partnership *n.* | 合夥 |
| **10.** | furnish *v.* | 提供 |
| **11.** | vocational *a.* | 職業上的 |
| **12.** | guardian *n.* | 監護人；保護人 |
| **13.** | majority age | 法定年齡；成年人年齡 |
| **14.** | title *n.* | 所有權 |
| **15.** | real estate | 房地產；不動產 |
| **16.** | minority *n.* | 不到法定年齡的狀態；未成年 |
| **17.** | waiver *v.* | 放棄 |
| **18.** | device *n.* | 手段 |
| **19.** | defraud *v.* | 騙取；欺騙 |
| **20.** | misrepresent *v.* | 錯誤地陳述；虛偽地陳述；不正確地說明 |
| **21.** | depreciation *n.* | 貶值 |
| **22.** | ratify *v.* | 確認；承認；認可；追認 |
| **23.** | ratification *n.* | 確認；承認；認可；追認 |
| **24.** | signify *v.* | 表示；表明 |
| **25.** | inaction *n.* | 無行動；無行為 |
| **26.** | insane *a.* | 有精神病的 |
| **27.** | incapacity *n.* | 無行為能力；無法定能力 |
| **28.** | comprehend *v.* | 理解 |
| **29.** | the status quo | 現狀 |
| **30.** | alternatively *adv.* | 兩者擇一地 |
| **31.** | intoxicated *a.* | 醉酒的；酗酒的 |
| **32.** | alien *n.* | 外國人 |
| **33.** | charter of incorporation | 公司章程；組成公司的特許狀 |
| **34.** | trustee *n.* | 受託人 |

| | |
|---|---|
| **35.** receiver *n.* | 破產事務官；破產管理人 |
| **36.** administrator *n.* | 管理人；遺產管理人 |
| **37.** executor *n.* | 執行人；實施者；遺囑執行人 |
| **38.** illegality *n.* | 非法；非法性 |
| **39.** positive law | 實在法（又譯：實證法）；制定法；成文法 |
| **40.** commission of a crime | 犯罪 |
| **41.** commission of tort | 犯了侵權行為 |
| **42.** criminal statutes | 刑事成文法規 |
| **43.** regulatory statute | 管理性成文法規 |
| **44.** wagering *n.* | 賭博 |
| **45.** stock market | 股票市場 |
| **46.** commodity market | 商品市場 |
| **47.** speculative *a.* | 投機的 |
| **48.** Sunday closing or blue laws | 禁止星期天營業法 |
| **49.** usury laws | 高利貸法 |
| **50.** forfeiture *n.* | 沒收 |
| **51.** practice of law | 開業做律師 |
| **52.** barbering *n.* | 理髮業務 |
| **53.** plumbing *n.* | 鉛管工業務 |
| **54.** the issuance of a license | 發許可證；發執照 |
| **55.** unlicensed person | 無執照人員 |
| **56.** nebulous *a.* | 模糊不清的 |
| **57.** mores *n.* | 習慣；慣例；道德態度 |
| **58.** breach of duty | 失職；不負責任 |
| **59.** fiduciary *n.* | 受信託人 |
| **60.** attributable *a.* | 可歸因的；可歸屬的 |
| **61.** wilful *a.* | 有意的；故意的 |
| **62.** ancillary *a.* | 附屬的；輔助的 |
| **63.** marital relation | 婚姻關係 |
| **64.** societal norm | 社會標準；社會規範 |
| **65.** divisible *a.* | 可分割的；可分開的 |
| **66.** unconscionable *a.* | 不合理的；不公平的 |
| **67.** superiority *a.* | 優越；優勢 |

**New Phrases and Idiomatic Expressions**

| | | |
|---|---|---|
| 1. | to accord sth. to sb. | 給予某人某物 |
| 2. | at one's option | 由……選擇 |
| 3. | in general | 一般地；大體上 |
| 4. | to be liable for | 對……負有責任的 |
| 5. | to be conditioned upon | 以……為條件 |
| 6. | from its inception | 從開始 |
| 7. | within the scope of | 在……範圍內 |
| 8. | to be contrary to | 與……相違背；與……背道而馳 |
| 9. | over time | 隨時間的變化 |
| 10. | on a case-by-case basis | 在因案而異的基礎上；在看情況而定的基礎上 |
| 11. | to deviate from | 偏離 |
| 12. | on an equal bargaining basis | 在平等的訂約基礎上 |
| 13. | in direct restraint of | 對……直接限制 |
| 14. | in contravention of | 違反…… |
| 15. | to run contrary to | 與……背道而馳；與……相違背 |
| 16. | to run the risk of | 冒……風險 |
| 17. | to be ignorant of | 不知道 |
| 18. | to drive an unreasonable and unfair bargain | 迫使對方接受不合理不公正的條件 |

 **Notes**

1. ...of course, there can be <u>more than one promisor</u>...

   注意：more than one 後要接單數，如more than one person

2. The law accords special protection to <u>minors</u>...

   minor（未成年人）有時也用 infant 來表示。

3. <u>The class of society</u> that the minor was born into...

   此處「the class of society」表示社會地位。

4. Some common examples of statutes declaring certain types of contracts illegal are <u>usury laws</u> and <u>Sunday closing or blue laws</u>.

   美國大多數州對放款時應收的最高利率都有具體規定。收取高於最高限額的利息就是高利貸，亦即犯法。但近若干年來，這方面的規定有所放寬；Sunday closing or blue laws（禁止星期天營業的法律）的制定受宗教法的影響。

**5.** ...contracts in violation of <u>positive law</u>...

positive law（實證法），即所謂嚴格意義上的法，是直接由作爲最高政治統治者的君主或權力機構制定的，也可以由處於對君主服從地位的次級政治統治者來制定，還可以由公民個人來制定，以保護他們的合法權益。所有實證法都是直接或間接的命令。

「positive law」有時也譯爲「制定法」或「成文法」。

## Exercises

## I. Answer the following questions:

**1.** How do you define the word of capacity?

**2.** What is the exact meaning of minor?

**3.** What are the common-law rules relating to minors' contracts?

**4.** What are necessaries for minors in the eyes of American law?

**5.** What is the usual test of insanity?

**6.** What sorts of contracts are illegal according to American law?

**7.** Is there any difference between wagering contracts and contracts to shift a risk?

**8.** What is meant by unconscionable contract under the U.C.C.?

## II. Translate the following Chinese passages into English:

**1.** 根據英美法，未成年人、精神病者、酗酒者，都屬於缺乏訂約能力的人。對於他們所訂立的契約，根據不同情況，可能產生三種不同的結果：(1)具有拘束力；(2)可以撤銷；(3)無效。

**2.** 根據美國法，凡是違反實證法（positive law）、成文法和公共政策的契約均屬不法契約。不法契約是不能強制執行的。

## III. Indicate whether each of the following statements is true or false by writing "T" or "F" in the space provided:

**1.** There is on legal limit to the number of persons who can be parties to a single contract.

**2.** Contracts entered into by a minor are void.

**3.** A minor may ratify a contract at any time before s/he reaches majority age.

**4.** The contract of an insane person may be ratified by his or her legal guardian.

**5.** Under old common law a married woman had the legal capacity to contract.

_____**6**. A corporation may enter into a contract on its own behalf.

_____**7**. Illegal contracts are generally void.

_____**8**. If a tort is committed during the performance of a contract, the contract is, by definition, illegal.

# 書面形式和第三人的權利
# Writing and Rights
# of Third Parties

## Writing

*1. Statute of frauds.* Under the statute of frauds, which is in effect in every state, certain types of contracts must be in writing signed by the party to be bound by his or her authorized agent and are not enforceable unless they are evidenced by such a writing. These classes of contracts include: (1) collateral contracts, (2) contracts for the sale of an interest in real property, (3) contracts which are not capable of performance within a year after they are made, (4) contracts for the sale of goods of a value above a certain fixed amount, (5) contracts to pay a commission for the sale of real estate, and (6) contracts agreeing to pay a debt barred by the statute of limitations or discharged in bankruptcy.

*2. Collateral contracts.* A collateral contract is one made with an obligee whereby a third person promises to pay the debt, default, or miscarriage of the obligor in the event the obligor fails to perform as obligated. Whether a contract is a collateral contract or is an original contract depends primarily on the intent of the parties. In an original contract the party in question has promised to perform in all events, whereas in the collateral contract the party's performance is required only upon the default of another promisor. Some examples of collateral contracts are the promise of a father to make good a debt owed by his son in the event the son fails to satisfy it, or the promise of an executor or administrator to be answerable from her own estate for a duty of the decedent's estate. A promise to answer for the debt, default, or miscarriage of another must be in writing to be enforceable under the statute of frauds.

*3. Interests in land.* Any contract which will affect the ownership rights in real property such as contracts to sell, to mortgage, to remove minerals, or to grant easements must be in writing to be enforceable. While leases fall into this category, they normally are covered separately by statute of frauds and whether or not a writing is required will depend on the length of the lease.

*4. Contracts not to be performed within a year.* Only those executory bilateral contracts that will not be performed within a year after the making of the contract fall under the statute of frauds and must be evidenced by a writing. However, the contract must be bilateral as opposed to unilateral and it can not have yet been fully performed. And no writing is required if the contract can be performed within a year of the time the contract is made. The one year period is computed from the time the contract comes into existence and not from the time that performance of it is to begin. When a contract is made extending the time in which to perform an existing contract, the time is computed from the day the contract to extend time is entered into until the time for performance under the extended contract will be completed; if this time period is more than a year, the contract to extend the time for performance must be in writing. Where the time for performance is stated in indefinite terms such as "for life," and under existing conditions it is possible to perform the contract within a year, then no writing is required even though the contract actually takes more than one year to complete.

*5. Contracts for the sale of goods.* Contracts for the sale of goods are subject to the U.C.C., which has its own statute of frauds provisions differing in some slight respects from the general statutes of frauds. The U.C.C. provisions will be discussed later in this lesson.

*6. Other contracts subject to the statute of frauds.* In most states, a contract made with a real estate broker or salesperson to pay a commission on the sale of real estate must be evidenced by a writing to be enforceable. And, in some states, a promise to pay a debt that is either barred by the statute of limitations or that was discharged in a bankruptcy proceeding must be evidenced by a writing to be enforceable.

*7. The writing required.* Although some states require a written contract, the statute of frauds of most states provides that a "memorandum" is required. The memorandum or contract may be made at any time up until the time when the suit is filed, and in the case of a memorandum may consist of several documents which show that they should be taken together as evidence of a single contract. The memorandum or contract must include the names of the parties to the contract, contain the material terms of the contract, and describe the subject matter of the contract with reasonable certainty. In addition, it must be signed by the party against whom enforcement of the contract is to be sought or by that party's authorized agent. An oral variation of a contract which is not evidenced by a sufficient writing or memorandum is not enforceable (although the original contract would be enforceable).

*8. Failure to comply with the statute of frauds.* An oral contract which comes within the statute of frauds is not made void or voidable; rather, it is unenforceable in that a court will not aid its enforcement. A party who has performed his or her duties under an oral contract can not recover on the contract; but s/he may recover in quasi contract for the value of the benefits conferred on the other party. Part performance of an oral contract for the sale of land where one party has entered into possession and made extensive improvements to the property takes the contract out of the statute of frauds. And an oral contract, once completed, can not be rescinded on the grounds that it was not evidenced by a writing.

*9. **The statute of frauds and the sale of goods.*** Under the U.C.C., the statute of frauds does not apply to an oral contract for the sale of goods unless the price of the goods is $500 or more. If the goods are of more than this price, then the contract will not be enforceable unless it is evidenced by a memorandum sufficient to indicate that a contract of sale has been entered into by the parties and has been signed by the party against whom enforcement is sought. It is not insufficient if it omits or incorrectly states a term, but if the quantity of goods is understated the contract is not enforceable beyond the quantity of goods so stated. Under the U.C.C., if an oral contract is made between two merchants, and within a reasonable time thereafter one of the merchants sends the other a written confirmation which would be sufficient as a writing, then the confirmation binds the other party, even though s/he does not sign it, if s/he does not object to it in writing within 10 days after its receipt. Part payment or delivery of goods takes the contract out of the statute of frauds but only with respect to the goods paid for or delivered and accepted. Oral contracts for the sale of specially manufactured goods are enforceable if the goods are not suitable for sale in the ordinary course of the seller's business and if the seller has made a substantial beginning on their manufacture of commitment for their procurement prior to repudiation of the oral contract by the buyer. The statute of frauds in the U.C.C. makes contracts unenforceable, not void or voidable, if the provisions of the statute are not complied with.

*10. **The parol evidence rule.*** Under the common law parol evidence rule, oral or extrinsic evidence is not admissible in court to add to, alter, or vary the terms of a written contract. Parol evidence is admissible to prove: (1) that a written contract is illegal or void, (2) that at the time it was executed it was agreed that it would not be operative except on the occurrence of a future, uncertain event, (3) that a subsequent contract was later entered into, or (4) to clear up ambiguities in a written contract. Under contracts for the sale of goods under the U.C.C., such parol evidence is admissible to supplement or to explain a written contract but not to contradict it unless the writing states that it is the exclusive agreement in which case parol evidence can not be used to supplement or explain.

# Rights of third parties

*1. **Assignment of contracts.*** Since the promisee on a contract can not demand performance of the contract in a manner which differs in any material respect from that promised, the promisee may not assign the promisee's interest in a contract if the duties of the promisor would be changed in any material respect by the assignment. Only those contracts the performance of which can be rendered by the promisor to the assignee without materially altering or increasing the burdens of performance may be assigned. Contracts which are personal in nature may not be assigned; thus, for example, any contract calling for personal skill, judgment, or character, or a contract to support another for life, can not be assigned. On the other hand, a contract calling for the payment of money is a common example of a contract which is assignable. The duties owed under a contract may not be assigned but may be delegated if they are impersonal in nature. Even though a promisor has delegated his or her duties to someone else, s/he remains liable for their performance in the event the delegatee fails to perform.

*2. Rights of an assignee.* The assignee of a contract can obtain no greater rights in the contract than the assignor had, since an assignment is essentially a sale of the assignor's contract rights. The assignee takes the contract subject to all defenses that the promisor has against the assignor on the contract. An assignee who wishes to protect the rights s/he acquired by assignment should give notice of the assignment to the promisor on the contract. When such notice is given to the promisor, s/he then becomes liable to render performance to the assignee. Where the promisee wrongfully makes two assignments of the same right without the second assignee realizing that a prior assignment of that right had already been made, the courts may follow one of two different rules: under the so-called "American rule," the first assignee has the better right; whereas under the so-called "English rule," the assignee who first gives notice of the assignment has the better right. In most states there are statutes regulating efforts to assign future wages.

*3. Assignor's liability to assignee.* When an assignor assigns a claim for value to an assignee, s/he makes certain implied warranties: (1) that the claim is valid, (2) that the parties have capacity to contract, (3) that the claim is not void for illegality, (4) that the claim has not been discharged, and (5) that s/he has, and is passing, good title to the claim to the assignee. The assignor also warrants that any written instrument involved is valid and that s/he will do nothing to impair the value of the assignment; at the same time the assignor does not warrant the solvency of the promisor. If an assignor should make two assignments of the same claim, s/he is liable for any damages sustained by any of the assignees because of such fraud.

*4. Third-party beneficiaries.* A contract may expressly provide that performance of the contract is to be rendered to a third person who is not a party to the contract, or a third person may benefit by the performance of a contract even though the third person is not named in it. A person so benefited is known as a third-party beneficiary. Three different categories of third party beneficiaries are recognized by the law: (1) donee beneficiaries, (2) creditor beneficiaries, and (3) incidental beneficiaries. If the primary purpose of the promisee, in requesting that performance of a contract be made to a third person, is to make a gift to that third person, then the third person is a donee beneficiary. As such, the donee (as well as the promisee) may bring suit to enforce the promise in the event the promisor defaults on his or her promise. A common example of a donee beneficiary is the beneficiary of a life insurance policy.

If the performance of a promise made to a promisee will satisfy an actual or supposed legal duty owed by the promisee to the beneficiary, then the beneficiary is a creditor beneficiary. For example, A, who owes B $10, promises C that he will give him a pair of shoes if C pays B $10; in this example B is a third-party creditor beneficiary of the agreement between A and C. A creditor beneficiary may also sue in his or her own name to enforce performance of the promise by the promisor. A person is an incidental beneficiary if s/he benefits from the performance of a contract to which s/he is not a party. An incidental beneficiary has no rights in the contract and can not sue to enforce it or to recover damages for nonperformance.

## ♣ New Words

| | | |
|---|---|---|
| **1.** | statute of frauds | 詐欺法（案）；禁止詐欺法 |
| **2.** | collateral contracts | 附擔保契約；保證契約 |
| **3.** | real property | 不動產 |
| **4.** | commission *n.* | 傭金 |
| **5.** | statute of limitations | 時效法 |
| **6.** | obligee *n.* | 債權人 |
| **7.** | obligor *n.* | 義務人；債務人 |
| **8.** | default *v.* | 不履行；拖欠 |
| **9.** | miscarrage *n.* | 失敗；不按契約規定履行義務（如運送貨物等） |
| **10.** | decedent *n.* | 死者；死亡人 |
| **11.** | easement *n.* | 地役權（指為因自己土地的利益而使用他人土地的權利） |
| **12.** | lease *n. v.* | 租賃 |
| **13.** | compute *v.* | 計算 |
| **14.** | broker *n.* | 經紀人 |
| **15.** | salesperson *n.* | 售貨員；營業員 |
| **16.** | memorandum *n.* | 備忘錄；書面紀錄 |
| **17.** | variation *n.* | 變更；改變 |
| **18.** | the parol evidence rule | 證言規則 |
| **19.** | extrinsic *a.* | 外來的；外部的 |
| **20.** | assignment *n.* | 轉讓；讓與 |
| **21.** | assignee *n.* | 受讓人 |

| | |
|---|---|
| **22.** assignor *n.* | 讓與人；轉讓人 |
| **23.** assignable *a.* | 可讓與的；可轉讓的 |
| **24.** delegate *v.* | 委託他人代行；授權 |
| **25.** delegatee *n.* | 代別人履行義務的人；代債務人向第三者還債的債務人 |
| **26.** warranty *n.* | 擔保 |
| **27.** impair *v.* | 損害；妨害 |
| **28.** solvency *n.* | 有清償能力；有償付能力 |

 **New Phrases and Idiomatic Expressions**

| | | |
|---|---|---|
| **1.** | upon default of sb. | 當某人不履行時 |
| **2.** | to make good a debt | 償還債務 |
| **3.** | to satisfy a debt | 償還債務 |
| **4.** | to answer for the debt of another | 為他人償還債務 |
| **5.** | to clear up ambiguities | 澄清含糊的意思 |
| **6.** | to object to sth. | 對……進行反對 |
| **7.** | to call for | 需要；要求 |
| **8.** | to benefit from | 從……受益 |
| **9.** | to extend time for sth. | 為……延長時間 |
| **10.** | up until the time when... | 直到……什麼時候 |

**Notes**

**1.** Under the statute of frauds...

statute of frauds — statutory requirement that certain contracts be in writing to be enforceable. Most such statutes in the U.S. are patterned after the English statute enacted in 1677.

**2.** Part performance of an oral contract for the sale of land where one party has entered into possession and made extensive improvements to the property takes the contract out of the statute of frauds.

...takes the contract out of the statute of frauds: is not governed by the statute of frauds.

**3.** Three different categories of third-party beneficiaries are recognized by the law: (1)donee beneficiaries, (2)creditor beneficiaries, (3)incidental beneficiaries.

美國有些教科書認為第三種 —— 附帶受益人契約，並非真正的第三人利益的契約。

**4.** ...contracts not to be performed within one year.

1年之內不能履行的契約，是指從訂約的那天起1年內不能履行的契約，而不是指從履行契約日起1年內不能被履行的契約。

**Exercises**

## I. Answer the following questions:

**1**. What types of contracts must be in writing under American statute of frauds? What must the writing contain?

**2**. What is a collateral contract?

**3**. What is meant by parol evidence rule?

**4**. How do you define assignment?

**5**. What are the two rules followed by American court where the promisee wrongfully makes two assignments of the same right?

**6**. What is a third-party beneficiaries contract? How many types of third-party beneficiaries contracts do you know?

**7**. Does an incidental beneficiary have the right to sue to enforce the contract? Why not?

## II. Translate the following Chinese passages into English:

**1**. 根據美國詐欺法的規定，爲他人清償債務的契約、以婚姻爲對價的契約、出售不動產權益的契約、從訂約日起1年內不予履行的契約、價金超過500美元的貨物買賣契約，都必須以書面形式作爲證據。

**2**. 一般說來，契約的權利是可以讓與的。讓與契約權利的人叫讓與人，被讓與契約權利的人是受讓人。

**3**. 爲了適應商業上的需要，美國法律上對債務移轉採取比較靈活務實的態度。美國法律雖然也認爲契約的債務原則上不能轉讓，但在某些情況下允許代行債務，即允許他人替原債務人履行債務。

**4**. 美國法律認爲，只要雙方當事人在訂立契約時，有意思使第三人享受契約利益，該第三人就可以憑契約向法院提起訴訟，要求取得契約所給予的利益。

## III. Indicate whether each of the following statements is true or false by writing "T" or "F" in the space provided:

____**1**. Certain types of contracts must be in writing in order to be enforceable under the provisions of the statute of frauds.

____**2**. In a collateral contract all parties promise to perform in all events.

_____**3**. A contract which affects the ownership rights in real property must be in writing to be enforceable.

_____**4**. All executory bilateral contracts must be evidenced by a writing.

_____**5**. A promise to pay a debt that is barred by the statute of limitations falls under the statute of frauds in some states.

_____**6**. Oral variations of a written contract which is required to be in writing are enforceable.

# 第十二課
## Lesson 12

# 履行和救濟
# Performance and Remedies

## Performance

*1. Conditions.* The parties to a contract may make their duties under a contract contingent on the happening of some future, uncertain event; such a contingency is known as a condition precedent. Likewise, the parties may provide that upon the occurrence of a future, uncertain event a party will be relieved of the performance of a duty that s/he otherwise would have to perform; such a condition is known as a condition subsequent. Some contracts provide that the parties are to perform their duties simultaneously; such a provision is a concurrent condition and more often arises by implication rather than by express provision.

*2. Architects' and engineers' certificates.* Construction contracts may provide that the production of an architect's or engineer's certificate is a condition precedent to the duty to make final payment on the contract. Failure to produce the certificate will be excused only on the death or incapacitating illness of the person who is to supply the certificate or if there is a fraudulent or unjustified withholding of the certificate.

*3. Performance and breach.* The promisor may or may not perform his or her obligations pursuant to the contract. The courts recognize three stages of performance: (1) complete or satisfactory performance, (2) substantial performance, and (3) material breach. Complete or satisfactory performance is achieved when the obligation is performed to the letter or to such a degree that it is all that could reasonably be expected. Substantial performance implies an honest effort to perform but a performance less than that reasonably expected. In such a case, the promisor is entitled to the contract price less any damage sustained by the promisee as a result of the defective performance. If there is a major defect in performance, there has been a material breach, and the promisor can not recover on the contract but may be entitled to some recovery in quasi contract for benefits conferred.

*4. Time of performance.* If time is of the essence in the performance of a contract, then failure to perform within the expected time is a material breach of the contract. On the other hand, if time is not of the essence, then as long as the promisor performs within a reasonable time the performance must be accepted although the promisee may be able to recover damages for late performance.

*5. Impossibility of performance.* Performance of a contract becomes impossible and is excused on the happening of the following events: (1) death or incapacitating illness of the promisor where his or her performance is personal in nature, (2) intervening illegality of the contract, and (3) destruction of the subject matter of the contract. Death of the promisor will always terminate a contract calling for personal service. Whether illness will terminate a contract depends on the length of the contract, the type of work involved, and the seriousness and probable length of the illness. Intervening illegality occurs when a government statute or regulation makes performance of the contract illegal; it is not enough that such a statute or regulation merely makes performance more difficult or less profitable. If the subject matter of the contract is destroyed prior to performance, then performance is excused; however, the destruction must be of something essential to the contract and not merely something of utility to its performance.

Under the U.C.C., nonperformance is excused if performance was made commercially impracticable by the occurrence of a contingency, the nonoccurrence of which was a basic assumption on which the contract was made.

*6. Discharge.* A contract is discharged when all parties to it are released from their obligations; this normally occurs when the contract is completely performed. Parties may be discharged by the occurrence or nonoccurrence of conditions subsequent and precedent as well as by impossibility of performance. If the other party is guilty of a material breach, a party is discharged from any duty to perform his part of the contract.

Since a contract is created by the agreement of the parties, it may also be discharged by agreement unless the rights of third parties will be adversely affected. The discharge of one party from his or her obligations by an agreement of the parties must be supported by consideration; however, mutual promises to rescind are supported by consideration since both parties have surrendered their rights under the contract. A party may specifically or impliedly relinquish a right s/he has under a contract; such a relinquishment is known as a "waiver." To avoid being considered to have waived his rights, the party should give prompt notice whenever s/he considers the other party's performance under the contract to be defective. So-called "statutes of limitations" commonly provide that a person must bring suit on a contract within a reasonable time after the cause of action arose or be barred from bringing the suit; each state sets a specific time within which suits on contracts must be brought and commonly distinguishes between oral and written contracts as far as the time allowed to bring suit.

Under the U.C.C., reasonable notice of cancellation must be given where a contract for the sale of goods provides for successive performances over an indefinite time. An agreement dispensing with notification of cancellation is not enforceable if its operation would be unconscionable. And the U.C.C. sets up a four-year statute of limitations for bringing suit for breach of contracts for the sale of goods.

# Remedies

*1. Nature of remedies.* When one of the parties to the contract fails to perform his or her obligations under the contract and the other party thereby sustains some injury, the injured party is entitled to be put, as nearly as possible, in the same position as if the contract had been performed. This may mean that s/he is given some measure of money damages such as the value of the thing s/he expected to receive or the profit that would have been made if the contract had been fully performed. If money damages would be insufficient to put the injured party in the same position s/he would have been in had the contract been fully performed, then the party may be granted the equitable remedy of specific performance, or allowed to rescind the contract, or granted some form of injunctive relief. To enforce a judgment for money damages, the creditor may have the sheriff execute the judgment on property owned by the debtor, or the creditor may proceed to garnishee the debtor's wages pursuant to the state garnishment statute. Under some circumstances, the creditor may have the sheriff seize property of the defendant to a suit for breach of contract at the time the suit is initiated; this is known as "attachment" and insures that property will be available to satisfy any judgment obtained against the defendant. The remedies available to aggrieved parties to contracts for the sale of goods are similar to those at common law and have the same objective; that is, putting the aggrieved party in the same position as if the contract had been performed.

*2. Damages.* A number of different types of damages may be awarded for breach of a contract: (1) compensatory, (2) consequential, (3) liquidated, and (4) nominal. Compensatory damages are those damages which would usually flow directly from the breach of contract and which are designed to make good or compensate for the wrong or injury sustained. Consequential damages are those damages which do not flow directly from the breach of contract but are due to the special circumstances of the contract; for example, a farmer sustains consequential damages when he is unable to harvest his crops because the combine he ordered did not arrive within the promised time for delivery. The term "liquidated damages" refers to a specific amount designated by the parties at the time of contracting which is to be recovered by the injured party in the event of a breach of contract. Nominal damages are awarded where there has been a technical breach of the contract but no damages or losses have been sustained as a result of the breach.

In order to recover damages, the aggrieved party must prove to a reasonable degree of certainty the amount of loss and that the loss was the direct result of the breach. Lost profits are recoverable only if they can be proved to a reasonable certainty and if they were within the contemplation of the parties at the time the contract was entered into; they are not recoverable if they are speculative in nature or if the person who breached the contract could not reasonably have been expected to realize that such damages would flow from his or her breach of the contract. The injured party owes a duty to make a reasonable effort to mitigate damages — that is, to minimize the damage s/he sustains. Liquidated damages can not be recovered unless the damages anticipated are uncertain in amount or difficult to prove, the parties intended to liquidate the damages in advance, and the amount agreed on is reasonable and not so large as to be considered a penalty.

*3. Equitable remedies.* As has been indicated, courts may decree specific performance of a contract when a damage remedy would be inadequate. Specific performance is most likely to be decreed where the sale of unique items such as pieces of land, antiques, or art objects are involved and where it would be difficult to place a value on the item or to acquire a satisfactory substitute for it. Specific performance is not granted where a contract for personal services is involved or where such a decree would require prolonged and detailed supervision by the court, such as where the contract called for the construction of a building. The remedy of an injunction may be available to prevent or protect against hardship, and is commonly used as a court directive to a person threatening to breach a contract to restrain from his threatened course of action.

## New Words

| | | |
|---|---|---|
| 1. | condition *n.* | 條件 |
| 2. | condition precedent | 停止條件 |
| 3. | condition subsequent | 解除條件 |
| 4. | concurrent condition | 同時履行條件 |
| 5. | contingency *n.* | 意外事故 |
| 6. | contingent *a.* | 偶然的；意外的 |
| 7. | simultaneously *adv.* | 同時發生地 |
| 8. | architect *n.* | 建築師；設計師 |
| 9. | incapacitating illness | 使人殘廢的疾病 |
| 10. | unjustified withholding | 不正當的扣留 |
| 11. | intervening illegality | 介入的非法性 |
| 12. | utility *n.* | 有用 |
| 13. | impracticable *a.* | 不能實行的 |
| 14. | adversely *adv.* | 有害地；不利地 |
| 15. | relinquish *v.* | 放棄；交出（權利……） |
| 16. | relinquishment *n.* | 放棄；交出（權利……） |

| | |
|---|---|
| **17.** cause of action | 案由；訴訟理由；訴訟原因 |
| **18.** successive *a.* | 連續的；接連的 |
| **19.** dispense *v.* | 免除 |
| **20.** the injured party | 受損害方 |
| **21.** equitable remedy | 衡平法上的救濟 |
| **22.** specific performance | 依約履行；實際履行；具體履行 |
| **23.** injunctive relief | 禁令救濟；禁止命令 |
| **24.** garnishee *v.* | 扣押在第三者手中之債務人財產 |
| **25.** garnishment statute | 扣押在第三者手中之債務人財產的法律 |
| **26.** attachment *n.* | 扣押；查封 |
| **27.** the aggrieved party | 受損方 |
| **28.** compensatory damages | 賠償金；應予以賠償的損害賠償金 |
| **29.** consequential damages | 間接損害賠償金 |
| **30.** liquidated damages | 違約金；預先約定的損害賠償金 |
| **31.** nominal damages | 名義賠償金 |
| **32.** combine *n.* | 聯合收割打穀機 |
| **33.** mitigate *v.* | 減輕 |
| **34.** decree *v.* | 判令；發布命令 |
| **35.** unique *a.* | 獨一無二的；舉世無雙的 |
| **36.** prolonged *a.* | 延長的 |
| **37.** directive *n.* | 命令；指示 |
| **38.** delivery *n.* | 交貨 |
| **39.** penalty *n.* | 罰金；懲罰 |
| **40.** art objects | 藝術品 |
| **41.** injunction | 禁令；禁止命令 |

## 🍀 New Phrases and Idiomatic Expressions

| | |
|---|---|
| **1.** to be contingent on | 依……而定 |
| **2.** to be pursuant to | 按照 |
| **3.** to the letter | 完全地；不折不扣地 |
| **4.** as a result of | 作為……結果 |
| **5.** to be released from | 被免除……（責任） |
| **6.** to be guilty of | 犯有……什麼罪 |
| **7.** to initiate a suit | 提起訴訟 |

| 8. | to set up a four year statute of limitation | 規定4年的消滅時效 |
|----|----|----|
| 9. | to harvest one's crops | 收割莊稼 |
| 10. | to dispense with | 省卻；免除 |
| 11. | to have sb. do sth. | 讓某人做某事 |
| 12. | in the event of | 如果……發生 |
| 13. | within the contemplation of | 在……期望（或打算）之內 |
| 14. | on the other hand | 另一方面 |
| 15. | on the happening of | 在……發生時 |

 **Notes**

1. condition：條件。

在英美法中「condition」一詞有三個意思：

(1)指契約的重要條款。按照英國法的解釋，凡屬契約中的重要條款，均稱爲「條件」，如果一方當事人違反了「條件」，即違反了契約的主要條款，對方有權解除契約，並可要求賠償損失；

(2)用它來表示某種不確定的事件發生與否來決定其是否生效的契約規定。從這個意義講英美法將條件分爲同時履行條件、停止條件和解除條件；

(3)用它來表示契約中的約定事項。從這個意義上說，英美法把契約的約定事項分爲兩種：一種叫明示條件（express condition），另一種叫默示條件（implied condition）。

2. ...then the party may be granted the equitable remedy...

在英美法中的補救分兩大類：一類叫普通法救濟，其中最常見的就是損害賠償（damages）；另一類是衡平法上的救濟（equitable remedies），其中主要包括：依約履行（specific performance）、禁令（injunction）、撤銷契約（rescission）和回復原狀（restitution）。

給予救濟的目的是爲了保護受允諾人的以下利益：

(1)期待利益（expectation interest）：即契約履行後給他帶來的利益；

(2)依賴利益（reliance interest）：即對契約依賴所致損失的賠償；

(3)回復原狀利益（restitution interest）：即收回自己給予對方的好處。

3. ...or allowed to rescind the contract, or granted some form of injunctive relief, ...

這裡的「injunctive relief」，是指禁令（injunction）。

 **Exercises**

## I. Answer the following questions:

**1.** How many types of conditions do you know?

2. How many stages of performance do American courts recognize?

3. In what case will failure to perform within the expected time constitute a material breach?

4. When will performance of a contract be excused?

5. Can you give an example of intervening illegality?

6. When will a contract be considered to be discharged?

7. How many types of damages do you know?

8. What are the rules regarding recovery of liquidated damages?

9. What are the common forms of equitable damages?

10. What is injunction? In what case will it be available to the injured party?

## II. Translate the following Chinese passages into English:

1. 按英國法的解釋，凡屬契約中的重要條款均稱爲「條件」，違反條件就是違反契約主要條款，就是違約。對方有權解除契約，並可要求損害賠償。

2. 在美國契約法中，有時還將條件分成明示條件（即契約當事人明確規定的條件）和默示條件（即指依照法律或按照解釋當事人的意思理應包括在契約中的條件）。

3. 最常見的消滅契約的方式是對契約的完全履行。當然還有其他方法，如：履行不可能、雙方達成協定、停止條件或解除條件的發生。

4. 英美法對待依約履行的態度與大陸法不一樣。英美法普遍認爲，如一方當事人不履行其契約義務，對方唯一的權利是提起違約之訴，要求獲得損害賠償金。因此，普通法中沒有依約履行這種救濟方式。但是，英美的衡平法院在處理某些案件時，如果原告能證明僅僅採用損害賠償金的辦法還不足以滿足他的要求，則可以考慮判決依約履行。

## III. Indicate whether each of the following statements is true or false by writing "T" or "F" in the space provided:

1. If the duties under a contract are contingent on the happening of some future, uncertain event, such a contingency is known as a condition subsequent.

2. A promisor who substantially performs the promise is entitled to the full contract price.

3. If time is of the essence, failure to perform within the expected time is a material breach of contract.

4. Death of the promisor in a contract for personal services terminates the contract and

excuses performance.

____**5**. When a contract is completely performed it is said to be discharged and all parties to it are released from their obligations.

____**6**. Under the common law, consideration is not necessary for a binding agreement to discharge one of the parties from his or her obligations under a contract.

____**7**. The specific or implied relinquishing of rights under a contract is known as a "waiver".

____**8**. Suit on a contract can be brought at any time after the cause of action arose.

____**9**. The seizure of the property of a defendant to a suit for breach of contract is known as an "attachment".

____**10**. The amount of any "liquidated damages" for breach of contract is specified at the inception of the contract.

____**11**. Lost profits are an example of compensatory damages.

____**12**. A court would decree specific performance of a contract to paint a picture if the aggrieved promisee could not find another artist to paint it for him.

# PART III

## 商業組織
## Business Organizations

## 英國商業組織
## UK Business Organizations

**Major Types of Business Organizations**. There are four main types of business organization under United Kingdom law, namely: the sole trader; the partnership; United Kingdom incorporated company limited by shares; United Kingdom branch of an oversea company.

There are some unlimited companies in existence, but they are rarely used because their shareholders may be liable to contribute all their assets to the company to the extent that it is unable to pay its debts. A number of old trading companies incorporated by royal charter still exist, as do statutory companies formed to run public utilities such as railways. Various other forms of business organization are also common, such as unincorporated associations, friendly societies and companies limited by guarantee, which are generally formed for charitable, social, or educational purposes, and are of lesser commercial importance.

Individuals or companies may also combine in consortia, syndicates and joint ventures, which have no separate legal personality distinct from that of their members.

### 1. The sole trader

A sole trader is an individual carrying on either a business or a profession on his own account. There are no legal requirements for a sole trader to keep accounts in any particular form, apart from those records which must be kept for value added tax and other taxation purposes. Nor do the accounts of a sole trader need to be either audited or publicly disclosed.

The individual businessman or professional person in business as a sole trader is not legally distinct from the business which he manages, and is therefore the owner of all the capital employed in the business. The corollary is that a sole trader is also liable for all the losses of his business. Thus the sole trader who is providing services, other than consultancy or advisory services for which he is insured, runs the risk of losing all his private capital in the business.

### 2. Partnership

There are two types of partnerships recognized by United Kingdom law, both governed principally by statute: a partnership in the ordinary sense of the word, which is governed by the Partnership Act 1890, and a limited partnership, which may be formed under the Limited Partnership Act 1907.

Certain professions, such as solicitors and accountants, have historically been prevented by law from being incorporated and must carry on business in partnership so that the public may rely on the unlimited liability of each of the partners for the firm's debts. Such professions are therefore exempt from the statutory prohibition on the formation of business associations consisting of more than 20 members. The law is however in the process of changing and it is likely that in future all professions will be able to practice through a limited company, although many may be reluctant to do so in view of the obligation to publish accounts.

*(1) Ordinary partnership*

A partnership comes into existence automatically without the need for any formalities, where two or more individuals or corporate bodies carry on business in common with a view to making a profit. In the absence of an express partnership agreement, the rights and duties of the partners are governed by the Partnership Act 1890, which refers to a partnership as a "firm".

The key legal consequence of the formation of a partnership is that the partners are personally liable, both jointly with their partners and individually, for the liabilities of the firm as a whole. A partnership is not a legal entity under English law separate from the identity of each of its constituent partners, though in Scotland a firm is a legal person distinct from the partners. However even a Scottish partner can be compelled to pay the firm's debts.

The liability of each partner is unlimited, each partner being an agent of the other partners with the authority to make contracts, undertake obligations and dispose of partnership property in the ordinary course of the business on behalf of the firm as a whole.

The Partnership Act 1890 regulates the relationship of the partners except to the extent that there is contrary agreement, which is why it is unusual for large partnerships to practice other than pursuant to a partnership deed, partnership agreement or set of partnership articles governing the division of capital, property, profits, management and providing for the distribution of assets on winding up. However the existence of such an express agreement does not affect the rights of third parties in their dealings with the firm, but merely governs the dealings of the partners as among themselves. There are also statutory provisions governing the use of firm names and publicity as to the names of individual partners both on the firm's stationery and at the firm's premises.

*(2) Limited partnership*

A limited partnership may be formed under and must be registered under the Limited Partnership Act 1907. The expression "limited partnership" is misleading, in that the liability of the firm to its creditors is unlimited, and it is simply the liability of some (but not all) of the partners which is limited. There must be at least one general partner who bears unlimited liability for the debts of the firm in the same way as any partner in an ordinary partnership. Some of the benefits of may be obtained by making the general partner a limited liability company, but even so limited partnerships are relatively rare in the United Kingdom.

In order to obtain limited liability for some of its members the limited partnership must be registered at the Companies Registry. Such registered particulars must include: the name; the general nature of the business; the principal place of business; the full name of each partner; the term (if any) of the partnership; the date of its commencement; a statement that the partnership is limited; and a description of every limited partner as such.

They must also specify the sum contributed by each limited partner and state whether it is in cash or otherwise. Failure to register means that the partnership will be considered to be an ordinary partnership and each limited partner will therefore be liable for all the debts and obligations of the firm.

A limited partner has no power to bind the firm and may not take part in the management of the business, on penalty of losing the benefits of limited liability. A limited partner may also be at risk if he directly or indirectly draws out or receives back any part of his contribution, in which case he becomes liable to third parties up to the amount so drawn out or received back. A limited partnership structure is normally selected for tax reasons.

### 3. Companies

*(1) Statutes governing corporation*

The main body of the law on public and private companies limited by shares is contained in the Companies Act 1985, as amended by the Companies Act 1989, which is now largely in force and was enacted partly in response to European Union legislation. The other two main statutes governing the activities of corporations are the Insolvency Act 1986, which covers both voluntary and compulsory liquidations, and the Financial Services Act 1986, which governs the conduct of investment business in the United Kingdom and provides a framework of investor protection. There are also numerous statutory instruments governing such areas as disclosure of interests in shares, the content of investment advertisements, the official listing of securities, merger pre-notification regulations, etc. While the law governing corporations is mainly statute-based, there is also a substantial body of case law in which the courts have interpreted and supplemented the relevant statutes.

*(2) Main forms of UK companies*

*Public limited company (PLC)*

A Public Limited Company is not necessarily a publicly quoted company, as there are certain public companies whose shares are not listed on the London Stock Exchange. However, a company whose ordinary shares are quoted on the Stock Exchange will invariably be a public company. A company may not be registered as a public company unless the Registrar of Companies is satisfied that the nominal value of the company's allotted share capital is not less than £50,000, or such other minimum sum as may be specified by statutory instrument. A public company must have at least two shareholders. Public companies are subject to stricter requirements than private companies on: ①payment and maintenance of capital; ② distribution of dividends; ③loans to directors and to persons connected with them; ④content and publication of accounts; ⑤purchase and redemption of their own shares; ⑥disclosure of interests in shares; and ⑦the granting of financial assistance for the acquisition of their shares.

The memorandum of a public company must state that it is to be a public company.

*Private company limited by shares (limited)*

A private company is any company registered under the Companies Act which is not a public company, the key difference being that it is an offence for a private company limited by shares to offer to the public (whether for cash or otherwise) any shares in or debentures of the company. There is no single definition in English law of what constitutes "the public", but there is some statutory guidance to the effect that an offer or invitation shall not be treated as made "to the public" if it not likely to result, directly or indirectly, in the shares or debentures becoming available for subscription of purchase by persons other than those receiving the offer or invitation. Further, the existing shareholders and employees of a company, together with the family members of such shareholders and employees, or an existing lender to the company, are not treated as constituting "the public".

*(3) Incorporation*

*The memorandum of association*

The Memorandum establishes the basis of a company's existence, setting out the fundamental provisions required by statute for the incorporation and continued operation of the company. The regulations governing the way in which the company's objects may be achieved, and the conduct of the internal management and affairs of the company, are set out in the Articles of Association .The Memorandum prevails over the Articles and may only be altered in limited circumstances.

The Memorandum must state: ①the name of the company, which must end with the *word limited* (or the Welsh equivalent) or an abbreviation thereof in the case of a private company, and with the words "public limited company" (or the Welsh equivalent) or an abbreviation thereof in the case of a public company; ②whether the registered office is to be situated in England and Wales, or in Scotland; ③the objects of the company; ④that the liability of its shareholders is limited; ⑤in the case of a company having a share capital, the amount of the share capital with which the company proposes to be registered and the division of that share capital into shares of a fixed amount.

The Memorandum of a public company must also state that the company is to be a public company. No subscriber of the Memorandum may take less than one share, and the number of shares taken must be shown opposite the name of each subscriber.

The single most important statutory particular required to be registered in the Memorandum used to be the "objects clause", which defines the nature and extent of the business which the company may transact, because a company may not do anything which is not expressly or impliedly authorised by the objects set out in the Memorandum. Therefore, in addition to the "main object" of the company, it is customary to add some 20 or 30 specific objects subsidiary to the main object, such as the power to invest or lend, and to do anything else which may be conducive to the attainment of the main object.

However, it has recently become possible for a company to be incorporated with an object to carry on business as a "general commercial company". Such a company has very wide statutory powers.

There is statutory protection for third parties who deal with a company in good faith, though the directors may be liable for acts which are *ultra vires* of the powers contained in the memorandum.

The Memorandum must be delivered to the Registrar of Companies for England and Wales (if the Memorandum states that the registered office is to be located in England and Wales) of the Registrar of Companies for Scotland (if it states that the registered of fice is to be situated in Scotland). The Memorandum so delivered must be subscribed by at least two persons (or only one in the case of a private company), who must each take at least one share. "Subscription" means the signing of the Memorandum by each subscriber in the presence of at least one witness who must attest the signature. The Memorandum may be subscribed by any individual or corporate body, and there is no prohibition on all or any of the subscribers being foreigners. There must also be delivered to the Registrar a statement of the identity of the first directors and secretary of the Company.

*The articles of association*

A company's management and administrative structure are set out in the Articles, which constitute a contract between each shareholder and the company. The Articles must be printed, divided into consecutively numbered paragraphs and, in the case of Articles registered on incorporation, must be signed by each subscriber. The formalities of subscribing the Articles are substantially the same as those relating to the Memorandum. Guidance on the content of the Articles is provided in the form of model regulations for limited companies, both public and private, known as Table A. A company may adopt as its Articles all or any of the regulations set out in Table A. However, it is common for a company to adopt Table A with modifications and exclusions.

The extent to which a company disapplies or varies Table A will depend, subject to the greater statutory constraints imposed on public companies, on the circumstances and wishes of the shareholders. Public limited companies quoted on the London Stock Exchange tend to disapply the whole of Table A and adopt long-form Articles, some provisions of which reproduce Table A and others are specially drafted. It is also common to adopt long-form Articles where the company is a United Kingdom subsidiary of a foreign corporation or a company with many non-resident shareholders, who find it more convenient to have the Articles set out in a single document rather than have to cross-refer to Table A. Subsidiaries of group companies will often have extended short-form articles enabling consistency of administration by the parent.

The Articles will regulate the following principal areas: ①share capital, and the rights and liabilities attaching to the shares; ②alteration of share capital, issue, transfer and transmission of shares; ③conduct of shareholders' meetings and exercise of voting rights; ④appointment and removal of directors; ⑤conduct of meetings of directors, exercise of their powers and their remuneration, expenses and other interests; ⑥general administrative and financial provisions for the keeping of minutes, notices, distribution of assets on winding up, declaration and payment of dividends, treatment of reserves and capitalisation of profits.

*Registered office*

The Memorandum must state whether the registered office is to be situated in England and Wales or in Scotland, or only in Wales. If it is to be only in Wales, the company may take advantage of the Welsh language provisions of the Companies Act. The part of Great Britain stated in the Memorandum to be the site of the registered office is important, as it dictates the place of jurisdiction. A company may not elect to move its registered office to another part of Great Britain, say from England and Wales to Scotland, as this would involve a change in the domicile of the company. However, it is possible for a company with its registered office in England and Wales to change its address to anywhere else within England and Wales.

Every company is required at all times to have a registered office to which all communications and notices may be addressed. It is a company's duty to keep at its registered office, of make available for public inspection there, any register, index or other document of the company. It is also its duty to mention the address of its registered office in any document, and to display legibly, on all business letters and order forms, the place of registration and the company number.

*Company name*

The name of a company, which must be stated in its Memorandum, must end in the case of a private company with the word "limited", or, in the case of a public company, the words "public limited company". If the registered office of the company is to be in Wales, the Welsh equivalents may be used, "cyfyngedig" and "cwmni cyfyngedig cyhoeddus". The statutory suffixes may be abbreviated by using the abbreviations "Ltd" and "PLC" or their Welsh equivalents "cyf" and "ccc".

There are a number of statutory restrictions on the use of certain words and expressions in business names generally without the consent of a named government department of professional body. Restricted names are generally those which may import a connection with the Crown, with a profession or with a particular trade or may otherwise be misleading, such as apothecary, assurance, chartered, English, European, international, royal or trust. Also, a name will not be accepted for registration if it is the same as one already appearing in the index kept by the Registrar of Companies. A company may also be required to change its name within 12 months of registration on the ground that its name is too similar to that of an existing company name. Nor will a name be accepted for registration if it is offensive or its use would constitute a criminal offence. There are further important restrictions on the use of either the company name or the business name of a company which has gone into insolvent liquidation.

*Duration*

Companies are normally set up for an unlimited period, although it is possible to provide in the Articles that the duration of the company will be for a limited period or that the company is to be dissolved on the occurrence of a particular event.

*(4) Shares*

The rights which a shareholder enjoys under the Memorandum and Articles determine the precise nature of the share itself. Different classes of shares may have different rights as to dividends, participation in surplus assets and voting. Shares are required to have a nominal or par value. Except for public company shares, shares may remain nil paid, partly paid or fully paid. However, where the shares are not fully paid up there remains an underlying liability on the part of the shareholder to pay up the nominal amount in the event of a call or on a winding up. Multi-currency share capital is lawful. A company may also, if it has the authority to do so in its Articles, issue a share warrant in respect of any fully paid shares.

It is almost impossible to classify every type of share in a company, but the most common classes of share, which are often used in combination, are: ①ordinary shares; ②preference shares; ③non-voting shares; ④redeemable shares; ⑤convertible shares; ⑥deferred shares.

It must be stated in the Articles how the various classes rank for any distribution by way of dividend or otherwise, and there are statutory restrictions on the variation of class rights.

*Share capital*

The share capital of a company must be stated in the Memorandum, but may be increased or reduced by following certain strict statutory procedures. The current minimum capital for a public company is £50,000 (of which £12,500 must be fully paid up), while there is no minimum for private companies.

*Transfer of shares*

The position at present is that the transfer of the legal title to shares can only be effected by means of a proper instrument of transfer known as a stock transfer form. This requirement may not be waived by anything to the contrary in the Articles, but does not apply to the transmission of shares on death or bankruptcy. The requirement for an instrument of transfer means that stamp duty must be paid on the value of shares transferred by the stock transfer form. This duty, currently at 0.5 percent of the price for the shares, is due to be abolished with the forthcoming dematerialisation of transactions on the Stock Exchange, whereby it will be possible to transfer shares held on a recognised computer system without the need for transfer forms or share certificates. Until the new system is implemented, a person to whom shares are transferred may not be registered as a shareholder until the instrument of transfer has been duly stamped with the requisite duty.

The Articles commonly provide that the directors may refuse to register the transfer of shares which are only partly paid or for other reasons, such as if the transfer form is not accompanied by the relevant share certificate or other evidence of title to the shares. A share certificate is *prima facie* evidence of the title of a shareholder to his shares. Share warrants however are negotiable instruments transferable by delivery.

The Articles of private companies often contain intricate preemption provisions designed to prevent control of the company passing out of the hands of a few founding or family shareholders, but public companies listed on the Stock Exchange are not permitted to impose restrictions on the transfer of their shares, as they would reduce marketability. If the Articles set out any pre-emption provisions on transfer, such provisions must be substantially complied with before a sale of the shares can be made to an outsider. Pre-emption provisions commonly require share valuations to be carried out by the auditors of the company in circumstances where the price is not agreed.

*Increase/reduction of capital*

**Increase.** The power for a company to alter its share capital must first of all be contained in the Articles. Provided a company has such a constitutional power, it then has a statutory power to increase its authorized share capital by such amount as it thinks fit. This statutory power must be exercised by the company in general meeting, and the Articles may provide either for majority voting or for 75 percent of votes in favour. A company may also consolidate and subdivide its share capital, convert shares into stock and cancel unissued shares.

The Articles may grant the directors the power to issue the newly created or any unissued shares, but this power is restricted by statute: whether the authority is given by the Articles or by a general meeting, it must state the maximum amount of shares which the directors may issue and the date when the authority will expire. The maximum period of the authority is generally five years, though this restriction can be waived for private companies.

There are also detailed legislative provisions restricting the issue of the new shares, so that a company may not issue the shares for cash without offering them first to its existing shareholders pro rata with their shareholdings. These statutory pre-emption rights may be excluded or varied by private companies. Any company whether public or private may also disapply the pre-emption rights provided that the directors have been given the requisite authority to issue shares and certain other stringent conditions have been met.

***Reduction of capital.*** There is under United Kingdom law a general prohibition on a reduction of capital. The corollary to the rule that capital must be maintained is that dividends may only be paid out of profits and that capital may only be returned to shareholders with the approval of the court or where the company redeems or purchases its own shares. Moreover if the net assets of a public company fall below 50 percent of its called up share capital, the directors must convene an extraordinary general meeting.

*Form of subscription*

Except in wholly exceptional cases, shares may not be issued at a discount. Where a company issues shares at a premium, whether for cash or otherwise, a sum equal to the aggregate amount or value of the premium must be transferred to a share premium account, which must be maintained in the same way as capital. In the case of a public company, one quarter of the nominal value of the shares plus the whole of any premium must be paid up before the shares are allotted.

The shares of a private company may be paid up in money or money's worth, including goodwill and know-how, but payment for public company shares otherwise than for cash must generally be supported by an expert's report in accordance with statutory rules.

*Purchase of own shares*

Both public and private companies are generally able, subject to statutory procedural requirements, to purchase their own shares, including any redeemable shares. The conditions for such a purchase include:

(i) the purchase monies may only be found out of distributable profits or the proceeds of a fresh issue of shares (with a limited exception in favour of private companies);

(ii) once purchased, the shares must be treated as cancelled and the issued share capital of the company reduced by their nominal amount;

(iii) following the purchase, there must be at least one shareholder who holds non-redeemable shares.

*Register of shareholders*

The register of shareholders is considered to be of fundamental importance as giving publicity to the identity of the shareholders and the extent of their liability, though shareholders are often nominees. The following information must be entered on the register:

(i) the names and addresses of shareholders;

(ii) a statement of the number and class of the shares held;

(iii) the amount paid up on the shares;

(iv) the date of entry on the register;

(v) the date of cessation of shareholding.

The register must be readily available, being kept either at the company's registered office or at some other publicised place. It must also be available for inspection during business hours by any shareholder, free of charge, and by any other person for a nominal fee.

*(5) The board of directors*

*Definition of a director*

There is no true definition of the term "director", although statute provides that a director includes any person occupying the position of the director, by whatever name called. A director is an officer of the company (but not necessarily an employee) and may be executive or non-executive, full or part-time.

A formal appointment to the Board is not necessary for a person to become a "director", and there is an important concept in English law of a "shadow director", defined as "any person in accordance with whose directions or instructions the directors of a company are accustomed to act". The existence of such a relationship is a question of fact rather than law. A person giving advice to the Board in a professional capacity is not however regarded as a shadow director merely because that advice is acted on. A number of statutory provisions affecting directors also apply to shadow directors.

*Appointment/dismissal of directors*

Although there is no maximum number of directors, a public company must have at least two directors, and a private company may have a sole director only if such a sole director is not also the secretary of the company.

The first directors are appointed by the subscribers to the Memorandum. The appointment of subsequent directors is primarily determined by the Articles, which usually confer the power of appointment both on the directors and on the company in general meeting. Table A provides that a third of all the directors shall retire by rotation at successive AGMs, at which they are then eligible for reappointment by the shareholders. It is usually specified however that a managing director or other director holding executive office shall not be subject to retirement by rotation.

Directors may resign from office at any time, and directors of public companies must retire at the age of 70 unless the continuance of their appointment is approved by a resolution in general meeting. It is also usual to provide in the Articles that directors shall be required to vacate their office on the occurrence of certain events, such as becoming a mental patient or being absent without leave for more than a certain period of time, or if they have been disqualified under the Company Directors Disqualification Act 1986.

Notwithstanding anything to the contrary in the Articles or in a separate contract between the company and a director, the company may remove a director by ordinary resolution (requiring over 50 percent of votes in favour) provided that special notice of 28 days has been given of such removal and certain other statutory procedures are followed. The board of directors also commonly has the power to remove one of their number from office, either by simple majority or by qualified majority set out in the Articles.

*Duties/powers of the board of directors*

The management of a company is usually delegated to its directors by the Articles, and the directors may exercise all the powers of the company through resolutions passed at duly convened board meetings. In practice, the day-to-day decision making is delegated to executive or managing directors or to committees of directors under empowering provisions in the Articles.

The relationship between a company and its directors is partly that of principal and agent. The directors are also trustees of the company's assets. The general role of the directors is to manage the business of the company for the benefit of the shareholders. For this reason, the directors have the power to bind the company.

When exercising his powers, a director must act not only in good faith and with honesty but also in the best interests of the company. He must not use company property or information gained in the course of his duties for his own personal gain. A director acting honestly and with reasonable care will usually be held to have performed his duty if he believed on reasonable grounds that the transaction he approved was for the benefit of the company. However, even this will not be sufficient if for example: ①the transaction is outside the scope of the company's objects or an abuse of the powers given to the directors; ②a personal profit was made by the director, even if the company also benefited; or③the director did not declare his interest in the transaction.

Certain conflicts of interest and duty may arise because of restrictions in company law.

The directors' duties are prescribed by both common law and statute. In common law, a director must exercise reasonable skill and care in carrying out his duties, must consider the position and interests of creditors if the company is insolvent, and must have regard to the interests of the company's employees in general as well as the interests of the company. Directors also owe a duty to the company's shareholders collectively rather than individually. Shareholders have important statutory rights to apply to the court on the ground that the company's affairs are being or have been conducted in a manner which is unfairly prejudicial to the interests of some or all of the shareholders.

In addition to these common law duties, the directors are responsible for the performance of the duties imposed by statute and non-compliance with any of these may give rise to a fine or to disqualification and even imprisonment if the default is serious or persistent. Their statutory duties are to maintain proper accounting and value added tax records, to ensure that the annual accounts are prepared in accordance with Companies Act requirements, and to maintain the various statutory books which must be kept at the company's registered office, *i.e.* the register of members, the register of directors and secretaries, the register of mortgages and charges, the register of debenture holders and the register of directors' interests, all of which must be open to public inspection.

The directors are also responsible for ensuring that the company complies with relevant legislation such as that relating to employees, health and safety at work and environmental protection.

*Board meetings*

Directors must ensure that the board meets sufficiently frequently to enable it to discharge its duties properly. Adequate notice should be given to allow the attendance of all directors and relevant papers should be circulated in advance. Minutes must be kept of all board meetings recording the names of the directors present, the decisions reached and the views expressed. The Articles usually prescribe such matters as period of notice, quorum, voting, chairman's casting vote, etc.

*Legal liability of directors*

The personal liabilities which can be imposed on directors for both civil and criminal offences are potentially very great and may arise in the following circumstances.

***Abuse of powers***. Directors must not act outside the objects of the company as set out in its Memorandum and must use the powers given to them only for their proper purpose, or else they may incur personal liability unless relieved by special resolution of the shareholders.

*Breach of duties.*  If a director is in breach of any of the duties imposed on him, he may be personally liable to pay to the company any profit he has made and/or reimburse the company for any loss suffered as a result of such breach. Relief is however available to any director who, although in breach of a non-statutory duty, has acted honestly and reasonably.

*Liabilities to shareholders.*  Directors may also be personally liable to the shareholders. Under criminal legislation, the directors are guilty as officers of the company of a criminal offence if they publish an account of the company's affairs with intent to deceive the shareholders or creditors and knowing that it is or may be false, misleading or deceptive. In addition, directors may be personally liable if a person suffers loss as a result of the directors knowingly permitting a contravention of any of the pre-emption rights on transfer of the existing shareholders.

*Liabilities to investors.*  Directors may incur liability for deceit or fraudulent misrepresentation, at common law in relation to dealings in the securities of a company, and under the Financial Services Act 1986 which requires prior authorisations to be obtained before any investment business (including offers and disposals of securities) may be lawfully conducted.

*Directors' transactions with the company*

In order to avoid any conflict of interest between the directors and the company, there is a wide range of statutory restrictions on directors, the principal ones being as follows:

*Loans.*  Subject to certain exceptions a company is prohibited from making loans to or providing guarantees for a director or a director of its parent company, or from making quasi-loans or providing credit to such directors, and to persons connected with them. A director receiving an unlawful loan is liable to account to the company for any gain made and to indemnify the company against any loss suffered as a result.

*Contracts of service.*  Broadly speaking, unless authorised by the shareholders in advance in general meeting, directors' contracts must not exceed five years and a register of contracts must be kept for inspection by the shareholders at any time.

*Substantial property transactions.*  Substantial property transactions by the company involving a director or connected persons must be first approved by the company in general meeting. Substantial property transactions include those in which the director or connected person buys from or sells an asset to the company the value of which exceeds a set amount.

*Interest in contracts.*  A director must disclose to the board any interest he may have, directly or indirectly, in a company contract. If the interest is material, it must also be disclosed in the accounts.

*Insider dealing.*  It is a criminal offence for a director of a listed company to deal in the securities of the company on the basis of unpublished price-sensitive information or to pass such information to a third party, if the director knows or has reason to believe that such third party may deal in the securities.

***Interests in shares or debentures.*** Directors have a duty to notify the company of any interests they and certain connected persons may have in its shares or debentures. Interests are defined to both beneficial and non-beneficial holdings and share options and similar rights.

*General meetings*

Meetings or shareholders fall into two categories: Annual General Meetings (AGMs) and Extraordinary General Meetings (EGMs). The rules governing the conduct of AGMs and EGMs are largely the same, though the length of the notice which must be given varies. All members may attend and vote at general meetings, unless they only hold shares of a particular class with no rights to attend. Meetings of debenture holders and creditors are often regulated in a similar way.

With some exceptions in favour of private companies, every company must hold an AGM in each calendar year and meetings must not be more than 15 months apart. The Articles may provide what business must be conducted at an AGM, but it is usual for AGMs to conduct only "ordinary business", meaning the declaration of dividends, consideration of the accounts, the election of directors who are required to retire by rotation, and the appointment and remuneration of auditors. Private companies may elect to dispense with the holding of AGMs. Any meeting which is not an AGM is an EGM. EGMs are held as and when necessary.

***The convening of meetings.*** If a company fails to hold an AGM when required, any shareholder may apply to the Department of Trade, which may then call an AGM and order that one person shall constitute a quorum for the meeting. Shareholders who are registered holders of not less than one tenth of such of the paid up capital as carries the right of voting at general meetings may requisition the holding of an EGM. Following such notice, the directors must then call a meeting for a date not later than 28 days following the notice. There is also a separate power for two or more members holding not less than one-tenth of the issued share capital (*i.e.* not necessarily the paid up capital) to call a meeting themselves, subject to proper notice. Shareholders with five percent or more of the voting rights may also insist that a particular resolution be included in the agenda of the next AGM, subject to notice.

The directors usually have the power under the Articles to decide when to call the AGM and to call an EGM at any time and the vast majority of meetings will be called in this way.

***Ordinary, special, extraordinary and elective resolutions.*** A company in general meeting may only transact business by passing the appropriate type of resolution. An ordinary resolution is one requiring a simple majority of votes in favour, in other words more votes in favour than against. An extraordinary resolution and a special resolution both require a three-quarters majority in favour for them to be passed.

The difference between an extraordinary resolution and a special resolution is that a special resolution requires 21 days' notice even if it is to be considered at an EGM, whereas an extraordinary resolution only requires the same length of notice as the meeting at which it is to be considered.

Statute generally requires a special resolution where minority shareholders might need protection, such as to alter the Articles or objects, or to exclude pre-emption rights.

Private companies have recently been given the power, by passing an elective resolution at a general meeting, to dispense with certain company law requirements. Under this elective regime, private companies may dispense with the holding of AGMs and with the annual laying of accounts and reports.

Private companies may also pass written resolutions to take certain decisions, which must be signed by all the share-holders，instead of having to hold formal meetings. Written resolutions may not be used to remove a director or an auditor from office.

***Notice of meetings.*** Business at a meeting cannot be properly transacted unless proper notice has been given of the meeting to every member required to be given notice under the Articles. This usually means all the members, although some Articles provide that shareholders with no registered address in the United Kingdom are not entitled to notice.

For an AGM, 21 days' notice is required. For an EGM, 14day's notice is required unless a special resolution or an elective resolution is to be proposed, in which case the period is 21 days. If all the shareholders agree to short notice, an AGM may be held without 21 days' notice. A majority in number owning at least 95 percent (or not less than 90 percent in the case of a private company which has so elected) of the voting shares may agree to shorter notice of an EGM.

Notices must specify the date, time and place of the meeting and describe the business to be considered in sufficient detail for shareholders to decide whether they wish to attend.

Certain resolutions, such as a shareholders' resolution to remove a director must be set out verbatim in the notice and require 28 days' notice, called "special notice".

Shareholders must also be informed in the notice of their right to appoint proxies.

***Duties/powers of meetings.*** A meeting cannot validly consider the business in hand unless a quorum is present. Without a provision to the contrary in the Articles two members personally present would constitute a quorum. Amendments may be proposed but only within the scope of the notice, which means that no amendment of substance is permitted to special, elective or extraordinary resolutions, and amendments to ordinary resolutions are limited. Proxies may speak at meetings of a private company in the same way as shareholders themselves.

Voting on resolutions may be decided on a show of hands, where each member personally present has one vote (regardless of the number of shares held) and proxies are not entitled to vote unless empowered to do so by the Articles. However, any five voting shareholders, or any shareholders with ten percent of the voting rights, or any shareholder with ten percent of the paid up voting capital, is entitled to demand a poll. Proxies have the same right to call for a poll as the shareholders whom they represent. On a poll, votes are counted according to the number of voting rights rather than the number of shareholders.

Minutes must be kept of all decisions taken at general meetings and remain available for inspection by shareholders at the registered office. Further, copies of certain resolutions must be sent to the Registrar of Companies within 15 days of being passed.

### 4. United Kingdom branch of an oversea company

An oversea company is any company incorporated outside Great Britain which establishes a "place of business" in Great Britain. A place of business is one which has some degree of permanence and consists of office premises of the company, rather than merely the presence of agents or sales representatives. Oversea companies must comply with certain provisions of company law within one month of establishment, which require them to deliver to the Registrar of Companies: (1) a certified copy of their articles of association or bylaws duly certified as true copies by an official of the Government of the country where the company is incorporated, or by a notary public, or under oath by anyone empowered to administer oaths; (2) a list of the directors and secretary, detailing their names, surnames, residential addresses, nationality, business occupation and directorships, together with the name of the secretary; (3) the names and addresses of one or more United Kingdom residents authorised to accept, on behalf of the company, service of any notice to be served on the company; (4) a formal notice of the balance sheet date; (5) the date of establishment.

The Registrar of Companies must also receive notice within 21 days of any change in the registered particulars. An oversea company may be refused permission to use its corporate name for trading in the United Kingdom.

Oversea companies are required to submit to the Registrar of Companies copies of their annual accounts, including group accounts, within 13 months of the end of their accounting period. The accounts so submitted must generally comply with United Kingdom company law, with certain exceptions.

An oversea company must display its name, the name of the country in which it is incorporated, and a statement that its liability is limited, at every place of business in the United Kingdom and on all invoices and letterheads and all publications of the company.

Certain charges over the United Kingdom assets of oversea companies need to be registered with the Registrar of Companies.

### 5. Audit/accounts

*Duties and powers of auditors*

United Kingdom company law requires that a company's accounts be examined and reported on by an independent, appropriately qualified person who must say whether such accounts comply with detailed statutory requirements and give a "true and fair view" of the company's affairs and results. United Kingdom company law has recently been substantially modified to reflect the former EC Eighth Company Law Directive.

For each financial year, the directors must prepare a profit and loss account and balance sheet (and group accounts where appropriate) and it is the duty of the auditors during their tenure of office to report to the shareholders on these accounts. However it must be emphasised that it is not the auditors who are responsible for preparing the accounts. This is the responsibility of the directors alone. The auditors are required to report on compliance with statutory requirements and whether the accounts show a true and fair view of the state of the company and its affairs. If they are not satisfied that this is the case, and the failure is material to the understanding of the accounts, they must qualify their report.

Apart from their responsibility to report on the accounts, the auditors are required to make reports in several other situations, such as when a public company allots shares otherwise than for cash, or a private company redeems or purchases its shares out of capital.

The auditors are entitled to receive all notices and other communications relating to general meetings which a shareholder is entitled to receive and to attend and be heard at any general meeting on any part of the business which concerns them as auditors, notably when a resolution for their removal is proposed.

Auditors may be held liable for their acts or omissions, either to the company in tort where they have been negligent in carrying out their duties or for breach of contract under the terms of their engagement by the company. Auditors will only be liable if they have failed to apply the proper standard of care in carrying out their duties and if they owed such a duty of care in the first place. A company and its shareholders may be owed a duty of care by the auditors in contract, by statute or in tort, but the position of third parties is quite different. It has recently been held that auditors do not owe a duty of care to protect the interests of potential investors, as distinct from existing shareholders.

It is currently proposed by regulatory bodies that the duties of auditors in relation to fraud and mismanagement be extended in the light of recent company failures. This may include making a judgment on a company's prospects for the ensuing financial year as well as actively reviewing management controls.

*Appointment/dismissal of auditors*

A specific resolution appointing or reappointing the auditors must be passed at every AGM for all public companies and for many private companies. Such resolution must provide that an auditor's term of office runs from the conclusion of the general meeting at which the accounts are laid until the conclusion of the next. The first auditors may be appointed by the directors at any time before the first AGM. The directors may, or the company may in general meeting, fill any subsequent vacancy. Where a general meeting is called to fill a casual vacancy, or to reappoint an auditor, or to appoint someone other than a retiring auditor, special notice of 28 days is required to be given to the company. Special notice must always be given for a resolution removing an auditor before the expiry of his term of office. An auditor can be removed by ordinary resolution of the company not withstanding any agreement to the contrary between the auditor and the company.

*Confidentiality*

The auditors are engaged by the shareholders and report to them. They are not empowered to disclose any information relating to the company's affairs without the company's permission, and their audit files are confidential. Audit files are however the property of the auditors and not of the company.

Auditors do not currently have a duty or the power to report to any third party on any aspect of a company's affairs without the authorisation of the company. There is not therefore any "public duty" to report irregularities to any legal, fiscal or other authority. However the proposed changes to auditors' duties mentioned above may impose such a duty to some extent in the future.

## 6. Costs of incorporation

The major expenses incurred in forming a private or a public company consist of a fee of £50, which must be sent to the Registrar of Companies on incorporation together with the Memorandum and Articles, the statement of first directors and secretary and intended situation of registered office, and the statutory declaration of compliance with requirements on application for registration. The fee for the oath will be £3.50. A further fee of £50 will usually be payable for a change of name of the company if a "ready made" company bought off the shelf is to be used. In addition to these costs there will be the legal costs incurred in the formation of the company. Clearly these will largely depend on the complexity of the shareholders' rights contained in the Articles of Association, and increasingly commonly in a Shareholders' Agreement, which will include specific protection for minority shareholders in respect of the day-to-day running of the company.

## 🍀 New Words

| | | |
|---|---|---|
| **1.** | incorporate *v.* | 使組成公司 |
| **2.** | unlimited companies | 無限公司 |
| **3.** | shareholders *n.* | 股東 |
| **4.** | royal charter | 皇家特許狀 |
| **5.** | unincorporated associations | 未組成公司的合夥或社團 |
| **6.** | consortia *n.* | （複）國際財團；聯合企業，（單）consortium |
| **7.** | syndicates *n.* | 企業聯合組織；財團 |
| **8.** | legal personality | 法律人格 |
| **9.** | sole trader | 獨家貿易商；個人營業者 |
| **10.** | corollary *n.* | 必然的結果 |
| **11.** | partnership articles | 合夥章程 |
| **12.** | general partner | 普通合夥人 |
| **13.** | the Companies Registry | 公司註冊處 |
| **14.** | premises *n.* | 房屋 |
| **15** | commencement *n.* | 開始；開端 |
| **16.** | the Registrar of Companies | 公司註冊員 |
| **17.** | redemption *n.* | 贖回；買回 |
| **18.** | subscription *n.* | 簽署；同意；認購 |
| **19.** | the Memorandum of Association | 公司章程；組織大綱 |
| **20.** | the Articles of Association | 公司辦事細則；內部細則 |
| **21.** | statutory powers | 法律規定的權力 |
| **22.** | ultra vires | 越權 |
| **23.** | attest *v.* | 證實 |
| **24.** | disapply *v.* | 不實施；不適用 |
| **25.** | the domicile of the company | 公司的住所（戶籍） |
| **26.** | legibly *adv.* | 字跡清楚地；可讀地 |
| **27.** | the Crown | 英王室 |
| **28.** | nominal or par value | 名義或票面價值 |
| **29.** | dissolve *v.* | 解散 |
| **30.** | a call | 催繳股款 |

| | | |
|---|---|---|
| **31.** shares *n.* | 股票 | |
| ordinary shares | 普通股 | |
| preference shares | 優先股；特別股 | |
| non-voting shares | 無投票選舉權的股票；無表決權股 | |
| redeemable shares | 可贖回的股票 | |
| convertible shares | 可轉換的股票 | |
| deferred shares | 遞延派息股票 | |
| **32.** class rights | 各種等級（股票）的權利 | |
| **33.** stock transfer form | 股票轉讓單 | |
| **34.** stamp duty | 印花稅 | |
| **35.** forthcoming dematerialisation | 即將到來的非物質化 | |
| **36.** share certificate | 股票；股票證券 | |
| **37.** intricate *a.* | 複雜的 | |
| **38.** preemption *n.* | 優先購買權 | |
| **39.** marketability *n.* | 可銷性 | |
| **40.** pro rata | 按比例 | |
| **41.** preemption rights | 優先購買權 | |
| **42.** stringent *a.* | 嚴格的 | |
| **43.** net assets | 淨資產 | |
| **44.** goodwill *n.* | 善意；企業聲譽；商譽 | |
| **45.** know-how *n.* | 專門知識；技術訣竅 | |
| **46.** cessation *n.* | 停止 | |
| **47.** executive *n.* | 行政管理人員；執事人員 | |
| **48.** non-executive *n.* | 非行政管理人員 | |
| **49.** shadow director | 影子董事；隱性董事 | |
| **50.** eligible *a.* | 有資格的 | |
| **51.** prescribe *v.* | 規定 | |
| **52.** quorum *n.* | 法定人數 | |
| **53.** abuse of powers | 濫用職權 | |
| **54.** contravention *n.* | 違反；觸犯 | |
| **55.** quasi-loans | 準貸款 | |
| **56.** indemnify *v.* | 補償 | |
| **57.** insider dealing | 內線交易；秘密交易 | |
| **58.** share options | 股票選擇權 | |
| **59.** declaration of dividends | 宣布分配股息 | |

**60.** requisition *v.* 　　　　　　要求；徵用

**61.** three-quarters majority 　　四分之三的多數

**62.** verbatim *adv.* 　　　　　　逐字地

**63.** bylaws *n.* 　　　　　　　　內部細則

**64.** group accounts 　　　　　　集團帳戶；分類帳戶

**65.** tenure of office 　　　　　　任職期；任期

**66.** regulatory bodies 　　　　　管理機構

**67.** the ensuing financial year 　接著而來的財政年度

**68.** irregularities *n.* 　　　　　不規則性；無規律性

**69.** confidentiality *n.* 　　　　保密性

**70.** non-resident shareholders 　非居民股東

**71** cross-refer *v.* 　　　　　　相互核對；對照

**72.** capitalisation of profits 　　利潤資本化

**73.** share warrant 　　　　　　　股份保證書；認股權

**74** called-up share capital 　　已催繳股本

**75.** proxy *n.* 　　　　　　　　代理人；代表；代理；委託書

**76.** notary public 　　　　　　　公證處；公證人

## ♣ New Phrases and Idiomatic Expressions

**1.** on one's own account 　　　自行負責；為自己的利益；依靠自己

**2.** with a view to doing sth. 　　以……做某事為目的

**3.** with the authority to do sth. 　授權做某事

**4.** to be conducive to 　　　　　有助於；有利於

**5.** in the presence of 　　　　　在……面前

**6.** to take advantage of 　　　　利用

**7.** at all times 　　　　　　　　隨時；總是

**8.** to be eligible 　　　　　　　有資格的；合格的

**9.** to be prejudicial to 　　　　對……有損害的；對……不利的

**10.** to account to sb. for sth. 　　對某人負責某事

**11.** under oath by sb. 　　　　　由某人發誓

**12.** during one's tenure of office 在某人任職期內

**13.** with or without the consent of sb. 在某人同意或不同意的情況下

**14.** by way of 　　　　　　　　透過……方法

**15**. at a premium 溢價
**16**. with intent to do sth. 有做某事的意圖

 **Notes**

**1**. ... though in Scotland a firm is a legal person...
儘管蘇格蘭是聯合王國的一個組成部分，但是由於歷史原因，在蘇格蘭存在著遠遠不同於英格蘭和威爾斯的法律結構和法律體系。在許多方面，蘇格蘭法（Scots Law）處於大陸法和習慣法體系中間的位置上。

**2**. the London Stock Exchange：倫敦證券交易所
a financial market in London. The London Stock Exchange was not created overnight nor was it brought into being by an Act of Parliament.

Historically the London Stock Exchange had assumed responsibility for the total regulation of its members — laying down strict standards to ensure an orderly market and the protection of investors.

Now the London Stock Exchange plays a key part in maintaining London's role as the leading international centre, with roots which stretch back to the 16th century when the first joint stock company was formed.

In addition to providing a market-place where listed securities can be traded efficiently, the Exchange provides the infrastructure to make the market work. That includes maintaining market rules and regulations, and providing services for market users, together with a secure and timely means of settling share transactions.

The Exchange provides a market for the buying and selling of more than 7,000 securities, with the main markets in U.K. and international equities.

Operating in the European time zone, the Exchange holds a vital position in the world of international finance, between the markets of New York and Tokyo.

More overseas companies are listed in London than on any other stock exchange and around 65 per cent of all shares traded outside their home country is done via London. The figure rises to more than 90 percent within Europe.

**3**. the Memorandum of Association
公司章程；公司組織大綱。美國用「Articles of Incorporation」來表示。

**4**. the Articles of Association
公司辦事細則（也譯為內部細則）。美國用「Bylaws」來表示。

**5**. insider dealing
秘密交易；內線交易。美國常用「insider trading」來表示。

**6.** United Kingdom company law requires that a company's accounts be examined...

由於動詞「require」的原因，在「be examined」前的「should」可以省略。在用另外一些動詞如：demand、suggest、insist時，也可以用類似的結構。

**7.** debentures of the company

公司債券。美國常用corporate bonds 來表示同樣的意思。

 **Exercises**

## I. Answer the following questions:

**1.** What are the four main types of business organizations under United Kingdom law?

**2.** What are the statutes governing the activities of corporations in the U.K.?

**3.** What is the Memorandum of Association and the Articles of Association? What is the difference between them?

**4.** What are the most common classes of share issued by companies?

**5.** How do you define a director?

**6.** What are the duties / powers of the Board of Directors?

**7.** What is insider dealing? Is it legal?

**8.** What are the duties / powers of the general meetings of shareholders?

**9.** What are the duties and powers of auditors?

**10.** What are the rules relating to the appointment and dismissal of auditors?

## II. Translate the following Chinese passages into English:

**1.** 公司是依法定程序設立以營利為目的法人組織。公司是法人，具有獨立的法律人格，這是公司最基本的特徵。

**2.** 公司組織大綱（公司章程）是公司存在的基礎，在該重要內容中通常載有：公司的名稱、註冊辦事處、公司的所在地、公司的目標和股份資本等。

**3.** 公司辦事細則（內部細則）是在公司組織大綱的基礎上制定的，它是一個規定公司管理、行政結構的重要文件。說得更具體一點，對股本、股本的變更、股東大會、董事的任命與免職、董事會、股利的分配等領域進行管理。

**4.** 英國的股東大會分為年度股東大會和特別股東大會兩種。股東大會一般由董事會召集，除無權參加大會的股東外，所有股東都能參加這樣的大會，並在大會上就公司的一些重大問題投票，表示贊成或反對。

## III. Indicate whether each of the following statements is true or false by writing "T" or "F" in the space provided:

_____1. A sole trader is an individual carrying on either a business or a profession on his own account.

_____2. A public limited company is always a publicly quoted company.

_____3. The Articles of Association prevails over the Memorandum of Association.

_____4. A company's management and administrative structures are set out in the Memorandum.

_____5. There is under United Kingdom law a general prohibition on a reduction of capital.

_____6. The auditors are engaged by the shareholder and report to them.

_____7. The share capital of a company must not be stated in the Memorandum.

_____8. Both public and private companies are generally able, subject to statutory procedural requirements, to purchase their own shares, including any redeemable shares.

# Principal Forms

Three principal categories of business are recognised: (1) sole proprietorship; (2) commercial (general or limited) partnership; (3) legal entities (company with limited liability; stock corporation company).

In addition to the above main forms, German law provides for civil partnerships which are in particular used for small enterprises, holding activities, joint ventures and the management of real estate. Of course, German law also knows the concept of sub-participations and silent partnerships (typical and non-typical, depending on their structure). Since the last mentioned organizations are of minor importance, they will not be reviewed here.

### 1. Sole proprietorship

A natural person doing business (*i.e.* not rendering professional services such as lawyers, auditors, physicians) himself is considered a merchant if, in principle, his business activities are of such size that a business organization is necessary. The sole proprietor, as owner, takes all the profits and losses and personally bears all risks. There is no distinction between his private and business capital so that both, private and business creditors, may take recourse to his entire assets. As a merchant he is subject to the provisions of the German Commercial Code (Handelsgesetzbuch: HGB). He has therefore to apply for registration in the commercial register, where his business as merchant is registered under his trade name (Firma). He is obliged to keep books and draw up a balance sheet once a year. As a merchant a sole proprietor is less protected than a private individual, i.e. consumer orientated laws, etc., do not apply to his benefit.

### Branch

A sole proprietor or a (domestic or foreign) company may set up a branch. A branch is not a legal entity, but rather a registered place of business. It does not have legal representatives of its own or own assets. It has , however, to be registered with the commercial register. In addition, a branch is subject to the same law as its owner.

### 2. Partnerships

The commercial partnerships (general and limited partnership) are governed by the Commercial Code and, secondarily, the Civil Code. Civil partnerships are merely subject to the Civil Code. There is no legal limitation to the number of partners in a civil or commercial partnership. Neither partnership requires a deed or a written partnership agreement. Hence, a notarization or the obtaining of a licence are not necessary. Where as partnership agreements as such do not have to be filed with the commercial register, commercial partnerships have to register their trade name, domicile, name and status (general of limited) of their partners and, in case of a limited partnership, the amount of the liable contributions of the limited partners. Although the applications to the commercial register do not require notarial form, the signatures of the partners have to be certified by a notary.

*(1) General partnership (offene handelsgesellschaft: OHG)*

An OHG consists of two or more persons, which may be legal entities, jointly establishing and running a business. It has no legal personality of its own, but it may sue or be sued in its own name. It may acquire rights including the title to real property and incur liabilities. But, despite its own assets, its partners are personally, jointly and severally liable for all debts incurred by the partnership. Registration (*cf.* above) is mandatory for reasons of publicity, but not necessary in a sense that the OHG's legal existence depends on it. The structure of an OHG is subject to rather few mandatory legal provisions. In principle, each partner is entitled and obliged to represent and manage the OHG. The partnership agreement may amend this principle. Unless the partnership agreement provides differently, any issue being of basic interest for an OHG must be decided upon unanimously by the partners'meeting. A statutory or minimum capital is not required. The partners are free to choose the amounts they are willing to invest. Usually, it is contractually stipulated that each partner has a fixed capital account in the amount of his contribution, which determines the ratio in which he participates in profits and losses, and a running account, where all contributions, profits, losses, withdrawals, etc., are recorded.

*(2) Limited partnership (kommanditgesellschaft: KG)*

The KG differs from an OHG in so far that it has one or more partners not being personally liable for the partnership's liabilities (limited partners: Kommanditisten). There must, however, be at least one general partner (Komplementar) being responsible for the management and representation of the KG. Whereas his liability is unlimited, the limited partners are liable for the partnership's liabilities only up to the amount of capital they are obliged to invest according to the provisions of the partnership agreement (liable contribution). There is no further liability once a limited partner has paid in this amount; his liability revives, however, when and in so far as the contribution is refunded to him. The partners are free to determine the amount of capital to be put up by the limited partners; there is no legal minimum. The name of the limited partners and the amount of their liability must be registered in the commercial register. This is fairly important since, before registration, the liability of a limited partner is unlimited. The limited partners have equal voting rights at the partners' meetings but do not participate in the partnership's management. The partnership agreement may, however, provide otherwise with respect to both. The limited partner's rights in the partners' meetings may be reduced, alternatively a limited partner may be appointed managing partner, without affecting the limitation of his liability.

*(3) The "GmbH & Co. KG"*

The most common form of business organization is the GmbH & Co. KG, *i.e.* a limited partnership, whose general partner is a company with limited liability. It combines the benefits of a partnership (great flexibility of structure, tax treatment as partner, somewhat restricted publicity) with those of a company with limited liability (*i.e.* liability limited to the assets of the limited company; as general partner, there would otherwise be unlimited liability). A GmbH & Co. KG is established by founding two companies. First, a GmbH (Gesellschaft mit beschrankter Haftung) is incorporated whereupon the newly established GmbH enters into a limited partnership agreement with the limited partner(s), which in practice are most often identical with the GmbH's shareholders. In recent years, there have been some decisions allowing the establishment of limited partnerships in which the general partner is a company incorporated under foreign law. Thus, for instance, a "Ltd. (British Law) & Co. KG" has been held admissible. For the time being, however, it is not certain to what extent German courts are willing to acknowledge all kinds of foreign companies to act as general partner of a German limited partnership. Legally, a GmbH & Co. KG is treated, in principle, as a limited partnership. However, certain rules on the protection of the share capital of a GmbH also apply to a GmbH & Co. KG.

*(4) The Civil partnership (gesellschaft burgerlichen rechtes: GbR)*

A civil partnership comes into existence ipso jure, if two or more persons associate for the purpose of operating an enterprise. A GbR does not have a corporate organization, legal capacity or a trade name. Typically, a GbR enters into legal relations with special assets serving the GbR's purpose. The GbR's assets are jointly owned by its partners. The contributions may be made in cash, in kind, with claims or intangible assets as well as services. Although the individual partner has his private assets, he is both jointly and liable without limit for all debts of the GbR. Such personal liability may, however, be excluded by agreement with the GbR's creditors so that only the partnership assets are subject to liability. In principle, the partners are jointly responsible for the management and, since the power of representation depends on the authority to manage, there is joint power of representation. Due to the permissive character of these provisions, it has to be noted that for practical purposes the partnership agreement usually provides differently.

### 3. The stock corporation (aktiengesellschaft: AG)

*(1) Introduction*

The law concerning Aktiengesellschaften (AG) is embodied in the Stock Corporation Act (Aktiengesetz: AktG) of 1965 as amended. Other laws of particular impact are the Co Determination Act of 1976, the Shop Constitution Act of 1952, both determining the representation of employees on the AG's supervisory board, and the Commercial Code (Handelsgesetzbuch: HGB) containing general provisions applicable to all fully qualified merchants such as an AG as well as general accounting and disclosure requirements. An AG is characterized by its own legal personality, the limited liability of its shareholders, a fixed share capital, incorporated organization (three tier system: general shareholders meeting; managing board; and supervisory board with mandatory representation of employees) and anonymous membership. Shareholders can be private individuals as well as corporate bodies, both domestic and foreign. All shares may be held by one shareholder. The form of an AG is the suitable legal form for large enterprises being able to turn to the public capital market. It offers to the investor relative protection by far reaching mandatory disclosure requirements, special protective provisions and its largely obligatory law thus preserving the (minority) shareholders' right, to a great extent.

*(2) Incorporation*

In principle, it is not necessary to obtain a licence in order to set up an AG (exceptions are the forming of banks, insurance and investment companies).The forming of an AG involves three steps:

The articles of association ("articles") and the minutes of the formation have to be set up in full notarial form (powers of attorney have to be certified by a notary public). The formation instrument includes the articles and must specify :A. the founders; B. the par-value, the issue price and, if any different classes of shares, those to which each incorporator subscribes; and C. the amount of the capital paid in.

Thereafter, the incorporators must subscribe in notarial form to all the shares (the future AG may not subscribe for its own shares), whereby a sort of pre-company without legal personality is established, i.e. is not yet an AG. With respect to the shares, at least one-fourth of the nominal value and, if any, the entire premium must be paid in. Any contributions in kind must be fully rendered prior to application for registration. Special mandatory precautionary measures require: A. the rendering of a written formation report by the incorporators; B. the examination of the formation process by the first managing board and first supervisory board; C. the making of a respective examination report; and D. under special circumstances (*e.g.* if incorporators are to be members of the supervisory/management board, the making of contributions in kind, etc.) a separate examination report by a court appointed auditor.

Finally, upon application to the commercial register (administered by the local district court) and approval of the formation process by the court, the company is entered into the commercial register, whereby it acquires its legal existence as an AG.

Registration in the commercial register along with details of the newly established AG are published in the official Federal Gazette (Bundesanzeiger) and the newspapers designated in the articles. All information filed with the commercial register is available for inspection by the public.

*Articles of association (satzung)*

The minimum contents are name, domicile and purpose of the AG, amount of share capital, par-value of each share, number of shares of each par-value, eventual classes of shares, issue of bearer or registered shares, number of members of the managing board and form of publications. Besides, the articles may contain provisions regarding the managing board, the supervisory board, general shareholders' meeting, annual financial reports and allocation of profits. The extent to which the articles may deviate from the principles contained in the AktG is rather limited, in particular the allocation of responsibility among the AG's three bodies may not be changed.

*Domicile (sitz)*

The domicile must be located in Germany and have an actual relationship to the business of the AG. It is sufficient that a business establishment of the AG or the location of the management is situated or the administration is carried out at the domicile. The legal domicile determines which commercial register is responsible for the AG's registration and other filing and registration matters.

*Company name (firma)*

The name selected has to include the full words "Aktiengesellschaft". The name itself is normally derived from the purpose of the enterprise, although an additional adaption of a personal name is permissible. Coined expressions are acceptable only if they conform with a known trademark or if they have acquired a secondary meaning. Of course the name has to be sufficiently different from all firms registered at the same place or community and may not contain deceptive elements.

*Duration*

German law allows the AG to be established for a limited period of time. Such limitation to be made by means of its articles is, however, a rare exception.

*(3) Shares (aktien)*

An AG may issue different classes of shares, *i.e.* common and preference shares

(Vorzugsaktien), the latter representing special rights with respect to dividends, liquidation proceeds and voting rights. Whereas preferred shares may be issued without voting rights provided they have preferential rights to dividends, preferential voting rights or multiple voting rights are in principle not admissible. Issue of shares and "interim certificates" (documents that may be issued as a preliminary substitute for the final share certificates) are not permissible prior to registration of the AG. All classes of shares must have a certain par-value to be DM 50.00 or DM 100.00 or a multiple of the latter, *e.g.* the issue of proportional/ fractional shares is not possible. An AG may issue convertible bonds (Wandelschuldverschreibu ngen) and option warrants.

*Share capital (grundkapital)*

The share capital must be stipulated in the articles and be denominated in Deutsche Marks. It has to amount to at least DM 100,000.00.Prior to application for registration all shares must be subscribed to and at least 25 percent of the nominal amount of the cash contributions, any premium of an over-par issue and all contributions in kind must have been made. Shares issued before paying in the full par-value must be registered shares.

The articles may authorise the board of management to increase the share capital up to a certain nominal amount (authorised capital) by issuing new shares against contributions during a period not exceeding five years. The nominal amount of the authorised capital may, however, not exceed one-half of the share capital existing at the date of the respective authorisation. There are strict rules on the preservation of the share capital including the prohibition to return paid contributions and, in principle, to acquire own shares, the rule that only retained earnings may be distributed, strict provisions on valuation and the requirement to form statutory reserves.

*Transfer of shares*

Bearer shares are transferred by agreement and delivery of the share certificate. Registered shares and interim certificates are legal instruments to order, whose transfer is effectuated by agreement and delivery with an endorsement of the certificates. Registered shares have to be registered in the share register book of the AG. The transfer of registered shares is contingent upon the consent of the AG which is granted by the managing board. The articles may, however, stipulate that such consent may only be granted if the supervisory board and/or the shareholders pass a consenting resolution.

*Increase/decrease of capital*

A capital increase to be specified in the articles and thus requiring an alteration of the statutes may be funded either by new funds, *i.e.* contributions by (new) shareholders, or from the AG's own funds, i.e. the conversion of capital reserves or revenue reserves into share capital (for authorised capital, *cf.* 2.3.1). All existing shareholders have a preemptive right on the issue of new shares, which can be excluded only: ① by an express resolution passed with a majority of at least 75 percent of the share capital represented; and ② if the exclusion is a suitable and necessary means for realizing the goal of the capital increase; and ③ the benefits for the AG resulting therefrom objectively outweigh the proportional loss of the excluded shareholders. A conditional increase is only permissible for certain objects.

Other means of increasing the financial means of the company are the issue of: ① bonds; ② convertible bonds granting the creditor a right of conversion or subscription to shares under certain conditions; ③ income bonds granting the holder/creditor a right to interest and repayment of the capital in linkage with the shareholder's share in the profit; and ④ usufructuary (participation) rights. Existing shareholders have a right of pre-emption.

Three forms of a capital reduction are available: ① An ordinary capital reduction may provide for a reduction of the nominal amount or for a consolidation of shares in order to distribute the released assets to the shareholders or to form a reserve as well as to numerically reduce the share capital in order to eliminate a deficit balance. ② A simplified capital reduction procedure is available to offset declines in the value of assets, to cover other losses or to transfer amounts to the capital reserve. ③ A redemption of shares is only permissible, if the shares to be redeemed have been acquired by the AG, or, if compulsory, if the redemption was provided for in the articles before the shareholders concerned acquired or subscribed to the shares. The AktG provides for strict protection of creditors.

*Form of subscription*

Subscription of shares to an AG can take place in cash or in kind. Contributions in the form of contracts of employment or services are not possible. Additional precautionary matters apply to contributions in kind, in particular the need for an audit and a certificate of evaluation to be prepared by a public accountant. It is not possible to issue shares under-par. If issued over par, which is permissible, the resulting premium is to be allocated to the capital reserves.

*Purchase of own shares*

An AG is not permitted to subscribe for its own shares. The purchase of own shares is permissible only if: ① it is necessary to protect the AG from severe damage; ② the shares are to be offered to the employees of the AG; ③ if the acquisition is made to indemnify shareholders in connection with a contract of domination or an integration by majority resolution; ④ if the nominal amount or a higher amount for the issue has been fully paid on the shares and the acquisition is free or the AG executes a purchase order therewith; ⑤

by means of legal succession; or ⑥ on the basis of a resolution of the shareholders' meeting concerning the redemption of shares.

In cases ① to ③ the number of shares to be acquired is limited to 10 percent of the share capital.

*Register of Shares*

Registered shares are registered in the share register book setting out the holder's name, residence and occupation, which is in principle not open to the public. It may be inspected only by shareholders (both of bearer or registered shares) and those persons who have a legal interest in inspection (§ 810 German Civil Code). Vis-a-vis the company only those who are registered are considered to be a stockholder. In the case of bearer shares, possession is sufficient proof of ownership.

*(4) Company's bodies*

The mandatory three-tier system separates the managing board being alone competent for the management and representation, the supervisory board competent for the supervision and controlling of the management and the shareholders' meeting, which is, in principle, excluded from the management of the AG and decides only on items assigned to it by the AktG or the articles.

*Managing board (vorstand)*

***Appointment/dismissal of managing directors.*** The managing board consisting of one or more persons (and a labour relations director with equal status if the AG employs more than 2,000 employees) is appointed by the supervisory board, i.e. it is not possible for the shareholder's meeting to appoint or revoke the appointment of members of the managing board. Only a natural person may be appointed. There are no residential or nationality requirements for the managing directors. The maximum term of office is five years, although an appointment is renewable. A removal from office may only be made by the supervisory board and only for good cause (gross violation of duties, incapability of proper management nonarbitrary withdrawal of confidence by the shareholders' meeting). Both appointment and removal must be registered in the commercial register.

***Duties/powers of the managing board.*** The main responsibilities for the management of the AG include all measures for realising the AG's purpose in the broadest sense. The managing board further represents the AG in and out of court. If the managing board consists of several members, all of them are, in principle, only jointly responsible for the management and representation. Unless sole power of representation is granted, an AG is typically represented by two members jointly or by one member together with a Prokurist. Whereas its power of representation is unlimited and not capable of limitation, the managing board is bound by internal rules with respect to its power of management. The articles or the supervisory board may order that certain transactions require the consent of the supervisory board. If such consent is not given, the shareholders' meeting has to decide thereon if requested by the managing board. German law does not know the "ultra vires doctrine" so that an AG is bound by all actions even if the managing board exceeds the internal rules or the objects of the AG. The only exception applies if the third party was acting in "bad faith", i.e. he knew the managing board was exceeding its internal power of management and was acting deliberately against the interests of the AG.

***Rules of procedure; board meetings.*** The specific allocation of rights and duties among the board members and the procedures to be observed are typically set out in internal rules of procedure (Geschäftsordnung), determined by the managing board itself unless the articles provide that only the supervisory board may determine such rules or the supervisory board does so. Resolutions of the managing board are taken unanimously unless the rules of procedure provide otherwise. In the case of a tie, the vote of one member (typically the chairman) may be the casting vote. It is not permissible that one or more board members may take decisions against the majority of the other members in the case of differences of opinion. The rules of procedure may also determine the number of board meetings, the quorum and all related procedural questions.

***Legal liability of managing directors.*** The managing directors have to apply a standard of care exercised by a "diligent and prudent manager" and are subject to a far reaching prohibition to compete. They are jointly and separately liable if they violate their duties. The strictness of liability is enhanced by a reversal of the burden of proof. The liability cannot be abrogated in advance nor may the AG, in principle, waive or settle a respective claim for damages. If a member grossly violates his duty of care, creditors who cannot obtain satisfaction from the AG are entitled to sue the managing directors. Finally, the AktG contains several provisions which, if violated by the managing board, result in their liability. The violation of certain statutory duties is a criminal offence.

*Supervisory board (aufsichtsrat)*

***Appointment, dismissal and composition.*** The supervisory board is composed of representatives of the shareholders and employees, both having the same rights and duties. For companies which employ more than 2,000 employees the supervisory board is to be composed of equal parts of representatives of shareholders and employees. For companies with a lesser amount of employees, only one-third of the members are employees' representatives. The supervisory board consists of at least three members up to 21 depending on the share capital. If the company is subject to full (equal number of representatives of shareholders and employees) co-determination the number is 12 to 20. Only natural persons may be elected with out restrictions on nationality or profession, unless the articles set personal requirements to be met by representatives of the shareholders .The accumulation of supervisory board posts is limited to 10 and interlocking boards are prohibited. The shareholders' representatives are elected by the shareholders' meeting for a maximum of four years (re-election is possible) unless the articles contain a right to delegate members to certain shareholders (limited to one-third of all members). The employees' representatives are, in principle, directly elected by the employees. Members of the supervisory board may be removed before the expiration of their term of office by a respective shareholders' resolution with a majority of 75 percent of the votes cast. In the case of representatives of the employees an approving resolution by a three-quarters' majority of all employees entitled to vote is necessary. The members of the supervisory board are not registered in the commercial register but their appointment, dismissal or resignation are published in the company's journals.

*Duties/powers of supervisory board.* The main duties are the supervision of the management by the managing board, and the appointment and removal of the managing board (for good cause only). The managing board is required to disclose all relevant information and to report regularly, at least once per calendar quarter, to the supervisory board, each member of which has extensive information rights. For certain kinds of transactions the supervisory board must grant its consent if so required by law, the articles or the supervisory board itself. An allocation of the management duties to the supervisory board is not possible. The power of representation is limited to the representation of the AG vis-a-vis the managing board.

*Rules of procedure; board meetings.* The internal organisation is determined by the AktG, where applicable the Co-Determination Act, the articles and, in addition, by rules of procedure as determined by the supervisory board itself. Decisions are taken by special resolutions to be passed, in principle, by a simple majority. In companies with full co determination the chairman has a casting vote in certain cases. Quarterly board meetings are the rule but ,if not, board meetings have to take place at least once per calendar half year. Meetings may be called by each member or the managing board.

*Legal liability of the supervisory board.* The liability of the members of the supervisory board follows the same pattern as those of the managing board. Members of the supervisory board are ,however, not subject to a prohibition against competition.

*The (annual) shareholders' meeting (hauptversammlung)*

*General provisions.* The AktG does not differentiate between an annual and an extra ordinary shareholders' meeting but at least one meeting must be held annually to decide on the appropriation of retained earnings, the appointment of the annual auditor and the release from responsibility of the managing and supervisory board.

***The convening of a shareholders' meeting.*** The shareholders' meeting is called by the managing board if required under the AktG, the articles or for the benefit of the AG. The supervisory board is also entitled and obliged to call a shareholders' meeting if necessary in the interest of the AG. Shareholders representing at least 5 percent of the share capital may request the calling of a shareholders' meeting. If such a request is not honoured, the minority shareholders may be authorised to convene the general meeting by a respective court order.

***Notices for the shareholders' meeting.*** The notice period for calling a shareholders' meeting is at least one month. The notice must be published in a prescribed form along with an announcement of the agenda, which has to contain the proposals of the administration on each item on which the shareholders' meeting should decide. Shareholders representing at least 5 percent of the share capital are entitled to have further items put on the agenda. No decision may be taken on items not properly published.

***Place of the shareholders' meeting.*** Unless the articles provide differently, the location will be at the domicile of the AG. However, the place of the meeting must, in principle, be located in Germany.

Duties/powers of the shareholders' meeting. The shareholders' meeting has no comprehensive competence but is restricted to the duties assigned to it by the AktG or the articles. Besides the items of the annual meeting (*cf.* 2.4.3.1), the shareholders' meeting decides exclusively on all questions related to the legal and economic organisation of the AG, in particular on amendments to the articles or in the capital base, so-called enterprise agreements (*e.g.* contracts of domination; profit and loss pooling agreements), integration, merger and transformation, transfer of all assets as well as the dissolution and liquidation of the AG. On questions of management the shareholders' meeting may only decide at the request of the managing board and in cases of extreme importance ("Holzmuller" case). All resolutions of the shareholders must be recorded in notarial form and, in principle, are passed by a simple majority of the votes cast. For certain resolutions of special significance (*e.g.* amendment to the articles) a qualified capital majority of at least three-quarters of the capital stock represented is also necessary. If several classes of shares have been issued, often special resolutions of the disadvantaged shareholders are required.

***Voting rights and restrictions.*** In principle, each issued share grants a voting right in accordance with the par-value of the share, If a preference dividend which is a prerequisite for the issue of nonvoting preference shares is not fully paid in a year and if the arrears are not paid up in the next year together with the full benefit of that year, then the preference shareholders have a voting right until the arrears have been paid up. Multiple voting rights are in principle impermissible. It is, however, possible to provide for a maximum number of votes to be exercised by a shareholder regardless of his actual shareholding or otherwise limit voting rights by graduation as long as such limitations do not aim at individual shareholders (*e.g.* foreign shareholders) only. The voting rights for own shares held by the AG or a controlled enterprise are fully suspended.

A voting right might be exercised by a holder of a written proxy. In most cases the articles make the exercise of the right to vote conditional upon the shareholder depositing his shares by a certain date prior to the meeting. All shareholders present are listed in a roster of participants available for inspection prior to the vote. In principle, contracts of shareholders stating how to exercise their voting rights (pooling agreement) are valid.

Each shareholder, including those holding non-voting preference shares, is entitled to participate in the meeting and has a right to information concerning the AG to the extent necessary for an appropriate evaluation of the items on the agenda. Resolutions may be contested in court, but there are special provisions on the right to rescind, the time limits to be observed and a possible ratification of resolutions.

*Works council (betriebsrat)*

A works council may be established in every enterprise with more than five employees. The works council is to be informed and consulted and partly has a certain right of co-determination on various internal matters effecting the employees. There is, however, no co-determination regarding the management of the company. The employees' rights are exercised through their representation on the supervisory board.

*(5) Accounting and auditing*

After the implementation of the former EC accounting directives, the German regulations concerning accounting, auditing and publications are basically the same as in the other former EC countries.

*Appointment and Dismissal of Auditors*

Each AG which is not considered to be a small company must be examined by a qualified auditor annually elected by the general meeting. If not appointed by the end of the financial year, a court will appoint an auditor. A small company is defined as not exceeding at least two of the following criteria: ① DM 3.9 million balance sheet total after deducting a deficit disclosed on the assets side; ② DM 8 million sales; ③ annual average of 50 employees.

*Duties and powers of auditors*

The auditor must report in writing on the results of his examination and, in the absence of objections, the examination must be confirmed by a respective statement to the effect that the accounting records and the financial statements comply with the legal regulations. Unless left to the determination by the shareholders' meeting, the annual financial statements are determined by being approved by the managing board and the supervisory board. In principle, the financial statements together with the auditor's certificate have to be filed with the commercial register where they are open for public inspection. In addition, details of which commercial register the documents have been filed have to be published in the Federal Gazette. The extent of the disclosure requirements varies according to the size of the AG. The auditors are obliged to perform a conscientious and independent audit and to maintain confidentiality. In case of a violation of such duties the auditor is liable to pay damages.

*Partnership Limited by Shares (Kommanditgesellschaft auf Aktien)*

The AktG provides for another legal form, namely the Kommanditgesellschaft auf Aktien which is a hybrid form of a limited partnership and an AG.

## 4. The limited liability company (gesellschaft mit beschrankter haftung:gmbH)

*(1) Introduction*

The limited liability company is one of the success stories in German business legislation. The newly created legal form, particularly designed to serve small and medium-sized enterprises or large enterprises with only a few shareholders, has won general acceptance within the business community. By the end of 1989,the number of GmbHs had risen to almost 400,000 with an aggregate share capital of approximately DM180 billion. The vast majority of all German subsidiaries of foreign corporations are GmbHs. The GmbH, more generally speaking, is also the adequate legal form for all enterprises which secure their financing from other sources than the public capital market. The GmbH is a legal entity (§ 13 sect.1 GmbH Act) which offers a wide range of flexibility in its structure. After a reform of the GmbH Act in 1980 (and in line with applicable former EC directives), it may now be formed from the outset as a one-person company with limited liability. The major advantage of the GmbH compared to the various existing forms of partnerships is the limited personal liability of its shareholders. Generally speaking, the shareholders are not liable to the company's creditors for the company's debts so that the entrepreneurial risk can effectively be limited to the minimum capital stock of DM 50,000.00.Compared to the AG, the GmbH offers more flexibility, simplified internal decisionmaking and, in principle, lower transaction costs. It affords the shareholder(s) better control of the company than they would have in case of an AG. The transfer of GmbH participations ("Geschä-ftsanteile", hereafter simply referred to as "shares") and the access to the capital market, on the other hand, are more difficult to accomplish than in case of an AG.

*(2) Formation of the company*

In comparison to the AG, the GmbH is procedurally less complicated to form. Three subsequent stages characterise the formation process: ① the execution of the articles of association; ② the subscription to the original capital contributions; and ③ the registration in the commercial register of the court district where the company has chosen its domicile. The latter must be within German national territory and is usually the place of its corporate office or principal place of business activity.

*Articles of association*

In order to assure a proper formation,§3 of the GmbH-Act demands certain minimum contents of the articles of association. They include the purpose of the business, the name of the company, its domicile, both the amount of the share capital and of the individual contributions. If appropriate, the articles should identify the duration of the company's existence.

**Company name.** Some attention has to be paid to the selection of the company's name. In order to facilitate identification of the company in business, its name must either be derived from the company's purpose, or contain the name(s) of (one or several) shareholder(s) together with an indication of a corporate relationship. Also a combination of both ways to name the company is possible. The use of foreign language elements, trademarks or proper names is permitted, subject to applicable legislation. In order to avoid confusion with existing companies, the selection of the name requires the approval of the local Chamber of Commerce at the company's domicile. This requirement and the commercial register's monitoring of the name selection often create problems to which non-German shareholders are not used.

**Share capital subscription and payment.** The shareholders have to subscribe to the entire original capital before registration. An application for entry of the company into the commercial register can only be made, if at least one-quarter of each original capital contribution has been paid in and the total amount of the paid-in contributions equals DM 25,000.00. For the formation of a one-shareholder company, the GmbH Act additionally requires a security for the remaining contribution(s).

*Formation procedure*

The articles of association must be signed by all shareholders and recorded by a notary. In addition, the shareholders' signatures must be authenticated by a notary. The notarial form may also be satisfied by a German consular officer acting outside of German territory.

**Appointment of managing directors.** Unless an appointment is already made in the articles, the managing directors have to be appointed before an application for registration can be filed. Each managing director has to give a sample signature in front of a notary or consular officer, who will also inform the director about the statutory obligations imposed on him in the new office. The managing directors may then apply for registration of the GmbH, once they have ensured payment of the minimum capital contributions (cf. 3.2.1.2).

***The application.*** The application has to contain information on the formation of the GmbH in compliance with the provisions of the GmbH-Act. It has to be accompanied by all documents necessary to enable the local court to control the proper formation. In particular, the articles, proof of the appointment of the managing directors and a list of all shareholders with their respective capital subscriptions have to be attached.

*Registration, costs and time-frame*

The local court of registration is obliged to examine all formal requirements for a GmbH formation. With the registration, the GmbH comes into existence as a legal entity. The following publication of the registration is merely for declaratory purposes. From the moment of registration, the concept of limited liability of the GmbH is applicable and the shareholders' unlimited liability during the period of formation (*cf.* 3.6) ceases.

The costs of registration include the notary's fees and the court fees for registration and publication. The fees vary depending on the stated capital of the company. For a GmbH with the (minimum) stated capital of DM 50,000.00, the total fees would generally amount to approximately DM 3,000.00, For companies with an elevated share capital, the fees may increase to, for instance, around DM 50,000.00 for a company with a share capital of DM 10,000,000.00. The legal fees of the lawyers involved will obviously depend on whether standard language can be used or whether any specific issues require in-depth consideration and drafting.

The process of formation, form the signing of the articles up to the registration in the commercial register, usually takes between four and six weeks.

*(3) Shares, shareholders and contributions*

*Share capital*

The basic function of the share capital is to ensure a minimum satisfaction of creditors' claims and to enable an evaluation of the company's standing. The minimum amount of share capital required is DM 50,000.00. The minimum participation of each shareholder is fixed at DM 500.00, but any amount may be agreed upon as long as it is a multiple of DM 100.00. The general rule of contributions to the GmbH is a share capital contribution in an amount of money, expressed in DM. Such a cash contribution may validly be made by crediting the company's bank account in Germany. The shareholders may not be released from their obligations to make the contributions. Equally, a set-off against the obligation to contribute is not possible.

*Contributions in kind*

As an exception to the rule of capital contributions in money, the GmbH-Act allows contributions in kind. This possibility has led to a variety of problems concerning the process of formation and shareholder liability. In order to constitute a valuable contribution in kind, transferable assets of whatever nature have to be definitely and fully placed to the free disposal of the managing directors prior to the registration. Furthermore, they have to be evaluated within the articles of association. In addition, it is necessary to prepare a formal report on the formation and consideration of contributions in kind which must set forth the essential circumstances from which the evaluation of these contributions results, a requirement which often leads to practical difficulties and inevitably to a substantial extension of the time period for the establishment of a GmbH. The local court of registration has to review the value stated in the articles and may reject an application for registration, if the value does not reach the stated amount of the share capital contribution(s).

*Transfer of shares*

The transfer of shares is subject to certain formalities. Both the agreement to transfer and the effective transfer require the notarial form. The lack of proper form of an agreement to undertake a transfer is remedied by a transfer agreement respecting the required notarial form. This requirement of notarial form applies as well to agreements containing options to sell or to purchase, preemptive rights or pre-contracts. It is even considered necessary for mere sale offers and respective acceptances. In principle, any transfer of GmbH shares must be notarised by a German notary. Under German regulations, the fees of the notary depend on the (actual, not stated) value of the shares. These fees may be astronomical, if interests in important companies are transferred. This is the reason why a significant practice has developed of having such transfers, particularly in the context of mergers and acquisitions, notarised by a non-German (notably Swiss or Dutch) notary. German courts have accepted this practice on a case-by-case basis. As their decisions continue to be challenged by lower courts and some commentators, it is essential to fully comply with the requirements established for a non-German notarisation (as otherwise the transaction may be held void by a German court of fiscal authority).

The articles of association can (and often do) require additional formalities or impose restrictions on the possibility of transfer. Such restrictions may require the prior consent of the company to any kind of transfer or impose a particular qualification upon the transfer. The transfer of shares may be subordinated to the approval of the company. In this case, the articles have to state which organ of the company is competent to pronounce such an approval.

Upon the transfer, the company has to be supplied with a copy of the transfer document. This notification may be performed by either party or by their representatives. Since the transfer of shares is not publicly registered, it is advisable to demand, prior to the conclusion of a transfer agreement, the presentation of an uninterrupted sequence of transfer documents in notarial form. This is the only way to ascertain that the transferor is in fact owner of the share.

*Acquisition of own shares*

If not otherwise stated in the articles, the company itself may acquire shares. A GmbH may only acquire own shares on which the share capital contributions have been fully paid is so far as the acquisition can be paid out of assets existing in excess of the amount of the share capital. Apart from this requirement, there is no limitation on the amount of own shares to be acquired by a GmbH.

*Shareholder rights and obligations*

***Shareholder rights.*** The shareholders' rights to be involved in the administration of the company essentially consist of the right to vote, the right to participate in shareholder meetings and the right to receive information on the activities of the company. Each of these rights may be defined in more detail in the company's articles. The right to vote can even be excluded by the issuance of nonvoting shares. The voting right is generally exercised according to the amount of capital share contributions and may be cast by proxy. A shareholder has no right to vote, if the passing of a resolution creates a particularly important conflict of interest, such as for a legal transaction between the company and himself. The individual shareholder is generally free in the way in which he exercises his voting right, but may not acquire advantages or abuse his majority position to the detriment of the company.

Share ownership also carries the right to receive a part of the profits according to the proportion of shares. §29 GmbH-Act states that this right may be modified or excluded by the articles or a resolution voted by the shareholders. The individual shareholder only has a right to receive payment, however, once a determination on the distribution of the annual profits has been made.

***Shareholder obligations.*** The principal obligation imposed on the shareholders is to fulfill the subscribed original capital contribution. In order to ensure this obligation, the GmbH-Act imposes a particular liability upon the shareholders. Defaulting shareholders must pay overdue interest. Furthermore, the articles may impose all kinds of duties upon the shareholders such as collaboration, availability as a consultant, service as a managing director and refraining from competition (the latter obligation may also exist as a statutory obligation without a specific provision in the articles).

*Repayments*

The GmbH-Act establishes the principle of preservation of the share capital. As far as the assets of the company are required for maintaining the share capital, the company is prevented from effecting payments to its shareholders, unless a full consideration for such payment is rendered to the company. The prohibition enters into force, if the net worth of the GmbH no longer equals the amount of the stated capital.

*Refund of prohibited payments.* If payments have been effected to a shareholder in violation of the prohibition to repay the share capital of the company, the recipient is obliged to refund what he has received. If he acted in good faith, the refund may only be claimed to the extent necessary for the satisfaction of the company's creditors. If a refund cannot be obtained from the recipient, the remaining shareholders are liable as far as is necessary to pay the company's creditors. Their liability depends on the proportion of their subscribed share capital contributions.

*"Capital replacing loans".* Once the shareholders have made their contributions they are no longer obliged to provide additional funds. If a shareholder nevertheless provides the company with extra funds by means of loans, his right to receive repayment is not a mere shareholder right, but a third party right equivalent to the rights of other creditors. The legal position of the respective shareholder, therefore, would be considerably stronger than in case of a supplementary contribution. In order to avoid abuse of this possibility, the GmbH-Act restricts the repayment of loans considered as "capital-replacing," if the company is in financial difficulties.

The definition of capital-replacing loans is quite broad. A loan is considered to have such an effect, if it is "made by a shareholder at a time when shareholders acting as orderly merchants would instead have provided capital to the company." The GmbH-Act even takes a further step and declares the limitation on repayments applicable for other legal transactions of a shareholder or a third party "which are the commercial equivalent of the granting of a loan." A legal transaction or a loan is of "capital-replacing" nature, if the company would not have been able to obtain the same conditions on the market from a third party.

Capital-replacing loans may not be re-claimed in case of bankruptcy or composition proceedings. If the company has repaid during the last year preceding bankruptcy proceedings a loan guaranteed or otherwise secured by a shareholder, this shareholder is obliged to refund the amount repaid by the company to the extent that a third party cannot be compensated from the bankruptcy proceeds.

*"Hidden contributions in kind".* If contributions in kind are to be made, the articles must clearly specify their nature and state the amount of the share capital contributions which they are intended to cover (see 3.3.2).If the articles provide for a cash contribution and the company subsequently purchases assets from a shareholder which would qualify for a contribution in kind, such purchase may be considered as a repayment of the share capital contribution and might give rise to a liability up to the amount of the repaid share capital

contribution. This doctrine which prohibits hidden contributions in kind intends to protect the strict rules on the raising of a GmbH's stated capital. It is of critical importance particularly in the context of leveraged buy-outs. The essential tests which the German courts apply to determine whether a transaction qualifies as a hidden contribution in kind is whether there is a correlation in time and substance between the fulfillment of the share capital contribution and the purchase of assets from a shareholder.

*(4) Corporate structure*

The structure of the GmbH is characterised by two main organs: the managing director(s) and the shareholder(s).The articles of association may additionally provide for a supervisory board. For companies with more than 500 employees, a supervisory board is mandatory.

*The Managing director(s) (geschäftsführer)*

The main task of the managing directors is to ensure management and representation of the company. If several managing directors are appointed, they may only jointly represent and act for the company. This legal principle can be altered by the articles. Individual representation of managing directors or joint representation of two managing directors or of one together with a holder of the power of Prokura (Prokurist) are all very common. The managing directors themselves have to follow instructions given by the shareholders and have to observe all limitations imposed upon them by the articles. Such limitations of the authority of the managing directors, however, remain without legal effect towards third persons. Additionally, the company is liable towards third persons for the acts of the managing directors.

*Liability.* Managing directors who violate their obligations are jointly and severally liable to the company for the resulting damage. The standard of diligence is the one of an orderly businessman. A particularly important example of liability to the company concerns any payments effected after an insolvency or over-indebtedness of the company.

*Appointment and dismissal.* Managing directors can either be appointed in the articles or by a resolution of the shareholders. The right of appointment may be transferred to another organ, such as the supervisory board. If a GmbH has a mandatory supervisory board, the competence to appoint the managing directors is with such a board. In general, the duration of the appointment of the managing directors is not limited in time. Dismissal of managing directors is permitted at any time notwithstanding claims resulting from employment contracts.

*Qualification.* In general, there is no particular qualification required for appointment as a managing director. Every natural person capable of contracting may serve, unless he has been convicted because of certain offences. Nationality, domicile or permissions from public authorities do not constitute obstacles to the appointment as managing directors, but the articles of association may establish additional requirements for an appointment.

*Shareholder meetings (gesellschafterversammlungen)*

Although control and management rights belong to the individual shareholder, their exercise in general is collective. With regard to all matters of the company, the shareholders constitute the ultimate authority of the GmbH. Shareholder resolutions are normally passed by simple majority votes, but different majorities may be stipulated in the articles.

The general procedure is to take resolutions in meetings. This is only mandatory for resolutions carrying amendments to the articles (such amendments have to be notarised). For all other kinds of resolutions no meeting is required, if all shareholders either consent in writing to a proposed resolution or agree to cast the votes in writing. Additional facilitations can be stated by the articles, e.g. the exchange of telefax messages as long as individual shareholders do not object.

A shareholder meeting has to be called by the managing directors or the supervisory board if it appears to be necessary in the interest of the company. The place of meeting, if not established by the articles, is determined at the reasonable discretion of the authority competent to call the meeting. It can take place on or out of German territory.

Notice of the meeting is to be sent by registered letter at least one week in advance. With the convocation, the purpose of the meeting shall be announced. If a procedural defect occurs, valid resolutions may nevertheless be passed, if all shareholders are present in the meeting.

*Supervision of the management*

GmbHs need not have a supervisory board. Frequently, shareholders nevertheless opt for the establishment of such a board in order to facilitate corporate governance and management control. Such a "voluntary" supervisory board may, but need not, be governed by the rules on supervisory boards of share corporations (see above 2.4.2). The shareholders have a large amount of discretion to determine the rules on the structure, competence, and decisionmaking of such board. If the board is not structured along the lines of an AG's supervisory board, it is often called an "advisory board" (Beirat).

***Mandatory supervisory board.*** The establishment of a supervisory board is mandatory in the following circumstances: ① GmbHs with more than 500 employees are obliged to establish a supervisory board composed of one-third of employee representatives (§76,§77 Shop Constitution Act). ② For even larger GmbHs with more than 2,000 employees, the Co-Determination Act of 1976 requires an equal number of representatives from the shareholders and from the employees (the details are the same as for the supervisory board of share corporations of that size, see above 2.4.1.1).

***Accounting and auditing.*** The statutory rules on the accounting and auditing of a GmbH are basically the same ones as for an AG. If the GmbH does not have a supervisory board, the annual financial statements have to be approved by the shareholders. If there is a supervisory board, the managing directors have to submit to the board the annual financial statement together with a business report. The supervisory board is then entitled to review the results and to report these in writing to the shareholders. The final adoption of the results is generally made by the shareholders.

*(5) Amendment of the articles of association*

Since the articles govern both the organizational structure and business activities of the company, an amendment is perceived as a major change. It is therefore subject to particular procedural requirements.

*Resolution, application, registration*

To effect an amendment, a shareholder resolution has to be voted by a majority of three quarters. In this respect, the articles may establish further requirements, but no facilitations so that the articles may not allow an amendment to be passed by smaller majorities than three quarters. Amendments concerning basic principles, such as the equal treatment of the granting of preferential rights need the consent of all shareholders. Furthermore, the amending resolution must be recorded in notarial form, registered by the local court and published.

*Increase and decrease of capital*

Increases and decreases of capital are, generally speaking, the most important amendments to be made to the articles. In case of an increase of capital, the minimum amount required by law has to be paid prior to registration. The provisions to assure a proper formation of the GmbH apply accordingly. The procedure to realise a reduction in capital is even more demanding. It has to be published three times together with the request to the creditors to report to the company. Additionally, a registration of the resolution to decrease the capital can only come into effect after a waiting period of one year.

*(6) Cases of unlimited shareholder liability*

Despite the fact that limited liability constitutes the principal characteristic of a GmbH, an unlimited liability of the shareholders is possible under certain circumstances.

*Pre-registration liability*

As described above (*cf.* 3.2.3), the GmbH comes into legal existence with registration. Even before this formal act, a company exists from the moment of adoption of the articles. This pre-incorporation company is liable to third parties with the company assets.

A quite different and far-reaching liability is on the managing directors during the process of formation. In this period, the managing directors are personally, jointly and severally liable to any third party. This liability is not limited to the amount of capital share contributions, and therefore constitutes a rather serious form of liability. Before the company's registration, it can only be excluded by explicit agreement with the third party concerned.

*Liability for pre-registration losses*

After registration, the shareholders remain liable for so-called pre-registration losses. If the net assets of the GmbH at the moment of registration do not equal the subscribed share capital contributions, the shareholders are liable for the difference in the amount of the underfunding.

*Piercing the corporate veil*

In a number of cases, the German courts have developed the circumstances in which a shareholder may not rely on a GmbH's limited liability. The most important ones of these are thin capitalisation and the mixing-up between the company's and the shareholders' assets. If a GmbH is a member of a group of companies (Konzern), the parent company may be liable for the subsidiary's obligations, if it exercises corporate governance on a permanent basis. The details of these liabilities are fairly complex and depend very much on the particular circumstances of a case.

*(7) Dissolution and liquidation*

Dissolution generally is caused by expiration of the company's determined duration, by a resolution of the shareholders voted with a three-quarters' majority, by judgment or following bankruptcy proceedings. Upon dissolution, liquidation takes place unless bankruptcy proceedings have been initiated. The liquidation is, in principle, executed by the managing directors; the applicable procedure is described in detail in the GmbH-Act.

## New Words

| | | |
|---|---|---|
| 1. | sole proprietorship | 個人企業；獨資 |
| 2. | commercial partnership | 商業合夥 |
| 3. | civil partnership | 民事合夥 |
| 4. | silent partnership | 隱名合夥 |
| 5. | notarisation *n.* | 公證人的證實；附在文件上的公證書 |
| 6. | notarial form | 公證形式 |
| 7. | notary *n.* | 公證人 |
| 8. | general partnership | 一般合夥 |
| 9. | legal entity | 法律實體；法人 |
| 10. | ipso jure | 按法律；根據法律 |
| 11. | anonymous *a.* | 匿名的；無名的；不具名的 |
| 12. | interim certificates | 臨時證明 |
| 13. | option warrants | 選購權證 |
| 14. | effectuate *v.* | 實現；完成 |

| **15.** outweigh *v.* | 超過 |
| **16.** usufructuary rights | 用益權 |
| **17.** vis-à-vis | （拉）關於；對於 |
| **18.** abrogate *v.* | 撤銷；廢除 |
| **19.** interlocking | 連鎖的 |
| **20.** contest *v.* | 爭論 |
| **21.** disclosure requirements | 資訊揭露規定或要求 |
| **22.** hybrid *n.* | 混合（體） |
| **23.** afford *v.* | 提供；給予 |
| **24.** authenticate *v.* | 認證 |
| **25.** in-depth *a.* | 深入的；徹底的 |
| **26.** refund *v.* | 償還；退款 |
| **27.** recipient *n.* | 收受人；接受人 |
| **28.** composition *n.* | 和解協議 |
| **29.** convocation *n.* | 召開；召集 |
| **30.** demanding *a.* | 要求高的 |
| **31.** piercing the corporate veil | 揭穿公司面紗原則 |
| **32.** dissolution *n.* | 解散 |
| **33.** liquidation *n.* | 清算 |
| **34.** arrears *n.* | 欠款 |
| **35.** roster *n.* | 名單；花名冊 |
| **36.** leveraged buy-outs | 負債買下 |

## ♣ New Phrases and Idiomatic Expressions

| **1.** to take recourse to | 求助於 |
| **2.** for the time being | 暫時 |
| **3.** in kind | 用實物 |
| **4.** to be characterised by | 以……為特徵 |
| **5.** in linkage with | 與……有聯繫 |
| **6.** to decide on sth. | 就……作出決定 |
| **7.** regardless of | 不論 |
| **8.** to the detriment of | 對……有損害 |
| **9.** to opt for | 選擇…… |
| **10.** upon dissolution | 解散後 |
| **11.** in detail | 詳細地 |

**Notes**

1. civil partnership and commercial partnership

   民事合夥與商業合夥。德國民法典第二編第705-740條對民事合夥有規定；關於商業合夥的規定包含在商法典第105-160條中。

2. stock corporation (company)

   股份公司，也譯爲股份有限公司。

3. The share capital must be stipulated in the Articles...Prior to application for registration all shares must be subscribed...

   德國和法國等大陸法國家採取「法定資本制」。根據這個制度，在申請登記註冊前，在公司章程中必須載明股本額，所有股份必須認購完畢。

4. DM：德國馬克，爲「Deutsche Mark」的縮寫。

5. to the effect that：大意是……

   在 that 後跟一個句子，例如：He spoke to the effect that we should all go with him.

6. business organizations：商業組織

   商業組織亦稱「商業企業」，指能夠以自己名義從事營利性活動，並且具有一定規模的經濟組織。

7. the former EEC accounting directives：前歐洲共同體財務會計指示。

   如前EEC178/660第四號指示。根據前歐洲共同體法，這類指示本身不能對各成員國公民或企業直接發生效力，但各成員國有義務透過制定或修改相應的國內法使「指示」變爲其國內法以約束其本國的公司和公民。

**Exercises**

## I. Answer the following questions:

1. What are the three principal categories of business recognised by law in Germany?

2. What are the advantages of the mandatory three-tier system of German stock companies?

3. What are the three steps involved in forming a stock corporation (AG)?

4. What are the rules relating to share capital of an AG?

5. What are the usual forms of subscription of shares of an AG?

6. What is the major advantage of limited lability company (GmbH)?

7. What is the difference between an AG and a GmbH?

8. When will dissolution and liquidation take place?

## II. Translate the following Chinese passages into English:

**1.** 股份公司的股本必須在公司章程中規定，並用德國馬克來表示。在申請註冊登記前，所有股份必須認購完畢。

**2.** 公司股東享有四種權利。它們是：投票表決的權利、參加股東大會的權利、獲得公司活動資訊的權利、分享公司利潤的權利。

**3.** 有限公司於1982年首創於德國，其目的在於融合合夥企業與股份（有限）公司的優點於一身，以適應中小型企業，特別是股東對很少的大型企業的客觀需要。

**4.** 由於公司規定的期限屆滿、股東投票產生的決議以及公司的破產都會導致公司的解散。

## III. Indicate whether each of the following statements is true or false by writing "T" or "F" in the space provided:

____ **1.** The sole proprietor, as owner, takes all the profits and losses and personally bears all risks.

____ **2.** Civil partnerships are merely subject to the Civil Code while the commercial partnerships are governed by both the Commercial Code and the Civil Code.

____ **3.** In Germany the most common form of business organisation is the limited liability company (GmbH).

____ **4.** The three-tier system of the stock corporation (AG) in Germany refers to general shareholders' meetings, managing board and supervisory board with mandatory representation of employees.

____ **5.** Subscription of shares to an AG can take place only in cash.

____ **6.** After the implementation of the former EC accounting directives, the German regulations concerning accounting, auditing and publication basically are the same as in the other EU countries.

____ **7.** The managing board consisting of one or more persons is appointed by the supervisory board.

____ **8.** The establishment of a supervisory board is not always mandatory for GmbHs.

# PART IV

## 國際貿易法
## International Trade Law

<table>
<tr><td>第十五課<br>Lesson 15</td><td>英國代理<br>U.K. Agency</td></tr>
</table>

An agent is a person who affects the legal position of another, called a principal, in dealings with third parties. This lesson is mostly concerned with agents making contracts on behalf of their principals but other legal consequences may arise from an agency relationship and some of these will be explained.

Since an agent does not make contracts on his own behalf, it is not necessary that he should have contractual capacity. A minor or a bankrupt may be an agent. The principal, however, must have full contractual capacity; if he does not have it, he cannot make a contract by employing an agent who does.

There are many different types of agents but familiar examples include: directors who are agents of their companies and partners who, in certain circumstances, are each other's agents and agents of their firms. Apart from these commercial examples, the use of an agent to effect a contract is common too in consumer transactions; a person may book a holiday through a travel agent. However, not all those who describe themselves as "agents" will be considered in law as so being. A car dealer, for example, may be referred to as an "agent" for Volvo motorcars. Such a dealer, however, would buy the cars from the manufacturer and would sell the cars on his own behalf, as a principal, to the customer. A statutory exception can arise in this context when a customer buys a Volvo on hire purchase terms; although there is a contract of sale (of a car) between the dealer and the finance company and another such contract between the finance company and the customer, the dealer is deemed by the Consumer Credit Act 1974, s.56 to be the agent of the finance company as well as being a seller of a car to the finance company.

General and special agents

When an agent is employed to act for his principal in all matters concerning a particular trade or business, he is termed a general agent. A special agent is one who is employed to make only a particular contract or series of particular contracts. A managing director of a company is the general agent of the company, but if a man sends a friend to bid for him at an auction, the friend is the special agent of the sender.

# Creation of Agency

The power of an agent to affect the legal position of a principal is derived either from the authority vested in the agent or from operation of law, i.e. where the law imposes an agency relationship in certain factual situations.

# Authority of The Agent

### 1. Actual authority

(1) Express authority. This type of authority is created by words, either written or oral. It often derives from a contract between the principal and agent, although an agent may act gratuitously. No particular form is required unless the agent is appointed to execute a deed, in which case he must be given authority in a deed, called a power of attorney. Powers of attorney are governed by the Powers of Attorney Act 1971, as amended by the Law of Property (Miscellaneous Provisions) Act 1989, s. 1, schedule 1 which dispenses with the requirement for a seal.

(2) Implied authority. The agent's implied authority permits him to perform all subordinate or incidental acts necessary to exercise his express authority.

Implied authority is sometimes divided into:

(a) *Usual authority*. This is a more specific form of implied authority which relates to agents of a certain type acting in the "usual" way of such agents. Unfortunately, the term usual authority has become confused due mainly to the case of Watteau v. Fenwick.

(b) *Customary authority*. Here, an agent's implied authority derives from a locality, market or business usage.

### 2. Apparent or ostensible authority

"An 'apparent' or 'ostensible' authority... is a legal relationship between the principal and the contractor (the third party) created by a representation, made by the principal to the contractor, intended to be and in fact acted on by the contractor, that the agent has authority to enter on behalf of the principal into a contract of a kind within the scope of the 'apparent' authority, so as to render the principal liable to perform any obligations imposed on him by such contract...".

Apparent authority may arise where there is or was an agency relationship in existence, but unknown to the third party, the actual authority has been limited or terminated.

Apparent authority clearly operates to protect third parties and may arise even where there has never been an agency relationship created between principal, and "agent." Provided the principal represents by words or conduct to the third party that the "agent" has authority to act on his behalf and the third party relies on this representation by entering into a contract, the principal will be prevented or estopped from denying the agency. Normally the principal's representation precedes the contract, but he may be bound by his behaviour subsequent to the contract.

# Operation of Law

### 1. Agency of Necessity

Agency of necessity occurs when a person is entrusted with another's property and it becomes necessary to do something to preserve that property. In such a case, although the person who is entrusted with the property has no express authority to do the act necessary to preserve it, because of the necessity such an authority is presumed. For example, if a horse is sent by train and on its arrival there is no one to receive it, the railway company, being bound to take reasonable steps to keep the horse alive, has been held to be the agent of necessity of the owner for the purpose of sending it to a livery stable for the night.

The master of a ship in cases of necessity can pledge the ship as security for the cost of repairs necessary to enable her to continue the voyage, provided that (a) there was a reasonable necessity according to the ordinary course of prudent conduct to pledge the ship; (b) the amount was advanced expressly for the use of the ship; and (c) the money was expended on the ship. If there is an agent of the shipowner on the spot, the master has no such authority.

But before any agency can be created by necessity, there conditions must be satisfied-

(1) It must be impossible to get the principal's instructions.

(2) There must be an actual and definite commercial necessity for the creation of the agency.

Generally, there is no agency of necessity unless there is a real emergency, such as may arise out of the possession of perishable goods or of livestock requiring to be fed.

(3) The agent of necessity must act bona fide in the interests of all parties concerned.

It is not possible to define all the situations in which an agency of necessity arises, but such an agency will be implied more easily when there is an existing agency which requires extending to provide for unforeseen events not dealt with in the original contract, than when there is no such agency. The relevant time for considering whether in particular circumstances there was a necessity or an emergency is the time when the existence of the supposed emergency became apparent.

### 2. Agency from cohabitation

At a time when the equality of sexes was not as clearly established as today and most wives looked after the common household and did not earn their own living, the common law developed the following principles. In modern times their application may be somewhat doubtful and it may well be that in appropriate cases the court may hold that it is the intention of the wife and the contracting party that the wife has not acted as agent of her husband and has made herself liable to the third party as principal.

At common law when a husband and wife are living together, the wife is presumed to have her husband's authority to pledge his credit for necessaries, judged according to his style and standard of living. The presumption of agency arises from cohabitation, not from marriage. The presumption can, however, be rebutted by the husband proving that:

(1) he expressly forbade his wife to pledge his credit; or

(2) he expressly warned the supplier not to supply his wife with goods on credit; or

(3) his wife was already sufficiently supplied with goods of the kind in question; or

(4) his wife was supplied with a sufficient allowance or sufficient means for the purpose of buying such goods without pledging the husband's credit; or

(5) the order, though for necessaries, was excessive in extent or, having regard to the husband's income, extravagant.

If the husband has been in the habit of paying his wife's bills with a particular supplier, his wife's agency will be presumed and he can only escape liability by expressly informing the supplier that his wife's authority is revoked. If the supplier gave credit to the wife personally and not to the wife as her husband's agent, the husband is not liable. In this connection, it is to be noted that the former rule that if a wife saved money from a housekeeping allowance made by the husband, such money belonged to the husband, has been changed by the Married Women's property Act 1964 with the result that, in the absence of any agreement to the contrary, such money is to be treated as belonging to the husband and wife in equal shares.

# Ratification

If an agent has no authority to contract on behalf of a principal or exceeds such authority as he has, the contract is not binding on the principal. The principal may, however, afterwards confirm and adopt the contract so made; this is known as ratification.

The effect of ratification is to render the contract as binding on the principal as if the agent had been actually authorised beforehand. Ratification relates back to the original making of the contract.

A contract can only be ratified under the following conditions:

(1) The agent must expressly have contracted as agent. If, having no authority in fact, he merely intended to contract as agent and did not disclose his intention to the other party, i.e. if without authority he purports to act for an undisclosed principal no ratification is possible.

(2) The contract can only be ratified by the principal who was named or ascertainable when the contract was made. If the principal was named, he can ratify the contract even if the agent never intended that he should do so, but wanted to keep the benefit of the contract for himself.

(3) The agent must have a principal who was in actual existence at the time of the contract. If, therefore, a person purports to enter into a contract as agent for a company which is not yet formed, then, subject to any agreement to the contrary, he will be personally liable in the contract as if it were his own.

(4) The principal must have had contractual capacity at the date of the contract and have it at the date of ratification. If the principal was, for example, an enemy at the date of the contract there can be no valid ratification.

(5) The principal must, at the time of ratification, have full knowledge of the material facts or intend to ratify the contract whatever the facts may be.

(6) The principal must ratify within the time set or within a reasonable time. Ratification may be either expressed or implied by the conduct of the principal.

# Breach of Implied Warranty of Authority

A person who professes to act as agent, but has no authority from the alleged principal or has exceeded his authority, is liable in an action for breach of warranty of authority at the suit of the party with whom he professed to make the contract (Collen v. Wright (1857) 8E. & B, 647). The action is based, not on the original contract, but on the implied representation by the agent that he had authority to make the original contract. Points to note:

1. The action can only be brought by the third party, not by the principal.

2. The agent is liable whether he has acted fraudulently, negligently or innocently, and even if his authority has been terminated, without his knowledge, by death or mental disorder of the principal.

3. The agent is not liable if his lack of authority was known to the third party, or if it was known that he did not warrant his authority or if the contract excludes his liability.

4. If the principal gives ambiguous instructions and the agent acts on them bona fide and in a reasonable way, he will not be liable in an action for breach of warranty of authority even if he has interpreted them wrongly.

In view of modern communication methods, however, if an agent receives instructions which are ambiguous and he realizes or ought to realize this, he may be under a duty to seek clarification.

5. The agent warrants his authority not only when he purports to contract on behalf of another but also when, purporting to act as an agent, he induces a third party to enter into any transaction with him on the faith of such agency.

6. Damages for breach of warranty are assessed by reference to the rules laid down in Hadley v. Baxendale (1854) 9 Ex. 341 for breach of contract, except that the liability is limited to the actual damage flowing from the agent's lack of authority and not for the breach of contract. If the agent is sued in tort (deceit or negligence or under the Misrepresentation Act 1967) damages will be awarded according to the rules relating to torts.

# Effect of Contracts Made by Agents

The effect of a contract made by an agent varies according to the circumstances under which the agent contracted.

### 1. Where the agent contracts as agent for a named principal

In this case the agent incurs neither rights nor liabilities under the contract.

Exceptions:

(1) Where the agent executes a deed in his own name he is liable on the deed, Note: the principal may also be liable.

(2) Where the agent signs a bill of exchange in his own name without indicating that he has signed as agent, he is liable on the bill.

(3) Where the nature of the contract and the surrounding circumstances make it clear that the agent is liable.

(4) Where the agent is in fact the principal but contracts as agent he is liable on the contract and can enforce it.

(5) Where the custom of a trade makes the agent liable.

It was once thought that an agent contracting on behalf of a foreign principal was personally liable, but it is now settled that there is no presumption of liability on the part of the agent.

It is possible that a person can be a party to a contract in two capacities i.e. as principal and as agent.

### 2. Where the agent contracts as agent for an unnamed principal

In this case the agent discloses the existence, but not the name, of his principal. As the agent expressly contracts as agent, he cannot be personally liable on the contract.

If, however, the agent does not, on the face of the contract, show that he is merely an agent, he will incur personal liability, and the third party may sue either him or his principal at his option. Descriptive words, e.g. on the heading of notepaper or following a signature, such as "broker" or "manager," are not sufficient of themselves to negative personal liability.

### 3. Where the agent contracts as agent for an undisclosed principal

In this case the agent discloses neither the existence nor the identity of the principal; he contracts with the third party as if he were the principal. Here: (1) the undisclosed principal has the right to intervene and claim, and if necessary sue, the third party directly. If he makes use of this right, he renders himself personally liable to the third party; and (2) the third party, after having discovered the principal, has an option. He may elect to hold liable and sue either the principal or the agent.

If the third party unequivocally elects to hold either the principal or the agent liable he cannot afterwards change his mind and sue the other. Commencement of proceedings against either is prima facie evidence of such election, but if that evidence is rebutted this does not bar subsequent proceedings against the other. On the other hand, obtaining judgment against either is conclusive evidence, even if unsatisfied, and bars proceedings against the other.

The ordinary rules that an undisclosed principal can intervene and that the third party can elect to sue the principal directly apply also where the undisclosed principal is a foreigner residing abroad; this fact is only one of the elements taken into consideration when determining whether he can sue.

The undisclosed principal may not intervene: (1) where it is contrary to the terms of the contract; (2) where the personality of the principal or agent is a significant factor; (3) where the third party made the contract with the agent to obtain the benefit of a setoff.

Where the rights relating to the undisclosed principal can be duly exercised, the principal can be met with any defence which was available to the third party against the agent before the third party discovered the existence of the principal.

If the third party did not believe the agent to be a principal, he cannot set off any claim he has against the agent against the principal.

If an agent borrows money without his principal's authority and applies it in payment of his principal's debts, the lender of the money is entitled to recover the loan as money had and received by the principal to the lender's use.

### 4. Torts of the agent

The principal is jointly and severally liable with his agent for any torts committed within the scope of his authority. Where the alleged act is performed by an agent acting within his actual authority, it is for the third party to prove that the principal did in fact authorise that particular act. Merely performing an act within the type or class authorised by the principal would not render the principal liable (*Kooragang Investments Property Ltd. v. Richardson and Wrench* [1981] 3 All E. R. 65). More often the wrongful act is performed by the agent acting within his apparent or ostensible authority.

# Rights and Duties between Principal and Agent

### 1. Duties of agent

The duties of an agent are:

(1) To exercise due diligence in the performance of his duties and to apply any special skill which he professes to have. If he is employed to sell, it is his duty to obtain the best price reasonably obtainable, and his duty does not cease when he has procured an offer which has been conditionally accepted.

He must disclose to his principal anything coming to his knowledge which is likely to influence the principal in the making of the contract.

The standard of care owed by a gratuitous agent is an objective standard i.e.: "that which may reasonably be expected of him in all the circumstances."

(2) To render an account when required.

(3) Not to become principal as against his employer. This is part of the more general duty that an agent must not let his interest conflict with his duty.

(4) Not to make any profit beyond the commission or other remuneration paid by his principal. So, for example, an agent is accountable to his principal for any profit which he makes, without the principal's consent, out of

① any property with which he has been entrusted by his principal.

② a position of authority, to which he has been appointed by his principal.

③ any information or knowledge, which he has been employed by his principal to collect or discover, or which he has otherwise acquired for the use of his principal. The reason for this is that such information or knowledge is the property of his principal, just as an invention would be.

An agent is, however, not so accountable when the information or knowledge is not of a special or secret character and he is not dealing with the property of his principal. This is because the agent cannot be prevented from taking advantage of an opportunity of earning money, although it is an opportunity which comes his way because of his employment as agent, provided he does not use his principal's property or break his contract by so doing.

If an agent does make a secret profit, the result is that the principal has the right to do all the following —

① The principal may recover the amount of the secret profit from the agent.

② The principal may refuse to pay the agent his commission or other remuneration. In Hippisley v. Knee, it was held that since the agents had not acted fraudulently they were entitled to their commission.

③ The principal may dismiss the agent without notice.

④ The principal may repudiate the contract.

⑤ Where the secret profit amounts to a bribe *i.e.* a payment made to the agent by the third party, the principal has in addition to (b), (c) and (d) above, alternative remedies: either for money had and received under which he can recover the amount of the bribe, or for damages for fraud, under which he can recover the amount of the actual loss arising from his entering into the transaction in respect of which the bribe was given, but he cannot recover both.

If the principal wishes to rescind the contract, he must establish that the third party had actual knowledge or was willfully blind to the fact that the agent intended to conceal his dealings from his principal. Where, on discovering the bribe, it is too late to rescind the contract, the principal may bring the transaction to an end for the future.

Both the agent and the person paying a bribe are guilty of a criminal offence under the Prevention of Corruption Acts 1906, 1916.

Where a person assumes the character of agent, i.e. takes it upon himself to act as if he were the duly authorised agent of another, he is liable to account to that other, as principal, for any profit made out of the property of that other person.

Before an agent can recover a commission from two principals whose interests are inconsistent he must make the fullest disclosure to each of his principals of his own position, and must obtain the consent of each of them to the double employment.

(5) Not to delegate his authority.

The relation between the principal and his agent being a personal one, the agent cannot employ another to do it for him except in the ordinary way of business, as by employing clerks and assistants. Delegation may take place in case of necessity or where it is customary or sanctioned by the principal. An estate agent who has been appointed "sole agent" has no implied authority to appoint a sub-agent.

(6) Not to disclose confidential information or documents entrusted to him by his principal. This is part of the agent's general duty of good faith. During the agency the agent must not act against the principal's interest.

In exceptional circumstances, where the principal fears that he may suffer damage if the agent destroys, or disposes of confidential information, the principal may obtain an ex parte injunction (i.e. an injunction granted on the application of one party, the principal, without the other party, the agent, being represented) authorising the principal's representative, usually a solicitor, to enter the agent's premises and to remove the confidential material. Such an injunction is called an **Anton Piller injunction** because it was first granted in *Anton Piller K.G. v. Manufacturing Processes Ltd*. [1976] Ch.55.

The burden of proving breach of duty by the agent is on the principal.

### 2. Duties of principal

The duties of the principal are:

(1) To pay the agent the commission or other remuneration agreed.

The amount of the commission and the terms under which it is payable depend entirely on the terms of the contract between the parties. There is no general rule by which the rights of the agent or the liabilities of the principal under commission contracts are to be determined, but when an agent claims commission from a principal:

① When an agent claims that he has earned the right to commission the test is whether on the proper interpretation of the contract between the principal and the agent the "event" has happened on which commission is to be paid.

② Once the "event" has happened it must be shown that it was the agent who was the "effective cause" of it.

The following are examples of such events with the implications. If the agent is to be paid a commission:

① on the sale of a particular thing, he is entitled to his commission if the thing is sold to a buyer whom he has introduced, although he may not have negotiated the terms of the sale and although the terms were accepted contrary to his advice. He need not be the first who introduced the buyer.

② on a sale being completed, it is not enough for the agent acting on behalf of the seller to find a buyer who signs an agreement to purchase but refuses to complete or to pay the purchase money. In such an even the seller is not obliged to sue for specific performance to enable the agent to obtain his commission. If it is the seller who refuses to complete, this will constitute the breach of an implied term of the agency contract that the principal (the seller) will not fail to perform the contract of sale with the buyer so as to deprive the agent of the commission due to him. If the buyer is able and willing to complete but signs an agreement "subject to contract" and the seller refuses to complete, no commission is payable. Neither is it payable if the seller refuses to sign the contract.

③ if he introduces a person "willing and able to purchase": he is not entitled to commission if he introduces one who is willing to purchase subject to contract or subject to satisfactory survey.

④ if he introduces a person ready, able and willing to purchase: it is payable when a person who is able to purchase is introduced and expresses readiness and willingness by an unqualified offer to purchase, though such offer has not been accepted and could be withdrawn.

⑤ if a "prospective purchaser" is found, the agent is entitled to commission if he finds a person who in good faith seriously contemplates the purchase and makes an offer, though, in the end, he might not be ready, willing and able to purchase.

A contract by which the owner of a house, wishing to dispose of it, puts it in the hands of an estate agent on commission terms, is not (in the absence of specific provisions) a contract of employment in the usual sense; for no obligation is imposed on the agent to do anything. The contract is merely a promise binding on the principal to pay a sum of money upon the happening of a specified event, which involves the rendering of some service by the agent. Nevertheless, the ostensible authority of an estate agent invited to find a purchaser for premises or a lessee for premises does not extend to entering into any contractual relationship on behalf of the person instructing him in respect of the premises.

When property is entrusted to an agent to sell there is, in the absence of any stipulation to the contrary, an implied term that the owner himself may sell or employ other agents to sell the property. But if an agent is employed as "sole agent" no other agent can be employed, although the owner may still sell the property himself without paying commission.

Where an estate agent is not the effective cause of the sale, although no commission is payable, he may be entitled to a quantum merit.

When an agency has been created for a fixed time, but is revoked before the expiration of that date, the agent is entitled to damages for being prevented from earning his commission if there is an obligation, express or implied, on the part of the principal to continue the agency for that time.

If the employment is one of agency merely, with no service and subordination, and the agent can act for other principals also, there is in general no obligation on the part of the principal to supply the agent with the means of earning his commission; but if the contract is one of service, then the commission is merely intended to be in the place of salary, and the contract cannot be determined without compensation to the servant.

If the sale had been made for the express purpose of defeating the agent's right to commission the principal could not have relieved himself from liability. An agreement to pay commission to an agent if a sale is effected at one price does not bind the principal to pay any commission if a sale is effected at a lower price.

Commission may be payable even after the termination of the agency. This, however, is exceptional. "Prima facie the liability to pay commission... ceases as to future trade with the cessation of the employment in the absence of a reasonably clear intention to the contrary."

An agreement to pay on "repeat" orders may show this intention. So may an agreement to pay commission as long as the principal does business with the customers introduced. An agent who received an advance on his commission from his principal is normally bound to account for any excess on termination of his contract.

(2) To indemnify the agent for acts lawfully done and liabilities incurred in the execution of his authority.

The agent loses his right to an indemnity if he acts beyond his authority or performs his duty negligently.

# Termination of Agency

Agency is terminated by:

(a)the act of the parties; and

(b)operation of law.

## 1. By act of the parties

The contract of agency can be terminated by mutual agreement between the parties, but the authority of the agent can be revoked at any time by the principal. If the revocation is a breach of his contract with the agent, the principal will be liable to pay damages for loss of the agent's commission or other remuneration. The power of the principal to revoke the authority of the agent is limited in two directions:

(1) If a principal has allowed an agent to assume authority, a revocation of that authority will only be effective as against third parties, if the third parties are informed of the revocation of authority. For example, if B. is the agent of C. to collect debts due to C., and C. revokes B.'s authority and then B., ostensibly on C.'s behalf, collects a debt from X. who has previously paid B. as C.'s agent, the payment will be good as between X. and C. unless X. knew at the time of payment that B. no longer had authority to collect debts.

(2) If the principal has given the agent an authority coupled with an interest, the authority is irrevocable. An example of such an authority is where X. sells the goodwill and book-debts of his business to Y. and appoints Y. his agent to collect the debts due to the business. In such a case, as the book-debts form part of the consideration for the sale, X. cannot revoke the authority he has given to Y.

The mere appointment of an agent to collect debts for five years on a commission is not an authority coupled with an interest.

## 2. By operation of law

The authority of an agent is revoked by the principal —

① having died;

② becoming bankrupt;

③ becoming mentally disordered; or

④ becoming an enemy.

Although the mental disorder of the principal revokes the authority of the agent, the principal will be bound by contracts made with third parties who have no notice of that incapacity.

When the principal becomes an enemy the authority of the agent ceases on the ground that it is not permissible to have intercourse with an enemy, and the existence of the relationship of principal and agent necessitates such intercourse.

# Types of Agent

### 1. Estate agents

The Estate Agents Act 1979 establishes procedures, within the competence of the Director General of Fair Trading, whereby a person can be adjudged and registered as unfit to do "estate agency work" (section 1(1)), and in consequence is prohibited from engaging in such work. An individuals unfitness or otherwise for such work may be determined by a number of criteria including, inter alia, his failure to give complete information on the likely charges and other liabilities at the time the agent is appointed, to disclose any personal interest in the property, to maintain a separate client deposit account, and to cover any clients money received by him by insurance against his failing to account for it. The Secretary of State may further impose by regulation standards of competence on those engaged in estate agency work (s.22(1)).

Estate agents may receive a deposit from the intending purchaser either as agents of the vendor or in an independent capacity, *e.g.* as stakeholders. The liability of the vendor to return the deposit if the agent is unable to do so arises only if the vendor has authorised the agent to receive a deposit on his behalf. If the vendor has given the agent no actual authority, there would be no liability because the estate agent does not have implied authority to receive a deposit as agent of the vendor.

The vendor is not liable for the return of the deposit. Estate agents who mislead buyers may be prosecuted under the Property Misdescriptions Act 1991.

### 2. Auctioneers

An auctioneer is an agent to sell goods at a public auction.

On a sale by auction there are three contracts:

(1) Between the owner of the goods (the vendor) and the highest bidder to whom the goods are knocked down (the purchaser). This is a simple contract of sale to which the auctioneer is not a party.

(2) Between the owner of the goods (the vendor) and the auctioneer. The vendor entrusts the auctioneer with the possession of the goods for sale by auction. The understanding is that the auctioneer should not part with the possession of them to the purchaser except against payment of the price: or, if the auctioneer should part with them without receiving payment, he is responsible to the vendor for the price. The auctioneer has, as against the vendor, a lien on the proceeds for his commission and charges.

(3) Between the auctioneer and the highest bidder (the purchaser). The auctioneer has possession of the goods and has a lien on them for the whole price. He is not bound to deliver the goods to the purchaser except on receiving the price in cash; or, if he is willing to accept a cheque, on receiving a cheque payable to himself, the auctioneer for the price. If he does allow the purchaser to take delivery without paying the price the auctioneer can, as he has a special property in the goods, sue in his own name for the full price. If the highest bidder refuses to take delivery of the goods the auctioneer can sue him for the price.

An auctioneer's implied authority is to sell without reserve price, and therefore a sale by him below the reserve will be binding on his principal even if the principal had instructed him not to sell below a definite price. On the other hand if the auctioneer states that the sale is subject to a reserve, but by mistake knocks the article down at a price below the reserve, the sale is not binding on the owner. In the latter case the buyer is informed that there is a limitation on the auctioneer's authority and therefore bids can only be accepted subject to the reserve being reached. The buyer will be entitled to sue the auctioneer for damages for breach of warranty of authority.

### 3. Mercantile agents

A mercantile agent, also called a factor, is a person who, in the customary course of his business as such agent, has authority either to sell goods, or to consign goods for the purpose of sale, or to buy goods, or to raise money on the security of goods (**Factors Act 1889**, s.1(1)). He has a general lien on goods in his possession and on the proceeds of sale of such goods for the balance of account between himself and his principal. Under the Factors Act, mercantile agents, who are not the owners of goods, can in certain circumstances, sell them and give good title to the buyer.

### 4. Confirming houses

In the export trade, when a supplier receives an order from a customer abroad, he sometimes asks for confirmation of that order by a person in the supplier's country. The confirmer "adds confirmation or assurance to the bargain which has been made by the primary contractor" and is personally liable to the supplier if the buyer abroad fails to perform the contract.

A confirmer has a particular, but not a general, lien on the goods or documents of title of his overseas principal.

If the confirmer fails to pay, the seller has still his claim for the purchase price against the buyer.

## 5. Brokers

A broker is an agent who is employed to buy or sell on behalf of another. He differs from a mercantile agent by not having possession of goods, and consequently he has no lien and he cannot sue in his own name on the contract. Brokers who are members of the Stock Exchange or a commercial exchange or other similar institution have an implied authority to make their contracts subject to the rules of such institution, but beyond that they have no implied or presumed authority of any kind. Brokers are not liable to their principal for the failure of a buyer to pay the price.

## 6. Del credere agents

A del credere agent is an agent employed to sell goods who undertakes for extra commission that purchasers he procures will pay for any goods they take. He only undertakes that he will pay, if the purchasers do not pay, owing to insolvency or an analogous cause. But he does not make himself liable to his principal if his buyer refuses to take delivery.

### New Words

| | | |
|---|---|---|
| 1. | hire purchase | 分期付款租購；租購；分期付款購買 |
| 2. | managing director | 總經理 |
| 3. | operation of law | 法律的作用；法律的實施；法律的運用 |
| 4. | gratuitously *adv.* | 無償地；免費地 |
| 5. | gratuitous *a.* | 無償的；免費的 |
| 6. | miscellaneous provisions | 各式各樣的規定；雜則 |
| 7. | undisclosed *a.* | 未被公開的；不披露姓名的 |
| 8. | precede *v.* | 處在……之前；先於 |
| 9. | agency of necessity | 客觀必須的代理；緊急處分的代理 |
| 10. | perishable *a.* | 易腐爛的；易變質的 |
| 11. | per *prep.* | 按照；根據 |
| 12. | cohabitation *n.* | 同居；姘居 |
| 13. | rebut *v.* | 反駁；駁回 |
| 14. | i.e. (id est) | （拉）那就是；即（相當於「that is」） |
| 15. | profess *v.* | 聲稱 |
| 16. | charter party *n.* | 租船契約；傭船契約 |

17. air compressors　　　　　　　空氣壓縮機

18. e.g. (exempli gratia)　　　　　（拉）例如（相當於「for example」）

19. unequivocally *adv.*　　　　　不含糊地；明確地

20. prima facie　　　　　　　　　初步的；表面的

21. principal *n.*　　　　　　　　（代理中的）本人

22. apparent or ostensible　　　　表見代理權或名義代理權
authority

23. confirming agent　　　　　　保付代理人

24. unroadworthy *a.*　　　　　　不適合於公路行駛的

25. estate agent　　　　　　　　不動產經紀人

26. terms of the contract　　　　契約條款

27. ex dividend　　　　　　　　無股息

28. cum dividend　　　　　　　有股息

29. ex parte　　　　　　　　　　單方面的（地）

30. colliery *n.*　　　　　　　　煤礦（包括建築物和設備等在內）

31. repeat orders　　　　　　　重複訂貨；繼續訂貨

32. book-debts　　　　　　　　帳面債務

33. inter alia　　　　　　　　　（拉）除了別的以外；特別

34. vendor *n.*　　　　　　　　賣主（與vendee（買主）相對）

35. documents of title　　　　　所有權狀

36. del credere agents　　　　　擔保代理人

37. wary *a.*　　　　　　　　　謹防的；唯恐的

38. quantum merit　　　　　　　依照服務計酬；相當的付給

## ☘ New Phrases and Idiomatic Expressions

1. to arise out of　　　　　　　由……產生；起源於……

2. to earn one's own living　　　謀生

3. in the habit of doing sth.　　有做某事的習慣

4. on credit　　　　　　　　　賒帳

5. by reference to　　　　　　參閱；參照

6. as follows　　　　　　　　如下

7. on the faith of sb.　　　　　憑……的保證；憑……的信用

8. to set off　　　　　　　　（債務）抵消；補償；相抵

9. to amount to　　　　　　　等於

10. to break out　　　　　　　發生

| | |
|---|---|
| **11.** in the absence of | 缺乏……；不存在 |
| **12.** to put an end to | 結束 |
| **13.** to be coupled with | 連同 |
| **14.** to knock down the goods | （拍賣時）擊錘賣出貨物；殺價 |
| **15.** to bid for | 為……出價 |
| **16.** to be wary in doing sth. | 謹防做某事；唯恐做某事 |
| **17.** to be entrusted with | 被……委託 |

## Notes

**1.** However, not all those who describe themselves as "agents" will be <u>considered in law as so being</u>.

But, not all those who call themselves as "agents" will be treated as agents.

"be considered in law as so being": be considered in law as being so.

**2.** Points to note: There are the following points to be noted.

**3.** We had committed a breach of duty <u>towards</u> K.

In American English "towards" is spelt as "toward" without "s". 一般來說，美國英語中的拼寫比英國英語中的拼寫簡單，例如：（英）labour＝（美）labor；（英）plough＝（美）plow等。

**4.** ...whose <u>books</u> were destroyed in the fire...

英語中的一個詞往往有幾個意思。根據上下文此句中的books當「帳冊」講。

**5.** Lloyd's：（英）勞埃德，指設在倫敦的保險商和保險經紀人的公會，是按1871年勞埃德法例組成的法人社團，起初在17世紀末從事海上保險業務，現在幾乎已成為經營任何種類保險的一個國際市場。

## Exercises

### I. Answer the following questions:

**1.** What is an agent? How many types of agents do you know?

**2.** Where does the power of an agent come from?

**3.** What is meant by express authority and implied authority?

**4.** What is agency of necessity? When will it arise?

**5.** Does apparent authority operate to protect third parties? How?

**6.** What does ratification mean in agency? Under what conditions an agency can be ratified?

**7.** What is the effect of contract made by agents for an undisclosed principal?

**8.** What are the main duties of agent?

**9.** What are the main duties of principal?

**10.** In what circumstances will agency be terminated?

## II. Translate the following Chinese passages into English:

**1.** 代理人是指在與第三人打交道中影響另一個人（本人）法律地位的人。在英國有各式各樣的代理人，大家比較熟悉的有：董事（公司的代理人）、合夥人（相互的代理人）、拍賣人（貨主的代理人）、銀行（儲戶的代理人）、房地產代理人、經紀人等。

**2.** 明示授權、默示授權、客觀必須的代理權（agency of necessity）都能產生代理。由於代理人不能代表自己簽訂契約，因此他不需要有行為能力。

**3.** 代理人有以下義務：

(1)勤勉地履行其代理職責；

(2)必要時開出帳目；

(3)除本人付給的佣金或其他報酬外，不得謀私利；

(4)不能成為反對其雇主的人；

(5)不得將其代理權委託給他人。

**4.** 本人的義務包括：向代理人支付佣金或其他報酬和對代理人完成的合法行為以及他在執行代理權中產生的債務進行補償。

## III. Indicate whether each of the following statements is true or false by writing "T" or "F" in the space provided:

**1.** An agent can make contract on his own behalf therefore he must have contractual capacity.

**2.** A managing director of a company is the special agent of the company.

**3.** Implied authority is sometimes divided into usual authority and customary authority.

**4.** The effect of ratification is to render the contract as binding on the principal as if the agent had been actually authorized before hand.

**5.** The principal is jointly and severally liable with his agent for any torts committed within the scope of his authority.

**6.** An agent can make a secrete profit for himself.

**7.** The contract of agency can be terminated by mutual agreement between the parties, but the authority of agent can be revoked at any time by the principal.

_____ **8.** An auctioneer is an agent to sell goods at a public auction.

_____ **9.** A broker is an agent who is employed to buy or sell on behalf of another.

_____ **10.** A del credere agent is an agent employed to sell goods who undertakes for extra commission that purchasers he procures will pay for any goods they take.

# 第十六課 Lesson 16

# 關貿總協定
# The General Agreement on Tariffs and Trade (GATT)

After World War II, several international measures were undertaken to liberalize trade and payments between nations. Plans for the creation of a liberal, multilateral system of world trade were started while the war was still in progress. Initiated for the most part by the United States, these plans envisaged the close economic cooperation of all nations in the fields of international trade, payments, and investment. At the time, it was widely believed that such cooperation, formalized by agreements, and implemented by international organizations, would avoid the mistakes of the past and lay the cornerstones for a progressive world economy. The two notable achievements of this wartime planning were the International Monetary Fund and the International Bank for Reconstruction and Development. The first institution was to insure the free convertibility of currencies; the second was to supplement and stimulate the international flow of private capital.

Once the war had ended, it soon became apparent that the difficulties of postwar reconstruction in Europe and elsewhere had been greatly underestimated. The weakness of the United Kingdom was dramatically highlighted by its failure to restore the convertibility of the pound in the summer of 1947, despite the assistance of the Anglo-American loan negotiated the previous year. Attention shifted from the now distant goal of a global system of multilateral trade to the immediate threat posed by Western Europe's economic distress and by the spread of Communism. The end of ambitious international planning was symbolized by the refusal of the United States Congress in 1950 to ratify the treaty establishing an International Trade Organization (ITO). As we shall see, the failure of the ITO was offset somewhat by the existence of the General Agreement on Tariffs and Trade. In the 1950's and 1960's new arrangements to liberalize trade and payments have been regional in nature and have focused primarily on Europe.

## 1. The birth of GATT

The effects of the failure of the ITO on international cooperation in commercial policy were considerably softened by the rise to prominence of the General Agreement on Tariffs and Trade, known as GATT. GATT was an almost casual offshoot of the international conference held at Geneva in 1947 to consider a draft charter for the ITO. There the United States initiated six months of continual negotiations with twenty-two other countries that led to commitments to bind or lower 45,000 tariff rates within the framework of principles and rules of procedure laid down by GATT.

Technically, GATT was viewed by the United States Administration as a trade agreement that came under the provisions of the Reciprocal Trade Agreements Act and, hence, did not require the approval of Congress. It was considered a provisional agreement that would lapse when the ITO was established to take over its functions. In the interim, GATT was to serve as a token of America's willingness to implement a liberal trade policy and thereby gain the adherence of other countries to the projected ITO. GATT began its "provisional" existence on January 1, 1948, when eight of its contracting parties, including the United States, put into effect the tariff concessions negotiated at Geneva.

### 2. Major provisions of GATT

The General Agreement is a document containing numerous articles and annexes. The tariff schedules listing the thousands of concessions that have been negotiated by the contracting parties are also part of the Agreement. Despite its complexity, GATT comprises four basic elements:

(1) The rule of nondiscrimination in trade relations between the participating countries.

(2) Commitments to observe the negotiated tariff concessions.

(3) Prohibitions against the use of quantitative restrictions (quotas) on exports and imports.

(4) Special provisions to promote the trade of developing countries.

The remaining provisions of GATT are concerned with exceptions to these general principles, trade measures other than tariffs and quotas, and sundry procedural matters.

*Tariffs.* GATT obligates each contracting party to accord nondiscriminatory, most-favored-nation treatment to all other contracting parties with respect to import and export duties (including allied charges), customs regulations, and internal taxes and regulations. An exception to the rule of nondiscrimination is made in the case of well-known tariff preferences, such as those between the countries of the British Commonwealth. No new preferences may be created, however, and existing preferences may not be increased. Frontier traffic, customs unions, and free trade areas are exempted from the general rule of nondiscrimination.

GATT legalizes the schedules of tariff concessions negotiated by the contracting parties and commits each contracting party to their observance. An escape clause, however, allows any contracting, party to withdraw or modify a tariff concession (or other obligation) if, as a result of the tariff concession (or obligation), there is such an increase in imports as to cause, or threaten to cause, serious injury to domestic producers of like or directly competitive products. When a member country uses the escape clause, it must consult with other member countries as to remedies; if agreement is not reached, those countries may withdraw equivalent concessions.

***Quantitative Restrictions.*** GATT sets forth a general rule prohibiting the use of quantitative import and export restrictions. There are, however, several exceptions to this rule. The four most important exceptions pertain to agriculture, the balance of payments, economic development, and national security.

The Agreement sanctions the use of import restrictions on any agricultural or fisheries product where restrictions are necessary for the enforcement of government programs in marketing, production control, or the removal of surpluses. This exception is important to the United States, which has placed import quotas on several agricultural products.

GATT also permits a member to apply import restrictions in order to safeguard its balance of payments when there is an imminent threat, or actual occurrence, of a serious decline in its monetary reserves or when its monetary reserves are very low. The member must consult with the contracting parties with respect to the continuation or intensification of such restrictions. Representatives of GATT must also consult with the International Monetary Fund when dealing with problems of monetary reserves, the balance of payments, and foreign exchange practices. Members of GATT are not to frustrate the intent of GATT by exchange action nor the intent of the Fund Agreement by trade restrictions. A country that adheres to GATT but is not a member of the Fund must conclude a special exchange agreement with the contracting parties.

GATT recognizes the special position of the developing countries and allows such countries to use nondiscriminatory import quotas to encourage infant industries. Prior approval, however, must be obtained from the collective GATT membership.

A member of GATT may use trade controls for purposes of national security. The strategic controls on United States exports come under this exception.

In addition to these four major exceptions, there are many of lesser importance. For example, members may use trade restrictions to protect public morals, to implement sanitary regulations, to prevent deceptive trade practices, and to protect patents and copyrights.

All quantitative restrictions permitted by GATT are to be applied in accordance with the most-favored-nation principle. Import licenses may not specify that goods be imported from a certain country.

***Special Provisions to Promote the Trade of Developing Countries.*** In 1965 the contracting parties added a new Part IV-Trade and Development-to the General Agreement in recognition of the need for a rapid and sustained expansion of the export earnings of the less-developed member countries. Under the terms of the three articles comprising Part IV, the developed countries agree to undertake the following positive action "to the fullest extent possible": (1) give high priority to the reduction and elimination of barriers to products currently or potentially of particular export interest to less-developed contracting parties; (2) refrain from introducing or increasing customs duties or nontariff import barriers on such products; and (3) refrain from imposing new internal taxes that significantly hamper the consumption of primary products produced in the developing countries, and accord high priority to the reduction or elimination of such taxes. In addition, the developed countries agree not to expect reciprocity for commitments made by them in trade negotiations to reduce or remove tariffs or other barriers to the trade of less-developed contracting parties.

In return, the developing countries commit themselves to take "appropriate action" to implement the provisions of Part IV for the benefit of the trade of other less-developed contracting parties.

The concluding article, Article XXXVIII, pledges the contracting parties to collaborate jointly to take action in a number of ways to further the objectives of Part IV. A new Committee on Trade and Development is charged with keeping under review the implementation of the provisions of Part IV.

*Other Provisions.*  Many other substantive matters are covered by the provisions of GATT: national treatment of internal taxation and regulation, motion picture films, antidumping and countervailing duties, customs valuation, customs formalities, marks of origin, subsidies, state trading, and the publication and administration of trade regulations. The intention of most of these provisions is to eliminate concealed protection and/or discrimination in international trade.

Several articles of GATT deal with procedural matters. In meetings, each member is entitled to one vote, and, unless otherwise specified, decisions are to the taken by majority vote. A two-thirds majority vote is required to waive any obligation imposed on a member by the General Agreement. Articles also cover consulation procedures and the settlement of disputes between members.

### 3. Activities of GATT

The members of GATT meet in regular annual sessions and special tariff conferences. A Council of Representatives deals with matters between sessions and prepares the agenda for each session. In addition, intersessional working groups have been appointed at regular sessions to report on specific topics at subsequent sessions.

Adding further to the continuous influence of GATT has been the practice of member governments to consult with each other before the regular sessions. The membership has obtained a secretariat from the United Nations that, among other things, publishes an annual report. In these and other ways, GATT has behaved like an international organization and, as a matter of fact, has been more effective than some legitimate organizations.

The main activities of GATT fall into three categories: (1) tariff bargaining, (2) quantitative restrictions, and (3) settlement of disputes.

***Tariff Bargaining.*** The parties to GATT have participated in six tariff conferences to negotiate mutual tariff concessions. Most of these conferences have lasted about six months and have involved scores of bilateral agreements and thousands of tariff concessions. The initial conference at Geneva negotiated 45,000 different tariff rates, and today the schedules of GATT include products that make up more than half the world's trade. All of these rates have been either reduced or bound against any increase in the future.

The magnitude of this accomplishment is unprecedented in tariff history; it represents a new approach to the task of lowering tariff barriers. Before World War II the most successful attempt to reduce tariffs by reciprocal bargaining was the trade agreements program of the United States. That program was limited, however, by its bilateral nature. GATT has overcome this disability by applying multilaterally the same principles and procedures that underlay the bilateral trade agreements of the 1930's.

Briefly, tariff negotiations at a GATT conference are conducted along the following lines. Each participating country prepares beforehand lists of products whose duties it is prepared to negotiate with other members of the conference. Actual negotiations are carried on by pairs of countries in accordance with the "chief supplier" principle; that is, each country negotiates with another country on tariff rates for those products that are mainly supplied by the latter country. Thus, there is a great number of bilateral negotiations at each conference.

The results of the round of tariff negotiations at each conference are not finalized until all of them are gathered into a single master agreement signed by the participating countries. The concessions in the master agreement then apply to trade between all members of GATT. In this way, each member receives the benefits of every tariff concession and becomes a party to every tariff agreement.

GATT has brilliantly overcome the difficulties of a purely bilateral trade agreements program: (1) the reluctance of nations to lower or bind tariff duties unless a large number of their trading partners are taking similar action; and (2) the time-consuming negotiation of individual trade agreements, each containing its own code of conduct and other provisions. While it is negotiating, each member knows that other members are also negotiating and that the results of those negotiations will accrue to its benefit. Countries are, therefore, apt to be more generous because the prospects of gain are greater. Moreover, one set of rules applies to every tariff concession and it is much more comprehensive in scope than would be possible in the case of individual bilateral agreements. GATT has also created an environment conducive to tariff bargaining, and it has often induced countries to bargain when they preferred to stand pat.

*Quantitative Restrictions.* Until 1959 GATT made only slow progress toward the elimination of import restrictions (quotas). The majority of GATT members took advantage of the balance of payments exception to the general prohibition of import quotas. The restoration of currency convertibility by Western European countries at the end of 1958 broke this logjam. At the Tokyo session of GATT in 1959, member governments reaffirmed their intention to abolish balance of payments restrictions as soon as possible. Since then, the major trading countries have abandoned quantitative import restrictions that were previously justified on grounds of a weak balance of payments or low monetary reserves. The problem has, therefore, shifted to the elimination of residual import restrictions no longer justified under the provisions of GATT, particularly those related to agricultural products.

Countries that continue to apply import restrictions for balance of payments reasons are required to hold periodical consultations with GATT. As a result, many countries have lowered or eliminated their restrictions or have removed objectionable features. Consultations are also mandatory when a member country introduces new restrictions or substantially modifies existing restrictions.

Perhaps the greatest contribution of GATT toward liberalizing import restrictions lies in its role as a forum for frank discussion between member countries. National measures in the field of commercial policy are now open to public scrutiny and criticism. Moreover, the close contact brought about by regular meetings, tariff conferences, and intersessional activities has helped to breed a common international viewpoint on trade policy. Hence, member governments take GATT into account when contemplating measures to protect their balance of payments and feel it necessary to explain and justify any action that is not in accord with the spirit of the Agreement.

*Settlement of Disputes.* One of the most striking but least publicized of GATT's accomplishments is the settlement of trade disputes between members. Historically trade disputes have been matters strictly between the disputants; there was no third party to which they might appeal for a just solution. As a consequence, trade disputes often went unresolved for years, all the while embittering international relations. When disputes were settled in the past, it was usually a case of the weaker country giving way to the stronger. GATT has improved matters tremendously by adopting complaint procedures and by affording through its periodic meetings a world stage on which an aggrieved nation may voice its complaint.

A large number of disputes have been resolved by bilateral consultations without ever coming before the collective membership. The mere presence of GATT was probably helpful in these instances. Thus, the British government repealed a requirement forbidding the manufacture of pure Virginia cigarettes when the United States protested the requirement as a violation of GATT.

When a dispute is not settled bilaterally, it may be taken by the complainant country to the collective membership at the next regular meeting on the basis that the treatment accorded to the commerce of the complainant country by the other disputant is impairing or nullifying benefits received under the Agreement. A panel on complaints hears the disputants, deliberates, and drafts a report. The report is then acted upon by the membership. In this way GATT resolved an extremely bitter disagreement between Pakistan and India.

In the event that the GATT recommendation is not observed, the aggrieved party may be authorized to suspend the application of certain of its obligations to the trade of the other party. Thus, the Netherlands was allowed to place a limitation on wheat flour from the United States because of the damage caused its exports by United States dairy quotas.

The most dramatic trade dispute erupted in 1963 between the United States and the former European Economic Community. In the middle of 1962 the former EEC countries sharply raised their duties on poultry imports, which came mostly from the United States. In Germany, the biggest United States poultry market, the duty was increased from 5 cents to 12.5 cents per pound. As a result, United States poultry exports to the former EEC tumbled 64 percent in 1963. The charges and countercharges between this country and the former EEC became known as the "chicken war." When bilateral negotiations between the two parties ended in a deadlock, a special panel of GATT experts was asked to arbitrate the question of damages to United States poultry exports. In October, 1963, the panel ruled that the United States had experienced a loss of $ 26 million (the United States had claimed damages of $ 46 million while the former EEC put the figure at $ 19 million) and could withdraw concessions to the former EEC of that amount if the parties could not reach a settlement. Both sides accepted the ruling but were unable to resolve the chicken war. In January, 1965, the United States imposed the high 1930 duties on imports of brandy, trucks, dextrine, and potato starch in retaliation for the former EEC poultry import duties. This action affected the former EEC exports to the United States valued at $ 25.4 million in 1962. (Compensatory tariff concessions were later made to third countries which also exported these products to this country.) In this instance the GATT settlement machinery did not succeed in modifying the former EEC duties on poultry, but it did limit the United States retaliation and prevented any counterretaliation by the former EEC.

### 4. The Future of GATT

GATT entered the 1970's with a membership of some eighty countries that together generated most of the world's trade. Nevertheless, the future role of GATT is clouded with uncertainty.

Despite its enormous success in liberalizing international trade in industrial products, GATT suffers from certain weaknesses that have become more prominent in recent years. GATT has failed to liberalize trade in agricultural products to any significant degree and, except for quantitative restrictions, it has not yet developed rules for the reduction or elimination of nontariff trade distortions. These two failures must be overcome if GATT is to spearhead the liberalization of trade in the 1970's.

Moreover, GATT has experienced only partial success in regulating trade measures adopted by member countries in response to balance of payments difficulties. As noted earlier, GATT has successfully limited the use of quantitative restrictions by the industrial countries for balance of payments purposes, but in recent years some of these countries have adopted import surcharges and export subsidies in violation of the rules. The most serious violation occurred in 1971 when the United States—the major trading country—imposed a 10 percent surcharge on its imports, thereby doubling its average level of duties.

Further, GATT has not been able to resist a steady erosion of the most-favored-nations principle, notably by the former European Economic Community (EEC). Article XXIV of GATT permits member countries to form a customs union or free trade area (which are inherently discriminatory) only when they do not raise new barriers to trade with outside countries. Nevertheless, the former EEC has created a highly protectionist system (variable import levies) to keep out agricultural products, and it has granted free entry or lower duties to many African and Mediterranean countries that are not extended to other GATT members. By undercutting GATT's basic rule of nondiscrimination, these former EEC policies threaten to supplant multilateral trading with a system of trade blocs practicing mutual discrimination.

Finally, GATT continues to exist as a mere executive agreement under the Protocol of Provisional Application which means, among other things, that member countries are not obligated to observe rules that are inconsistent with their domestic legislation existing at the time of their entry into GATT. GATT would be greatly strengthened as an instrument of trade liberalization if it were transformed into a permanent legal organization by the legislative approval of its member countries.

The future of GATT is dependent on the foreign economic policies of its members, particularly the United States and the former European Economic Community. Only these two economic units have the capacity to lead GATT toward freer trade in the 1970's. GATT has been described as a "church with a congregation of sinners," but if the sinning gets out of hand, then the whole purpose of GATT is "cast into darkness." If the United States sincerely desires a liberal, multilateral trading system embracing the entire world, then it must take the initiative to overcome the weaknesses of GATT which, in the last analysis, flow from the protectionist policies of its members, including the United States.

## ♣ New Words

| | | |
|---|---|---|
| 1. | envisage *v.* | 展望；設想 |
| 2. | formalize *v.* | 使正式；使定形 |
| 3. | apparent *a.* | 明顯的 |
| 4. | postwar *a.* | 戰後 |
| 5. | underestimate *v.* | 低估 |
| 6. | highlight *v.* | 著重；突出 |
| 7. | distant *a.* | 遙遠的 |
| 8. | distress *n.* | 不幸 |
| 9. | symbolize *v.* | 象徵；代表 |
| 10. | soften *v.* | 使溫和 |
| 11. | prominence *n.* | 突起；聲望 |
| 12. | casual offshoot | 偶然的支流 |
| 13. | draft charter | 憲章草案 |
| 14. | reciprocal *a.* | 互惠的 |
| 15. | annexes *n.* | 附加；附錄；附件 |
| 16. | tariff schedules | 稅率表；稅則 |
| 17. | contracting parties | 締約國 |
| 18. | sundry *a.* | 各式各樣的 |
| 19. | nondiscriminatory *a.* | 非歧視的 |
| 20. | most favored nation treatment | 最惠國待遇 |
| 21. | allied charges | 聯合徵稅 |
| 22. | customs regulations | 海關管理 |
| 23. | tariff preferences | 關稅特惠 |
| 24. | frontier traffic | 邊境交通 |
| 25. | customs unions | 關稅同盟 |
| 26. | legalize *v.* | 使合法 |
| 27. | escape clause | 退出條款；例外條款；免責條款 |
| 28. | sanction *n.* | 制裁 |
| 29. | imminent *a.* | 迫近的 |
| 30. | balance of payments (bop) | 國際收支 |
| 31. | monetary reserves | 貨幣儲備 |
| 32. | intensification *n.* | 增強；強化 |
| 33. | infant industries | 幼稚工業；新生產業 |

| | | |
|---|---|---|
| **34.** national security | 國家安全 |
| **35.** sanitary regulations | 衛生條例；衛生管理規則 |
| **36.** import licenses | 進口許可證 |
| **37.** deceptive *a.* | 騙人的；容易使人誤解的 |
| **38.** hamper *v.* | 妨礙；阻礙 |
| **39.** substantive matters | 實質性問題 |
| **40.** antidumping *a.* | 反傾銷的 |
| **41.** countervailing duties | 抵銷關稅；反補貼稅 |
| **42.** customs valuation | 海關估價 |
| **43.** customs formalities | 海關手續 |
| **44.** subsidies *n.* | 補貼；補助 |
| **45.** secretariat *n.* | 秘書處 |
| **46.** unprecedented *a.* | 空前的；史無前例的 |
| **47.** magnitude *n.* | 重要性 |
| **48.** underlay *v.* | 從下面支撐 |
| **49.** tariff negotiations | 關稅談判 |
| **50.** public scrutiny | 公衆檢查 |
| **51.** forum *n.* | 論壇 |
| **52.** intersessional *a.* | 屆會之間；會期之間 |
| **53.** breed *v.* | 產生 |
| **54.** striking *a.* | 明顯的 |
| **55.** accomplishment *n.* | 成就 |
| **56.** embitter *v.* | 加重 |
| **57.** impair *v.* | 破壞 |
| **58.** nullify *v.* | 使無效 |
| **59.** deliberate *v.* | 仔細考慮 |
| **60.** erupt *v.* | 爆發 |
| **61.** poultry *n.* | 家禽 |
| **62.** dextrin(e) *n.* | 糊精 |
| **63.** potato starch | 馬鈴薯澱粉 |
| **64.** compensatory *a.* | 補償的 |
| **65.** settlement machinery | （爭議）解決方式 |
| **66.** counterretaliation *n.* | 反報復 |
| **67.** enormous *a.* | 巨大的 |
| **68.** prominent *a.* | 突出的；顯著的；傑出的 |

| 69. | trade distortions | 貿易異常現象；貿易畸形發展 |
|---|---|---|
| 70. | spearhead *v.* | 當……先鋒 |
| 71. | erosion *n.* | 侵害；侵蝕 |
| 72. | .import levies | 進口稅 |
| 73. | Mediterranean countries | 地中海國家 |
| 74. | undercut *v.* | 削價與……搶生意 |
| 75. | trade blocs | 貿易同盟 |
| 76. | embrace *v.* | 包括 |
| 77. | congregation of sinners | 犯罪者的人群 |

### ☘ New Phrases and Idiomatic Expressions

| 1. | to lay the cornerstones for | 為……打下基礎 |
|---|---|---|
| 2. | to take over | 接替 |
| 3. | within the framework of | 在……框架內 |
| 4. | in the interim | 在間歇的空檔；在過渡期間 |
| 5. | to serve as a token of | 作為……一種象徵 |
| 6. | to cause injury to | 對……造成損害 |
| 7. | to give high priority to | 給予……最先優先權 |
| 8. | to commit oneself to do sth. | 承諾做某事 |
| 9. | to be charged with doing sth. | 承擔做某事的任務 |
| 10. | to be conducive to | 有助於…… |
| 11. | to stand pat | 堅持；不改變主張 |
| 12. | as a consequence | 作為後果 |
| 13. | to give way to | 讓步 |
| 14. | in the event that…… | 若發生……（that後面接一個句子） |
| 15. | to end in a deadlock | 結果陷入僵局 |
| 16. | to be clouded with uncertainty | 蒙上不確定的陰影 |
| 17. | in response to | 作為……的反應 |
| 18. | to be dependent on | 依靠 |
| 19. | in the last analysis | 追根究底 |

### ☘ Notes

**1**. the General Agreement on Tariffs and Trade (GATT)：關貿總協定。

Strictly speaking GATT was not a full international trade organization yet. It is an international agreement which was designed to try to limit government intervention that restricts international trade. This agreement was signed in October 1947 by 23 countries including China. The GATT itself is a small organization located in Geneva, Switzerland.

**2**. the International Monetary Fund (also IMF)：國際貨幣基金。

A special agency of the United Nations, established in 1945 to promote international monetary cooperation and expand international trade, stabilize exchange rates, and help countries experiencing short-term balance of payments difficulties to maintain their exchange rates. The IMF assists a member by supplying the amount of foreign currency it wishes to purchase in exchange for the equivalent amount of its own currency. The member repays this amount by buying back its own currency in a currency acceptable to the IMF, usually within three to five years. The IMF is financed by subscriptions from its members, the amount determined by an estimate of their means. Voting power is related to the amount of the subscription. The higher the contribution the higher the voting rights. The head office of the IMF is in Washington.

**3**. the International Bank for Reconstruction and Development (IBRD)

Specialized agency working in coordination with the United Nations, established in 1945 to help finance postwar reconstruction and to help raise standards of living in developing countries, by making loans to governments or guaranteeing outside loans. It lends on broadly commercial terms, either for specific projects or for more general social purposes, funds are raised on the international capital markets. The Bank and its affiliates, the International Development Association and the International Finance Corporation, are often known as the World Bank. It is owned by the governments of 151 countries. Members must also be members of the IMF. The headquarters of the Bank are in Washington, with offices in Paris and Tokyo.

**4**. British Commonwealth：英聯邦。

Also the British Commonwealth of Nations which is an association of the U.K. with the states that were previously part of British Empire, but are now sovereign nations.

**5**. European Economic Community (also EEC or EC or Common Market)：歐共體；共同市場。現被「歐盟」（EU）取代。

An economic union which was established in 1958. It had 12 member states (Belgium, Denmark, France, Germany now reunified, Greece, Ireland, Italy, Luxemburg, the Netherlands, Spain and the U.K.) To promote its economic growth, the four freedoms were encouraged in dealings among the member nations, i.e. freedom of movement of goods, freedom to provide service, freedom of movement of persons and freedom of movement of capital.

**Exercises**

## I. Answer the following questions:

**1**. What was the background against which GATT was born?

**2**. What are the four basic elements of GATT?

**3**. What are the four most important exceptions to the general rule prohibiting the use of quantitative import and export restrictions?

**4**. What are the main activities carried out by GATT?

**5**. Does GATT recognizes the special position of the developing countries? How?

**6**. What are the special provisions to promote the trade of developing countries.

**7**. How did you predict the future of GATT before the birth of WTO?

## II. Translate the following English passages into Chinese:

**1**. Thus, at the start of the 1980s, tariff levels throughout the world economy were probably as low as they had ever been. And world trade has seen three decades of rapid growth, arising at least in part from the success of GATT in removing trade restrictions. But the threat of protection had not been abolished for ever. With increasing unemployment in the industrial economies in the early 1980s, there has been renewed pressure for tariffs. The United States imposed a quota on steel imports from Japan and Europe, and the Japanese have agreed to restrict their car exports to Europe and the United States.

**2**. Since the formation of the GATT, several rounds of negotiations had taken place and these had resulted in general tariff reductions. One of these, the Kennedy Round that began in the early 1960s, resulted in large tariff cuts. Yet further tariff cuts resulted from the Tokyo Round that took place between 1973 and 1979. The most recent GATT tariff round was the Uruguay Round, which ended in the first half of 1994. The main purpose of this Round was to achieve less restricted trade in service and agricultural products.

**3**. GATT's purpose has been to stipulate a basic set of rules under which trade negotiations can occur. Participating countries agreed to three basic principles: (1) nondiscrimination in trade through unconditional most-favored-nation treatment; (2) the reduction of tariffs by multilateral negotiations; (3)elimination of most import quotas with exceptions such as protection of domestic agriculture or safeguarding of country's bop position.

## III. Indicate whether each of the following statements is true or false by writing "T" or "F" in the space provided:

_____ 1. Legally speaking GATT has an international trade organization.

_____ 2. China was one of the 23 countries which singed GATT in 1947.

_____ 3. GATT set forth a general rule prohibiting all uses of quantitative import and export restrictions regardless of the purpose.

_____ 4. One of the most important accomplishments made by GATT was tariff cuts.

_____ 5. The future of GATT was clouded with uncertainty despite its achievements.

## IV. Translate the following Chinese passages into English:

1. 關稅與貿易總協定於1947年10月30日在日內瓦簽訂，是關於調整各國在國際貿易政策方面的相互權利與義務的一項多邊條約。

2. 關貿總協定的基本原則可概括成以下幾點：(1)無差別原則；(2)互惠與平等的關稅減讓；(3)消除進口數量限額；(4)禁止傾銷和限制出口補貼。

3. 關貿總協定在促進戰後國際貿易發展、緩和各締約國之間矛盾，形成一套有關國際貿易政策規章等方面發揮了重要作用。

4. 關貿總協定所發揮的作用被公認的有以下幾點：(1)促進了戰後國際貿易的發展；(2)緩和了各締約國之間的矛盾；(3)形成了一套有關國際貿易政策的規章。

# 第十七課 Lesson 17　國際貨物買賣 The International Sale of Goods

In the international sale of goods, the use of special trade terms is customary. These trade terms, though universally used, have sometimes a different meaning in various countries with respect to the obligations of the seller and the buyer. In order to avoid a misunderstanding between the parties to the contract and to promote uniformity of law, the International Chamber of Commerce has published "Incoterms," the present edition of which is dated 1990. Incoterms apply to a contract of international sale of goods only if the parties have incorporated them into their contract. Incoterms 1990 are frequently adopted by the parties.

The present edition of Incoterms lists the following special trade terms:

ex works (the seller's works, factory or warehouse, where the goods are situated);

free carrier (named point);

f.a.s. (free alongside; named port of shipment);

f.o.b. (free on board; named port of shipment);

c.f.r. (cost and freight; named port of destination);

c.i.f. (cost, insurance and freight; named port of destination);

c.p.t. (carriage paid to; named port of destination);

d.a.f. (delivered at frontier, named place of delivery at frontier.

This clause can only be used in terrestrial sales and the two countries separated by the frontier should be indicated);

d.e.s. (delivered ex ship; named port of destination);

d.e.q. (delivered ex quay; duty paid by the seller or duty on buyers account, according to the agreement of the parties);

d.d.u. (delivered duty unpaid; named port of destination);

d.d.p. (delivered duty paid; named port of destination in country of importation).

The trade term "free carrier" under the 1990 Incoterms refers to t.o.b. in ordinary sea transport, f.o.r. (free on rail) for rail transport, and f.o.t. (free on truck) for ordinary truck transport.

The adoption of any of these trade terms indicates at which point the delivery of the goods shall take place. Sometimes the trade terms indicate the calculation of the purchase price and the incidental charges included in it.

## 1. F.O.B. Contracts

In an f.o.b. contract it is the duty of the seller to place the goods over the ship's rail and to deposit them on board the ship. The contract of carriage by sea has to be made by, or on behalf of the buyer, and the cost of freight and likewise of insurance has to be borne by the buyer if the buyer wishes to insure the goods.

There are two types of f.o.b. contracts, the strict or classic type and the f.o.b. contract providing for additional services. Under the strict f.o.b. contract, the arrangements for shipment and, if he so wishes, for insurance are made by the buyer direct. He is a party to the contracts of carriage by sea and marine insurance, if he insures the goods in transit. Under this type of contract the buyer has to name to the seller an effective ship, i.e. a ship ready, willing and able to carry the goods away from the port of shipment within the stipulated shipping time. If the buyer fails to nominate an effective ship, the seller cannot make such nomination. In this case the seller's remedy is an action for damages for non-acceptance of the goods but not an action for the price.

In an f.o.b. contract with additional services the parties have agreed that the arrangements for the carriage by sea and insurance shall be made by the seller, but for and on behalf of the buyer and for his account. If after the conclusion of the contract of sale these charges are increased, the buyer has to bear the increase. If the seller has paid the increased charges, he is entitled to have them refunded by the buyer.

In all types of f.o.b. contracts the cost of putting the good on board ship have to be borne by the seller. Delivery is complete when the goods are put on board ship. The risk of accidental loss under section 20(1) of the Sale of Goods Act 1979 passes to the buyer when the seller has placed the goods safely on board ship. The seller should give notice of the shipment to the buyer so as to enable him to insure; if the seller fails to do this, the goods will be at his risk.

Unless the parties otherwise agree, the property in goods sold under an f.o.b. contract passes to the buyer when the goods are placed on board ship.

Where the seller has taken out a bill of lading, as will always be the case where the contract is on f.o.b. terms with additional services, the common intention of the parties is that property in the goods shall pass on the delivery of the bill of lading unless the facts disclose a different intention as illustrated in Mitsui & Co. Ltd. u. Flota, Mercante Grancolombiana S.A. [1988]2 Lloyd's Rep. 208; the Court of Appeal held that according to the intention of the parties, the passing of the property was postponed until the balance of the purchase price was paid.

There is no general rule that, in the absence of a specific provision in an f.o.b. contract, the duty of obtaining an export licence falls on the buyer: the obligation depends in each case on the construction of the contract and the surrounding circumstances and, if there are so indications to the contrary, this obligation will fall on the seller.

## 2. C.I.F. Contracts

The central feature of the c.i.f. contract is that this contract is performed by the seller by delivery of the shipping documents to the buyer, and not by delivery of the goods. The normal shipping documents are:

(1)the bill of lading, representing the contract of carriage by sea;

(2)the insurance policy or certificate, representing the contract of marine insurance; and

(3)the invoice, representing the contract of sale.

The c.i.f. contract has been described by McNair J. in *Gardano and Giampieri v. Greek Petroleum George Mamidakis & Co.* [1962] **I W. L. R.**40, 52 as a contract in which "the seller discharges his obligations as regards delivery by tendering a bill of lading covering the goods." The c.i.f. price includes the freight and insurance premium. If there is an increase in these charges, the seller must bear them. The cost of unloading and the import duties have to be borne by the buyer. Under the c.i.f. contract, it is immaterial whether the goods arrive safely at the port of destination. If they are lost or damaged in transit, the marine insurance policy should cover the loss or damage and, by the virtue of the transfer of the bill of lading and the insurance policy, the buyer has direct contractual claims against the shipowner or the insurer.

The duties of a seller under such a contract are:

(1) To ship at the port of shipment goods of the description contained in the contract.

(2) To procure a contract of carriage by sea, under which the goods will be delivered at the destination contemplated by the contract.

(3) To arrange for an insurance upon the terms current in the trade which will be available for the benefit of the buyer.

(4) To make out an invoice of the goods.

(5) To tender, within a reasonable time after shipment, the bill of lading, the policy or certificate of insurance and the invoice to the buyer so that the buyer may obtain delivery of the goods, if they arrive, or recover for their loss, if they are lost on the voyage. The bill of lading tendered must correctly state the date of shipment, otherwise the buyer can reject the goods.

Under a c.i.f. contract the buyer has a right to reject the documents and also a right to reject the goods. These two rights are quite distinct.

But if the buyer accepts the documents, knowing that they are not in order, he is estopped from later trying to reject them.

The duties of the c.i.f. buyer are:

(1) to pay the price, less the freight, on delivery of the documents. He cannot defer payment until after he has inspected the goods (*Clemens Horst Co. v. Biddell Bros.* [1912] A. C. 18)；

(2) to pay the cost of unloading, lighterage and landing at the port of destination according to the bill of lading; and

(3) to pay all import duties and wharfage charges, if any.

During the voyage the goods are at the risk of the buyer. This risk will in ordinary cases be covered by the insurance, but if the goods are lost from a peril not covered by the ordinary policy of insurance current in trade, the buyer must nevertheless pay the full price on delivery of the documents.

Even if the seller knows that the goods have been lost at the time the shipping documents are tendered, he can still compel the buyer to take and pay for them.

The property passes when the documents are taken up by the buyer, but "what the buyer obtains, when the title under the documents is given to him, is the property in the goods, subject to the conditions that they revest if upon examination he finds them to be not in accordance with the contract". If, however, the goods are not ascertained at the time the documents are taken up, no property in the goods will pass until the goods become ascertained.

As has been seen, under a c.i.f. contract property passes normally to the buyer when the bill of lading is transferred to him. What if, after the risk has passed to the buyer but before property has passed to him, the goods are damaged by the negligence of some third party, such as the carrier? This situation may arise if, for one reason or another, the buyer has not become the holder of the bill of lading. In such a case the buyer, not having had title to the goods at the time of the damage, cannot maintain an action for the tort of negligence against the third party.

In a c. & f. (c. f. r.) contract the seller is obliged to arrange for the carriage of the goods to the place of destination and to pay the freight, but he need not insure the goods. The buyer may insure them if he is so minded. Sometimes the c. & f. contract provides that the buyer shall be obliged to insure the goods in transit.

### 3. Arrival and Ex Ship Contracts

Under an arrival contract the goods themselves must arrive at the place of destination and it is insufficient that documents evidencing the shipment of the goods to that destination are made available to the buyer. When examining whether a particular contract is a c.i.f. contract or an arrival contract, attention has to be paid to the intention of the parties, as contained in their agreement; the designation of the contract used by the parties is not decisive.

When goods are sold ex ship, the duties of the seller are:

(1)to deliver the goods to the buyer from a ship which has arrived at the port of delivery at a place from which it is usual for goods of that kind to be delivered;

(2)to pay the freight or otherwise release the shipowner's lien; and

(3)to furnish the buyer with a delivery order, or some other effectual direction to the ship to deliver.

The goods are at the seller's risk during the voyage and there is no obligation on the seller to effect an insurance on the buyer's behalf.

### 4. International Sales and the Unfair Contract Terms Act 1977

The Unfair Contract Terms Act 1977 does not normally apply to contracts for the international sale of goods. Such contracts qualify normally as international supply contracts and are, as such, exempt from the operation of the Act. An international supply contract is defined in section 26 (3) and (4) as follows:

(1) either it is a contract of sale of goods or it is one under or in pursuance of which the possession or ownership passes; and

(2) it is made by parties whose places of business (or, if they have none, habitual residences) are in the territories of different States (the Channel Islands and the Isle of Man being treated for this purpose as different States from the United Kingdom).

In addition, the contract must satisfy the following requirements:

(1) the goods in question are, at the time of the conclusion of the contract, in the course of carriage, or will be carried, from the territory of one State to the territory of another; or

(2) the acts constituting the offer and acceptance have been done in the territories of different States; or

(3) the contract provides for the goods to be delivered to the territory of a State other than that within whose territory those acts were done.

### 5. The Uniform Laws on International Sales Act 1967

This Act gives effect on two Conventions signed at a conference at the Hague in 1964, which were designed to achieve some uniformity in the laws which in different states apply to contracts for the international sale of goods. The two Conventions are incorporated in the Act as Schedules. The first Convention, the Uniform Law on the International Sale of Goods, is in Schedule 1 and the second Convention, the Uniform Law on the Formation of Contracts for the International Sale of Goods, is in Schedule 2. The Act is part of English law and whenever a contract of sale of goods is governed by English law as the law governing the contract, the Uniform Law in Schedule 1 will apply to that contract, provided the parties to the contract have expressly chosen the Uniform Law as the law of the contract s. 1(3) and Uniform Laws on International Sales Order 1972 (S.I. 1972 No. 973, art. 2(b)).

*The Uniform Laws and home transactions*

Although the Uniform Laws are conceived of as applying to contracts of international sale, there is nothing to stop the parties to a home transaction expressly adopting them (Sched.

1, art. 4). The only limitation is that the parties cannot in the case of a home transaction avoid the mandatory provisions of English law (Sched. 1, art. 4). The only such mandatory provisions are sections 12-15 of the Sale of Goods Act 1979 (1967 Act, s. 1(4), as amended by the 1979 Act, Sched.2, para.15). Thus, where in a home transaction the parties expressly adopt the Uniform Laws, the latter will apply except in so far as they are inconsistent with those mandatory provisions of the Sale of Goods Act. Apart from that restriction relating to home sales, the parties are free to contract out of any of the provisions of the Uniform Laws (Sched. 1, art. 3).

*The Uniform Law on the International Sale of Goods*

The Uniform Law (Sched. 1) contains provisions governing the seller's obligations as to the time and place of delivery, the insurance and carriage of the goods, the conformity of the goods with the contract, and the giving of good title. Other provisions govern the passing of risk and the buyer's obligations as to payment and the taking delivery of the goods. These rules are in several respects different from ordinary English law. In particular, the Uniform Laws do not recognise the concept of the "condition" which exists in English law, for the breach of which the buyer can reject the goods even though the breach causes him no loss. The Uniform Laws instead introduce a concept of "fundamental breach." Thus, in order to determine whether the buyer has the right to reject, one must examine the breach that has actually occurred together with its consequences. The lawyer will be able to reject the goods only if the breach is "fundamental," *i.e.* if a reasonable person in the position of the buyer "would not have entered into the contract if he had foreseen the breach and its effects" (Sched. 1, art. 10).

The Uniform Law does not prevent a contract of a well recognised type, e.g. c.i.f. or f.o.b. taking effect as such, or from agreeing on a uniform interpretation of these trade terms, e.g. by embodying into their contract Incoterms. The parties are "bound by any usage which they have expressly or impliedly made applicable" (Sched. 1, art.9).

The Uniform Law on the Formation of Contracts for the International Sale of Goods

Schedule 2, which contains this Uniform Law, applies to the formation of contracts of sale which if they were concluded would be governed by the Uniform Law in Schedule 1. Its provisions relate to offer and acceptance. In particular, it contains the following rules. An offer is in general revocable until the offeree has despatched his acceptance. However, an offer is not revocable if it either states a fixed time for acceptance or else indicates that it is irrevocable (Sched. 2, art. 5). A qualified acceptance will normally be construed as a rejection of the offer and a counter-offer. However, if the qualification consists of additional or different terms which do not materially alter the terms of the offer, it will constitute a binding acceptance unless the offeror promptly objects to the discrepancy (Sched. 2, art. 7). A late acceptance may be treated by the buyer as having arrived in time, provided the offeror promptly informs the acceptor that he regards it as binding. A late acceptance which suffers an unusual delay in transit and which would in normal transit have arrived in time is regarded as being in time unless the offeror promptly informs the acceptor that he considers his offer has lapsed (Sched. 2, art.9).

**6. The UN Convention on Contracts for the International Sale of Goods**

On April 11, 1980 this Convention, promoted by UNCITRAL (UN Commission on International Trade Law), was signed in Vienna. The Vienna Convention is a further development of the attempt to unify the law relating to the international sale of goods. The Convention is founded on the two Hague Conventions of 1964, discussed above, and is intended to supersede them. The Vienna Convention combines the topics treated in the two Hague Conventions in one document.

The Vienna Convention came into operation on January 1, 1988 and has been ratified or acceded to by such states as China and the U. S. A. However, at the date of going to press the United Kingdom has not given effect to it.

## New Words

| | | |
|---|---|---|
| **1.** | trade terms | 貿易術語 |
| **2.** | the International Chamber of Commerce | 國際商會 |
| **3.** | Incoterms | 解釋通則（又譯成《國際貿易術語》或《貿易術語的國際通例》） |
| **4.** | ex works | 工廠交貨 |
| **5.** | free carrier | 船工交貨（按1990《解釋通則》） |
| **6.** | f. a. s. | 船邊交貨（指定裝運港） |
| **7.** | f. o. b. | 船上交貨（指定裝運港） |
| **8.** | c. f. r. | 成本加運費（指定裝運港） |
| **9.** | c. i. f. | 成本加運費及保險費（指定目的地港） |
| **10.** | c. p. t. | 運費付至目的地港 |
| **11.** | d. a. f. | 邊境交貨（在邊境指定交貨地點） |
| **12.** | d. e. s. | 船上交貨（指定目的地港） |
| **13.** | d. e. q. | 碼頭交貨 |
| **14.** | d. d. u. | 指定目的地港交貨（稅未付） |
| **15.** | d. d. p. | 進口國指定目的地港交貨（稅已付） |
| **16.** | tender *v.* | 提供 |
| **17.** | forge *v.* | 偽造 |

**18.** superintendent *a.*     監督的；管理的

**19.** lighterage *n.*      駁船費

**20.** wharfage *n.*      碼頭費

**21.** revest *v.*       使恢復原狀

**22.** copra *n.*       椰子仁乾；乾椰肉

**23.** ascertained *a.*     被確定的

**24.** delivery order      小提單

**25.** arrival contract     貨物到達契約

**26.** convention *n.*      公約

**27.** conceive *v.*      抱有想法

**28.** despatch *v.*      發送

**29.** discrepancy *n.*     差異；不一致

**30.** Vienna *n.*       維也納

**31.** accede *v.*       同意；加入

**32.** supersede *v.*      代替；取代

## ♣ New Phrases and Idiomatic Expressions

**1.** with respect to      關於

**2.** to make out       書寫；填寫（發票，支票等）；簽發

**3.** at the risk of       風險由……承擔；風險由……負責

**4.** to be destined for     指定給……；預定去……

**5.** to arrange for      為……作安排

**6.** to be exempt from     免除……

**7.** to be inconsistent with    與……不一致

**8.** in transit        在運輸中

**9.** to come into operation    使……實施或生效

**10.** to go to press      出版

**11.** to give effect to      使……生效

**12.** by the virtue of      憑藉；由於；因為

**13.** to take up       接受

## ♣ Notes

**1.** Incoterms：《國際貿易術語》又譯成「解釋通則」或「貿易術語的國際通例」。

Glossary of terms used in international trade published by the International Chamber of Commerce. It gives precise definitions to eliminate misunderstandings between traders in different countries. The sub-title is International Rules for the Interpretation of Trade Terms.

**2**. the International Chamber of Commerce (also ICC)：國際商會。

An international business organization that represents business interests in international affairs. Its office is in Paris.

**3**. bill of lading：提單。它有以下三個作用：

From the legal point of view, a bill of lading is —

(1) a formal receipt by the shipowner acknowledging that the goods of the stated species, quantity and condition are shipped to a stated destination in a certain ship, or at least received in the custody of the shipowner for the purpose of shipment;

(2) a memorandum of the contract of carriage, repeating in detail the terms of the contract which was in fact concluded prior to the signing of the bill; and

(3) a document of title to the goods enabling the consignee to dispose of the goods by indorsement and delivery of the bill of lading.

**4**. As the market had fallen...

As the market prices had fallen...

**5**. This Act gives effect on two Conventions signed at a conference at the Hague in 1964...

The two Conventions mentioned here are the two Uniform Laws known as The Uniform Law on International Sale of Goods (Uniform Law on Sales) and The Uniform Law on the Formation of Contracts for the International sale of Goods (Uniform Law on Formation). The Former aims at the unification of the substantive law of international sales; apart from its general provisions, it is divided into four major parts, viz. the obligations of the buyer, the obligation of the seller, provisions common to the obligations of the seller and the buyer, and the passing of the risk. The latter is complementary to the former; it attempts to reconcile the considerable differences of the common law and European continental law on offer and acceptance leading to the conclusion of an international contract of sale. The provisions of the Uniform Laws differ in many important aspects from English law but represent, as such, an acceptable and logical code of the law of international sales.

 **Exercises**

## I. Answer the following questions:

**1**. What is Incoterms?

**2**. What are the normal shipping documents?

**3**. What is bill of lading from legal point of view?

**4**. What are the duties of the seller and the buyer under a c.i.f. contract?

**5**. What are the two types of f.o.b. contracts mentioned in this lesson? What is the difference between them?

**6**. Ho does the Unfair Contract Terms Act 1977 define an international supply contract?

**7**. What are the purposes of the two Conventions?

**8**. Can you give examples to show that The Uniform Law on the International Sale of Goods is different from ordinary English law?

## II. Translate the following Chinese passages into English:

**1**. 《解釋通則》最初於1953年發表，即人所共知的1953年《解釋通則》。1967年增加了兩個術語，即「過境交貨」和「目的地交貨」。1976年又增加了一個術語，即「F.O.B 船上交貨」。1977年4月，出版了包括上述增加的術語在內的所有術語的《解釋通則》。

**2**. 主要裝運單據包括提單、保險單、發票、產地證明書、裝箱單。通常應向賣方航寄兩套裝運單據。

**3**. 1964年4月在海牙召開了由28個國家參加的外交會議，會上簽訂了兩個公約，即《國際貨物買賣統一法公約》和《國際貨物買賣契約訂立統一法公約》。這兩個公約雖於1972年8月生效，但並沒有被廣泛接受。

**4**. 1980年4月11日在維也納召開的由62個國家代表參加的外交會議上，通過了《聯合國國際貨物買賣契約公約》(以下簡稱「公約」)，該公約於1988年1月1日生效。中國和美國都已批准此公約。

## III. Indicate whether each of the following statements is true or false by writing "T" or "F" in the space provided:

_____ **1**. In the international sale of good, the use of special trade terms is customary.

_____ **2**. In an f.o.b. contract it is the duty of the buyer to place the goods over the ship's rail and to deposit them on board the ship.

_____ **3**. In a c. & f. contract the seller is obligated to arrange for the carriage of the goods to the place of destination and to pay the freight, but he need not insure the goods.

_____ **4**. Under a c.i.f. contract, during the voyage the goods are always at the risk of the buyer.

_____ **5**. The Vienna Convention is a further development of the attempt to unify the law relating to the international sale of goods.

___**6**. China so far has not given effect to the Vienna Convention.

## IV. Translate the following English passages into Chinese:

**1**. In 1980, representatives of 62 countries, including the United States, assembled in Vienna for a United Nations' Diplomatic Conference. The objective was to complete work dating back to the 1930s seeking to establish a Uniform Law of International Sales.

**2**. The Law Society of England and Wales have made the following objections to the Vienna Convention:

(1)that it will not produce uniformity because it will be subject to differing national interpretations;

(2)that sophisticated commercial trades will find it easy to avoid the provisions of the Convention;

(3)the Convention will more commonly apply by default, given the working of the Convention "s" opt-out provision;

(4)that the Convention will result in a diminished role for English law within the international trade arena.

# 第十八課 Lesson 18 | 國際貿易融資 The Finance of International Trade

In the international sale of goods various methods of paying the purchase price are used. The buyer may pay the seller on open account or the seller may allow the buyer credit. The two most common methods are payment under a collection agreement and payment under a letter of credit, also called a documentary credit. In both cases banks are used as intermediaries and the shipping documents are used as collateral security for the banks. In the former case payment is effected by a bank in the buyer's country and in the latter case by a bank in the seller's country.

It is usual in international sales transactions for the seller to draw a bill of exchange, either on the buyer or on a bank. The bill of exchange may be a sight bill, which has to be paid at sight, or a time bill, which is payable usually a certain number of days after sight, *e.g.* 90 days after sight; a time bill requires acceptance.

Collection arrangements and letters of credit are governed by international regulations sponsored by the International Chamber of Commerce and applied by most banks in the world. Collection arrangements are governed by the *Uniform Rules for the Collection of Commercial Paper* (1978 Revision) and documentary credits by the *Uniform Customs and Practice for Documentary Credits* (1983 Revision).

## Collection Arrangements

If the collection of the price at the buyer's place is arranged, the seller hands the shipping documents, including the bill of lading to his own bank, the remitting bank, which passes them on to a bank at the buyer's place, the collecting bank. The collecting bank then presents the bill of exchange to the buyer and requests him to pay or to accept the bill. When the buyer has done so, the collecting bank releases the shipping documents to the buyer. The buyer thus receives the original bill of lading which enables him to obtain the goods from the carrier on arrival of the ship.

The collecting bank must not release the shipping documents to the buyer unless it obtains finance from him. If it does so contrary to the instructions of the seller, it renders itself liable to him. Sometimes, however, the collecting bank, of which the buyer may be a customer, takes this risk and, notwithstanding the contrary instructions of the seller, releases the bill of lading to the buyer. It will try to protect itself by releasing the bill of lading under a trust receipt. This document provides that the buyer constitutes himself a trustee for the bank in three respects: a trustee for the bills of lading, for the goods which he receives from the ship, and for the proceeds of sale, when he resells the goods. He will then pay the original purchase price to the collecting bank and retain the profits which he has made on the resale of the goods. If the buyer, in breach of his obligations under the trust receipt, pledges the bill of lading to another bank as a security for a loan and the second bank accepts the bill of lading in good faith, the second bank acquires a good title to the bill and the goods, by virtue of the Factors Act 1889, s.2 (i) and the first bank has lost its title: *Lloyds Bank v. Bank of America Association* [1938] 2 K.B.147. The buyer will be liable to the bank for breach of contract and for conversion of the bill of lading.

# Letters of Credit

Of particular importance are letters of credit. This method of payment applies only if the parties to an export transaction have agreed to it in their contract of sale. The buyer instructs a bank in his country (the issuing bank) to open a credit with a bank in the seller's country (the advising bank) in favour of the seller, specifying the documents which the seller has to deliver to the bank if he wishes to receive finance. The instructions also specify the date of expiry of the credit.

If the documents tendered by the seller are correct and tendered before the credit has expired, the advising bank pays the seller the purchase price, or accepts his bill of exchange drawn on it, or negotiates his bill of exchange which is drawn on the buyer. Whether the credit is a payment, acceptance, negotiation or deferred payment credit, depends on the arrangements between the seller and the buyer.

# Types of Letters of Credit

Various types of letters of credit are used according to the agreement of the parties to the contract of sale. Whether the credit is revocable or irrevocable, depends on the commitment of the issuing bank. Whether it is confirmed or unconfirmed depends on the commitment of the advising bank. These commitments are undertaken to the seller, who is the beneficiary under the credit.

The following are the main types of letters of credit.

*1. The revocable and unconfirmed letter of credit.* Here neither the issuing nor the advising bank enters into a commitment to the seller. The credit may be revoked at any time. A revocable and unconfirmed credit affords little security to the seller that he will receive the purchase price through a bank.

*2. The irrevocable and unconfirmed letter of credit.* Here the authority which the buyer gives the issuing bank is irrevocable and the issuing bank enters into an obligation to the seller to pay; this obligation is likewise irrevocable; the bank has to honour the credit. This, from the point of view of the seller, is a more valuable method of payment than a revocable and unconfirmed letter of credit. The seller can claim that the issuing bank honours the credit, provided that he tenders the correct documents before the date of expiry of the credit. If the issuing bank refuses to honour the credit, the seller may sue it in the country in which the issuing bank has its seat. If the issuing bank has a branch office in the seller's country, the seller may in certain circumstances even sue the issuing bank in his own country.

*3. The irrevocable and confirmed letter of credit.* If the advising bank adds its own confirmation of the credit to the seller, the latter has the certainty that a bank in his own locality will provide him with finance if he delivers the correct shipping documents in the stipulated time (*Hamzeh Malas & Sons v. British Imex Industries Ltd.*, below). A "reliable paymaster" in his own country has been substituted for the overseas buyer. A confirmed credit constitutes "a direct undertaking by the banker that the seller, if he presents the documents as required in the required time, will receive payment". The confirmation thus constitutes a conditional debt of the banker, i.e. a debt subject to the condition precedent that the seller tenders the specified documents. The buyer need not open the credit as confirmed unless he has undertaken to do so in the contract of sale. A confirmed credit which has been notified to the seller cannot be cancelled by the bank on the buyer's instructions.

*4. The transferable letter of credit.* The parties to the contract of sale may agree that the credit shall be transferable. The seller can use such a credit to finance the supply transaction. The buyer opens the credit in favour of the seller and the seller (who in the supply transaction is the buyer) transfers the same credit to the supplier (who in the supply transaction is the seller). The credit is transferred on the same terms on which the buyer has opened it, except that the amount payable to the supplier is made smaller because the seller wishes to retain his profit from the export transaction. Every transferable credit is thus automatically divisible because it is transferred in a smaller amount than the amount in which it is opened by the issuing bank.

*The Uniform Customs and Practice for Documentary Credits* (1983 Revision), issued by the International Chamber of Commerce, provide in article 54(e) that a transferable credit can be transferred only once.

# The Autonomy of The Credit

The credit constitutes a separate banking transaction and the issuing and advising banks are, in principle, not involved in the underlying transactions, *e.g.* the contract of export sale.

*The Uniform Customs and Practice for Documentary Credits* (1983 Revision) express this principle in the *General Provisions and Definitions* article 3, as follows:

"Credits, by their nature, are separate transactions from the sales or other contract(s) on which they may be based and banks are in no way connected with or bound by such contracts, even if any reference whatsoever to such contract(s) is intended in the credit."

# The Doctrine of Strict Compliance

The banks which operate the documentary credit act as agents for the buyer who is the principal. If they exceed his instructions, they have acted without authority and he need not ratify their act; the loss would then fall on the bank in question. This has led to the development of **the doctrine of strict compliance** under which the correspondent bank will, on principle, refuse documents tendered by the seller which do not correspond strictly with the instructions "There is no room for documents which are almost the same of which will do just as well".

Article 41 (c) states that it is sufficient if all the documents taken together contain the particulars of the bank's mandate and it is not necessary that every document in the set should contain them.

# Opening of a Letter of Credit

The credit must be made available to the seller at the beginning of the shipment period (*Pavia & Co. v. Thurmann-Nielsen* [1952] 2 Q.B. 84). If the parties have not laid down in their contract a time for opening the credit, it must be opened a reasonable time before the seller has to make shipment (*Sinason-Teicher Inter American Grain Corporation v. Oilcakes and Oilseeds Trading Co. Ltd.* [1954] I. W. L. R. 935). If an intermediary bank has become insolvent, the buyer or another person involved in the transaction may make direct payment to the seller.

# Fraud in Letter of Credit Transactions

Letters of credit have been described by English judges as "the lifeblood of commerce".

The defence of the bank that it need not honour the credit because a fraud has occurred is therefore admitted only in very limited circumstances. Such a fraud may occur if the shipment of the goods is fraudulent or if the bills of lading tendered under the credit are falsified or forged.

Three cases have to be distinguished here. First, there is only a suspicion — perhaps a grave suspicion — that a forgery has occurred. In this case the bank must pay. Megarry J. said in Discount Records Ltd. v. Barclays Bank Ltd.: "I would be slow to interfere with bankers' irrevocable credits, and not least in the sphere of international banking, unless a sufficiently grave cause is shown."

Secondly, it is proved to the satisfaction of the Bank that the documents tendered are fraudulent but it cannot be established that the seller was a party to the fraud or knew of it. In this case, according to the decision of the House of Lords in United City Merchants (Investments) Ltd. v. Royal Bank of Canada, (see below), the bank should honour the credit.

Thirdly, it is proved to the bank that the documents are fraudulent and, in addition, that the seller was a party to the fraud or knew of it. In this case the bank should refuse to honour the credit.

# Performance Guarantees

Sometimes an overseas buyer arranges with the seller that the latter shall provide a performance guarantee safeguarding the due performance of the contract by the seller. Such a performance guarantee may be given by a bank, an insurance company or a surety company.

There are two types of performance guarantees, conditional and on demand guarantees.

A conditional guarantee is conditional on the buyer obtaining a judgment or an arbitration award against the seller or on the production of a certificate of default on the part of the seller by a neutral person.

A demand guarantee is payable on mere demand on the bank or other guarantor by the buyer. Banks prefer to issue on demand guarantees. In the case of an on demand guarantee the bank or other guarantor must honour the guarantee even if it is manifestly clear that the demand was unfair. The obligations of a bank which has issued an on demand guarantee are similar to those of a bank which has confirmed a letter of credit. The defence of fraud is available to the bank only on the same conditions which would entitle a bank to refuse to honour a confirmed letter of credit.

**New Words**

| | | |
|---|---|---|
| **1.** | collection agreement | 託收協議（或契約） |
| **2.** | documentary credit | 跟單信用證（狀） |
| **3.** | collateral security | 抵押品 |
| **4.** | sight bill | 即期匯票 |
| **5.** | time bill | 定期匯票 |
| **6.** | the remitting bank | 匯款銀行；寄單銀行 |
| **7.** | the collecting bank | 託收銀行 |
| **8.** | rust receipt | 信託收據 |
| **9.** | conversion *n.* | 侵占罪 |
| **10.** | the issuing bank | 開證（狀）銀行 |
| **11.** | the advising bank | 通知銀行 |
| **12.** | deferred payment | 延期付款 |
| **13.** | revocable *a.* | 可撤銷的 |
| **14.** | unconfirmed *a.* | 未保兌的 |
| **15.** | confirmed *a.* | 保兌的 |
| **16.** | irrevocable *a.* | 不可撤銷的 |
| **17.** | honour *v.* | 兌現；承兌 |
| **18.** | seat *n.* | 所在地；活動中心 |
| **19.** | paymaster *n.* | 會計員；主計官；付（發）款員；出納員 |
| **20.** | the doctrine of strict compliance | 嚴格符合原則（理論） |
| **21.** | debit *v.* | 將……記入借方 |
| **22.** | protein *n.* | 蛋白質 |
| **23.** | the lifeblood of commerce | 商業的生命線 |
| **24.** | falsify *v.* | 偽造 |
| **25.** | grave *a.* | 嚴重的；重大的 |
| **26.** | backdate *v.* | 回溯；寫上比實際日期早的日期 |
| **27.** | performance guarantees | 履約保證 |
| **28.** | conditional guarantee | 有條件的履約保證 |
| **29.** | on demand guarantees | 即期履約保證 |
| **30.** | manifestly *adv.* | 顯然地；明瞭地 |
| **31.** | thereupon *adv.* | 關於那；在其 |
| **32.** | non-performance *n.* | 不履行 |
| **33.** | surety company | 擔保公司 |

**34.** correspondent bank　　　　　代理銀行；往來銀行；關係銀行

 **New Phrases and Idiomatic Expressions**

| | | |
|---|---|---|
| **1.** | to pay on open account | 以記帳形式支付 |
| **2.** | to honour the credit | 承兌信用證（狀） |
| **3.** | by instalments | 分期裝運或付款 |
| **4.** | by means of | 用……方式 |
| **5.** | to interfere with | 干預 |
| **6.** | on board | 在船上 |
| **7.** | without the knowledge of | 不瞭解；不知道 |
| **8.** | to make a demand on the bank | 向銀行提出（付款）要求 |
| **9.** | under the performance bond | 根據履約保證金（協定） |

 **Notes**

1. the Uniform Rules for the Collection of Commercial Paper (1978 Revision)

   商業票據統一託收規則（1978年修改本）。

   該規則自1956年首次公布後，已修改兩次，一次在1967年，1978年6月又修改一次。經國際商會理事會批准，1978年修改本於1979年1月1日生效，並作爲322號出版物出版。

2. the Uniform Customs and Practice for Documentary Credits (1983 Revision)

   跟單信用證（狀）統一慣例（1983年修改版）。

   該慣例當時作爲400號出版物由國際商會出版。到1993年，該商會再次對它進行修改，然後以500號出版物出版，與UCP400相比，其條文變化頗大。

3. the doctrine of strict compliance：嚴格符合理論（原則）。

   按UCP500號第13條的規定，該理論有新的發展。新版本的解釋是：「本慣例所體現的國際標準實務是確定信用證（狀）所規定單據表面與信用證（狀）條款相符爲依據。單據之間表面互不一致，即視爲表面與信用證（狀）條款不符。」

   (...Documents which appear on their face to be inconsistent with one another will be considered as not appearing on their face to be in compliance with the terms and conditions of the credit.)

**Exercises**

## I. Answer the following Questions:

**1.** What are the common methods of paying the purchase price in the international sale of goods?

**2.** How do you define a letter of credit? What are the main types of letters of credit used in the international sale of goods?

**3.** How do you explain the doctrine of strict compliance? Any new development in this area?

**4.** When should the letter of credit be opened?

**5.** What does the autonomy of the credit mean?

**6.** What is performance guarantee? How many types of performance guarantees do you know?

## II. Translate the following phrases into Chinese:

| | |
|---|---|
| on opened credit | to honour the credit |
| collateral security | in favour of the seller |
| sight bill | bill of exchange |
| time bill | performance guarantee |
| issuing bank | performance bond |
| deferred payment | autonomy of credit |
| acceptance | the doctrine of strict compliance |
| negotiation | |

## III. Indicate whether each of the following statements is true or false by writing "T" or "F" in the space provided:

____**1.** The two most common methods of paying the purchase price are payment under a collection agreement and payment under a letter of credit.

____**2.** A revocable and unconfirmed credit affords much security to the seller.

____**3.** The credit constitutes a separate banking transaction and the issuing and advising banks are, in principle, not involved in the contract of export sale.

____**4.** If the advising bank adds its own confirmation of the credit to the seller, the latter has the certainty that a bank in his locality will provide him with the finance if he delivers the correct shipping documents in the stipulated time.

_____ **5.** The letter of credit is opened usually after the seller has made shipment.

_____ **6.** The obligations of a bank which has issued an on demand guarantee are similar to those of a bank which has confirmed a letter of credit.

## IV. Translate the following Chinese passages into English:

**1.** 英國法官常常把信用證（狀）形容成商業的生命線。可見信用證（狀）在國際貿易中發揮十分重要的作用。

**2.** 在國際貨物買賣中有兩種常用的付款方法。它們是託收安排和跟單信用證（狀）。在這兩種情況下，銀行充當中間人的角色，裝船單據用來作為對銀行的抵押。

**3.** 在國際貿易中常見的信用證（狀）有：可撤銷的未保兌信用證（狀）、不可撤銷的未保兌信用證（狀）、不可撤銷的保兌信用證（狀）和可轉讓的信用證（狀）。不管使用哪種信用證（狀），它必須在裝船期的開始時讓賣方得到。

**4.** 有時外國買方與賣方會作出這樣的安排：賣方向買方提供履約保證，保證賣方履行其契約。這樣的履約保證可由銀行、保險公司或擔保公司提供。

# 海上保險
# Marine Insurance

A contract of marine insurance is a contract whereby the insurer undertakes to indemnify the assured against marine losses, that is to say, the losses incident to a marine adventure (s.1.). There is a marine adventure when:

1. any ship or goods are exposed to maritime perils;

2. the earning or acquisition of any freight, passage money, commission, profit, or other pecuniary benefit or the security for any advances is endangered by the exposure of insurable property to maritime perils;

3. liability to a third party may be incurred by the owner of or a person interested in insurable property by reason of maritime perils.

"Maritime perils" means the perils consequent on or incidental to the navigation of the sea, but a marine insurance contract may, by express terms or by usage of a trade, be extended to protect the assured against losses on inland waters (s.2).

## Insurable Interest

A contract of marine insurance where the assured has no insurable interest is a gaming or wagering contract and is void. Policies are void when they are made:

1. interest or no interest; or

2. without further proof of interest than the policy itself; or

3. without benefit of salvage to the insurer, except where there is no possibility of salvage (s.4).

A person has an insurable interest if he is interested in a marine adventure in consequence of which he may benefit by the safe arrival of insurable property or be prejudiced by its loss, damage or detention. The following persons have an insurable interest:

1. The lender of money on bottomry or respondentia, to the extent of the loan. Bottomry is a pledge of the ship and freight to secure a loan to enable the ship to continue the voyage. It is named after the bottom or keel of the ship, which is figuratively used to express the whole ship. Respondentia is a pledge of the cargo only and not of the ship.

2. The master and crew to the extent of their wages.

3. A person advancing freight to the extent that the freight is not repayable in case of loss.

4. A mortgagor, to the extent of the full value of the property, and a mortgagee for the sum due under the mortgage.

5. The owner, to the extent of the full value, notwithstanding that a third party has agreed to indemnify him from loss.

6. A reinsurer, to the extent of his risk.

Defeasible, contingent and partial interests are insurable.

The assured must have the insurable interest at the time of the loss, although he need not have it when the insurance is effected. If he insures property "lost or not lost" the insurance is good although the property may in fact be lost at the date when the insurance is effected, provided the assured did not know that it was lost. If the assured assigns his interest in the property insured he does not transfer his rights in the insurance to the assignee, unless there is an agreement to that effect.

# Disclosure and Representations

A contract of marine insurance is one in which the utmost good faith (uberrima fides) must be observed, and if it is not, the contract is voidable (s.17). The assured must disclose to the insurer every material circumstance which is known to him, and he is deemed to know everything which he ought to know in the ordinary course of business. A circumstance is material if it would influence the judgment of a prudent insurer in fixing the premium or determining whether to take the risk (s.18). It is not necessary that the prudent insurer would have acted differently if he had known the circumstance, merely that he would have wanted to know of it when making his decision. The following are examples of the concealment of facts, which have been held to be material:

The fact that the ship had grounded and sprung a leak before the insurance was effected.

A merchant, on hearing that a vessel similar to his own was captured, effected an insurance without disclosing this information.

The nationality of the assured concealed at a time when his nationality was important.

In an insurance on a ship, the fact that the goods carried were insured at a value greatly exceeding their real value.

In every case, however, whether a circumstance is material or not depends on the particular facts. The following circumstances need not be disclosed:

1. Those diminishing the risk.

2. Those known or presumed to be known by the insurer in the ordinary course of his business.

3. Those which are waived by the insurer.

If the insurance is effected by an agent, the agent must disclose to the insurer every fact which the assured himself ought to disclose and also every material circumstance known to the agent. The agent is deemed to know every fact which he ought to know in the ordinary way of business or which ought to have been communicated to him (s.19).

In addition to his duty to make a full disclosure, the assured is under a duty to see that every material representation made during the negotiations for the contract is true. If any material representation be untrue the insurer may avoid the contract (s.20).

# The Policy

The contract of marine insurance is made as soon as the proposal is accepted by the insurer, although the policy may not be issued until later. Before the policy is issued it is usual to issue a document called **the slip** which, when accepted by the underwriter, is a short memorandum of the contract evidencing the date of the commencement of the insurance (s.21). The contract is constituted in the following manner. The broker, who acts as agent of the insured, offers the slip to various insurers, such as underwriting syndicates at Lloyd's, and the agent of each of these syndicates writes "a line," i.e., accepts to a limited amount (pro tanto), until the full amount stated on the slip is covered. The slip thus constitutes an offer and the signature of each of the underwriters, through their agents, is the acceptance pro tanto. Consequently separate binding contracts are concluded by the underwriters when they each accept pro tanto and the validity of these contracts is not conditional on the completion of the slip. This legal position becomes relevant when a loss occurs before the slip is fully underwritten. In this case the insured can hold those underwriters who have already written a line liable pro tanto but, on the other hand, the insured cannot cancel the contracts concluded with them, if such cancellation would be advantageous to him for one reason or another.

No action against the insurer can be brought by the insured until the policy is issued; the slip cannot be sued upon, but where there is a duly stamped policy reference may be made to the slip in any legal proceedings (s.89). The policy must be signed by the insurer, or, if the insurer is a corporation, it may be sealed, and must specify:

1. The name of the assured or of some person who effects the insurance on his behalf;

2. the subject-matter insured and the risk insured against;

3. the voyage or period of time or both, as the case may be, covered by the insurance;

4. the sum or sums insured;

5. the name or names of the insurers.

The subject-matter of the insurance must be described with reasonable certainty, regard being had to any trade usage. The nature and extent of the assured's interest in the subject-matter need not be specified (s.26).

The Marine Insurance Act 1906 sets out in Schedule 1 the form of a Lloyd's S. G. Policy and Rules for Construction of Policy. As from January 1, 1982 Lloyd's S.G. Policy is no longer used by the practice. It is superseded by the so-called Lloyd's Marine Policy, which is supplemented, as required, by the Institute Cargo Clauses A, B or C. The Rule for Construction of Policy still apply, where appropriate.

Lloyd's Marine Policy does not contain any insurance clauses, except the clause "This insurance is subject to English jurisdiction." This clause links the whole policy with the provisions of the Marine Insurance Act 1906. Apart therefrom, Lloyd's Marine Policy is merely the vehicle for the Institute Cargo Clauses, which define the risks covered and the exclusions of liability on the part of the insurers. These documents are called "Institute Cargo Clauses" because they are sponsored by the Institute of London Underwriters.

Policies are of the following kinds:

*1. Voyage policies*, where the contract is to insure "at and from" or from one place to another. The subject-matter is then insured for a particular voyage only.

*2. Time policies*, where the contract is to insure for "a definite period of time" (s.25(1)). A policy for a period of time and not for a voyage does not cease to be a time policy merely because that period may thereafter be extended or curtailed pursuant to one of the policy's provisions. The duration of the policy is defined by its own times and is thus for "a definite period of time." By the Stamp Act 1891, s.93, no time policy can be made for a period exceeding 12 months, but by virtue of section 11 of the Finance Act 1901 a time policy may contain a "continuation clause" providing that if at the end of the period the ship is at sea the insurance shall continue until the ship's arrival at her port of destination or for a reasonable time thereafter. A time policy sometimes contains restrictions as to locality, *e.g.* "from June 1, 1984, to April 1, 1985, no Baltic." A contract for both voyage and time may be included in the same policy (s.25.) This is known as a **mixed policy**. The underwriter is only liable under it when the loss occurs within the insured period and while the ship is on the described voyage.

*3. Valued policies*, where the policy specifies the agreed value of the subject-matter insured. In the absence of fraud, this value is conclusive as between the insurer and the assured, whether the loss be partial or total; but it is not conclusive in determining whether there has been a constructive total loss (s.27). Mere over-valuation is not fraudulent unless it is of a very gross nature. Without fraud, over-valuation is not a ground for repudiation.

*4. Unvalued policies*, where the value of the subject-matter is not specified, but is left to be subsequently ascertained, subject to the limit of the sum insured. The insurable value is ascertained as follows —

(1) As to the ship, the value includes her outfit, provisions and stores, money advanced for wages and disbursement to make the ship fit for the voyage, plus the charges of insurance on the whole. In the case of a steamship, it also includes the machinery, boilers, coals and engine stores.

(2) As to the freight, the value is the gross freight at the risk of the assured, plus the charges of insurance.

(3) As to the goods and merchandise, the value is the prime cost of the property insured, plus the expenses of and incidental to shipping and the charges of insurance (s.16).

5. *Floating policies*, where the insurance is described in general terms, leaving the name of the ship and other particulars to be defined by subsequent declaration. The subsequent declarations may be made by indorsement on the policy or in other customary manner and must be made in order of shipment. They must, in the case of goods, comprise all consignments within the terms of the policy and the value of the goods must be stated. If the value is not stated until after notice of loss or arrival, the policy must be treated as unvalued as regards those goods (s.29).

*Open cover* is not a policy, but is an agreement by the underwriter to issue an appropriate policy within the terms of the cover. To this extent it resembles a floating policy.

*Reinsurance* is where the insurer himself insures the whole or part of the risk he has undertaken with another insurer. In such a case the ordinary law as to insurer and assured applies as between the reinsurer and the insurer. Unless the policy provides otherwise, the original assured has no right or interest in the reinsurance (s.9). When a constructive total loss occurs, the insurer need not give notice of abandonment to the reinsurer (s.62(9)).

*Double insurance* is where two or more policies are effected by or on behalf of the assured on the same adventure and interest and the sums assured exceed the indemnity allowed by the Act, e.g. if X. insures property worth £1,000 with Y. for £750 and Z. for £500, there is a double insurance, because the measure of X's indemnity, viz. £1,000, has been exceeded. If X. had insured with Y. for £450 and Z. for £550 there would be no double insurance.

Where the assured is over-insured by double insurance he may, unless the policy otherwise provides, claim payment from the insurers in such order as he may think fit, provided he does not recover more than his indemnity. If the policy is a valued policy, the assured must give credit as against the valuation for any sum received under any other policy without regard to the value of the subject-matter insured. If the policy is unvalued, the assured must give credit, as against the full insurable value, for any sum received under any other policy. If the assured receives any sum in excess of his indemnity, he is deemed to hold it in trust for the insurers according to their rights amongst themselves (s.32).

As between the insurers, each is liable to contribute to the loss in proportion to the amount for which he is liable. If any insurer pays more than his proportion he can sue the others for contribution (s.80).

# Warranties

In contracts of marine insurance the term "warranty" has a different meaning from that in the Sale of Goods Act 1979. In the Marine Insurance Act 1906 it means that the assured undertakes that some particular thing shall or shall not be done, or that some condition shall be fulfilled, or whereby he affirms or negatives the existence of a particular state of facts. A warranty must be exactly complied with whether it be material or not. The effect of non-compliance is to discharge the insurer from liability as from the date of the breach (s.33). The result is not dependent on the insurer taking a decision, although a breach of warranty may be waived by the insurer.

The following warranties are implied:

1. In a voyage policy, that at the commencement of the voyage the ship is seaworthy for the purpose of the particular adventure insured. A ship is deemed to be seaworthy when she is reasonably fit in all respects to encounter the ordinary perils of the seas of the adventure insured (s.39(1),(4)).

2. In a voyage policy, where the voyage is to be performed in stages, during which the ship requires different kinds of or further equipment or preparation, that at the commencement of each stage the ship is seaworthy in respect of such preparation or equipment for the purpose of that stage.

3. Where the policy attaches while the ship is in port, that the ship shall, at the commencement of the risk, be reasonably fit to encounter the ordinary perils of the port (s.39(2)).

4. In a voyage policy on goods or other movables, that at the commencement of the voyage the ship is not only seaworthy as a ship, but also that she is reasonably fit to carry the goods to the destination contemplated by the policy.

5. That the adventure is a legal one and will be carried out in a lawful manner (s.41).

There is no implied warranty in the following cases:

1. As to the nationality of the ship or that her nationality shall not be changed during the risk (s.37).

2. In a time policy, that the ship shall be seaworthy at any stage of the adventure, but where, with the privity of the assured, the ship is sent to sea in an unseaworthy state, the insurer is not liable for any loss attributable to seaworthiness (s.39(5)).

If the loss is not attributable to the unseaworthiness to which the assured was privy, the insurer will be liable on the policy.

3. In a policy on goods or other movables, that the goods or movables are seaworthy (s.40(1)).

# The Voyage

In a voyage policy, if the voyage is altered, the insurer is discharged from liability. If, when the contract is made, the ship is said to be at a particular place, it is not necessary that it should be at that place, but the voyage must be commenced within a reasonable time (s.42). If the ship does not sail from the place of departure specified in the policy or does not go to the destination so specified or does not prosecute the voyage with reasonable dispatch, in all these cases the insurer is not liable on the policy.

If the ship deviates from the voyage contemplated by the policy, the insurer is discharged from liability as from the time of deviation, and it is immaterial that the ship may have regained her route before any loss occurs (s.46). Deviation, however, is excused in the following cases:

1. where authorised by the policy;

2. where caused by circumstances beyond the control of the master and his employer;

3. where reasonably necessary to comply with an express or implied warranty;

4. where reasonably necessary for the safety of the ship or subject-matter insured;

5. for the purpose of saving human life of aiding a ship in distress where human life may be in danger; but not for saving property;

6. where reasonably necessary to obtain medical aid for any person on board the ship; and

7. where caused by the barratrous conduct of the master or crew if barratry be one of the perils insured against.

When the cause excusing the deviation ceases to operate, the ship must resume her course and prosecute her voyage with reasonable dispatch (s.49).

If the policy specifies several ports of discharge, the ship must proceed to such of them as she goes to in the order designated by the policy; if she does not, there is a deviation (s.47).

# Assignment of Policy

A marine policy is assignable by indorsement, and the assignee can sue on it in his own name subject to any defence which would have been available against the person who effected the policy. The assignment may be made either before or after loss, but an assured who has parted with or lost his interest in the subject-matter assured cannot assign.

# The Premium

The insurer is not bound to issue the policy until the payment of the premium. If the insurance is effected through a broker, the broker is responsible to the insurer for the premium. He has, however, a lien on the policy for the premium and his charges. If he has dealt with the person who employs him as a principal, he has a lien on the policy for his general balance of insurance account. When a broker effects the insurance and the policy acknowledges the receipt of the premium, the acknowledgment is, in the absence of fraud, conclusive as between the insurer and the assured, but not as between the insurer and the broker (s.54).

# Risks Covered

Lloyds' Marine Policy does not contain insurance clauses, except a clause providing for English jurisdiction. The risks covered are stated in the Institute Cargo Clauses A, B and C.

Institute Cargo Clauses (A) cover:

all risks of loss or of damage to the subject-matter insured.

Institute Cargo Clauses (B) cover:

1. loss of or damage to the subject-matter insured reasonably attributable to

(1)fire or explosion,

(2)vessel or craft being stranded ground sunk or capsized,

(3)overturning or derailment of land conveyance,

(4)collision or contact of vessel craft or conveyance with any external object other than water,

(5)discharge of cargo at a port of distress,

(6)earthquake volcanic eruption or lightning,

2.loss of or damage to the subject-matter insured caused by

(1)general average sacrifice,

(2)jettison or washing overboard,

(3)entry of sea lake or river water into vessel craft hold conveyance container liftvan or place of storage,

3. total loss of any package lost overboard or dropped whilst loading on to, or unloading from, vessel or craft.

Institute Cargo Clauses (C) cover:

1. loss of or damage to the subject-matter insured reasonably attributable to

(1)fire or explosion,

(2)vessel or craft being stranded grounded sunk or capsized,

(3)overturning or derailment of land conveyance,

(4)collision or contact of vessel craft or conveyance with any external object other than water,

(5) discharge of cargo at a port of distress,

2. loss of or damage to the subject-matter insured caused by

(1)general average sacrifice,

(2)jettison.

All three sets of Institute Cargo Clauses contain a general average clause and a "both to blame collision" clause. In all three cases the risks covered are subject to a long list of "exclusions," specifying the cases in which the insurer is not liable. This list contains, inter alia, a war exclusion clause and a strikes exclusion clause but it is possible to obtain additional cover under the Institute War Clauses and the Institute Strikes Riots and Civil Commotion Clauses. It will be noted that Set A covers "all risks," but excluded from this cover is damage or loss caused by delay, inherent vice or insufficient packing. Set B. covers in clause 1.2.3 loss or damage caused by "entry of sea lake or river water into the vessel craft hold conveyance container liftvan or place of storage" but this risk is not covered by Set C.

# Burden of Proof

Whether the burden of proof is upon the insured or the insurer is often a matter of practical importance in that a case may be determined one way or the other according to where the burden lies owing to the paucity of evidence. Thus, when a plaintiff claims for loss under a policy of marine insurance asserting that the loss was caused by one of the perils of the sea specified in the policy, the onus is on him to prove that the loss was accidental. Accordingly, if on the available evidence the loss is equally consistent with accidental loss by perils of the sea as with scuttling, the plaintiff fails. It follows therefore that if the plaintiff in such a case does not disprove scuttling on a balance of probabilities, he has failed to prove his loss was caused accidentally and fortuitously by one of the specified risks.

The position is different, however, in the case of a claim under a policy for "loss by fire." The risk of fire insured against is not confined to an accidental fire. Thus, if a ship has been set alight by some mischievous person but without the insured's connivance, the insured will be entitled to recover. The insured cannot, of course, recover if he was the person who fired the ship or was a party to the ship being fired, because of the principle of insurance law that no man can recover for a loss which he himself has deliberately or fraudulently caused. However, the fact that the insured cannot recover does not prevent an innocent mortgagee from recovering. As to the burden of proof, once it is shown that the loss has been caused by fire, the plaintiff has made out a prima facie case and the onus is upon the defendant to show on a balance of probabilities that the fire was caused or connived at by the plaintiff. Accordingly, if the court comes to the conclusion that the loss is equally consistent with arson as it is with an accidental fire, the onus being on the defendant, the plaintiff will succeed.

# Loss and Abandonment

The insurer is only liable for those losses which are proximately caused by a peril insured against.

The fact that the loss would not have happened but for the negligence of the master or crew does not relieve the insurer from liability, but he is not liable for loss attributable to the wilful misconduct of the assured. He is not liable for loss through delay, even though caused by a risk insured against, or for wear and tear, leakage or breakage, or inherent vice of the subject-matter insured (s.55).

A loss may be either total or partial. A partial loss is any loss other than a total loss. A total loss may be actual or constructive.

An actual total loss is where the subject-matter insured is (1) destroyed, (2) so damaged as to cease to be a thing of the kind insured against, or (3) where the assured is irretrievably deprived thereof.

An actual total loss may be presumed if a ship is missing and, after a reasonable time, no news of her has been received (s.58).

A constructive total loss is where the subject-matter insured is reasonably abandoned because its actual total loss appears to be unavoidable, or because the expenditure to prevent an actual total loss would be greater than the value of the subject-matter when saved. For example, there is a constructive total loss where a ship has sunk and the cost of raising her exceeds her value when recovered; where a ship is damaged and the cost of repairs exceeds the value of the ship when repaired; where goods are damaged and the cost of repair and forwarding them to their destination exceeds their value on arrival (s.60).

Where there is a constructive total loss, the assured may either treat the loss as a partial loss, or abandon the subject-matter to the insurer and treat the loss as an actual loss. In the latter case notice of abandonment must be given. No notice of abandonment need be given in the case of actual total loss.

*Notice of abandonment* may be either in writing or by word of mouth, and may take any form as long as it indicates clearly that the assured abandons unconditionally the subject-matter of the insurance to the insured. If notice is not given the loss will be considered as partial. The notice must be given with reasonable diligence after the receipt of reliable information of the loss, time being allowed to make inquiries in a doubtful case. When notice of abandonment is accepted the acceptance conclusively admits liability for the loss, but if the insurer refuses to accept the notice the assured is not prejudiced if the notice has been properly given (s.62).

On abandonment of the subject-matter the insurer is entitled to take over the interest of the assured in whatever may remain of the subject-matter insured, and consequently would be entitled to any freight earned subsequent to the casualty causing the loss (s.63).

# General Average

If a general average loss has been incurred in connection with a peril insured against, the assured may recover the whole amount from the insurer without having recourse to the other parties liable to contribute (s.66). The insurer can recover this amount from the others.

A particular average loss is a partial loss of the subject-matter insured, caused by a risk insured against, which is not a general average loss. It gives no right of contribution from the other parties interested in the adventure. Such a loss can be recovered from the insurers if it is caused in connection with a peril insured against.

# Measure of Indemnity

Marine insurance being a contract of indemnity, the assured is only entitled to recover from the insurer such loss as he actually sustains. In the case of a total loss, the measure of indemnity is the sum fixed by the policy in the case of a valued policy, and the insurable value of the subject-matter in the case of an unvalued policy (s.68).

In the case of a partial loss to the ship the measure of indemnity is:

1. Where the ship has been repaired, the cost of repairs less the customary deductions which are usually one-third of the cost of new materials replacing old.

2. Where the ship has been partially repaired, the cost of repairs as above, and the amount of depreciation arising from the unrepaired damage.

3. Where the damage has not been repaired, the amount of depreciation from the unrepaired damage (s.69).

In the case of a partial loss of goods the measure of indemnity is:

1. Where part of the goods is lost and the policy is valued, such proportion of the fixed value as the value of the lost goods bears to the whole value of the insured goods.

2. Where part of the goods is lost and the policy is unvalued, the insurable value of the part lost.

3. Where the goods have been damaged, such proportion of the fixed value in the case of a valued policy, or of the insurable value in the case of an unvalued policy, as the difference between the gross sound and damaged values at the place of arrival bears to the gross sound value (s.71).

An insurer is liable for successive losses, although the total amount may exceed the sum insured; but if a partial loss, which has not been made good, is followed by a total loss, the assured can only recover in respect of the total loss (s.77).

It is the duty of the assured to take reasonable measures to avert or minimise a loss, and to prevent him from being prejudiced by anything he does to preserve the insured property after an accident, the policy usually contains a "suing and labouring" clause. This provides that it shall be lawful for the assured "to sue, labour and travel for, in and about the defence, safeguards, and recovery of the goods, ship, etc. without prejudice to this insurance." Under the clause the assured can recover from the insurer any expenses properly incurred pursuant to the clause, notwithstanding that the insurer has paid for a total loss (s.78).

# Rights of Insurer on Payment

When the insurer pays for a total loss, he is entitled to whatever remains the subject-matter insured, but if he pays for a partial loss he is entitled to no part of the subject-matter. In both cases, however, he is subrogated to the rights of the assured, i.e. he can bring an action in the assured's name against any person responsible for the loss.

# Return of Premium

Where the consideration for the payment of the premium totally fails, and there has been no fraud or illegality on the part of the assured, the premium is returnable to the assured, e.g. if the assured insured goods on the wrong ship by mistake. If the consideration is apportionable, and there is a total failure of an apportionable part of the consideration, a proportionate part of the premium is returnable.

The premium is returnable in the following cases:

1. Where the policy is void or is avoided by the insurer as from the commencement of the risk, if there has been no fraud or illegality on the part of the assured.

2. Where the subject-matter insured has never been imperiled.

But if a ship is insured "lost or not lost," and has arrived safely when the insurance is effected, the premium is not returnable unless the insurer knew of the safe arrival.

3. Where the assured has no insurable interest, unless the policy is a gaming or wagering policy.

4. Where the assured has over-insured under an unvalued policy, a proportionate part of the premium is recoverable.

5. When the assured has over-insured by double insurance, a proportionate part of the several premiums is returnable, except when the double insurance was effected knowingly by the assured (s.84).

# Mutual Insurance

Mutual insurance is where two or more persons agree to insure each other against marine losses. In such a case no premium is usually payable, but each party agrees to contribute to a loss in a certain proportion. The rights and duties between the parties depend on agreement, usually embodied in the rules of an association, and the ordinary law of marine insurance applies, subject to any such agreement.

Protection and Indemnity Associations, usually referred to as P.&I. Clubs, are a most common example of mutual insurance. It is a usual practice of shipowners to enter their tonnage in a P. & I. Club, contributing to its funds on an agreed basis of mutuality, in return for which the Association, on behalf of its members and within the framework of its rules, undertakes to meet the cost of various kinds of liabilities incidental to shipowning, usually those which would otherwise not be covered by the ordinary form of marine hull insurance policy, e.g. liabilities for injuries to passengers and crew, damages to piers, docks and harbours and quarantine expenses.

Frequently the rules of P. & I. Clubs contain a "pay to be paid" clause , the effect of which is that the club is liable to indemnify a member only where the latter has paid the claim against it. The presence of such a clause means that the third party will be unable to use the provisions of the Third Parties (Rights Against Insurers) Act 1930 in the event of the member becoming bankrupt.

### ♣ New Words

| | | |
|---|---|---|
| 1. | marine insurance | 海上保險 |
| 2. | marine adventure | 海上風險；海上冒險 |
| 3. | maritime perils | 海上險；海上危險 |
| 4. | passage money | 通行費用 |
| 5. | pecuniary benefit | 金錢利益 |
| 6. | the assured | 被保險人；投保人；要保人 |
| 7. | insurable interest | 可保利益；可保險權益；保險利益 |
| 8. | insurable property | 保險財產；可保險財產 |
| 9. | gaming contract | 賭博契約 |
| 10. | benefit of salvage | 海上打撈救助報酬 |
| 11. | bottomry of respondentia | 押船借貸契約或貨船抵押貸款 |
| 12. | keel of the ship | 船的龍骨 |
| 13. | the master *n.* | 船長 |
| 14. | the crew *n.* | 全體船員 |
| 15. | figuratively *adv.* | 比喻地 |
| 16. | mortgagor *n.* | 抵押人 |
| 17. | mortgagee *n.* | 被抵押人；抵押權人 |
| 18. | reinsurer *n.* | 再保險人 |
| 19. | defeasible *a.* | 可作廢的；可塗銷的 |
| 20. | uberrima fides | （拉）最大誠信 |
| 21. | premium *n.* | 保險費；保險金 |
| 22. | concealment *n.* | 隱瞞 |
| 23. | underwriting syndicate | 保險業組織 |
| 24. | voyage policy | 航程保險單 |
| 25. | time policy | 定期保險單 |
| | mixed policy | 混合保險單 |
| 26. | valued policy | 定值保險單 |
| 27. | unvalued policy | 不定值保險單 |
| 28. | open cover | 預約保險單；承保單 |
| 29. | floating policy | 流動保險單 |
| 30. | reinsurance *n.* | 再保險 |
| 31. | double insurance | 雙重保險；複保險 |
| 32. | over-insure *v.* | 超額保險 |
| 33. | seaworthy *a.* | 適合海上航行的 |

**34.** the ship's fittings and spars　　船的設備與圓杆

**35.** the privity of the assured　　被保險人契約關係

**36.** prosecute *v.*　　實行；徹底執行

**37.** deviate *v.*　　偏離航道

**38.** barratrous *a.*　　船長或海員的非法行為的

**39.** barratry *n.*　　船長或海員的非法行為

**40.** ports of discharge　　卸貨港

**41.** strand *v.*　　使船擱淺

**42.** capsized *a.*　　（船）被傾覆的

**43.** overturning *n.*　　使傾覆

**44.** derailment *n.*　　出軌；脫軌

**45.** land conveyance　　陸上運載工具

**46.** collision *n.*　　碰撞

**47.** port of distress　　避難港

**48.** earthquake volcanic eruption　　地震火山噴發

**49.** lightning *n.*　　閃電

**50.** jettison *n.*　　船遇險時投棄貨物；拋棄

**51.** vessel craft hold　　船艙

**52.** liftvan *n.*　　起重車

**53.** general average　　共同海損

**54.** strike *n.*　　罷工

**55.** riots *n.*　　暴動；騷亂

**56.** civil commotion　　民眾騷亂

**57.** inherent vice　　固有的瑕疵

**58.** general average loss　　共同海損

**59.** all risks　　一切風險

**60.** paucity *n.*　　缺乏

**61.** scuttling *n.*　　完全毀壞；全部放棄

**62.** disprove *v.*　　反駁；證明……不成立

**63.** fortuitously *adv.*　　偶然地

**64.** mischievous *a.*　　惡作劇的

**65.** connivance *n.*　　默許

**66.** balance of probabilities　　可能差額

**67.** particular average loss　　單獨海損

| | |
|---|---|
| **68.** imperil *v.* | 危害；使處於危險 |
| **69.** quarantine expenses | 檢疫費用 |
| **70.** pier *n.* | 直碼頭；（凸式）碼頭；（橋）墩 |
| **71.** returnable *a.* | 可退還的 |
| **72.** abandonment *n.* | 委付；放棄，拋棄 |
| **73.** right of subrogation | 代位權 |
| **74.** privy *n.* | 當事人；利害關係人；合約關係 |
| **75.** lost or not | 無論滅失與否 |
| **76.** outfit *n.* | 裝配 |
| **77.** actual total loss | 實際全損 |
| **78.** constructive total loss | 推定全損 |
| **79.** notice of abandonment | 委付通知；放棄通知 |
| **80.** avert *v.* | 防止 |
| **81.** pro tanto | （拉）到此；到這個程度；以此為限 |

## ♣ New Phrases and Idiomatic Expressions

| | | |
|---|---|---|
| **1.** | be incident to | 易發生的；伴隨而來的 |
| **2.** | in consequence of | 由於……緣故 |
| **3.** | be conditional on | 決定於…… |
| **4.** | for one reason or another | 因為這樣或那樣的原因 |
| **5.** | to be sponsored by | 由……主辦（倡議） |
| **6.** | in excess of | 超過 |
| **7.** | be attributable to | 可歸因於 |
| **8.** | without prejudice to | 不使……受損害 |
| **9.** | to recover from | 從……獲得 |
| **10.** | in the ordinary course of business | 在通常的交易過程中 |
| **11.** | on the part of | 就……而言 |
| **12.** | to be bound to do sth. | 有義務做某事 |
| **13.** | except when... | 除非……當 |
| **14.** | to effect the insurance | 進行保險 |
| **15.** | to act as... | 充當；擔當…… |
| **16.** | on hearing that... | 當聽到…… |
| **17.** | as to... | ……至於 |
| **18.** | a ground for... | ……的根據 |

**19.** to have a lien on sth.　　　　有對……的留置權
**20.** to part with sth.　　　　　　放棄某物

 **Notes**

1. Lloyd's S.G. policy：勞氏船貨保險單。

   這裡「S」代表ship，「G」代表goods。

2. Institute Cargo Clauses：協會貨物保險條款。

   Clauses issued by the Institute of London Underwriters that are added to standard marine insurance policies for cargo to widen or restrict the cover given. Each clause has a wording agreed by a committee of insurance companies and Lloyd's underwriters. By attaching particular clauses to the policy the insurers are able to create an individual policy to suit the clients' requirements.

3. the Institute of London Underwriters (also ILU)：倫敦保險業協會。

   association of UK insurance companies that cooperate with each other in providing a market for marine insurance and aviation insurance. Although Lloyd's underwriters are not members of the institute, the two organizations work closely with each other. The ILU appoints agents to settle claims, provides certificates of insurance for cargo shippers insured by members and is responsible for drawing up its own insurance contracts for the use of members.

4. warranty：擔保；保證。

   海上保險法中的「擔保」在含義上與買賣法中的「擔保」不一樣。在買賣法中，違反擔保發生時，受害人僅能請求損害賠償；而在海上保險法中，如被保險人違反擔保，無論其是否重要，保險人均可解除契約（參看1906年英國海上保險法第33條）。

5. Marine insurance being a contract of indemnity, the assured is only entitled to recover from the insurer such loss as he actually sustains.

   句中劃線部分可釋義為：Because marine insurance is a contract of indemnity...

6. The subject-matter of the insurance must be described with reasonable certainty, regard being had to any trade usage.

   句子劃線部分可釋義為：and regard should be given to any trade usage.

7. the ship must proceed to such of them as she goes to in the order designated by the policy.

   句中劃線部分的「such of them」可理解成「such ports」。

## Exercises

### I. Answer the following questions:

**1.** What is your definition of a contract of marine insurance? And what is the most important feature of it?

**2.** What is meant by insurable interest? Why is it so important?

**3.** What material circumstances must be disclosed to the insurer and what need not?

**4.** What content must be specified in the policy?

**5.** How many types of policies do you know?

**6.** What is the exact meaning of warranty in contracts of marine insurance? Is the meaning the same as that in sales law?

**7.** In what case is premium returnable?

**8.** What is mutual insurance?

**9.** What are Institute Cargo Clauses?

**10.** What do you know about the Institute of London Underwriters?

### II. Translate the following Chinese passages into English:

**1.** 海上保險契約是一個保險人承擔向被保險人賠償海上風險造成的海上損失的契約。

**2.** 按英國1906年保險法第24條的規定，保險單必須載明：

(1)被保險人或代其投保人的姓名；

(2)被保險的標的物和承保的風險；

(3)保險的航次或期間或兼有兩者；

(4)保險價額；

(5)保險人的姓名。

**3.** 在未付保險金前，保險人沒有簽發保險單的義務，如果透過保險經紀人取得保險，經紀人可留置保險單以獲得欠他的保險金和費用。

**4.** 海上保險契約是最大誠意契約，被保險人必須將規定的一切重要情況揭露給保險人，若有隱瞞或遺漏，保險人可據以解除契約。

## III. Indicate whether each of the following statements is true or false by writing "T" or "F" in the space provided:

_____ 1. A contract of marine insurance is a contract whereby the insurer undertakes to indemnify the assured against all sorts of losses.

_____ 2. Maritime perils mainly mean perils consequent on or incidental to the navigation of the sea.

_____ 3. Insurable interest is vital for a contract of insurance to be legally effective.

_____ 4. One of the most important features of a insurance contract is the observation of utmost good faith.

_____ 5. The insurer is bound to issue the policy before the payment of the premium.

_____ 6. The assured is only entitled to recover from the insurer such loss as he actually sustains.

_____ 7. When the insurer pays for a total loss, he is entitled to whatever remains the subject-matter insured.

_____ 8. Mutual insurance is where two or more persons agree to insure each other against marine losses.

_____ 9. A marine policy is assignable by indorsement, and the assignee can sue on it in his own name subject to any defence which would have been available against the person who effected the policy.

_____ 10. When the insurer pays for a total loss, he is entitled to whatever remains the subject-matter insured, but if he pays for partial loss he is entitled to no part of the subject-matter.

# 第二十課 Lesson 20

# 烏拉圭回合介紹
# Introduction to the Uruguay Round

On 1 January 1995 a new international economic organization came into being. Depending on one's perspective, the World Trade Organization (WTO) is either a modest enhancement of the General Agreement on Tariffs and Trade (GATT) that preceded it, or a watershed moment for the institutions of world economic relations reflected in the Bretton Woods system. After more than three years of the WTO's existence, it now looks highly probable that the latter conclusion will prevail.

The Uruguay Round (UR) Agreement of the GATT/WTO has been described as "the most important event in recent world economic history". In addition, the WTO is already being described as the "central international economic institution", and nations are becoming ever more engaged with the detailed processes of the WTO, especially its dispute settlement procedures, than had been contemplated at the time of signing. Indeed, the WTO Agreement, including all its elaborate Annexes, is probably fully understood by no nation that has accepted it, including some of the richest and most powerful trading nations that are members.

For twelve years preceding 1995, over 120 nations of the world participated in the largest and most complex negotiation in history concerning international economics. The Round was launched formally under GATT auspices in Punta del Este, Uruguay, in September 1986 (after some years of preparation). with a Ministerial Declaration setting forth the agenda. The Uruguay Round negotiating results were formally signed at Marrakesh, Morocco, on 15 April 1994 and were ratified by a sufficient number of nations to bring those results into force on 1 January 1995.The results are embodied in a "document" of some 26,000 pages! Most of these pages are detailed schedules of tariffs, services trade and other concessions, but the basic texts of the Agreement alone can approach 1,000 pages.

From its beginning, a most important objective of this trade round was to extend a GATT-type treaty rule-oriented discipline to three new subject areas: trade in services, agriculture product trade, and intellectual property matters. Of these three, services and intellectual property were truly new for the GATT. Although the GATT had always formally applied to agriculture product trade, for a variety of reasons this sector had largely escaped GATT discipline. Attempts to bring it "into the GATT fold" had failed in the two previous negotiating rounds (the Kennedy Round of 1962-1967 and the Tokyo Round of 1973-79).

In addition, the 1986 Punta declaration expressed priority for subsidy rules, changes in the dispute settlement procedures, new attention to the problems of textile trade and more elaboration of rules relating to product standards. A number of other measures were also targeted for attention.

The Uruguay Round result is remarkably fulfilling of the original intentions, although with some gaps. A list of the important achievements of the Round includes:

(1) *Services*. The services agreement (GATS — General Agreement on Trade in Services) is a major new chapter in GATT history. Although in some ways flawed, it offers an overall "umbrella" concept for trade in services that, it is hoped, will allow an ongoing negotiating process (probably lasting at least fifty years) for additional detail to occur. For more than a decade, various policy groups and interested enterprises had foreseen the need for some kind of international rule discipline for trade in services. The service "sector" is extraordinarily complex, consisting of some 150 specific service sectors, but in the aggregate services are beginning to represent a larger portion of gross domestic product of many of the Western industrialized countries than the production of goods. Service providers have begun to encounter government actions designed to restrict their commercial activity and presence, and so they have begun to urge an international cooperative mechanism that would develop rules against such protectionist activity. The Uruguay Round text must be deemed a worthy beginning.

(2) *Intellectual property*. The TRIPS agreement (Trade Related Intellectual Property) is an excellent new achievement, bringing new international rule discipline to the level of protection for patents, copyrights, trade secrets and similar intellectual property subjects, even though some of the specialists or particular interest groups appear disappointed by certain gaps in the text.

(3) *Agriculture*. The result in agriculture is in many respects meager, certainly as measured against the 1986 Punta del Este (and US!) aspirations. Nevertheless, there is now some realistic expectation for trade rule discipline over agricultural trade (especially subsidies and border quantitative restrictions). Like many subjects of the Uruguay Round, further attention will be needed over the years ahead, but the Uruguay Round achieved an important beginning which is already impacting on national agricultural policies.

(4) *Subsidies/countervailing duties*. Results include a new subsidies "Code", again not without flaw, but with an overall conceptual approach that improves the Tokyo Round code. Worries about this text focus on the ambiguity of several "exceptions" clauses which could lead to abuse.

(5) *Textiles*. For decades, trade in textiles has escaped normal GATT discipline and has been

governed by a byzantine fine set of embarrassing rules providing quantitative restrictions that are actually inconsistent with the normal GATT rules. The Uruguay Round provides a "phase-out" agreement for the special textile regime, to be accomplished over a decade. Again, many feel the Textile Agreement is flawed-the phase-out is considered either too slow or too fast-but the direction seems right.

(6) *Standards*. Trade rules for product standards have been further addressed, after the accomplishment of the Tokyo Round Code. It has become obvious that standards questions are much more complex than many thought, with some fundamental policy differences (such as the clash of environmentalist interests with trade policy goals, and questions about which government institutions should make decisions regarding difficult scientific evidence).

(7) *Safeguards*. One of the major failures of the Tokyo Round in 1979 was its inability to achieve an agreement on safeguards and escape clause measures. Here the Uruguay Round succeeded where the Tokyo Round failed, and a very impressive and ambitious Safeguards Code is part of the UR results. This not only provides guidelines and criteria for normal escape clause use, but also establishes a rule against the use of voluntary export restraints of various kinds. If this agreement is satisfactorily implemented, it could be a needed addition to world trading discipline.

(8) *Market access*. The Uruguay Round results include impressive advances in so-called "market access", with a reduction in the use of quotas (and a shift from quotas to tariffs). as well as very substantial tariff-cutting (some say the most of any round). Some of the most substantial tariff-cutting has been accomplished by developing countries, but there have also been some important achievements in reducing tariffs of certain industry sectors to zero for important groups of countries.

(9) *Integration of developing countries and economies in transition*. Developing countries are more fully integrated into the GATT/WTO system than before, with a requirement that all countries have tariff and service schedules, and with constraints on certain less developed country (LDC) exceptions. This measure could be one of the most important features of the Uruguay Round result, bringing a discipline at least to the "newly industrializing countries", (NICs). and the "economies in transition". A "soft membership" track through sponsorship of newly independent states has been eliminated to avoid certain abuses.

(10) *Preshipment and rules of origin*. Several interesting additions to the international trade rules are contained in a new treaty text of the Uruguay Round relating to pre-shipment inspections and to rules of origin. The text on pre-shipment inspections is designed to allow governments to establish procedures whereby a foreign buyer can obtain an inspection of goods ordered before those goods are shipped, with the possibility of a certification that the goods meet contractual criteria and standards, and to prevent fraud. But the text is also

designed to prevent such procedures from being abused for discriminatory or other purposes. The text on rules of origin, although fairly limited (but calling for further negotiation of such rules with a "work program for the harmonization" of such rules). sets out certain disciplines during a transition period. Particularly relevant to regional preference arrangements, rules of origin are recognized to have the potential to damage the principles of liberal trade.

(11) *Regional trade agreements*. One of the more troublesome chapters of the GATT is its provisions (in Article XXIV) regarding free trade agreements, customs unions and interim agreements leading to a free trade area (FTA) or customs union (CU). This article grants a rather broad exception to some of the GATT rules, especially the most-favoured nation (MFN) principle of non-discrimination, for agreements that meet certain criteria spelled out in the article. Because the criteria are not very precise, the GATT discipline on regional trade agreements has been quite loose and has been subject to dispute and possible abuse. The UR texts take a small first step towards the creation of greater discipline in this regard, providing some definitions and interpretations of clauses in GATT Article XXIV.

(12) *GATT grandfather rights*. Because the GATT had been applied only "provisionally", there existed a certain number of "grandfather rights", derived from a treaty clause in the Protocol of Provisional Application that allowed certain "existing legislation" to prevail legally over certain GATT rules. These exceptions created some difficulties and perceptions of unfairness. With the new WTO and its "definitive" application of treaty rules, these grandfather rights have now been abolished although some of them reappear in other legal forms.

(13) *Dispute settlement procedures*. Despite its "birth defects", one of the many achievements of the GATT has been the four-decade development of a reasonably sophisticated dispute settlement process. However, a certain number of flaws have been recognized in these procedures. The Uruguay Round, for the first time, establishes an overall unified dispute settlement system for all portions of the UR Agreements, and a legal text (rather than just customary practice) to carry out those procedures. These new procedures include measures to avoid "blocking", which occurred under previous consensus decision-making rules, and for the first time a new "appellate procedure", which will replace some of the procedures that were vulnerable to blocking.

(14) *WTO Charter*. Finally, one of the interesting achievements of the Uruguay Round is the development of a new institutional Charter for an organization that will help facilitate international cooperation concerning trade and economic relations, and will fundamentally change the GATT system to accommodate the vast new terrain of trade competence thrust on the trading system by the Uruguay Round. Some people have even said that this may be the most important element of the Uruguay Round result.

Interestingly enough, the original 1986 Punta del Este agenda did not refer to the possibility of a new international trade organization. Official proposals for such an organization were first made early in 1990. It was only in the December 1991 composite draft text of potential treaty clauses of the various UR negotiating groups that there was included in the official negotiating draft texts a tentative draft agreement for a new organization, at that time titled "Multilateral Trade Organization" (MTO). This draft had a number of flaws which were recognized by some governments, but through hard work the negotiators were able to revise the draft and iron out most of them. Thus, in the December 1993 (nearly) final draft of the Uruguay Round, a "Charter" for the new organization — entitled the World Trade Organization — was agreed, and later came into force.

## New Words

1. perspective *n.* 觀點；看法
2. watershed *n.* 轉捩點；重要關頭
3. probable *a.* 很可能發生的
4. contemplate *a.* 對……作周密考慮
5. elaborate *a.* 詳盡的
6. annexes *n.* 附件；附錄
7. objective *n.* 目的；目標；宗旨
8. concession *n.* 讓步
9. rule-oriented *a.* 以規則為導向的（類似的複合形容詞有：export-oriented）
10. meager *a.* 不足的
11. aspiration(s) *n.* 渴望達到的目的
12. ambiguity *n.* 不明確；模稜兩可
13. abuse *n.* 濫用
14. byzantine *a.* 死板的
15. flawed *a.* 有缺陷的
16. phase-out *n.* 分階段地停止或結束
17. market access 市場准入
18. appellate procedure 上訴程序
19. terrain *n.* 領域；範圍
20. composite *a.* 綜合的；複合的
21. tentative *a.* 暫時性的
22. ratify *vt.* 正式批准；認可

**New Phrases and Idiomatic Expressions**

| | | |
|---|---|---|
| 1. | come into being | 出現；產生；形成（有時也用「come into existence」表示同樣意思） |
| 2. | under GATT auspices | 在關貿總協定的支持下 |
| 3. | Punta Del Este | 烏拉圭的埃斯特角城 |
| 4. | set forth | 陳述；闡明 |
| 5. | not without flaw | 不是沒有缺點的 |
| 6. | be embodied in | 表現在；包含在；包括在 |
| 7. | be inconsistent with | 與……不一致（反義詞為「be consistent with」） |
| 8. | be fully integrated into | 完全與……一體化 |
| 9. | through sponsorship of | 透過……的贊助 |
| 10. | derive form | 從……衍生出來 |
| 11. | come into force | 生效（相同意思的表達方法還有 enter into force; be put into force, become effective） |
| 12. | impact on | 對……產生不良影響The cost of energy impacts heavily on every essential in the family budget. |

 **Notes**

**1.** for twelve years preceding：1995年前的12年裡

**2.** Marrakesh *n.*：馬拉喀什（摩洛哥的一個城市）

**3.** Morocco *n.*：摩洛哥

**4.** quantitative restrictions：數量限制
它多指防止或限制進口數額的措施，其形式有：(1)配額（quotas）；(2)進口許可（import licenses）；(3)自動出口約束 voluntary export restraint；(4)禁止（prohibition）。

**5.** Uruguay Round (RU)：烏拉圭回合
指1986年9月15日在烏拉圭埃斯特角城 Punta Del Este 的第八輪多邊貿易談判。

**6.** countervailing duties
抵消關稅，反補貼稅（countervailing duties are intended to affect any unfair competitive advantage that foreign manufacturers of exports might gain over the importing nation's producers because of foreign subsidies）。

**7.** subsidies *n.*：補貼
指政府給予本國出口商的補貼。可分為：Direct and indirect subsidies: direct subsidy in the form of an outright cash disbursement is prohibited by GATT principles; indirect subsidies include tax concessions, insurance arrangements and loans at below-market interest rate.

8. grandfather rights：「祖父權利」

它指根據GATT的Article I (2) 繼續享受新法頒布前所獲得的最惠國待遇（most favored nation treatment）the WTO 成立以後已將這種權利取消。

 **Exercises**

## I. Answer the following questions:

**1**. What is Uruguay Round (UR)? Why is it called so?

**2**. Why has UR been described as the most important event in recent world economic history?

**3**. Can you tell briefly all the important achievements of the UR?

**4**. Do you know anything about grandfather rights?

## II. Translate the following English passages into Chinese:

**1**. Article VI(3) of the GATT limits the amount of a countervailing duty to amount of foreign subsidy — interestingly enough regardless of whether the subsidy was legal or not under Article XVI.

**2**. General Agreement on Trade in Service (GATS) is a major new chapter in GATT history. Although in some ways flawed, it offers an overall "umbrella" concept for trade in services that, it is hoped, will allow an ongoing negotiating process (probably lasting at least fifty years) for additional detail to occur.

## III. Translate the following Chinese passages into English:

**1**. 烏拉圭回合的目的有三個：

(1)制止和扭轉保護主義，消除貿易扭曲現象；

(2)維護關貿總協定的基本原則（如：無歧視待遇原則，用多邊談判減少關稅原則和取消大多數進口配額原則）；

(3)建立一個更加開放，具有生命力的和持久的多邊貿易體制。

**2**. 中國根據「烏拉圭回合」部長會議宣言（Ministerial Declaration）的有關規定，全面參加了「烏拉圭回合」所有15個議題的談判。但由於中國創始締約國的地位未能恢復，中國在該輪多邊談判中的作用受到了很大限制。

# 世界貿易組織機構介紹
# Introduction to the WTO as an Institution

Perhaps the most dramatic result of the Uruguay Round negotiation was the establishment of a new organization to replace the GATT institutional function. This result was achieved by the Agreement Establishing the WTO, which informally is called the "charter" of the WTO.

## Structure

The governing structure of the WTO follows the GATT 1947 model in part, but departs from it substantially. At the top there is a "Ministerial Conference" (MC) which meets at least every two years. Next, there are not one but four "councils". These include one "General Council", which seems to have overall supervisory authority, can carry out many of the functions of the MC between MC sessions, and meets approximately every two months. In addition there are Council for Trade in Goods, Council for Trade in Services, and Council for Trade-Related Aspects of Intellectual Property Rights.

## Decision-making

The WTO decision-making procedures are very complex. But basically, there are five different techniques for making decisions or formulating new or amended rules of trade policy in the WTO: decision on various matters, "interpretations", waivers, amendments, and finally the negotiation of new agreements.

## Functions

1. To facilitate the implementation, administration and operation, and further the objects, of the Agreement for establishing the WTO.

2. To provide the forum for negotiations among its members concerning their multilateral trade relations in matters dealt with under the agreement for establishing the WTO.

3. To administer the Understanding on Rules and Procedures Governing the settlement of Disputes.

4. To administer the Trade Policy Review Mechanism.

5. To cooperate with the IMF and the International Bank for Reconstruction and Development and its affiliated agencies.

# Status

The WTO shall have legal personality, and shall be accorded by each of its members such legal capacity as may be necessary for the exercise of its functions mentioned above; the WTO shall be accorded by each of its Members such privileges and immunities as are necessary for the exercise of its functions.

## New Words

| | | |
|---|---|---|
| 1. | charter *n.* | 憲章 |
| 2. | institutional *a.* | 機構的 |
| 3. | Council *n.* | 委員會 |
| 4. | approximately *adv.* | 大約地 |
| 5. | amended *a.* | 修改的；修正的 |
| 6. | waiver *n.* | 棄權 |
| 7. | forum *n.* | 論壇 |
| 8. | procedure(s) *n.* | 程序 |
| 9. | amendments *n.* | 修正；修正案 |
| 10. | facilitate *vt.* | 促進 |
| 11. | privileges *n.* | 特權 |
| 12. | immunities *n.* | 豁免權 |
| 13. | legal personality | 法人資格 |
| 14. | legal capacity | 行為能力；法定資格 |

## New Phrases and Idiomatic Expressions

| | | |
|---|---|---|
| 1. | in part | 部分地（也可用「partly」或「partially」） |
| 2. | between sessions | 在閉會期間（指部長委員會閉會期間） |
| 3. | provide a forum for | 為……提供一個論壇 |
| 4. | be accorded by | 被授予…… |

**Notes**

**1.** the WTO  The full name is the World Trade Organization which came into being on January 1, 1995.

**2.** the Uruguay Round  The Round was launched formally under GATT auspices in Punta del Este, Uruguay, in September 1986. A most important objective of this trade round was to extend a GATT-type treaty rule-oriented discipline to three new subject areas: trade in services, agriculture product trade, and intellectual property matters. Of these three services and intellectual property（知識產權）were truly new for the GATT.

**3.** IMF指國際貨幣基金組織（the International Monetary Fund）。

**4.** the International Bank for Reconstruction and Development
國際復興開發銀行，簡稱世界銀行，1947年成為聯合國的專門金融機構，總部設在美國首都華盛頓。1980年，中國在該行合法席位得到恢復。其主要任務是幫助會員國解決發展經濟所需資金。

**5.** 文章最後一句話中的as是法律英語，表示which。

 **Exercises**

## I. Answer the following questions:

**1.** What is WTO? Its main functions?

**2.** How much do you know about the Uruguay Round?

**3.** What is the organizational structure of the WTO?

**4.** What is the status of the WTO?

## II. Translate the following English passages into Chinese?

**1.** The Marrakesh Agreement establishing the WTO sets out the purposes and objectives of the WTO and its institutional framework. The primary purposes of the WTO are two-fold: to ensure the reduction of tariffs and other barriers to trade, and the elimination of discriminatory in international trade relations.

**2.** The WTO is to ensure these primary purposes in order to facilitate in the economics of member states higher standards of living, full employment, a growing volume of real income and effective demand, and an expansion of production and trade in goods and services. These national objectives correspond to those of the IMF.

**3.** The functions of the WTO may be described as follows: First, the WTO provides a substantive code of conduct directed at the reduction of tariffs and other barriers to trade, and the elimination of discrimination in international trade relations. Second, the WTO provides the institutional framework for the administration of the substantive code. Third, the WTO ensures the implementation of the substantive code. Fourth, the WTO acts as a medium for the conduct of international trade relations among member states.

## III. Indicate whether each of the following statements is true or false by writing "T" or "F" in the space provided:

_____ **1**. The WTO is an enhancement of GATT.

_____ **2**. The most dramatic result of the Uruguay Round was GATT.

_____ **3**. The governing structure of the WTO completely follows the GATT 1947 model.

_____ **4**. The Council for Trade in Goods seems to have overall supervising authority.

_____ **5**. Negotiation of new agreement is one of the basic techniques used by the WTO to make decisions.

## The EU's policy needs reform. But not in the way the European Commission is proposing

BUREAUCRATS, not least those in Brussels, tend to guard their powers jealously. So it is surprising — nay, astonishing — that the European Commission is proposing to hand back some of its antitrust powers to national governments. Such a willingness to devolve power is most refreshing. Perhaps the commission, so often a byword for meddling, bungling and even corruption, is starting to put its house in order following the forced resignation of the previous lot of commissioners last year. It may finally even be converted to "subsidarity", the ugly name for the doctrine that decisions are to be taken at European level only when they cannot be better taken at lower levels. Unfortunately, in this case it is a mistake to devolve power. Competition policy, without which Europe's single market cannot function effectively, is one of those rare areas that is usually best dealt with in Brussels rather than Paris or London.

Even Eurosceptics concede that the EU's handling of competition policy has been an unexpected success. When, in 1992, border barriers within the European Union were torn down to form a single market, there were fears that companies would soon find new ways of stifling competition. After all, cosy corporatism is more in keeping with the traditional European way than is the vigorous promotion of consumer welfare. Yet Karel Van Miert, a Belgian socialist who was until last year the EU's competition commissioner, was not afraid to go after national monopolists or restrictive practices. Longsuffering consumers could scarcely stifle their cheers when, for instance, he slapped a record fine on Volkswagen, Germany's biggest car maker, for breaching single-market rules.

## Do the right thing

Yet for all its merits, EU antitrust policy is not without its faults. It is still too lenient towards big business. It is not tough enough on illegal government subsidies. It relies too little on economic analysis and too much on arbitrary rules enforced with plenty of discretion and little transparency. And it is far too regulatory and bureaucratic. Trustbusters spend most of their time processing paperwork about deals between minnows rather than chasing big fish.

Reform, then, is clearly needed. But the changes that Mario Monti, the new EU competition supremo, is proposing, and that the European parliament approved this week, will do more harm than good. On the plus side, firms will no longer have to notify all their commercial agreements to the commission, cutting down on unnecessary red tape. But on the minus side, Mr. Monti wants to farm out most of the enforcement of rules against restrictive practices, such as price-fixing, to national watchdogs and courts. The aim is to allow the commission, which has only 150 trustbusters, compared with a total of 1,200 in EU member states, to concentrate on the most serious breaches of competition law.

That is laudable. But there are big drawbacks to having national authorities taking on a bigger role. Some countries, such as France, have a bad record of turning blind eyes to anticompetitive behaviour by national champions. Others, such as Britain, have often allowed politics an undue sway over policy. More generally, businessmen have good grounds to fear that the simplicity and certainty of a "one-stop shop" will be replaced by a morass of duplicate hearings and conflicting rulings. A better solution to the commission's overload is to streamline its procedures, as well as to give it more resources, if necessary at the expense of national watchdogs.

But there is a bigger point. Though Mr. Monti, a former economics professor, hints that EU antitrust policy will be more based on economic criteria, rightly further limiting the scope for political meddling, his proposed reforms fail to deal with its biggest flaw. Currently, it is inconceivable that a European Microsoft would be investigated as openly and as rigorously as Bill Gates's firm has been in America, let alone that its break-up would be considered. This needs to change.

## ♣ New Words

| | | |
|---|---|---|
| 1. | bureaucrat(s) *n.* | 官僚 |
| 2. | jealously *adv.* | 妒忌地 |
| 3. | nay *adv.* | 不 |
| 4. | refreshing *a.* | 使人精神振作的 |
| 5. | byword *n.* | 俗語；綽號 |
| 6. | meddling *n.* | 干預；干涉 |
| 7. | bungling *n.* | 耽誤 |
| 8. | subsidarity *n.* | 附屬性 |
| 9. | devolve *vt.* | 移交 |
| 10. | Eurosceptics *n.* | 歐洲懷疑主義者 |
| 11. | concede *vt.* | （退一步）承認 |

| | | |
|---|---|---|
| **12.** | cosy *a.* | 舒適的 |
| **13.** | corporatism *a.* | 各階級合作主義 |
| **14.** | commissioner *n.* | （此處指歐洲委員會的）委員 |
| **15.** | long-suffering *a.* | 長期受苦的；長期遭難的 |
| **16.** | stifle *vt.* | 抑制 |
| **17.** | arbitrary *a.* | 專制的；武斷的 |
| **18.** | trustbuster *n.* | 要求解散托拉斯的人 |
| **19.** | minnow *n.* | 小魚；微不足道的人（與「big fish」相對） |
| **20.** | supremo *n.* | 最高領導人 |
| **21.** | red tape | 煩瑣和拖拉的工作作風；官僚作風 |
| **22.** | laudable *a.* | 值得稱讚的 |
| **23.** | draw back *n.* | 障礙；缺陷 |
| **24.** | streamline *vt.* | 精簡……使效率更高 |
| **25.** | inconceivable *a.* | 不可思議的；難以相信的 |

## 🍀 New Phrases and Idiomatic Expressions

| | | |
|---|---|---|
| **1.** | put one's house in order | 進行必要的改革 |
| **2.** | in keeping with | 與……一致；與……協調 |
| **3.** | slap a record fine on sb. | 向某人強制徵收破紀錄的罰款 |
| **4.** | not without its faults | 不是沒有缺點的 |
| **5.** | on the plus side | （在）好的方面 |
| **6.** | cut down on sth. | 減少…… |
| **7.** | on the minus side | （在）壞的方面 |
| **8.** | farm out | 將……交給他人做 |
| **9.** | concentrate on | 全神貫注…… |
| **10.** | take on (a bigger role) | 承擔 |
| **11.** | have a bad record of | 在……方面有壞的紀錄 |
| **12.** | turn blind eyes to sth. 或 turn a blind eye to sth. | 對……視而不見；對……裝作不見 |
| **13.** | allow sth. an undue sway over sth. else | 允許某事支配另外一件事 |
| **14.** | a morass of | 一大堆亂七八糟的…… |
| **15.** | let alone | 更不用說 |
| **16.** | be tough on sth. | 對……態度強硬 |
| **17.** | take a decision | 作決定；作決策 |

**Notes**

**1.** antitrust *a. n.*：反托拉斯的；反托拉斯（attacking monopolies and encouraging competition）。

**2.** the EU：歐盟（全名爲European Union, it was established by the Treaty of Rome.）

Today's union was originally called the European Economic Community (EEC) and was after informally referred to as the Common Market.

現歐盟共有27個成員。

**3.** the European Commission

歐洲委員會（the administrative body of the EU，歐盟的行政管理機構）

**4.** the European Parliament

歐洲議會（parliament of members elected in each member country of the EU.）

 **Exercises**

## I. Answer the following questions:

**1.** How much do you know about the EU?

**2.** Do you agree with the view that the EU's handling of competition policy has been an unexpected success? (give facts to support your opinion.)

**3.** What are the faults of the EU's antitrust policy?

**4.** What should the EU's antitrust policy be based on?

## II. Indicate whether each of the following statements is true or false by putting "T" or "F" in the space provided:

_____ **1.** The EU's antitrust policy is perfect.

_____ **2.** A record fine was slapped on Volkswagon for breaching single-market rules.

_____ **3.** According to Mr. Monti, EU's antitrust policy should be more based on economic criteria.

_____ **4.** Britain has often allowed politics an undue sway over policy.

_____ **5.** The European Commission is the law-making body of the EU.

# 第二十三課 Lesson 23

# 歐盟的競爭政策
# Competition Policy of the EU

If you wanted to do some serious rigging of European Union markets by means of an illegal cartel, pushing up prices or sharing out customers, chances are that you would not send an advance memorandum describing your intentions to the EU's anti-trust authorities. You would keep your head down and pile up the profits until the day when the authorities came to find you.

But say, on the other hand, you ran a big, law-abiding firm that was planning an entirely fair and commercial distribution arrangement with another firm. Your plan might, at first glance, seem to fall within the very broad prohibitions set down in the EU's treaty of Rome designed to catch restrictive practices and abusive monopolies.

Very probably, your plan would qualify for one of many exemptions, whether the sweeping ones included in those same articles or more specific ones in rules added later. These include special rules for "vertical" agreements between distributors at different levels in a market, which the European Commission is currently simplifying. This week the commission said it was also considering new rules for some "horizontal"

**The powers that be:** Article 81 of the Treaty of Rome prohibits all "agreements" and "concerted practices" which "may affect trade between Member States and which have as their object or effect the prevention, restriction or distortion of competition". But exceptions may be made for agreements and practices which contribute "to improving the production or distribution of goods", or to other forms of "technical and economic progress", and which give consumers "a fair share of the resulting benefit". Article 82 bans any "abuse of a dominant position" in a market by a firm or group of firms, particularly abuses involving price-fixing or market-sharing arrangements, and which "may affect trade between Member States".

agreements between competing firms.

In practice, you would follow your lawyer's advice and play safe. You would notify your plan to the sole authority able to grant you an exemption, the European Commission in Brussels, and you would ask for confirmation that your plan was indeed legal. You would be encouraged in this course by the knowledge that the application to Brussels also shielded your deal from legal challenge at home.

The result is that competition officials at the commission-153 civil servants-have been deluged with hundreds of dossiers each year describing perfectly unobjectionable trading arrangements that they have scarcely time to read, let alone analyse fully. Usually, an official writes a quick letter back saying the plan looks all right at first glance, and both sides are happy. The plan goes ahead, and the dossier gets filed away.

But every hour officials spend rubberstamping these routine applications is an hour less they have available for seeking out the secretive and harmful cartels that ought to have first claim on their attention. The need for change of some sort has long been obvious. At last it is coming, if slowly, and not necessarily surely.

This week the European Parliament debated and approved radical plans from the commission which would abolish the centralised notification system. The commission wants to share out to national courts and antitrust authorities the power to grant exemptions under articles 81 and 82, ending its own monopoly in this area. Firms that want clearance can seek it at home, not in Brussels. Commission staff will have much more time to pursue the firms with something to hide. (Mergers are dealt with under a different regulation, and the commission's rules for investigating them would not be affected by this reform.)

The proposed changes will not pass into law until next year (2000) at best, and only then if governments agree. They also require all EU countries to allow national competition authorities to apply community law as well as national law. Only eight of the 15 do so far.

One deep worry voiced this week by Euro-MPS, and also by some industry groups, concerns the uniformity of the new system. Can national authorities be relied on to implement EU rules identically? Or will some countries prove more lenient than others? If they do, that would threaten the integrity of the EU as a "single market".

The EU's competition commissioner, Mario Monti, says the reforms address this danger adequately. Under the new rules, the commission would still set competition policy for the whole EU. It would issue notices and regulations to advise or bind national authorities when needed. It would have the power to overrule national proceedings and to impose its own decisions if it thought national authorities were handling cases the wrong way. But mainly, the new system presumes that the principles of EU competition policy are already well established, well understood and well accepted by national authorities. That assumption may be sorely tested over time.

## New Words

1. law-binding *a.*      守法的
2. exemption *n.*      例外
3. article *n.*      此文中表示法律的「條」

| | |
|---|---|
| **4.** vertical *a.* | 豎式的；垂直的 |
| **5.** horizontal *a.* | 橫式的；水平的 |
| **6.** concerted *a.* | 一致的；商定的 |
| **7.** dossier *n.* | 一宗檔案材料 |
| **8.** secretive *a.* | 守口如瓶的；遮遮掩掩的 |
| **9.** lenient *a.* | 寬大的 |
| **10.** integrity *n.* | 完整 |
| **11.** address *vt.* | 著手解決（一個問題……） |
| **12.** overrule *vt.* | 駁回；否決 |

## New Phrases and Idiomatic Expressions

| | |
|---|---|
| **1.** do some rigging of a market | 操縱市場 |
| **2.** by means of | 用；依靠 |
| **3.** share out | 分配；分發 |
| **4.** keep one's head down | 不公開地做 |
| **5.** pile up | 積累 |
| **6.** at first glance | 第一眼 |
| **7.** fall within | 在……範圍內 |
| **8.** set down | 規定 |
| **9.** quality for | 勝任 |
| **10.** play safe | 求穩；不冒險 |
| **11.** be deluged with sth. | 被……所淹沒 |
| **12.** go ahead | 開始被實施 |
| **13.** get filed away | 歸檔並放在一起 |
| **14.** pass into law | 使……成為法律 |
| **15.** at best | 充其量；至多 |
| **16.** shield from | 保護……不受侵襲 |

## Notes

**1.** cartel：卡特爾。

An agreement among the producers of goods or services to fix prices of their products. Cartels are not unknown among banks and other financial institutions, but they are notoriously hard to detect.

2. public servants：公務員。

3. arrangements：非正式協議。

4. national proceedings：（成員）國（家）的訴訟。

5. impose its own decisions：給予它自己的裁決。

 **Exercises**

**Answer the following questions:**

1. What is the usual purpose of forming a cartel?

2. What changes have been proposed for the EU's competition policy?

3. What worry has been voiced by Euro-MPS and some industry groups concerning such changes?

4. What can the European Commission do in making the competition policy when the reforms are carried out?

# 貿易秘密、專利和商標
# Trade Secrets, Patents and Trade Marks

## Trade Secrets

Trade secrets form one aspect of intellectual property law, which also includes patents, trade marks, copyrights and designs. In today's competitive business environment, with so many businesses exploiting innovative products, the intangible assets protected by this area of the law are often the most valuable assets that a business owns. Intellectual property rights overlap, protecting different facets of a product, for example the product itself may be patented; its method of manufacture may be protected as a trade secret; sales literature, and software used to run the product, may be protected by copyright; its shape or configuration may be protected by the new design right; and its name by a trade mark.

### 1. Elements of an action for breach of confidence

Trade secrets are protected by the civil laws of confidentiality. Criminal law does not really play a part. Three conditions must be satisfied before an action for breach of confidence can succeed: (1) The information must be confidential; (2) The information must have been imparted in circumstances imposing an obligation of confidence; and (3) There must be an actual or threatened unauthorised use or disclosure of the information.

### 2. Remedies

The final remedies are the usual civil ones of injunction, damages, account, etc., but interlocutory procedures such as Anton Piller orders and interlocutory injunctions are particularly important, for intellectual property cases rarely go to full trial. An unusual feature of the injunction in these cases is the "springboard doctrine," which holds that a person who has acquired confidential information in breach of an obligation cannot use it to obtain a "head start" on other trade rivals. He is therefore restrained from using the information for the length of time the court judges that it will take the trade rivals to catch up, or for the information to enter the public domain.

### 3. Confidential information

The main test for assessing whether information is confidential was given by Sir Robert Megarry in *Thomas Marshall v. Guinle* [1978] 3All E.R. 193,209. He said that there were four factors which might be of assistance in identifying confidential information in a trade or industrial setting: (1) The information must be such that the owner believes its release would be injurious to him or of advantage to his rivals or others; (2) The owner must believe the information is confidential or secret, *i.e.* not already in the public domain; (3) The owner's belief under the two previous headings must be reasonable; (4) The information must be judged in the light of the usages and practices of the particular industry concerned.

### 4. When will an obligation be imposed?

As a general rule, an obligation of confidence will be imposed whenever confidential information is disclosed for a limited purpose. The cases have not limited the range of circumstances in which an obligation can arise. Common situations which give rise to the obligation in a commercial context are pre-contractual disclosures, *e.g.* for the purpose of negotiations; contracts; licences; employment; and the professional relationships lawyers, bankers and accountants have with their clients and customers. In *Coco v. Clark* [1969] R.P.C.41, 48, Megarry J. said that where information of commercial or industrial value is given on a business-like basis, or with some avowed common object in mind, such as the manufacture of articles by one party for another, the recipient will find it difficult to deny that he is bound by an obligation of confidence. The test is whether a reasonable man standing in the shoes of the recipient would realize on reasonable grounds that information was being given to him in confidence.

It is not necessary for the obligation of confidence to be set out in writing, but for evidential reasons, writing is often preferable, and also a written statement can serve as a strong warning to the disclosee that the discloser is serious about protecting his secrets.

### 5. Employees and independent contractors

The position of employees and independent contractors warrants special attention. Confidential information acquired by an employee in the course of his employment (or by an independent contractor performing a contract for services) will be protected either by an express undertaking of confidentiality, or by the duty of fidelity which is implied into every contract of employment (or contract for services, as the case may be). Express and implied duties to respect confidentiality can continue even after termination of the contract. Express covenants to respect confidentiality are often combined with agreements not to compete with a former employer, when they are known as covenants in restraint of trade. These are prima facie void as being contrary to public policy, unless they are no wider than is reasonably necessary to protect the employer's interest in terms of the information and activities covered, the geographical area over which the restriction extends, and the length of time it is to last.

While an ex-employee (or independent contractor) should not use or disclose his former employer's trade secrets unless authorised to do so, he is however free to exploit general knowledge and skill acquired in the course of his former employment. It is very difficult to draw the line between general knowledge and skill, and trade secrets. In *Faccenda Chicken v. Fowler* [1986] 1All E.R.617, a case concerning the duty owed by ex-employees, Neill L. J. said that the following matters must be taken into account, (1) the nature of the employment: was confidential information habitually, normally or only occasionally handled; (2) the nature of the information itself: only trade secrets or information of a highly confidential information would be protected; (3) whether the employer impressed upon the employee the confidential nature of the information; (4) whether the relevant information could be isolated easily from other information which the employee is free to use or disclose.

### 6. Third parties

Third parties can also be bound by an obligation of confidence. For example, if an ex-employee, in breach of an obligation of confidence owed to his former employer, discloses a trade secret to his new employer, the second employer will also be bound to respect the confidentiality of the information. He can be restrained by injunction from using or further disclosing it, or be required to pay damages for use after he has been informed of its confidential nature.

# Patents

*A patent* is the name given to a bundle of monopoly rights which give the patentee the exclusive right to exploit an invention for a stated period of time. It is important to realize that a patent is a right to stop others; an inventor does not need permission to exploit his invention. The right is a true monopoly giving the patentee the right to prevent another exploiting the invention even though devised independently. A patent lasts for 20 years from the date an application for the grant of a patent is made to the Patent Office.

Originally, a patent was a royal grant in the form of Letters Patent — hence the name — but now the rights granted are purely statutory and are set out in the Patents **Act** 1977. The rationale of the patent system is to encourage technological development. In return for disclosing the invention, the patentee is granted a temporary monopoly of 20 years, during which period he can, in theory, recoup his investment in research and development through exploitation of the invention. Competitors faced with the patent often seek to design round it, thus achieving further innovation. Patenting is not compulsory and some companies can and do rely on trade secrecy to protect their innovations.

### 1. Applying for a patent

An application for the grant of a patent for an invention must be made to the Patent Office. The application procedure is governed entirely by the Patents Act 1977 and its associated Patent Rules. The application is accompanied by a specification which consists of a detailed description of the invention and a set of claims. The claims define the scope of the invention for which the patentee seeks his monopoly. It is the invention as defined in the claims which is tested for patentability and against which alleged infringements are considered.

The Patent Office carries out **a search** in the relevant technical literature ("prior art") to test for "novelty" and "inventive step." The applicant is sent the result of the search usually within about 12 to 15 months from the date of the application. According to the results of the search the applicant may decide to abandon or modify his application or to request a substantive **examination**. The request for the examination must be made within six months from the date the application is published by the Patent Office. This publication must take place within 18 months from the date of filing the application. This is to give an early warning to competitors that a patent is being sought. If an application is withdrawn in time before the publication date it will not be published, thus preserving for the applicant the secrecy of its contents.

At the examination stage, the application is examined by a technically qualified Patent Office Examiner to see whether it complies with the requirements of patentability and certain other technical requirements laid down by the Act. Fees are payable on the initial application, for the search, for the examination and on grant. The application must comply with the requirements of the Act within the period of 4 years from the date of filing, otherwise a patent will be refused. Once granted, the patent lasts 20 years from the date of filing (note not the date of grant) provided renewal fees are paid every year from the fourth year onwards.

### 2. Priority date

Where two or more applications are made independently for the same or for overlapping inventions, it is necessary to have a system for working out which application is to be granted and which rejected. In the United Kingdom, priority is given to the first to file and not to the first to invent. So, the application with the earlier date of filing will have priority.

As a variant to the application procedure described above, an applicant may file an application accompanied only by a description of his invention. If he files a second application within a year from the first, he may claim as his **priority date** the date of filing the earlier application, even though in the intervening period he has further developed his invention. The only requirement is that his second application be "supported by," *i.e.* reasonably related to, the matter disclosed in the earlier application. It is the priority date which is the relevant date for testing the patentability of an invention.

Where an applicant, who is resident in a country which is a member of the Paris Convention (most are). files an application in that country and within 12 months files an application in the United Kingdom, he may claim as his priority date, the date of filing abroad, provided again that his United Kingdom application is supported by the matter disclosed in the foreign filing.

*Illustration:*

*A. files an application for an invention in the United States on January 1, 1990.*

*B. files an application for the same invention in the United Kingdom on May 1, 1990.*

*A. files a United Kingdom application claiming priority from his United States application on December 1, 1990.*

*A's invention has the earlier priority date and B's application will be refused.*

In practice, of course, the problems are far more complex.

Note that, for security reasons, a U.K. resident must file his patent application in the British Patent Office first. He may then apply for patents abroad.

### 3. International application procedures

An application made at the British Patent Office will result in the grant of a British patent only. An applicant who wished to obtain patent protection in several countries had, until recently, to file separate applications and pay separate fees in each country in which he sought a patent. Not only was this costly, but it resulted in the application being searched and examined with varying degrees of thoroughness in different countries depending on the competence of the local Patent Office. Two international systems have been devised to minimise the need for separate national applications.

The **Patent Co-operation Treaty** provides for the filing of a single application, designating the countries for which the applicant seeks protection. A single search is carried out and the application is then sent to each of the designated countries for separate examination as a national application according to their local laws. A variant provides for a single search and examination before the application is transmitted to the designated countries which may then carry out a supplemental examination if required. The system is operated under the auspices of the **World International Property Organisation** (WIPO) in Geneva. Some 45 countries, including the United States, the Soviet Union, the United Kingdom and most European States, are members.

The second system is the **European Patent Convention** to which all of the former EEC member states plus Austria, Switzerland and Sweden belong. Here an application is filed at the **European Patent Office** and the member states in which the applicant requires protection are specified. The application is searched and examined and if the invention satisfies the requirements of the Convention, separate national patents are granted for the specified countries. Thus a single application results in a bundle of national patents. Apart from a period of the first nine months after grant, when the validity of the European patent can be challenged at the European Patent Office, validity and infringement can be contested only before the separate national courts. The Patents Act 1977 contains provisions for treating European patents (United Kingdom). i.e. a European patent which specified the United Kingdom, as being in all respects the same as patents applied for and granted under the Act itself.

## 4. Patentability and patentable inventions

Patents are granted only for inventions which fulfil certain criteria. The invention must be new, it must involve an inventive step and be capable of industrial application. Each of these criteria is discussed more fully below.

Curiously, the Patents Act 1977 does not define what is a patentable invention; instead it sets out a non-exhaustive list of what are not inventions for the purposes of the Act. The exclusions are there as a matter of public policy as certain matters should be freely available to all. Non-patentable inventions include:

(1) discoveries, scientific theories or mathematical methods (s. 1(2) (a));

(2) literary, dramatic, musical or artistic works or any other aesthetic creations (s. 1(2) (b)). These are protected by copyright;

(3) schemes, rules or methods for performing a mental act, playing a game, doing business; or a program for a computer (s. 1(2) (c));

(4) the presentation of information (s. 1(2) (d)).

In addition, a patent may not be granted for any variety of plant or animal nor for an essentially biological process for their production (s. 1(3) (b)).However, a patent may be granted for a microbiological process, or for the product of such a process (s. 1 (3) (b)).

## 5. Novelty

An invention must be "new" to be patentable. It is new (or "novel") if it does not form part of the state of the art at the priority date (s. 2(1)). The state of the art comprises all matter (whether a product, a process, information about either, or anything else) which has at any time before that date, been made available to the public anywhere in the world by written or oral description, by use or in any other way (s. 2(2)). Case law under earlier patent legislation has interpreted the phrase "made available to the public" as meaning disclosure to one person who was free in law and equity to use the information as he pleased. Thus disclosure to another under an obligation of confidence will not affect patentability.

Where the art is a crowded one, two or more inventors may arrive at the invention at the same time and each file patent applications. To avoid the grant of a patent to two patentees, the earlier application is deemed to be part of the prior art when considering the novelty of the later application (s. 2(3)).

Certain prior disclosures will not invalidate a patent. These are:

(1) where the disclosure was made in breach of confidence (s. 2(4) (a). (b)) *e.g.* A. discloses his invention to B. in confidence. B. publishes the information in breach of confidence. A. can still patent his invention providing he files his application within six months of the disclosure (s. 2(4));

(2) where the invention was disclosed at an "international exhibition," *i.e.* one falling within the terms of the Convention on International Exhibitions (s. 2 (4) (c)). This exception is very narrow as the Convention excludes trade fairs; or

(3) where the invention is the use of a substance or composition for the treatment of the human or animal body, the fact that the substance or composition is already known may be disregarded if it has not previously been known to have pharmaceutical or veterinary properties (s. 2 (6)).

Where an invention has been disclosed in the prior art it is said to have been "anticipated." To test for **anticipation** it is necessary to compare the invention as defined in the claims with the alleged prior publication. The prior publication must be interpreted as at its date of publication in the light of the then existing knowledge without regard to subsequent events. The claims must likewise be construed as at their priority date. If the prior publication, so construed, contains a clear description of, or clear instructions to make the alleged invention, or if carrying out the directions contained in the prior publication will inevitably result in something being made or done which, if the patent were valid would amount to an infringement, the claim has been anticipated. An anticipation must be clear: "a signpost, however clear, upon the road to the patentee's invention will not suffice. The prior inventor must be clearly shown to have planted his flag at the precise destination before the patentee".

## 6. Inventive step

An invention is taken to involve an inventive step if it is not obvious to a person skilled in the art having regard to the prior art (s. 3). other than co-pending patent applications which are deemed to be prior art for the purpose of testing for novelty only (s. 3). Whether an invention is obvious is the most litigious question of all, as a patentee will not defend his patent if shown a clear anticipation. It is the "nearly but not quite" piece of prior art that is the most troublesome. The issue is particularly difficult to resolve as it is often fought years after the invention was made and the benefit of hindsight must somehow be discounted. "I confess that I view with suspicion arguments to the effect that a new combination, bringing with it new and important consequences in the shape of practical machines, is not an invention, because, when it has once been established, it is easy to show how it might be arrived at by starting from something known, and taking a series of apparently easy steps. This ex post facto analysis of invention is unfair to the inventors and, in my opinion, it is not countenanced by English patent law".

The test is directed to a hypothetical addressee: the man skilled in the art. He has been described as "a skilled technician who is well acquainted with workshop technique and who has carefully read all the relevant literature. He is supposed to have an unlimited capacity to assimilate the contents of, it may be, scores of specifications but to be incapable of a scintilla of invention". The notional addressee is also supposed to have read every piece of prior art which has been diligently unearthed in order to attack the patent. Much will be old, and in obscure languages.

The route by which the European Patent Office assesses obviousness is different from that traditionally adopted by British courts. It is more like the German approach, which uses as a yardstick a person who has only reasonable knowledge of the prior art, but who is capable of original thought. U. K. patents granted or litigated domestically are therefore currently measured by different tests than those coming before the European Patent Office or Board of Appeal.

## 7. Infringement

Two main questions arise. Does the scope of the invention as defined in the claims cover the product or process concerned? Does the defendant's act fall within the lists of acts prescribed by the Patents Act 1977?

### (1) Construction of claims

The claims must not be construed in isolation from the rest of the specification. The correct approach is to read the specification first, looking to see whether any terms are given a particular meaning, and having understood the specification, the claims must then be construed in the light of the whole specification, including the drawings, if any, (s. 125). In order for there to be infringement, all the essential features of the claim must have been taken; inessential features added or omitted do not take a product or process out of infringement. The claims must not be given a purely literal meaning but must be given a purposive construction. The question in each case is: "whether persons with practical knowledge and experience of the kind of work in which the invention was intended to be used, would understand that strict compliance with a particular descriptive word or phrase appearing in a claim was intended by the patentee to be an essential requirement of the invention so that any variant would fall outside the monopoly claimed, even though it could have no material effect upon the way the invention worked".

*(2) Prescribed Acts*

A person infringes a patent if, but only if, while the patent is in force, he does any of the following things in the United Kingdom, without the consent of the proprietor of the patent:

(1) where the invention is a product, he makes, disposes of, uses or imports the product or keeps it for disposal or otherwise (s. 60 (1) (a));

(2) where the invention is a process, he uses the process or he offers it for use when he knows, or it is obvious to a reasonable person in the circumstances, that its use there would be an infringement, (s. 60 (1) (b)) or he disposes of, offers to dispose of, uses or imports any product obtained directly by means of that process or keeps any such product whether for disposal or otherwise (s. 60 (1) (c)).

It is also an infringement for a person to supply or offer to supply "means essential for putting an invention into effect" to a person not entitled to work the patent, when he knows or it is obvious to a reasonable person in the circumstances, that those means are suitable for putting and are intended to put the invention into effect in the United Kingdom, (s. 60 (2)). This is sometimes referred to as contributory infringement. As an example, suppose there is a patent for a mixture of chemical A with chemical B in a herbicidal composition. The supply of chemical A to a person who, the supplier knows, is going to mix it with B and sell the mixture as a herbicide is an infringement.

There are certain limited exceptions to infringement including acts done for private, non-commercial purposes (s. 60 (5) (a)). acts done for experimental purposes (s. 60 (5) (b)). acts done on ships and aircraft temporarily or accidentally within the territorial waters or airspace (s. 60 (5) (d) (e) (f)). A person who has himself used the invention before the priority date of the patent may do so again or continue to do the acts he did before that date (s. 64). Obviously, the prior use must have been secret, otherwise the patent would be bad for lack of novelty. The right to continue the use is personal and may be assigned only with the business in connection with which the invention was used (s. 64 (2)).

Only a valid patent can be infringed and a defendant may attack validity in the defence and in addition counterclaim for revocation of the patent.

*(3) Remedies for infringement*

A patentee whose patent is valid and infringed is entitled to an injunction, delivery up of infringing articles and damages or an account of profits. Damages are assessed on a loss of profits or on a royalty basis.

## 8. Ownership, assignment and licensing

A patent or an application for a patent is personal property (without being a chose in action) (s. 30(1)). Any assignment must be in writing signed by or on behalf of both parties to the transaction; otherwise it is void (s. 30(6)). A licence may be granted orally and may be non-exclusive or exclusive (i.e. excludes even the patentee from working the invention). An exclusive licensee can bring infringement proceedings in his own name without joining the patentee (s. 67). All transactions must be registered at the Patent Office (s. 32). Penalties for non-registration include loss of priority over subsequent transactions (s. 33) and restrictions on the right to recover damages against infringers (s. 68).

## 9. Employee inventions

Where an invention is made by an employee in the course of his normal duties as an employee, or in the course of duties falling outside his normal ones but specifically assigned to him and, in either case, an invention might reasonably be expected to result from his carrying out those duties, that invention belongs to the employer (s. 39 (1) (a)). Where an invention is made by an employee who, because of the nature of his duties and particular responsibilities arising therefrom, is under a special obligation to further the employer's business, that invention also belongs to the employer (s. 39 (1) (b)). All other employee inventions belong to the employee (s. 39 (2)). Where a patent granted on an employee invention is of outstanding benefit to the employer, the employee may be entitled to a fair compensation (s. 40). A contract entered into before the invention was made and which diminishes the employee's rights in his inventions is to that extent unenforceable (s. 42).

# Trade Marks

Trade marks are protected both under the common law of passing off and under the Trade Marks Acts 1938 and 1984. A trade mark is essentially any word or symbol or combination of both which is used to indicate a connection in the course of trade between the goods or services in relation to which the mark is used and the owner of the mark. Trade names and get-up are also protectable by a passing off action. The law relating to registered trade marks is about to be changed. At the time of writing, the Government has produced a White Paper on Reform of Trade Marks Law (Cm. 1203). Reference will be made to the proposals in the white Paper, for English law must be amended before the end of 1992 to comply with an EEC Directive (first Council Directive of December 21, 1988); and also to allow the U.K. to ratify as soon as possible the Protocol to the Madrid Agreement Concerning the International Registration of Trade Marks; and move us further down the road towards the establishment of a Community Trade Mark System.

### 1. Registered trade marks

The Trade Marks Acts provide a system of registration for certain marks and entitles the owner of the mark to its exclusive use.

Since 1986 marks used in connection with goods and with services can be registered.

*(1) Registrability*

At the moment the Trade Marks Register is divided into part A and Part B. It is easier to secure registration in Part B but a more restricted protection is obtained. Under the White Paper it is proposed to combine the two parts of the Register into one single part. Turning to the definition of a registrable trade mark, Article 2 of the Directive states that "A trade mark may consist of any sign capable of being represented graphically, particularly words, including personal names, designs, letters, numerals, the shape of goods or of their packaging, provided such signs are capable of distinguishing the goods or services of one undertaking from those of other undertakings." The inclusion of the "shape of goods or of their packaging" is important, as it removes the anomaly introduce by the House of Lords, that a Coca Cola bottle cannot, however distinctive its shape, be registered as a trade mark.

Returning to the present position, to be registrable in Part A, a mark must consist of or contain at least one of the following:

(1) the name of a company, individual or firm, represented in a special or particular manner (s. 9 (1) (a));

(2) the signature of the applicant for registration or some predecessor of his in business (s. 9 (1) (b));

(3) an invented word or words (s. 9 (1) (c));

(4) a word or words having no direct reference to the character or quality of the goods, and not being according to its ordinary meaning, a geographical name or surname (s. 9 (1) (d));

(5) any other distinctive mark, but a name, signature or word, other than those covered by (a) to (d) above, is not registrable except on evidence of distinctiveness (s. 9 (1) (e)).

There is no similar list of requirements for registration in Part B of the register. The limitations set out in section 9 (1) (d) and in Article 2 of the Directive are to ensure that no one trader can monopolize, through his trade mark registration, words which other traders may legitimately want to use in connection with their products, such as descriptive words, or the name of the area in which they trade, or laudatory epithets or phrases. All trade marks must be distinctive, *i.e.* distinguish the goods or services of the trade mark proprietor (owner) from those of other traders. There are differences in this requirement as between Part A and Part B registrations, but once again these are to be swept away in the reforms and will not be considered here.

If the reforms are implemented, it should also be easier to register a trade mark. Currently the onus is on the applicant to show that his mark ought to be registered. However, there is evidence that the law is too strict and prevents the registration of marks which ought to be capable of registration. In future there is to be a presumption that a mark is registrable unless there is some specific objection to it. Objections might be raised if, as under current law, a mark is likely to deceive or cause confusion or would be contrary to law or morality, or contain any scandalous design (s. 11). This prevents, inter alia, registration of marks which are confusingly similar to existing unregistered marks which by use have acquired some goodwill and reputation. It also prevents registration of marks which would be deceptive in use, such as, for example, the use of "Orwoola" for non-woollen materials. In addition, under section 12 (1) no trade mark may be registered if it is identical with or confusingly similar to a mark which is already registered for the same goods or description of goods or services for which registration is sought. It is proposed to broaden protection under this heading so as also to protect against registration in respect of similar goods or services; or in respect of goods and services which are not similar, but where use of the mark by another would take unfair advantage of the reputation of a registered mark or be detrimental to the reputation or distinctive character of the mark. The Registrar may however permit registration where in his opinion there has been honest concurrent use of the two marks in question (s. 12(2)). The matter is one for the discretion of the Registrar and factors to be taken into account are: the extent of use in time, quantity and area of trade; the degree of confusion likely to ensue: the honesty of the concurrent use; and the relative inconvenience which would be caused if the mark were registered.

*(2) Infringement*

The owner of a valid trade mark or service mark has the exclusive right to use that trade mark in relation to the goods or services for which it is registered. That right is infringed by any person who, without permission, uses in the course of trade, a mark identical with the registered trade mark or a mark so nearly resembling it as to be likely to deceive or cause confusion (s. 4 (1) (a)).

In considering whether a mark is confusingly similar, the resemblance of the two marks must be considered with reference to the ear as well as to the eye. Also, the idea conveyed by the mark must be regarded. Thus two marks which, when placed side by side, can be seen to be different may yet leave the same impression on the mind.

Also, some account must be taken of imperfect recollection. It is not to be supposed that a person has the two marks side by side but whether in view of his general recollection of the one mark he would be likely to be deceived and to think that the trade mark before him is the same as the other.

A second type of infringement is by "importing a reference" to a trade mark (s.4 (1) (b)). This type of infringement occurs where an infringer uses the mark not to describe his own goods, but compares his own goods with those of the trade mark proprietor and refers to the latter's goods by the trade mark. Thus comparative price lists issued to the public which set out the trader's own brand and price in comparison with a famous named product and its price will be an infringement under section 4 (1) (b).

The test for infringement of a Part B mark is the same as for a Part A mark, except that it is a defence for the alleged infringer to show that his use of the mark (or one objectively confusingly similar) was not such as to be likely to deceive or cause confusion (s. 10).

## 2. Defences to infringement

The defences commonly available are:

(1) that the mark is invalid, *e.g.* for non-use for a period of five years (s. 26) or that its registration contravened sections 9-12;

(2) that there is no infringement;

(3) that the defendant used his mark prior to the first use by the proprietor of the mark sued upon or prior to its registration, whichever is the earlier (s. 7);

(4) that the defendant is bona fide using his own name or that of his place of business (s. 8 (a));

(5) that the defendant is using a bona fide description of the character or quality of his goods (s. 8 (b));

(6) that the defendant is himself the registered proprietor of the mark complained of (s. 4 (4));

(7) that the plaintiff has no title;

(8) general defences, such as acquiescence, estoppel or that the plaintiff's use of the mark is fraudulent or deceptive.

### (1) Remedies for infringement

A successful plaintiff is entitled to bring the usual interlocutory procedures, or to obtain an injunction, damages or an account of profits for infringement and to an order for destruction or modification of the offending material. It is not to be assumed that every article sold by the defendant would have been sold by the plaintiff for some customers may have purchased the defendant's goods for other reasons such as lower price, but the plaintiff may claim damages for the general lowering of his trade reputation if the spurious goods are of a much inferior quality.

### (2) Ownership, assignment and licensing

Any person who claims to be the owner of a mark used or intended to be used by him may apply for registration (s. 17 (1)). Once registered, the mark may be assigned either in connection with the goodwill of the business in which it is used or separately (s. 22 (1)).

Where the assignment is without the goodwill of the business, it does not take effect unless the assignee applies to the Registrar of Trade Marks within six months from the date of the assignment for directions with respect to advertising the assignment in a suitable trade journal (s. 22 (7)). There are no formal requirements for the grant of licences to use a trade mark, save that some form of quality control should be exercised by the trade mark owner over the licensee's goods or there should be some other connection between them, such as being associated companies, so that a connection in the course of trade is still maintained between the registered proprietor and the goods. There is provision for entry of a licensee as a registered user on the Register (s. 28) and a registered user may institute proceedings in his own name if the trade mark proprietor neglects or refuses to do so within two months of being called upon (s. 28 (3)). The rules relating to licensing are likely to be changed in line with recommendations in the White Paper.

### 3. Passing off

The purpose of an action for passing off is to prevent one trader from misappropriating the goodwill and reputation which has been built up by another. What is protected is not a proprietary right in a name, mark or get-up which has been improperly used, but the goodwill in the business in which the name, mark or get-up is used. The basic principle behind every passing off action is that no man is entitled to represent that his goods or his business are the goods or business of another. As Lord Diplock said in Warninck v. Townend [1980] R. P. C. 31, 93, it is possible to identify five characteristics which must be present in order to create a valid cause of action for passing off:

(1) a misrepresentation;

(2) made by a trader in the course of trade;

(3) to prospective customers of his or ultimate consumers of goods or services supplied by him;

(4) which is calculated to injure the business or goodwill of another trader (in the sense that this is a reasonably foreseeable consequence); and

(5) which causes actual damage to the business or goodwill of the trader by whom the action is brought will probably do so.

Whether or not a trader is guilty of passing off is not necessarily to be decided by reference to precedents. Rather, the tort is capable of development to meet the times and could sometimes be regarded as a remedy against unfair trading actionable at the suit of other traders who thereby suffer loss of business or goodwill. For example, the goodwill may be injured by someone who sells genuine goods of an inferior quality as being goods of a superior quality. Thus, in *Spalding v. Gamage*, [1915] 32R. P. C. 273, Spalding's lower grade footballs were sold by Gamage in such a way as to mislead purchasers into thinking they were buying the higher grade Spalding footballs. Or the goodwill may be injured by someone who falsely applies a trade description to a product. Thus, in *Bollinger v. Costa Brava Wine Co.*, [1960] R. P. C. 16, and 116 it was held that a sparkling Spanish wine sold as "Spanish Champagne" was a misrepresentation, as the name "champagne" denoted the sparkling white wine produced in the Champagne region of France and not just any sparkling white wine.

A plaintiff must first establish his reputation in the name, mark or get-up complained of. It is possible, though not common, for a name which ordinarily has a descriptive meaning to acquire a secondary meaning, i.e. that it has become distinctive of the goods of a particular trader.

Normally, the court requires a great deal of persuading to accept that a descriptive term has lost its primary meaning and is in fact distinctive of the plaintiff's goods or business.

The misrepresentation may be made not only by using names or marks the same as or confusingly similar to that of the plaintiff, but also by adopting a packaging or get-up which is very close. For example, in *Reckitt & Colman Products Ltd. v. Borden Inc*. [1990]1 All E. R. 873, the defendants were prevented from marketing their lemon juice in lemon-shaped containers which closely resembled those of the plaintiffs. as to do otherwise would cause confusion among consumers as to the origin of the product.

It is not necessary for the plaintiff's and defendant's trade to be identical. Provided there is a sufficient similarity for the one to be thought connected with the other. The test is whether there is confusion of a common consuming public.

*(1) Defences to an action for passing off*

The following defences are commonly raised:

①that the name or mark or get-up is not distinctive of the plaintiff, or that it is descriptive and the plaintiff cannot establish a secondary meaning;

②that there is no real likelihood of confusion or, if there is confusion, there is no real likelihood of damage to the plaintiff;

③that the defendant has a concurrent right to use the mark or name or get-up;

④that the defendant is trading bona fide under his own name;

⑤general defences such as acquiescence, estoppel and delay.

*(2) Remedies*

A successful plaintiff is entitled to an injunction and to damages or an account of profits and to an order for obliteration or modification of the mark name or get-up complained of. Interlocutory procedures, such as interlocutory injunctions and Anton Piller orders, are also important.

*(3) Ownership, assignment and licensing*

There is no proprietary right in an unregistered mark, trade name or get-up. What may be assigned is the goodwill of the business in connection with which the name, mark or get-up is used. A licence to use the name, mark or get-up is, strictly speaking, merely an agreed immunity from a passing off action capable of being brought by the licensor.

## ♣ New Words

| | | |
|---|---|---|
| 1. | intellectual property law | 知識產權法；智慧財產權法 |
| 2. | patents *n.* | 專利權 |
| 3. | trade marks | 商標 |
| 4. | copyrights *n.* | 著作權 |
| 5. | designs *n.* | 設計 |
| 6. | overlap *v.* | 與……交叉；與……重疊 |
| 7. | trade secret | 商業秘密 |
| 8. | sales literature | 銷售廣告（或宣傳品） |
| 9. | software *n.* | 軟體 |
| 10. | breach of confidence | 破壞信用；洩密 |
| 11. | impart *v.* | 把……分給；給予；傳遞 |
| 12. | interlocutory *a.* | 在訴訟期間宣告的；中間裁決的 |
| 13. | "springboard doctrine" | 「跳板理論」 |
| 14. | pre-contractual *a.* | 契約前的 |
| 15. | business-like *a.* | 事務式的；有條理的 |
| 16. | avowed *a.* | 公開宣稱的 |
| 17. | discloser *n.* | 揭露人 |
| 18. | disclosee *n.* | 被揭露人 |
| 19. | fidelity *n.* | 忠誠；忠實 |
| 20. | covenants *n.* | 契約 |
| 21. | ex-employees *n.* | 過去的雇員 |
| 22. | patentee *n.* | 專利權人 |
| 23. | Letters Patent | 專利證書 |
| 24. | recoup *v.* | 扣除；補償 |
| 25. | patentability *n.* | 專利性；專利條件 |
| 26. | patentable *a.* | 可取得專利的 |
| 27. | technical literature | 技術宣傳品 |
| 28. | prior art | 已有技術；現有技術 |

| | | |
|---|---|---|
| **29.** novelty *n.* | 新穎性 | |
| **30.** inventive step | 創造性 | |
| **31.** variant *n.* | 變體；變種 | |
| **32.** non-exhaustive *a.* | 非詳盡的 | |
| **33.** non-patentable *a.* | 不可取得專利的 | |
| **34.** aesthetic *a.* | 美學的 | |
| **35.** biological *a.* | 生物學上的 | |
| **36.** microbiological *a.* | 微生物學上的 | |
| **37.** the state of the art | 技術水平 | |
| **38.** pharmaceutical *a.* | 藥物的 | |
| **39.** veterinary *a.* | 獸醫的 | |
| **40.** signpost *n.* | （十字路口的）路標 | |
| **41.** co-pending *a.* | 聯合未決的 | |
| **42.** hindsight *n.* | 事後的認識 | |
| **43.** ex post racto | 事後的；溯及既往的 | |
| **44.** hypothetical *a.* | 假設的 | |
| **45.** assimilate *v.* | 吸收；同化 | |
| **46.** scintilla *n.* | 一點點 | |
| **47.** unearth *v.* | 發現 | |
| **48.** obscure *a.* | 難解的；含糊的 | |
| **49.** lintel *n.* | 過梁 | |
| **50.** vertically *adv.* | 垂直地；豎式地 | |
| **51.** adjacent *a.* | 鄰近的 | |
| **52.** horizontal *a.* | 水平面的；臥式的 | |
| **53.** herbicidal *a.* | 除莠的；阻礙植物生長的 | |
| **54.** chose in action | 無形財產；訴訟上的財產 | |
| **55.** diminish *v.* | 使變減少；使變小 | |
| **56.** get-up *n.* | 裝訂；式樣 | |
| **57.** passing off | 騙賣；出售假貨 | |
| **58.** White Paper | 白皮書 | |
| **59.** Madrid Agreement | 馬德里協議 | |
| **60.** registrability *n.* | 可登記註冊性 | |
| **61.** registrable *a.* | 可註冊登記的 | |
| **62.** graphically *adv.* | 用圖式表示地 | |
| **63.** anomaly *n.* | 不按常規；破格 | |

64. laudatory epithets      讚美的短語

65. onus *n.*      義務；責任

66. scandalous *a.*      惡意中傷的

67. headlamps *n.*      （汽車等的）前燈

68. recollection *n.*      回憶

69. acquiescence *n.*      默認；默許

70. misappropriate *n.*      濫用；盜用

71. sparkling *a.*      起泡沫的

72. countenance *v.*      支持；鼓勵

## ♣ New Phrases and Idiomatic Expressions

1. in breach of      違反……

2. in the public domain      受公共支配

3. in the light of      根據

4. to be accompanied by      與……一起；被伴隨

5. to give warning to      向……提出警告

6. under the auspices of      在……主持或領導下

7. without regard to      不考慮

8. to use sth. as a yardstick      用……作為衡量標準

9. in isolation from      從……割裂開來

10. in force      生效

11. to put into effect      使……生效；使……實施

12. in one's own name      以……自己的名義

13. for the discretion of      由……斟酌決定

14. to call upon      傳訊

15. to be capable of      能做……

16. at the suit of      在投訴……時

17. in the course of      在……過程中

18. to put sth. into effect      使……開始生效或實施

19. to raise objections      提出反對（意見）

20. to take account of sth.      考慮某事；重視某事

## ♣ Notes

1. the Paris Convention：巴黎公約。

　　它是以保護工業產權為目的的一個國際公約。該公約於1883年在巴黎召開的外交會議上通過。

當時在該公約上簽字的只有11個國家（比利時、巴西、薩爾瓦多、法國、瓜地馬拉、義大利、荷蘭、葡萄牙、塞爾維亞、西班牙和瑞士）。巴黎公約於1884年7月7日生效，後來英國、突尼西亞和厄瓜多爾也相繼參加。該公約保護的物件不僅包括專利權，也包括商標以及其他形式的智慧財產權。

**2.** the World International Property Organization (WIPO)：世界智慧財產權組織。

世界智慧財產權組織是聯合國組織系統下16個專門機構之一。建立該組織的公約於1967年在斯德哥爾摩簽訂，1970年生效。該組織總部設在日內瓦。該組織的總目標是：在全世界維護和加強對知識產權的尊重，以便透過鼓勵創造性活動、便利技術的轉移和文化藝術作品的傳播，促進工業和文化的發展。

**3.** the European Patent Convention (EPC)：歐洲專利公約。

歐洲專利公約是一些歐洲國家在1973年10月在慕尼黑簽訂的，所以又稱為慕尼黑公約。該公約的目的是採用單一的程序來取代向各國分別申請專利的多重程序。按公約規定，申請人毋需向每個歐洲國家分別提出專利申請，而只需向歐洲專利局提出一申請即可。

**4.** the European Patent Office：歐洲專利局。

**5.** Anton Piller Orders：安東‧皮賴爾命令（或裁定）。

該裁定以 Anton Piller K.G.V. Manufacturing Processes, Ltd (1976) 一案命名。該裁定允許對據信被用以進行某種侵犯原告著作權活動的作案場所實施檢查。

**6.** the Patent Co-operation Treaty：專利合作條約。

該條約於1970年6月19日在美國華盛頓簽訂，1978年生效。該條約的主旨是規定單一的申請（provides the filing of a single application）和單一的審查（a single search），但是否給予專利權，還得由各國根據國內法自行決定。截止1980年11月，已有30個國家加入這一條約，其中包括英國、美國、法國和聯邦德國等發達國家。

## Exercises

### I. Answer the following questions:

**1.** What does intellectual property law include?

**2.** Can you give some examples of trade secrets?

**3.** What conditions must be satisfied before an action for breach of confidence can succeed?

**4.** What is patent? What is the rationale of patent system?

**5.** How do you apply for the grant of a patent in the U. K.?

**6.** Can you say something about the Paris Convention?

**7.** What criteria should be fulfilled before patents are granted for inventions?

**8.** What are the usual remedies available for patent infringement?

## II. Translate the following Chinese passages into English:

1. 專利是由政府主管部門根據發明人的申請，認爲其發明符合法律規定的條件，而授予發明人在一定時期內使用發明的專有權。

2. 在英國，一項發明要取得專利權必須具備兩個最基本的條件：(1)新穎性；(2)創造性。其他條件還有先進性和實用性。

3. 從本質上講，商標是任何一個詞或標誌或它們兩者的組合，用來表示在貿易過程中貨物或服務與商標所有者之間的一種聯繫。

4. 爲便於一國公民在其他國家取得專利保護，各國先後簽訂了一些有關保護工業產權或專利權的國際公約。其中著名的有：《巴黎公約》、《專利合作條約》和《歐洲專利公約》等。

## III. Indicate whether each of the following statements is true of false by writing "T" or "F" in the space provided：

_____ 1. In the U. K. the patent lasts 20 years from the date of grant provided renewal fees are paid every year from the fourth year onwards.

_____ 2. In the U. K., priority is given to the first to file and not the first to invent. So, the patent application for an invention with the earlier date of filing will have priority.

_____ 3. Whether an invention is obvious is the most litigious question of all.

_____ 4. Only a valid patent can be infringed.

_____ 5. The English law relating to registered trade marks is about to be changed.

_____ 6. All trade marks must be distinctive, i.e. distinguish the goods or services of the trade mark proprietor (owner) from those of other traders.

_____ 7. The owner of a valid trade mark or service mark has no exclusive right to use that trade mark in relation to the goods or services for which it is registered.

_____ 8. Whether or not a trader is guilty of passing off is not necessarily to be decided by reference to precedents.

# 著作權和有關的權利
# Copyright and Related Rights

Unlike the monopoly granted by a patent, which enables the patentee to exclude independent but later originators from working the invention, the rights comprised by copyright give protection only against copying. Copyright protects the independent skill, labour and effort which have been expended in producing a copyright work and prevents another from taking a short cut to the end result by helping himself to too liberal a portion of that skill, labour and effort. Copyright is acquired simply by bringing a work into existence which has the appropriate degree of originality and a qualifying connection with the United Kingdom. There is no need and, indeed, no provision for registration.

Copyright is purely statutory and the governing legislation is the Copyright, Designs and Patents Act 1988. This statute codified and amended the law; one of the aims of the legislature was to express existing law in more comprehensible form. There are thus many changes of expression as well as substantive changes over earlier legislation.

Copyright protects literary, dramatic, musical and artistic works, films, sound recordings, broadcasts, cable programmes and the typographical arrangement of published editions. The 1988 Act gives to the copyright owner the exclusive right to do or to authorise others to do so-called "restricted acts." These differ according to the nature of the work protected by copyright and define the scope of the protection afforded to that work.

## Subsistence of Copyright

### 1. Qualification or "connecting factor"

A work may qualify for copyright protection in the United Kingdom by authorship or by first publication:

Authorship. If at the material time the author is a national of, resident or incorporated in the UK, a colony or a state belonging to an appropriate Convention, the work will enjoy UK copyright. For literary, dramatic, musical and artistic works and films, the Berne Convention is of paramount importance. This Convention guarantees a minimum level of protection and national treatment of foreign works as between signatory states. Most countries are members either of Berne, or of the Universal Copyright Convention of 1952, or of both. For sound recordings and broadcasts the Rome Convention of 1961, with more limited membership, applies. Typefaces are governed by the Vienna Agreement.

Publication. First publication in the UK or another country to which the Act extends or applies will also qualify a literary, dramatic, musical or artistic work, film or typographical arrangement for copyright protection. Broadcasts and cable programmes qualify by transmission. "Published" is defined in s.175 as meaning the issue of copies of the work to the public or making certain works available to the public by means of an electronic retrieval system.

A work which is copyright in the United Kingdom will enjoy national copyright protection in other Convention countries.

Crown and Parliamentary copyright are available where a work is made by officers of the Crown or under the direction or control of Parliament; protection is also given to works made under the auspices of certain international organizations.

## 2. Literary, dramatic and musical works

Copyright subsists in original works of these descriptions. The meaning of "original" is discussed on p.661, post. A literary work means any work, other than a dramatic or musical work, which is written, spoken or sung. The definition (s.3 (1)) includes tables, compilations and computer programs. "Writing" includes any form of notation or code, regardless of the method or medium of recording. There is no requirement of literary merit in order for a work to be protected and such diverse works as street directories, logarithm tables, examination papers, advertising brochures, football pool coupons and series of bingo numbers are entitled to copyright. It is possible for more than one copyright to exist in a work: thus in the case of a published anthology of poetry there will be separate copyrights in the individual poems as well as an additional compilation copyright, and typographical arrangement copyright in the anthology as a whole. "Dramatic work" is defined as including works of dance or mime and "musical work" means a work consisting of music, exclusive of any words or action.

There appears to be a quantitative minimum below which creations of these kinds do not constitute "works." In Exxon, that word was held not to be a literary work. Copyright does not exist in literary, dramatic or musical works until they are recorded, in writing or otherwise.

## 3. Originality

It can be seen that copyright only subsists in "original" literary, dramatic, musical and artistic works. Originality here does not have the same meaning as novel or unique in the sense that an invention must be novel to be patentable. Original merely means that the work must be the product of the independent skill and labour of the author and must not have been slavishly copied or derived from some pre-existing work. Even though a work contains a substantial part derived from earlier material it will still attract copyright provided further independent skill, labour, knowledge, taste or judgment have been expended upon it. However, if a derived work has been made in infringement of another's copyright, it may not be possible to exploit the later work without consent.

## 4. Artistic works

This important category includes: (1) graphic works (paintings, drawings, maps, engravings etc.). photographs (wide definition). sculptures and collages *irrespective of artistic quality*; (2) works of architecture being buildings (fixed structures or parts) or models; (3) works of artistic craftsmanship.

The phrase "irrespective of artistic quality" enabled the courts to hold that engineering production drawings were entitled to copyright. Copying a product which had been manufactured from engineering drawings amounted to indirectly copying the drawings. Copyright actions were fought (and won) on production drawings for spare parts for cars, such as exhaust systems, light fittings, solid fuel gravity feed boilers, plastic knock-down drawers for furniture and even lavatory pan connectors. In this respect copyright protection was as valuable, if not more so, than patent protection. Other growth areas of copyright litigation included the fashion trade since fashion sketches, cutting patterns and point patterns for knitted garments were protected as "artistic works."

Such use of copyright in two-dimensional works to prevent plagiarism of three-dimensional articles has been curtailed by the 1988 Act. It is still possible for copyright in a two-dimensional work to be infringed by a three-dimensional copy, and vice versa. However, where an artistic work records or embodies the design for the shape or configuration of an article which is not in itself an artistic work or typeface, s.51 now permits others to make articles to the design or to copy articles made to the design. Thus copyright in production drawings for a pump component may not be used to prevent others from manufacturing the component. Other forms of protection for designers' artefacts may be available — design right or registered designs. Where the article depicted in a sketch or drawing is an artistic work, such as a sculpture, copyright in the graphic work may be used to control copying of the work depicted. The same result may be obtained if the drawing or sketch was not *intended* to be a design drawing. However, once an artistic work is applied industrially in the manufacture and marketing of articles, s.52 limits to 25 years the copyright owner's ability to control manufacture.

Designs for the surface decoration of an article are not affected by s.51, so that copyright in the design document may be used to restrain copying of the design. However, s.52 applies in relation to the surface of articles, although not to truly two-dimensional articles such as calendars or posters.

A work of artistic craftsmanship is not defined and the leading case , *Hensher (George) Ltd. v. Restawile Upholstery (Lancs.) Ltd.* [1976] A. C. 64 (H.L.) gives no clear guidance except as to what is not a work of artistic craftsmanship. The intention of sub-section 4 (1) (c) is to give protection to such works as stained glass, pottery and other forms of artistic endeavor not covered by the previous categories of "artistic work".

*Authorship of literary, dramatic, musical and artistic works*

Section 9 (1) defines the author of a work as "the person who creates it." Usually there is no difficulty in identifying that person. Sometimes two or more individuals collaborate in the creation of the work in such a way that their respective contributions cannot be distinguished; in those circumstances the work is treated as a work of joint authorship. Some works are originated by computers in such a way that no particular human author can be identified. In these circumstances a work may be accorded copyright as a computer — generated work; the person who undertook the arrangements for creating the work is given the status of author.

### 5. Films

A film is defined by s.5 (1) as "a recording on any medium from which a moving image may by any means be produced." This encompasses celluloid and video recordings. It should be noted that the making of a film very frequently involves the use of other copyright works such as books, scripts, music, for which copyright clearance must be obtained. The sound track of a film is treated under the 1988 Act as a sound recording — a separate work. The author of the film is the person who makes arrangements necessary for its creation — usually the producer, although the director of a film is responsible for its cultural merit. It is the director and not the producer who enjoys moral rights in the film — the right to be named as creator and to object to derogatory treatment. Because film is a species of work recognized by the Berne Convention, films can enjoy copyright virtually worldwide. Copyright does not subsist in a film or part of a film which is copied from a previous film: s.5 (2).

### 6. Sound recordings

Most sound recordings embody literary, dramatic or musical works, spoken or performed, and the recording provides a means for reproducing the work in sound. This type of recording is included in the definition of sound recording at s.5 (1) (b). The first limb of the definition at s.5 (1) (a) embraces reproducible recordings of sound such as birdsong or industrial noise. The definition applies regardless of recording medium or means of reproduction but does not appear to include a computer program capable of generating non-musical sounds *ab initio*.

The author of a sound recording is the person who makes the arrangements necessary for its creation: s.9 (2) (a). This probably achieves the same effect in most cases as s.12 (4) of the Copyright Act 1956, by which the first owner of copyright in a sound recording was the person who owned the master. Sound recordings do not enjoy copyright if or to the extent that they are copies of previous sound recordings.

### 7. Broadcasts and cable programmes

These "works" enjoy an evanescent existence in the form of electromagnetic waves. The medium through which the waves travel is the criterion for distinguishing between the two types of work. If the signals are sent along a cable, optical fibre or other specially adapted medium, they may constitute a cable programme but not a broadcast. If the signals are transmitted through free space, by "wireless telegraphy," they may constitute a broadcast but not a cable programme. In each case the purpose and recipients of the transmission establish its status as a work. A broadcast is either capable of lawful receipt by members of the public or transmitted for presentation to members of the public. Lawful receipt of an encrypted broadcast requires use of authorized decoding equipment. There are two types of author of a broadcast — the person making the transmission and the person having responsibility for its contents to any extent. This means that joint authorship and ownership of broadcast copyright are likely to be common. As broadcasting is also a means of infringing copyright, copyright in works included in a broadcast without consent is likely to be infringed by joint tortfeasors.

The complex definition of "cable programme service" in section 7 confers copyright on transmissions of visual, sound and teletext material. It is designed to include public transmissions for passive reception and to exclude private and domestic transmissions and services internal to a business or media organization. The definition probably includes transmissions sent to those who consult databases online. The Secretary of State has power to add exceptions to the definition or remove them.

Qualifying broadcasts and cable programmes will enjoy copyright to the extent that they do not infringe copyright in another broadcast or cable programme:ss.6(6) and 7(6). This low threshold of originality means that repeat transmissions attract copyright, the duration of which is tied to that of copyright in the original transmission: s.14(3).

# Duration of Copyright

Unless a work enjoys Crown or Parliamentary copyright, to which special rules apply, copyright endures as follows:

For literary, dramatic, musical and artistic works, copyright expires 50 years from the end of the calendar year in which the author dies:s.12 (1). If an original work has been created by computer in circumstances where there is no human author, copyright expires 50 years from the end of the year of making.

Copyright in sound recordings and films subsists for 50 years from the end of the calendar year in which the work was made; if released during that period, 50 years of copyright run from the end of the year of release: s.13. "Release" includes authorized publication, broadcasting or cablecasting and the public showing of a film and its soundtrack.

Broadcasts and cables programmes enjoy copyright for 50 years from the end of the year of first transmission: s.14.

Copyright in the typographical arrangement of published editions expires 25 years from the end of the year of publication: s.15.

# Infringement

The acts restricted by copyright are spelt out in s.16 and subsequent sections. Copyright is infringed by doing any of the restricted acts in relation to a work without the licence of the copyright owner and by authorizing others to do so. For there to be infringement of copyright, there must be a sufficient objective similarity between the copyright work and the alleged infringing work such that the original work or a "substantial" part of it has been reproduced (performed in public, broadcast, etc.) Also the copyright work must be the source from which the infringing work is derived — there must be a causal connection between the copyright work and the infringement. "Substantial" is not necessarily measured in terms of the quantity taken, for a short extract may be a very important part of the work and it is often said that whether a substantial part has been copied depends more on the quality rather than the quantity. Difficult questions arise when a defendant acknowledges that he used the plaintiff's work as a source but says he has taken no more than the idea. There is no copyright in ideas as such because ideas are not literary, dramatic, musical or artistic works. It has been said that copyright is confined to the expression of ideas and it is only if the expression has been copied that there is infringement. In reality most copyright works consist of a detailed interlocking interplay of ideas and if that detailed pattern has been taken then there will be infringement.

If there has been substantial taking it is immaterial whether copying has been direct or indirect or whether intervening acts constitute infringement or not. Infringement by "authorization" was at issue in C.B.S. v. Amstrad. The House of Lords held in Amstrad that "to authorize" means "to grant or purport to grant, expressly or by implication, the right to do the act complained of."

### 1. Acts Restricted by Copyright

The acts restricted by copyright are as follows:

(1) Copying — all works. Section 17 provides that in relation to literary, dramatic, musical

and artistic works, copying means reproducing the work in any material form or storing on any medium by electronic means. Copies may be permanent or transient, deliberate or incidental. A two-dimensional representation of a three dimensional artistic work constitutes a copy and vice versa. Films, television broadcasts or cable programmes may be "copied" by photographing the whole or substantial part of any image. Typographical arrangements are "copied" by making facsimile copies.

Collective licensing schemes exist under which published literary, musical and other works may be reproduced upon the payment of royalties to a central agency.

(2) Issue of copies to the public — all works. Section 18 replaces the former restricted act of publication — putting a work before the public for the first time — with a distribution right. The copyright owner gains the right to put a given copy of the work into circulation. Once this has occurred, anywhere in the world, distribution of that copy is no longer restricted by s.18 unless the work is a sound recording, film or computer program. For these species of work, the copyright owner may control the commercial rental of copies. If the copy concerned is an infringing copy, however, commercial importation or dealing may constitute "secondary" infringement (ss. 22-24, seep.668 post) where the actor has actual or constructive knowledge that the copies are infringing.

(3) Public performance, showing or playing — s.19. Copyright in a literary, dramatic or musical work (but not an artistic work) is infringed by its unauthorized performance in public. Copyright in sound recordings, films, broadcasts and cableprogrammes restricts their playing in public. It is the person who organizes the public performance or playing who infringes, rather than the performer or operator of equipment. Performing rights are administered by collecting societies. It is wise for the occupier of premises used for public entertainment to ensure that the societies' tariffs have been paid: section 25 renders it tortious to permit premises to be used for an infringing performance unless it is believed on reasonable grounds that copyright would not be infringed. A similar burden is imposed upon suppliers of equipment: s. 26.

(4) Broadcasting a work or including it in a cable programme service-section 20. These activities are restricted by copyright in all works except typographical arrangements.

(5) Adaptations. Section 21 provides that making an adaptation is restricted by copyright in literary, dramatic, musical and artistic works. Modes of adaptation include translation, dramatisation, arrangement and transcription. Where, in the course of running, a computer program is incidentally converted into or out of language, subs. 21 (4) spares the translation from infringement. Acts restricted by copyright in the original work are also restricted in relation to an adaptation.

(6) Secondary infringement — ss. 22-27. An "infringing copy" is one which has been made in the UK in infringement of copyright or has been made abroad but whose manufacture in the UK either would have infringed or would have constituted a breach of exclusive licence:s.27 (3). "Parallel imports" may thus be deemed infringing copies, unless made in the EC: s.27 (5). Commercial imports, dealings with and possession of infringing copies and noncommercial but prejudicial distributions will infringe if the doer knows or has reason to believe that the copies are infringing. The usual way of fixing an importer or other dealer with actual knowledge is to write a letter before action. It is also infringement with knowledge to provide certain means for making infringing copies. Secondary infringement in relation to performances has already been noted.

## 2. Offences

Making or dealing with infringing copies is also a criminal offence if actual or constructive knowledge is present: other offences relate to supplying the means to infringe and to infringing performances. The penalties are not trivial and there are provisions for delivery up and search warrants in the 1988 Act.

## 3. Exceptions to infringement — the "permitted acts"

The 1988 Act lists a number of exceptions to infringement in ss.28-76. Some of the more important activities which are permitted notwithstanding the subsistence of copyright are: (1) fair dealing with a literary, dramatic, musical or artistic work for the purpose of research or private study (s.29); a number of detailed provisions in ss. 32-36 provide further scope for using works in education without the copyright owner's consent. (2) fair dealing with a work for the purposes of criticism, review or reporting current events, providing that sufficient acknowledgement is made (acknowledgement is not required for news reporting by audio, film, broadcast or cable). (3) use of works for the purposes of judicial and parliamentary proceedings (s.45). A number of other acts are permitted, to smooth the path of public administration (s.46-50). (4) copying by librarians and archivists is permitted in a number of circumstances (ss.37-44, 61 and 75) whilst scientific and technical abstracts may be used (s.60). (5) the use of designs embodied in artistic works (ss.51-55; see p.662, *ante*).

## 4. Remedies for infringement

In addition to the usual remedies of an injunction and damages or an account of profits for infringement, a copyright owner may be entitled to additional statutory damages having regard to the flagrancy of the infringement and the benefit the defendant has derived from it (s. 97 (2)).

"Conversion damages," formerly awarded on the basis that the copyright owner was deemed also to own infringing copies, have been abolished save in actions starting prior to August 1, 1989 for infringements committed before that date. There are now special provisions for delivery up in copyright actions. These, it is submitted, do not affect the court's equitable jurisdiction to order delivery up in support of an injunction, or to grant Anton Piller orders.

## 5. Ownership, assignment and licensing

The general rule is that the author of a work is the first owner of copyright. The most important exception to this principle is that where a literary, dramatic, musical or artistic work is created in the course of employment under a contract of service, the employer is first owner of copyright. This exception is subject to any agreement to the contrary. In fact copyright may be assigned prospectively, in advance of creation of the work; s.91 operates to vest copyright in the assignee upon creation of the work. Crown Copyright, Parliamentary copyright and that belonging to international organizations fall outside the general rule.

Copyright is transmissible as personal property (s.90). An assignment has no effect unless it is in writing, signed by or on behalf of the assignor (s.90 (3)). The assignment may be complete or partial only (s. 90 (2)) and may be limited as to the type of rights assigned (reproduction rights, publishing rights which, by custom of the trade are further split into serialization, paperback and hardback rights, translation rights, performing rights, film rights, broadcasting rights, etc.). as to time and geographically, country by country. In this way there can be a multiplicity of rights all stemming from the original work and all capable of separate assignment or licensing. A licence may be created orally or in writing and may be exclusive or nonexclusive. An exclusive licensee whose licence is in writing may sue for infringement in his own name and be entitled to damages, although the copyright owner must at some stage be joined in the action, either as plaintiff or as defendant (s. 102 (1)).

# Right of the Copyrights Owner

## 1. Public lending right

The Public Lending Right Act 1979 gives authors of books the right to receive payments from time to time out of a Central Fund in respect of their books lent out to the public by locallibrary authorities in the United Kingdom. A Registrar of Public Lending Right is established; his office is at Stockton-on-Tees. The right applies only to books but not to gramophone records or cassettes. The author's entitlement to public lending right depends on loans of his books over thecounter at local libraries. Loans from academic, private or commercial libraries are excluded. The Central Fund is constituted by the Secretary of State and placed under the control and management of the Registrar of Public Lending Right.

## 2. Moral rights

In addition to restricting economic control over works to the copyright owner, the 1988 act confers certain "moral" rights upon the authors of literary, dramatic, musical and artistic works and upon the directors of films. Previously a right was given to non-authors to object when works were wrongly attributed. This is retained.

Three new forms of moral right are as follows. The first new right, to be identified as author or director when a work is put before the public, has to be asserted before it is effective. Assertion may be upon assignment or by a separate instrument. The second new right is the right to object to derogatory treatment of a work. This involves actual mutilation of the work by addition or deletion. It is the putting of a mutilated work before the public, rather than the act of mutilation, which is tortious. Both these forms of moral right are subject to catalogues of exceptions. Computer programs are excluded; the moral rights of employees are curtailed. Fair dealing and certain other "permitted acts" may be carried out.

Thirdly the commissioner of private and domestic photographs and films has a limited right of privacy; s.85 restricts the distribution, exhibition, broadcasting or cablecasting of the photograph or film. This was enacted to compensate for repeal of provisions vesting copyright in the commissioner of photographs.

All varieties of moral right may be waived formally or informally, although they may not be assigned. The new moral rights endure as long as copyright in the works in question and devolve after the author's death. The right to object to false attribution endures 20 years after death.

### 3. Rights in performances

In the United Kingdom, dramatic and musical performances have been protected since 1925 by penal statutes, which were held in Rickless v. United Artists Corp. to confer civil rights of action on performers and (after death) their personal representatives. Part II of the 1988 Act introduced express civil rights of action in favour of dramatic and musical performers, those who recite literary works and performers of variety acts (ss.180,182). Rights are also given to those who enjoy the benefit of exclusive recording contracts with such performers (s.185).

The performer's consent is required (s.182) for the non-domestic recording or re-recording of the whole or a substantial part of a qualifying performance — one given by a qualifying individual or taking place in a qualifying country (s.181). Consent is also required for the live broadcasting or cablecasting of the performance (s.182). Activities of these kinds are actionable by performers as breach of statutory duty (s.194). A former requirement that consent be in writing has been repealed, although written consent is desirable for evidential purposes. It is a defence to a claim for damages that the defendant believed on reasonable grounds that consent had been given (s.182 (2)). Public use of an illicit recording without consent is also actionable if the user has actual or constructive knowledge of its illicit status, as is the knowing import (other than for private and domestic purposes). commercial possession or dealing with illicit copies. Damages only are available against an innocent acquirer (s.184 (3)). There is a list of "permitted acts" (s.189 and Sched, 2) like those in the copyright part of the Act.

Similar rights are granted to persons with exclusive recording rights (ss. 185-188). The record companies' rights are infringed where neither they nor the performer consents. Where a performer gives consent to a third party in breach of an exclusive recording agreement, the remedy lies in contract or for the tort of procuring breach of contract but not under the 1988, Act.

Rights in performance subsist for 50 years from the end of the year in which the performance takes place:s.191. The rights as such may not be assigned, but devolve upon the death of the performer and are effectively transferred along with the benefit of an exclusive recording contract: ss.185 and 192 (4).

Making, using or dealing with illicit recordings is an offence: s.198; it is also an offence falsely to represent authority to give consent: s.201.

### 4. Protection for product design

The original design of a three-dimensional artistic work such as a sculpture or building will be protected by copyright. Any two dimensional or surface design which is created through the medium of a drawing or other original artistic work will also enjoy protection, by virtue of copyright in the design drawing (see p.000, *ante*). Prior to commencement of the 1988 Act, copyright in design drawings was also widely used to prevent the plagiarism of three-dimensional product design. Now, where a three\|dimensional design has been created after July 31, 1989 for a comparatively mundane product, which is not an artistic work in its own right, the removal of copyright protection by s.51 of the 1988 Act means that protection must be sought elsewhere. Two possibilities exist: design registration and exercise of unregistered design right. Both may protect computer-generated designs as well as those of identifiable human designers.

*(1) Registered designs*

There exists a system of design registration under the Registered Designs Act 1949, which was overhauled by the 1988 Act. Two-and three-dimensional designs which are new and have eye-appeal may be registered for an initial period of 5 years, plus a maximum of four 5 year extensions. Registrable features are those of shape, configuration, pattern or ornament (s.1 (1)). Methods or principles of construction are excluded by s.1 (1) (a). which means that a registrable design has to be depicted or defined in detail. Purely functional features are excluded from registration:s.1 (1) (b) (i). The design of parts which are made and sold separately may be registered separately-the definition of "article" in s.44 includes such parts- but the "part" registration cannot protect features which are dependant on the appearance of the larger whole:s.1 (1) (b) (ii).

A registrable design is one which is applied to an article by any industrial process. Rule 35 of the Registered Designs Rules 1989 states that a design shall be regarded as "applied industrially" if it is applied to more than 50 articles which do not constitute a single set, or to goods manufactured in lengths or pieces, not being handmade goods. Rule 26 excludes designs for certain works of sculpture, plaques, medallions and printed matter of a primarily literary or artistic character, such as calendars or post cards. The appeal of the design to the eye of the consumer must be material, appearance being normally or actually taken into account by acquirers or users: s.1 (3). The requirement of novelty relates only to the United Kingdom. If the design or a trade variant has been published or registered in the UK before, it is not "new": s.1 (4).

A design is registered for a particular article or description of articles. It is in the proprietor's interest to describe the product in wide terms. If a proprietor wishes to gain protection for the same design as applied to further articles, subsequent applications may be made, but the later registrations cannot outlive the original: s. 4.

The registration of a design gives its proprietor the exclusive right commercially to manufacture or to deal in an article for which the design is registered and which bears that design or a design not substantially different from it (s.7(1)). Thus, in relation to a particular description of article, the proprietor is given an absolute monopoly; there is no need to prove that the alleged infringer copied. The manufacture, supply or assembly of a kit may infringe the registration of a design for an assembled article (s. 7(4)). Actual registration is necessary to found an action for infringement: s.7 (5). One cannot sue upon an application to register. Both the Chancery Division of the High Court and the Patents County Court have jurisdiction over infringement proceedings. Validity and ownership may be challenged in these proceedings.

All the usual remedies for infringement are available. However, a defendant may not be liable to pay damages if innocence can be shown of the registration; it is always wise to mark articles with the registered design number (s.9). Unjustified threats of infringement proceedings against defendants other than manufacturers or importers are actionable (s.26); care must therefore be taken in drafting any letter before action. Compulsory licences (s.10) and licences of right (s. 11A) may be made available. There are provisions for Crown use (s.12 and Sched.1)

Where a design is created under a commission for value, the commissioner is entitled as proprietor to apply for registration. Otherwise, designs created in the course of employment belong to the employer, whilst the design's author is first owner in the absence of commission or employment (s.2). In the case of a computer generated design, The person who made arrangements necessary for the creation of the design is regarded as author (s.2 (4)). There is no qualification requirement for prospective applicants, but a person who has first applied to register the design in a Convention country may use the date of that earlier application as the "priority date" for the UK application; such a priority date may be up to six months earlier than the date of the UK application.

Registered designs may be assigned, transmitted, licensed, or mortgaged, subject to any such prior interest recorded on the register (s.19).

*(2) Design right*

A new system of unregistered rights in three-dimensional designs was introduced By ss.213-235 of the 1988 Act. Provided an original design has been recorded in some way, in a "design document" (s.263 (1)). prototype article or model, the design right subsists with no formality (s.213 (1)). Design right therefore operates rather like artistic copyright, but free from the requirement of an original artistic work. However, the provisions whereby foreign creations may qualify for design right in the UK (ss.217, 221, 256) are much more limited than those for copyright. Designs qualify for design right if the designer, his or her employer or a commissioner for value is a qualifying individual or other qualifying legal person (ss.218,219). A design will also qualify if it is first marketed in the UK, EC or another country to which the Act extends by a qualifying person who is exclusively authorized to market in the UK (s.220).

"Design" is defined as meaning any aspect of the internal or external shape or Configuration of the whole or part of an article (s. 213 (2)). As for registered designs, design right is not available for a method or principle of construction (s.213 (3) (a)). Such principles are to be protected by patent, if at all. Also excluded from protection are features which enable the article to fit in, around or against another article so that either may perform its function — the so-called "must-fit" exclusion of s.213 (3) (b) (i) — or which are dependant upon the appearance of another article of which the article in question is intended by its designer to form an integral part — the so-called "must-match" exception of s.213 (3) (b) (ii). These exceptions ensure that motor spares are not protected by design right. Subject to the exceptions, however, design right may subsist in functional design; there is no requirement of artistic merit or eye appeal.

The threshold of originality is somewhat higher than for copyright; s.213 (4) states that a design is not original if it is commonplace in the design field in question at the time of its creation.

The rules for first ownership of design right mirror those for registered designs; the designer's right is displaced by that of his employer where the design was created in the course of employment. Both are displaced by the right of a person who has commissioned the design for value (s.215 and 263 (1)). Like copyright, design right may be assigned prospectively, so that it vests in the assignee upon the creation of the design (s.223).

Design right may be assigned or transmitted as personal property (s.222). The assignment may be partial either in the sense of assignment for less than the whole term, or in the sense that the assignment relates to some but not all of the activities reserved to the design right holder (s.222 (2)). Assignment of a registered design will carry a presumption that any unregistered design right subsisting in the same design is also assigned, in the absence of contrary intention (s.224).

Design right may be licensed; an exclusive licence in writing and signed by or on behalf of the design right owner gives the licensee rights of action for infringement which are concurrent with those of the right owner (ss.225, 234-235).

The duration of design right may be difficult for third parties to estimate. The right endures for the shorter of 15 years from the recording of the design or ten years from first marketing, anywhere in the world, by or with the licence of the design right owner: s.216. During the last five years of design right protection, licences are to be available as of right (s.237). There are also provisions for Crown use (s.240-4) and earlier licences of right when the monopolies

and Mergers Commission have reported adversely upon the conduct of the right owner (s.238).

Like copyright, design right is infringed by copying without licence — by making articles to the design or by making a design document recording the design for the purpose of making the articles (s.226 (1)). The copying can be direct or indirect; it does not matter if the process involves intermediate stages which do not infringe (s.226 (4)). The infringing articles may be made exactly or substantially to the design. Primary infringement may be effected either by doing these acts or by authorizing another to do them (s. 226 (3)).

Apart from these "primary" forms of infringement, there are also "secondary" infringements — importing or dealing with infringing articles (s.227). Such activities infringe if the actor knows or has reason to believe that the article is an infringing one. An "infringing article" (s.228) is one whose making infringed design right. Where an article has been imported into the UK or its import is proposed, the article is deemed to be "infringing" if its manufacture in the UK would have infringed design right or breached an exclusive licence agreement. Subsection.228 (5) ensures that this provision cannot operate in contravention of European Union law. The definition of infringing article excludes design documents made in infringement of design right. The rules on subsistence and infringement of design right apply to kits as they do to assembled articles (s.260). The remedies for infringement of design right (ss. 229-233) are modelled upon those for infringement of copyright.

It is not an infringement of design right to do anything which is an infringement of copyright (s.236). This provision may give rise to problems where copyright in a design document belongs to one person and design right to another. It would be wise for anyone commissioning a design or taking an assignment to contract for ownership of copyright in design documents or models.

The commission of the European Union is taking an interest in the harmonization of design law; further changes to the law can be anticipated.

## 🍀 New Words

| | | |
|---|---|---|
| **1.** | originality *n.* | 原創性 |
| **2.** | typographical *n.* | 印刷上；活版印刷 |
| **3.** | typeface *n.* | 鉛字面；鉛字印出的字樣 |
| **4.** | electronic retrieval system | 電子補救系統 |
| **5.** | subsist *v.* | 存在 |
| **6.** | logarithm *n.* | 對數 |
| **7.** | bingo *n.* | 賓果（一種賭博遊戲） |
| **8.** | anthology *n.* | 選集 |
| **9.** | mime *n.* | 笑劇；默劇 |
| **10.** | engravings *n.* | 雕刻 |
| **11.** | sculptures *n.* | 雕塑 |
| **12.** | collages *n.* | 抽象派拼貼畫 |
| **13.** | exhaust system | 排氣系統 |
| **14.** | gravity feed boilers | 引力輸送鍋爐 |
| **15.** | knock-down drawers | 可拆開的抽屜 |
| **16.** | lavatory pan connectors | 廁所瓷質馬桶連接器 |
| **17.** | plagiarism *n.* | 剽竊；抄襲；剽竊物 |
| **18.** | configuration *n.* | 外型；外觀 |
| **19.** | artefacts *n.* | 人工製造；製造物 |
| **20.** | depict *v.* | 描述；描寫 |
| **21.** | graphic work | 圖解作品 |
| **22.** | celluloid *n.* | 賽璐珞；電影 |
| **23.** | derogatory treatment | 貶損待遇 |
| **24.** | limb *n.* | 突出物 |
| **25.** | ab initio | 自始；從頭開始 |
| **26.** | the master | 母片；原版錄音片 |
| **27.** | evanescent *a.* | 短暫的 |
| **28.** | optical fibre | 光學纖維 |
| **29.** | wireless telegraphy | 無線電報機 |

| | | |
|---|---|---|
| **30.** decoding equipment | 解碼設備 |
| **31.** encrypted *a.* | 被譯成密碼的 |
| **32.** tortfeasors *n.* | 侵權行為人 |
| **33.** teletext *n.* | 電視文字廣播 |
| **34.** databases online | 資料庫聯機密碼系統 |
| **35.** threshold *n.* | 界限 |
| **36.** interplay *n.* | 相互影響；相互作用 |
| **37.** delivery up | 交出 |
| **38.** search warrants | 搜索票 |
| **39.** flagrancy *n.* | 明目張膽 |
| **40.** gramophone records | 留聲機唱片 |
| **41.** attribute *v.* | 將……歸因於 |
| **42.** assertion *n.* | 主張自己是作品的作者 |
| **43.** derogatory *a.* | 貶低的；貶損的 |
| **44.** mutilation *n.* | 刪改得支離破碎 |
| **45.** right of privacy | 隱私權 |
| **46.** cablecasting *n.* | 有線電視播送 |
| **47.** devolve *v.* | 轉移；移交 |
| **48.** illicit *a.* | 違法的；違禁的；不正當的 |
| **49.** conversion damage | 侵占損害賠償 |
| **50.** mundane *a.* | 庸俗的 |
| **51.** overhaul *v.* | 大修改；徹底修改 |
| **52.** eye-appeal *n.* | 悅目的東西 |
| **53.** plaques *n.* | 匾；飾板 |
| **54.** medallions *n.* | 大紀念章 |
| **55.** outlive *v.* | 比……活得久 |
| **56.** prototype *n.* | 原型 |
| **57.** subsistence *n.* | 生存；存在 |
| **58.** mirror *v.* | 反映 |
| **59.** displace *v.* | 取代 |
| **60.** kits *n.* | 成套工具 |
| **61.** harmonization *n.* | 協調 |

## New Phrases and Idiomatic Expressions

| | | |
|---|---|---|
| **1.** | to define sth. as | 將……解釋成…… |
| **2.** | in its own right | 憑它本身的品質、資格…… |
| **3.** | to vest in | 授權給…… |
| **4.** | to be modelled upon | 以……爲樣式 |
| **5.** | to take an interest in | 對……感興趣 |
| **6.** | to stem from | 發生於……；起源於…… |
| **7.** | to take a short cut | 走捷徑 |
| **8.** | in infringement of | 侵犯…… |
| **9.** | to derive from | 從……而來 |
| **10.** | in terms of | 根據；按照；用……的話；以……措辭 |
| **11.** | to provide means for doing sth. | 提供做某事的手段 |
| **12.** | to be imported into | 向……進口 |
| **13.** | upon the death of sb. | 在某人死亡時 |
| **14.** | in the absence of | 在缺少……情況下 |
| **15.** | in contravention of | 與……相違背；在違反……的情況下 |

## Notes

**1.** the Berne Convention：伯恩公約。

它是版權領域內最老的國際條約。自1886年簽訂後已多次被修改（1928年在羅馬，1948年在布魯塞爾，1967年在斯德哥爾摩，1971年在巴黎）。至1992年1月，已有93個國家成爲這個最早最全面的國際著作權公約的成員國。該公約於1992年10月15日在中國生效。這表明中國智慧財產權保護體系已全面進入與世界同步水平。該公約的全名爲：The Berne Convention for the Protection of Literary and Artistic Works, 1886。

**2.** the Rome Convention of 1961：1961年羅馬公約。

該公約於1961年10月26日在羅馬締結，於1964年3月18日生效，保護對象爲表演者、唱片製作者和廣播組織，其成員國一半以上是發展中國家。該公約規定的最低保護期限爲20年。

**3.** moral rights：精神權。

伯爾尼公約要求成員國向作者授予的權利之一。該權利包括：(1)主張自己是作品的作者的權利（assertion）；(2)反對對作品進行貶損的權利（the right to object to derogatory treatment of a work）。

**4.** Stockton-on-Tees：（提茲河畔）斯托克頓（英國英格蘭東北部港口城市）。

**5.** the Chancery Division of the High Court

（英）高等法院的一部分：衡平法庭；有人也將它譯爲高等法院的「大法官法庭」。

**6.** Convention country：這裡指巴黎公約成員國。

**7.** ...earlier legislation

這裡指：the Copyright Act 1956, as amended by the Design Copyright Act 1968 and the Copyright (Amendment) Acts 1971, 1982 and 1983, the Criminal Justice Act 1982, the Cable and Broadcasting Act 1984 and the Copyright (computer software) Amendment Act 1985.

 **Exercises**

## I. Answer the following questions:

**1.** What is the difference between monopoly granted by a patent and the rights comprised by copyright?

**2.** What does copyright protect?

**3.** How can your work enjoy U.K. copyright?

**4.** What are the acts restricted by copyright?

**5.** What exceptions are listed by the 1988 Act to infringement of copyright?

**6.** What are the remedies for copyright infringement?

**7.** Can a design right be assigned?

**8.** What are the forms of protection available for designs?

## II. Translate the following Chinese passages into English:

**1.** 著作權保護文學、戲劇、音樂、藝術作品、電影、錄音、廣播、有線電視播送和對出版物的版面安排等。英國提供保護這方面最重要的法律爲《1988年版權、設計和專利法》。

**2.** 伯恩公約是最早最全面的國際性著作權保護公約，它保證最低限度的保護和國民待遇。

截止1992年，已有93個國家成爲該公約的成員國，其中也包括中國。

**3.** 著作權法限制的行爲包括抄襲、向公衆發行、公開表演、廣播和改編等。

**4.** 在英國，著作權侵犯發生後，所給予的補救除正常的禁令、損害賠償外，著作權所有者還有權獲得法定損失賠償，以及被告從著作權侵犯中所獲得的利潤。

## III. Indicate whether each of the following statements is true or false by writing "T" or "F" in the space provided:

_____ **1**. Copyright is acquired simply by bringing a work into existence, which has The appropriate degree of originality and a qualifying connection with the U.K..

_____ **2**. Copyright does not exist in literary, dramatic or musical works until they are recorded in writing or otherwise.

_____ **3**. The author of a work is defined by English law as the person who creates it.

_____ **4**. For literary, dramatic, musical and artistic work, copyright expires 40 years from the end of the calender year in which the author dies or the last of joint author dies.

_____ **5**. Copyright is transmissible as personal property. An assignment has no effect unless it is in writing, signed, by or on behalf of the assignor.

_____ **6**. Making, using or dealing with illicit recordings is an offence.

_____ **7**. The general rule is that the author of a work is the first owner of copyright.

_____ **8**. Copyright is purely statutory and the governing legislation in the U.K. is the Copyright, Designs and Patents Act 1988.

# PART VI

## 產品責任法
## Products Liability Law

---

### 第二十六課 Lesson 26

## 美國產品責任法
## The U.S. Product Liability Law

---

Warranties, negligence, and strict liability are the grounds on which sellers and manufacturers of goods are held liable to the buyers of the goods for the quality, suitability, and character of the goods. Warranties are contractual grounds for this liability, whereas negligence and strict liability are usually considered to be tort grounds for it. Warranties may be either express, that is, based on representations of the seller; or implied, that is, imposed on the seller by operation of law. And warranties may pertain to the quality of goods or to title to them.

*Express warranties.* When any affirmation of fact or promise is made by the seller to the buyer which relates to the goods and becomes part of the basis of the bargain, an express warranty is created that the goods will conform to the promise or affirmation of fact. Likewise, any description of the goods or sample or model, which is made part of the basis of the bargain, creates an express warranty that the goods will conform to the description, sample, or model. It is not necessary to the creation of an express warranty that the seller use formal words such as "warrant" or "guarantee" or that s/he intends to make a warranty; however, a mere affirmation of the value of the goods or a statement which purports to be merely the seller's opinion or commendation of the goods does not create an express warranty.

*Implied warranty of title.* The seller of goods impliedly warrants that: (1) the title being passed is good, (2) the transfer is legal, and (3) the goods are free from any security interest or lien that the buyer does not have knowledge of at the time of contracting. This warranty attaches unless the buyer is aware that the seller is acting in some official capacity (such as a sheriff at a judicial sale) and cannot be excluded except by clear and unequivocal language in the contract which indicates the seller is not warranting a clear and unencumbered title.

*Implied warranty of merchantability.* There are two implied warranties of the quality of goods, the warranties of merchantability and of fitness for a particular purpose, which are imposed on the seller of goods by operation of law unless they are excluded or modified by the contract of sale. The implied warranty of merchantability is made by merchants dealing in goods of the kind sold, and means that in order for the goods to be up to the warranted standard they must: (1) pass in the trade under the contract description; (2) be of fair average quality within the contract description if they are fungible goods; (3) be fit for the ordinary purposes for which such goods are sold; (4) be of even kind, quality, and quantity within each unit and among all units involved; (5) be adequately contained, packaged, and labeled; and (6) conform to promises or affirmations of fact, if any, contained on the label or container. Under the U.C.C., the serving of food and drink to be consumed either on the premises or elsewhere is a sale of goods and subject to the implied warranty of merchantability.

*Implied warranty of fitness for a particular purpose.* If the seller at the time of contracting knows the purpose for which the goods are required by the buyer and that the buyer is relying on the seller's skill and judgment to pick out suitable goods, the seller makes an implied warranty that the goods will be suitable or fit for the intended purpose. This warranty may, apply even to nonmerchant sellers; however, in all cases, it is necessary to show that the buyer was relying on the seller and that the seller knew this as well as knowing the desired purpose for which the goods are sought.

*Exclusion and modification of warranties.* Since warranties are considered to be part of the contract for the sale of goods, the parties are free (within certain restraints of public policy) to exclude or modify them. However, the courts are of the interests of the buyers and are reluctant to allow them to contract away their rights in the warranty area unless it is clear that the buyers: (1) were aware that they were doing so and freely consented to the exclusion or modification; and (2) were not in a take-it-or-leave-it situation with a seller of considerably larger economic power. To exclude the implied warranty of merchantability, the word "merchantability" must be used, and if the exclusion is in a written contract it must be conspicuous, that is, set out in larger or different colored type so that it is likely to be noticed. To exclude the implied warranty of fitness for a particular purpose, the exclusion must be in writing and must be conspicuous. If the buyer was given an opportunity to inspect the goods and did so or refused to do so, then the implied warranties do not include those defects which should have been apparent from the inspection. Implied warranties can also be excluded or modified by course of dealing, course of performance, or trade usage. And where the contract contains both express and implied warranties, they are to be construed as consistent with each other and cumulative unless such a construction is unreasonable, in which case the intent of the parties controls.

*Beneficiaries of warranties.* Since warranties are part of the contractual relationship between buyer and seller, the courts for some time displayed a reluctance for anyone to be able to claim the benefits of the warranty unless this person was in *privity of contract* with the actual seller of goods. Today, through statutory and decisional law changes, the rule of privity of contract is no longer adhered to. The demise of the rule of privity of contract is important in two areas: (1) in determining whether someone other than the buyer (*e.g.*, someone in the buyer's family who is injured by a defective product) can sue the seller of the product, and (2) in determining whether the actual buyer of goods who is injured or has sustained other damage because of a defective product can sue not only the immediate seller, but also the manufacturer who put the product into the stream of commerce.

The U.C.C. specifically provides that a seller's warranty runs not only to the buyer of goods but that it also runs to any natural person in the family or household of the buyer, or who is a guest in the buyer's house, if it is reasonable to expect that such a person may use, consume, or be affected by the use of the goods and who is injured in his person by breach of the warranty. And the U.C.C. provides that the seller may not exclude or limit his or her liability for breach of warranty to members of the buyer's family or household or guests.

The U.C.C. does not take a position on whether a buyer may sue the manufacturer directly for breach of warranty even though the buyer did not purchase the goods directly from the manufacturer. However, virtually all courts allow recovery directly form the manufacturer. This is justified on the grounds that the manufacturer has control over the quality of the product and should be held responsible for the quality or lack thereof. In most modern marketing situations, the retailer and wholesaler are mere conduits for the product that is manufactured and advertised by the manufacturer. In those cases where the buyer recovers from the retailer for breach of warranty, the retailer usually has a right back against the manufacturer, so by allowing a direct suit against the manufacturer an unnecessary step in the litigation process is avoided.

***Magnuson-Moss Warranty Act.*** In 1975 the Magnuson-Moss Warranty Act was enacted. This Act, which is enforced by the Federal Trade Commission, is designed (1) to provide minimum warranty protection for consumers; (2) to increase consumer understanding of warranties; (3) to assure warranty performance by providing meaningful remedies ; and (4) to promote better product reliability by making it easier for consumers to chose between products on the basis of their likely reliability. Under the Act and the F.T.C.'s regulations any seller of a consumer product that costs more than $15 who gives a written warranty to the consumer is required to clearly disclose a number of items of information concerning the warranty and to designate it as a "full warranty" or a "limited warranty." Failure to comply with the Act subjects the seller to a lawsuit for damages.

***Liability based on negligence.*** The seller owes a duty to the buyer to use due care in the production, packaging, and sale of his or her goods so that foreseeable harm, which might proximately result from the seller's failure to use due care, will be avoided. Failure to exercise this duty of due care, which results in injury to the buyer, is the basis for a suit in negligence to recover the damages sustained by the breach of duty. Liability for negligence has been found in cases where there was: (1) a failure to adequately inspect the goods prior to sale; (2) misrepresentation as to the character of the goods and their fitness for a particular purpose; (3) failure to disclose known defects or to warn about known dangers; and (4) failure to use due care in designing and preparing the goods for sale .Lack of privity of contract is no defense to an action for negligence because it is based on tort law, not contract law, and courts do not look with favor on efforts of sellers to disclaim liability for their own negligence because it is considered to be against public policy to allow them to do so.

***Strict liability.*** Strict liability is a means of holding a seller liable for the safety of the seller's product even though all reasonable care may have been exercised in producing and selling it — thus making the seller an insurer of the safety of the product. Strict liability arises when a product reaches customers in a defective state that presents an unreasonable danger to them; that is, more danger than they would normally expect from a product of that type. Lack of privity of contract is no defense to an action premised on strict liability, and the seller cannot defend on the grounds that s/he exercised all reasonable care. Strict liability is not accepted by all states with respect to all types of products. At present, it finds its most common acceptance with sales of food and drink, but is gradually being extended to all types of products than can be considered to be unreasonably dangerous if defectively manufactured.

## ♣ New Words

| | | |
|---|---|---|
| **1.** | warranty *n.* | 擔保；保證 |
| **2.** | negligence *n.* | 疏忽；過失 |
| **3.** | strict liability | 嚴格責任；結果責任 |
| **4.** | suitability *n.* | 適合性 |
| **5.** | express warranties | 明示擔保；明示保證 |
| **6.** | affirmation *n.* | 確認 |
| **7.** | title *n.* | 所有權 |
| **8.** | attach *v.* | 附加；隸屬 |
| **9.** | unencumbered *a.* | 不受妨礙的；沒有負擔的 |
| **10.** | unequivocal *a.* | 不含混的；明確的 |
| **11.** | implied warranty | 默示擔保；默示保證 |
| **12.** | merchantability *n.* | 商銷性 |
| **13.** | fitness *n.* | 適合 |
| **14.** | fair average quality | 平均中等品質 |

15. fungible goods      可代替的貨物；可互換的貨物

16. non-merchant seller      非商人的賣主

17. conspicuous a.      明顯的；顯著的

18. privity of contract      契約關係

19. statutory law      成文法；制定法

20. decisional law      判例法

21. demise *n.*      死亡；終止

22. natural person      自然人

23. Magnuson-Moss Warranty Act      1975年馬格努森—莫斯保固法

24. product reliability      產品可靠性

25. full warranty      完全擔保

26. limited warranty      有限擔保

27. disclaim *v.*      排除

28. seek *v.*      尋找

29. exclusion of warranties      擔保的排除

30. modification of warranties      擔保的修改

31. course of dealing      慣常交易方式

32. course of performance      履行方法

33. trade usage      商業習慣；貿易慣例

34. immediate seller      直接賣主

## New Phrases and Idiomatic Expressions

1. to pertain to      與……有關

2. to be fit for      適合於……

3. on the premises to be drunk (or consumed) on the premises      在房屋內只供酒類飲品（指酒等）

4. to pick out      挑選

5. in a take-it-or-leave-it situation      處於一種買或者不買的狀況

6. to contract away sth.      訂約放棄某物

7. to be construed as      被解釋成；被理解成

8. to put the product into the stream of commerce      將產品投入源源不斷的商業供應

9. to run to      使……獲得；使……得到

**10.** to take a position on sth.　　　　表明對某事的立場

**11.** to be the conduits for　　　　　成為……渠道

**12.** to chose between...　　　　　　在……此間進行挑選

**13.** to owe a duty to sb.　　　　　　對某人負有責任

**14.** to exercise the duty of due care　　履行應有的注意責任

**15.** to be solicitous of　　　　　　對……表示關心

**16.** to look on　　　　　　　　　考慮

**17.** in a defective state　　　　　　處於有缺陷的狀態

**18.** to be premised on　　　　　　以……為前提

 **Notes**

**1.** product liability：產品責任。

Refers to the legal liability of manufacturers and suppliers and sellers to compensate buyers, users and even bystanders, for damages or injuries suffered because of defects in goods purchased.

**2.** ..., in which cases the intent of the parties controls

此句子的control，表示in a controlling position（處於支配地位）。

**3.** The demise of the rule of privity of contract is important in two areas.

在此句中的demise表示a cessation of existence（終止存在）。

**4.** the Federal Trade Commission：（美）聯邦貿易委員會

Agency of the federal government created in 1914.The principal functions of this Commission are to promote free and fair competition in interstate Commerce through prevention of general trade restraints such as price-fixing agreements, false advertising, boycotts, illegal combination of competitors and other unfair methods of competition.

**5.** ...the courts for some time displayed a reluctance...

...the courts for some time showed an unwillingness.

 **Exercises**

## I. Answer the following questions:

**1.** On what grounds are the sellers and manufacturers of goods held liable to the buyers of the goods for the quality, suitability, and character of the goods?

**2.** What are the two types of warranties mentioned in the text?

3. What does the seller of goods impliedly warrant?

4. What are the two types of implied warranties of the quality of goods?

5. In what cases will the courts allow the buyers to contract away their rights in the warranty area?

6. In what areas is the demise of the rule of privity of contract is important?

7. What are the purposes of Magnuson-Moss Warranty Act?

8. When will there be liability for negligence?

9. When will strict liability arise?

10. Is strict liability accepted everywhere in the United States?

## II. Translate the following Chinese passages into English:

1. 產品責任法是確定生產者和銷售者對其生產或銷售的產品應承擔之責任的法律，其目的是爲了防止危險產品的流傳。

2. 美國產品責任法是在民事侵權法的基礎上發展起來的一個歷史較短而又對商業活動具有深遠影響的法律。根據這種法律，只要證明投入市場的產品有缺陷，並且這個缺陷對購買者或消費者或旁觀者造成人身或財產方面的損害，該產品的製造者或出售者就要對此承擔民事侵權責任。

3. 美國法庭認爲，作爲產品的製造者或裝配者，在製造或裝配產品前，必須做到小心謹慎地設計，一絲不苟地選擇材料和部件，以保證產品使用者的安全。

4. 美國產品責任法以下三種理論爲依據：(1)疏忽說；(2)違反擔保說；(3)嚴格責任說。凡原告由於使用有缺陷的產品遭受損害向法院起訴要求賠償損失時，他必須引上述三種理由之一作爲要求該產品的生產廠商或銷售者承擔責任的依據。

## III. Indicate whether each of the following statements is true or false by writing "T" or "F" in the space provided:

_____ 1. Implied warranty is imposed on the seller by operation of law.

_____ 2. Express warranty is based on the buyer's intent.

_____ 3. Warranties are tort grounds on which sellers and manufacturers of goods can be held liable to buyers of goods.

_____ 4. The words "warrant" or "guarantee" are necessary to the creation of an express warranty of quality.

_____ 5. The implied warranty of merchantability means, in essence, that the goods will be fit for the ordinary purpose for which they are used.

___ 6. The statement "the seller makes no implied warranties" in regular black type in a contract is sufficient to exclude the implied warranty of merchantbility.

___ 7. Under the U.C.C, the rule of privity of contract bars members of the buyer's family from recovering for injuries they sustained because of a breach of warranty.

___ 8. The U.C.C. does not take a position on whether a buyer may sue the manufacturer directly for breach of warranty when the buyer purchased the goods directly from a retailer.

___ 9. Lack of privity of contract is not a defense to a negligence action.

___ 10. Strict liability may be imposed when a defective product is more dangerous than the buyer would normally expect.

## IV. Translate the following English passages into Chinese:

1. Like many areas of law, the scope of the law of products liability is quite broad and not easy to define. A sound definition of product liability is Tebbens's phrase liability of a professional supplier of a product for damage caused by that product.

2. Modern American products liability law essentially consists of two parallel regimes, a negligence theory and a strict liability theory, both belonging to the law of torts.

3. In addition to, and in contrast with, the claims under tort law, the buyer (and certain other persons) can resort to claims for breach of warranty against the seller. The elements of the claims and the scope of the remedies are codified in article 2 of the U.C.C., which has been adopted in all states except Louisiana.

4. Under the Consumer Protection Act (1987). passed to conform with the requirements of the European Union (EU) law, the producer of a defective product that causes death or personal injury or damage to property is strictly liable for the damage.

# PART VII

國際仲裁法
**Arbitration**

<table>
<tr><td>第二十七課<br>Lesson 27</td><td>仲裁<br>Arbitration</td></tr>
</table>

## Arbitration Acts

The statutory regulation of the law relating to arbitration is contained in the Arbitration Acts 1950, 1975 and 1979.

1. The Arbitration Act 1950 is the principal Act. It also gives effect to two international measures, *viz.* the Geneva Protocol on Arbitration Clauses of 1923 and the Geneva Convention on the Execution of Foreign Arbitral Awards of 1927, appended to the 1950 Act as Schedules 1 and 2. The two Geneva measures are in the process of being superseded by the New York Convention on the Recognition and Enforcement of Foreign Arbitral Awards of 1958, which was promoted by the United Nations.

2. The object of the Arbitration Act 1975 is to give effect to the New York Convention in the United Kingdom. The 1975 Act came into operation on December 23, 1975 (S.I.1975, No.1662).The purpose of the New York Convention is to provide for the enforcement of international arbitration agreements and the enforcement of foreign arbitration awards.

3. The 1979 Act was introduced strictly to limit judicial intervention in arbitral proceedings, to eliminate the former stated case procedure for judicial review on a question of law and to allow for the parties to exclude any right of appeal in certain types of cases. This is consistent with an international trend towards giving greater finality to arbitral awards.

The Arbitration Acts 1950 to 1979 provide, *inter alia*, for: (1) the enforcement arbitration agreements; (2) judicial assistance in the formation of the arbitral tribunal; (3) judicial assistance during the reference (especially in matters which may affect third parties such as the issue of a subpoena or an order for the preservation of property); (4) judicial supervision during the reference (*e.g.*, in cases where an arbitrator has misconducted himself); (5) judicial review of arbitration awards; and; (6) the enforcement of arbitration awards.

# Reference to Arbitration

A reference to arbitration may be made in one of three ways: (1) Under order of the court; (2) Under an Act of Parliament; (3) By agreement of the parties.

## 1. Under order of the court

The court may refer any question arising in any matter before it to an official or special referee for inquiry or report. It may also refer the whole question before it to be tired by an official or special referee if: (1) all the parties consent; (2) the case requires prolonged examination of documents or scientific or local investigation; (3) the question in dispute consists wholly or in part of matters of account.

## 2. Under an Act of Parliament

Various Acts of Parliament provide for the settlement of disputes arising out of their provisions by arbitration. These Acts usually describe how the arbitration is to be conducted; but in all other cases the Arbitration Acts 1950 to 1979 apply (Arbitration Act 1950, s.31; Arbitration Act 1979, s.3 (5); 7(1)).

## 3. By agreement of the parties

A reference by agreement of the parties must originate in an arbitration agreement. Such an agreement may be made verbally or in writing. The Arbitration Acts 1950 to 1979 apply only to written agreements, but an agreement by telex is "an agreement in writing" (*Arab African Energy Corporation Ltd. v. Olieprodukten Nederland B.V.* [1983] Com. L. R. 195). This would presumably apply to communications by FAX. A tacit acceptance of a written quotation which contained an arbitration clause is sufficient to comply with the requirement for an agreement in writing.

An arbitration agreement is defined by section 32 as "a written agreement to submit present or future differences to arbitration, whether an arbitrator is named therein or not."

An arbitration must be distinguished from a valuation. It is an arbitration if the parties intend that any dispute between them shall be settled by an inquiry held in a quasi-judicial manner, usually but not necessarily, after hearing argument or evidence.

On the other hand, it is a **valuation** if the object of the activity of the appointed person is to value or appraise something but no dispute exists between the parties on the facts or the law. Examples of valuers are an architect who certifies the sums payable by the building owner to the builder, as the work performed by the builder progresses; or an accountant who, in accordance with the agreement between shareholders of a company, fixes the "fair value" of the shares sold by one of them to another. A valuer is liable for negligence in the performance of his duties but an arbitrator enjoys the same immunity as a judge and cannot be held liable in negligence.

However, it should not be inferred from the Arenson case that an accountant is a valuer in all circumstances; if a dispute on facts or a legal question has arisen and is referred by the parties to their accountant, the latter would act as an arbitrator even if in the course of his arbitration he has to make an appraisal, and he would enjoy quasi-judicial immunity unless he acts fraudulently.

If the parties have agreed that the valuation shall be "final, binding and conclusive," a "speaking valuation," *i.e.* a valuation giving reasons, it can be impugned in court proceedings if it is clear from the reasons expressed in the valuation that the valuer proceeded on a fundamentally erroneous basis.

# Effect of Arbitration Agreement

### 1. Award to be condition precedent to court proceedings

An arbitration agreement may be framed in such a manner as to prevent any right to court proceedings from accruing under the contract until an award is first made. In such a case an award is a condition precedent to a right to sue. A clause which is framed in such a manner is known as a **Scott v. Avery clause** (below).

It is provided by section 25 (4) that if the court orders that the agreement to refer the dispute to arbitration shall cease to have effect, it may also order that the condition precedent shall cease to have effect.

### 2. Power of court to break arbitration agreement

If a party to an arbitration agreement commences proceedings in court, contrary to his undertaking to submit to arbitration, the court, on the application of the other party, may either order a stay of court proceedings, thus allowing the arbitration to proceed, or refuse the application for a stay, thus breaking the arbitration agreement (s.4). If the only point in issue is a point of law, the court may be inclined to refuse a stay of proceedings. It is increasingly rare for a court to refuse to give effect to an arbitration agreement.

Two cases have to be distinguished here: if the arbitration agreement is a domestic arbitration agreement, the discretion of the court to order or refuse a stay of court proceedings is wide (s.4 (1)). but if it is a non-domestic arbitration agreement its discretion is limited (Arbitration Act 1975, s.1).

An arbitration agreement is domestic if at the time the proceedings are commenced:(1) it does not provide, expressly or by implication, for arbitration in a state other than the United Kingdom; and (2) all parties to it are: ① United Kingdom citizens or natural persons habitually resident in the United Kingdom; or ② corporations incorporated in the United

Kingdom or having their central management and control exercised in the United Kingdom (1975 Act, s.1 (4)). Both conditions must be satisfied for an arbitration agreement to be classified as domestic.

*Domestic arbitrations*

A stay of court proceedings **may** only be granted if all the following requirements are satisfied (s.4 (1)): (1) The matter in question must be within the scope of the arbitration agreement; (2) The applicant must have taken no step in the court proceedings. If he delivers a defence, makes an application to the court, or does anything else of a like nature, he cannot have the proceedings stayed; (3) The applicant must have been ready and willing from the commencement to do everything necessary for the proper conduct of the arbitration; and (4) There must be no sufficient reason why the dispute should not be referred to arbitration.

The burden of proof is upon the party opposing the stay to satisfy the court there are strong reasons for proceeding with the action and not granting the stay, because when parties have agreed that their disputes are to be decided by a particular tribunal the court is inclined to hold them to their agreement, unless there is some strong reason why they should not be so held. Factors relevant to the exercise of the discretion to stay court proceedings include: whether there are complex issues of law; the delay and expense that might arise if there are other court proceedings involving the same issues or parties and a multiplicity of proceedings might result if the arbitration is allowed to proceed; and the efficiency and economy generally of court proceedings compared to arbitration in the circumstances of the case. The same principles apply where the parties have agreed on an **exclusive jurisdiction clause**, and not on an arbitration clause. An exclusive jurisdiction clause provides that the courts of a particular country shall have exclusive jurisdiction to decide disputes between the parties.

The court may, in particular, refuse a stay (s.24): (1) After a dispute has arisen, if the arbitrator is or may not be impartial by reason of his relation to one of the parties or of his connection with the subject referred; (2) If the dispute involves the question whether any of the parties have been guilty of fraud, so far as necessary to enable that question to be determined.

*Non-domestic arbitrations*

Here the court must order a stay of proceedings, unless it is satisfied: (1) that the arbitration agreement is null and void, inoperative or incapable of being performed; or (2) that there is not in fact any dispute between the parties with regard to the matters agreed to be referred (1975 Act, s.1 (1)).

A party who wishes the court to stay court proceedings so that the arbitration will proceed, must apply to the court after entering an appearance and before delivering any pleadings or taking any other step in the court proceedings (1975 Act, s.1 (1)). That party must prove the existence of an arbitration agreement. The party bringing court proceedings in breach of the alleged arbitration agreement would have the onus of proving that the agreement was null and void (for example, because it was induced by fraud or duress) or that the agreement was inoperative (for example, because arbitral proceedings were not brought within a contractual time limit) or that the agreement is incapable of being performed (for example, because the arbitrator named therein died before the dispute arose).

Summary judgment procedures are available, even under the Arbitration Act 1975 in relation to international arbitration agreements, where there is no arguable defence to a claim, on the premise that there is not in fact any dispute between the parties with regard to the matters agreed to be referred.

### 3. Whether the arbitrator can determine the validity of the arbitration agreement

The question whether or not an arbitrator has power to determine the validity of the agreement by virtue of which he has been appointed as arbitrator is determined in accordance with the following principles:

(1) An arbitration clause is a written submission, agreed to by the parties to the contract, and, like other written agreements, must be construed according to its language and in the light of the circumstances in which it is made.

(2) If the dispute is whether the contract which contains the clause has ever been entered into at all, that issue cannot go to arbitration under the clause, for the party who denies that he has ever entered into the contract is thereby denying that he has ever joined in the submission.

(3) Similarly, if one party to the alleged contract contends that it is void ab initio (because, for example, the making of such a contract is illegal). the arbitration clause cannot operate, for on this view the clause itself is also void.

(4) But where the parties are at one in asserting that they entered into a binding contract, but a difference arises between them whether there has been a breach by one side or the other, or whether circumstances have arisen which have discharged one or both parties from further performance, the arbitration clause is binding.

(5) Where there is an application to the court to stay proceedings, if the agreement is on the face of it perfectly valid and effective, the application will generally be granted as the court will be unwilling to treat the agreement or the submission to arbitration as void until the matter has been decided by a court or by an arbitrator.

"It is not the law that arbitrators, if their jurisdiction is challenged or questioned, are bound immediately to refuse to act until their jurisdiction has been determined by some court which has power to determine it finally. Nor is it the law that they are bound to go on without investigating the merits of the challenge and to determine the matter in dispute, leaving the question of their jurisdiction to be held over until it is determined by some court which had power to determine it. They might then be merely wasting their time and everybody else's. They are not obliged to take either of those courses. They are entitled to inquire into the merits of the issue whether they have jurisdiction or not, not for the purpose of reaching any conclusion which will be binding upon the parties — because that they cannot do — but for the purpose of satisfying themselves as a preliminary matter about whether they ought to go on with the reference or not."

### 4. Separability of the arbitration agreement

An arbitration clause constitutes a separate agreement independent of the substantive contract in which it is embedded. It will survive the invalidity or termination of the main contract unless the main contract was void ab initio or never came into existence. The arbitrator has jurisdiction to adjudicate on the validity of the main contract unless the (separate) arbitration agreement itself is affected by a vitiating event.

### 5. Scope of the arbitration agreement

An arbitral tribunal may consider only claims which are encompassed by the wording of the arbitration agreement. An agreement to refer all disputes to arbitration arising "under this contract" will be construed narrowly and will not cover claims in tort. But an agreement to refer all disputes to arbitration arising "under or in connection with this contract" will cover claims in tort (*Ashville Investments Ltd. v. Elmer Contractors Ltd.* [1989] 2 Q. B. 488).The words "arising out of this contract" will also be given a wide interpretation and will encompass a plea for rectification of the contract. If a contract contains an arbitration clause and a claim is made in negligence — a tort — which is coextensive with a claim for breach of the contract containing the clause, the claim in tort is within the jurisdiction of the arbitrators who can dispose of it. The position is the same in other cases in which a sufficiently close connection exists between the tort and the breach of contract.

### 6. Arbitration agreement in apprenticeship deed

An arbitration clause in an apprenticeship deed between a minor and his employer is for the minor's benefit (see p.70, *ante*). and is binding on the minor (*Slade v. Metrodent Ltd.* [1953] 2 Q. B. 112).

### 7. Assignment of contract containing arbitration agreement

When a contract is assignable, the benefit of an arbitration clause contained in it is assignable as part of the contract (*Shayler v. Woolf* [1946] Ch. 320).But an assignment of all money due under a contract does not include an arbitration clause in the contract.

# The Arbitration Agreement

Every arbitration agreement is assumed to include the following provisions, unless a contrary intention is expressed in it —

1. If no other mode of reference is provided, the reference is to a single arbitrator (s.6).

2. If the reference is to two arbitrators, they may appoint an umpire at any time after they are themselves appointed and shall do so forthwith if they cannot agree (s.8(1). amended by the Arbitration Act 1979, s.6 (1)).

3. If the arbitrators have delivered to any party or to the umpire a notice in writing stating that they cannot agree, the umpire may enter on the reference (s.8(2)).

4. The parties to the arbitration must submit to be examined on oath before the arbitrator or umpire and must produce all books, deeds, papers, accounts, writings and documents in their possession which may be called for, and must do all other things which, during the reference, the arbitrators or umpire may require (s.12(1)).

5. The witnesses on the reference must, if the arbitrators or umpire think fit, be examined on oath (s.12 (2)).

6. The award to be made by the arbitrators or umpire is final and binding on the parties (s.16).

7. The costs of the reference and award are in the discretion of the arbitrators or umpire, who can direct who shall pay the costs and can tax or settle the amount of costs to be paid (s.18(1)). A provision in the arbitration agreement that a party shall pay his own costs in any event is void unless the provision is in an agreement to submit to arbitration a dispute which has already arisen (s. 18(3)).

8. The arbitrators or umpire can order specific performance of any contract, except a contract relating to land (s.15).

9. An interim award may be made (s.14).

An arbitration agreement may be altered or amended by consent of the parties, but the arbitrator or umpire has no power to alter it.

The authority of an arbitrator or umpire appointed under an arbitration agreement is irrevocable except by leave of the court (s.1). An arbitration agreement is not discharged by the death of any party to the agreement, and the authority of an arbitrator is not revoked by the death of the party appointing him (s.2). On the bankruptcy of a party, an arbitration clause in a contract is enforceable by or against his trustee in bankruptcy if he adopts the contract (s.3). There is no similar provision dealing with the liquidator of a company. The court may revoke an agreement, after a dispute has arisen, on the ground that the arbitrator is not impartial by reason of his relation to one of the parties to the agreement, or of his connection with the subject referred, or when a question of fraud arises (s.24).

# The Applicable law

Where an international contract contains an arbitration clause but does not define the proper law of the contract, the presumption is that the law of the place at which the arbitration is to be held is the proper law of the contract (*Tzortzis v. Monark Line A/B* [1968] 1 W. L. R. 406) but this presumption may be rebutted by the surrounding circumstances (*Cie Tunisienne de Navigation S. A. v. Cie d' Armement Maritime S. A.*, see pp. 207-208, ante).

The law applicable to the arbitration procedure, or *lex arbitri*, may be different from the substantive law governing the contract. The lex arbitri which governs the conduct of the arbitration is the law of the place where the arbitration takes place unless the parties expressly and clearly agree that the arbitration is to be subject to the procedural law of some other country. Such a provision would, however, produce a highly complex and possibly unworkable result.

The validity, effect and interpretation of an arbitration agreement are determined by the proper law of the arbitration agreement itself. In most cases this will be the same law as the proper (or applicable) law of the substantive contract in which an arbitration clause is embedded. The parties may, however, choose to have the main contract and the arbitration agreement governed by different laws. The arbitration procedure may be governed by a third law. Thus, for example, an arbitration in London would be governed by English procedural law but the arbitrators might have to apply Swiss law to the merits of the dispute and French law to questions relating to the scope of the arbitration agreement. The provision of the Arbitration Act 1950 which gives the court power to extend the time for commencing arbitration proceedings in case of undue hardship (s.27) forms part of the substantive law governing the arbitration agreement and can be invoked if the arbitration agreement is governed by English law even though the arbitration procedure may be governed by a foreign law.

# Appointment of Arbitrator

The parties may refer their dispute to a single named arbitrator, to two arbitrators — one to be appointed by each party — or to two arbitrators and an umpire or chairman. A High Court judge may be appointed arbitrator or umpire; he is known as a judge-arbitrator or judge-umpire (Administration of Justice Act 1970, s.4).

In the following cases: (1) where the reference is to a single arbitrator and the parties do not concur in the appointment of an arbitrator; (2) if the appointed arbitrator dies or refuses to act and the parties do not supply the vacancy; (3) where the parties or two arbitrators are required or are at liberty to appoint an umpire and do not appoint him; (4) where the umpire dies or refuses to act and the parties do not supply a vacancy. Any party may serve the others with a written notice to make an appointment, and if the appointment is not made within seven days the court will make the appointment (s.10).

Sometimes the arbitrator or umpire is to be appointed by a third person, e.g. by a chamber of commerce or the president of a professional association. If the organisation or person who is to make the appointment, declines or fails to do so, any party to the arbitration agreement may give the organisation or person in question written notice to make the appointment and if it is not made within seven days, the party may apply to the court for the appointment of the arbitrator or umpire (Arbitration Act 1979, s.6 (4)).

A clause worded "suitable arbitration clause" in an English contract is not void on the ground of uncertainty but means an arbitration which reasonable men in this type of business would consider suitable, the court being empowered to appoint an arbitrator under the Arbitration Act 1950. Where the arbitration clause provides for the appointment of "commercial men" as arbitrators and umpire, a practising member of the Bar can not be appointed umpire by the arbitrators.

Where the agreement provides that the reference shall be to two arbitrators, one to be appointed by each party, and one party appoints an arbitrator who subsequently dies or refuses to act, such party may appoint a new arbitrator. If he fails to do so or fails to appoint an arbitrator in the first instance, the other party may serve notice on him to make an appointment within seven days, and, in default of such appointment, the arbitrator appointed by the other party will be the sole arbitrator and his award will be binding on both parties. An appointment made under these circumstances may be set aside by the court (s.7). As already observed, the two arbitrators may appoint an umpire and shall do so forthwith, if they can not agree.

If the agreement for reference is to three arbitrators the award of any two is binding unless a contrary intention is expressed (Arbitration Act 1950, s.9 as amended by the 1979 Act, s.6 (2)).

The appointment of an arbitrator is constituted by (1) nominating the arbitrator to the other party, (2) informing the arbitrator of his nomination, and (3) an intimation by him that he is willing to accept the nomination.

The court may remove an arbitrator or umpire who fails to use reasonable dispatch in proceeding with the reference and making an award. No remuneration is payable to an arbitrator or an umpire who is removed (s.13).

# Judicial Review

The Arbitration Act 1979 admits the judicial review of arbitration awards on questions of law, but this review is severely restricted and admitted only subject to stringent conditions. If these conditions are not satisfied the court has no power to review the award on its merits. In certain well-defined cases the parties to the arbitration may even exclude judicial review completely.

## 1. Reasoned awards

A party is entitled to an award which contains sufficient reasons to enable the court to carry out a judicial review. If an appeal is brought from the award to the court and the judge is unable to consider any question of law arising out of the award, he may order the arbitrator or umpire to state the reasons for his award in sufficient detail or to supplement the reasons given in the award. The judge can make such an order only if: (1) a party has notified the arbitrator or umpire before the award was made that a reasoned award is required; or (2) there is some special reason why such a notice was not given. (1979 Act, s.1 (5) and (6)).

The court will be vigilant to ensure that the power to order further reasons is used only for its proper purpose and not as an indirect way of obtaining a review of the merits of an award (*Universal Petroleum Co. Ltd. v. Handels-und Transport Gesellschaft m. b. H.* [1987] 1 Lloyd's Rep.517.)

## 2. Judicial review procedure

The procedure for a review of the award by the court is as follows. An appeal may be brought to the High Court on any question of law arising out of the award by any party to the arbitration: (1) with the consent of all other parties; or (2) by leave of the court but the court shall not grant leave unless it considers that "the determination of the question of law concerned could substantially affect the rights of one or more of the parties to the arbitration agreement." (1979 Act, s.1 (3) and (4)).

According to the guidelines laid down by the House of Lords in the Nema, the requirements under (2) should be applied very strictly and leave to appeal should be granted by the court only sparingly, particularly in so-called "**one-off**" contracts, *i.e.* contracts of singular occurrence and not concluded on standard contract forms. "In a 'one-off' case, in the absence of special circumstances, leave should not be given unless on the conclusion of argument on the application for leave the court has formed the provisional view that the arbitrator was wrong and considers that it would need a great deal of convincing that he was right".

The philosophy now adopted by the courts is to prefer finality over legality. It is presumed that the parties intended to take the risk that the arbitrators might make an error in fact or law. The appeal court will grant leave to appeal on a question of law only in a case where the interests of justice to the parties or the integrity of the arbitral process demand that a court consider the question or if a matter of general legal import is involved.

An arbitrator can not refer a question of EU law to the Court of the European Communities in Luxembourg by virtue of article 177 of the former EEC Treaty. But where such a question arises in arbitration, the court will allow an appeal from the award if the point is new, is capable of serious argument, and is potentially of great importance and far-reaching effect.

### 3. Preliminary Points of law

An application may be made to the High Court to determine any question of law arising in the course of the arbitration. The High Court shall not entertain the application unless: (1) the determination might produce substantial savings in costs; and (2) the conditions on which the court may give leave to appeal from an arbitration award under section 1 (3) and (4) of the 1979 Act (see above) are satisfied. (1979 Act, s.2 (2)).

The application for the determination of a preliminary point of law by the court is made either by a party with the consent of the arbitrator or umpire, or with the consent of all other parties (1979 Act, s.2 (1)).

### 4. Appeals from the decision of the High Court

Appeals from the decision of the High Court to the Court of Appeal are greatly restricted, both in cases concerning an appeal from the award (1979 Act, s.1 (6A) and (7)) and in those concerning the determination of a preliminary point of law (1979 Act, s.2 (2A) and (3)).

Appeals to the Court of Appeal are only admitted if: (1) the High Court or the Court of Appeal gives leave; and (2) a certificate is given by the High Court that the question of law in issue is either of general public importance or is one which for some other special reason should be considered by the Court of Appeal.

### 5. Exclusion agreements

The parties to the arbitration may in certain circumstances exclude judicial review completely. Where they have done so lawfully, no appeal from the award on a point of law is admitted and the court has no power to determine a preliminary point of law.

*Domestic, non-domestic and special category arbitrations*

For the purposes of exclusion clauses, arbitrations are arranged into:

domestic arbitrations,

non-domestic arbitrations, and

special category arbitrations.

The definition of domestic and non-domestic arbitrations in this connection is the same as that for the purposes of the Arbitration Act 1975 (see p.721, *ante*). except that the requirements must be satisfied at the time the arbitration agreement is entered into (1979 Act, s.3 (7)). and not, as under the 1975 Act, at the time the arbitration proceedings are commenced.

Special category proceedings concern: (1) a question or claim falling within the Admiralty jurisdiction of the High Court; or (2) a dispute arising out of a contract of insurance; or (3) a dispute arising out of a commodity contract. (1979 Act, s.4 (1)).

A commodity contract is defined as a contract: (1) for the sale of goods dealt with on a commodity market or exchange in England and Wales, which is specified by an order made by the Secretary of State; and (2) of a description as specified. (1979 Act, s.4 (2)).

The Arbitration (Commodity Contracts) Order 1979 (S.I.1979 No.754) specifies the commodity markets and exchanges to which these provisions apply. They include, e.g. the London Metal Exchange, the Grain and Feed Trade Association Limited (GAFTA) and the Federation of Oils, Seeds and Fats Association of London (FOSFA).

### 6. Domestic arbitrations

In domestic arbitrations parties may exclude judicial review by an exclusion agreement only if the agreement is entered after the commencement of the arbitration (1979 Act, s.3 (6)).

### 7. Non-domestic arbitrations (other than special category arbitrations)

Here the parties may enter into an exclusion agreement *before or after* the commencement of the arbitration (1979 Act, s.4 (1)).

In these cases it would be possible to combine the exclusion agreement with the arbitration clause in the original contract. The admission of exclusion agreements before the commencement of the arbitration in this class of cases should be of particular value in international "one-off" contracts.

When parties agree on arbitration under the Rules of the Court of Arbitration of the International Chamber of Commerce — as they frequently do in international "one-off" contracts — they are taken to have concluded an exclusion agreement because the ICC Rules provide that "the arbitral award shall be final".

### 8. Special category arbitrations

Here an exclusion agreement is only admitted: (1) *after* the commencement of the arbitration; or (2) if the contract is governed by a law other than that of England and Wales. (1979 Act, s.4 (1)).

Special category arbitrations will often be non-domestic arbitrations. Nevertheless, they are, at least for the time being (1979 Act, s.4 (3)) subject to a special regulation which constitutes an exception to the general treatment of non-domestic arbitrations.

# Conduct of an Arbitration

The duty of an arbitrator is to make an award on the matters of dispute or difference between the parties submitted for his decision. An arbitrator or an umpire can not delegate the powers conferred on him by the agreement.

A lay arbitrator may in a proper case, in the absence of an objection by the parties, hear the arbitration with a legal assessor. In all cases he may employ legal assistance in drawing up his award.

The arbitrator should fix a time and place for the hearing of the arbitration and give notice to all parties. Should one of the parties fail to attend after notice, the arbitrator can proceed with the reference, notwithstanding his absence. The arbitrator can administer oaths to the witnesses appearing before him (s.12 (3)). and with respect to their testimony he is bound to observe the rules of evidence. Unless the submission provides to the contrary he should hear the witnesses tendered in the presence of both parties. He has no power to call a witness himself without the consent of the parties. An arbitrator may order that pleadings be filed or that there be discovery and inspection of documents but has no power to order security for costs unless specifically granted such power by the parties. A court may order security for costs (s.12 (6)) but as a general rule will decline to do so against a foreign claimant in an international arbitration.

A commercial arbitrator is entitled to rely on his own knowledge and experience in deciding on the quality of the goods which form the subject-matter of the arbitration, and can also assess the damages, even though there has been no evidence before him as to the amount of the damages. But if intending to rely on his own knowledge of the trade, he must not take the parties by surprise but invite them, if he thinks they have missed a point, to deal with it; further, if he has knowledge of facts which do not appear to be known to the parties, he must disclose those facts to them and give them an opportunity to plead to them.

In commercial arbitrations where an umpire has been appointed the arbitrators can give evidence before the umpire.

The arbitrator must decide according to the law; the parties can not give him power to decide according to an equitable rather than a strictly legal interpretation because the adoption of such an extra-legal criterion would make it impossible for the court, when a judicial review is called for, to ascertain whether the arbitrator had fallen into an error when deciding a question of law.

"I have no hesitation in accepting...that a clause which purported to free arbitrators to decide without reference to law and according, for example, to their own motions of what would be fair would not be a valid arbitration clause."

However, a decision by the arbitrators to apply internationally accepted principles of law governing contractual relations in an arbitration subject to Swiss law was not so uncertain as to preclude enforcement of the award by an English court.

The arbitrator has no power to dismiss a case for want of prosecution, even if inordinate and inexcusable delay on the part of the parties occurs in the proceedings before him. But an arbitration agreement, like every other contract, might be terminated by frustration, abandonment by both parties, or a repudiatory breach by one party which is accepted by the other. Frustration of the arbitration agreement does not occur if the parties are in default with their mutual obligation to apply to the arbitrator for directions in order to prevent inordinate delay. If inordinate delay occurs, the arbitrator or umpire may make an order and if the parties fail to comply with it, he may apply to the court under section 5 of the Arbitration Act 1979. The court has power under this section to allow the arbitrator or umpire to continue with the proceedings in the same manner as a High Court judge may do. Under this provision the court might empower the arbitrator or umpire to dismiss the case for want of prosecution.

# The Award

The award may be in writing or made verbally, unless the arbitration agreement provides that it must be in writing. To be valid, the award should comply with the following:

1. It must follow the agreement and not purport to decide matters not within the agreement. An award on something outside the agreement is void, and if the void part can not be severed from the rest of the award, the whole award is void.

2. It must be certain. If it is uncertain it can not be enforced. For example, an award that A. or B. shall do a certain act is void for uncertainty.

3. It must be final. An award, therefore, that a third party shall certify the loss arising from a breach of contract is void for want of finality.

4. It must be reasonable, legal and possible. An award that one of the parties should do something beyond his power, as to deliver up a deed which is in the custody of X., is void.

5. It must dispose of all the differences submitted to arbitration. If, however, all matters in dispute between the parties are submitted to arbitration, the award is good if it deals with all matters submitted to the arbitrator, although there may be other differences between the parties.

6. The award must be reasoned in the circumstances explained earlier.

An arbitrator has jurisdiction to make his award in a foreign currency where that currency is the currency of the contract.

An arbitrator is entitled to award interest on the sum he finds to be due. In a commercial arbitration, interest should always be awarded, except for good reason.

When the award is ready the arbitrator gives notice to the parties, who can take it up on paying the arbitrator's costs. After the award is made the arbitrator is functus officio, and can not alter or vary his award. He may, however, correct any clerical mistake or error arising from any accidental slip or omission (s.17).

For the purposes of the Arbitration Act 1975 and the New York Convention, an award is made at the place where it is signed. If an arbitrator in an arbitration which takes place in England according to English procedural law, decides to sign the award in a different country then it becomes an award made in that country and may only be set aside, if at all, under the law and by the courts of that country.

*Effect of the award*

When an award is made it is final, and no appeal can be made to the courts, except in the limited cases when the judicial review of the award is admitted or when the award can be remitted to the arbitrator or set aside by the court. The agreement for arbitration may provide for an appeal to an appeal committee or other tribunal, but except when it does so, the arbitrator's decision on the facts is final and conclusive, and it is his duty to state the facts, as found by him, in the award; a mere reference to the evidence, e.g. to the transcript of evidence is insufficient.

# The Costs of the Arbitration

The costs of the arbitration, unless a contrary intention is expressed in the agreement, are in the discretion of the arbitrator (s.18). This discretion must be exercised judicially. In the absence of special circumstances, it is settled practice that the successful party should be awarded costs. If there are special circumstances before the arbitrator justifying the exercise of his discretion in favour of the unsuccessful party, he need not follow the settled practice. The arbitrator may award a lump sum for costs, or may direct that the costs shall be taxed in the High Court or by himself. The costs include all the costs of the arbitration including the arbitrator's own costs.

The arbitrator may fix the amount of his own remuneration and include it in the award. It is then payable on the taking up of the award. The fees of an arbitrator and an umpire may be taxed, and only so much as is found to be reasonable on taxation need to be paid (s.19). If the reference is to two arbitrators and an umpire and the umpire, owing to the disagreement of the arbitrators, draws up the award, he should include the fees of the arbitrators as well as his own fees, specifying the amount of each. In exceptional cases if it is apparent that the umpire, when settling his own and the arbitrator's remuneration, misunderstood his duties and settled it in a wholly extravagant manner, this might amount to misconduct and the whole award be set aside.

An arbitrator is entitled to reasonable fees but may not insist upon a commitment fee unless it was agreed before appointment. It would be misconduct for an arbitrator to insist upon a commitment fee as a condition of continuing to act in the absence of such prior agreement. It would also probably constitute misconduct for an arbitrator to conclude an agreement as to fees with one party, after appointment, if the other party refuses to join in the agreement.

# Enforcement of Awards

An award on an arbitration agreement may, by leave of the court, be enforced in the same manner as a judgment (s.26). Leave will be granted unless it can be shown that the award is a nullity, or is bad on the face of it, or is ultra vires.

An alternative method of enforcing an award is to bring an action on it. If the submission is oral, an action is the only method of enforcing the award.

# Remission to Arbitrator

In all cases of reference to arbitration, the court may remit the whole or part of the matter for reconsideration by the arbitrators or umpire. When an award is remitted the award must be made within three months of the order of remission (s.22). but the time may be enlarged by the court (s.13 (2)).

An award may be remitted for reconsideration on the following grounds:

1. Where the arbitrator has made a mistake with respect to his jurisdiction.

2. Where, since the making of the award, material evidence has been discovered which might have affected the arbitrator's decision.

3. Where there has been misconduct on the part of the arbitrator. In such a case the court may either set the award aside or remit it to the arbitrator.

Misconduct, sometimes called technical misconduct, does not imply a moral reprobation. It occurs if the arbitrator has failed "to act fairly and to be seen to act fairly. This is not to say that [the arbitrator] intended to be unfair or was aware that [he] might appear to have acted unfairly. Such cases are, happily, very rare because the commercial community is fortunate in the skill and conscientiousness of those who devote time to the resolution of commercial disputes by arbitration".

The court has an unlimited jurisdiction to remit an arbitral award as a safety net to prevent injustice but it is usually invoked, if at all, in relation to procedural mishaps or misunderstandings. A court has no jurisdiction to remit or set aside an award on the ground of errors of fact or law on the face of the award except in accordance with the appeal provisions of the Arbitration Act 1979 (s.1).

# Setting Aside the Award

Where an arbitrator or umpire has misconducted himself, or any arbitration or award has been improperly procured, the court may set aside the award (s.23). An award is improperly procured if it is obtained by fraud or by concealment of material facts.

An award can be set aside for misconduct if the arbitrator has received bribes, or if he is secretly interested in the subject-matter of the dispute. Misconduct, however, may exist where no improper motives are imputed to the arbitrator. It is misconduct, for example, to make an award on an illegal contract. It is also misconduct to make his award before hearing all the evidence, or allowing a party to finish his case; to examine a witness in the absence of either of the parties; to inspect property, the subject of the arbitration accompanied by only one party. to fail to give notice to the parties of the time and place of meeting; or to hear the evidence of each party in the absence of the other; or where one of three arbitrators signs the award in blank without deliberating with the other arbitrators, but if all three have considered their decision, the arbitrators need not sign the award at the same time.

# Foreign Awards

Foreign awards, as defined in section 35, can be enforced in England either by action or in the same manner as the award of an arbitrator under section 26, provided that the conditions laid down in section 37 are complied with.

One of these conditions is that the award has become final in the country in which it was made. Whether an award has become final in this way is a matter of English law when enforcement is being sought in England and it matters not, for example, if the award could not be enforced in the country where it was made until some further step had been taken, such as an order of the local court.

# Convention Awards

A Convention award is an award made in pursuance of an arbitration agreement in the territory of a foreign state which is a party to the New York Convention on the Recognition and Enforcement of Foreign Arbitral Awards of 1958. These awards are subject to the Arbitration Act 1975, ss.2 to 6.

A Convention award is enforced in the same manner as an English award (1976 Act, s.3). Enforcement of such an award can be refused only if the party against whom it is made proves: (1) that a party to the arbitration agreement was (under the law applicable to him) under some incapacity; or (2) that the arbitration agreement was not valid under the law to which the parties subjected it or, failing any indication thereon, under the law of the country where the award was made; or (3) that he was not given proper notice of the appointment of the arbitrator or of the arbitration proceedings or was otherwise unable to present his case; or (4) that the award deals with a difference not covered by the arbitration agreement; or (5) that the composition of the arbitral authority or the arbitral procedure was not in accordance with the agreement of the parties, or failing such agreement, with the law of the country where the arbitration took place; or (6) that the award has not yet become binding on the parties, or has been set aside or suspended by a competent authority of the country in which, or under the law of which, it was made (1975 Act, s.5 (1)).

The enforcement of a Convention award may also be refused if the subject-matter of the award is not capable of settlement by arbitration or it would be contrary to public policy to enforce it (1975 Act, s.5 (3)).

As of 1991 more than 80 countries have acceded to the New York Convention (for a list of these countries see the Arbitration (Foreign Awards) Order 1975 (No.1709). as amended).

# International Investment Disputes

Legal disputes arising directly out of an investment between a state (or a department or agency of a state) and a national of another state may be settled by arbitration under the rules of the International Centre for Settlement of Investment Disputes, established at the International Bank for Reconstruction and Development in Washington. The Centre has jurisdiction only if both parties have consented in writing to submit the dispute to the Centre.

The provisions relating to arbitration over international investment disputes are contained in an international convention of 1965, which is set out in the Schedule to the **Arbitration (International Investment Disputes) Act 1966**. A person seeking recognition or enforcement of such an award is entitled to have the award registered in the High Court (s.1 (2)). If the award is in a foreign currency, the currency is converted on the basis of the rate of exchange prevailing at the date when the award was rendered (s.1 (3)). The Act came into force on January 18, 1967.

### New Words

| | | |
|---|---|---|
| 1. | arbitration *n.* | 仲裁 |
| 2. | arbitrator *n.* | 仲裁人 |
| 3. | umpire *n.* | 裁決人；首席仲裁人 |
| 4. | arbitral awards | 仲裁裁決 |
| 5. | reference *n.* | 提交仲裁；交仲裁人裁定 |
| 6. | referee *n.* | 仲裁人 |
| 7. | certify *v.* | 證明 |
| 8. | building owner | 建築所有者 |
| 9. | builder *n.* | 建築者 |
| 10. | speaking valuation | 說明理由的估價 |
| 11. | impugn *v.* | 駁斥；指責；表示懷疑；非難 |
| 12. | accruing *n.* | 自然增長 |
| 13. | stay *n.* | 審判的延緩或推遲；中止訴訟程序 |
| 14. | turpentine *n.* | 松油；松脂 |
| 15. | writ *n.* | 書面命令；傳票；法院的令狀 |
| 16. | inoperative *a.* | 不發揮作用；不生效的；無效的 |
| 17. | ab initio | （拉）自始；從頭開始；從開始起 |
| 18. | embed *v.* | 包含在……裡 |
| 19. | apprenticeship deed | 學徒契據 |
| 20. | forthwith *adv.* | 立即地 |
| 21. | encompass *v.* | 包括 |
| 22. | plea *n.* | 請求 |
| 23. | coextensive *a.* | 共同擴張的 |
| 24. | charterparty *n.* | 租船契約；傭船契約 |
| 25. | charterer *n.* | 租船人 |
| 26. | sequel *n.* | 餘波；結局 |
| 27. | liquidator *n.* | 公司清算人 |
| 28. | lex arbitri | （拉）仲裁法 |
| 29. | intimation *n.* | 告知；通知；暗示 |

**30.** stringent *a.*      嚴格的；嚴厲的；嚴苛的

**31.** vigilant *a.*      警戒的；注意的

**32.** one-off contract      一次性發生的不是在標準契約格式基礎上訂立的契約

**33.** sparingly *adv.*      少量地

**34.** icebound *a.*      冰封住的

**35.** transatlantic *a.*      橫跨大西洋的

**36.** frustration *n.*      落空；契約的受挫失效

**37.** reverse *v.*      反轉；撤銷

**38.** legal import      法律含義或重要性

**39.** the admiralty jurisdiction      海事法管轄權

**40.** exclusion agreement      排他性仲裁協議

**41.** lay arbitrator      外行的仲裁人；非專業性的仲裁人

**42.** legal assessor      法定估價人

**43.** inordinate *a.*      過分的；無限制的

**44.** inexcusable *a.*      不可原諒的

**45.** repudiatory breach      因拒絕承擔義務而毀約

**46.** functus officio      履行職責

**47.** lump sum      總額；總數

**48.** remission to arbitration      重新仲裁

**49.** moral reprobation      道德上的譴責或指責

**50.** safety net      安全網

**51.** mishaps *n.*      不幸的事

**52.** impute *v.*      把……歸因於；歸咎於……

## ♣ New Phrases and Idiomatic Expressions

**1.** to be appended to      附加於……

**2.** to bring an action on sth.      就……提起訴訟

**3.** to give finality to arbitral awards      給予仲裁裁決終局性

**4.** to originate in      發生於……

**5.** in a quasi-judicial manner      以一種準司法方式

**6.** to enjoy the same immunity      享受同樣的豁免權

**7.** to be inferred from      從……推斷出

**8.** in issue      在爭論中

9. to order a stay of court proceedings　下令停止法庭訴訟

10. to be inclined to do sth.　傾向於做某事

11. as the result of　作為……的結果

12. in the affirmative　肯定地

13. on the premise that......　在……前提下

14. on the face of　在表面上

15. by leave of the court　法院的允許

16. to serve notice on sb.　向某人發通知

17. for want of　缺乏

18. to be severed from　從……分離開

19. in the custody of　被託交某人保管中

20. to deliberate with　與……商議

21. to waive one's right to any form of appeal　放棄任何形式的上訴權

22. to set aside the award　宣布裁決無效

 **Notes**

1. the Geneva Protocol on Arbitration Clauses of 1923：1923年《日內瓦仲裁條款議定書》。
它是在國際聯盟主持下締結的。該議定書除規定各締約國相互承認契約當事人訂立的仲裁協議有效性外，還規定各締約國在一定條件下承認和執行外國仲裁裁決。

2. the Geneva Convention on the Execution of Foreign Arbitral Awards of 1927：1927年《關於執行外國仲裁裁決的日內瓦公約》。
該公約肯定了1923年《日內瓦仲裁條款議定書》的內容，同時對承認和執行外國仲裁裁決的條件以及拒絕執行外國裁決的條件作了詳細規定。

3. the New York Convention on the Recognition and Enforcement of Foreign Arbitral Awards of 1958：1958年《承認和執行外國仲裁裁決的紐約公約》（簡稱為《紐約公約》）。
該公約吸收了1923年《日內瓦仲裁條款議定書》和1927年《關於執行外國仲裁裁決的日內瓦公約》兩個法律條約的基本內容，但比前者有了新的發展。前兩個法律是以互惠為基礎的，兩國之間必須首先締結一項雙邊協議，然後才能在各國的管轄範圍內實行這兩項公約。而《紐約公約》則放棄了互惠要求。原則上，它可適用於任何一個外國的裁決。但每一個國家在簽署或參加此公約時，可以聲明它只願意對公約的締約國所作出的裁決實行該公約。目前《紐約公約》已取代前兩項公約成為有關執行外國仲裁裁決的一個重要國際公約。截至1991年，80多個國家已加入該公約。

4. the Rules of the Court of Arbitration of the International Chamber of Commerce (ICC Rules)：
《國際商會仲裁法院規則》。

國際商會仲裁法院成立於1932年，它是一個處理國際性商事爭議的仲裁機構。凡擬採用該法院規則進行仲裁的當事人都要在契約仲裁條款中明確規定：一切有關該合同所引起的爭議應按國際商會仲裁法院規則進行仲裁，作出最後的處理。

5. the International Centre for Settlement of Investment Disputes (ICSID)：解決投資爭議國際中心。

該中心是根據「the Convention on the Settlement of Investment Disputes between States and Nationals of Other States」所設立。該中心是現代處理國家投資爭議的專門國際仲裁機構，並制定了一套比較完善的仲裁規則。

 **Exercises**

## I. Answer the following questions:

1. What is the purpose of the New York Convention?
   Has the U.K. given effect to this Convention?

2. In what ways may a reference to arbitration be made?

3. How do you distinguish an arbitration from a valuation?

4. In what cases will an arbitration be considered domestic?

5. What are the factors to be taken into consideration when the court exercises its discretion to stay court proceedings?

6. What are the principles in accordance with which an arbitrator has power to determine the validity of the arbitration agreement?

7. What are the main provisions contained in an arbitration agreement?

8. What law will be normally the applicable law of the contract where an international contract contains an arbitration clause but without defining the proper law of the contract?

9. What procedures must be followed by a court to review the arbitral award?

10. In what kind of arbitrations, parties may exclude judicial review by an exclusion agreement?

11. What are the duties of an arbitrator?

12. What principles must be complied with for an award to be valid?

## II. Translate the following Chinese passages into English:

**1.** 大多數國家的仲裁法認爲，仲裁協議有三個作用：(1)雙方當事人均須受仲裁協定的約束，如果發生爭議，應以仲裁解決，不向法庭起訴；(2)可使仲裁人和仲裁庭取得對有關爭議案件的管轄權；(3)排除法院對有關爭議的管轄權。

**2.** 1958年在聯合國主持下，在紐約締結了《承認和執行外國仲裁裁決的公約》，簡稱爲紐約公約。該公約現在已取代了1923年的《日內瓦仲裁條款議定書》和1927年的《關於執行外國仲裁裁決的公約》，成爲有關執行外國仲裁裁決的一個主要國際公約。截止1991年，參加該公約的國家已有80多國。

**3.** 仲裁人的職責是對雙方的爭議作出裁決。無論是仲裁人還是裁判人，不能將給予他們的權力交給他人行使。

**4.** 要使一項仲裁裁決有效，它必須符合以下條件：(1)必須符合仲裁協議；(2)必須肯定；(3)必須有終局性；(4)必須合理、合法和有可能性；(5)必須解決了提交仲裁的所有分歧。

## III. Indicate whether each of the following statements is true or false by writing "T" or "F" in the space provided:

_____ **1.** The Arbitration Act 1950 is the principal law relating to arbitration in the U.K..

_____ **2.** The New York Convention is one of the principal conventions on the Recognition and Enforcement of foreign arbitral awards.

_____ **3.** The international trend is towards giving greater finality to arbitral awards.

_____ **4.** An arbitration agreement is defined as an oral agreement to submit present or future difference to arbitration, whether an arbitrator is named therein or not.

_____ **5.** An arbitration clause in an apprenticeship deed between a minor and his employer is binding on the minor.

_____ **6.** The arbitrator or umpire has power to alter an arbitration agreement.

_____ **7.** According to English law a High Court judge may be appointed arbitrator or umpire.

_____ **8.** The ICC Rules provide that "the arbitral award shall be final" therefore the parties are deemed to have waived their right to any form of appeal.

_____ **9.** The arbitral award may be in writing or made verbally, unless the arbitration agreement provides that it must be in writing.

_____ **10.** When an arbitral award is made final, no appeal can be made to the court except in limited cases.

## IV. Translate and define the following terms into Chinese:

1. Convention award

2. foreign award

3. arbitration agreement

4. umpire

5. arbitrator

6. reference

7. exclusion agreement

8. exclusive jurisdiction clause

9. arbitral tribunal

10. one-off contracts

中 篇
國際金融法

## 第二十八課 Lesson 28

## 匯票
## Bills of Exchange

A BILL of exchange is an instrument of the class called "negotiable." The characteristics of a negotiable instrument are:

1. The title to it passes on delivery if it is a bearer instrument, and on delivery and indorsement if it is an order instrument. This distinguishes it from such things as a fire insurance policy, a bill of sale and a right to recover a debt.

2. The holder for the time being can sue in his own name.

3. No notice of assignment need be given to the person liable thereon.

4. A bona fide holder for value takes free from any defect in the title of his predecessors. This quality distinguishes a negotiable instrument from an assignable contract. Chooses in action, for example, can be assigned, either at law under section 136 of the Law of Property Act 1925 or in equity, but in each case the assignee takes subject to any defences available against the assignor. In the case of a negotiable instrument, however, the assignee takes free from any such defences.

Examples of negotiable instruments are; bills of exchange, cheques, promissory notes, dividend warrants, share warrants and debentures payable to bearer. On the other hand, postal orders, share certificates, bills of lading and dock warrants are not negotiable.

A bill of exchange is —
— an unconditional order in writing
— addressed by one person to another
— signed by the person giving it
— requiring the person to whom it is addressed
— to pay
— on demand, or at a fixed or determinable future time
— a sum certain in money
— to or to the order of a specified person or to bearer

The following are common forms of bills of exchange:

*Order bill payable on demand*

---

£400                                    London, October 1,1991
    On demand pay John Jones or order the sum of
    £400 for value received.      WILLIAM SMITH
To Thomas Robinson.

---

*Bearer bill payable at future fixed time*

---

£300                                    Newcastle, October 1,1991
    Three months after date pay bearer the sum of
    £300 for value received.      WILLIAM SMITH
To Thomas Robinson.

---

*Bill payable 90 days after acceptance*

---

£200                                    Manchester, October 1,1991
    Ten days after sight pay to my order £200 for
    value received.      WILLIAM SMITH
To Thomas Robinson.

---

From these forms it will be seen that there are three parties to a bill:

(1) the person who gives the order to pay—the **drawer**;

(2) the person to whom the order to pay is given—the **drawee**;

(3) the person to whom payment is to be made—the **payee**.

In the examples given, "William Smith" is the drawer, "Thomas Robinson" is the drawee, and "John Jones" is the payee. The drawer and the payee may be the same person, as may also be the drawee and the payee. If the drawer and the drawee are the same or the drawee is a fictitious person, the instrument may be treated as a bill of exchange or a promissory note at the holder's option. The holder is the payee or indorsee who is in possession of the bill, or the bearer in the case of a bearer bill.

Both the drawee and the payee must be named or indicated with reasonable certainty. If the payee is a fictitious or non-existing person the bill may be treated as payable to bearer. A bill drawn in favour of an existing person may be in favour of a "fictitious" person if the person named was never intended by the drawer to take under the bill.

If, however, the drawer intends the payee to take under the bill, although he is induced by fraud to form that intention, the payee is not fictitious.

"Cash" cannot be said to be a fictitious or non-existing person and so an instrument made out "cash" cannot be read as payable to bearer. Accordingly, an instrument in the terms "pay cash or order" is not a bill of exchange because it is not to or to the order of a specified person or to bearer; but by virtue of the Cheques Act 1957, s.4, a banker collecting payment on such a document may be protected.

The bill must be an order, not a request. Accordingly, a document in the terms, "We hereby authorise you to pay on our account to the order of G £6,000," is not a bill of exchange.

The order must be unconditional, It must not order any act to be done in addition to the payment of money. If these conditions are not complied with, the instrument is not a bill of exchange. An order for payment out of a particular fund is not unconditional, but an order which is coupled with: (1) an indication of a fund from which the drawee is to refund himself; or (2) a statement of the transaction which gives rise to the bill, is unconditional.

A bill at the end of which is written "provided the receipt form at foot hereof is signed" is not unconditional.

On the other hand, a dividend warrant which ends with the words, "This warrant will not be honoured after three months from date unless specially indorsed by the secretary," is unconditional, the words merely denoting what the company thinks is a reasonable time for presenting the warrant.

Similarly, where the words "to be retained" were written on a cheque, it was held that the cheque was unconditional, on the ground that the words merely imported a condition between the drawer and the payee, and did not affect the order on the bankers.

A bill is payable on demand if it is expressed to be payable on demand, or at sight, or on presentation, or if no time for payment is expressed.

A bill is payable at a determinable future time when it is expressed to be payable at a fixed period after date or sight, or after the occurrence of a specified event which is certain to happen, although the time of happening may be uncertain. For example, an order to pay three months after X's death will be a valid bill, but an order to pay three months after X's marriage will not. Even though X. does in fact marry, the order will not be a bill. Furthermore, where a document expresses the sum to be payable "on or before" a stated date, the option thus reserved to pay at an earlier date than the fixed date creates an uncertainty and contingency in the time for payment and the document is not a bill. It has been held by the Court of Appeal in *Korea Exchange Bank v. Debenhams (Central Buying) Ltd.*, [1979] 1 Lloyd's Rep.548,that a bill of exchange payable at a certain time after "acceptance" was not a bill payable at a determinable future time but the correctness of this decision is respectfully doubted.

A sum is certain although it may be payable: (1) with interest; (2) by instalments, with or without a provision that upon default in payment of may instalment the whole shall be due; (3) according to an indicated rate of exchange.

If there is a difference between the sum payable as expressed in words and as expressed in figures, the sum expressed in words is the amount payable.

A bill is **payable to order** when: (1) it is expressed to be payable to order; (2) it is payable to a particular person and does not contain words prohibiting transfer, e.g. a bill in the form "to pay A.B. £500" is an order bill, but a bill "to pay A.B. only" or "pay A.B. personally £500" is not an order bill; (3) it is payable to the order of a particular person. In such a case it is payable either to the person in question or his order (s.8). e.g. a bill payable to "the order of A.B." is payable either to A.B. or to A.B's order.

A bill is **payable to bearer** when it is expressed to be so payable or when the only or last indorsement is an indorsement in blank.

An **inland bill** is one which is: (1) both drawn and payable within the British Isles, or (2) drawn within the British Isles upon some person resident therein.

A **foreign bill** is any other bill.

A bill which is payable at a fixed period after date may be issued undated. In such a case any holder may insert the true date of issue, and if by mistake the wrong date is inserted, the bill is payable as if the date so inserted had been the true date. The date on a bill is presumed to be the true date unless the contrary is proved.

A bill may contain words prohibiting its transfer. In such a case it is valid between the parties, but is not negotiable.

*Incomplete bills*

When a bill is wanting in any material particular, the person in possession of it has prima facie authority to fill up the omission in any way he thinks fit.

# Acceptance

If the bill is a **sight bill**, i.e. if it is payable at sight or on demand, it must be paid by the drawee when seen by him and the question of acceptance of such a bill cannot arise. But different is the position if the bill is a **time bill**, i.e. if it is payable at a future fixed time or a fixed time after acceptance. After a time bill has been issued, the holder should present it to the drawee for acceptance to find out whether the drawee is willing to carry out the order of the drawer. If the drawee agrees to obey the drawer's order he is said to accept the bill, which he does by signing his name on the bill, with or without the word "accepted". Acceptance is defined as the signification by the drawee of his assent to the order of the drawer. After acceptance, the drawee is known as the **acceptor**. It is not essential for the holder to present the bill for acceptance, although it is to his advantage to do so as he thereby gains the additional security of the acceptor's name and, if acceptance is refused, the antecedent parties become liable immediately. In three cases, however, a bill must be presented for acceptance: 1. When it is payable after sight, presentment for acceptance is necessary to fix the date of payment. 2. When it expressly stipulates that it shall be presented for acceptance.3.Where it is payable elsewhere than at the place of residence or business of the drawee.

A bill may be accepted before it has been signed by the drawer or while otherwise incomplete, and even if it is overdue or has been dishonoured by a previous non-acceptance or non-payment.

The rules as to **presentment for acceptance** are: 1. Presentment must be made at a reasonable hour on a business day and before the bill is overdue. 2. When the bill is addressed to two or more drawees who are not partners, presentment must be made to them all, unless one has authority to accept for all. 3. Where the drawee is dead, presentment may be made to his personal representative. 4. Where the drawee is bankrupt, presentment may be made to him or to his trustee. 5. Where authorised by agreement or usage, presentment may be made through the post.

On the presentment the drawee may give either a general or a qualified acceptance, or he may refuse an acceptance.

A **general** acceptance assents without qualification to the order of the drawer.

A **qualified** acceptance in express terms varies the effect of the bill as drawn. An acceptance is qualified which is: (1) conditional; (2) partial, i.e. for part only of the amount of the bill; (3) local, i.e. to pay only at a particular place. An acceptance to pay at a particular place is a general acceptance, unless it expressly states that the bill is to be paid there only and not elsewhere; (4) qualified as to time; (5) the acceptance of some of the drawees, but not all.

The holder of the bill may refuse to take a qualified acceptance and may treat the bill as dishonoured by non-acceptance. If the holder does take a qualified acceptance,the drawer and indorsers are discharged unless they have assented to it. They are deemed to assent to a qualified acceptance if, after notice, they do not dissent within a reasonable time.

A bill may therefore be treated as dishonoured by non-acceptance when: 1. The drawee does not, after presentment, accept the bill within the customary time, which is generally 24 hours. 2. The drawee gives a qualified acceptance. 3. The drawee is dead or bankrupt, or is a fictitious person or a person not having capacity to contract by bill. 4. Presentment, cannot be effected, after the exercise of reasonable diligence. 5. Although the presentment has been irregular, acceptance has been refused on some other ground.

When a bill is treated as dishonoured by non-acceptance, notice of dishonour must be given in the manner stated below, otherwise the holder will lose his right of recourse against the drawer and indorsers.

If the acceptance is procured by fraud, the acceptor is only liable to a holder in due course and not to other holders.

A bill drawn on M. in favour of A. was accepted by M. through the fraud of F. Held, M. was not liable on the bill to A.: Ayres v. Moore [1940] 1K.B.278.

# Acceptance for Honour

If a bill is dishonoured by a non-acceptance, the holder may nevertheless allow any other person to accept it for the honour of the drawer. The bill itself sometimes has inserted in it the name of a person to whom the holder may resort in case the bill is dishonoured. Such a person is called **the referee in case of need**, but there is no obligation on the holder to resort to the referee in case of need.

To be valid, an acceptance for honour can only take place after the bill has been protested for non-acceptance and is not overdue.

The acceptance for honour supra protest must: (1) be written on the bill and indicate that it is an acceptance for honour; and (2) be signed by the acceptor for honour.

It may state for whose honour the bill is accepted, but if it does not so state it is deemed to be accepted for the honour or the drawer.

The effect of accepting a bill for honour is that the acceptor for honour becomes liable to pay the bill, provided that: (1) it is presented to the drawee for payment; (2) it is not paid by the drawee; (3) it is protested for non-payment; and (4) he has notice of these facts.

Every person who has accepted a bill becomes liable to pay it according to the tenor of his acceptance.

# Negotiation

A bill is said to be negotiated when it is transferred from one person to another in such a manner as to constitute the transferee the holder of the bill. It may be negotiated by the holder at any time either before or after acceptance in the following manner: (1) In the case of a bearer bill, by delivery. (2) In the case of an order bill, by indorsement followed by delivery, if an order bill is delivered without indorsement, the transferee acquires such title as the transferor had in the bill, and in addition the right to have the indorsement of the transferor.

# Indorsements

An indorsement, in order to operate as negotiation, must be written on the bill itself and signed by the indorser. It must be an indorsement of the entire bill, i.e. if the bill is for £100 it is not possible to indorse it as to £25 to X. and as to £75 to Y. Where there are two or more indorsements on a bill, they are presumed to have been made in the order in which they appear on the bill, but the liability of an indorser is not affected if he inadvertently puts his signature above instead of below the indorsement of the payee, provided that it is the intention of the parties that the indorser shall be liable on his signature. Each indorser is in the nature of a new drawer, so far as those taking the bill after his indorsement are concerned.

Indorsements are of four kinds: (1) in blank; (2) special; (3) conditional; and (4) restrictive.

## 1. Blank indorsement

A blank indorsement is effected by the simple signature of the payee on the back of the bill. If the payee's name is wrongly spelt, he may indorse according to the spelling on the bill, adding, if he thinks fit, his proper signature. A blank indorsement specifies no indorsee and the bill in consequence becomes payable to bearer.

## 2. Special indorsement

A special indorsement is when the payee writes on the back "pay A.B." or "pay A.B. or order," both of these having the same meaning. If a bill has been indorsed in blank, any holder may insert some person's name above the signature and so convert the indorsement into a special indorsement.

## 3. Conditional indorsement

A conditional indorsement is where a condition is attached to the signature, as, for example, where the indorser adds the words "*sans recours,*" which has the effect of negativing his personal liability on the bill. When a bill is so indorsed, the condition may be disregarded by the payer and payment to the indorsee is valid whether the condition has been fulfilled or not.

## 4. Restrictive indorsement

A restrictive indorsement is one which prohibits further negotiation of the bill, as, for example, "pay D. only" or "pay D. for the account of X.", or "pay D. or order for collection." This gives the indorsee the right to receive payment of the bill, but no right to transfer his rights.

A holder transferring a bill after indorsement incurs the liabilities of an indorser as set out below. The transferor of a bearer bill incurs no liability except that he warrants to his immediate transferee for value: (1) that the bill is what it purports to be; (2) that he has a right to transfer it; and (3) that he is not aware of any fact rendering it valueless.

A bill which is negotiable in its origin continues to be negotiable until it has been: (1) restrictively indorsed; or (2) discharged by payment or otherwise.

# Holder in Due Course

The effect of the negotiation of a bill is to give the transferee, if he took the bill bona fide and for value, a good title to the bill notwithstanding any defects in the title of his predecessors. This attribute is the characteristic of negotiability, and it only attaches to a transferee who is **a holder in due course**.

A holder in due course is a holder who has taken a bill: (1) complete and regular on the face of it; (2) before it was overdue; (3) without notice that it had been previously dishonoured, if such was the fact; (4) in good faith and for value; (5) without notice,at the time the bill was negotiated to him, of any defect in the title of the person who negotiated it.

Every holder is prima facie deemed to be a holder in due course. But if in an action on a bill it is established that the acceptance, issue or subsequent negotiation of the bill is affected with fraud, duress or illegality, the burden of proof shifts. This means that to be a holder in due course, the holder must prove that, subsequent to the alleged fraud or illegality, value has in good faith been given for the bill. In this context fraud means common law fraud.

The original payee is not a holder in due course.

The holder of a cheque who had a lien on it is deemed to have taken it for value to the extent of the sum for which he had a lien. Accordingly, provided such a holder satisfies the other conditions of section 29(1). he can be a holder in due course.

A holder, whether for value or not, who derives his title through a holder in due course has all the rights of a holder in due course as regards the acceptor and all parties prior to such holder if he was not a party to any fraud of illegality affecting the bill; such a person may be the drawer of a bill which has been dishonoured and returned to him by way of recourse.

The rights and powers of the holder of a bill are: (1) He may sue on the bill in his own name. (2) Where he is a holder in due course he holds free from any defect of title of prior parties.

Where his title is defective. (1) if he negotiates the bill to a holder in due course, that holder obtains a good title; (2) if he obtains payment, the person who pays him in due course gets a valid discharge.

# Valuable consideration

Valuable consideration is presumed in the case of negotiable instruments, but the presumption may be rebutted. Thus, in the case of a cheque the onus is upon the drawer of it to show that it was not for value. The consideration to support a bill is either: (1) any consideration sufficient to support a simple contract; or (2) any antecedent debt or liability.

The antecedent debt or liability must be the debt or liability of the drawer. A cheque drawn to pay an existing debt owed by the drawer is accordingly drawn for valuable consideration, but a cheque drawn to pay another's debt is not.

Where value has at any time been given for a bill the holder is deemed to be a holder for value as regards the acceptor and all parties to the bill who became parties prior to such time.

Consequently the holder may sue the acceptor and all such parties. Further, there is no requirement that the consideration must have passed directly between one party to the bill and another party to the bill. The requirement of the subsection is met if consideration has been given by a third person.

A payee gives consideration for a negotiable instrument by impliedly agreeing to forgo a debt which is owed to the payee. Even where the debt is owed to others as well as the payee, the payee will still furnish consideration so as to enable the payee to sue the drawer bank where the cheque is dishonoured.

From the description of a holder in due course it follows:

(1) When an overdue bill is negotiated,the holder takes it subject to any defect of title affecting it at its maturity. A bill payable on demand is overdue when it appears on the face of it to have been in circulation for an unreasonable length of time.

(2) When a bill which is not overdue has been dishonoured, any person taking it with notice of dishonour takes it subject to any defect of title attaching to it at the time of dishonour.

# Payment

In order to make the drawer and indorsers liable on a bill it must be presented for payment. But presentment for payment is not necessary to make the acceptor liable when the bill is accepted generally. Presentment for payment must comply with the following rules:

1. Presentment is made by exhibiting the bill to the person from whom payment is demanded. On payment the holder must deliver up the bill to the payer.

2. When the bill is payable on demand, presentment must be made within a reasonable time from issue to make the drawer liable, and within a reasonable time from indorsement to make

the indorser liable. What is a reasonable time depends on the nature of the bills, the usage of trade with regard to similar bills, and the circumstances of the case.

3. When the bill is not payable on demand, presentment must be made on the date payment is due. Three days of grace must be added to the time of payment, but when the last day of grace is a non-business day, the bill is payable on the succeeding business day. Non-business days are: Saturday, Sunday, Good Friday, Christmas Day, a day declared to be a non-business day by an order made under the Banking and Financial Dealings Act 1971, s.2, and a day appointed by Royal proclamation as a public fast or thanksgivings day.

4. Presentment must be made at a reasonable hour on a business day to the payer or some person authorised to make payment on his behalf.

5. Presentment must be made: (1) at the place of payment specified in the bill; (2) if no place is specified, at the address of the drawee or acceptor as given in the bill; (3) if neither of these are present, at the acceptor's place of business, if known, and , if not, at his ordinary residence; (4) in any other case, if presented to the acceptor wherever he can be found or at his last known place of business or residence.

6. Presentment may be made through the post where agreement or usage authorises that course.

7. Delay in making presentation will be excused it if is imputable to circumstances beyond the holder's control, and presentment is effected with reasonable diligence after the cause of the delay has ceased to operate.

**1. Presentment for payment may be dispensed with:**

(1) where, after the exercise of reasonable diligence, it cannot be effected;

(2) where the drawee is a fictitious person;

(3) as regards the drawer, where the drawee is not bound as between himself and the drawer to accept or pay the bill, and the drawer has no reason to believe that the bill would be paid if presented. This occurs when the bill is an accommodation bill;

(4) as regards an indorser, where the bill was accepted or made for the accommodation of that indorser, and he has no reason to expect that the bill would be paid if presented;

(5) by waiver of presentment, express or implied.

If a bill is not paid when it is presented for payment of if, presentment for payment being excused, it is overdue and unpaid, the bill is said to be dishonoured by non-payment and the holder has an immediate right of recourse against the drawer and indorsers. But whether the bill is dishonoured by non-acceptance or by non-payment,the drawer and indorsers cannot be sued until notice or dishonour is given.

## 2. Notice of dishonour

This notice must be given by the holder to the last indorser and to everyone on whom he wishes to impose liability. If he merely gives notice to the last indorser, the latter must give notice to any preceding indorsers whom he may wish to make liable, and they in turn must give notice to their predecessors in title. No particular form of notice is essential. The notice may be verbal or in writing or partly one and partly the other, provided that it is given in terms which sufficiently identify the bill and that it intimates that the bill has been dishonoured by non-acceptance or non-payment. The return of the dishonoured bill is a sufficient notice of dishonour. The notice may be given as soon as the bill is dishonoured and must be given within a reasonable time.

In the absence of special circumstances, a reasonable time is as follows: (1) Where the parties live in the same place, the notice must be given or sent off in time to reach the recipient on the day after the dishonour of the bill. (2) Where the parties live in different places, the notice must be sent off on the day after the dishonour of the bill, if there be a post on a convenient hour on that day, and if there be none, then by the next post thereafter.

Non-business days are excluded. Notice of dishonour which is duly addressed and posted is effective although the letter may be lost or delayed in the post. Further, the notice is effective at the date when it is received, i.e. when it is opened or would be opened in the ordinary course of business. The notice must become effective after the bill is dishonoured. If the notice is received before the dishonour of the bill it is bad, but if it is sent out before dishonour and received after that event it is a good notice.

Delay in giving notice of dishonour will be excused if it is caused by circumstances beyond the control of the giver of the notice and is not imputable to his misconduct or negligence. But when the cause of the delay has ceased to operate, notice must be given with reasonable diligence.

Notice of dishonour is dispensed with:

(1) When after the exercise of reasonable diligence, notice cannot be given or does not reach the person sought to be charged.

(2) By waiver, express or implied.

(3) As regards the drawer, where: (a) the drawer and the drawee are the same person; (b) the drawee is a fictitious person or person not having capacity to contract; (c) the drawer is the person to whom the bill is presented for payment; (d) the drawee is as between himself and the drawer under no obligation to accept or pay the bill; (e) where the drawer has countermanded payment.

(4) As regards the indorser, where: (a) the drawee is a fictitious person or a person not

having capacity to contract and the indorser was aware of the fact at the time he indorsed the bill; (b) where the indorser is the person to whom the bill is presented for payment; (c) where the bill was accepted or made for his accommodation.

If a bill has been dishonoured by non-acceptance and notice of dishonour is given, it is not necessary to give a fresh notice of dishonour on non-payment of the bill, unless in the meantime it has been accepted.

Where a **foreign bill** has been dishonoured by non-acceptance or non-payment, in addition to notice of dishonour the bill must be **protested**. If it is not protested, the drawer and indorsers are discharged. An inland bill need not be protested.

A protest is a document drawn up by a notary, or, if no notary is available at the place of dishonour, by a householder in the presence of two witnesses, certifying that the bill was duly presented for payment and that payment was refused. It must be signed by the notary making it and must specify: (1) the person at whose request the bill is protested; (2) the date and place of protest and the reason for protesting the bill; (3) the demand made and the answer given, if any, or the fact that the drawee or acceptor could not be found.

The protest must also contain a copy of the bill. It must be made at the place where the bill was dishonoured, except that: (1) when the bill is presented through the post office and returned by post dishonoured, it may be protested at the place to which it was returned; (2) when the bill is payable at the place of business or residence of some person other than the drawee and has been dishonoured by non-acceptance, it must be protested for nonpayment at the place where it is expressed to be payable.

Protest may be dispensed with by any circumstances dispensing with notice of dishonour. It must be made promptly, but it is sufficient if the bill has been noted for protest within the specified time, and the formal protest may be extended at any time afterwards as of the date of the noting. A bill may be noted on the day of its dishonour and must be noted not later than the next succeeding business day (Bills of Exchange (Time of Noting) Act 1917); non-business days are excluded.

### 3. Payment for honour

If a bill has been accepted for honour supra protest or contains a reference in case of need, it must at maturity be presented to the acceptor for payment. If the acceptor dishonours it, it must be protested for non-payment and then presented to the acceptor for honour or referee in case of need, The presentment must be made in accordance with the following rules:

(1) Where the address of the acceptor for honour is in the same place as where the bill is protested for non-payment, the bill must be presented not later than the day following its maturity.

(2) Where his address is in some other place, the bill must be forwarded not later than the day following its maturity.

When a bill has been protested for non-payment, any person may intervene and pay it. Such a payment, in order not to operate as a mere voluntary payment, must be attested by a notarial act of honour which may be appended to the protest. The notarial act of honour must declare the intention to pay the bill for honour and for whose honour it is paid. The effect of a payment for honour supra protest being made is to discharge all parties subsequent to the party for whose honour it is paid and to subrogate the payer for honour for the holder. On paying the bill and the notarial expenses incident to the protest, the payer for honour is entitled to receive both the bill and the protest. If the holder of the bill refuses to receive payment supra protest, he loses his right of recourse against any party who would have been discharged by the payment.

# Liability of Parties

No person is liable on a bill whether as drawer, indorser or acceptor who has not signed it, but the fact of his signing it in a trade or assumed name does not absolve him from liability. Where a cheque drawn on a partnership account bears the printed name of the partnership and the signature of one partner, the other partners are likewise liable (Ringham v. Hackett (1980) 124 S.J.201). A signature by procuration operates as notice that the agent has only a limited authority to sign, and therefore the principal will not be bound unless the agent was acting within the scope of his authority. Accordingly, if the payee receives payment of a bill drawn by an agent without authority and knows that it is so drawn, he is liable to refund the amount received to the drawer.

If a person signs a bill and adds words to his signature indicating that he signs for or on behalf of a principal or in a representative character, he is not personally liable on the bill; but the words must clearly show that he signs as agent, a mere description of himself as an agent does not negative his personal liability. When it is doubtful whether the signature is that of a principal or of an agent, the construction most favourable to the validity of the instrument is to be adopted.

The Companies Act 1985 s.349 (4). provides that an officer of a company or another person who signs or authorises to be signed on behalf of a company a bill of exchange, promissory note or cheque in a name other than the proper name of the company, shall be personally liable. Thus, where the directors of the L. & R. Agencies Ltd. signed a cheque for the company by writing "L. & R. Agencies Ltd.," omitting the connecting ampersand, they were held to be personally liable. But the use of the abbreviation "Ltd." or a similar abbreviation for "Limited"—or possibly the use of an ampersand for "and"—does not attract personal liability.

The court will not allow rectification of such an instrument so as to nullify the effect of the statutory provisions.

Further, where the statutory requirements are not complied with, an officer of that company will not be able to rely on the doctrine of estoppel where there is simply no compliance with the statutory provisions.

This statutory provision (Companies Act 1985 s.349 (4)) is entirely consistent with the general law relating to bills of exchange whereby a person who signs a bill of exchange will be personally liable if there is nothing to indicate that the instrument is signed as agent for the company.

A person who accepts a bill engages to pay it according to the tenor of his acceptance.He is precluded from denying to a holder in due course the existence of the drawer, the genuineness of his signature or his capacity to draw the bill, also he is precluded from denying the capacity of the drawer or payee to indorse the bill, but not the genuineness of their indorsements.

The drawer engages that on due presentment the bill shall be accepted and paid according to its tenor, and that if it be dishonoured he will compensate the holder or any indorser who is compelled to pay it, provided that the requisite proceedings on dishonour be taken. He is precluded from denying to a holder in due course the existence of the payee or his capacity to indorse.

The indorser engages that on due presentment the bill shall be accepted and paid according to its tenor, and that if it be dishonoured he will compensate the holder or a subsequent indorser who is compelled to pay it, provided that the requisite proceeding on dishonour be taken. He is precluded from denying to a holder in due course the genuineness of the drawer's signature and all previous indorsements, and to his immediate or a subsequent indorsee that the bill was at the time of his indorsement a valid bill and that he had a good title thereto.

Any person who signs a bill otherwise than as drawer or acceptor incurs the liabilities of an indorser. If a person has signed a bill as drawer, acceptor or indorser without receiving value therefor, he is known as an **accommodation party**. He incurs full liability on the bill to a holder for value, and it is immaterial whether, when the holder took the bill, he knew the party to be an accommodation party or not.

The **measure of damages** on a dishonoured bill is: (1) the amount of the bill; (2) interest from the time of presentment for payment if the bill is payable on demand and from the maturity of the bill in any other case; (3) the expenses of noting, and, when protest is necessary, the expenses of protest.

When the bill is dishonoured abroad, the measure of damages is the amount of the re-exchange with interest until the time of payment. This is the sum for which a sight bill, drawn at the time and place where the drawer or indorser sought to be charged resides, must be drawn to realise at the place of dishonour the amount of the dishonoured bill and the expenses consequent on its dishonour.

A claim on a bill may be met with the defence that acceptance was procured by fraud, duress of for a consideration which has failed, but not with a counterclaim for unliquidated damages.

# Forged Signatures

If any of the signatures on a bill are forged, the signature in question is wholly inoperative and no person, even if acting in good faith, can acquire rights under it.

# Exceptions

1. If a banker pays a bill which is drawn on a banker and payable to order on demand, in good faith and in the ordinary course of business, he is protected from liability for his act if the indorsement has been forged or made without authority.

The person receiving payment will, however, be liable to refund any money received under a forged indorsement to the true owner.

2. If a transferee taking under a forged instrument in a foreign country obtains, by the law of that country, a good title, his title will be treated as good in England.

# Discharges of the Bill

A bill is discharged by —

*1. Payment* in due course by or on behalf of the drawee or acceptor. Payment in due course means payment made at or after the maturity of the bill to the holder in good faith and without notice that his title is defective. Payment by the drawer or an indorser does not discharge the bill, but: (1) where a bill payable to or to the order of a third party is paid by the drawer, the drawer may enforce payment against the acceptor, but may not reissue the bill; (2) where a bill is paid by an indorser, or where a bill payable to the drawer's order is paid by the drawer, the party paying it is remitted to his former rights as regards the acceptor or antecedent parties, and he may, if he thinks fit, strike out his own and subsequent indorsements and again negotiate the bill.

When an accommodation bill is paid by the party accommodated the bill is discharged.

*2. The acceptor* of the bill becoming the holder of it at or after maturity in his own right. (s.61).

*3. Waiver*, where the holder renounces his rights under it. Renunciation must be in writing, unless the bill is delivered up to the acceptor.

*4. Cancellation*, where it is done intentionally by the holder or his agent and the cancellation is apparent.

*5. Alteration* of the bill in a material particular without the assent of all parties liable on it. The following alterations are material; the date, the sum payable, the time of payment, the place of payment, and, where the bill has been accepted generally, the addition of a place of payment without the acceptor's assent. It is also material to alter an inland bill into a foreign bill. The alteration of the number on a banknote is a material alteration, and avoids the note even in the hands of an innocent holder. But if the alteration is made accidentally, the note is not avoided.

The effect of a material alteration is only to discharge those who became parties prior to the alteration. The person who made the alteration and all subsequent indorsers are bound by the bill as altered.

If the alteration is not apparent and the bill is in the hands of a holder in due course, the holder may enforce the bill as if it had never been altered.

An alteration is apparent if it is of such a kind that it would be noticed by an intending holder scrutinising the document which he intends to take with reasonable care (Woollatt v. Stanley (1928) 138L.T.620).

# Lost Bill

If a bill is lost before it is overdue, the holder may apply to the drawer to give him another bill of the same tenor, and the drawer is bound to do so on receiving from the holder security indemnifying the drawer against loss.

# Bill in a Set

When a bill is drawn in a set, i.e. in duplicate or triplicate, then if each part of the set is numbered and contains a reference to the others, the whole of the parts only constitute one bill. The acceptor should only accept one part, and if he accepts more than one and the different parts get into the hands of different holders in due course, he is liable on each part. On payment, he should require the part bearing his signature to be delivered up to him, because, if he does not do so, he will be liable on it if it is outstanding in the hands of a holder in due course. If the holder indorses two or more parts to different persons, he is liable on each. Except in the cases just mentioned, payment of one part discharges the whole bill.

# Conflict of Laws

The form of a bill is determined by the law of the place of issue, but if a bill issued out of the United Kingdom conforms as regards its form to the law of the United Kingdom, it is valid as between all persons who negotiate, hold or become parties to it in the United Kingdom.

The form and the interpretation of the acceptance, indorsement or acceptance supra protest and the interpretation of the drawing of a bill is according to the law of the country where it took place.

But if an inland bill is indorsed abroad, the interpretation of the indorsement is according to the law of the United Kingdom. The duty of the holder with respect to presentment for acceptance or payment is determined by the law of the place where it is to be done. The duty of the holder with regard to protest of notice of dishonour is determined by the law of the country where the bill was dishonoured. When a bill is drawn in one country and is payable in another, the time when it is payable is determined by the law of the place of payment.

Where a bill is expressed in foreign currency, the holder, when suing on it, has a choice: he may either sue in sterling, converting, in the absence of some express stipulation, the foreign currency at the date when the bill matured, or he may sue in the foreign currency; in the latter case the English court will give judgment in the foreign currency and the judgment debt will be converted into sterling either at the date of payment of the judgment or at the date of execution.

## New Words

| | | |
|---|---|---|
| 1. | bill of exchange | 匯票 |
| 2. | negotiable instrument | 流通票據 |
| 3. | indorsement *n.* | 背書 |
| 4. | order instrument | 指示票據；記名票據 |
| 5. | bill of sale | 銷售證；賣契；（動產）抵押證券 |
| 6. | bona fide holder | 誠實持票人 |
| 7. | predecessor *n.* | 前輩 |
| 8. | postal orders and dock warrants | 郵政匯票和倉單 |

| | | |
|---|---|---|
| **9.** | drawer *n.* | 出票人；發票人；開票人 |
| **10.** | drawee *n.* | 付款人；受票人 |
| **11.** | payee *n.* | 受款人 |
| **12.** | receipt form | 收條 |
| **13.** | order bill | 指示票據；記名票據 |
| **14.** | inland bill | 國內票據 |
| **15.** | foreign bill | 外國票據 |
| **16.** | incomplete bill | 不完整票據 |
| **17.** | time bill | 遠期匯票 |
| **18.** | sight bill | 即期匯票 |
| **19.** | antecedent parties | 前當事人 |
| **20.** | presentment *n.* | 提示 |
| **21.** | acceptance *n.* | 承兌 |
| **22.** | general acceptance | 普通承兌 |
| **23.** | qualified acceptance | 附有限制條件的承兌；非單純承兌 |
| **24.** | dishonour *v.* | 拒付 |
| **25.** | holder in due course | 正當執票人；票據合法持有人 |
| **26.** | presentment for acceptance | 提示承兌 |
| **27.** | acceptance for honour | 參加承兌 |
| **28.** | the referee in case of need | 預備支付人；需要時的支付人 |
| **29.** | supra protest | 參與承兌；第三者代為承兌 |
| **30.** | negotiation *n.* | 議付 |
| **31.** | inadvertently *adv.* | 疏忽地；出於無心地 |
| **32.** | blank indorsement | 空白背書 |
| **33.** | special indorsement | 特別背書；完全背書 |
| **34.** | conditional indorse-ment | 附有條件的背書 |
| **35.** | sans recours | （拉）無追索權 |
| **36.** | restrictive indorsement | 限制性背書 |
| **37.** | attribute *n.* | 屬性；特徵 |
| **38.** | delivery up | 讓給；交給 |
| **39.** | accommodation bill | 通融匯票 |
| **40.** | accommodation party | 通融當事人 |
| **41.** | intimate *v.* | 暗示；提示；通知 |
| **42.** | vitiate *v.* | 使……無效；使……有缺陷 |

**43.** countermand *v.*            召回；取消

**44.** attest *v.*                 證明

**45.** append *v.*               附加

**46.** subrogate *v.*             代位行使；代替

**47.** procuration *n.*           代理（權）；委任；賦予權力

**48.** churchwarden *n.*        教會執事

**49.** ampersand              表示「and」的符號：&

**50.** rectification *n.*         糾正；改正

**51.** engage *v.*               保證

**52.** unliquidated damages    未確定的損害賠償；等待法庭裁定的損害賠償

**53.** renounce *v.*             放棄

**54.** scrutinise *v.*            仔細檢查

**55.** judgment debt           判決確定債務

**56.** requisite *a.*             必要的；必不可少的

**57.** protest *n.*               （匯票的）拒付；拒付證書

## ☘ New Phrases and Idiomatic Expressions

**1.** payable to bearer         應付持票人

**2.** pay cash or order        付現金或其指定人

**3.** payable to or to the order of        對某人或其指定的人付款

**4.** by virtue of             憑藉；依靠；由於……

**5.** on one's account        為某人的緣故；為某人的利益

**6.** to deliver up            交給；交出；讓給

**7.** to dispense with        免除

**8.** to have a right of recourse against sb.      對某人行使追索權

**9.** in liquidation           正在被清理（清算、清償……）

**10.** on balance of probabilities    可能差額的情況下

**11.** to make inquiries       作詢問

**12.** to absolve sb. from sth.    免除某人或開脫某人的某事

**13.** to be precluded from doing sth.      阻止某人做某件事

**14.** under no liability       沒有義務；沒有責任

**15.** in duplicate            一式兩份

| 16. in triplicate | 一式三份 |
| 17. to get into the hands of sb. | 落入某人之手 |
| 18. to be bound to do sth. | 有義務做某事 |

## Notes

**1**. A bona fide holder for value takes free from any defect in the title of his predecessors.
善意而又付對價的持有人不受前手所有權缺陷的影響。

**2**. payable to bearer：交付來人。
若匯票上載有這樣的字樣，該匯票爲無記名匯票。英美法承認這樣的匯票。

**3**. pay cash or order：付現金或指定人。
載有這樣字樣的票據不被英國法承認爲匯票。

**4**. a holder in due course
正當執（持）票人；合法持有人。

**5**. the referee in case of need
預備支付人。
指在匯票上加一個人的名字，當匯票被拒付時，執票人可求助於他（她）來給付。

**6**. three days of grace
三天的寬限期；三天的優惠日。
英國票據法規定，非即期匯票的付款期可另加三天，如寬限期最後一天爲非營業日，還可順延到隨後的一個營業日。

**7**. as of the date of
這是法律英語用法。「as of」表示在……（某一天），「on or at」。

##  Exercises

### I. Answer the following questions:

**1**. What characteristics does a negotiable instrument have?

**2**. What are the common examples of negotiable instruments?

**3**. What is a bill of exchange?

**4**. In what cases must a bill be presented for acceptance?

**5**. What are the rules regarding presentment for acceptance?

**6**. When will a bill be treated as dishonoured by non-acceptance?

**7**. What is the legal effect of accepting a bill for honour?

**8.** What is indorsement? How many kinds of indorsements do you know?

**9.** What are the rights and powers of the holder of a bill?

**10.**What rules must be complied with when presenting for payment?

**11.**When will a bill be discharged?

## II. Translate the following Chinese passages into English:

**1.**匯票是一個人向另一個人開立的，要求對方於見票時或於一定時間內對某人或其指定人或持票人支付一定金額的無條件書面支付命令。

**2.**匯票當事人有三：(1)給予支付命令的人：發票人；(2)接受支付命令的人：付款人；(3)接受付款的人：受款人。

**3.**英國票據法規定，當匯票不是即期匯票時，可給付款時間加三天的寬限期。當寬限期最後一天爲非營業日時，匯票可在隨後的那個營業日支付。

**4.**在下列情況下，可能毋需提示付款：

(1)當經過勤奮努力，不可能提示付款；

(2)當付款人是虛擬人時；

(3)當付款人無義務承兌支付匯票，出票人無理由相信提示可付款時；

(4)當以明示或默示方式放棄提示時；

(5)當背書人無理由相信，提示可使匯票照付時。

## III. Indicate whether each of the following statements is true of false by writing "T" or "F" in the space provided.

**1.** The bill must be an order, not just a request.

**2.** Postal orders, share certificates, bills of lading and dock warrants are also negotiable instruments.

**3.** Normally, there are three parties to a bill: (a) the drawer; (b) the drawee; and (c) the payee.

**4.** Acceptance of a bill is defined as the signification by the drawee of his assent to the order of the drawer.

**5.** Not all holders in prima facie are deemed to be holders in due course according to Bills of Exchange Act 1882.

**6.** Presentment for payment must comply with certain rules.

**7.** A bill can be dishonoured by non-acceptance of non-payment.

**8.** The form and the interpretation of the acceptance, indorsement or acceptance supra protest and the interpretation of the drawing of a bill is according to the law of the country where it took place.

# 第二十九課 Lesson 29 支票和本票 Cheques and Promissory Notes

**A cheque is**

— a bill of exchange;

— drawn on a banker;

— payable on demand.

It therefore follows that the law relating to bills of exchange set out in the preceding lesson applies equally to cheques.

A cheque form was filled up "Pay cash or order", the word "cash" being in writing and "or order" printed. *Held*, not a cheque, because it was not payable to a specified person or to bearer but a direction to pay cash to bearer, the printed "or order" being neglected in favour of the written word "cash": *North and South Insurance Co. v. National Provincial Bank* [1936] 1K. B. 328.

A bank is not bound to honour an undated cheque. The holder of such a cheque is authorised by section 20 to fill in the date, but he must do so within a reasonable time (*Griffiths v. Dalton* [1940]2. K. B. 264).

A cheque may be postdated. A cheque is not usually accepted. Marking or certification is not an acceptance.

A cheque drawn on the B. bank on June 13, postdated to June 20, was certified by the manager "marked good for payment on 20.6.39." The P. bank became holders in due course and on June 20 presented the cheque for payment, which was refused owing to the state of the drawer's account. Held, (1) the certification was not an acceptance of the cheque; (2) the manager had no authority to certify postdated cheques; (3) the B. bank was not liable: *Bank of Baroda Ltd. v. Punjab National Bank*[1944]A. C. 176.

The holder of a cheque must present it for payment within a reasonable time of its issue, and failure to do this will discharge the drawer to the extent of any damage he may suffer from the delay. Damage will only be suffered when the bank on which the cheque is drawn is unable, for any reason, to honour the cheque.

In such a case the holder of the cheque is a creditor of the bank to the extent of the discharge of the drawer.

If a bank wrongly dishonours a cheque, it is liable to pay damages to its customer, but only nominal damages can be recovered by persons who are not traders.

The relationship of banker and customer is that of debtor and creditor, with the modification that the banker is only liable to repay the customer on payment being demanded, while the ordinary debtor is under an obligation to pay without any demand being made. The consequence of this is that a banker can not successfully plead the bar provided by the Limitation Act to any action for money standing to a customer's credit, until six years from a demand of payment has elapsed. If, however, the account has not been operated upon for a number of years, payment may be presumed.

Where a deposit account is kept between a customer and a banker, there is not a new contract every time money is paid in.

An unindorsed cheque—like an indorsed one—which appears to have been paid by the banker on whom it is drawn is evidence of the receipt by the payee of the sum payable by the cheque (Cheques Act 1957, s. 3).

The authority of a banker to pay a cheque is terminated by:

1. Countermand of payment. An oral countermand is sufficient, but whether oral or written it must actually reach the banker.

But where a bank, under a mistake of fact, pays a cheque drawn on it by a custome, it is prima facie entitled to recover payment from the payee if it has acted without mandate (e.g. if it has overlooked a notice of countermand given by the customer) unless the payee has changed his position in good faith or is deemed in law to have done so.

2. Notice of the customer's death.

3. Notice of a winding up petition against the drawer.

4. Notice of the presentation of a bankruptcy petition against the drawer.

# Crossed Cheques

A cheque is a crossed cheque when two parallel lines are drawn across it; in addition to the parallel lines, words may be written across the cheque.

Crossings are of four kinds: 1. General: consisting only of the parallel lines, or with the addition of the words "and company." 2. Special: when the name of a banker is written between the parallel lines. 3, Not negotiable: when these words are written across the cheque, either with or without the name of a banker. 4. A / c payee: when these words are written across the cheque, whether in addition to the other crossings or not.

The use of such words on a cheque imposes no duties upon a banker to its customer.

The crossing is a material part of the cheque and must not be obliterated or added to or altered except in the following cases:

1. Where a cheque is uncrossed, the holder may cross it generally or specially.

2. Where a cheque is crossed generally, the holder may cross it specially or add the words "not negotiable."

3. A banker to whom a cheque is crossed specially may cross it specially to another banker for collection.

4. Where a cheque is sent to a banker for collection he may cross it specially to himself.

When a cheque is crossed it can only be paid to a banker, and if crossed specially, only to the banker named in the crossing. If the banker on whom the cheque is drawn pays it otherwise than in accordance with the crossing, he is liable to the true owner of the cheque for any loss he may sustain owing to the payment. But if the cheque does not appear to be crossed or to have had a crossing which has been obliterated or to have been added to or altered, and the banker pays the cheque in good faith and without negligence, he does not incur any liability.

When a cheque is crossed "not negotiable", the person taking it does not have and is not capable of giving a better title to the cheque than that which the person from whom he took it had (s.81). Where a non-negotiable cheque is given for an illegal consideration, e.g. in exchange for tokens to be used at a casino for gaming, a person to whom the cheque is indorsed has no better title than the person who took the cheque.

The words "account payee" on a cheque are a direction to the bankers collecting payment that the proceeds when collected are to be applied to the credit of the account of the payee designated on the face of the cheque. If, therefore, the bankers credit the proceeds to different account, they are prima facie guilty of negligence and will be liable to the true owner for the amount of the cheque. This prima facie liability can be displaced on their proving that they made proper inquiry as to the authority of the person, to whose account the cheque was credited, to receive the amount.

If a bank collects the cheque on behalf of another bank, they are not bound to see that the other bank credits the payee with the amount of the cheque.

The duty of the collecting banker must be carefully distinguished from that of the paying banker.

A cheque crossed "account payee" is still negotiable (*National Bank v. silke* [1891]1Q. B. 435). but a bill payable to "payee only "is not negotiable.

# Provisions Protecting Bankers

The Bills of Exchange Act 1882 and the Cheques Act 1957 afford bankers special protection from liability when paying a crossed cheque to a banker; or receiving payment of a crossed cheque for a customer; or paying a cheque that is not indorsed. However, no definition is given of a banker save that it *includes* a body of persons, whether incorporated or not, *who carry on the business of banking*.

Characteristics which are usually found in bankers today were identified in *United Dominions Trust Ltd. v. Kirkwood*[1966]2 Q. B. 431, as follows : (1) they accept money from, and collect cheques for, their customers and place them to their credit; (2) they honour cheques or orders drawn on them by their customers when presented for payment and debit their customers accordingly; and (3) they keep current accounts, or something of that nature, in their books in which the credits and debits are entered.

A banker, but not other persons, is protected:

1. If, when there is a forged indorsement, the banker pays: (1) a bill drawn on him payable to order on demand ; (2) in good faith and in the ordinary course of business, he is deemed to have paid the bill in due course.

A banker can act negligently although he is acting in the ordinary course of business. "The common aphorism that a banker is under a duty to know his customer's signature is in fact incorrect even as between the banker and his customer. The principle is simply that a banker cannot debit his customer's account on the basis of a forged signature, since he has in that event no mandate from the customer for doing so". Where a banker, without acting negligently, pays a cheque on which the signature of his customer (the drawer) is forged, he can recover the amount paid from the collecting bank and the payee.

Further, if, in the absence of an indorsement or where there is an irregular indorsement, a banker pays: (1) a cheque drawn on him; (2) in good faith and in the ordinary course of business, he is protected (Cheques Act 1957, s.1).

2. If, *when a cheque is crossed,* the banker pays : (1) the cheque drawn on him ; (2) in good faith and without negligence; (3) if crossed generally, to a banker, and, if crossed specially, to the banker to whom it is crossed, he is placed in the same position as if he had paid the true owner.

The drawer is also protected if the cheque has come into the hands of the payee.

3. A banker who receives an unindorsed cheque "for collection" and has given value for, or has a lien on it, has the same rights as if the cheque had been indorsed to him in blank (Cheques Act 1957, s.2).

Section 2 applies even if the cheque is collected not for the payee's account but for another account, but the banker can successfully sue the drawer of an unindorsed cheque only if he gave value for the cheque or had a lien on it; otherwise the cheque must be indorsed to him.

4. If, when a customer has no title or a defective title to a cheque, the banker receives

payment of a cheque *whether crossed or not crossed*: (1) for the customer ; (2) in good faith and without negligence, the banker does not incur any liability by reason only of having received payment (Cheques Act 1957, s.4).

This section (which takes the place of the repealed s. 82 of the Act of 1882) applies to cheques and to any document issued by a customer of a banker which, though not a bill of exchange, is intended to enable a person to obtain payment from that banker of the sum mentioned in the document. It therefore applies, *inter alia*, to bankers' drafts, dividend warrants and cheques payable "cash or order." Further, where an agent having a customer's ostensible authority to sign and issue an instrument, the instrument is a document "issued by a customer" even where the agent signs it and puts it into circulation in fraud of his principal.

A banker is not protected if a cheque ceases to be a cheque by reason of a material alteration.

A person becomes a customer of a banker when he goes to the banker with money or a cheque and asks to have an account opened, and the banker accepts the money or cheque and agrees to open an account. The duration of the relationship is immaterial. But mere casual acts of service, such as cashing a cheque for a friend of a customer, do not create the relationship of banker and customer.

A bank may be a "customer" of another bank if it has a drawing account with it.

What amounts to negligence depends on the facts of the particular case and the practice of bankers. In *Marfani & Co. v. Midland Bank*[1968]1W. L. R. 956, Nield J. formulated four principles which should guide a court in such cases, namely :

1. The standard of care required of bankers is that to be derived from the ordinary practice of careful bankers.

2. The standard of care required of bankers does not include the duty to subject an account to microscopic examination.

3. In considering whether a bank has been negligent in receiving a cheque and collecting the money for it, a court has to scrutinise the circumstances in which a bank accepts a new customer and opens a new account.

4. The onus is on the defendant to show that he acted without negligence.

The principles that should guide a court in deciding whether a bank was negligent were further formulated by Hutchinson J. in *Thackwell v. Barclays Bank Plc*[1986]1All E. R. 676.

1. It was reaffirmed that in order for a bank to establish a defence under Section 4 Cheques Act 1957, the bank must show that it received payment of the cheque in good faith and without negligence. The onus is on the bank to establish this.

2. In deciding whether a bank has acted negligently, there were two tests that have been applied by the courts.

3. The first test is that based on the ordinary practice of banks. The court must look at the transaction and decide whether the circumstances surrounding the paying in of the cheque in question would have aroused suspicion in a banker's mind so that the bank in question would have made further inquiry. The test is an objective one.

4. Furthermore, it is no defence to a bank, which has been guilty of negligence in the collection of a cheque, to show that had they made further inquiries, then a reassuring answer would have been given to them.

5. In this particular case the court applied the first test.

6. The second test is that based on the practice of banks to protect themselves and others against fraud. A bank should act in a way which furthers this aim.

It is negligence:

(1) To open an account without inquiring as to the identity and circumstances of the customer (*Ladbroke & Co. v. Todd* (1914) 111L. T. 43). Among the circumstances to be inquired into are the nature of the customer's employment and the name of his employer.

(2) To receive payment of a cheque for a customer, when the cheque is drawn in favour of the customer's employer, without inquiring as to his title to the cheque.

If a cheque payable to a customer in his official capacity is paid into the customer's private account, the bank should make similar inquiries. The same applies if the instrument bears a clear indication that it is payable to the customer as agent of another person.

(3) To receive payment of a cheque for a customer, when the cheque is drawn by the customer's employer in favour of a third party of bearer, without inquiring as to the customer's title to the cheque.

(4) To receive payment of a cheque for a customer, when the cheque is drawn by the customer as agent for a third party in his own favour, without inquiring as to the customer's title to the cheque.

(5) Where the circumstances would put a reasonable banker on enquiry and the banker does not make any inquiries.

(6) Not to notice the account of the customer from time to time and consider whether it is a proper or a suspicious one.

If an open cheque for a large amount payable to bearer is presented to a bank for payment over the counter, it is not negligence for the bank to pay the cheque without making inquiries "in the absence of very special circumstances of suspicion, such as presentation by a tramp, or a postman or an office boy "(*per* Wright J.).

If a banker pays a cheque on the forged signature of his customer he cannot debit his customer with that amount. Similarly, if the amount of a cheque properly drawn by the customer has been fraudulently increased and the banker pays the altered amount, he can only debit his customer with the amount of the cheque as originally drawn. But the customer owes a duty to his banker in drawing a cheque to take reasonable and ordinary precautions against forgery, and, if as the natural and direct result of the neglect of these precautions, the amount of the cheque is increased by forgery, the customer must bear the loss as between himself and the banker.

It is not normally a breach of duty on the part of the customer to use reasonable care in leaving a space between the name of the payee and the words "or order "but if the customer abbreviates the name of the payee in a manner which makes forgery more easily possible, that may be contributory negligence (*Lumsden & Co. v. London Trustee Savings Bank* [1971]1Lloyd's Rep. 114).

There is no corresponding duty to be careful imposed on the drawer or acceptor of a bill of exchange.

The customer is under a duty to disclose to the bank any forgeries which he has discovered.

Whilst a customer owes its bank a duty to take care in the drawing of cheques, and a duty to inform the bank of any forgeries of which the customer knows, the customer does not owe a duty to its bank to take precautions in the carrying on of its business so as to prevent its employees committing fraud in relation to the cheques of the company.

In modern practice banks use computers to sort out cheques on which the branch and account number of the customers are printed in magnetic ink. Where a customer alters the printed branch to another one by ordinary ink (which the computer cannot read) and then countermands the cheque but the computer dispatches the cheque to the original branch which pays it, the bank might be liable.

# Promissory Notes

Promissory note is
— an unconditional promise in writing
— made by one person to another
— signed by the maker
— engaging to pay
— on demand or at a fixed or determinable future time
— a sum certain in money
— to or to the order of a specified person or to bearer.
As to certainty of time of payment, it has been held that a document expressing a sum to be

payable "on or before"a stated date introduced uncertainty and so was not a promissory note.

The following is one form of promissory note:

Newcastle,

*June* 1, 1991

I promise to pay on demand A B or order the sum of £100 for value received.

XY.

An instrument, which is void as a bill of exchange because it is not addressed to anyone, may nevertheless be valid as a promissory note.

An instrument in the form of a note payable to the maker's order is not a note unless and until it is indorsed by the maker. A note which is made and payable within the British Isles is an inland note: any other note is a foreign note. A promissory note is not complete until it has been delivered to the payee or bearer.

A note may be made by two or more makers, who may be liable on it jointly or severally. If it is payable on demand it need not be presented for payment within a reasonable time to render the maker liable; but it must be presented within a reasonable time after indorsement to render the indorser liable.

Even if it appears that a reasonable time has elapsed since the note was issued, the holder is not, on that account, affected by defects of title of which he had no notice.

Presentment for payment is not necessary to render the maker liable, but it is necessary to make the indorser liable. If, however a note is, in the body of it, made payable at a particular place, it must be presented for payment at that place in order to render the maker liable.

The maker of a promissory note by making it:

(1) engages that he will pay it according to its tenor;

(2) is precluded from denying to a holder in due course the existence of the payee and his then capacity to indorse (s. 88).

The law as to bills of exchange applies to promissory notes, the maker of a note corresponding with the acceptor of a bill, and the first indorser of a note corresponding with the drawer of an accepted bill payable to the drawer's order. When a foreign note is dishonoured, protest is unnecessary.

## New Words

| | | |
|---|---|---|
| 1. | undated *a.* | 無日期的；未填日期的 |
| 2. | postdated *a.* | 填遲日期的 |
| 3. | crossed cheques | 劃線支票 |
| 4. | deposit receipt | 存單；存款收據 |
| 5. | deposit account | 存款帳戶 |
| 6. | petition *n.* | 請求；申請 |
| 7. | humiliation *n.* | 丟臉、羞辱 |
| 8. | general crossing | 普通劃線 |
| 9. | special crossing | 記名劃線 |
| 10. | not negotiable crossing | 不能轉讓劃線 |
| 11. | A / c payee crossing | 帳戶受款人劃線 |
| 12. | obliterate *v.* | 塗抹 |
| 13. | banker *n.* | 銀行；銀行家 |
| 14. | casino *n.* | 賭場 |
| 15. | aphorism *n.* | 格言；警句 |
| 16. | National Westminster Bank | 國民西敏寺銀行 |
| 17. | undetectable *a.* | 不能被發現的 |
| 18. | drawing account | 提款帳戶 |
| 19. | further *v.* | 促進；推動 |
| 20. | private account | 私人帳戶 |
| 21. | contributory negligence | 被害人本身的過失；與有過失 |
| 22. | take-over *n.* | 兼併 |
| 23. | overdraft *n.* | 透支 |
| 24. | tramp *n.* | 流浪乞丐 |
| 25. | computer banking | 電腦銀行（業務） |
| 26. | statutory defence | 法定抗辯 |
| 27. | microscopic *a.* | 顯微鏡的 |
| 28. | magnetic *a.* | 有磁性的 |

## New Phrases and Idiomatic Expressions

| | | |
|---|---|---|
| 1. | having regard to | 注意 |
| 2. | to bank with a banker | 與銀行發生業務關係；在銀行開戶 |
| 3. | to have a lien on | 對……有留置權 |

| | | |
|---|---|---|
| **4.** | to have a drawing account with a bank | 在銀行有提款帳戶 |
| **5.** | to pay in | 存款 |
| **6.** | to pay out | 付出 |
| **7.** | to open an account with a bank | 在銀行開帳戶 |
| **8.** | to know nothing of | 對……一無所知 |
| **9.** | to leave the employment of | 停止被……聘用 |
| **10.** | to pay for | 償還 |
| **11.** | to inquire into | 對……進行詢問或調查 |
| **12.** | through the clearing house | 通過票據交換所 |
| **13.** | to take reasonable and ordinary precautions against | 採取合理的、通常的預防……的措施 |
| **14.** | to sort out | 整理；挑出 |
| **15.** | to clear the cheque to | 為……對支票進行結算 |
| **16.** | in full | 充分地；完全地 |
| **17.** | to give a mortgage on some property to sb. | 向某人提供財產抵押貸款 |
| **18.** | to correspond with | 與……一致 |

## Notes

**1**. cheque：支票，這是英國英語，美國用check。

**2**. ...there being on such thing as ... there is no such a thing as ...

**3**. A /c payee: account payee：帳戶受款人。

**4**. Midland Bank：米特蘭銀行。

該行於1993年被匯豐銀行兼併，但原名未變。該銀行是英國四大商業銀行之一，其他三個為 National Westminster Bank, Barclays Bank and Lloyds Bank，即國民西敏寺銀行，巴克萊銀行和勞埃德銀行，其中國民西敏寺銀行實力最強。

**5**. British Isles：不列顛群島。

主要指不列顛和愛爾蘭（Ireland and Britain）兩大島以及附近的許多小島。

It should not be confused with the following:

(1) Great Britain — the larger of the above two islands, and it is divided into three parts: Scotland, Wales and England;

(2) The United Kingdom — that part of the British Isles ruled over by the Queen. It consists of Scotland, Wales and England, also about one sixth of Ireland, the Northern part.

The Full title of the U.K. is: The United Kingdom of Great Britain and Norther Ireland.

**Exercises**

## I. Answer the following questions:

**1.** What is a cheque?

**2.** Is a bank liable to pay damages to its customer when it wrongly dishonours a cheque?

**3.** In what circumstances can a bank's authority to pay a cheque be terminated?

**4.** What is a crossed cheque? In what cases can it be obliterated or added to or altered?

**5.** What are the provisions protecting bankers?

**6.** What are the four principles formulated by the court in deciding whether a bank was negligent?

**7.** What duties does a customer owe to his bank?

**8.** What is a promissory note? In what way is it different from a cheque?

## II. Translate the following Chinese passages into English:

**1.** 英國票據法認爲支票是以銀行爲付款人的即期支付的匯票，因此它受票據法的管轄。

**2.** 如果銀行錯誤地拒付支票，它必須向其客戶支付損害賠償金，但對非貿易者只支付名義賠償金。

**3.** 如果發票人、背書人或執票人在支票正面劃兩道平行橫線，這樣的支票即稱之爲劃線支票。劃線支票只能向銀行支付，如果是記名劃線只能向兩邊劃線所指定的銀行支付。

**4.** 本票是發票人約定於見票時或於一定日期，向受款人或其指定人支付一定金額的無條件書面允諾。

## III. Indicate whether each of the following statements is true or false by writing "T" or "F" in the space provided:

**1.** A bank is bound to honour an undated cheque.

**2.** A cheque may be postdated.

**3.** A holder of a cheque must present it for payment within a reasonable time of its issue and failure to do this will discharge the drawer to the extent of any damages he may suffer from the delay.

**4.** When a cheque is crossed it can only be paid to a banker, and if crossed specially, only to the banker named in the crossing.

**5.** A banker is protected oven if a cheque ceases to be a cheque by reason of a material alteration.

**6.** To open an account without inquiring as to the identity and circumstances of the customer constitutes n egligence of a banker.

**7.** If a banker pays a cheque on the forged signature of his customer he can debit his cheque with that amount.

**8.** A promissory note which is made and payable within the British Isles is an inland note; any other note is a foreign note.

# 德國銀行法
# German Banking Law

## General

The general law on the regulation and supervision of banks is set out in the Banking Act of July 10, 1961. The Act came into effect on January 1, 1962 and superseded the Banking Act of 1934, which with some amendments had been in effect until then.

The introduction of general regulation and official supervision of banks was a consequence of the break-down of the German banking system in the banking crisis of 1931. In 1931 and 1932 a number of Emergency Regulations (*Notverordnungen*) of the President of the Reich set up for the first time a system of governmental supervision of banks on a general scale which was consolidated by the Banking Act of 1934. Prior to 1931 only sketchy legislation had existed in this field: the Mortgage Bank Act of 1899 provided for special governmental supervision of these specialized institutions and the Act Regarding Custody and Deposit Business of 1925, which had been planned as a temporary measure and expired at the end of 1929, introduced a licencing system for banks organized as corporations carrying out securities custody and deposit business and established certain reporting duties, but did not provide for a general system of governmental supervision.

The Banking Act of 1961 remained essentially unaltered for fifteen years. The first substantial changes were brought about by the Second Act to Amend the Banking Act, which came into effect on May 1, 1976, and incorporated various attempts to remedy certain weaknesses in the banking system which had become apparent in connection with the collapse in the immediately preceding years of several small and medium-sized banks, including *I. D. Herstatt KGaA*. The 1976 amendments had been preceded or were accompanied by other, non-legislative, measures to improve the security of the banking system.

The second overhaul of the Banking Act came about by the Third Act to Amend the Banking Act which came into effect in part on January 1, 1985 and as to the remainder on July 1, 1985. Legislative action which led to the 1985 amendments was expedited by the financial difficulties of the private bank *Schroeder, Munchmeyer, Hengst & Co.* (SMH-Bank) in the autumn of 1983, a case which had not only revealed disregard of the existing regulatory system, but also shortcomings of that system which long-pending legislative proposals were designed to cure and which resulted in a remarkable rescue operation by the private banking community in concert with the authorities.

The 1985 amendments introduced far-reaching changes to the regulatory system. Most importantly, they prescribed consolidation of groups of banks, including foreign subsidiaries, both for purposes of equity-lending ratios and large-scale credit ratios, reduced the ceiling for large-scale credits from 75 percent to 50 percent of the equity capital, supplemented the provisions on equity capital by providing stricter requirements for silent capital contributions and by recognizing within limits participation capital as equity capital, narrowed the possibilities of investing in fixed assets, provided new rules designed to facilitate and improve international cooperation in the field of banking supervision and, among many further changes, introduced the right of the Banking Supervisory Authority to refuse the issuance of a banking licence to branches of foreign banks if reciprocity is not guaranteed by treaty.

Other recent and important changes affecting bank operations were made entirely outside of the Banking Act and have become known as "*Restliberalisierung*" of the DM capital markets. In December 1984, parliament abolished the coupon tax, i.e., the withholding tax on interest income derived by non-residents from bonds of German issuers, that had been introduced in 1965. Effective as of May 1, 1985, the committee of leading German banks which controlled the calendar and volume of DM-denominated bond issues of non-German issuers and which had been establi" shed in 1968 by a gentlemen's agreement between the Federal Bank and these banks, was disbanded. Simultaneously, German incorporated banking subsidiaries (but not German branches) of foreign banks were allowed to act as lead managers of DM-denominated bond issues of non-German issuers. In addition, the permitted types of DM bonds were expanded to include floating rate, zero-coupon, and dual currency bonds as well as bonds issued in conjunction with the conclusion of interest rate and currency swaps. Moreover, with effect from May 1, 1986, German banks, including German branches of foreign banks, were permitted to issue DM-denominated certificates of deposit. As of the same date, the minimum reserve regulations were amended so as to provide in effect that the banks' liabilities to nonresidents denominated in foreign currencies are largely exempt from minimum reserve requirements by virtue of an offsetting arrangement. Finally, in June, 1986 the Federal Bank invited 16 banking subsidiaries of foreign banks to join the Federal Bond Consortium responsible for the underwriting of bond issues of the Federal Republic, the Federal Post Office and the Federal Railways. Most of these changes constitute simply a change of central bank policy and did not require a change of, and are not laid down in, any provision of law. The policy change was prompted by the Federal Bank's desire to further the use of the Deutsche Mark as an international investment currency and to help to stimulate the growth of Germany as an international financial center.

# Enterprises Subject to Regulation and Supervision

The Banking Act subjects to regulation and official supervision all enterprises which fall within the definition of "banking institutions" (*Kreditinstitute*) as set forth in §1 (1) Banking Act, unless they are specifically exempted under §2 Banking Act.

## 1. The definition of "banking institutions"

§1 (1) Banking Act defines the term "banking institutions" as meaning enterprises engaged in "banking business" (*Bankges-chafte*) if the scope of such banking business necessitates a commercially organized business operation.

"Banking Business" means any of the following activities: (1) the acceptance of monies from others as deposits, irrespective of whether interest is paid thereon (deposit business; *Einlagengeschafe*); (2) the granting of loans and acceptance credits (credit business; Kreditgeschft); (3) the purchase of bills of exchange, promissory notes and cheques (discount business; *Diskontgeschiift*); (4) the purchase and sale of securities for the account of others (securities business; *Effektengeschaft*); (5) the custody and administration of securities for the account of others (custody business; *Depotgeschaft*); (6) the transactions designated in §1 of the Investment Companies Act (investment business; *Investmentgeschaft*); (7) the incurring of the obligation to acquire claims in respect of loans prior to their maturity; (8) the assumption for others of guarantees and other indemnities (guarantee business; *Garantiegeschaft*); and (9) the effecting of transfers and clearings (giro business; *Cirogeschaft*).

Any enterprise, regardless of its legal form and whether incorporated under private or public law, which conducts any one or more of these types of business, even if only as a side-line, on a scale which requires a commercially organized business operation constitutes a "banking institution" and is, therefore, subject to regulation and supervision pursuant to the terms of the Banking Act, notwithstanding the fact that it may additionally be subject to bank regulation by special statute (such as savings banks, building loan savings banks, mortgage banks, ship mortgage banks, or investment companies).

## 2. The definition of "banking business"

§1 (1) Banking Act specifies nine types of transactions as "banking business". These types of transactions will be briefly dealt with in the following paragraphs.

"*Deposit business*" is defined as the acceptance of monies from others as deposits, irrespective of whether interest in paid thereon. The term "deposit" and its distinction from other funds received (such as loans, advances or prepayments), the acceptance of which does not constitute "banking business", remains undefined in the Act. For purposes of bank supervision, particularly for determining whether or not an enterprise is engaged in "deposit business", the

Banking supervisory Authority has adopted a definition in its administrative practice which is shared by the courts. According to such definition, deposit business constitutes the continuous acceptance of monies from a multitude of persons who are not banking institutions on the basis of standardized contracts in the form of loans or irregular deposits (§700 Civil Code) without the giving of security of a kind customary in banking and without making a written agreement in the individual case.

"*Credit business*" comprises the extension of loans and acceptance credits. Only the extension of loans, not the acquisition of already existing money debts, constitutes "credit business", so as to exclude in particular factoring and forfaiting from the definition of banking business. However, for purposes of financial reporting of banking institutions pursuant to §§13 ff. Banking Act,§19 (1) No. 1 Banking Act provides that the term "credit" includes money debts acquired for consideration, which transactions are accordingly subject to bank regulation if carried on by a "banking institution".

"*Discount business*" is defined as the purchase of bills of exchange, promissory notes and cheques. The discounting of such paper constitutes, in terms of private law, not a credit transaction, but a purchase contract. The purchase of securities other than bills, notes and cheques or of book receivables does not constitute discount business.

"*Securities business*" is defined as the purchase and sale of securities for the account of others, *i.e.* is securities broking. The purchase and sale of securities for own account does not constitute banking business. According to the definition, it is irrelevant whether the securities are purchased or sold in the name of the banking institution or in the name of its customers. As a rule, German banks purchase and sell securities on behalf of their customers in their own name, regularly as commission agents, in certain cases also as dealers. The securities business is regulated by the provisions of the Act Concerning the Custody and Acquisition of Securities and is subject to special control of the Banking Supervisory Authority by means of securities deposit audits pursuant to § 30 Banking Act.

The management and underwriting of securities issues does not constitute banking business, unless the underwriter acts for the account of others. However, underwriting will often be accompanied by transactions which constitute deposit business or credit business under §1 (1) No. 1 and No.2 Banking Act.

"*Custody business*" comprises the custody and administration of securities for the account of others (§ 1 (1) No. 5 Banking Act). Bank custody operations occasionally take the form of separate deposits (Sonderverwahrung), but more commonly that of collective deposits (Sammelverwahrung), whereby the custodian bank may either keep the customer's securities itself or entrust them to a sub-custodian bank (Drittverwahrung), such sub-custodian generally being a securities clearance bank. Custodian operations are governed by the Act Concerning the Custody and Acquisition of Securities. The administration of securities includes primarily the detaching and collection of maturing coupons, the procuring of new sheets of coupons, the attendance to drawings and notices of repayment and the cashing of maturing securities. The custody business is subject to special control of the Banking Supervisory Authority by means of securities deposit audits pursuant to § 30 Banking Act.

"*Investment business*" is defined by reference to §1 of the Investment Companies Act. "Investment business" may only be carried on by investment companies which may not conduct any other banking or other business, although any bank may establish or hold shares in an investment company. Investment companies are corporations in the form of AGs or GmbHs engaged in the setting up and administration of investment funds.

§1 (1) No.7 Banking Act designates as banking business the "*incurring of the obligation to acquire claims in respect of loans prior to their maturity*". This definition relates to a special kind of revolving credit transaction, commonly referred to as "7-M-business", by which a party sells long-term loan claims to one or several institutions granting short-term refinancing and undertakes to repurchase such loan claims on a short-term basis (e.g., upon the expiration of three months) with the aim to re-sell the loan claims again for short-term refinancing upon re-purchase.

"*Guarantee business*" is the issuance for others of guarantees and indemnities of any other kind such as suretyships (*Bürgschaften*), guarantees (*Garantien*) of any nature, and includes bid bonds, prepayment bonds, performance bonds and guarantee bonds, the opening or confirming of documentary letters of credit, the endorsement of bills of exchange and cheques and the granting of any other indemnity for others.

Finally, "*giro business*" is defined as the effecting of transfers and clearings.

### 3. Designation of further transactions as "banking business"

The catalogue of the various types of banking business listed in §1 (1) Banking Act is exhaustive. The catalogue does not include certain kinds of transactions frequently carried on by banks, such as the management and underwriting of securities issues, the trading in securities as principal, factoring, forfaiting, financial leasing or the brokerage of transactions falling under the definition of banking business; these transactions consequently do not constitute "banking business", and could thus be carried out without licence or supervision if not accompanied by transactions which do constitute "banking business".

Under §1 (1) Banking Act, the Federal Minister of Finance is empowered to designate by regulation further transactions than those listed in §1 (1) of the Act as banking business. However, such power has up to now never been exercised.

### 4. Exempted Enterprises

Specifically exempted from regulation and supervision pursuant to the terms of the Banking Act are the Federal Bank, the *Kreditanstalt fur Wiederaufbau*, which is subject to the direct supervision of the Federal Government, insurance companies, insofar as they do not conduct banking business not forming part of their typical business, and the other institutions mentioned in § 2 Banking Act (such as the Federal Post Office with respect to its savings banks and giro operations and the social security authorities).

# Supervisory Authorities

### 1. Banking supervisory authority

Official supervision over banking institutions is exercised by the Banking Supervisory Authority (*Bundesaufsichtsamt für das Kreditwesen*).

The Banking Supervisory Authority maintains its offices in Berlin. It is headed by a President who is appointed by the President of the Federal Republic upon nomination by the Federal Government which must consult the Federal Bank prior to making its nomination. The Authority falls within the responsibility of the Federal Minister of Finance and is subject to his instructions. The Authority at present consists of five divisions, of which Division I is entrusted with policy matters regarding bank supervision, while the other four divisions are responsible for the supervision of banks within specific sectors of the banking industry; the supervision of branches, subsidiaries and representative offices of foreign banks falls within the jurisdiction of Division V.

The functions of the Banking Supervisory Authority are twofold, namely (i) to supervise the operation of banks and (ii) generally "to prevent abuses in the banking system which might jeopardize the security of the assets entrusted to banking institutions, adversely affect the proper conduct of banking business or substantially prejudice the economy generally". These functions extend to the entire banking industry and relate not only to the various groups of universal banks, such as private commercial banks, savings banks and credit associations, but also to the specialist banks and to banks with special functions, irrespective of whether incorporated under private of public law.

In connection with its function as overseer of bank operations, the Banking Supervisory Authority has the rights, powers and duties outlined in more detail below. It supervises in particular compliance of operations with the provisions of the Banking Act and the special banking laws pertaining to the specialist banks. The Authority is the licensing agency for all banks and has as such defined rights of information, investigation and intervention. It has significant policy making powers, e.g., in determining, in accordance with §§ 10, 10a and 11 Banking Act, the principles governing equity capital and liquidity requirements, and important regulatory functions in that it may, where the Banking Act so provides or where the Minister of Finance pursuant to authorization in the Banking Act has delegated his authority to issue regulations to the Banking Supervisory Authority, issue regulations pertaining to matters specified in the Act. The Minister of Finance has made use of his power to delegate to the Authority the authority to issue regulations in respect of reporting procedures generally, monthly returns, general provisions for bad and doubtful debts, the format of audit reports, the securities deposit audit and the exemption from certain reporting duties. The Authority co

operates in matters concerning banking supervision with the appropriate authorities of the other member countries of the European Union.

### 2. Federal bank

The Banking Act calls for the close cooperation of the Banking Supervisory Authority and the Federal Bank in the field of bank supervision pursuant to the terms of the Act and binds both authorities to exchange observations and findings which may be of significance for the fulfillment of their respective functions.

Many of the financial and other reports required to be given by banking institutions under the Banking Act and the Federal Bank Act must be submitted both to the Banking Supervisory Authority and the Federal Bank, others must be filed with the Federal Bank which in turn must pass them on to the Banking Supervisory Authority with its comments, whereas still others must be submitted to the Federal Bank only. While the Federal Bank is involved in the collection, examination and evaluation of such reports, it is generally the responsibility of the Banking Supervisory Authority, either on its own initiative or at the request of the Federal Bank, to take appropriate steps in the light of such reports.

The Banking Supervisory Authority needs the consent of the Federal Bank for the Promulgation of the important principles governing equity capital and liquidity requirements pursuant to §§10, 10a and 11 Banking Act and for various regulations which it may issue under the Banking Act, such as regulations regarding reporting, submission of documents, monthly returns, general provisions for bad and doubtful debts and other matters. The Authority may also require the assistance of the Federal Bank in carrying out special audits of banking institutions pursuant to § 44 (1) No. 1 Banking Act.

# Admission to Business

Any enterprise falling within the definition of "banking institution" pursuant to §1 (1)

Banking Act and which is not specifically exempted from the provisions of the Act must obtain a banking licence from the Banking Supervisory Authority prior to the commencement of operations.

A banking licence is likewise required for any foreign enterprise conducting the business of a "banking institution" through a branch in Germany.

The Authority may grant the licence subject to the applicant's fulfillment of specified conditions set by the Authority or may limit the licence to certain types of banking business within the meaning of §1 (1) Banking Act. Prior to the issuance of a licence permitting the conduct of deposit business, the Authority must consult the appropriate association of banks. In the case of private commercial banks the Authority will normally subject the licence, insofar as it allows the conduct of deposit business with non-banks, to the condition that the applicant bank becomes a member of the Deposit Protection Fund.

### 1. Banking licence for banks incorporated in Germany

Pursuant to §33 Banking Act, the banking licence for German incorporated banks may only be refused by the Banking Supervisory Authority if: (i) adequate capital necessary for the operations is not available within Germany; (ii) the bank does not appoint at least two managers (*Geschäftsleiter*); (iii) the managers are not "reliable" (*zuverlassig*); (iv) the managers are not "professionally qualified" (*fachlich geeignet*) to direct the affairs of the bank; or (v) the application for the licence is not accompanied by a business plan.

The issuance of the banking licence is thus not a matter of the Authority's discretion. In the absence of the aforementioned five negative criteria there exists a right in law to the licence which can be enforced in court.

The initial minimum capital of banking institutions is not fixed by statute or regulation but is set from time to time by the Banking Supervisory Authority as a matter of administrative practice. The initial minimum capital required by the Authority for private commercial banks has been DM6,000,000 for some years. Once a bank is in operation, Principle I of the "Principles Concerning the Equity Capital and Liquidity of Banking Institutions" issued by the Banking Supervisory Authority which lays down the required ratio between credits extended by a bank and its equity capital determines in effect the necessary minimum capital.

The term "manager" (*Geschäftsleiter*) is defined in §1 (2) Banking Act and refers to the legal representatives of the banking institution, i.e., in the case of banks incorporated under private law, the general partners of a general partnership (*OHG*), limited partnership (*KG*) or partnership limited by shares (*KGaA*), the members of the board of management (*Vorstand*) of a stock corporation (*AG*) and the managing directors (*Geschäftsfhrer*) of a limited liability company (*GmbH*). The Banking Act contains a number of provisions, under which the managers of a bank are personally responsible for observing the rules set forth in the Banking Act, or which impose special obligations on them, or which create special duties with respect to them.

The managers need not be German citizens but they must be resident in Germany and must, according to the administrative practice of the Banking Supervisory Authority, be conversant with the German language. The requirement of "professional qualification" (§33 (1) No. 3 Banking Act) of a manager is normally deemed fulfilled if he has served prior to his appointment for at least three years in an executive position with a bank of comparable size engaged in a comparable type of business.

The term "business plan" (*Geschäftsplan*) means a description of the kind of business which the bank wishes to carry out and of the proposed organizational structure of the bank.

With a few exceptions, banks incorporated under private law may be organized in any one of the five forms offered by German company and partnership law, namely as a general partnership (*OHG*), limited partnership (*KG*), partnership limited by shares (*KGaA*), stock corporation (*AG*), or limited liability company (*GmbH*). It is not permitted, however, to set up a new bank as a sole proprietorship. All the five forms mentioned are found in practice. However, the GmbH which constitutes by far the most widely used corporate vehicle in Germany is less often found in banking. Large and important banks, even if closely-held, prefer in general the form of the AG. For certain specialized banking institutions the freedom of choice of the legal form of incorporation is restricted. Thus, private law mortgage banks, ship mortgage banks and investment companies may only be organized as AGs or GmbHs. Private law building loan savings banks may only be incorporated as AGs.

There exist no nationality or residence requirements regarding the shareholders of banks incorporated in Germany and no condition of reciprocity. Accordingly, foreign corporations may freely incorporate banks in Germany.

## 2. Banking licence for German branches of foreign banks

A branch of a foreign bank carrying on "banking business" within the meaning of § 1 (1) Banking Act within Germany is deemed, for purposes of the application of the Banking Act, to be a "banking institution". Consequently, all provisions of the Banking Act apply mutatis mutandis to such branch, subject to certain modifications as provided in § 53 Banking Act. If a foreign bank maintains several branches in Germany, all such branches together are deemed, for banking regulatory purposes, to constitute a single "banking institution".

Thus, prior to the commencement of the operations of the branch, a banking licence must be obtained. The requirements to be met in order to obtain the licence correspond to those which must be fulfilled by German incorporated banks.

The foreign bank must appoint at least two persons who are authorized to manage the business of the branch and to represent the foreign bank. Such persons are deemed to be managers (*Geschäftsleiter*) which means that all provisions of the Banking Act regarding the managers of German banks apply likewise to them. The managers must fulfill the personal and professional qualifications described above for managers of German banks. At least one of them must have served prior to his appointment for at least three years in an executive position with a bank in Germany, which may be a German branch of a foreign bank, of comparable size engaged in a comparable type of business. For the others it generally suffices if they have served in such position with a bank abroad, but in any event they must have had not less than one year of banking experience in Germany.

Furthermore, the minimum initial capitalization requirements applicable to German private commercial banks apply in the form that the foreign bank must supply the branch with the appropriate amount of donation capital.

The Banking Supervisory Authority may refuse the granting of the banking licence if reciprocity in the country of incorporation of the foreign bank "is not assured on the basis of international agreements". This reciprocity requirement, which in the past was alien to German law, was introduced by the 1985 amendments of the Banking Act. It is particularly unfortunate that the discretionary-authority to refuse the licence exists if reciprocity is not assured by virtue of "international agreements", as this means that the licence may be denied notwithstanding that there may exist de facto reciprocity or reciprocity may be assured under the municipal law of the foreign country or otherwise. It is hardly conceivable, however, for legal reasons as well as on grounds of international comity, that in such circumstances the Authority would invoke the absence of the assurance of reciprocity by "international agreement" as ground for refusal. Moreover it must be expected that foreign banks desiring to set up a banking facility in Germany will in lieu of establishing branches choose to incorporate banking subsidiaries as reciprocity requirements do not apply to them. Such a development would not necessarily be desirable, even under banking regulatory considerations.

The authority to refuse the banking licence for a branch on grounds of lack of reciprocity does not apply for banks incorporated in the EU member countries or in countries with which a treaty of friendship and commerce has been concluded which provides for such countries' banks to be treated on an equal footing with German banks.

Notwithstanding the principle that several German branches of a foreign bank constitute one "banking institution" for banking regulatory purposes, a banking licence must nevertheless be obtained for each of the several branches. This requirement does not, however, apply in the case of foreign banks incorporated in the EU member countries. Where it is applicable, the licence for the second or even further branches is generally granted as a routine matter.

The branch must be registered in the Commercial Register. In connection with such registration the managers (*Geschäftsleiter*) of the branch must also be entered in the Commercial Register.

The Banking Supervisory Authority will normally subject the licence to the conditions that the branch must, prior to commencement of operations, be registered as a branch in the Commercial Register and that deposit business with non-banks may only be taken up after the branch has become a member of the Deposit Protection Fund.

3. Expiration or Revocation of the Banking Licence

A banking licence granted expires automatically if banking operations are not commenced within one year after issue. The Banking Supervisory Authority may revoke the licence only under specified circumstances, e.g., if banking operations have been discontinued for a period of one year, if the bank ceases to have at least two managers, if the bank's managers are not "professionally qualified" or "reliable", or if the fulfillment of the bank's obligations to its creditors, in particular the security of the assets entrusted to the bank, is jeopardized and such jeopardy cannot be averted by other measures. A jeopardy of the security of such assets is presumed to exist in the event of a loss of 50 percent of the bank's equity capital or of more than 10 percent of the bank's equity capital in each of the three preceding consecutive business years. In the case of the expiration or revocation of the licence, the Banking Supervisory Authority may order that the bank be wound up.

# Regulation of Bank Operations

The rules on bank operations relate principally to the maintenance of adequate equity capital and liquidity, consolidation for banking supervision purposes, investments, the extension of credits, the securities and deposit business, minimum reserve requirements, reporting requirements, the preparation, auditing and publication of the annual financial statements, audits and rights of information, investigation and intervention of the Banking Supervisory Authority.

## 1. Provisions regarding equity capital and liquidity

(1) *Equity Capital*. Pursuant to § 10 Banking Act banks must maintain adequate equity capital. The Act contains detailed definitions of the term equity capital for the various legal forms of banks.

For *corporations (i.e. AGs, KGaAs and GmbHs)* such term is defined in the Act in principle as the paid-in share capital (including paid-in surplus) plus retained earnings less the nominal amount of shares held by the corporation itself. Credits to affiliates which are not extended at market conditions or are not adequately collateralized although collateralization would be required by sound banking practice are to be deducted from the equity capital. Capital contributions of silent partners (*Vermögenseinlagen stiller Gesellschafter*) and, within limits, the provision of participation capital (*Genuβscheinkapital*) may be added to the equity capital if prescribed conditions are fulfilled. Subordinated loans, on the other hand, do not in any event qualify as equity for regulatory purposes. Capital contributions of silent partners qualify if they: ① share up to their full amount in any losses; ② are subordinated; ③ are put at the disposal of the bank for a minimum term of five years; and ④ do not mature within less than two years. Participation capital qualifies under the same conditions, but only up to 25 percent of the equity capital (exclusive of capital contributions of silent partners).

For *branches of foreign banks* the equity capital is deemed to comprise the operating capital made available to the branch by the foreign bank plus any retained operating surplus minus the credit balance on inter-branch account (*aktiver Verrechnungssaldo*), if any.

The computation of the equity capital is made on the basis of the last approved annual balance sheet, except in the case of branches of foreign banks, where the latest monthly return from time to time is used.

On the basis of the statutory authorization set out in § 10 (1) Banking Act, the Banking Supervisory Authority has issued Principles I and Ia forming part of the "Principles Concerning the Equity Capital and Liquidity of Banking Institutions" (*Grundsätze für die Angemessenheit des Eigenkapitals und der Liquidität der Kreditinstitute*).

Under *Principle I* the basic rule is that credits extended and participations held by a bank may not exceed 18 -times the equity capital, whereby detailed rules apply as to the definition of the term credits and the credits not to be included, or to be included only in part, in the computation of such ratio. The term "credit" as used in Principle I includes primarily: ① all money claims on other banks and customers; ② bills of exchange and promissory notes on hand; ③ assets with respect to which the bank, as lessor, has entered into leasing agreements; and ④ contingent claims arising from guarantees and other indemnities of any kind, the provision of security for the liabilities of others, endorsements of rediscounted bills of exchange, and from bills in circulation drawn by the bank, discounted and credited to borrowers. For purposes of the ratio requirement of Principle I, credits to German banks (including public law banks and German branches of foreign banks) are to be included in the credit volume only at 20 percent, while credits to foreign banks and contingent claims on customers arising from guarantees and other indemnities and from the provision of security for the liabilities of others are to be included at 50 percent. Credits to German public entities (excluding public law banks) are not included, as are commitments to extend credit, except for commitments resulting from standby or back-up agreements in respect of revolving underwriting or note issuance facilities which according to a ruling of the Banking Supervisory Authority are regarded as amounting to an indemnity.

*Principle Ia* limits the open positions in foreign currencies to specified percentages of the equity capital in order to prevent the incurrence of foreign currency risks disproportionate to equity capitalization. The Principle requires that at the close of business on each business day a bank's open position ① in foreign currencies irrespective of maturities and precious metals shall not exceed 30 percent of its equity capital, ② in foreign currencies maturing in any one calendar month shall not exceed 40 percent of the equity capital, and ③ in foreign currencies maturing in any one calendar half-year shall not exceed 40 percent of the equity capital.

§ 10a Banking Act prescribes that banks forming part of a group must as a group maintain adequate equity capital. Principle I provides, accordingly, that the fundamental rule pursuant to which credits extended and participations held may not exceed 18-times the equity capital applies on a consolidated basis also to a group of banks. The determination as to whether a group of banks has adequate capital is to be made on the basis of consolidation of the equity capital on the one hand and the risk assets, i.e. the credits and participations pursuant to Principle I, on the other. Such consolidation of group equity capital and group risk assets is to be made in proportion to the share of nominal capital held by the parent bank in the respective affiliates. Included in the consolidation are all domestic and foreign banking, factoring and leasing affiliates in which the parent bank holds directly or indirectly 40 percent or more of the share capital or of the voting rights or over which the parent bank can exercise directly or indirectly a controlling influence.

No consolidation is required in respect of open positions in foreign currencies pursuant to Principle Ia.

(2) *Liquidity*. Under § 11 Banking Act, banks must at all times maintain sufficient liquidity. Based on the statutory authorization contained in § 11 Banking Act, the Banking Supervisory Authority has issued Principles II and III of the "Principles Concerning the Equity Capital and Liquidity of Banking Institutions".

*Principle II* aims at keeping long-term lending and investments in a reasonable relationship to long-term financial resources by providing that the aggregate of certain specified long-term asset items shall not exceed the aggregate of certain specified long-term liability items. *Principle III* limits the use of outside resources for assets that cannot at all times be relatively easily mobilized.

(3) *Failure to Comply with Equity Capital and Liquidity Requirements*. A bank's failure to comply

with the equity capital or liquidity requirements laid down by the Banking Supervisory Authority creates a rebuttable presumption that the equity capital of the bank is inadequate or its liquidity is insufficient. The bank must either establish to the satisfaction of the Authority that specific reasons justify lesser requirements with respect to its equity capital or liquidity or must remedy such failure within a reasonable time. If it fails to do so, the Authority may proceed under § 45 (1) Banking Act and prohibit or restrict the distribution of profits or the extension of further credits by the bank. If the liquidity is insufficient, the Authority may in addition prohibit the bank from investing available funds in assets falling under § 12 Banking Act (See (b) below).

### 2. Limitations on investments

Under § 12 Banking Act, the aggregate book value of the investments of a bank in real estate, buildings, equipment, ships participations in banks or other enterprises and in capital contributions as silent partner and participation rights (*Genußrechte*) may not exceed the amount of the bank's equity capital. The Act exempts certain investments from this ruls as provided in detail in § 12 (2). If a bank fails to observe the restrictions regarding investments, the Banking Supervisory Authority may intervene pursuant to § 45 (1) Banking Act and prohibit or restrict the distribution of profits, the extension of further credits and the investment in assets covered by § 12 Banking Act.

### 3. Rules on the extension of credits

The Banking Act contains in § §13 to 20 detailed rules regarding the extension of credits. The terms "credit" ("*Kredit*") and "borrower" ("*Kreditnehmer*") as used in these provisions are defined in §19 Banking Act.

"Credit" includes *inter alia*: loans of any kind; debts acquired for a consideration; acceptance credits; the discounting of bills of exchange, promissory notes and cheques; money claims from other commercial transactions of the bank; guarantees or other indemnities; the liability arising from the provision of security for the liabilities of others; participations of the bank in a borrower's enterprise amounting to 25 percent or more of the share capital of such enterprise; and assets with respect to which the bank as lessor has entered into leasing agreements.

Under the definition of "borrower" certain related persons or entities are deemed to be a single borrower; in particular, all companies which belong to the same group of companies count as one borrower.

(1) *Large-scale Credits (Groβkredite)*. Large-scale credits are by definition credits to any one borrower which exceed 15 percent of the equity capital of the bank. § 13 Banking Act deals with large-scale credits of an individual bank, § 13a thereof with their consolidation within a group of banks.

No single large-scale credit may exceed 50 percent of the bank's equity capital. The aggregate of all large-scale credits together may not exceed eight times the equity capital of the bank; in the application of the "eight-times" rule, credit commitments not yet utilized are not counted, but only amounts actually taken up. Guarantees of any kind are normally to be taken into account at their full nominal amount, but in certain cases only at one-half of their nominal amount.

Each large-scale credit must be reported forthwith to the Federal Bank which in turn must transmit the report to the Banking Supervisory Authority. Large-scale credits may only be extended upon a unanimous resolution of all managers.

§13a Banking Act requires consolidation of large-scale credits and prescribes essentially that the rules applicable to large-scale credits of an individual bank, pursuant to which any credit may not exceed 50 percent of the equity capital and all large-scale credits together may not exceed eight-times the equity capital of a bank, apply on a consolidated basis also to a group of banks. Consolidation is to be made in proportion to the share of nominal capital held by the parent bank in the respective affiliates. Included in the consolidation are all domestic and foreign banking, factoring and leasing affiliates in which the parent bank holds directly or indirectly 50 percent (as opposed to 40 percent in the case of capital adequacy) or more of the share capital or of the voting rights or over which the parent bank can exercise directly or indirectly a controlling influence. The parent bank is required to report large-scale credits on consolidated basis to the Federal Bank which in turn must forward such reports to the Banking Supervisory Authority.

(2) *Million Mark Credits* (*Millionenkredite*). pursuant to § 14 Banking Act a bank must report to the Federal Bank every three months the names of those borrowers who have had at any time during the preceding three months obligations to the bank amounting to DM 1,000,000 or over from credits extended, stating the amount of such obligation on the last day of the month preceding the date of the report and giving certain information on the term and type of the credit obligation (s). Where the reporting bank has a non-German subsidiary which is to be included in the consolidation of large-scale credits (see (1) above), such report must include the respective information on million mark credits of such subsidiary. If a borrower has taken up million mark credits with more than one reporting bank, each bank will be advised by the Federal Bank of the aggregate obligations of such borrower arising from such credits, the number of banks involved (but not of their names or the individual amounts) and of certain details on the term and type of the obligations. Upon conclusion of pertinent international agreements or the entry into force of a relevant directive of the European Union, the Federal Bank may give information on million mark credits reported to it to the

international institution set up pursuant to such agreements or directive for passing on to the banks participating in such reporting system.

(3) *Credits to Related Persons or Entities (Organkredite)*. Special rules apply to credits extended to persons or entities having a special relationship with the bank, such as companies which are affiliated with the bank or its managers or members of its supervisory board, by way of participation or otherwise, managers, partners, executive employees, supervisory board members, spouses and minor children of such persons, all as set out at length in § 15 Banking Act (so-called "*Organkredit*").

An *Organkredit* may only be extended upon a unanimous resolution of all managers which sets out the terms of the credit. It must be expressly approved by the bank's supervisory board (if any). In the event of failure to comply with these rules, the credit must be repaid immediately. Furthermore, if these rules are violated, managers and supervisory board members are under certain circumstances jointly and severally liable to compensate the bank for damages incurred in connection with the granting of an *Organkredit*. The bank's claim for compensation may be enforced by a creditor of the bank to the extent that such creditor cannot obtain satisfaction from the bank.

Each *Organkredit* must be reported promptly to the Banking Supervisory Authority and the Federal Bank if: ① it exceeds DM250,000 where the borrower is an individual; or ② where the borrower is an enterprise, it exceeds both DM 250,000 and 5 percent of the equity capital of the bank.

(4) *Information to be Required of Borrowers*. Under § 18 Banking Act, a bank must require any borrower to whom credits amounting to more than DM 100,000 are extended to disclose his financial position, in particular by submission of annual financial statements. The bank may dispense with this requirement, if the request for disclosure would be unfounded in view of the security provided or the co-obligors.

### 4. Provisions regarding securities and custody business

The securities and custody business of banks within the meaning of §1 (1) Banking Act is subject to special rules and control by the Banking Supervisory Authority.

### 5. Management and underwriting of securities issues

As has been mentioned above, the management and underwriting of securities issues does not constitute banking business within the meaning of §1 (1) Banking Act and is as such not subject to any special banking regulatory provisions. Under current policies of the Federal Bank, however, the lead management of DM-denominated bond issues of foreign issuers may be carried out only by banks incorporated in Germany (so as to exclude German branches of foreign banks). The Federal Bank requires further that such issues, if publicly placed, must have a minimum term of five years and, if privately placed, a minimum term of three years. Pursuant to such policies any such issue must be governed by German law, the principal paying agent for such issue must be a bank incorporated in Germany, and the securities must be included in the German securities clearance system. Public issues must, in addition, be listed on a German stock exchange.

### 6. Minimum reserves

The rules on minimum reserves are laid down in § 16 Federal Bank Act and in the Directive of the Federal Bank regarding Minimum Reserves of 1983 as amended (the "Directive"). Regard must also be given to the comprehensive Rulings of the Federal Bank concerning Specific Questions on Minimum Reserves.

§16 Federal Bank Act authorizes the Federal Bank to require all banks to maintain with it minimum reserves equal to a certain percentage rate of their liabilities from demand, term and savings deposits and from short and medium-term borrowings, excluding, however, liabilities to banks which are themselves subject to minimum reserves. The reserve rates to be fixed by the Federal Bank may not exceed 30 percent for demand liabilities, 20 percent for term liabilities and 10 percent for savings deposits; for liabilities to non-residents, however, the rate may be set at up to 100 percent. Within these limits the Federal Bank may fix the reserve rates at various levels in accordance with general principles (which includes the authority to set different rates for different categories of banks and to apply higher rates to any increase in a bank's liabilities as compared to the position at a particular date) and may exclude certain kinds of liabilities from minimum reserve requirements.

In principle, all German banks, including German branches of foreign banks, are subject to minimum reserve requirements. Exempt from such requirements are only a few categories of banking institutions as provided in the Directive. These include, inter alia, investment companies, securities clearance banks, and banks in liquidation.

Pursuant to the provisions of the Directive, minimum reserve requirements apply to all liabilities which: ① arise from deposits or borrowings，including liabilities from registered bonds and from global bonds payable to order, and have a maturity of less than four years; ② arise from bonds payable to bearer and have a maturity of less than two years; ③ arise from bonds payable to order which form part of a larger issue and have a maturity of less than two years; provided, in each of the cases mentioned in ① to ③, that such liabilities are not due to banks which themselves are subject to German minimum reserve requirements. Liabilities from repurchase transactions are also subject to reserve requirements if certain circumstances are met.

Certificates of deposits issued to bearer or to order, as follows from ② and ③ above, are subject to minimum reserve requirements if they have an original maturity of less than two years, and are not so subject if their term is two years or over. Certificates of deposit issued in registered form or as a global bond to order are subject to minimum reserve requirements if their original maturity is less than four years. No minimum reserves need be maintained in respect of certificates of deposit, in whatever form of issue, which are held by German banks subject to the reserve requirement. The Rulings set out procedures which facilitate proof that certificates of deposit are held by German banks and thus exempt from minimum reserves.

In the case of German branches of foreign banks, the reserve requirement applies also to the liabilities of the branch to its head office and sister branches shown as debit balance on interbranch account. For minimum reserve purposes such liabilities are deemed to be demand liabilities irrespective of their agreed maturities.

The Directive exempts certain liabilities otherwise subject to the reserve requirement from such requirement, such as liabilities ① to the Federal Bank, ② from certain earmarked funds received and already passed on to the ultimate recipient or a bank acting as intermediary, ③ from building loan savings deposits, and ④ from certain other deposits or borrowings, all as specified in the Directive. The most important exemption, however, relates to liabilities to non-residents denominated in foreign currencies. It has been inspired by elements of the International Banking Facilities and became effective on May 1, 1986. It provides that foreign currency denominated liabilities to non-residents arising from deposits and borrowings, including liabilities from registered bonds and global bonds payable to order, with maturities of less than four years are exempt from reserve requirements up to the amount of the claims of the bank on non-residents denominated in foreign currencies with maturities of less than four years. Such exemption is not available in respect of DM-denominated liabilities, liabilities expressed in units of account (such as Special Drawing Rights) and liabilities (in whatever currency) under certificates of deposit issued to bearer or to order.

Among the liabilities subject to reserve requirement, the Directive distinguishes between ① demand liabilities which are defined as liabilities maturing daily or with an agreed notice period or maturity of less than one month, ② term liabilities which are defined as liabilities with an agreed notice period or maturity of one month or longer, and ③ savings deposits.

The minimum reserve rates are at present graded by the Federal Bank as follows: ① according to the type and term of liabilities (demand liabilities, term liabilities or savings deposits); ② according to the amount of the various types of liabilities subject to minimum reserves (up to DM 10 million; over DM 10 million up to DM 100 Million; over DM 100 million); and ③ according to the source of funds (liabilities to residents or non-residents).

The minimum reserves required to be kept by a bank are determined by applying the reserve rates to the monthly average of that bank's liabilities subject to minimum reserves. The banks have the option of computing such monthly average either on the basis of the position at the end of each day (including non-business days) during the period from the 16th day of the preceding month to the 15th day of the current month. It may also be computed on the basis of the position on the 23rd and last day of the preceding month and the 7th and 15th day of the current month. This method of computation allows the banks considerable flexibility in the management of their minimum reserve holdings. Since the minimum reserve requirement must be complied with only on the basis of a monthly average, the banks can use their central bank deposits to effect payments and can draw on such deposits freely so long as the reserves are correspondingly increased on other days of the relevant period. Accordingly, the banks need not maintain with the central bank any other special deposits for the purpose of making current payments. Rather, the deposits which they keep with the Federal Bank to meet their minimum reserve requirements also serve as working balances.

Under §16 (3) Federal Bank Act, the Federal Bank may charge special interest at a rate up to 3 percent from time to time above the prevailing lombard interest rate on the amount by which the actual reserve kept by a bank falls short of the reserve required to be kept by it. The Federal Bank has usually set this rate at the maximum level of 3 percent above the lombard interest rate.

### 7. Reporting obligations

As a further material aspect of bank regulation and supervision, all banks are subject to most comprehensive reporting obligations which are established by the Banking Act and the Federal Bank Act and numerous regulations or directives of the Banking Supervisory Authority and the Federal Bank issued under those acts. Most of the reporting obligations，which must as a rule be fulfilled on prescribed forms, naturally relate to financial matters，but reports must also be given on certain organizational and administrative matters. A comprehensive enumeration of these reporting obligations would go beyond the scope of this introduction into the bank regulatory system and reference can accordingly only be made to the most important reporting requirements.

*Inter alia*, the following *reports on financial matters* must be furnished to the Federal Bank or the Banking Supervisory Authority or to both institutions:

(1) Monthly returns (*Monatsausweise*) under §25 Banking Act which take the form of monthly balance sheet statistical reports (*Monatliche Bilanzstatistik*) pursuant to §18 Federal Bank Act. These extremely detailed reports are required to be submitted by the 5th business day of each month and constitute the core of the financial reporting system. The reports must be given to the Federal Bank on prescribed forms in accordance with comprehensive guidelines issued by

the Federal Bank. The Federal Bank transmits a copy of the monthly returns to the Banking Supervisory Authority. Parent banks must in addition submit consolidated monthly returns by the last business day of each month for the preceding month.

(2) Monthly reports concerning compliance with Principles I, Ia, II and III, to be submitted together with the monthly returns.

(3) Monthly reports showing the credit commitments to German resident borrowers and the amounts drawn thereon (*Monatliche Kreditzusagenstatistik*). These reports are to be submitted to the Federal Bank by the 15th day of each month for the preceding month.

(4) Quarterly summary reports on credits extended to German resident borrowers as per the end of each calendar quarter (*Vierteljährliche Kreditnehmerstatistik*). These quarterly reports must be submitted to the Federal Bank by the 10th business day after the end of the respective calendar quarter. The Federal Bank forwards a copy of such report to the Banking Supervisory Authority.

(5) Monthly reports showing the foreign assets and liabilities (*Monatliche Meldung "Auslandsstatuts"*). These comprehensive reports are to the submitted to the Federal Bank by the 5th business day of each month. In addition, less comprehensive weekly status reports showing the short term receivables and payables to non-residents are to be made to the Federal Bank (*Bankwöchentliche Kurzmeldung "Auslandsstatus"*).

(6) Monthly minimum reserve reports (*Reservemeldung*) pursuant to §9 of the Directive of the Federal Bank regarding Minimum Reserves. These reports are to be submitted to the Federal Bank by the 5th business day following the 15th day of each month.

(7) Quarterly reports pursuant to the Country Risk Regulation (*Länderrisikoverordnung*) on credits extended to foreign borrowers. Parent banks must furnish these reports also on a consolidated basis. These reports are to be made by banks whose volume of credits to foreign borrowers, in the case of groups of banks on a consolidated basis, exceeds DM 100 million. They are to be given to the Federal Bank by the last business day of the month following the respective calendar quarter.

(8) Separate reports on the extension of each large-scale credit, certain credits to related persons and entities and three-monthly reports on million mark credits. In respect of large scale credits an annual summary report must also be given, in the cases of private commercial banks and branches of foreign banks as at September 30 of each year. The details regarding the procedure for these reports, including the forms to be used, are provided in the Regulation on Reporting issued by the Banking Supervisory Authority. Certain exemptions from the duty to report on these matters are set out in the Authority's Exemption Regulation.

Apart from these reports on financial matters, certain *reports on organizational* or administrative matters must be made promptly to the Banking Supervisory Authority and the Federal Bank under §24 Banking Act. Such reports are to be given, *interalia*, on the appointment and removal of managers, the purchase and sale, or changes in the extent, of a participation in another company, changes of legal form, capital or articles of association, a loss of 25 percent of the equity capital, the commencement and discontinuation of business activities not constituting banking business as defined in §1 (1) Banking Act, and intended mergers with other banks. The details concerning the procedure for these reports are set out in §8 of the Regulation on Reporting. In respect of the duty to report the commencement and discontinuation of business activities not constituting banking business regard must be given to §9 of the Exemption Regulation setting out a wide catalogue of those activities which need not be reported.

### 8. Annual financial statements

Specific requirements apply to the preparation, auditing, reporting and publication of the annual financial statements of banks. As a rule, the annual financial statements must be prepared within the first three months following the end of the business year and must be filed promptly after their preparation with the Banking Supervisory Authority and the Federal Bank. Format presentation and contents of the annual financial statements are regulated by numerous regulations, guidelines and prescribed forms; for banks organized as corporations (*i.e., AGs, KGaAs and GmbHs*), the pertinent rules are primarily contained in the Regulation on the Forms for the Layout of the Annual Financial Statements of Banking Institutions of December 20, 1967, as amended, the Form for the Annual Financial Statements of Banking Institutions Incorporated as Stock Corporations, Partnerships Limited by Shares and Limited Liability Companies, and the Guidelines of the Banking Supervisory Authority for the Preparation of the Annual Balance Sheet and Profit and Loss Statement of Banking Institutions Incorporated as Stock Corporations, Partnerships Limited by Shares and Limited Liability Companies. Branches of foreign banks must submit to the Banking Supervisory Authority and the Federal Bank the annual financial statements of the foreign bank in addition to the branch's annual accounts.

Within five month after the end of the business year, the annual financial statements must be audited by an independent public accountant and, upon completion of such audit, they must promptly be approved by the appropriate organ of the bank. The format, presentation and contents of the audit report are again prescribed by fairly extensive guidelines of the Banking Supervisory Authority. The audit report must promptly upon completion of the audit be submitted to the Banking Supervisory Authority and the Federal Bank. The auditor appointed by the bank must be notified to the Authority which may require the appointment of another auditor if this is necessary in order to achieve the purpose of the audit.

Promptly after their approval, the certified and approved financial statements and the annual report of the bank must be filed with the Banking Supervisory Authority and the Federal Bank.

The annual financial statements and the annual report must be published in the Federal Gazette (*Bundesanzeiger*) not later than nine months after the end of the business year.

Finally, the approved annual financial statements and annual report of the bank are to be filed with the Commercial Register where there are open to public inspection.

### 9. Audits

Bank operations are subject to various prescribed external audits as mentioned below.

The annual financial statements of banks must be audited by independent public accountants as outlined under (h) above.

Banks which are members of a deposit protection scheme may be audited by the auditing agency of the respective banking association. The report on any such audit must be submitted by the auditor to the Banking Supervisory Authority and the Federal Bank.

All banks are subject to audits by the Federal Bank regarding their compliance with minimum reserve requirements (minimum reserve audit-*Mindestreserveprüfung*). Although these audits are supposed to be carried out annually, in practice they are not performed on an annual basis due to staff shortages at the Federal Bank.

Banks which are engaged in securities business or in custody business within the meaning of §1 (1) Banking Act must observe the provisions of the Act Concerning the Custody and Acquisition of Securities and are subject to statutory audits in respect of these businesses (securities deposit audit-*Depotprüfung*).The securities deposit audit is normally conducted on an annual basis. The audit is carried out by special auditors, in the case of private commercial banks normally by independent public accountants, who are appointed by the Banking Supervisory Authority or by the Federal Bank. The auditor's report is submitted to the Banking Supervisory Authority and the Federal Bank. Details regarding the securities deposit audit are set forth in comprehensive provisions issued by the Banking Supervisory Authority.

Finally, under §44 (1) No. 1 Banking Act the Banking Supervisory Authority may at any time conduct special audits of bank operations "with or without specific cause". The Authority may carry out such audits itself or entrust the conduct of the audit to the Federal Bank or independent public accountants. In recent years the Authority has made increasing use of its power to conduct audits under §44 (1) No. 1 Banking Act.

In addition to external audits, the Banking Supervisory Authority requires the banks conduct internal audits on a regular basis. They may be carried out by internal auditors of the bank or by independent public accountants. The requirements regarding internal audits have been laid down in a ruling of the Authority.

## 10. Rights of information, investigation and intervention of the banking supervisory authority

(1) *Rights of Information and Investigation.* Under §44 Banking Act the Banking Supervisory Authority may: ① request from a bank any and all information pertaining to the bank's operations; ② inspect all books and records of the bank; ③ carry out an audit, even without specific cause; ④ attend shareholders' meetings and meetings of supervisory boards of banks organized as corporations and speak at such meetings; ⑤ require from banks organized as corporations the calling of shareholders' meetings and meetings of the supervisory board. The Authority may request that items specified by it for deliberation and resolution be placed on the agenda of such meetings.

(2) *Rights of Intervention.* The rights of the Banking Supervisory Authority to intervene in the operations of a bank are briefly summarized below.

If a bank fails to maintain adequate equity capital or liquidity or to observe the restrictions on investments and does not remedy such failure, the Banking Supervisory Authority has the rights of intervention set out in §45 of the Banking Act.

If the fulfillment of a bank's obligations towards its creditors, in particular if the security of the assets entrusted to the bank, is jeopardized, the Banking Supervisory Authority may take appropriate action under §46 Banking Act. In particular, it may: ① issue directives concerning the management of the bank's operations; ② prohibit or restrict the acceptance of deposits and the extension of credits; ③ prohibit or restrict the managers' administration of the bank's operations; and ④ appoint supervisors.

In such event the Authority may also proceed under §46a Banking Act and take the following temporary actions, for the purpose of preventing the bankruptcy of the bank: ① prohibit transfer of assets and payments; ② close the bank for business with customers; and ③ unless one of the deposit protection schemes undertakes to satisfy those making such payments, prohibit the acceptance of payments not made in or towards the settlement of debts owing to the bank (*i.e.*, deposits).

The authority to move for bankruptcy proceedings against a bank is exclusively vested in the Banking Supervisory Authority. Also, a petition for judicial composition proceedings requires the consent of the Authority.

If a manager of a bank is not "professionally qualified "of "reliable" or if the fulfillment of a bank's obligation to its creditors is jeopardized, and if such jeopardy cannot be averted by other means, the Banking Supervisory Authority may require his removal and prohibit him from exercising his functions. The same applies if a manager intentionally or because of gross negligence violates provisions of the Banking Act, the regulations issued thereunder, or directives of the Banking Supervisory Authority.

## New Words

| | | |
|---|---|---|
| 1. | break-down *n.* | 分類；分析 |
| 2. | sketchy *a.* | 不完全的；粗略的 |
| 3. | overhaul *n.* | 全面修訂 |
| 4. | rescue *n.* | 營救 |
| 5. | far-reaching *a.* | 深遠的；廣泛的 |
| 6. | reciprocity *n.* | 互惠；對等 |
| 7. | gentlemen's agree-ment | 君子協定 |
| 8. | disband *v.* | 解散 |
| 9. | lead managers | 領先的商行（銀行） |
| 10. | coupon tax | 息票利息稅 |
| 11. | zero-coupon bonds | 零息票債券 |
| 12. | reserve requirements | 準備金要求 |
| 13. | commission agents | 佣金代理商或經紀人 |
| 14. | refinancing *n.* | 再募集資金 |
| 15. | suretyships *n.* | 保證人的地位（資格責任）；保證契約 |
| 16. | overseer *n.* | 監督者 |
| 17. | liquidity requirements | 流動性要求 |
| 18. | format *n.* | 格式；樣式 |
| 19. | bad debts | 呆帳；壞帳 |
| 20. | donation capital | 捐贈或饋贈資本 |
| 21. | comity *n.* | 大家庭 |
| 22. | jeopardy *n.* | 危險；風險 |
| 23. | jeopardize *v.* | 使處於危險境地；危及 |
| 24. | silent partners | 隱名合夥人 |
| 25. | collateralize *v.* | 提供抵押 |
| 26. | collateralization *n.* | 提供抵押 |
| 27. | open position | 末結清期貨契約 |
| 28. | rebuttable *a.* | 反駁的 |
| 29. | place *v.* | 銷售 |
| 30. | clearance system | 結算系統 |
| 31. | list *v.* | （在證券交易所）上市 |
| 32. | public accountant | 公共會計師；會計師 |
| 33. | Federal Gazette | 聯邦公報 |
| 34. | transfer of assets | 資產的轉讓 |

**35.** judicial composition proceedings 　司法和解協議訴訟

**36.** detach *v.* 　使分開；使分離

## New Phrases and Idiomatic Expressions

**1.** in concert with 　與……協力一齊

**2.** up to now 　至今

**3.** insofar as 　在……的範圍內；到……程度

**4.** to delegate one's authority to do sth. 　授權某人做某事

**5.** to be exempted from 　免除……

**6.** to be conversant with 　熟悉；精通

**7.** on an equal footing with 　在……平等基礎上

**8.** to share in 　分享

**9.** on the one hand...on the other 　一方面……另一方面

**10.** at all times 　隨時；總是

**11.** to the satisfaction 　到……滿意程度；使……確信的程度

**12.** to be affiliated with 　隸屬於……

**13.** to compensate sb. for sth. 　對某人的某事進行補償

**14.** within the meaning of 　在……含義內

**15.** to be publicly (or privately) placed 　公開（私下）銷售

**16.** to have the option of doing sth. 　有做某事的選擇

**17.** in practice 　在實踐中；實際上

**18.** to be placed on the agenda 　列入議事日程

## Notes

**1.** factoring：客帳代理業務。

Buying of the trade debts of a manufacturer, assuming the task of debt collection and accepting the credit risk, thus providing the manufacturer with working capital.

**2.** forfaiting：福費廷。

Form of debt discounting for exporters in which forfaiter accepts at a discount, and without recourse, a promissory note, bill of exchange, letter of credit, etc. received from a foreign buyer by an exporter. Maturities are normally from one to three years. Thus the exporter receives payments without risk at the cost of the discount.

3. financial leasing (or financial lease)：金融租賃。

Under a financial lease, the lessee agrees to make a series of payments to the lessor for the use of equipment. Of course all the payments must cover both the full purchase price of the leased asset and a rate of return on capital. The contract cannot be cancelled or terminated by either party during the initial term of the lease — a period of seven years.

Therefore with this type of lease, the lessee — although not the legal owner — holds all the risks of asset ownership (e.g. the risk of technological obsolescence and the risk that the demand for the asset's services will be below expectations). The lessor holds no risk other than the risk of the lessee's default on the lease payments. Hence, a financial lease is virtually indistinguishable from more normal debt capital — both in theory and in practice.

4. the Federal Bank：聯邦銀行（德國中央銀行），又稱德意志聯邦銀行，the Deutsche Bundesbank which is in Frankfurt on maine.

5. Lombard interest rate (also Lonbard rate)：倫巴第貸款利率；短期放款利率。

Rate of interest at which the German central bank lends to German commercial banks, usu, 1/2% above the discount rate. It is also used to mean interest rate charged by a German commercial bank lending against security.

6. the International Banking Facilities (IBFs)：國際銀行設施。

International Banking Facilities were first introduced in the US in December 1981. These offices enable banks to establish international banking free trade zones within geographic confines of the United States and for regulatory purposes they are treated as though they were located abroad. Transactions of IBFs are considered as "offshore" transactions and, as such, are free from reserve requirements and interest rate ceilings. Domestic US residents are not allowed to deal with IBFs and their business is strictly limited to the international sector. IBFs are permitted only to accept funds (deposits) from and to lend to, foreign-based individuals, corporations, governments and banks. Foreign subsidiaries of American and other multinationals, as well as other IBFs, can deal directly as long as the funds are not obtained from within the US or used for domestic (i.e. US) purposes. Transactions must be in minimum amounts of $100,000 and may be denominated in any currency. IBFs are not allowed to issue certificates of deposit (CDs) or other bearer instruments.

7. ECU (European Currency Unit)：歐洲貨幣單位，現已被歐元（EURO）所取代。

Currency medium and unit of account created in 1979 to act as the reserve asset and accounting unit of the European Monetary System. The value of ECU is calculated as a weighted average of a basket of specified amounts of the former EC currencies; its value is reviewed periodically as currencies change in importance and membership of the EC expands. It also acts as the unit of account for all EC transactions. It has some similarities with the special drawing rights of the International Monetary Fund; however, ECU reserves are not allocated to individual countries but are held in the European Monetary Cooperation Fund. Private transactions using the ECU as the denomination for borrowing and lending have proved popular. It has been suggested that the ECU will be the basis for a future European currency to replace all national currencies.

8. Special Drawing Right (SDR)：特別提款權。

Standard unit of account used by the IMF. In 1970 members of the IMF were allocated SDRs in proportion to the quotas of currency that they had subscribed to the Fund on its formation. There have since been further allocations. SDRs can be used to settle international trade balances and to repay debts to the IMF itself. On the instructions of the IMF a member country must supply its own currency to another member, in exchange for SDRs, unless it already holds more than three times its original allocation. The value of SDRs was originally expressed in terms of gold but since 1974 it has been valued in terms of its members' currencies. SDRs provide a credit facilities; unlike these existing facilities they do not have to be repaid, thus forming a permanent addition to members' reserves and functioning as an international reserve currency.

9. private commercial banks：私人商業銀行。

Among the private commercial banks are the three largest banks：德意志銀行、德勒斯登銀行和商業銀行（Deutsche Bank, Dresdner Bank and Commerzbank.）

10. Reich：帝國。

 **Exercises**

## I. Answer the following Questions:

1. What does "Banking Business" mean?

2. How does the Banking Act define "deposit business" "discount business" and "securities business"?

3. What organ supervises over banking institutions?

4. What are the major functions of the Banking Supervisory Authority? And what are the responsibilities of its five divisions?

5. In what case may the banking licence for German incorporated banks be refused by the Banking Supervisory Authority?

6. Under what circumstances may the Banking Supervisory Authority revoke the banking

licence?

7. The Banking Supervisory Authority has issued Principle I. What is this principle about?

8. What are the Banking Act rules on the extention of credits?

9. What is the most important characteristic of German Banking law?

10.What sort of reports on financial matters must be furnished to the Federal Bank or the Banking Supervisory Authority or to both institutions?

11.How many types of audits the Banking Supervisory Authority requires?

12.What rights does the Banking Supervisory Authority have?

## II. Translate the following Chinese passages into English:

1. 在德國，對銀行機構進行監管的機構是銀行監管局。該局下設五個處：一處負責銀行監管政策；二處、三處、四處負責銀行業某一個體領域的監管；五處負責對分行、支行、外國銀行的代表處進行監管。

2. 只有在以下情況下，德國銀行監督局才會拒發營業執照：(1)在德國沒有足夠的必要的經營資本；(2)銀行未任命至少兩名行長；(3)銀行不可靠；(4)行長業務上不合格，無法勝任對銀行業務的指導；(5)申請執照時未附上業務計畫。

3. 對銀行經營的規定主要與保持足夠的股本和流動性、銀行兼併、投資、信貸的發放、證券和存款業務、最低準備金要求、報告要求、審計和年度財務報表的公布，以及銀行監督局的資訊權、調查和干預權有關。

4. 對德國銀行的管理與監督的主要法律是1961年銀行法。該法於1962年1月1日生效。

## III. Indicate whether each of the following statements is true or false by writing "T" or "F" in the space provided:

1. The general law on the regulation and supervision of banks is set out in the Banking Act of July 10, 1961.

2. According to German Law, investment business may only be carried on by investment companies which may not conduct any other banking or other business, although any bank may establish or hold shares in an investment company.

3. Official supervision over banking institutions in Germany has never been exercised by the Banking Supervisory Authority.

4. Foreign corporations may not freely incorporate banks in Germany.

5. The authority to refuse the banking licence for a branch on grounds of lack of

reciprocity applies for banks incorporated in the EU member countries.

6. The Federal Bank is exempted from regulation and supervision pursuant to the terms of the Banking Act.

7. In principle, all German banks, including German branches of foreign banks, are subject to minimum reserve requirements.

8. Audits by the Federal Bank are supposed to be carried out annually, in practice, they are not performed on an annual basis.

## State "Blue Sky Laws"

A prolegomenon on American securities regulation for a Japanese audience, if not for a considerable number of Americans as well, must begin with an aphorism and an enigma. The aphorism — which is common to both countries if not universally true — is that the life of the law is not logic, as Lord Coke insisted in the early seventeenth century, but experience, as Justice Holmes emphasized in the early twentieth. The enigma — which today is peculiar to the United States and a few other countries but is probably destined to puzzle future generations of lawyers in the new federalisms that are on the horizon — is the interaction of local and national law in a federal system.

The fact is that the United States has operated under a dual system of federal and state securities regulation since 1933. If the period 1887-1914, which saw the introduction of federal regulation of the railroads and the passage of the two great antitrust statutes, had also produced federal regulation of the securities markets, probably there would never have been any state legislation in this field. But, as the political history of the United States turned out, there was no federal regulation of the issuance of securities until the Interstate Commerce Commission was given control over railroad issues in 1920, and beyond that area the country had first to endure the stock market crash of 1929, followed by the Great Depression, and then to elect in late 1932 an Administration under President Franklin D. Roosevelt that was dedicated to widespread socio — economic reform within the capitalist system.

By then virtually every state had enacted some form of "blue sky law" — so called because the proponent of the Kansas statute of 1911, one of the first, said that the legislation was aimed at promoters who "would sell building lots in the blue sky." As a matter of constitutional power, Congress could have "preempted" the state statutes, as it had done with respect to railroad securities in 1920. But it chose instead specifically to preserve them against an implication of displacement by the new federal legislation.

Today there are blue sky laws in all 50 states, the District of Columbia, and Puerto Rico. In 1956, the National Conference of Commissioners on Uniform State Laws promulgated, and recommended to the state legislatures, the Uniform Securities Act, which the author of this lesson had drafted at the Conference's request after conducting a two-year Study of State Securities Regulation at the Harvard Law School. That Act is now law — with greater or lesser modifications — in Some 39 jurisdictions; and it has had varying impacts on the legislation elsewhere, notably the California Corporate Securities Law of 1968.

The Uniform Act reflects all three of the interrelated approaches that have characterized most blue sky laws from the beginning: (1) prevention of fraud in the sale of securities generally by giving the blue sky administrator broad authority to conduct investigations, sue for injunctions, and recommend criminal prosecutions; (2) registration and regulation of brokers, dealers, and, more recently, investment advisers; and (3) registration of securities. Indeed, this is equally true of the statutes in most of the states that have not adopted the Uniform Act, except that they tend to suffer from both poor draftsmanship and obsolescence.

When Congress came to grips in 1933 with the problem or regulating distributions of securities, it chose the disclosure philosophy of the British Companies Act's prospectus provisions rather than the home-grown philosophy of the blue sky laws, which in most states subjected issuers of securities (as they still do) to various substantive standards. In the Uniform Act those standards refer principally to (1) unreasonable underwriters "or sellers" compensation, (2) unreasonable promoters' profits or participation, and (3) unreasonable amounts or kinds of options. But some blue sky laws go further. California and a number of other states go to the extreme of speaking (at least in some cases) in terms of whether the offering and the proposed method of doing business are "fair, just, and equitable."

One cannot assume, of course, that Congress would have been satisfied with a disclosure statute if it had not also preserved the state blue sky laws, most of which went further. This is something that is apt to be overlooked when suggestions are made today that Congress should preempt the field. In any event, the theory is that one is free to sell shares in a "hole in the ground" as long as he does not represent it to be a gold mine.

It should also be stated that legislation is one thing and enforcement another. Whereas some states — again, notably California — have considerable administrative staffs and enforce their laws strictly, both the competence and the level of enforcement in other states are not what they might be. This is apart from the fact — which is one of the very reasons for federal legislation — that the American economy has become increasingly national in scope so that a single state is often powerless effectively to enforce its statute against persons who make offerings from places outside its borders.

# The Securities and Exchange Commission

The federal securities legislation under which the Securities and Exchange Commission functions consists of eight separate statutes passed since 1933 and frequently amended. The SEC is one of the major "independent," multimember, and bipartisan commissions in Washington, along with a few others like the Federal Communications Commission, the Federal Trade Commission, the Interstate Commerce Commission, and the National Labor Relations Board. There are five Commissioners, appointed by the President with the consent of the Senate for staggered five-year terms. Although it is provided that "in making appointments members of different political parties shall be appointed alternately as nearly as may be practicable." not surprisingly no President of either party has ever found it "practicable" to have more than two members of the opposition Party. Nevertheless, the Statute does contain a further provision, which is categorical, that not more than three Commissioners may be members of the same party. And no Commissioner may be engaged in any other employment or business.

Independence is, of course, a relative thing. These "independent" commissions have access to appropriations only through the Office of Management and Budget, which is an arm of the White House; all filing and other fees are paid directly into the Treasury .Again, although the Commission is represented in the lower courts (except in criminal cases) by its own lawyers, it may appear in the Supreme Court of the United States only through the Solicitor General of the United States, through whom all Government litigation in the Supreme Court is channeled. Moreover, the Chairman is appointed by the President without the necessity of Senate confirmation, although he must be confirmed as a Commissioner. On the other hand, the legislative committees of the two Houses of Congress that are in charge of SEC legislation tend to think of the Commission as being more under their tutelage, if anything, than that of the White House. And this very attitude tends to prevent the Commission from becoming a mere arm of the Administration.

The independence of the SEC and similar agencies is considered to be important precisely because they have been called "a fourth branch" of government, cutting across Montesquieu's neat trilogy of the Executive, the Legislative, and the Judicial. Insofar as the Commission *enforces the statutes* — for example, when it investigates a suspected market manipulation or goes to court to seek a receivership against an insolvent broker — it is acting in an executive capacity. Insofar as it *adopts rules*, which have all the force of criminal law — when, for example, it adopts a 30-page proxy regulation under a brief statutory provision that simply makes it unlawful for any person to solicit proxies in contravention of whatever rules the Commission may adopt "in the public interest or for the protection of investors" — it is legislating just as surely as Congress does. Insofar as it *holds hearings* through its "administrative law judges" (with full right of counsel and cross-examination) and enters orders that are subject to judicial review (like orders of the federal trial courts) in one of the United States Courts of Appeals — as it does, for example, to revoke a broker's registration for willful violation of one of the statutory provisions or to deny an investment company's application for an exemption from one or more provisions — it is clearly acting in a judicial capacity.

To be sure, there is another side to the coin: As matters stand, the Commission, in a sense, acts as both prosecutor and judge in the same case. It acts as prosecutor when it approves a motion of the proper staff division that an administrative proceeding be instituted to discipline a broker; and it then acts as judge when it sits on review of the proposed findings of its trial examiner who has heard the evidence. The fact that all final orders of the Commission are subject to judicial review in a Court of Appeals does not afford a complete answer; for, although the review is plenary on questions of law, the Commission's findings of fact are conclusive if supported by "substantial evidence."

For this reason suggestions are still heard on occasion that the SEC and similar agencies ought to be confined to the *initiation* of proceedings of this sort, and that there ought to be one or more specialized administrative courts to hear and decide the cases. But the administrative law judges are required by the Administrative Procedure Act to be independent; and the staff lawyers who prosecute administrative proceedings do not, of course, approach either the administrative law judge or the Commission once the Commission, acting *ex parte* on the staff's recommendation, determines that the staff's evidence warrants the institution of a proceeding. There is also fear that the very separation of the prosecutory and judicial functions, with the relegation of the latter to a specialized administrative court, would unduly formalize matters and reduce the efficiency of administration in so highly complex and specialized an area as securities regulation,

In short, the present system — after varying periods ranging from 95 years in the case of the Interstate Commerce Commission, which is the grandfather of all these agencies, to 48 years in the case of the SEC — seems reasonably well entrenched.

# The Federal Securities Statutes

The substantive provisions of the eight federal statutes touching on securities regulation are at the same time disparate and closely interrelated.

### 1. Securities Act of 1933

The 1933 Act is concerned essentially with the initial distribution of securities (or their secondary distribution by persons in a control relationship with the issuer, which is to say, parents, subsidiaries, or sister companies that are under common control), rather than with subsequent trading. Securities that are offered to the public must be registered with the SEC by the issuer, and a prospectus (which is the principal portion of the registration statement) must be given to each offeree.

As we have already noted, the Commission has no authority to approve any security or pass on its merits. Its sole function is to ensure complete and accurate disclosure. Every registration statement is thoroughly examined by staff personnel consisting of financial analysts, accountants, lawyers, and, when necessary, engineers or geologists. If the staff considers that a registration statement is materially defective, it may recommend that the Commission institute an administrative proceeding looking toward the issuance of a "stop order," which prevents the registration statement from becoming effective automatically under the statute 20 days after the filing of the last amendment. In practice, however, stop-order proceedings are rare; for the issuer simply files one or more amendments in response to the staff's letters of comment, and meanwhile, in substance, waives the statutory provision on automatic effectiveness.

Willful misstatements in a registration statement are also criminal. And, more significantly in practice, any person who buys a registered security — even one who buys in the market prior to the expiration of the statute of limitations — may recover damages, on proof of a material misstatement or omission, against a variety of persons: the issuer, its directors and principal officers, its underwriters, the independent accountant who certified the financial statements, and any geologists or other experts who consented to the inclusion of their "expertized" information in the registration statement.

The constitutional nexus is afforded by the federal postal and commerce powers. That is to say, the registration requirement applies only if some use is made of the mails or of an instrumentality of interstate or foreign commerce in offering, selling, or delivering the security; but there is seldom difficulty on that account.

### 2. Securities Exchange Act of 1934

The 1934 Act is directed at post-registration trading. It has four basic purposes:

(1) to afford a measure of continual disclosure to people who buy and sell securities;

(2) to prevent, and afford remedies for, fraudulent practices in securities trading and manipulation of the markets;

(3) to regulate the markets generally (including, since the extensive amendments of 1975,the development of national market and clearance-settlement systems); and

(4) to control the amount of the nation's credit that goes into those markets.

All stock exchanges, brokers, dealers, transfer agents, clearing agencies, and "securities information processors" must register. So must any "national securities association" of brokers and dealers in the over-the-counter market; the only such association registered is the National Association of Securities Dealers, Inc. (NASD)

The credit provisions of this statute give the Board of Governors of the Federal Reserve System authority to promulgate margin rules and the SEC the task of enforcing them. The Board's rules now extend not only to brokers and banks but also to other substantial lenders. And since a 1970 amendment of the statute a new regulation for the first time applies to borrowers if they are citizens or residents of the United States or companies organized under the laws of a state, whether the loan is made in the United States or, in the case of a "United States security," abroad.

Securities must be registered with the SEC under the 1934 Act (quite independently of the registration requirement under the 1933 Act) either if they are listed on an exchange or (since 1964) if they are equity securities with at least 500 holders of record issued by a company with at least $1 million of gross assets (increased to $3 million by an exemptive rule in 1982). Companies with securities so registered are subject to periodic reporting requirements, proxy regulation, insider trading controls, and (since 1968) regulation with respect to tender offers.

One of the more controversial — but symbolically important — proxy rules, Rule 14a-8, gives a shareholder the right to submit any proposal that is proper for shareholder action under the law of the state of incorporation and requires the management to include in its own proxy statement not only the shareholder proposal, together with yes and no boxes, but also a 200-word statement by the shareholder in support of the proposal. In recent years that rule has been used by shareholder groups in a number of the largest companies, such as General Motors Corporation, in an attempt to further the goals of cleaner environment, fair employment practices, automobile safety, and so on.

With specific reference to environmental controls, the Commission presumably influenced to some extent by the National Environmental Policy Act of 1969, which requires that all federal statutes and policies be interpreted and administered "to the fullest extent possible" in accordance with the statute's policy of mobilizing the resources of the Government behind a consistent policy of environmental protection — not only has required the inclusion of some of these proposals in management proxy statements but also is developing general disclosure requirements in the registration and report forms with respect to significant capital outlays that are likely to be required to meet antipollution and safety standards.

### 3. Public Utility Holding Company Act of 1935

Whereas the 1933 Act is purely a disclosure statute and the 1934 Act is to some extent a regulatory statute, the Holding Company Act contemplates pervasive SEC regulation of electric and gas holding companies and their subsidiaries, with elaborate provisions that required their geographical integration and corporate simplification. In December 1981, the Commission recommended repeal of this statute as having served its basic purpose.

### 4. Trust Indenture Act of 1939

The 1939 Act, which is in substance an appendage of the 1933 Act but in form a separate statute, applies to the public offering of debt securities. Debt securities that are offered to the public must be issued under a "qualified indenture," which contains specific provisions and provides for a corporate trustee meeting rigorous standards of independence.

### 5. Investment Company Act of 1940

This Act, like the Holding Company Act, is not merely disclosure legislation but a highly articulated regulatory statute. It is the longest and most elaborate of the SEC series. It was amended in a number of significant respects in late 1970, notably by tightening the fiduciary obligations of management companies.

For example, Section 36 had provided from the beginning that, on a showing by the Commission that an officer, director, or investment adviser of a registered investment company had been guilty of "gross misconduct or gross misuse of trust" with respect to his company, a federal court should enjoin him either temporarily or permanently from acting in any of those capacities. This provision had been applied in a number of cases. Indeed, it was one of the provisions under which the courts implied private rights of action even though technically the conduct described in Section 36 was not unlawful in the criminal sense.

Section 36 was considerably expanded, however, in 1970. For one thing, the "gross misconduct or gross misuse of trust" language was liberalized to "a breach of fiduciary duty involving personal misconduct." Beyond that, Section 36 (b) now provides that the investment adviser is "deemed to have a fiduciary duty with respect to the receipt of compensation for services"; that an action may be brought by the commission, or by a security holder of the registered investment company on behalf of the company, for breach of that duty; and that ratification of the compensation arrangement by the investment company's shareholders, instead of being considered conclusive or well-nigh conclusive as at common law, "shall be given such consideration by the court as is deemed appropriate under all the circumstances." This language was a compromise, which did not go as far as the Commission had desired, but it is nevertheless a considerable step toward the goal of keeping management companies' compensation within reasonable limits.

In 1980, the Investment Company Act was further amended by the Small Business Investment Incentive Act in order to relieve from a number of the statutory restrictions in the interest of financing relatively small business ventures.

### 6. Investment Advisers Act of 1940

This Act. the simplest of the series, requires the registration with the SEC of investment advisers. It also regulates their methods of compensation and a few other activities.

### 7. Chapter 11 of the Bankruptcy Statute

The Commission has unique but important functions under a seventh measure. Chapter 11 of the new bankruptcy statute effective October 1,1979, which provides for corporate reorganizations in the bankruptcy courts. Because a corporate reorganization is apt to require a combination of legal, financial, and accounting skills beyond the competence of a single federal judge, this chapter — successor to the Chapter X that had been added to the predecessor Bankruptcy Act in 1938 — marks an interesting and highly successful experiment in judicial-administrative collaboration (what the late Judge Jerome Frank called "administrative law in the courts") by making the Commission an impartial adviser to the reorganization court. The Commission may appear in a reorganization proceeding and be heard on any issue. And the courts have found the Commission's participation to be very helpful.

### 8. Securities Investor Protection Act of 1970

The Commission, finally, has certain functions under the Securities Investor Protection Act of 1970,as revised in 1978. The Securities Investor Protection Corporation, which was created by that statute and is funded by assessments against all the broker-dealers in the country (with minor exceptions) as well as a ＄1 billion backing from the United States Treasury if needed, insures customer accounts against broker-dealer insolvency to a limit of ＄500,000 in cash and securities claims, of which the maximum cash component is ＄100,000.

### 9. The Foreign Corrupt Practices Act of 1977

The Foreign Corrupt Practices Act of 1977 (FCPA) amended the Exchange Act so as to require SEC－reporting companies to make and keep books, records and accounts that, in reasonable detail, accurately and fairly reflect the transactions and dispositions of the assets of the issuer.

Reporting companies are also required to devise and maintain a system of internal accounting controls sufficient to provide reasonable assurances that: (1) Transactions are executed in accordance with management's specific authorization; (2) Transactions are recorded as necessary to permit preparation of financial statements in conformity with generally accepted accounting principles or other applicable criteria and to maintain accountability for assets; (3) Access to assets is permitted only in accordance with management's authorization; (4) The recorded accountability for assets is compared with existing assets at reasonable intervals, and appropriate action is taken with respect to any differences.

The FCPA also makes it unlawful for any reporting company (or its officers, directors, employees, agents or stockholders acting on its behalf) to corruptly further a payment, offer to pay, or give anything of value to: (1) A foreign official in his official capacity; (2) A foreign political party or candidate for foreign political office; or (3) Any person knowing or having reason to know that a portion of such money or thing of value will be offered, given, or promised to any foreign official, political party, or candidate if the purpose of the payment or proposed payment to any of the foregoing persons is to influence a decision or act of the foreign government (or an instrumentality thereof) and to assist in retaining or directing business. A foreign official is defined so as to exclude employees whose duties are essentially ministerial or clerical. Therefore, the FCPA does not cover so-called "grease payments" to minor officials.

The SEC staff interprets the FCPA as applying to foreign private issuers — that is, foreign securities issuers that are not governments — that are required to report under the Exchange Act. Consequently, foreign private issuers — as defined by the SEC — who are considering entering the U.S. securities market are advised to consult their independent accountants and legal counsel about the applicability and effects of the FCPA.

# Development of a "Federal Corporation Law"

Although the Commission completed a Herculean task, which required some 25 years, when it reorganized the nation's electric and gas holding company systems in accordance with the geographical integration and corporate simplification standards of the Public Utility Holding Company Act and although the Commission continues to spend a considerable portion of its time administering the Investment company Act, it seems clear, when one considers that those are both statutes of specialized application, that the most significant developments of general application in the corporate and securities would have occurred increasingly under the Securities Exchange Act.

To a large extent this has happened in an altogether unanticipated way — through the implication by the courts of private rights of action — partly under a provision of the Act that makes illegal contracts voidable and partly under the common law doctrine to the effect that a member of a class who is injured by the violation of a criminal law passed for his benefit (in the case of the SEC statutes, any investor) can recover damages in a tort action. Strangely enough, the latter doctrine — though it has withered in England, the country of its origin, except with respect to industrial welfare legislation — has flowered as a matter of federal law under the SEC statutes, to the point where courts and commentators are now speaking of a "federal corporation law".

In a proper sense, of course, there is no federal corporation law. All corporations except national banks and federal savings and loan associations (there are also state banks and savings and loan associations) and an occasional federally chartered company like the Communications Satellite Corporation are incorporated by the states. Thus the basic corporation law, both common law and statutory, is state law. Nevertheless, the Supremacy Clause of the Constitution gives the federal law precedence over the state law when there is a clash. And, when the courts (federal or state) construe such broad terms as "fraud" and "material" that appear in federal statutes or rules, or when they decide to what extent such common law concepts as scienter, reliance, and causation inhere in the private rights of action that they have invented, they are not bound by state common law precedents but, in any realistic view are creating a new federal common law.

This is the sense in which we speak today of a "federal corporation law." The situation here is more than a little reminiscent of the British professor of constitutional law who is said to have started his lecture by stating. "There is no British Constitution," and immediately to have added. "The British Constitution is the greatest constitution there ever was."

The Investment Company Act aside, the development has centered primarily around two provisions in the Securities Exchange Act. One is the proxy section, already mentioned, pursuant to which the Commission has gradually evolved a complex regulation that, among other things, requires the filing, examination, and delivery of a "proxy statement," more or less comparable to a prospectus; and also broadly prohibits misstatements and half-truths in the solicitation of proxies. The other is the famous Rule 10b-5 — which is to say, the fifth rule under Section 10 (b) of the act — the catchall antifraud rule, which in the most general terms prohibits deceptive practices, misstatements, and half-truths in connection with the purchase or sale of any security as long as there is some tangential use of the mails or an instrumentality of interstate or foreign commerce. Although the only statutory sanctions for violation of these sections and rules are public, the Supreme Court in the late 1960s and early 1970s stamped its approval on the lower courts' earlier implication of private rights of action.

In the proxy area this means — when proxies have been solicited to approve a merger, for example — that an opposition stockholder who can prove a violation of the proxy regulation (usually a misstatement in the solicitation or perhaps a failure to deliver a copy of the proxy statement) has a private right of action. More than that, the court, once its jurisdiction has been properly invoked, has all the traditional powers of a court of equity that American courts inherited from the British Chancellors.

Thus, although the only conduct made unlawful by the statute is the solicitation of proxies in violation of the commission's rules, a court has inherent authority to prevent the violator from enjoying the fruits of his violation by enjoining him from voting the proxies that he illegally solicited. Indeed, in an appropriate case the court may go so far as to declare the proxies to be void, to set aside the action taken by their use if they have already been voted, to require a re-solicitation and the holding of a new meeting, or, if the hypothetical merger has actually been consummated before the court has had an opportunity to act, to order the unwinding of the merger. Moreover, all this will be decided as a matter of federal law — which is to say, judge-made law — regardless of whatever the state statutory or common law may be with reference to the setting aside of action approved by a vote of stockholders.

In the area of Rule 10b-5 — which the author has elsewhere called "a dark horse of dubious pedigree, but very fleet of foot" — the judicial development has been even more startling. For example, although the common law traditionally has considered directors and officers to be fiduciaries in dealing with *their corporation*, it has not considered them to occupy a fiduciary relation to individual *shareholders*. It is a strange dichotomy. For the corporation as a separate "person" is, after all, a fiction — however convenient or even essential a fiction in an industrialized society — and to treat an officer, director, or controlling shareholder like a fiduciary in dealing with the artificial entity, the *persona ficta*, the ghost, but not in dealing with the flesh-and-blood shareholders who *own* the corporation, is nothing less than a monument to the ability of lawyers and judges to hypnotize themselves with their own creations.

Nevertheless, this anomaly led the courts at common law — at least a few decades ago — to treat a director, officer, or controlling shareholder who buys shares as if he were a stranger dealing at arm's length with the selling shareholders. That is to say, he must not lie; for even a stranger may be liable in a common law deceit action if he knowingly misstates a material fact. But he has no affirmative obligation, such as an agent has in dealing with his principal, to disclose all material facts bearing on his adverse interest in the transaction.

Admittedly, even at common law a few courts in the United States have not been able to stomach this anomalous result; and, one way or another, the courts as a matter of common law gradually have come over to a fiduciary standard in these cases so that an "insider" is not permitted to buy shares for himself on the eve of consummation of a favorable merger of on the basis of a freshly discovered and not yet announced discovery of oil on the company's property.

But the significant judicial development is that Rule 10b-5 has now been construed, in effect, to place "insiders" (as well as persons receiving inside information from insiders) on a fiduciary basis in dealing with shareholders as a matter of federal law. The result is that plaintiffs in cases of this type seldom bother anymore with bringing actions under state law.

Again, by holding that the issuance of a security involves a "sale" and "purchase" for purposes of Rule 10b-5,many stockholders' derivative actions that would normally be mismanagement lawsuits under state law have been federalized. And in the process, the law has been liberalized on the theory that it was the purpose of Congress in the Securities Exchange Act to elevate the standards of doing business generally as far as securities are concerned. Since a securities transaction of one sort or another is apt to lurk in most mismanagement cases, one can readily appreciate why courts and commentators have come to refer to a "federal corporation law" in this area.

All this, inevitably, has solved some problems at the cost of creating others, notably the uncertainty and unpredictability resulting from the fact that this elaborate development has been based on a short rule adopted under an even shorter Section 10 (b) of the Securities Exchange Act, whose somewhat broader version in the 1934 bill was described during the course of the legislative hearings by the administration's spokesman as saying, "Thou shalt not devise any other cunning devices."

## Codification: The Federal Securities Code

By now the hundreds of decided cases — indeed, two whole treatises have been written on Rule 10b-5 — should make it possible, without necessarily foreclosing further judicial development, to codify (and thus lend a greater degree of certainty to) some of the basic jurisprudence that has developed under the rule. In the process, moreover, something should be done about the almost chaotic state of civil liability generally that has been caused by the judicial implication of private rights of action, however salutary that development has been in reforming an important branch of the law of corporations.

There are other areas that cry equally for legislative reform−indeed, for a general restructuring and codification of the seven securities statutes (Chapter 11 being essentially bankruptcy rather than securities legislation). And in 1969, The American Law Institute undertook to do precisely that by preparing an integrated Federal Securities Code that would not only replace all seven statutes but also systematize a considerable portion of the administrative regulations and the jurisprudence.

The author of this lesson, as the "Reporter," worked with 30 odd consultants and advisers, who included two United States Court of Appeals judges; several academics (among them

Professor Gower, the outstanding British authority on company law and a former member of the Law Commission); a current member of the SEC; several former SEC Chairmen, Commissioners, and counsel; a state blue sky commissioner; and a nationwide group of distinguished practicing lawyers.

In May 1978, the membership of the Institute, after considering portions of the Code at its annual meetings of 1972-1977, approved the proposed final draft, which extends to some 700 pages. The Code was subsequently endorsed, and its enactment urged, by the House of Delegates of the American Bar Association. The official draft, with extensive commentary by the Reporter, was published in two volumes by the Institute in April 1980.And, after extensive negotiations by the Reporter and a few of the advisory group with the SEC and its staff, the Commission in September 1980 announced its support of the Code with a number of changes not going to its basic structure or substantially affecting its major reforms.

The national elections of November 1980 resulted in a change in control of the Senate committee, as well as the defeat or reassignment of those members of the House committee who had been following the Code's progress, so that the educational process had to begin again with a new cast of characters. In January 1982, however, a "new" Commission three of whose members had been appointed by President Reagan "strongly" reaffirmed its support for the Code, which it called "an enormous simplification." And the courts seem to be treating the Code. when possible, as if it were a restatement of existing law.

The Code is in 20 parts:

1. Legislative Findings and Declarations
2. Definitions
3. Exemptions
4. Issuer Registration
5. Distributions
6. Postregistration Provisions
7. Broker, Dealer, and Investment Adviser Registration and Qualifications
8. Self-Regulatory Organizations
9. Market Regulation
10. National Market and Clearance-Settlement Systems
11. Municipal Securities
12. Broker-Dealer Insolvency
13. Trust Indentures
14. Investment Companies
15. Utility Holding Companies

16. Fraud, Misrepresentation, and Manipulation

17. Civil Liability

18. Administration and Enforcement

19. Scope of the Code

20. General

To mention but a few of the major problems and areas of reform:

(1) First of all, the very fact that the seven statutes were passed at different sittings of Congress, and have been amended a number of times since, has resulted in legislative gaps on the one hand and a good deal of needlessly complex overlapping on the other. The same term is sometimes defined in two or three different ways when a single definition would suffice. The result has been an unhealthy prevalence of theological hair-splitting, which should be relegated to history not only by the very process of codification but also, more specifically, by the attendant elimination or simplification of some of today's arcane concepts like "private offering," "control", and "restricted securities."

(2) With the gradual development of more effective disclosure devices than the prospectus — for example, the proxy statement and the annual report to shareholders — the registration and prospectus provisions in the 1933 Act should no longer be treated as if they were the center of the SEC universe. The very dependence of those provisions on the concept of an "offer" or a "sale" has resulted in a series of overly sophistic rules, such as the complex Rule 133 (reversed in 1972 by the equally complex Rule 145) that governed the necessity of registration in connection with mergers, consolidations, sales of assets for securities, and corporate reclassifications.

The need today is for a rational system of continual disclosure — whose seed was planted in 1964 when the Securities Exchange Act was amended to require registration of all equity securities held by more than 500 persons and issued by companies with at least ＄1 million (since 1982, ＄3 million by rule) of gross assets — instead of continuing to rely on the hit-or-miss registration process under the 1933 Act, which depends on the financing needs of particular issuers or their controlling persons. The philosophy of the 1964 amendment is of considerable significance; for it is the first instance of compulsory registration in the 1933 and 1934 Acts. Previously, companies (other than investment companies or public utility holding companies) could avoid registration — at a price, of course — by not going to the public or listing on an exchange. But a company that meets the size and ownership standards of the 1964 amendment has no choice. This new registration requirement — with one of its standards broadened in the Code from 500 equity security holders of a class to 500 holders in the aggregate — is one of the pegs (the other is a "distribution" of a given size by any person) on which the Code bases a continual disclosure system through the permanent registration of companies rather than the registration of securities.

(3) The Code also affords a rational treatment of secondary distributions, gives the SEC direct authority over reports to security holders, rationalizes a good deal of the vast and complex body of "federal corporation law" that has evolved around Rule 10b-5, synchronizes the whole areas of fraudulent and manipulative acts (Part XVI) and civil liability (Part XVⅡ), prescribes standards for the further implication of private rights of action, and harmonizes the scattered accounting provisions into a single section (§1805) as a result of extensive discussions with representatives of the Commission (including its Chief Accountant) and the American Institute of Certified Public Accountants.

(4) There has been a considerable amount of litigation in recent years with respect to the variegated problems of extraterritorial application of the SEC statutes. Section 30 (b) of the 1934 Act — a not very satisfactory provision never implemented by Commission rules — has been interpreted to exclude from the statutory coverage the transacting of "a business in securities" but not an isolated act outside the territorial limits of the United States when there are substantial contacts with the United states. Since it would not be practicable to spell out and codify the extraterritorial application of the statutes generally on a section-by-section basis, as was done in the much simpler Uniform Securities Act, the Code's solution is a series of general principles, which are not inconsistent with the American Law Institute's Restatement of Foreign Relations Law of the United States (now under revision), with rulemaking authority in the Commission to vary those principles and to provide for cases that they do not cover.

(5) To complete this inventory of problems, as any good symphony should, with a variation of the theme that began this introduction, the Code contains a general reassessment of the relationship between the SEC statutes and the state blue sky laws. Complete preemption, quite probably, is neither desirable nor politically feasible. But a majority of the states have already adopted the Uniform Securities Act's system of "registration by coordination," under which the procedure of federal and state registration is coordinated without sacrificing the substantive standards of the state statutes to the federal disclosure philosophy. That is to say, whenever an offering is registered with the SEC, the issuer need only file with the state authorities whatever information and documents it files with the SEC, and then registration becomes effective at the state level the moment it becomes effective in Washington unless the state authorities institute an administrative proceeding under their own substantive standards to prevent the local registration from becoming effective. In most cases, of course, there is no proceeding, and therefore the issuer that contemplates a nationwide offering is spared the necessity of

frantically clearing with several dozen state blue sky administrators in order to make sure that it is free to proceed in the respective states when registration becomes effective in Washington.

The Code requires substantially this procedure as a matter of federal law by preempting those state laws whose procedure is not substantially coordinated by a certain date with that of the SEC. This much, it seems, is the barely decent minimum that the states owe to the Union in so complex an area of the economy as securities distributions. Moreover, the states are precluded from second-guessing the SEC on the contents of a prospectus or from any regulation at all of securities that meet prescribed quality standards. And, there is complete preemption in the tender offer field, which has spawned 30-odd state statutes largely since the 1968 amendment of the 1934 Act.

The time does seem ripe for codification. There will undoubtedly be opposition to many of the proposed changes, for it is of the nature of codification that existing law will be tightened in some respects and loosened in others. Surely the Reporter is painfully aware of the danger that the solution of one problem may create two new ones. But one can only hope that most informed persons will conclude that on balance they have more to gain from the Code generally than they have to lose from particular changes that may not be to their liking. Meanwhile one nurtures his faith.

 **New Words**

| | | |
|---|---|---|
| 1. | synopsis *n.* | 概要；提要 |
| 2. | securities *n.* | 證券 |
| 3. | the Securities and Exchange Commission (the SEC) | 證券交易委員會 |
| 4. | codification *n.* | 法典化 |
| 5. | code *n.* | 法典 |
| 6. | codify *v.* | 使法典化 |
| 7. | prolegomenon *n.* | 序；前言；緒論 |
| 8. | "Blue Sky Laws" | 「藍天法」；美國州一級的證券法 |
| 9. | aphorism *n.* | 格言；警句 |
| 10. | enigma *n.* | 謎；曖昧不明的話 |
| 11. | federalism *n.* | 聯邦制 |
| 12. | proponent *n.* | 建設者；提議者；支持者；辯護者 |
| 13. | preempt *v.* | 先占；先取；以先買權取得 |
| 14. | prospectus *n.* | 公開說明書；招股章程 |

15. disclosure philosophy 　　　　揭露哲學

16. multimember *n*. 　　　　多成員

17. bipartisan *a*. 　　　　由兩黨組成的；被兩黨支持的

18. staggered *a*. 　　　　交錯的

19. alternately *adv*. 　　　　輪流地；交替地

20. categorical *a*. 　　　　無條件的；絕對的；明白的；明確的

21. the Solicitor General 　　　　首席檢察官

22. Montesquieu *n*. 　　　　孟德斯鳩（法國法學家、哲學家）

23. trilogy *n*. 　　　　三部曲；（本課文中作）三權分立

24. receivership *n*. 　　　　破產管理人的職務（或職位）

25. plenary *a*. 　　　　完全的；充分的

26. ex parte 　　　　單方面地；片面地

27. prosecutory function 　　　　起訴的或檢舉的作用（職能）

28. judicial function 　　　　司法職能

29. judicial review 　　　　司法檢查；司法審查

30. formalize *v*. 　　　　使正式；使定形；使具有形式

31. entrench *v*. 　　　　使……處於牢固地位

32. disparate *a*. 　　　　全異的；根本不相同的；無聯繫的

33. stop order 　　　　停止交易令

34. nexus *n*. 　　　　連接；聯繫；關係

35. clearance-settlement systems 　　　　清算結算系統

36. transfer agents 　　　　過戶代理人

37. clearing agencies 　　　　交換代理；清算代理

38. the over-the-counter market 　　　　場外交易市場；櫃檯交易市場

39. the National Association of Securities Dealers, Inc 　　　　全國證券交易商協會（NASD）

40. equity securities 　　　　股票；產權股票；普通股

41. gross assets 　　　　總資產

42. proxy statement 　　　　委託書

43. proxy rules 　　　　委託規則

44. proxy regulation 　　　　委託管理

45. insider trading controls 　　　　對內線交易的控制

46. tender offers 　　　　收購股權；招標

47. environmental controls 　　　　環境控制

| | | |
|---|---|---|
| **48.** capital outlays | 資本支出 | |
| **49.** holding company | 控股公司；股權公司 | |
| **50.** trust indenture | 信託契約；委託書 | |
| **51.** appendage *n.* | 附屬物；附加物 | |
| **52.** debt securities | 債務證券；債券 | |
| **53.** well-nigh *adv.* | 幾乎；近乎 | |
| **54.** herculean *a.* | 艱難的；費力的；艱巨的 | |
| **55.** altogether *adv.* | 完全地；全部地 | |
| **56.** wither *v.* | 使消亡；使衰落；使畏縮 | |
| **57.** scienter *n.* | 故意；知情；明知 | |
| **58.** inhere *v.* | 生來即存在於；本質上即屬於 | |
| **59.** reminiscent *a.* | 回憶往事的；懷舊的；提醒的 | |
| **60.** evolve *v.* | 使逐漸形成；使逐步演變；使發展 | |
| **61.** solicitation of proxies | 委託請求 | |
| **62.** catchall *a.* | 包含甚廣的 | |
| **63.** tangential *a.* | 離開正題的；扯得很遠的 | |
| **64.** resolicitation *n.* | 再請求 | |
| **65.** consummate *v.* | 使完美 | |
| **66.** unwinding *n.* | 解開；鬆開 | |
| **67.** dark horse | 競爭中出人意料的獲勝者 | |
| **68.** dubious pedigree | 可疑的家世 | |
| **69.** fleet of foot | 走路快的；捷足的；轉瞬即逝的 | |
| **70.** dichotomy *n.* | 二分法 | |
| **71.** persona ficta | 虛構的人 | |
| **72.** anomaly *n.* | 破格；不按常規 | |
| **73.** adverse *a.* | 相反的 | |
| **74.** admittedly *adv.* | 公認地 | |
| **75.** anomalous *a.* | 不規則的；異常的；破格的 | |
| **76.** consummation *n.* | 完成 | |
| **77.** derivative *a.* | 派生的；被引出的 | |
| **78.** federalized *a.* | 使結成聯邦 | |
| **79.** unpredictability *n.* | 無可預見性 | |
| **80.** bill *n.* | 法案 | |
| **81.** treatises *n.* | 論文 | |
| **82.** foreclose *v.* | 妨礙；阻止 | |

| | | |
|---|---|---|
| **83.** | salutary *a.* | 表示歡迎的 |
| **84.** | systematize *v.* | 使系統化；使成體系 |
| **85.** | academics *n.* | 學者；學究式的人物 |
| **86.** | distinguished *a.* | 著名的；傑出的 |
| **87.** | endorse *v.* | 贊同；認可；擔保 |
| **88.** | a new cast of characters | 角色表 |
| **89.** | overlapping *n.* | 重疊 |
| **90.** | suffice *v.* | 足夠 |
| **91.** | sittings *n.* | 開會；開庭 |
| **92.** | prevalence *n.* | 流行；盛行；優勢 |
| **93.** | theological *a.* | 神學上的 |
| **94.** | hair-splitting *n.a.* | 作無益而瑣細分析（的） |
| **95.** | relegate *v.* | 使湮沒無聞 |
| **96.** | attendant *a.* | 伴隨的 |
| **97.** | arcane *a.* | 秘密的；神祕的 |
| **98.** | sophistic *a.* | 詭辯的 |
| **99.** | peg *n.* | 藉口；遁詞 |
| **100.** | synchronize *v.* | 同時發生；同步 |
| **101.** | variegated *a.* | 多樣化的 |
| **102.** | extraterritorial *a.* | 治外法權的 |
| **103.** | symphony *n.* | 交響樂；調和 |
| **104.** | spawn *v.* | 引起；釀成 |
| **105.** | 30-odd | 三十多個 |
| **106.** | liking *n.* | 愛；喜歡 |
| **107.** | nurture *v.* | 養育；哺育 |

### ♣ New Phrases and Idiomatic Expressions

| | | |
|---|---|---|
| **1.** | to be apt to do sth. | 易於……的；有做……傾向的 |
| **2.** | to come to grips with | 千方百計解決……；開始盡力對付…… |
| **3.** | to go to the extreme of doing sth. | 走做某事的極端 |
| **4.** | to cut across | 抄近路穿過；穿過 |
| **5.** | in a sense | 一定意義上 |
| **6.** | under one's tutelage | 在……監護或教導下 |
| **7.** | to be directed at | 針對…… |

| | | |
|---|---|---|
| **8.** in an attempt to do sth. | 試圖做某事 |
| **9.** in substance | 本質上；實質上 |
| **10.** to enjoin sb. from doing sth. | 禁止某人做某事 |
| **11.** for one thing | 其一 |
| **12.** to spend time doing sth. | 花時間做某事 |
| **13.** to give...precedence over | 給……優先於……的地位 |
| **14.** to inhere in | 生來即屬於；本質上即屬於 |
| **15.** to center around | 圍繞 |
| **16.** to go so far as to do sth. | 走得如此之遠以致於做某事 |
| **17.** at arm's length | 保持一定距離的 |
| **18.** to cry for | 要求 |
| **19.** to give authority over | 給予……的權力 |
| **20.** to gain from | 從……獲益 |
| **21.** to lurk in | 潛藏在；潛在於…… |

 **Notes**

**1.** Blue Sky Laws：藍天法；州一級證券法。

a popular name for state statutes providing for the regulation and supervision of securities offerings and sales, for the protection of citizen-investors from investing in fraudulent companies. Laws intended to stop the sale of stock in fly－by-night concerns, visionary oil wells, distant gold mines, and other like fraudulent exploitations. A statute is called a "Blue Sky Law" because it pertains to speculative schemes which have no more basis than so many feet of blue sky.

**2.** the Great Depression of 1903-1933 or of the 1930s：1930年代大蕭條。

It was a worldwide depression where output fell 30% below the peak value reached in 1929. In Europe, it caused political demonstration that contributed to the rise of Nazism and set the world marching toward the Second World War. In the chain of events that brought the world depression, the depression in the United States, and the collapse of the U.S. banking system seem to have been major links.

**3.** the stock market crash of 1929：1929年股市大崩潰。

It refers to the 1929 panic and crash in Wall Street. When the black October Crash of 1929 came everyone was caught by the dramatic decline in securities prices. Billions of dollars of security values were wiped out every month.

**4.** ...to elect in late 1932 an Administration under President

Franklin D. Roosevelt that was dedicated to widespread socioeconomic reform within the capitalist system:

His socio-economic reform mainly refers to the "New Deal" program. Roosevelt summarized New Deal in three words:

relief — to assist distressed persons

recovery — to lift the nation out of the depression

reform — to eliminate abuses in the economy

**5.** the American Law Institute

Group of American legal scholars who are responsible for the Restatements in the various disciplines of the law and, who, jointly with the National Conference of Commissioners on Uniform State Laws prepare some of the Uniform State Laws, e.g. Uniform Commercial Code.

**6.** hit-or-miss or hit-and-miss

時而打中時而打不中；時而成功時而不成功。

**7.** right of action：訴訟權。the right to bring suit.

private right of action：私人訴訟權。

**8.** the National Association of Securities Dealers, Inc (NASD)：全國證券交易商協會。

the Maloney Act, passed in 1938,which amended the Securities Exchange Act of 1934,provides for self-regulation of the over-the-counter securities market by associations registered with the SEC. The NASD is the only association so registered. Most companies offering variable annuities are NASD members.

**9.** insider trading (insider dealing)：內線交易。

Buying and selling of corporate shares by officers, directors and stockholder who own more than 10% of the stock of a corporation listed on a national exchange. Such transactions must be reported monthly to the SEC.

## Exercises

### I. Answer the following Questions:

**1.** What does "Blue Sky Law" mean?

**2.** Explain the reasons for the United States to use federal legislation to regulate securities distributions.

**3.** How much do you know about the SEC?

4. What are the basic objectives of the Securities Act of 1933 and the basic purposes of Securities Exchange Act of 1934?

5. What is insider trading ? Is it against the securities law?

6. What are the component parts of the Federal Securities Code?

## II. Translate the following Chinese passages into English:

1. 對美國一級證券市場管理的法律是1933年證券法。制定該法的兩個目的是：(1)向投資者提供資訊，幫助他們對向公衆出售證券的價值進行正確的評估；(2)防止證券買賣中的虛假說明和詐欺行爲的發生。

2. 1934年證券交易法是對美國證券市場二級市場進行管理的重要法律。制定該法有四個基本目的：(1)向買賣證券的人提供繼續資訊揭露的衡量標準；(2)防止證券交易中詐欺做法的發生和對市場的操縱，並爲其提供救濟；(3)對證券市場進行全面管理；(4)對國家進入證券市場信貸量進行控制。

## III. Indicate whether each of the following statements is true or false by writing "T" of "F" in the space provided:

1. There was no federal regulation of the issuance of securities until 1920.

2. The first stock market crash of the United States took place in 1929, followed by the Great Depression.

3. The disclosure philosophy chosen by American Congress for regulating distribution of securities originated in the British Company Act's prospectus provisions.

4. The SEC has authority to approve on security or pass on its merits.

5. Whereas the 1933 Act is purely a disclosure statute and the 1934 Act is to some extent a regulatory statute.

6. The United States has been trying hard to codify its securities legislation.

7. The SEC was established in 1933 to help regulate the United States securities market.

8. The SEC has no legislative power.

# 第三十二課 Lesson 32

# 信用狀法
# Letter of Credit Law

In letter of credit disputes, the courts often apply the standard of strict compliance in conjunction with other principles derived from contract law, equity, and banking custom. The author analyzes thirteen such principles: (1) the rule of contra proferentem; (2) the "render performance possible" rule; (3) the "plain meaning" rule; (4) provisions of the Uniform Customs and Practice for Documentary Credits; (5) reformation of the written terms of a letter of credit; (6) the parol evidence rule; (7) waiver; (8) estoppel; (9) course of dealing and course of performance; (10) banking customs; (11) good faith; (12) duty to notify the beneficiary of oppressive terms; and (13) the UCC presentment warranty. He demonstrates, with reference to leading cases, how the application of these principles frequently dilutes the baseline strict compliance standard of letter of credit law and creates a standard of compliance that is akin to substantial compliance. He sees a real danger that the seeming willingness of courts to accept a substantial compliance standard may be confused with a willingness to accept so-called non-documentary payment conditions as well.

There are over $250 billion of standby letters of credit outstanding in the United States. Although there are no readily available statistics on commercial letters of credit, there must be outstanding at the present time hundreds of millions of dollars of these letters of credit as well.

Creditors who are beneficiaries of standby letters of credit and sellers who are beneficiaries of commercial letters of credit rely on these financial instruments as ironclad payment guarantees. Beneficiaries assume that if they present documents that strictly comply with the terms of their credits, they will be paid quickly and without protest by the various banks that have issued them.

Whereas this doctrine of strict documentary compliance is basic to letter of credit law, this article shows that courts do not always apply it in isolation. Often, courts apply strict compliance in conjunction with other principles derived from contract law, equity, and banking custom. In many cases, the interaction between strict compliance and these other principles softens the rigors of strict compliance and results in the application of a standard of documentary compliance that is perhaps more akin to substantial compliance than to strict compliance. It is important for all parties to a letter of credit transaction to keep this interaction in mind because it has an important impact on how letters of credit are drafted and enforced.

To probe this interaction in some detail, this lesson briefly describes the doctrine of strict documentary compliance. It then enumerates those principles that tend to soften the rigors of strict documentary compliance. The concluding section of this lesson shows that even if courts sometimes apply what is essentially a substantial compliance standard under the rubric of strict compliance, this should not be used as an argument for relaxing the prohibition against "non-documentary payment conditions" in letters of credit. A substantial compliance standard to test *documentary* conditions in letters of credit is one thing; a substantial compliance standard to test *factual* (*nondocumentary*) conditions in letters of credit is entirely something else.

# The Doctrine of Strict Documentary Compliance

To describe what is meant by the doctrine of strict documentary compliance, the author hypothesizes a typical standby letter of credit transaction. Creditor X is willing to lend debtor Q $1 million as long as X is guaranteed that the loan will be repaid. Instead of taking a security interest in collateral of Q, X may agree to accept a standby letter of credit from debtor Q's bank.

Once they agree to use a standby letter of credit, creditor X and debtor Q enter into their basic loan agreement. For the purposes of this analysis, this loan agreement is dubbed Contract I. Before the loan is actually made, however, Q has to provide X with the requisite letter of credit. Q goes to bank V and applies for the issuance of either a documentary or a clean standby letter of credit in X's favor. Assuming Q applies for the issuance of a documentary standby credit. Q requests in his application that bank V issue a credit, obligating itself to pay X $1 million if X presents his draft for that amount and a signed certificate attesting to the fact that Q has failed to repay the $1 million loan at maturity. If bank V agrees to issue the documentary credit on these terms, it enters into a contract with Q by co-signing Q's application. As part of this contract, Q agrees to reimburse bank V for all payments made under the credit. The resulting contract between bank V (the issuing bank) and Q (the customer or applicant for the credit) is dubbed Contract II. Finally, bank V issues the standby credit to X, obligating itself to pay X $1 million if X strictly complies with the documentary terms of payment (e.g., presentation of a draft for $1 million and a signed certificate attesting to Q's default). The standby letter of credit itself represents a contract between bank V (the issuing bank) and creditor X (the beneficiary of the credit). Once the credit is "established" in regard to X, bank V is obligated to pay X, regardless of any disputes that may arise either between Q and X over the terms of the loan agreement (Contract I) or between itself and Q over the terms of the application and reimbursement agreement (Contract II). In other words, upon "establishment," the standby letter of credit contract (Contract III) becomes separate from and independent of both Contracts I and II.

Assume that Q fails to repay the loan at maturity; X had demanded the standby letter of credit to protect against this very eventuality. Standby letters of credit are usually structured so that they are triggered by the presentation of a document attesting to the default of the applicant. It is at the very moment when X presents a certificate of default that the doctrine of strict documentary compliance takes on its greatest importance. Bank V will obviously realize that if it pays the credit, it may have difficulty obtaining reimbursement from Q under Contract II. If Q defaulted on its repayment obligation to X under Contract I, it is very likely that Q will also default on its reimbursement obligation to the bank under Contract II. Thus, bank V will carefully scrutinize the draft and certificate of default to make sure that they strictly comply with the terms of the credit in all details.

### 1. The crucial question

How strictly must X's documents comply with the terms of bank V's letter of credit? This is the crucial question. Few would argue that strict compliance means absolute literal compliance. In Tosco v. FDIC, for example, a bank refused to honor its letter of credit commitment because, as alleged by the bank, the beneficiary's draft did not strictly comply with the terms of the credit. The letter of credit required, inter alia, that the beneficiary's draft state that it was drawn under the bank's "Letter of Credit Number 105." When presented, the beneficiary's draft stated that it was drawn under "letter of Credit No.105." The court rejected the bank's strict compliance argument, finding that these discrepancies in the draft were trivial and did not justify dishonor.

But if strict compliance does not mean absolute literal compliance, it also does not mean substantial compliance. If a standby credit, for example, required a certificate that stated that the loan had not been repaid "on or before June 30," a certificate that stated that the loan had not been repaid "before June 30" would not strictly comply with the terms of the credit. In fact, because the certificate did not rule out payment on June 30, it is doubtful whether this certificate would even substantially comply with the terms of the credit.

### 2. The conservative stance

The standard of strict documentary compliance requires the issuing bank to compare the documents presented with the terms of the letter of credit and, based on this comparison, assess reasonably and in good faith whether any discrepancies between the two are consequential. Obvious typographical errors (Smithh for Smith) or obvious alternative phrasings ("debtor Q has not repaid the $1 million loan due on June 1" for "debtor Q has not repaid the $1 million loan maturing on June 1") should not affect payment. But, realistically, whenever there is any doubt about the relevance of a discrepancy, the issuing bank should adopt a conservative stance. The bank should refuse to pay and as required by Article 16 of the Uniform Customs and Practice for Documentary Credits (UCP), promptly notify the beneficiary of any discrepancies. By receiving prompt notice of discrepancies, the beneficiary may be able to cure these discrepancies and represent complying documents before the credit expires. This Article 16 rule that the issuing bank must notify the beneficiary of documentary discrepancies is a prudent requirement because it often leads to the quick resolution of interparty disputes over the wording of required documents.

# Rules of Contract Law, Equity, and Banking Custom Affecting Strict Compliance

What happens if the documentary discrepancies cannot be cured before the expiration date of the letter of credit? If the issuing bank dishonors the beneficiary's draft, the beneficiary may sue the issuing bank, claiming that the discrepancies do not justify the issuing bank in refusing to honor the credit. In determining whether the beneficiary's documents strictly comply, courts frequently apply principles drawn from contract law, equity, and banking custom in conjunction with the strict compliance standard. In actual effect, however, these principles often dilute the stringency of the strict compliance standard. In the end, these principles rather than the strict compliance standard itself may determine whether the beneficiary or the issuing bank will prevail in the lawsuit.

Article 5 of the UCC does not preclude the use of these "diluting" principles. Section 5-102 (3) of the UCC provides that Article 5 "deals with some *but not all* of the rules and concepts of letters of credit as such rules or concepts have developed prior to this act or may hereafter develop" (emphasis supplied). Among the more important areas of letter of credit law not covered by Article 5 is the issue of documentary compliance. The drafters of Article 5 purposely left this issue to be worked out in future adjudication. Thus, the question whether to apply "diluting" principles in the context of strict documentary compliance will not be answered by reading Article 5. It will be answered only by reading court opinions.

## 1. The rule of contra proferentem

Although a letter of credit is frequently referred to as a specialty contract, courts still treat it as a contract. A basic rule of contract interpretation requires that in the case of an ambiguity in the language of a contract, the ambiguity should be interpreted against the party who drafted or proffered the contract. Since a letter of credit is drafted by the issuing bank and not by the beneficiary, this rule of *contra proferentem* requires that in a suit between the beneficiary and the issuing bank, all ambiguities in the credit should be construed against the issuing bank.

*Marino Industries, Inc. v. Chase Manhattan Bank, N. A.* provides a good example of how the rule of *contra proferentem* impacts on the strict compliance standard. In *Marino*, the beneficiary was required to present a certificate of receipt signed by a Mdica representative in order to obtain payment under a commercial letter of credit. The beneficiary presented a certificate of receipt signed by a Mdica representative, but the signature on the receipt was not one of the signatures on file with Chase. Chase refused to pay based on the doctrine of strict compliance. The beneficiary, however, sued Chase for wrongful dishonor of the credit. The Court of Appeals for the Second Circuit ruled that since there was an ambiguity in the letter of credit as to whether the receipts could be signed by any Mdica representative or only by one of the three Mdica representatives whose signatures were on file with Chase. The letter of credit had to be interpreted against the party generating the credit — here, Chase. Consequently, if the beneficiary presented receipts signed by any Mdica representative, the receipts would strictly comply with the terms of the letter of credit, entitling the beneficiary to payment.

It should be recognized, however, that it is up to a court to determine whether the terms of a letter of credit are ambiguous, and courts will frequently disagree as to whether an ambiguity exists. *Fair pavilions, Inc. v. First National City Bank* is a case in point. In Fair pavilions, the applicant for a letter of credit had the power to cancel the credit if, at least ten days prior to any drawing date under the credit, an officer (or one describing himself as an officer) of the applicant presented the issuing bank with an affidavit certifying that "one or more of the events described in clause XV" of the underlying contract had occurred. The applicant presented the necessary affidavit to cancel the credit but did not specify in the affidavit which particular event described in clause XV of the underlying contract had occurred. The issuing bank proceeded to cancel the credit. When the beneficiary sued the issuing bank for wrongful dishonor, both the beneficiary and the bank moved for summary judgment. The New York trial court denied both motions for summary judgment, because the court felt that there was an issue presented as to whether any of the events specified in clause XV had occurred and thus whether the credit had been validly canceled. On appeal, however, the New York appellate division reversed and granted summary judgment to the issuing bank. Although the appellate division recognized that the words of the credit must be taken "as strongly against the issuer as a reasonable reading will justify," it could not find any ambiguity in the credit. According to the appellate division, the credit required the affidavit to state only that one or more of the events described in clause XV of the contract had occurred, not which of the events had occurred. To require that the event be specified in the affidavit would have required a modification of the credit.

The case did not end with the appellate division; however, it was appealed to the New York Court of Appeals, New York's highest court. The court of appeals reversed the appellate division's decision, finding in essence that the terms of the credit were ambiguous. According to the court of appeals, the text of the credit, read in conjunction with clause XV of the underlying contract, contemplated that if the applicant certified that one of the events in clause XV had occurred (these events were acts of default by the beneficiary), the beneficiary would be given an opportunity to correct its defective performance. To provide the beneficiary with a meaningful right of cure, it was necessary, said the court of appeals, to interpret the credit as requiring the applicant to state in the affidavit which specific event or events enumerated in clause XV had occurred. Since the affidavit as presented by the applicant did not specify which event had occurred, the bank could not cancel the credit. Summary judgment was granted to the beneficiary. The *Fair Pavilions* case is a good example of how courts can differ over whether the terms of a credit are ambiguous.

The rule of *contra proferentem* can also be used to prevent issuing banks from adding payment conditions to letters of credit. In *United Bank of Denver, N.A. v. Citibank, N.A.*, the particular credit required a signed, written statement certifying that "[the applicant for the credit] has failed to pay U.S. $ 200,000 on the due date pursuant to Section 4 of the Technology Sale Agreement...". Subsequent to the issuance of the credit, an arbitral tribunal declared the Technology Sale Agreement void due to mutual mistake of the parties. After complex procedural maneuverings in the courts of two states, the beneficiary finally drew on the credit. The beneficiary presented the necessary signed written statement certifying that "[the applicant]" has failed to pay U.S. $ 200,000 on the due date [April 12, 1985] pursuant to Section 4 of the Technology Sale Agreement...". Citibank, which had issued the credit, refused to pay, arguing that because of the arbitral decision, the Technology Sale Agreement did not exist on April 12, 1985, and thus payment under this agreement could not be due on this date.

A New York federal district court rejected Citibank's argument. In the court's view, what Citibank was claiming was that the terms of the letter of credit required the beneficiary to certify two things: first, that the applicant had not paid on April 12 and second, that the applicant was legally required to pay on April 12. The letter of credit, however, required the beneficiary to certify only the first point and the rule of *contra proferentem* prevented Citibank as the issuer of the credit from making the second point a condition of payment. Therefore, since the credit explicitly required the beneficiary to certify only nonpayment on April 12, the court ruled that Citibank could not also require the beneficiary to certify that payment was in fact legally due on that date.

Before concluding this discussion of the rule of *contra proferentem*, the Court of Appeals for the Fifth Circuit's decision in *Exxon Co., U.S.A. v. Banque de paris et des pays bas* should be mentioned. According to the Fifth Circuit, the rule of *contra proferentem* can be used when there are ambiguous terms in a credit but not when there are *inconsistent* terms in a credit. In *Exxon*, a standby letter of credit was issued to protect Exxon in the event Houston Oil & Refining, Inc. "Failed to deliver to Exxon Company, U.S.A. 558,000 barrels [of oil]...between September and December, 1981." Even though the credit stated that Houston could deliver oil to Exxon through December 1981,the credit went on to require that payment documents "must be presented not later than October 31,1981." In essence, the October 31 expiration date required Exxon to draw on the credit before Houston's full delivery period was over on December 31. When Houston told Exxon in November that it would not be able to deliver the required oil by the end of December, Exxon drew on the letter of credit on November 31 and again on December 1.Paribas, the issuer of the credit, however, refused to honor Exxon's drawings on the ground that they were untimely. Paribas pointed out that, by its terms, the credit expired on October 31. The federal district court found for Exxon, construing the seemingly inconsistent provisions in the credit against Paribas, the drafter of the credit. The Fifth Circuit, however, reversed ruling (somewhat questionably in this author's opinion) that the expiration date in the letter of credit "[was] as certain as words permit." As a result, there was no textual uncertainty as to when the letter of credit expired. In dictum, however, the Fifth Circuit went beyond merely overruling the district court on the facts. According to the Fifth Circuit, even if there had been inconsistent terms in the letter of credit, the district court would have been wrong in applying the rule of contra proferentem. The rule should be applied only when there are ambiguous as opposed to inconsistent terms in a credit. The Fifth Circuit offered no analysis to explain its distinction.

## 2. The "render performance possible" rule

It is a standard rule of contract construction that when a contract is susceptible to two interpretations — one that will render performance possible and the other impossible — the former interpretation should be preferred. This principle is frequently cited by courts in assessing whether the doctrine of strict compliance has been satisfied.

In the Exxon case discussed earlier, the federal district court had applied this principle to permit Exxon to draw on the letter of credit after the October 31 expiration date. In the district court's mind, since the credit allowed Houston to satisfy its delivery obligation through the end of December, Exxon could not certify Houston's default by the October 31 expiration date. Thus, the inconsistent terms of the credit should be construed so as to render Exxon's performance under the credit possible. The simplest way to do this was to extend the expiration date of the credit. In overruling the district court, the Fifth Circuit did not reject the principle that inconsistent terms should be construed so as to render performance possible. The Fifth Circuit simply found no inconsistent terms that required application of this principle.

A Texas state court of appeals applied a variant of this "render performance possible" rule in *Willow Bend National Bank v. Commonwealth Mortgage Corporation*. In *Willow Bend*, the letter of credit did not contain two inconsistent terms as in the Exxon case; the credit contained instead two terms, one of which was susceptible to two constructions. The letter of credit (1) stated that it was available through sight drafts drawn on the issuing bank and (2) required that "the amount of the draft must be endorsed on [the] reverse hereof by [a] negotiating bank." When the beneficiary presented an unindorsed draft, the issuing bank refused to honor it, claiming that the draft required an indorsement by a negotiating bank.

In the court's view, the indorsement term was susceptible to two constructions. On the one hand, the indorsement term could be construed as a condition precedent requiring that all sight drafts drawn under the credit had to be negotiated to a second bank before being presented to the issuing bank for payment. On the other hand, the indorsement term could be construed as requiring an indorsement by a negotiating bank only if the beneficiary decided to negotiate the draft.

To avoid a forfeiture and to render the beneficiary's performance in compliance with the terms of the credit, the court construed the indorsement terms as requiring an indorsement by a negotiating bank only when the beneficiary chose to present its sight draft through a negotiating bank, which the beneficiary had not chosen to do in this case.

### 3. The "plain meaning" rule

In Travis Bank & Trust v. State, a standby credit required the presentation of "drafts." When the beneficiary presented a nonnegotiable draft, the issuing bank refused to pay, claiming that the letter of credit required the presentation of a negotiable draft. The Texas court applied the plain meaning rule of contract interpretation and rejected the issuing bank's argument. According to the court "[A] word used in a contract is to be given its ordinary meaning unless the contract reveals a strong reason for assigning to the word a different meaning." The ordinary meaning of "draft" covers both a negotiable and a nonnegotiable draft. Thus, using the plain meaning rule, the beneficiary strictly complied with the terms of the letter of credit when it presented a nonnegotiable draft.

But the plain meaning rule could not save the draft presented by the beneficiary in *Armac Industries. Ltd. v. Citytrust. In Armac*, the credit required the presentation of a draft but the draft presented was not signed by the drawer. Article 5 of the UCC expressly incorporates the UCC's Section 3-104 definition of draft. Under this definition, the signature of the drawer is necessary to validate a negotiable draft. Thus, what the beneficiary presented in *Armac* could not satisfy the plain meaning of the word "draft." At best, the beneficiary's payment demand was an incomplete negotiable instrument that was not enforceable as a draft until completed.

### 4. Provisions of the UCP

The UCP is normally incorporated into the text of bank letters of credit by specific reference. Many articles of the UCP set forth interpretative rules aimed at clarifying such matters as the documentary conditions of the credit, the quantity and amount of goods shipped, and date terms in the credit. These UCP provisions necessarily affect how the strict compliance doctrine is applied. Three examples should suffice to demonstrate the point.

(1) *Article 41 (c) of the UCP* provides that in the commercial invoice, the description of the goods "must correspond with the description in the credit." But in documents other than the commercial invoice (e.g., a bill of lading), "the goods may be described in general terms not inconsistent with the description of the goods in the credit." Article 41 (c) is usually interpreted to mean that a very strict degree of compliance is required with respect to the description of the goods in the commercial invoice — the document prepared by the beneficiary of a commercial credit — but a more relaxed standard of compliance may be applied to the description of the goods in a bill of lading or certificate of inspection.

(2) *Article 43 (b) of the UCP* states that, in general, any quantity of goods described in a letter of credit that is subject to the UCP allows for a tolerance of 5 percent, more or less. Thus, if a commercial letter of credit called for a certificate of inspection covering 50,000 tons of wheat, a certificate covering any amount of wheat from 47,500 to 52,000 tons would strictly comply with the terms of the credit. This 5 percent tolerance rule, however, will not be applied if the quantity of goods in the credit is expressed in terms of a stated number of individual items, such as 50,000 suede coats.

(3) *Article 45 of the UCP* provides that if a commercial letter of credit stipulates shipments by installments within given periods and any installment is not shipped within a given period, the credit ceases to be available for that and for all future installments. Thus, if a commercial letter of credit required the shipment of 30,000 tons of grain in each of six consecutive ten — day periods beginning on June 1 and the June 21-30 shipment was missed, any presentation by the beneficiary for the July 1-10 shipment would not strictly comply with the terms of the credit. The credit would have terminated. Article 45 is of obvious importance in evaluating whether there has been strict documentary compliance with the terms of certain installment credits.

### 5. Reformation of the written terms of a letter of credit

Reformation "is the remedy by which writings are rectified to conform to the actual agreement of the parties." Sometimes two parties wish to enter into a contract on certain specified terms but mistakenly express one or more of these terms in their writing. Sometimes one party to a contract is charged with reducing the contract to writing and in so doing, fraudulently changes one or more terms of the agreement. In these cases of mutual mistake or fraud, the law permits the aggrieved party to reform the terms of the writing to reflect the true agreement of the parties.

The equitable doctrine of reformation, however, cannot be easily integrated with letter of credit law. As necessary prerequisites for reformation, there must be both a prior agreement between the parties and a writing that is at variance with the terms of that prior agreement. Although a letter of credit is an independent contract between the issuing bank and the beneficiary, the actual terms of a letter of credit are not directly negotiated between the issuing bank and the beneficiary. The beneficiary and the applicant for the credit agree on the payment terms of the credit and the applicant then instructs the issuing bank to include these terms in the credit. Even though the letter of credit is an independent contract and there is no direct agreement between the issuing bank and the beneficiary with respect to the payment terms of the credit, mistaken or fraudulent instructions by the applicant as to what to include in the credit might persuade a court to allow reformation of the written terms of the credit as against the issuing bank. For these purposes, the issuing bank would have to be deemed the agent of the applicant for the credit.

In *Fina Supply, Inc. v. Abilene National Bank*, the Supreme Court of Texas considered whether the beneficiary could reform the terms of an amendment to a letter of credit based on the alleged fraud of a representative of the issuing bank. In Fina Supply, Fina entered into an oil exchange agreement with Brio. To cover any oil exchange imbalances, Brio requested that Abilene National Bank issue a standby letter of credit in Fina's favor. The original letter of credit covered exchange imbalances during October 1981 and expired in November 1981. An amendment specifically extended the coverage of the letter of credit to include exchange imbalances during both November and December 1981 and extended the expiration date of the credit to January 1982. Subsequent amendments extended the expiration date of the credit to May 31, 1982, but unlike the first amendment, these subsequent amendments did not specifically extend the credit to cover oil imbalances arising after December 1981. A representative of Abilene Bank stated, however, that by extending the expiration date of the credit, the number of months of oil imbalances covered by the credit was extended as well. As it turned out, however, the representative was wrong and the extension of the expiration date did not automatically extend the credit to cover post-December oil imbalances. Thus, when Fina sought payment under the credit for oil imbalances that arose after December 1981, Abilene refused to honor Fina's draw, contending that the draw did not strictly comply with the terms of the amended credit because the amended credit only covered oil imbalances arising prior to December 1981.

Fina sued Abilene and sought to reform the credit for fraud and mistake. The Supreme Court of Texas made short shrift of Fina's fraud argument. The court ruled that the bank representative's statements as to the effect of extending the expiration date were "mere statements of opinion which will not support an action for fraud." The court was also not persuaded by Fina's mistake argument. Fina could have determined on its own the effect of the extension of the expiration date. Since Fina did not make its own determination (Fina, remember, had its own legal counsel), Fina did not really make a mistake as to the legal effect of the amendments; it made a mistake in relying on the opinions of Abilene's representative. This was not the type of mistake that triggers reformation of a credit.

Although it rejected the use of reformation in this case, still the Supreme Court of Texas in Fina Supply implicitly accepted the notion that reformation would be an acceptable remedy in an appropriate letter of credit case.

### 6. The parol evidence rule

In general, terms in a written contract that are intended by the parties to be the final expression of their agreement cannot be varied or contradicted by prior oral or written agreements or by contemporaneous oral agreements. The parol evidence rule, however, does not preclude a written contract from being modified or affected by a contemporaneous written agreement executed as part of the same transaction. Thus, if at the time the letter of credit is issued, a side covenant is agreed to in writing between the issuing bank and the beneficiary, this covenant may affect the terms of the letter of credit. For example, assume a side covenant requires the beneficiary to give the issuing bank a ten-day written notice before making any draw under the letter of credit. Assume the beneficiary fails to give this ten-day notice but presents the issuing bank with complying documents two days before the credit is set to expire. Based on the side covenant, a court will most likely permit the issuing bank to refuse to pay the letter of credit despite the fact that the documents presented strictly comply with the payment terms stated in the credit.

The existence of side covenants between the issuing bank and the beneficiary is not typical in letter of credit practice, however. An issuing bank will be loathe to enter into a covenant with the beneficiary because any covenant that changes the terms of the letter of credit will in all probability affect the bank's ability to obtain reimbursement from its customer/applicant.

Instead of entering into a side covenant with the beneficiary, it would be more prudent for the issuing bank to obtain the consent of the customer to the terms of the side covenant and incorporate these terms into an amended letter of credit. Obtaining the consent of the customer will preclude the customer from successfully objecting to any change in the terms of the credit.

Occasionally, however, documents other than issuing bankbeneficiary covenants may create parol evidence problems. For example, in *American Airlines, Inc. v. FDIC*, a letter of credit required the presentation of a sight draft. The beneficiary, in fact, presented a draft, but a draft that did not mention the issuing bank as the drawee. Along with the draft, however, the beneficiary presented the issuing bank with the letter of credit and a covering letter, both of which mentioned the proper drawee. The court allowed the accompanying documents to supply the name of the drawee, which had not been written on the draft itself. Since "there was no possibility that the [issuing bank] could have been misled by the documents submitted to it by [the beneficiary]," the federal district court ruled that when read to gather the draft and accompanying documents satisfied the strict compliance standard.

Not all courts, however, will require an issuing bank to consider collateral documents not specified by the terms of the credit in assessing whether the beneficiary has strictly complied with the terms of the credit. In *Courtaulds North America, Inc. v. North Carolina National Bank*, the letter of credit required the presentation of an invoice stating that the goods were "100% acrylic yarn." Although the invoices presented stated that the goods were "imported acrylic yarn," packing lists which referred to the goods as "100% acrylic" were stapled to these invoices. The Court of Appeals for the Fourth Circuit ruled that the invoices with the packing lists stapled to them did not strictly comply with the terms of the credit. According to the court, the invoices themselves had to comply with the terms of the credit and the bank "was not expected to scrutinize the collateral papers, such as the packing lists."

### 7. Waiver

A waiver is the intentional surrender of a known right. At discussed earlier, before honoring the beneficiary's draft, a bank issuer of a letter of credit has the right to insist on documents that strictly comply with the terms of the credit. But under the equitable doctrine of waiver, an issuing bank, by word or by action, may intentionally relinquish its right to insist on strictly complying documents.

*Chase Manhattan Bank v. Equibank* graphically demonstrates how waiver may be able to dilute the rigors of strict documentary compliance. In *Equibank*, beneficiary Chase presented the necessary documents to Equibank ten days after the expiration date of the credit. Equibank refused to honor them, giving as its reason their late presentation. Chase argued, however, that Equibank had waived timely presentment. According to an affidavit presented by Chase, an Equibank employee had telephoned Chase on the due date of the credit and agreed that the necessary documents required by the credit "could be forwarded through domestic collections," a process that was commonly known to take several days.

An employee of Equibank in his affidavit, however, maintained that he "never waived the requirements necessary to draw on the credit." Despite this factual disagreement in the parties' respective affidavits, the federal district court granted summary judgment for issuer Equibank. The Court of Appeals for the Third Circuit, however, reversed and remanded the case for a hearing on the waiver question. "We decide only," the court noted, "that the possibility of an estoppel or waiver on the part of Equibank has been raised and it was error to enter summary judgment with that issue unresolved."

## 8. Estoppel

Like waiver, the equitable doctrine of estoppel can also affect how a court will apply the doctrine of strict documentary compliance. But in the area of letter of credit practice, a distinction must be drawn between two different forms of estoppel — what might be termed notice estoppel and what might be termed prior conduct estoppel.

*Notice Estoppel*. Article 16 (d) of the UCP requires the issuing bank to give expeditious notice of documentary discrepancies to the beneficiary or to the bank presenting the documents for payment. Under Article 16 (e), failure to do so will preclude the issuing bank from relying on these discrepancies to justify dishonor. Thus, if the issuing bank rejects the documents, citing X and Y discrepancies as its reasons for rejection, the issuing bank will be precluded from relying on Z discrepancy to justify its dishonor. Although there is some dispute in the case law, the preclusion in Article 16 (e) will presumably estop the issuing bank from relying on Z discrepancy even if the beneficiary knew about Z discrepancy when it presented the documents and even if the beneficiary could not have cured Z discrepancy had the proper notice been given.

*Prior Conduct Estoppel*. Unlike notice estoppel, "prior conduct estoppel" is not predicated on the issuing bank's failure to give expeditious notice of discrepancies. Even if the issuing bank, pursuant to Article 16 (d) of the UCP, did notify the beneficiary of X, Y, and Z discrepancies, the issuing bank might still be estopped from relying on these discrepancies if on prior occasions, it had accepted from the beneficiary documents containing X, Y, and Z discrepancies. No matter whether it intended to relinquish any of its rights, if an issuing bank has consistently accepted nonconforming documents in the past, it may be estopped from refusing such documents in the future — at least until such time as it notifies the beneficiary of a change in its policy.

In *Schweibish v. Pontchartrain State Bank*, for example, the issuing bank dishonored the beneficiary's draw because the beneficiary failed to present a sight draft drawn on the bank as required by the terms of the letter of credit. Under the strict compliance standard, the absence of the required sight draft was enough to justify dishonor. But on prior occasions, the issuing bank had paid the beneficiary even though the beneficiary had not strictly complied with the documentary terms of the credits. In one case, the bank had paid even though the beneficiary had not presented a necessary sight draft — the exact situation under litigation. Given this prior conduct, the court ruled that the bank was estopped from demanding strict compliance in this case. To quote the court: "While the bank can impose conditions in the credit and demand complete compliance with them, it cannot, in a series of dealings based upon credits, arbitrarily select those credits which must conform to the requirements therein stated and those which may be paid without complete compliance."

But in *Security State Bank v. Basin Petroleum Services, Inc.*, the Supreme Court of Wyoming (with two judges in dissent) refused to apply estoppel in circumstances similar to those in Schweibish. In Basin, the issuing bank had not insisted on strict compliance with respect to discrepancies in four prior purchase orders. Nonetheless, the court refused to rule that the bank was estopped from insisting on strict compliance with respect to a fifth purchase order. Looking at the elements necessary for estoppel, the Wyoming court noted that the beneficiary — the party asserting estoppel — had to prove, inter alia, a lack of knowledge about the documentary terms of the letter of credit or an inability to discover the nature of these terms. Since the beneficiary could not meet this burden of proof, the court refused to estop the issuing bank from insisting on strict compliance.

Even when a court is predisposed to apply estoppel principles, however, an issuing bank may still prevail if it can justify its prior inconsistent conduct. In *Courtaulds*, for example, the beneficiary proved that in the past, the issuing bank had honored noncomplying drafts. The issuing bank , however, countered this evidence by showing that before honoring these drafts, it had always followed customary letter of credit practice and checked with its customer regarding any discrepancies in the drafts. In each prior case, the issuing bank had received the customer's authorization to waive the discrepancies. Whenever a customer waived discrepancies, it was the usual practice for the issuing bank not to notify the beneficiary that there had been discrepancies and that these discrepancies had been waived. But when the bank sought a waiver of discrepancies regarding the draft in *Courtaulds*, the customer refused. Because of this refusal, the issuing bank proceeded to notify the beneficiary of the discrepancies. From the evidence presented, it was clear that in *Courtaulds*, the bank's prior practice of paying over discrepant drafts should not be deemed to constitute an estoppel.

### 9. Course of dealing and course of performance

The concept of "course of dealing" may be used as an alternative mode of analysis in many strict compliance estoppel cases. If an issuing bank has consistently paid over discrepant documents presented by a particular beneficiary and then without notifying the beneficiary, it suddenly insists on strict documentary compliance, a court might find either that the bank is estopped from refusing to accept the noncomplying documents due to its prior inconsistent conduct or that the bank's course of dealing with the beneficiary regarding discrepancies in prior letters of credit must be read as an integral part of its agreement with the beneficiary regarding discrepancies in this letter of credit.

Section 1-205 (1) of the UCC defines a course of dealing as "a sequence of previous conduct between the parties to a particular transaction which is fairly to be regarded as establishing a common basis of understanding for interpreting their expressions and other conduct." The UCC then goes on to state that whereas express terms (the terms of a letter of credit) will control an inconsistent course of dealing, a course of dealing can still "give particular meaning to and supplement or qualify terms of an agreement [a letter of credit]." By giving particular meaning to documentary terms in a letter of credit, a course of dealing can obviously affect how a court will apply the doctrine of strict documentary compliance.

If a course of dealing involves a sequence of previous conduct between the issuing bank and the beneficiary regarding prior letters of credit, a "course of performance" involves repeated occasions of performance regarding one letter of credit. For example, if a commercial letter of credit permits five consecutive monthly drawings, the performance of the two parties with respect to the initial drawings under the credit will be regarded as part of their agreement with respect to subsequent drawings under the credit.

*Titanium Metals Corporation v. Space Metals, Inc.* illustrates how both a course of dealing and a course of performance can dilute the rigors of the strict compliance standard. In *Titanium Metals*, three letters of credit, each allowing for multiple presentations, had been issued to the beneficiary by the issuing bank. Although the text of the credits seemed to require that drafts be presented to obtain payment, the issuing bank processed all of the beneficiary's invoices with respect to the first two letters of credit and one invoice with respect to the third letter of credit without demanding separate drafts from the beneficiary. Instead the bank simply stamped the invoices presented as "paid" and also filled out a voucher calling the completed transaction a "sales draft." Suddenly, however, the bank refused to pay the six remaining invoices presented under the third letter of credit, claiming that the beneficiary failed to present a draft. The beneficiary argued, however, that by its previous course of conduct with respect to the first two letters of credit and with respect to the first invoice of the third letter of credit, the bank had waived the need for the beneficiary to present a separate draft. The trial court ruled in favor of the beneficiary on the ground that the bank had in fact waived the need for a separate draft.

The Supreme Court of Utah upheld the trial court but not on a waiver theory. According to the supreme court, "[T] he long course of conduct of the parties, with numerous shipments, acceptances, orders to remit and compliances therewith" reflected a clear manifestation of what the beneficiary and issuing bank thought the terms of the letter of credit to be. In essence, the court was stating that the parties' course of dealing (with respect to the first two letters of credit) and their course of performance (with respect to the first invoice of the third letter of credit) had to be read as permitting the draft called for by the credit to be incorporated into the invoice itself. No separate draft was required to be presented. Thus, the issuing bank had to pay the six remaining invoices presented under the third letter of credit because the beneficiary had strictly complied with the terms of the credit.

## 10. Banking customs

In addition to a course of prior dealing or a course of prior performance, trade customs may also impact on how a court will apply the doctrine of strict compliance. In this context, the relevant trade customs are banking customs. Suppose, for example, that the beneficiary presents a document to the issuing bank that does not strictly comply with the terms of the letter of credit. According to local banking customs, however, banks routinely accept what is presented in lieu of what should be presented under the terms of the credit. If this is the local banking custom, the issuing bank will most likely have to accept the noncomplying document.

This is the rule gleaned from the famous case *Dixom Irmaos & Cia v.Chase National Bank*. In *Dixon*, the beneficiary presented the issuing bank with a guarantee from a leading New York bank in lieu of a missing bill of lading. Expert testimony showed that it was a "general and uniform" custom of New York banks to accept such a guarantee. Given this custom, Chase could not use strict compliance to justify rejecting the guarantee in lieu of the bill of lading.

## 11. Good faith

Section 5-114 (1) of the UCC requires that an issuing bank "honor a draft...which complies with the terms of the relevant credit..." This provision creates a duty in the issuing bank to honor the beneficiary's draft upon the presentation of a facially complying draft and facially complying documents. In carrying out this duty, Section 1-203 of the UCC imposes on the bank an obligation to act in good faith.

Like so many of the other contract and equitable doctrines previously discussed, this obligation to act in good faith can significantly impact on the way in which the strict compliance standard is judicially applied. Suppose the beneficiary presents documents that strictly comply with the terms of the credit. The issuing bank, however, "flyspecks" the documents and points to trivial discrepancies to justify its refusal to honor the credit. If the beneficiary can show that the bank has acted dishonestly in raising these trivial discrepancies (usually because the customer no longer has the wherewithal to reimburse the issuing bank), a court should hold that the bank has violated its Section 1-203 obligation of good faith by rejecting the documents. Once an obligation declared by the UCC has been violated, Section 1-106 (2) affords the aggrieved party (here the beneficiary of the credit) a cause of action to enforce that obligation. If there is a bad-faith refusal to honor a credit, the beneficiary should be able to enforce Section 1-203 through a wrongful dishonor suit and require the issuing bank to accept the documents even though they contain trivial discrepancies.

It should be recognized, however, that a wrongful dishonor suit based on the issuing bank's refusal to act in good faith can be a particularly potent weapon. If a beneficiary can show that the issuing bank not only wrongfully dishonored the credit but did so dishonestly, the beneficiary may be able to recover punitive damages from the issuing bank.

### 12. Duty to notify the beneficiary of oppressive terms

Occasionally, banks issue irrevocable letters of credit that condition payment on the presentation of a document executed by the applicant for the credit. Because of their internal inconsistency, these credits have troubled some. On one hand, the issuing bank states to the beneficiary that its letter of credit is irrevocable; on the other hand, however, the bank includes a documentary payment condition in the credit that allows the applicant to "veto irrevocability" simply by refusing to execute a required document. While the existing case law contains little careful analysis of these credits, the appellate division in *Fair Pavilions* did express serious reservations about one such credit. In *Fair Pavilions*, the credit was particularly one-sided because it allowed the applicant to cancel the credit simply by submitting an affidavit certifying the occurrence of one or more events specified in a collateral contract. According to the court, this provision was so broad and its potential for abuse so vast that "the characterization of [the credit's] irrevocability becomes either a misnomer or an overgenerous description." The court went on to state that given this and certain other terms of the credit, the issuing bank might "have had at least a moral obligation to point out the possible deficiency to the beneficiary in view of [the beneficiary's] risk and exposure to possible damage. [The beneficiary] could then have elected to accept or reject the proffered credit."

To this author, imposing a duty on issuing banks to notify beneficiaries of oppressive or one-sided letter of credit terms does not seem to be a wise policy decision. Letter of credit beneficiaries are generally sophisticated business entities, well advised by legal counsel. They should be able to understand the impact of the credit's terms. Still, the concern expressed by the appellate division in Fair Pavilions might conceive a court in an appropriate case to impose such a duty on an issuing bank. Imposing notification obligations on issuing banks is not totally without precedent in letter of credit litigation. If such a notification obligation were imposed and the issuing bank failed to live up to it, the bank might be forced to accept discrepant documents, particularly if the discrepancies related to the oppressive payment terms that were the subject of the notification obligation.

### 13. The UCC presentment warranty

Section 5-111 (1) of the UCC provides: "Unless otherwise agreed the beneficiary by transferring or presenting a documentary draft or demand for payment warrants to all interested parties that the necessary conditions of the credit have been complied with. This is in addition to any warranties arising under Articles 3, 4, 7 and 8."

Section 5-111 (1) does not deal directly with the strict compliance doctrine. The section, however, does deal with the issue of who — beneficiary or issuing bank — must bear losses resulting from the presentation of discrepant documents. For this reason, Section 5-111 (1) will be discussed in this context.

Assume the beneficiary presents documents that contain patent (on the surface) discrepancies. The issuing bank gives the documents a cursory examination and fails to discover the discrepancies. The bank honors the credit but the applicant discovers the discrepancies and refuses to reimburse the bank. One interpretation of Section 5-111 (1) would allow the issuing bank (an "interested party") to sue the beneficiary for breach of warranty regarding the discrepant documents. By presenting documents, the beneficiary warrants that "the necessary conditions of the credit have been complied with." Since a letter of credit contains documentary conditions, the beneficiary arguably warrants that the documents presented facially comply with the documentary requirements of the credit. If the beneficiary breaches this warranty, the bank can have recourse against the beneficiary. It is important for an issuing bank to focus on the implications of this interpretation of Section 5-111 (1). Despite its own negligence, an issuing bank may have a breach of warranty action against the beneficiary of the credit in cases in which the bank honors a credit without discovering patent documentary discrepancies and as a consequence is denied reimbursement from its customer.

Several caveats should be mentioned, however, about this interpretation of the Section 5-111 (1) warranty provision.

There is not a great deal of case law interpreting Section 5-111 (1).One influential commentator argues that the section should not be interpreted to allow a bank recourse against the beneficiary if it pays over documents that contain patent as opposed to latent defects. As more courts focus on Section 5-111 (1), a more authoritative body of case law will inevitably develop.

Even if Section 5-111 (1) is generally interpreted to cover patent discrepancies, the beneficiary should still be able to raise many of the principles discussed in this article to block the bank's recovery. For example, if the issuing bank (1) fails to discover a discrepancy and pays the beneficiary and then (2) cannot obtain reimbursement from its customer, the bank should not be able to recover from the beneficiary for breach of warranty if the beneficiary can prove that the discrepancy in the document resulted from an ambiguity in the terms of the credit. The rule of contra proferentem provides that an ambiguity in the terms of the letter of credit is to be construed against the issuing bank. If this rule is applied, the documents presented by the beneficiary should be deemed in compliance with the terms of the credit, thus precluding the bank from using the Section 5-111 (1) warranty provision to obtain recourse from the beneficiary.

# Non-documentary Conditions and Strict Compliance

A letter of credit is a payment mechanism that conditions payment against the presentation of a stipulated draft and/or stipulated documents. Strict compliance developed as a rule for determining whether the beneficiary's draft and documents formally complied with the terms of the letter of credit. A guarantee, however, is not a letter of credit and as a result, it can condition payment against the performance of facts. Substantial compliance can be used to determine whether the "beneficiary" of a guarantee has sufficiently complied with the factual conditions of the guarantee. This distinction between the letter of credit strict compliance standard and the guarantee substantial compliance standard was recognized in *BA Commercial Corporation v. Hynutek, Inc*.

In Hynutek, the plaintiff received an instrument called a "standby guarantee of payment." This instrument required the plaintiff to make a draw before December 31, 1983. Plaintiff, however, missed the December 31 expiration date and submitted its draw in January 1984. The court agreed with the plaintiff that it could make its draw in January. The court ruled that this "standby guarantee of payment" did not satisfy the UCC definition of a letter of credit. Strict compliance with the expiration date is the rule for letters of credit, but as the court noted, "[W] e have before us a guaranty, not a letter of credit, and we are cited to no such require-ment covering guaranties."

But does the analysis developed in this lesson blur this classic distinction between a letter of credit with its strict compliance standard and a guarantee with its substantial compliance standard? Properly understood, the analysis should not affect this distinction.

This lesson has demonstrated that in some situations, contract and equity rules can dilute the baseline strict compliance standard of letter of credit law and create a standard of compliance that is akin to substantial compliance. But this does not represent a blurring of the distinction between a letter of credit and a guarantee. In the letter of credit cases discussed, the substantial compliance standard is used to test the sufficiency of the *documents* presented by the beneficiary. In guarantee cases, however, the substantial compliance standard is used to test the sufficiency of the beneficiary's *factual* performance. A substantial compliance standard for *documentary* conditions and a substantial compliance standard for *nondocumentary* conditions are two quite different standards.

There is a real danger, however, that in the letter of credit area, the seeming willingness of courts to accept a substantial compliance standard may be confused with a willingness to accept so-called non-documentary payment conditions as well. A non-documentary payment condition is a payment condition that requires an issuing bank to verify a fact — not to examine the text of a document — before honoring a letter of credit. *Guilford Pattern Work*, Inc. v. United Bank shows what could result from an acceptance of non-documentary payment conditions in letters of credit.

In *Guilford*, the beneficiary sued the issuing bank for wrongful dishonor of a standby credit. The bank's defense was that the beneficiary had failed to deliver goods by the delivery date in the credit. The beneficiary countered the bank's defense by claiming that the delivery date constituted a non-documentary payment condition, requiring only substantial compliance. The beneficiary argued that it had satisfied this substantial compliance standard.

The Colorado federal district court rejected the beneficiary's attempt to characterize the delivery date as a non-documentary payment condition. But, relying on prior Colorado decisions, the federal district court appeared willing to accept the idea that a non-documentary payment condition can properly be included in a letter of credit and once included, might be governed by the less stringent substantial compliance standard. To quote the court:

These [prior Colorado] cases can be read to require strict compliance only with *documentary* terms and conditions. *Nondocumentary* terms might then require only substantial compliance if the courts were convinced a different and lower standard should apply to the distinction... [But because the delivery term in this credit was determined to be a documentary condition], it becomes unnecessary...to decide whether a standard other than strict compliance is necessary...for non-documentary terms of the agreement.

If the *Guilford* court speculation is correct that a letter of credit may contain both documentary terms governed by strict compliance and non-documentary terms governed by substantial compliance, the job of determining whether to honor a letter of credit will become much more complex and time-consuming. The major problem is with non-documentary payment conditions because they may require a lengthy analysis of facts. It is important to recognize, however, that neither the UCC, the UCP, nor regulatory definitions of letters of credit sanction including non-documentary payment conditions in letters of credit. In fact, the documentary nature of a letter of credit constitutes the fundamental difference between a valid bank letter of credit and an ultra vires bank guarantee.

Thus, a judicial willingness to accept a de facto substantial compliance standard in letter of credit cases should not blur the fundamental distinction between a letter of credit and a guarantee. When a substantial compliance standard is used in a letter of credit case, it is used to test the sufficiency of documents. When a substantial compliance standard is used in a guarantee case, it is used to test the sufficiency of factual performances, not the textual accuracy of documents. What does blur the fundamental distinction between a letter of credit and a guarantee is the acceptance of non-documentary payment conditions in letters of credit.

# Conclusion

This lesson has shown that principles derived from contract, equity, and banking custom such as the plain meaning rule, reformation, and estoppel can work to soften the rigors of strict compliance. When these principles interact with strict compliance, what results is often a standard of documentary compliance that is akin to substantial compliance.

Several conclusions can be drawn from this article. First, although letters of credit are specialty contracts, courts refuse to treat them as somehow immune from common contract and equity principles. But principles such as reformation, estoppel, and good faith necessarily dilute the rigors of strict documentary compliance, thereby contributing a degree of unpredictability to letter of credit transactions. Although certainty and predictability are important in letter of credit practice, it seems unrealistic to expect courts to refrain from applying general contract and equity principles when disputes arise over the sufficiency of documentary presentations.

Second, questions of waiver, estoppel, and reformation necessarily affect how fast documentary compliance disputes will be resolved. Frequently, documentary compliance issues are handled through summary judgment motions. Issues such as waiver and estoppel, however, are fact-specific and cannot be appropriately resolved through summary judgment motions. Thus, when these issues are raised, they necessarily delay the time within which letters of credit will be honored.

Third, given these facts, issuing banks should take steps to prevent documentary disputes from arising. The risk of future disputes can be reduced if issuing banks draft their credits carefully and precisely and avoid putting excessive detail in the text. Where feasible, it is also advisable for banks to include in their letters of credit the exact form and wording of any document required to trigger payment.

Fourth, in cases where beneficiaries are seeking to have an equitable principle such as reformation applied, issuing banks should remind courts that since equitable remedies are discretionary, they should be applied in a way consistent with fundamental letter of credit policy. Because the wholesale application of equitable principles could undermine the predictability of letter of credit payments, a persuasive case can be made that a burden of proof even more stringent than that required of ordinary parties should be imposed on letter of credit beneficiaries seeking equitable relief.

Fifth, issuing banks should avoid including non-documentary payment conditions in their letters of credit. There are two reasons for this: (1) because these conditions may be subject to a substantial compliance standard, issuing banks may be required to make more burdensome judgment calls than under a strict compliance standard; and (2) because these conditions blur the distinction between a valid letter of credit and an ultra vires bank guarantee, they may lead to challenges by bank regulatory authorities.

## ♣ New Words

| | | |
|---|---|---|
| **1.** | contra proferentem | 反（契約）起草人 |
| **2.** | oppressive terms | 令人難以忍受的條件 |
| **3.** | standby letters of credit | 備用信用狀 |
| **4.** | commercial letters of credit | 商業信用狀 |
| **5.** | financial instruments | 金融工具 |
| **6.** | ironclad *a.* | 打不破的 |
| **7.** | letter of credit law | 信用狀法 |
| **8.** | rigors *n.* | 嚴格性 |
| **9.** | hypothesize *v.* | 假設；假定 |
| **10.** | security interest | 擔保利益 |
| **11.** | collateral *a. n.* | 附屬的；擔保的；附屬；擔保物 |
| **12.** | requisite *a.* | 必要的 |
| **13.** | attest *v.* | 證實；證明 |
| **14.** | co-signing *n.* | 會簽 |
| **15.** | reimburse *v.* | 償還；付還 |

16. default *n. v.*　　　　　　　不履行；拖欠

17. literal *a.*　　　　　　　　按詞文義的；逐字的

18. discrepancies *n.*　　　　　差異；不一致

19. complying documents　　　相符的單據

20. stance *n.*　　　　　　　　態度

21. typographical *a.*　　　　印刷上的

22. relevance *n.*　　　　　　關聯

23. realistically *adv.*　　　　現實地；實際地

24. dilute *v.*　　　　　　　　沖淡

25. affidavit *n.*　　　　　　　保證書；宣誓書

26. summary judgment　　　　即決審判

27. motion *n.*　　　　　　　（訴訟人向法院提出的）請求

28. arbitral tribunal　　　　　仲裁庭

29. untimely *adv.*　　　　　　不及時地

30. expiration date　　　　　　期滿日

31. variant *n.a.*　　　　　　　變種；不同的

32. forfeiture *n.*　　　　　　沒收；罰款；權利喪失

33. validate *v.*　　　　　　　使生效，使有法律效力

34. negotiable *a.*　　　　　　可轉讓的

35. nonnegotiable *a.*　　　　不可轉讓的

36. certificate of inspection　　檢驗證明

37. suede *n.*　　　　　　　　小山羊皮

38. shipments by install-ments　分期裝運

39. rectify *v.*　　　　　　　　糾正；調整

40. trigger *v.*　　　　　　　引起；引發

41. contemporaneous *a.*　　　同時發生的

42. side covenant　　　　　　附帶的契約

43. acrylic yarn　　　　　　　丙烯酸紗

44. packing lists　　　　　　　裝箱單

45. relinquish *v.*　　　　　　放棄

46. reverse *v.*　　　　　　　顛倒

47. remand *v.*　　　　　　　發回給下級法院

48. nonconforming *a.*　　　　不符的

49. Wyoming *n.*　　　　　　　懷俄明（美國州名）

50. inter alia　　　　　　　　（拉）除了別的以外

**51.** predispose *v.*                  預先安排；使先傾向於

**52.** course of dealing             慣常交易

**53.** course of performance       慣常履行

**54.** voucher *n.*                    擔保人；收據

**55.** sales draft                   銷售匯票

**56.** course of conduct            慣常行為

**57.** trade customs              貿易習慣

**58.** routinely *adv.*                例行的；常規的

**59.** facially *adv.*                 表面上的

**60.** flyspeck *v.*                  找出小錯誤

**61.** wherewithal *n.*              必要的效力

**62.** potent *a.*                    強有力的

**63.** irrevocable letters of credit    不可撤銷的信用狀

**64.** irrevocability *n.*            不可撤銷性

**65.** one-sided *a.*                片面的

**66.** misnomer *n.*               用詞不當

**67.** overgenerous *a.*           過分慷慨的

**68.** the proffered credit         所起草的信用狀

**69.** sophisticated business      非常有經驗的企業實體
     entities

**70.** conceive *v.*                 構想出；設想

**71.** patent discrepancies       顯然的差異

**72.** caveats *n.*                  防止誤解的說明

**73.** latent defects             隱而不見的缺陷

**74.** Inc. abbr.: incorporate     組成公司的

**75.** counter *v.*                  反擊

**76.** Colorado *n.*              科羅拉多（美國州名）

**77.** stringent *a.*               嚴格的

**78.** speculation *n.*            推測

**79.** ultra vires                 （拉）越權

**80.** textual accuracy           原文的準確

**81.** predictability *n.*           可預料性

**82.** unpredictability *n.*       不可預料性

**83.** persuasive *a.*            有說服力的

**84.** burdensome *a.*           難以負擔的；累贅的

| | | |
|---|---|---|
| **85.** | baseline *n.* | 基線 |
| **86.** | trivial *a.* | 輕微的；不重要的 |
| **87.** | dishonor *v.* | 不兌付 |
| **88.** | unindorsed *a.* | 未背書的 |
| **89.** | specialty contract | 蓋印契約；書面要式契約 |

## ♣ New Phrases and Idiomatic Expressions

| | | |
|---|---|---|
| **1.** | in conjunction with | 與……共同；連同 |
| **2.** | to be akin to sth. | 與……相近似 |
| **3.** | to derive from | 從……演變；從……引申出 |
| **4.** | to soften the rigors of sth. | 使變得不嚴格 |
| **5.** | under the rubric | 在……標題下 |
| **6.** | to default on sth. | 不履行 |
| **7.** | to be separate from | 與……分割開 |
| **8.** | to be independent of | 獨立於…… |
| **9.** | in good faith | 誠信地 |
| **10.** | rather than | 而不是 |
| **11.** | to draw on the credit | 提取信用狀項下的款項 |
| **12.** | in the event | 如果 |
| **13.** | to find for sb. | 作出有利於某人的裁決 |
| **14.** | to be susceptible to | 易受……影響 |
| **15.** | on the one hand...on the other hand | 一方面……另一方面…… |
| **16.** | at best | 充其量；最多 |
| **17.** | at variance with sth. | 與……不符 |
| **18.** | to make a draw under the letter of credit | 從信用狀項下取款 |
| **19.** | to preclude sb. from doing sth. | 阻止某人做某事 |
| **20.** | in all probability | 完全可能 |
| **21.** | to glean from | 從……找到或發現 |
| **22.** | to blur the distinction | 使區別變得模糊 |
| **23.** | to be immune from | 不受……影響 |
| **24.** | to put detail in the text | 在文中加入細節 |
| **25.** | in isolation | 孤立地 |

**Notes**

1. UCP：統一慣例。

其全名為Uniform Customs and Practice for Documentary Credits (UCP)，初版於1933年，後來經過多次修改（1951年、1962年、1975年），1983年的修改本簡稱為UCP400，為適應近年來發展的需要，國際商會經過幾年努力，又對UCP400進行了修改，制定了現在被廣泛採用的UCP500。

2. letter of credit：信用證；信用狀。

有時也用 credit 或 L/C 來表示。Normally a letter of credit is defined as a letter from one banker to another authorizing the payment of a specified sum to the person named in the letter on specified conditions. Commercially, letters of credit are widely used in the international import and export trade as a means of payment. According to the definition of UCP 500 "Documentary Credit (s)" and "Standby Letter (s) of Credit" mean any arrangement, however named or described, whereby a bank (the "issuing Bank") acting at the request and on the instructions of a customer (the "Applicant") or on its own behalf,

   a. is to make a payment to or to the order of a third party (the "Beneficiary"), or is to accept and pay bills of exchange (drafts drawn by the Beneficiary). or

   b. authorises another bank to effect such payment, or to accept and pay such bills of exchange (drafts), or

   c. authorises another bank to negotiate, against stipulated document (s), provided that the terms and conditions of the Credit are complied with.

3. prior agreement：先前的協議。

prior 可當形容詞用，如 prior letter of credit；也可當副詞用，如 prior to my arrival。

4. ...an action for fraud：詐欺訴訟。

有時可簡化成 fraud action。

5. Section 1-203 of the UCC

Every contract or duty within this Act imposes an obligation of good faith in its performance or enforcement.

本法的每一個契約或責任都強加以善意履行或強制執行的義務。

6. Section 5-114 (1) of the UCC

An issuer must honor a draft or demand for payment which complies with terms of the relevant credit regardless of whether the goods or documents conform to the underlying contract for sale or other contracts between the customer and beneficiary. The issuer is not excused from honor of such a draft or demand by reason of an additional general term that all documents must be satisfactory to the issuer, but an issuer may require that specified documents must be satisfactory to it.

不論貨物或單據是否與基本買賣契約或顧客與受益人之間的其他契約相符，只要匯票或要求付款書與有關信用狀相符，開狀人必須付款。開狀人不得附加一般條件，規定所有單據必須使開狀人滿意爲由，而免除對匯票或要求付款書的付款，但開狀人可要求特定單據必須使其滿意。

7. Section 5-111 (1) of the UCC provides: "Unless otherwise agreed the beneficiary by transferring or presenting a documentary draft or demand for payment warrants to all interested parties that the necessary conditions of the credit have been complied with.This is in addition to any warranties arising under Articles 3, 4, and 8."

統一商法典第5-111(1)條規定：「除另有規定外，受益人轉讓或提示跟單匯票或要求付款書，向所有利害關係方保證，業已符合信用狀上所有必要條件。這是對第3、4和8條項下保證所作的補充。」

8. It is up to sb. to do sth.

某人有責任做某事。

 **Exercises**

## I. Answer the following questions:

**1**. How do you define a letter of credit and a documentary letter of credit?

**2**. What is UCP about?

**3**. What is meant by the doctrine of strict documentary compliance?

**4**. What is the rule of Contra Proferentem? What is the use of it?

**5**. What are the two constructions to which the indorsement term was susceptible?

**6**. How is the Parol Evidence Rule applied in letter of credit issues?

**7**. What is a waiver?

**8**. What are the two different forms of estoppel? What is the difference between them?

**9**. What is the content of Section 5-111 (1) of the UCC?

**10**. What are the conclusions drawn from this lesson by the author?

## II. Translate the following Chinese passages into English:

**1**. 跟單信用狀和備用信用狀作爲一項約定，不論其如何命名或描述，是指一家銀行（「開狀行」）應客戶（「申請人」）的要求和指示或以其自身的名義，在與信用狀條款相符的條件下，憑規定的單據：

(1)向第三者（「受益人」）或其指定人付款，或承兌並支付受益人出具的匯票；

(2)授權另一家銀行付款，或承兌並支付該匯票；

(3)授權另一家銀行議付。

2. 在信用狀業務中，各有關當事人所處理的只是單據，而不是單據所涉及的貨物、服務或者其他行為。

3. UCP500的第14條規定，開狀行及／或保兌行（如有），代其行事的指定銀行，當收到單據時，必須僅以單據為依據，確定單據是否表面與信用狀條款相符。如單據表面與信用狀條款不符，可以拒絕接受。

4. 美國法院在處理信用狀爭議方面除常常採用嚴格符合原則外，還採用其他一些原則。它們是：(1)反起草人原則；(2)使契約履行成為可能原則；(3)誠信原則；(4)統一商法典提示保證原則；(5)不可反悔原則；(6)意思清楚原則；(7)證言規則；(8)慣常交易和慣常履行；(9)書面信用狀條款的再形成；(10)有責任將難以忍受的條件通知給受益人；(11)銀行習慣做法；(12)放棄；(13)跟單信用狀統一慣例。

## III. Indicate whether each of the following statements is true or false by writing "T" or "F" in the space provided:

1. Whereas this doctrine of strict documentary compliance is basic to letter of credit law, the courts do not always apply it in isolation.

2. If strict compliance does not mean absolute literal compliance, it also does not mean substantial compliance.

3. A letter of credit is frequently referred to as a specialty contract, courts still treat it as a contract.

4. The rule of contra proferentem can not be used to prevent issuing banks from adding payment conditions to letters of credit.

5. When a contract is susceptible to two interpretations one that will render performance possible and the other impossible － － the former interpretation should be preferred. This is a standard rule of contract construction.

6. UCP 500 is old and it is not in wide use by banks.

7. The equitable doctrine of reformation can be easily integrated with letter of credit law.

8. In general, terms in a written contract that are intended by the parties to be the final expression of their agreement can be varied or contradicted by prior oral or written agreements or by contemporaneous oral agreements.

9. According to the author, imposing a duty on issuing banks to notify beneficiaries of oppressive or one-side letter of credit terms seems to be a wise policy decision.

____**10.** A letter of credit is a payment mechanism that conditions payment against the presentation of a stipulated draft and or stipulated documents.

第三十三課
Lesson 33

# 外國直接投資待遇準則
# Guidelines on the Treatment of Foreign Direct Investment

## The Development Committee Recognizing

That a greater flow of foreign direct investment brings substantial benefits to bear on the world economy and on the economies of developing countries in particular, in terms of improving the long term efficiency of the host country through greater competition, transfer of capital, technology and managerial skills and enhancement of market access and in terms of the expansion of international trade;

That the promotion of private foreign investment is a common purpose of the International Bank for Reconstruction and Development, the International Finance Corporation and the Multilateral Investment Guarantee Agency;

That these institutions have pursued this common objective through their operations, advisory services and research;

That at the request of the Development Committee, a working group established by the President of these institutions and consisting of their respective General Counsel has, after reviewing existing legal instruments and literature, as well as best available practice identified by these institutions, prepared a set of guidelines representing a desirable overall framework which embodies essential principles meant to promote foreign direct investment in the common interest of all members;

That these guidelines, which have benefited from a process of broad consultation inside and outside these institutions, constitute a further step in the evolutionary process where several international efforts aim to establish a favorable investment environment free from non-commercial risks in all countries, and thereby foster the confidence of international investors; and

That these guidelines are not ultimate standards but an important step in the evolution of generally acceptable international standards which complement, but do not substitute for, bilateral investment treaties,

Therefore *calls the attention* of member countries to the following Guidelines as useful parameters in the admission and treatment of private foreign investment in their territories, without prejudice to the binding rules of international law at this stage of its development.

# Scope of Application

1. These Guidelines may be applied by members of the World Bank Group institutions to private foreign investment in their respective territories, as a complement to applicable bilateral and multilateral treaties and other international instruments, to the extent that these Guidelines do not conflict with such treaties and binding instruments, and as a possible source on which national legislation governing the treatment of private foreign investment may draw. Reference to the "State" in these Guidelines, unless the context otherwise indicates, includes the State or any constituent subdivision, agency or instrumentality of the State and reference to "nationals" includes natural and juridical persons who enjoy the nationality of the State.

2. The application of these Guidelines extends to existing and new investments established and operating at all times as *bona fide* private foreign investments, in full conformity with the laws and regulations of the host State.

3. These Guidelines are based on the general premise that equal treatment of investors in similar circumstances and free competition among them are prerequisites of a positive investment environment. Nothing in these Guidelines therefore suggests that foreign investors should receive a privileged treatment denied to national investors in similar circumstances.

# Admission

1. Each State will encourage nationals of other States to invest capital, technology and managerial skill in its territory and, to that end, is expected to admit such investments in accordance with the following provisions.

2. In furtherance of the foregoing principle, each State will: (1) facilitate the admission and establishment of investments by nationals of other States; and (2) avoid making unduly cumbersome or complicated procedural regulations for, or imposing unnecessary conditions on, the admission of such investments.

3. Each State maintains the right to make regulations to govern the admission of private foreign investments. In the formulation and application of such regulations, States will note that experience suggests that certain performance requirements introduced as conditions of admission are often counterproductive and that open admission, possibly subject to a restricted list of investments (which are either prohibited or require screening and licensing), is a more effective approach. Such performance requirements often discourage foreign investors from initiating investment in the State concerned or encourage evasion and corruption. Under the restricted list approach, investments in non-listed activities, which proceed without approval,

remain subject to the laws and regulations applicable to investments in the State concerned.

4. Without prejudice to the general approach of free admission recommended in Section 3 above, a State may, as an exception, refuse admission to a proposed investment; (1) which is, in the considered opinion of the State, inconsistent with clearly defined requirements of national security; or (2) which belongs to sectors reserved by the law of the State to its nationals on account of the State's economic development objectives or the strict exigencies of its national interest.

5. Restrictions applicable to national investment on account of public policy (*ordre public*), public health and the protection of the environment will equally apply to foreign investment.

6. Each State is encouraged to publish, in the form of a handbook or other medium easily accessible to other States and their investors, adequate and regularly updated information about its legislation, regulations and procedures relevant to foreign investment and other information relating to its investment policies including, inter alia, an indication of any classes of investment which it regards as falling under Sections 4 and 5 of this Guideline.

# Treatment

1. For the promotion of international economic cooperation through the medium of private foreign investment, the establishment, operation, management, control, and exercise of rights in such an investment, as well as such other associated activities necessary therefor or incidental thereto, will be consistent with the following standards which are meant to apply simultaneously to all States without prejudice to the provisions of applicable international instruments, and to firmly established rules of customary international law.

2. Each State will extend to investments established in its territory by nationals of any other State fair and equitable treatment according to the standards recommended in these Guidelines.

3. (1) With respect to the protection and security of their person, property rights and interests, and to the granting of permits, import and export licenses and the authorization to employ, and the issuance of the necessary entry and stay visas to their foreign personnel, and other legal matters relevant to the treatment of foreign investors as described in Section 1 above, such treatment will, subject to the requirement of fair and equitable treatment mentioned above, be as favorable as that accorded by the State to national investors in similar circumstances. In all cases, full protection and security will be accorded to the investor's rights regarding ownership, control and substantial benefits over his property, including intellectual property.

(2) As concerns such other matters as are not relevant to national investors, treatment under the State's legislation and regulations will not discriminate among foreign investors on grounds of nationality.

4. Nothing in this Guideline will automatically entitle nationals of other States to the more favorable standards of treatment accorded to the nationals of certain States under any customs union or free trade area agreement.

5. Without restricting the generality of the foregoing, each State will:

(1) promptly issue such licenses and permits and grant such concessions as may be necessary for the uninterrupted operation of the admitted investment; and

(2) to the extent necessary for the efficient operation of the investment, authorize the employment of foreign personnel. While a State may require the foreign investor to reasonably establish his inability to recruit the required personnel locally, e.g., through local advertisement, before he resorts to the recruitment of foreign personnel, labor market flexibility in this and other areas is recognized as an important element in a positive investment environment. Of particular importance in this respect is the investor's freedom to employ top managers regardless of their nationality.

6. (1) Each State will, with respect to private investment in its territory by nationals of the other States:

(a) freely allow regular periodic transfer of a reasonable part of the salaries and wages of foreign personnel; and, on liquidation of the investment or earlier termination of the employment, allow immediate transfer of all savings from such salaries and wages;

(b) freely allow transfer of the net revenues realized from the investment;

(c) allow the transfer of such sums as may be necessary for the payment of debts contracted, or the discharge of other contractual obligations incurred in connection with the investment as they fall due;

(d) on liquidation or sale of the investment (whether covering the investment as a whole or a part thereof), allow the repatriation and transfer of the net proceeds of such liquidation or sale and all accretions thereto all at once; in the exceptional cases where the State faces foreign exchange stringencies, such transfer may as an exception be made in installments within a period which will be as short as possible and will not in any case exceed five years from the date of liquidation or sale, subject to interest as provided for in Section 6 (3) of this Guideline; and

(e) allow the transfer of any other amounts to which the investor is entitled such as those which become due under the conditions provided for in Guidelines IV and V.

(2) Such transfer as provided for in Section 6 (1) of this Guideline will be made (a) in

the currency brought in by the investor where it remains convertible, in another currency designated as freely usable currency by the International Monetary Fund or in any other currency accepted by the investor, and (b) at the applicable market rate of exchange at the time of the transfer.

(3) In the case of transfers under Section 6 (1) of this Guideline, and without prejudice to Sections 7 and 8 of Guideline IV where they apply, any delay in effecting the transfers to be made through the central bank (or another authorized public authority) of the host State will be subject to interest at the normal rate applicable to the local currency involved in respect of any period intervening between the date on which such local currency has been provided to the central bank (or the other authorized public authority) for transfer and the date on which the transfer is actually effected.

(4) The provisions set forth in this Guideline with regard to the transfer of capital will also apply to the transfer of any compensation for loss due to war, armed conflict, revolution or insurrection to the extent that such compensation may be due to the investor under applicable law.

7. Each State will permit and facilitate the reinvestment in its territory of the profits realized from existing investments and the proceeds of sale or liquidation of such investments.

8. Each State will take appropriate measures for the prevention and control of corrupt business practices and the promotion of accountability and transparency in its dealings with foreign investors, and will cooperate with other States in developing international procedures and mechanisms to ensure the same.

9. Nothing in this Guideline suggests that a State should provide foreign investors with tax exemptions or other fiscal incentives. Where such incentives are deemed to be justified by the State, they may to the extent possible be automatically granted, directly linked to the type of activity to be encouraged and equally extended to national investors in similar circumstances. Competition among States in providing such incentives, especially tax exemptions, is not recommended. Reasonable and stable tax rates are deemed to provide a better incentive than exemptions followed by uncertain or excessive rates.

10. Developed and capital surplus States will not obstruct flows of investment from their territories to developing States and are encouraged to adopt appropriate measures to facilitate such flows, including taxation agreements, investment guarantees, technical assistance and the provision of information. Fiscal incentives provided by some investors' governments for the purpose of encouraging investment in developing States are recognized in particular as a possibly effective element in promoting such investment.

# Expropriation and Unilateral Alterations or Termination of Contracts

1. A State may not expropriate or otherwise take in whole or in part a foreign private investment in its territory, or take measures which have similar effects, except where this is done in accordance with applicable legal procedures, in pursuance in good faith of a public purpose, without discrimination on the basis of nationality and against the payment of appropriate compensation.

2. Compensation for a specific investment taken by the State will, according to the details provided below, be deemed "appropriate" if it is adequate, effective and prompt.

3. Compensation will be deemed "adequate" if it is based on the fair market value of the taken asset as such value is determined immediately before the time at which the taking occurred or the decision to take the asset became publicly known.

4. Determination of the "fair market value" will be acceptable if conducted according to a method agreed by the State and the foreign investor (hereinafter referred to as the parties) or by a tribunal or another body designated by the parties.

5. In the absence of a determination agreed by, or based on the agreement of, the parties, the fair market value will be acceptable if determined by the State according to reasonable criteria related to the market value of the investment, i.e., in an amount that a willing buyer would normally pay to a willing seller after taking into account the nature of the investment, the circumstances in which it would operate in the future and its specific characteristics, including the period in which it has been in existence, the proportion of tangible assets in the total investment and other relevant factors pertinent to the specific circumstances of each case.

6. Without implying the exclusive validity of a single standard for the fairness by which compensation is to be determined and as an illustration of the reasonable determination by a State of the market value of the investment under Section 5 above, such determination will be deemed reasonable if conducted as follows: (1) for a going concern with a proven record of profitability, on the basis of the discounted cash flow value; (2) for an enterprise which, not being a proven going concern, demonstrates lack of profitability, on the basis of the liquidation value; (3) for other assets, on the basis of (i) the replacement value or (ii) the book value in case such value has been recently assessed or has been determined as of the date of the taking and can therefore be deemed to represent a reasonable replacement value.

For the purpose of this provision:

— "a going concern" means an enterprise consisting of income producing assets which has been in operation for a sufficient period of time to generate the data required for the calculation of future income and which could have been expected with reasonable certainty, if the taking had not occurred, to continue producing legitimate income over the course of its economic life in the general circumstances following the taking by the State;

— "discounted cash flow value" means the cash receipts realistically expected from the enterprise in each future year of its economic life as reasonably projected minus that year's expected cash expenditure, after discounting this net cash flow for each year by a factor which reflects the time value of money, expected inflation, and the risk associated with such cash flow under realistic circumstances. Such discount rate may be measured by examining the rate of return available in the same market on alternative investments of comparable risk on the basis of their present value;

— "liquidation value" means the amounts at which individual assets comprising the enterprise or the entire assets of the enterprise could be sold under conditions of liquidation to a willing buyer less any liabilities which the enterprise has to meet;

— "replacement value" means the cash amount required to replace the individual assets of the enterprise in their actual state as of the date of the taking; and

— "book value" means the difference between the enterprise's assets and liabilities as recorded on its financial statements or the amount at which the taken tangible assets appear on the balance sheet of the enterprise, representing their cost after deducting accumulated depreciation in accordance with generally accepted accounting principles.

7. Compensation will be deemed "effective" if it is paid in the currency brought in by the investor where it remains convertible, in another currency designated as freely usable by the International Monetary Fund or in any other currency accepted by the investor.

8. Compensation will be deemed to be "prompt" in normal circumstances if paid without delay. In cases where the State faces exceptional circumstances, as reflected in an arrangement for the use of the resources of the International Monetary Fund or under similar objective circumstances of established foreign exchange stringencies, compensation in the currency designated under Section 7 above may be paid in installments within a period which will be as short as possible and which will not in any case exceed five years from the time of the taking, provided that reasonable, market-related interest applies to the deferred payments in the same currency.

9. Compensation according to the above criteria will not be due, or will be reduced in case the investment is taken by the State as a sanction against an investor who has violated the State's law and regulations which have been in force prior to the taking, as such violation is determined by a court of law. Further disputes regarding claims for compensation in such a case will be settled in accordance with the provisions of Guideline V.

10. In case of comprehensive non-discriminatory nationalizations effected in the process of large scale social reforms under exceptional circumstances of revolution, war and similar exigencies, the compensation may be determined through negotiations between the host State and the investors' home State and failing this, through international arbitration.

11. The provisions of Section 1 of this Guideline will apply with respect to the conditions under which a State may unilaterally terminate, amend or otherwise disclaim liability under a contract with a foreign private investor for other than commercial reasons, i.e., where the State acts as a sovereign and not as a contracting party. Compensation due to the investor in such cases will be determined in the light of the provisions of Sections 2 to 9 of this Guideline. Liability for repudiation of contract for commercial reasons, i.e., where the State acts as a contracting party, will be determined under the applicable law of the contract.

# Settlement of Disputes

1. Disputes between private foreign investors and the host State will normally be settled through negotiations between them and failing this, through national courts or through other agreed mechanisms including conciliation and binding independent arbitration.

2. Independent arbitration for the purpose of this Guideline will include any ad hoc or institutional arbitration agreed upon in writing by the State and the investor or between the State and the investor's home State where the majority of the arbitrators are not solely appointed by one party to the dispute.

3. In case of agreement on independent arbitration, each State is encouraged to accept the settlement of such disputes through arbitration under the Convention establishing the International Centre for Settlement of Investment Disputes (ICSID) if it is a party to the ICSID Convention or through the "ICSID Additional Facility" if it is not a party to the ICSID Convention.

## New Words

| | | |
|---|---|---|
| 1. | host country | 東道國；地主國 |
| 2. | legal instruments | 法律文書；法律文據 |
| 3. | foster v. | 促進；鼓勵；培養 |
| 4. | parameter n. | 起限定作用的因素 |
| 5. | juridical person | 法人 |
| 6. | constituent a. | 構成的 |
| 7. | privileged treatment | 特權待遇 |

| | | |
|---|---|---|
| **8.** | performance requirements | 履行要求；履約條件 |
| **9.** | counterproductive *a.* | 產生相反結果（或效果）的 |
| **10.** | screening *n.* | 審查；檢查 |
| **11.** | strict exigencies | 急切需要；迫切要求 |
| **12.** | ordre public | （拉）公共政策 |
| **13.** | international instru-ments | 國際文書；國際證書 |
| **14.** | stay visas | 逗留簽證 |
| **15.** | accord *v.* | 給予 |
| **16.** | discriminate *v.* | 歧視 |
| **17.** | generality *n.* | 一般規則 |
| **18.** | concessions *n.* | 讓步 |
| **19.** | net revenues | 淨收入 |
| **20.** | repatriation *n.* | 調回 |
| **21.** | accretions *n.* | 財產的自然增值 |
| **22.** | stringencies *n.* | 吃緊；短缺；不足 |
| **23.** | armed conflict | 武裝衝突 |
| **24.** | insurrection *n.* | 叛亂；暴動；造反 |
| **25.** | tax exemptions | 免稅 |
| **26.** | fiscal incentives | 財政刺激；財政鼓勵 |
| **27.** | obstruct *v.* | 阻止；妨礙 |
| **28.** | appropriate *a.* | 合適的 |
| **29.** | adequate *a.* | 充足的 |
| **30.** | effective *a.* | 有效的 |
| **31.** | prompt *a.* | 即時的 |
| **32.** | fair market value | 公平市場價值 |
| **33.** | going concern | 繼續經營的企業；辦得成功的企業 |
| **34.** | discounted cash flow value | 現金流轉貼現價值 |
| **35.** | realistically *adv.* | 現實地 |
| **36.** | liquidation value | 變現價值 |
| **37.** | replacement value | 重置價值 |
| **38.** | book value | 帳面價值 |
| **39.** | social reforms | 社會改革 |
| **40.** | ad hoc | （拉）特別；臨時；特設 |
| **41.** | exigency *n.* | 緊急狀態；危急（關頭） |
| **42.** | disclaim *v.* | 放棄；否認 |

**New Phrases and Idiomatic Expressions**

| | | |
|---|---|---|
| **1.** | to bear on | 對……有影響 |
| **2.** | to aim to do sth. | 打算或企圖做某事 |
| **3.** | without prejudice to | 在不損害……的情況下 |
| **4.** | as a complement to | 作為……的補充 |
| **5.** | to conflict with | 與……發生衝突 |
| **6.** | to be based on the general premise that... | 根據一般前提 |
| **7.** | to that end | 為達到那個目的 |
| **8.** | on account of | 因為……；由於…… |
| **9.** | to be accessible to sb. | 使某人可得到 |
| **10.** | through the medium of | 透過……機制 |
| **11.** | to resort to | 採用；求助於 |
| **12.** | in whole | 全部 |
| **13.** | in part | 部分 |
| **14.** | to be associated with | 與……有聯繫 |
| **15.** | in the common interest of | 為了……共同的利益 |

 **Notes**

**1**. foreign direct investment：外國直接投資。

Foreign investment is of two kinds, portfolio investment（有價證券投資）and direct investment. Direct investment is a long-term equity investment in a foreign company that gives the investor managerial control over that company. Portfolio investment is a long-term investment in which the investor does not exercise any managerial control.

**2**. the International Bank for Reconstruction and Development
「國際復興開發銀行」（又稱「世界銀行」）。

It is also known as World Bank

**3**. international law：國際法（又稱國際公法，古稱萬國法或萬國公法）。

The law which regulates the intercourse of nations; the law of nations. The customary law which determines the rights and regulates the intercourse of independent nations in peace and war.

**4**. failing this：如果沒有這一點；若無此點。

"failing" here is a preposition which means "without".

**Exercises**

## I. Answer the following questions:

**1.** What attitude does the Development Committee take towards foreign direct investment?

**2.** How many types of foreign investments do you know and what is the essential difference between them?

**3.** What should each state do in order to further the principle of free admission of private investment?

**4.** According the Guidelines what sort of treatment should be granted to foreign investors?

**5.** What kind of compensation will be deemed "adequate, effective and prompt" for a specific investment taken by the host state?

**6.** What guideline is offered on expropriation?

**7.** In what case "adequate effective and prompt" compensation for a specific investment will not be due or will be reduced?

**8.** What are the normal means of settling investment disputes?

## II. Translate the following Chinese passages into English:

**1.** 依國際法關於國家間主權平等原則，外國投資者在他所投資的國家應當服從該國法律的管轄，在法律上與本國國民享受同等待遇和同等保護。這就是所謂國民待遇問題。

**2.** 由於公共政策、公共衛生和保護環境，適用於本國投資的限制也同樣適用於外國投資，外國投資者不應要求獲得特權。

**3.** 該準則認為對外國投資的沒收必須進行「合適」的賠償 —— 即「充分、有效」和「即時」的賠償。

**4.** 正確處理投資爭議是調整國際投資環境的一個重要措施。解決國際投資爭議的方法有司法訴訟（透過法院）、仲裁和解和談判。到底用哪種方式要視具體情況而定。

## III. Indicate whether each of the following statements is true or false by writing "T" or "F" in the space provided:

**1.** Equal treatment of investors plus a positive free competition among them are prerequisites of a positive investment environment.

**2.** The Guidelines suggest that foreign investors should receive a privileged treatment.

**3.** The Guidelines automatically entitle nationals of other states to the more favorable standards of treatment accorded to the nationals of certain states under any customs union or free trade area agreement.

_____ **4.** A state may expropriate or otherwise take in whole or in part a foreign private investment in its territory.

_____ **5.** Developed and capital surplus states will be encouraged to obstruct flows of investment from their territories to developing states.

_____ **6.** Compensation for specific investment taken by the host state is quite necessary.

_____ **7.** The criteria for compensation can be summarized into three words: adequate, effective and prompt.

_____ **8.** Investment disputes can only be settled by arbitration.

# 美國侵權法
## American Tort Law

## Definition of Tort and Tort Law

Tort is a French word for a "Wrong". Tort law is the law that protects a variety of injuries and provides remedies for them.

Under tort law, an injured party can bring a civil lawsuit to seek compensation for a wrong done to the party or the party's property.

Many torts have their origin in Common Law. The Courts and legislatures have extended tort law to reflect changes in modern society.

## History of Tort law

The history of Anglo-American tort law can be traced back to the action for trespass to property or to the person. Not until the late 18th cent. was the currently observed distinction made between injury willfully inflicted and that which is unintentional, and both types were punished equally. In the early 19th cent. Negligence was distinguished as a separate tort, and it has come to supply the bulk of tortuous litigation.

The general tendency today is to rule that the breach of any duty constitutes a tort, rather than to rule that an alleged tort must fit into some previously recognized variety, such as assault, false imprisonment, or libel. Some courts treat any willful unjustified injury as tortious. (e.g. erect a wall on one's property solely to shut off a neighbor's light), while others hold that the act must be defined as tortuous by law, regardless of the perpetrator's motive.

# Classification of Tort Laws

Tort Laws can be classified into five types: **Intentional Torts Against Persons, Intentional Torts Against Property, Unintentional Torts (Negligence), Business Torts and Strict Liability**. The focus of our attention will be turned to: ① unintentional torts (negligence); ② business torts and; ③ strict liability. But other torts will be touched on briefly.

**1. Intentional torts against persons include the following:**

**Assault, battery, false imprisonment intentional infliction of emotional distress** and **malicious prosecution**.

**2. Intentional torts against property which include: trespass to land, trespass to personal property and conversion of personal property**.

**3. Unintentional torts (Negligence)**

**3.1 Concept**

Unintentional torts, commonly referred to as negligence is a doctrine that says a person is liable for harm that is the foreseeable consequence of his or her actions.

**3.2 Elements**

To be successful in a negligence lawsuit, the plaintiff must prove the following four points:

(1) The defendant owed a duty of care to the plaintiff. "Duty of care" means the obligation we all owe each other not to cause any unreasonable harm or risk of harm. For example, a mortgage's duty of care is to sell assets to obtain a fair and reasonable price. As a director of a company he or she has the duty of care to protect the company from exposing it to a risk of insolvency.

(2) The defendant breached his duty of care. "A breach of the duty of care" is the failure to act as a reasonable person would act. Throwing a lit match on the ground in a forest and causing a fire or a failure to act when there is a duty to act (e.g. a fire fighter who refuses to put out a fire).

(3) The plaintiff suffered injury. Here it means the plaintiff must suffer personal injury or damage to his or her property in order to recover monetary damages for the defendant's negligence.

(4) The defendant's negligent act caused the plaintiff's injury. In other words the defendant's negligence or negligent act is the cause of the injury to the plaintiff. Courts have divided causation into two categories-causation in fact and proximate cause-and require each to be shown before the plaintiff may recover damage.

**3.3 Special Negligence Doctrines**

The courts have developed many special negligence doctrines. The most important of them are listed below:

**(1) Negligence per se**

Statutes often establish duties owed by one person to another. The violation of a statute that proximately cause an injury is **negligence per se**. A homeowner in the U.S. is liable if he or she fails to repair a damaged sidewalk in front of his or her home and a pedestrian trips and is injured because of the damage.

**(2) Res Ipas Loquitur** （事情不言自明, These are Latin words for "thing speaks for itself"）. This doctrine raises an inference or presumption of negligence and places the burden on the defendant to prove that he was not negligent. Res Ipas Loquitur applies in cases where (a) the defendant had exclusive control of the instrumentality or situation that caused the injury and (b) the injury would not have ordinarily occurred "but for" someone's negligence (e.g. a surgical instruments are not ordinarily left in patient's bodies). Other typical Res Ipas Loquitur cases involve commercial airplane crashes, falling elevators, and the like.

**(3) Guest statutes** They are statutes that provide that if a driver of a vehicle voluntarily and without compensation gives a ride to another person (e.g. a hitch hiker), the driver is not liable to the passenger for injuries caused by the driver's ordinary negligence. But the driver is always liable to the passenger for wanton and gross negligence, for example, injuries caused because of excessive speed.

**(4) Fireman's rule** It is the rule that provides that fireman, policeman, and other government workers who are injured while providing the service they are trained and paid to perform cannot sue the person who negligently caused the emergency situation to which they responded.

**(5) Duty of utmost care** It is a duty of care that goes beyond ordinary care that says common carriers and innkeepers have a responsibility to provide security to their passengers or guest. For example, a large hotel must provide greater security to guests than a "mon-and-pop" motel. （家庭經營的汽車旅館）

**3.4 Defenses against Negligence**

Even if the plaintiff can prove the existence of all the four elements of negligence, the defendant will still be not liable if he or she can establishes defenses to the plaintiff's claim, e.g. contributory negligence（被害人本身過失）, voluntary consumption of risk on the part of the plaintiff, or the damaged suffered by the plaintiff is too remote, and superseding or intervening event.

**(1) Contributory negligence** A defense（美）/defence（英）that says a person who is injured by a defective product but has been negligent and has contributed to his or her own injuries cannot recover from the defendant.

**(2) Voluntary Assumption of risk** If a plaintiff knows of and voluntarily enters into or <u>participates</u> in a risky activity that results in injury, the law recognizes that the plaintiff assumed, or took on, the risk involved. Thus, the defendant can raise the defense/defence of voluntary assumption of the risk against the plaintiff. For example, a race car driver voluntarily assumes the risk of being injured or killed in a crash.

**(3) Remoteness of damage**   A defendant is liable only for the damage caused "directly" or "indirectly" by him, not for remote consequences. Remoteness of damage=legal principle that damage that is insufficiently connected or foreseeable by a defendant should not make the defendant liable to the plaintiff.

**(4) Supervening or intervening event**   Under negligence, a person is liable only for foreseeable events. Therefore, an original negligent party can raise a superseding (or intervening) event as defense/defence to liability. For example, an injured person, while lying on the ground waiting for an <u>ambulance</u> to come, he is struck by a <u>bolt of lightening</u> and killed. The <u>care-taker</u> for the injured person is not liable for the death of the injured person he is taking care of, because the lightening was an unforeseen intervening event.

### 4. Business Torts

#### 4.1 Concept

Loosely speaking all torts, whether committed by or against business or torts involving businesses can be regarded as business torts.

#### 4.2 Important types

Three types of such torts are discussed in the following paragraphs.

#### Entering Certain Business and professions without a Licence

In a lot of countries, esp. those ruled by law, there are government restrictions and prohibitions on the freedom of entry into certain business and professions. These restrictions are made for the purpose of protecting the public from unqualified <u>practioners</u> and to promote the efficient operation of the economy.

For example, a person cannot <u>erect</u> a television or radio transmitter and start broadcasting. Many <u>occupations</u>, such as lawyers, dentists, <u>real estate</u> brokers and <u>the like</u>, require state licenses. To obtain them, certain requirements must be met.

#### Intentional Misrepresentation (Fraud)

#### Concept

According to Some American law experts, intentional misrepresentation (also known as <u>fraud</u> or <u>deceit</u>) is one of the most <u>pervasive torts</u>. It occurs when a <u>wrongdoer</u> <u>deceives</u> <u>another</u> <u>person out of money</u>, property, or something else of value.

#### Conditions for recovering damages

A person who has been injured by an intentional misrepresentation can recover damages from the wrongdoer. When the following four conditions are satisfied:

(1) The wrongdoer made a false representation of a <u>material fact</u>;

(2) The wrongdoer had knowledge that the representation was false and intended to deceive that <u>innocent party</u>;

(3) The innocent party justifiably relied on the misrepresentation;

(4) The innocent party was injured.

**Civil <u>RICO</u>**

RICO is the short form of <u>Racketeer Influenced and Corruption Organizations Act</u> which <u>outlaws</u> a pattern of "racketeering activities" including <u>arson</u>, <u>counterfeiting</u>, gambling, dealing in <u>narcotics</u>, bribery, <u>embezzlement</u>, mail and wire fraud, securities fraud, and other <u>enumerated</u> criminal activities.

Persons injured by a RICO violation can bring a private civil action against the violator. RICO permits recovery only for injury to business or property.

**5. Strict liability**

Strict liability is another category of torts. Strict liability is defined as liability without fault. Sometimes it is also defined as liability that is imposed without a finding of fault (as negligence or intent). According to this definition, a participant in a <u>covered</u> activity will be held liable for any injuries caused by the activity even if he or she was not negligent. This doctrine holds that (1) there are certain activities that can <u>place the public at risk</u> of injury even if reasonable care is taken, and (2) the public should have some means of compensation if such injury occurs.

For example, if a dangerous animal escaped from somebody's land and got a person injured, the owner of the dangerous animal must bear strict liability. In other words the injured person can hold the owner of the animal liable without having to show that the defendant was negligent or at fault.

 **New Words**

| | | |
|---|---|---|
| **1.** | tort *n.* | 侵權行為 |
| | tort law | 侵權行為法 |
| **2.** | wrong *n.* | 法律上的不法行為 |
| | civil wrong | 民事不法行為 |
| | criminal wrong | 刑事不法行為＝犯罪 |
| **3.** | remedy *n.* | 補救 |
| **4.** | injury *n.* | 傷害；侵害 |
| **5.** | legislature *n.* | 立法機構 ＝ law-making body |
| **6.** | inflict *vt.* | 予以（打擊）；使遭受（損傷、傷害……） |
| **7.** | alleged *a.* | 被指稱的 |

| | | |
|---|---|---|
| **8.** | to erect *vt.* | 建立；建起 |
| **9.** | perpetrator *n.* | 作惡者；行兇者；犯罪者 |
| **10.** | motive *n.* | 動機 |
| **11.** | doctrine *n.* | 原則；學說 |
| **12.** | foreseeable *a.* | 可料到的；可預見的 |
| **13.** | mortgagee *n.* | 承受抵押人（與「mortgagor」（抵押人）相對） |
| **14.** | insolvency *n.* | 破產；無力償還債務 |
| **15.** | to breach *vt.* | 不履行（契約、義務……） |
| **16.** | causation *n.* | 原因 |
| **17.** | statutes *n.* | 成文法；法規 |
| **18.** | pedestrian *n.* | 步行者；行人 |
| **19.** | to trip *vi.* | 絆倒 |
| **20.** | inference *n.* | 推理 |
| **21.** | instrumentality *n.* | 工具 |
| **22.** | elevator *n.* | （美）電梯＝（英）lift |
| **23.** | innkeeper *n.* | 小旅館老闆 |
| **24.** | motel *n.* | 汽車旅館 |
| **25.** | ambulance *n.* | 救護車 |
| **26.** | to reflect *vt.* | 反映；表現 |
| **27.** | enumerated *a.* | 列舉的 |

## ♣ New Phrases and Idiomatic Expressions

| | | |
|---|---|---|
| **1.** | to fit into | 適合 |
| **2.** | to touch on | 提及 |
| **3.** | to expose sth. to sth. else | 將……暴露給 |
| **4.** | to participate in... | 參加……；參與…… |
| **5.** | to give a ride to sb. | 讓某人搭車 |
| **6.** | a bolt of lightening | 一陣閃電 |
| **7.** | to place sb. at risk of sth. | 使某人處於……風險之中 |
| **8.** | to bring a lawsuit | 進行起訴＝bring a legal action |
| **9.** | the bulk of | 大部分；大多數 |
| **10.** | to shut off | 擋住 |
| **11.** | at fault | 有錯 |

## Notes

| | | |
|---|---|---|
| **1.** | injured party | 受傷害一方的當事人；受害當事人 |
| **2.** | assault *n.* | 對他人身體使用武力或暴力 |
| **3.** | false imprisonment | 私禁；非法監禁；錯誤扣留 |
| **4.** | libel *n.* | 誹謗（罪） |
| **5.** | intentional torts against persons | 針對人的意圖侵權行為 |
| **6.** | intentional torts against property | 針對不動產的意圖侵權行為 |
| **7.** | unintentional torts | 非意圖侵權行為（又稱negligence疏忽、過失） |
| **8.** | business torts | 商業侵權行為 |
| **9.** | strict liability | 嚴格責任 |
| **10.** | battery *n.* | 毆打罪（既遂） |
| **11.** | intentional infliction of emotional distress | 意圖使人遭受感情上的憂傷 |
| **12.** | malicious prosecution | 惡意告發；誣告 |
| **13.** | trespass to land | 侵犯他人土地 |
| **14.** | trespass to personal property | 對個人財產的侵犯行為 |
| **15.** | conversion of personal property | 侵占個人財產 |
| **16.** | monetary damages | 損害賠償金 |
| **17.** | proximate cause | 近因；最近的原因 |
| **18.** | causation in fact | 事實上的因果關係 |
| **19.** | negligence per se | 自身的過失 |
| **20.** | res ipsa loquitur (the thing speaks for itself) | 事實不言自明 |
| **21.** | home *n.* | 房子（美國人用法） |
| **22.** | wanton and gross | 任性和嚴重的疏忽 |
| **23.** | common carriers | 公共運送人 |
| **24.** | contributory negligence | 互有過失；共同過失；與有過失 |
| **25.** | voluutary assumption of risk | 自願承擔風險 |
| **26.** | remote and superseding or intervening event | 間接遙遠的不可預測的或者介入的事件 |
| **27.** | license *n.* | 許可（證） |
| **28.** | real estate | 不動產；房地產 |
| **29.** | intentional misrepresentation | 故意的錯誤說明（=「fraud」欺詐） |
| **30.** | pervasive torts | 普遍發生的侵權行為 |
| **31.** | material fact | 重大事實；重要事實 |

| 32. innocent party | 無辜的當事人 |
| 33. RICO (Racketeer Influenced and Corruption Organization Act) | 敲詐勒索影響和腐敗組織法（美國聯邦法律之一，它授權受損害人可提起針對進行敲詐勒索活動的被告的民事訴訟） |
| 34. arson *n.* | 縱火 |
| 35. counterfeiting *n.* | 生產仿冒產品 |
| 36. bribery *n.* | 行賄；受賄；賄賂 |
| 37. embezzlement *n.* | 貪污公款 |
| 38. dealing in narcotics | 販毒 |

 **Exercises**

## I. Answer the following questions:

**1**. What's tort? tort law?

**2**. How do you classify torts?

**3**. Define unintentional tort (negligence).

**4**. What are the four elements of unintentional tort?

**5**. Can you mane a few special negligence doctrines?

**6**. What are the common defenses against negligence?

**7**. What is your understanding of a business tort?

**8**. Can you name some of the important types of business torts with examples?

**9**. What is strict liability? Can you give an example to show it?

## II. Put the following into English:

**1**. tort這一詞是法語，意思是：「不法行為」或「不規行為」。「不法行為」分為兩種：民事不法行為和刑事不法行為，刑事不法行為就是犯罪。法律英語中可用它表示侵權行為（tortious act）。

**2**. 根據侵權法，受傷害的一方可以提起民事上的訴訟尋求給自己或自己財產造成損害的賠償。

**3**. 特殊疏忽理論或原則包括「被告自身的過失」原則、「事實不言自明」原則、「最大小心」原則、「消防員規則」等。

## III. Indicate whether each of the following statements is true or false by putting "T" or "F" in the space provided.

_____ **1.** Negligence was distinguished as a separate tort, and it has come to supply the bulk of tortuous litigation.

_____ **2.** The common defences against negligence are contributory negligence, voluntary assumption of risk and remoteness of damage.

_____ **3.** Business torts have nothing to do with business.

_____ **4.** Entering certain business without a license is regarded as one type of business torts.

_____ **5.** A person who has been injured by an intentional misrepresentation can recover damages from the wrongdoer very easily.

第三十五課
Lesson 35

英國財產法
English Property Law

## Definition of property

The word "property" has several meanings, and in law therefore we must make a careful distinction, especially the distinction between the following two meanings:

1. The thing or things capable of ownership. In this sense the word "property" includes not only physical things, such as a pen, a watch and land, but also non-physical things such as copyrights, debts, and patent rights.

2. Ownership The word "property" may be used to denote ownership or the relationship between a person and an object. Thus, we may say in law that "A has the property in this watch", or in other words, "A owns this watch". Both statements mean the same. In a sale of goods where, for example, a student buys a camera, the shop assistant hands the camera to the buyer, and at the same time, passes "the property" in the camera (the ownership) to the buyer by delivery on the sale.

## Classification of Property (things capable of ownership)

English law has classified property in various ways. But the most common way is to divide property into the following two classes:

**1. Real property** (something also referred to as realty)

Real property consists of

• **Land** which includes (1) land covered by water; (2) any estate, right, interest or easement in or over any land; (3) the whole or part of an undivided share in land and any estate, right, interest or easement in or over the whole or part of an undivided share in land.

• **Buildings and fixtures** According to English property law land also includes things attached to land or permanently fastened to land.

The term "land" in narrow sense also refers to a flat owned by an individual in a multi-storey building. Hence the sales of a second-floor flat is a sale of land in the eyes of law.

In English property law, real property is divided into corporeal hereditament and incorporeal hereditament. A hereditament is real property which can be inherited. A corporeal hereditament is tangible real property, i.e. the land itself and objects attached to it, e.g. buildings, trees. An incorporeal hereditament is intangible objects, e.g. easements, covenants.

**2. personal property** (also known a personalty)

personal property under English property law consists of the following:

• **Chattles real,** *i.e.* movable property such as choses in possession and choses in action. The word "chose", derived from the French, means in law "a thing". The characteristic of a "chose in possession" is that it is a physical thing and can be touched. For example, a chair, a horse, a book and a pen are all examples of "choses in possession". As each has a physical existence, they are sometimes called corporeal (i.e. material) chattels to distinguish them from the so-called choses in action. The main characteristic of a chose in action is that it can be owned but not touched. It has no physical existence (It is incorporeal). Accounts receivable rights, copyrights, trade marks, shares, good will are all examples of choses in action.

# Ownership and Possession

### 1. Concept

Ownership can be defined as "the most extensive right allowed by the law of dealing with a thing to the exclusion of all others". It is both a legal and theoretical concept. For example the owner of a thing has an aggregate of rights, namely (1) the right of enjoyment; (2) the right of destruction; (3) the right of disposition, subject to the right of others.

### 2. Acquisition of Ownership

Ownership may be obtained by

• creating something e.g. painting a picture or writing a book.

• occupation, where a person claims something not owned by anyone, e.g. a wild bird or animal, or by occupation of property abandoned by another.

• accession, e.g. if A owns an animal which begets young, the young animals become the property of A by accession.

• sale. Though sale you can acquire ownership of a good.

• compulsory acquisition by law, e.g. where goods or land are compulsorily acquired by statute, or taken by execution of judgment.

• Succession. On the death of a previous owner another person may succeed to the property and thus acquire ownership, e.g. a beneficiary under a will.

### 3. Transfer of ownership

**Concept**

Since ownership is a collection of rights, a transfer of ownership involves a transfer of rights.

**Basic Rule**

The basic rule is: <u>nemo dat quod non habet</u> (no one can give away what is not his). Thus, if Peter buys a stolen car, Peter is not the car's owner, even though he obtains possession of the car.

However there are some important exceptions to this rule, such as transfer of <u>negotiable instruments</u>.

**Transfer of personalty**

Transfer of choose in possession, if they take place by sale and not <u>by way of</u> gift or <u>barter</u>, is governed by the **Sale of Goods Ordinance**. This ordinance <u>codifies</u> the rules of customary <u>merchantile law</u> concerning such matters as:

- the moment when the property in goods passes from the seller to the buyer;
- the conditions and warranties to be implied in the contracts of sale;
- the rights and remedies of buyers and sellers.

**Transfer of Realty (<u>conveyancing</u>)**

The sale of land raises problems which are not <u>encountered in the case of</u> the sale of goods, as land is <u>by nature</u> <u>immovable</u> and there can not be any <u>physical delivery</u> as in the case of goods. The transaction would therefore rely very much on documents themselves to <u>arrange for</u> transfer of ownership.

For instance, **the Conveyancing and Property Ordinance** — the main piece of legislation for governing the sale of land, <u>provides</u> that an agreement for the sale and purchase of land must <u>be evidenced in writing</u> and signed by the party <u>to be charged</u>, otherwise it is unenforceable in the courts of law.

The procedure for the transfer of realty such as land or the land conveyancing process normally involves the following 4 steps:

(1) the <u>pre-contract</u> negotiation  This concerns the inspection of the <u>subject property</u>, its <u>surrounding environment</u>, planning control and building structures.

(2) the contract for the sale of land  As mentioned above such a contract must be in writing to be enforceable.

(3) post contract stage.

Once the contract for sale of land has been signed and exchanged on both sides, the vendor/seller remains the <u>legal owner</u> but the contract of sale gives the purchaser an <u>equitable interest</u> in land. From that time, he is entitled to any increase in value but must also <u>bear the risk of</u>

loss and should therefore <u>insure</u> the property. The vendor/seller has a right to a <u>lien over the land</u> until he is paid <u>the balance of the purchase money</u>. If either party refuses to complete the transaction, the other party may apply to court for <u>a decree of specific performance</u>.

(4) the conveyance stage.

Conveyance of land can only be <u>effected</u> by deed under seal called an <u>assignment</u>. This will be done when the buyer/purchaser is satisfied as to <u>the title</u> of the vendor/seller and the existence of other <u>interests</u>. The consignment is <u>composed of</u> the following parts:

• the date;

• the names of the parties;

• the consideration;

• the receipt clause;

• the operative (the conveyancing)clause, by which the title is actually conveyed;

• the <u>parcels</u> (describing the property);

• the <u>habendum</u>, stating the interest that is to pass;

• exceptions and reservations, if any covenants, i.e. the lease and the deed of mutual covenant;

• the attestation clause.

At completion, the vendor/seller will <u>hand over</u> to the buyer/purchaser the <u>title deeds</u> and the assignment which he has <u>executed</u> under seal in return for the payment of the purchase price by the purchaser who also executed the same under seal so that he is <u>bound</u> by the lease covenants contained in the assignment.

Transfer of land ownership sometimes happen where no sale or purchase of land is involved and the land ownership is being transferred as a gift from the <u>donor</u> to the <u>donee</u> and as such the whole conveyancing process would not be needed, one single document known as <u>a deed of gift</u> is required to be <u>drawn up</u> and executed by the donor under seal giving particulars of the property to be transferred and the identity of the donee.

### Possession

### 1. Concept

Possession is defined as the visible form of exercising physical control over a thing with the intention of doing so to the exclusion of all others. So possession in law is based on possession in fact. It involves three concepts:

(1) the <u>corpus possessionis</u>, meaning the control over the thing itself which may be exercised by a person, their servant or agent, and

(2) the <u>animus possidendi</u>, which is intent to exercise <u>exclusive possession</u> of the thing itself and thus to <u>prevent others from using</u> it.

Possession is, therefore, largely a question of fact, as is <u>borne out</u> by common experience.

(3) evidence that the thing concerned is under control.

## 2. ways of obtaining possession

Possession may be obtained lawfully and unlawfully.

### 2.1 by lawful means

Lawful possession needs no explanation. For example if Marry lends a car to Peter for use, Peter is in temporary physical possession of the car. Such possession apparently is lawful.

### 2.2 by unlawful means

Sometimes possession may be obtained by unlawful means. Such possession is what we call unlawful possession. For example, if A steals a pen from B, A's possession of the pen is unlawful.

### Mortgages

### 1. Definition

A mortgage may be defined as a conveyance of property as <u>security</u> to <u>discharge</u> an obligation (e.g. the payment of a debt). The person who mortgages property is called a mortgagor. The person or the party to whom or in whose favour property is mortgaged is known as a mortgagee. So a mortgage involves two parties as mentioned above.

### 2. Types of property offered as a security against repayment of debt

Two types of property are offered as a security when a person borrows money from somebody including a bank. In other words personal property or real property can be offered as a security against bank loans or money borrowed.

**(1) personal property**, such as a gold watch which is a simple form of security; it is easily <u>deliverable</u> and is the kind sometimes transferred to a <u>pawnbroker</u> as security for a loan which the latter is prepared to advance to the borrower/the pawner. When the loan is repaid with interest on the date agreed the property (the gold watch) is returned to the borrower.

**(2) Real property**, such as a valuable piece of land or a house which also provides a good form of security acceptable to the money lender.

<u>The forms</u> of mortgages of land today are (1) legal mortgages and (2) equitable mortgages. In other words mortgages of land may be either legal or equitable.

### Legal mortgages

First let's have a look at legal mortgages.

At common law, a legal mortgage may be created in two ways. The first is to grant <u>a legal estate</u> to the mortgagee in the form of an assignment with a <u>proviso</u> that the lease shall come to an end on repayment of the loan. The second method is by creating a <u>sub-lease</u> for a slightly shorter period than the original <u>leasehold term</u>. Normally, the mortgagee does not take possession of the property, which remains with the mortgagor.

**(A) Remedies for the mortgagee under a legal mortgage**

The mortgagee of a legal mortgage has the following rights:

• (a) To sue for debt

The amount due on the mortgagor's covenant to repay is the principal sum plus interest. Where the date fixed for redemption has passed, the mortgagee may sue for that amount. This remedy is comparably less effective unless there are reasons to believe that the borrower will repay the debt if threatened with bankruptcy or winding-up proceedings.

• (b) To take possession of the land

This remedy is available to the mortgagee as the legal tenant of the land. Possession may be taken at once or before the ink is dry on the mortgage. If the land is let to a tenant whose tenancy is binding on the mortgagee, the mortgagee can require the tenant to pay the rent to him directly.

A mortgagee's right to obtain possession of a dwelling house is restricted by the Administration of Justice Acts of 1970 and 1973.

• (c) To foreclose

That means the mortgagee can obtain a court order removing or extinguishing the mortgagor's equitable right to redeem the property and vesting the full legal estate in the mortgagee if the mortgagor fails to pay the sum due for an unreasonable time. According to law experts in the U.K., such remedy is not normally sought as it involves a cumbersome procedure and is subject to reopening by the mortgagor in some circumstances.

• (d) To sell the land

The mortgagee must exercise his power to sell in good faith and must not sell to himself on his nominee and the sale is usually effected by public auction. If there is any surplus after deducting the costs of the sale from the proceeds, the mortgagee is obliged to return the same to the mortgagor.

• (e) To appoint a receiver

The power to appoint a receiver is implied in all mortgages by deed, unless a contrary intention is expressed. The receiver's duties are to receive the rents and profits on the mortgagee's behalf in order to discharge the sum due.

**What about the remedies for the mortgagor under legal mortgage?** The main weapon of the mortgage is the right to redeem the mortgaged property on repayment of the principal sum borrowed, plus interest.

**(B) Equitable Mortgage**

**Concept**

An equitable mortgage is one in which the mortgagee receives merely an equitable interest in the land.

**Types**

There are two distinct types of equitable mortgages:

• A mortgage of an equitable interest owned by the mortgagor, e.g. a life interest or other interest under trust. In these cases the mortgagor may assign their equitable interest to the mortgagee with a proviso for reassignment of the equitable interest on repayment of the debt, plus interest.

• An informal mortgage of a legal estate or legal interest. Sometimes a borrower requires a loan urgently and wishes to avoid the trouble and expense of drawing up a formal legal mortgage. In case of his type, an agreement in writing to create a mortgage or the deposit of title deeds as an act of part performance of an oral agreement operates to create an equitable mortgage. This will be treated in equity as a mortgage since "equity looks upon that as done which ought to be done".

**Methods of creating equitable mortgages**

There are three common ways of creating equitable mortgages. The three usual methods of doing so are:

• (a) A written agreement (signed as required by section 40 of the Law of Property Act) which is not accompanied by a deposit of title deeds.

• (b) A deposit of deeds alone, without written agreement, if the deposit of the deeds amounts to part performance of an agreement to give security.

• (c) A combination of (a) and (b) above, i.e. a written agreement plus a deposit of deeds.

The agreement is usually by deed as this gives the mortgagee certain valuable remedies under the Law of Property Act, 1925.

# Remedies of the mortgagee under an equitable mortgage

**1. An equitable mortgagee by deed** enjoys the same remedies as a legal mortgagee except that the equitable mortgagee and the receiver so appointed do not have the right to sell the mortgaged property to the purchaser. However, this particular problem can be cured where the equitable mortgagee is given:

(a) an irrevocable power of attorney to act on behalf of the mortgagor concerning the land, including the power to sell; or

(b) a declaration of trust by the mortgagor declaring that he holds the mortgaged property in trust for the mortgagee with express power conferred on the mortgagee to nominate another person as trustee in place of the mortgagor.

**2. An equitable mortgage in writing** gives no authority to sell the mortgaged property even though the memorandum of mortgage contains an undertaking by the mortgagor to sell the land when called upon to do so. Therefore, the mortgagee will have to apply for a court order so that the sale can be effected.

 **New Words**

| | | |
|---|---|---|
| **1.** | class *n.* | 種類 |
| **2.** | estate *n.* | 個人地產；資產上的所有權 |
| **3.** | easement *n.* | 地役權；使用他人土地權 |
| **4.** | fixtures *n.* | 附著物；不動產的附屬物 |
| **5.** | object *n.* | 物體 |
| **6.** | multi-storey *a.* | 多層的（當複合形容詞用） |
| **7.** | flat *n.* | 一套公寓房間（這是英式表達方式＝美式「apartment」） |
| **8.** | hence *adv.* | 因此 |
| **9.** | tangible *a.* | 有形的；實體的（反義詞為「intangible」） |
| **10.** | covenant *n.* | 專約契約 |
| **11.** | acquisition *n.* | 取得；獲得 |
| **12.** | accession *n.* | 添附；增加 |
| **13.** | to beget *vt.* | 生（下） |
| **14.** | compulsory *a.* | 強制性的 |
| **15.** | barter *n.* | 易貨；以物易物 |
| **16.** | to codify *vt.* | 將⋯⋯編成典 |
| **17.** | to encounter *vt.* | 碰到 |
| **18.** | pre-contract *n.* | 訂約前（的） |
| **19.** | assignment *n.* | （權利，財產）轉讓；讓與 |
| **20.** | parcel *n.* | （土地的）一塊 |
| **21.** | habendum *n.* | （拉）權利取得（~clause） |
| **22.** | to execute *vt.* | 經簽名蓋章使其生效 |
| **23.** | to be bound by... | 受⋯⋯所拘束／約束 |
| **24.** | donor *n.* | 贈與人；捐贈人 |
| **25.** | donee *n.* | 受贈人 |
| **26.** | particulars *n.* | 詳況；細節 |

| 27. security *n.* | 擔保 |
|---|---|
| 28. to discharge *vt.* | 清償（如to ~ an obligation清償債務） |
| 29. deliverable *a.* | 可交付的 |
| 30. pawnbroker *n.* | 當鋪老闆 |
| 31. pawner *n.* | 出典人；出當人 |
| 32. proviso *n.* | （契約等的）附件；但書 |
| 33. redemption *n.* | 贖回 |
| 34. to let *vt.* | 出租；租給 |
| 35. to foreclose | 取消對抵押品的贖回權 |
| 36. cumbersome *a.* | 麻煩的 |
| 37. to redeem *vt.* | 贖回 |
| 38. express *a.* | 明示的（與implied「默示的」相對） |
| 39. undertaking *n.* | 承擔；許諾；保證 |
| 40. to denote *vt.* | 表示 |

## ♣ New Phrases and Idiomatic Expressions

| 1. physical things *a.* | 有形物 |
|---|---|
| 2. non-physical *a.* | 無形物的 |
| 3. shop assistant | 店員；售貨員 |
| 4. to hand sth. to sb. | 將……交給某人 = to hand sth. over to sb. |
| 5. to be attached to | 使附屬於 |
| 6. to be permanently fastened to sth. | 使永久地附著在……上 |
| 7. good will | 善意 |
| 8. an aggregate of | 綜合一起的……；合在一起的…… |
| 9. execution of judgment | 執行判決；判決的執行 |
| 10. to bear the risk to | 承擔……風險 |
| 11. a lien over the land | 土地上的留置權 |
| 12. to draw up | 寫出；草擬 |
| 13. in good faith | 善意地；誠意地 |
| 14. to deduct the costs of...from... | 從……中扣掉……的成本 |
| 15. to amount to | 等於 |
| 16. in place of | 取代 |
| 17. by way of... | 用……方法；透過……方法 |

| **18.** | in the case of... | 就⋯⋯來說 |
| **19.** | be evidenced in writing | 以書面形式作證 |
| **20.** | to prevent sb. (from) doing sth. | 阻止某人做某事（現代英語中from可省掉） |

### Notes

| | | |
|---|---|---|
| **1.** | copyright *n.* | 著作權 |
| **2.** | patent right | 專利權 |
| **3.** | to pass the property in sth. to sb. | 將⋯⋯的所有權轉移給某人 |
| **4.** | English law | 英國法（注意不能用British law來取代，因為英國的蘇格蘭採用的是大陸法） |
| **5.** | corporeal hereditaments | 有形可繼承的財產（指不動產） |
| **6.** | incorporeal hereditaments | 無形的遺產（如地役權等） |
| **7.** | personalty *n.* | 動產（與「personal property」意同） |
| **8.** | chattels real | 準不動產 |
| **9.** | an action in rem | 物權訴訟 |
| **10.** | chattels personal | 動產；私人動產 |
| **11.** | choses in possession | 所有物；實際占有的動產 |
| **12.** | choses in action | 無形財產（無體所有物）；訴訟上的財產 |
| **13.** | account receivable | 應收帳款 |
| **14.** | shares *n.* | （英）股票＝（美）stocks |
| **15.** | the right of disposition | 處置權 |
| **16.** | nemo dat quod non habet | （拉）任何人不能給予他人不是（屬）自己的東西（No one can give away what is not his.）又譯成：自己無有者不得與人 |
| **17.** | negotiable instruments | 可轉讓票據 |
| **18.** | the Sale of Goods Ordinance | 貨物銷售條例 |
| **19.** | the Conveyancing and Property Ordinance | 轉讓與房地產條例 |
| **20.** | legal owner | 合法所有人 |
| **21.** | equitable interest | 衡平法上的權益 |
| **22.** | a decree of specific performance | 依約履行的法令 |
| **23.** | the corpus possessionis | （拉）對物本身的控制 |
| **24.** | the animus possidendi | （拉）（對某物）占有意圖／向 |

| | |
|---|---|
| **25.** legal mortgages | 普通法上的抵押 |
| **26.** equitable mortgages | 衡平法上的抵押 |
| **27.** legal estate | 普通法上的不動產權益；普通法地產權 |
| **28.** leasehold term | 租賃保有期限 |
| **29.** winding-up proceedings | 結束營業程序 |
| **30.** life interest | 終身利益 |
| **31.** title deeds | 所有權契約 |
| **32.** irrevocable power of attorney | 不可撤銷的授權書 |
| **33.** memorandum of mortgage | 抵押備忘錄 |

## Exercises

## I. Answer the following questions:

**1**. What is property? Is it important for law students to make a careful distinction between the two major meanings it has?

**2**. Can you tell the difference between real property and personal property?

**3**. How do you distinguish between ownership and possession?

**4**. How many steps are involved when transferring realty?

**5**. What are the three concepts possession involves?

**6**. What are the usual ways of obtaining possession?

**7**. Can you tell the methods of creating legal mortgages and equitable mortgages?

**8**. What remedies are available for mortgagee under legal mortgage and equitable mortgages?

**9**. What is your definition of mortgage?

## II. Put the following into Chinese:

**1**. The person who mortgage property is called mortgagor and the person or the party to whom or in whose favour property is mortgaged is known as mortgagee.

**2**. The two important meanings of the word "property" a law student must know are (1) the thing or things capable of ownership. (2) it is used to denote "ownership", or the relationship between a person and an object.

**3**. "to foreclose" in property law means the mortgagee can obtain a court order removing or extinguishing the mortgagor's equitable right to redeem the property and vesting the full legal estate in the mortgagee.

**4**. The main weapon for the mortgagor is the right to redeem the mortgaged property on repayment of the principal sum borrowed plus interest.

## III. Indicate whether each of the following statement is true of false by putting "T" of "F" in the space provided.

_____ **1.** The word "property" does not have several meanings.

_____ **2.** Realty, real estate, real property are synonyms.

_____ **3.** The term "land" in narrow sense also refers to a flat owned by an individual.

_____ **4.** A corporeal hereditament is intangible real property.

_____ **5.** Accounts receivable, patent rights, copyrights trademarks are examples of choses in action.

_____ **6.** "Nemo dat quod non habet" is the basic rule for transferring ownership.

## 第三十六課 Lesson 36 — 英國繼承法 English Law of Succession

## The Meaning of Succession

Here in law, succession means the act of process by which a person becomes entitled to the property or property interest of a deceased person and esp. an intestate: the transmission of the estate of a decedent to his or her heirs, legatees, or devisees.

## The Concept of Law of Succession

What is the law of succession about? It is a law which deals with the transfer of property when a person dies. The two important issues discussed in this law are: (1) who is entitled to receive the property of a deceased person; and (2) how the property of the deceased is to be distributed.

## Personal Representatives

What is meant by "personal representative"?

"Personal representative" has the following two meanings: (1) one recognized as the representative of another party or his or her interest; (2) an executor or administrator who may bring or be subject to an action or proceeding for or against a deceased person and his or her estate (when a person who has brought an action for personal injury dies pending the action, such action may be revived in the name of his personal representative.)

The two important types of personal representatives in the law of succession are:

**(a) An executor** (or an executrix for a female) An executor is the personal representative appointed to administer an estate under a will, or by the testator (who disposes of his property by will). The testator may appoint anyone (or more than one person) as his executor(s), but under the Probate and Administration Ordinance, <u>probate</u> will not to be granted to more than four executors nor will it be granted to a minor until he <u>becomes of full age</u>. If the last surviving executor <u>dies testate</u>, then his executors will take his place and be responsible for administering not only the estate of the deceased executor but also the estate of the deceased person who appointed the deceased executor.

**(b) An administrator** (or administratrix for a female)

An administrator is personal representative for the estate of a deceased person. He is appointed by the court under the following circumstances:

If the deceased had left no will appointing an executor, or if the appointment fails (e.g. the person appointed as an executor is unsuitable or refuses to act).Such an administrator is called <u>an administrator cum testamento annexo</u>.

When the deceased had died intestate or had not made a valid will, the administrator appointed in this case is called <u>an administrator upon intestacy</u>.

When the legal proceedings touching the validity of the will have not been settled.

# Statutory Duties of Personal Representatives

Apart from the common law duties imposed on a personal representative which are similar to those imposed on a <u>trustee</u>, **the Probate and Administration Ordinance imposes** further statutory duties on the personal representative which include

(1) Collection of all the assets e.g. by suing for debts if necessary.

(2) Payment of all the deceased's debts in the following order:

• **Preferred debts** such as funeral and <u>testamentary</u> and administration expenses.

• **Ordinary debts**

• **Deferred debts** such as loans owing to a <u>spouse</u>, etc.

# Wills

### 1. Definition

A will is a legal declaration of a person's wishes regarding the disposal of his or her property after death. The declaration is made when the person is still alive. It does not have any effect till the time of death.

### 2. Nature

A will is said to be <u>ambulatory</u> (i.e. not permanent subject to <u>revocation</u> or <u>alteration</u> until the death of the <u>testator</u>. In other words the will speaks from death. If A makes a <u>disposition</u>

of "All my property to Z", the successor (Z) will receive all the property which A owns at the moment of death. The gift will include property which A acquires between the time of making the will and death. It will not, however, include property which A has disposed of between these times.

### 3. Testamentary capacity

The general rule is that any person of full age and sound mind may make a valid will. The testator is presumed same at the time when the will was made; but if the will is contested on the ground that the testator was of unsound mind, the person propounding the will has the burden of proving the sanity of the testator.

Married women were formerly incapable of making valid wills, but legislation in the past century has amended this, so that now they have full testamentary capacity **(Married Women's Property Act, 1882 and 1892, and the Law Reform (Married Women's and Torteasors) Act, 1935).**

An infant (i.e. a person under the age of 18) cannot make a valid will, but there is an exception in regard to infant soldiers, sailors, and airmen. In other words, a person in actual naval, military or air force service, and a mariner or seaman at sea, may make a valid will even though they are minors.

**4. Testamentary intent**    It means an intention to make a revocable ambulatory disposition of the testator's property taking effect on death; to possess the necessary intent, the testator must intend that the disposition comes into play immediately and is not postponed by some future event or condition.

### 5. Formalities to be complied by a valid will

According to the Wills Act, 1837, — the main legislation governing this important matter, for a will to be valid, it has to comply with the following formalities:

**(a) Writing**.    A will must be in the form of a written document. Any document, e.g. a letter, can suffice and may include other documents exiting at the time the will was made and referred to in the will. Here "writing" includes handwriting, print and typescript.

**(b) Signature**.    The will must be signed by the testator, initials, a partial signature, a mark (e.g. a cross) or a thumb print in ink may be used, as long as the mark is clearly ascribable to the testator. A seal stamped with the testator's initials has been held to be a signature.

**6. Attestation**.    The signature of the testator, "shall be made or acknowledged by the testator in the presence of two or more witnesses present at the same time, and each witness either attests and signs the will or acknowledges their signature in the presence of the testator (but not necessarily in the presence of any other witnesses)".

**7. Addition and alterations**.    A will having been made is alterable. Any changes may be made in the body of an existing will, provided that they are: initialed by the testator and the witnesses. Moreover, additions may be made even below the testator's signature if they are signed and attested in the same manner as the will itself. Further, a will may be supplemented or added to by properly signed and attested <u>codicils</u>.

**8. Revocation.**  It is of the very nature of a will, according to English law, that a will shall be revocable until the testator dies. <u>Revocation</u> may be express or it may be implied from the conduct of the testator.

Revocation may be <u>effected</u> by (a) subsequent will or codicil; (b) a writing executed like a will; (c) subsequent marriage or (d) destruction of the will.

# Family Provision

Until 1938 a testator according to **the Inheritance Act 1938** had complete freedom to dispose of property, in any manner thought fit. But in 1978, this Act was replaced by **the Inheritance (Provision for Family and Dependents Act 1975).** In accordance with this Act, the following persons may apply to the Court for an order to make <u>reasonable provisions</u> for them.

(a) the wife or husband of the deceased;

(b) a former <u>spouse</u> who has not remarried;

(c) a child;

(d) any person who was treated by the deceased as a child of the family (in relation to any marriage of his);

(e) any person who immediately before the death of the deceased was being <u>maintained</u> by the deceased without <u>reciprocal</u> consideration.

A partner or other person with whom the deceased was <u>cohabiting</u> may claim under (e) above. Any such person (a) to (e) may apply to the court for an order on the ground that the disposition of the deceased's estate effected by the will or the law relating to <u>intestacy</u> is not such as to make reasonable financial provision for such person.

## New Words

| | | |
|---|---|---|
| **1.** | deceased *a.* | 死去的；已死的 |
| **2.** | intestate *n.* | 未留遺囑的死亡者 |
| **3.** | heir *n.* | 繼承人（男）；女繼承人＝heiress |
| **4.** | legatee *n.* | 遺產繼承人 |
| **5.** | devisee *n.* | 受遺贈人 |
| **6.** | asset *n.* | 資產 |

| | | |
|---|---|---|
| **7.** | liability | 負債 |
| **8.** | to distribute *vt.* | 分配（財產……） |
| **9.** | pending *prep.* | 在……期間，如：pending the negotiation在談判期間 |
| **10.** | to revive *vt.* | 使復活 |
| **11.** | probate *n.* | 遺囑檢驗 |
| **12.** | testator *n.* | 留遺囑的人；立遺囑人 |
| **13.** | administrator cum testamento annexo | 附帶遺囑遺產管理人 |
| **14.** | trustee *n.* | 受託人 |
| **15.** | ambulatory *a.* | 可變更的 |
| **16.** | revocation *n.* | 撤銷 |
| **17.** | alteration *n.* | 改動 |
| **18.** | to contest *vt.* | （產生）爭議 |
| **19.** | to propound *vt.* | 提出有關（遺囑）合法性 |
| **20.** | to amend *vt.* | 修正 |
| **21.** | revocable *a.* | 可撤銷的 |
| **22.** | to suffice *vi.* One word will ~ | 足夠 一句話就足夠了 |
| **23.** | typescript *n.* | 打字稿（文件） |
| **24.** | initials *n.* | 姓名的開頭字母 |
| **25.** | thumb print | 拇指紋 |
| **26.** | seal *n.* | 印章；圖章 |
| **27.** | witness *n.* | 證人 |
| **28.** | to authenticate *vt.* | 使……生效 |
| **29.** | to subscribe *vt.* | 簽署 |
| **30.** | to effect *vt.* | 產生 |
| **31.** | to maintain *vt.* | 扶養；供養 |
| **32.** | reciprocal *a.* | 報答的 |
| **33.** | to cohabit *vi.* | 同住（男女）；同居 |
| **34.** | spouse *n.* | 配偶 |

## ♣ New Phrases and Idiomatic Expressions

| | | |
|---|---|---|
| **1.** | pending the action | 在訴訟期間 |
| **2.** | in the name of... | 以……的名義 |
| **3.** | under a will | 根據遺囑 |

| | |
|---|---|
| **4.** to dispose of | 處理；處置 |
| **5.** to become of full age | 成年 = reach full age |
| **6.** to die testate | 死時留有遺囑（與「die intestate」（死時未留遺囑）相對） |
| **7.** upon intestacy | 在未留遺囑情況下 |
| **8.** statutory duties | 成文法上規定的義務 |
| **9.** testamentary expenses | 遺囑方面的開支 |
| **10.** on the ground that... | 以……為理由；以……為藉口 |
| **11.** to take effect | 生效 |
| **12.** to come into play | 開始發揮作用 |
| **13.** to be ascribable to... | 起因於 |

## Notes

| | |
|---|---|
| **1.** the Probate and Administration Ordinance | 遺囑檢驗與管理條例 |
| **2.** preferred debts | 優先債務 |
| **3.** deferred debts | 遞延的債務 |
| **4.** infant *n.* | 未達法定年齡的人 = minor |
| **5.** air force | 空軍 |
| **6.** mariner *n.* | 水手；海員 |
| **7.** reasonable provision | 本文中當「合理供養」講 |

## Exercises

### I. Answer the following questions:

**1**. What is succession law about?

**2**. What is meant by personal representative?

**3**. What are the main statutory duties for the personal representatives to perform?

**4**. Can you define the word "will"? What is the nature of a will?

**5**. What kind of will is a valid will?

**6**. What are the benefits of making a will?

**7**. What is the purpose of "attestation"?

**8**. What persons can apply to the court for an order to make reasonable provision for them?

## II. Put the following into Chinese:

**1.** Until 1938 a testator had complete freedom to dispose of property, in any manner thought fit.

**2.** It is of the very nature of a will, according to English law, that a will shall be revocable until the testator dies.

## III. Indicate whether each of the following statements is true or false by writing "T" or "F" in the space provided:

_____**1.** In Succession law "Succession" means the act or process by which a person becomes entitled to the property or property interest of a deceased person and esp. an intestate.

_____**2.** The general rule is that any person of full age and sound mind may make a valid will.

_____**3.** A valid will must not be in writing and signed by the testator.

_____**4.** A testator has complete freedom to dispose of property in any manner thought fit.

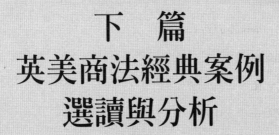

下　篇
英美商法經典案例
選讀與分析

# The List of References

The foregoing sixty odd classical cases are taken from the following law books:

1. Case book on Contract Law

   *by W. T Major*

   *published of by Pitman in* 1990

2. Contemporary Business Law

   *by Henry R. Cheeseman*

   *published in* 1997 *by Prentice Hall Inc.*

3. Charlesworth's Business Law

   *by Pawl Dobson,Clive M. Schmittnoff*

   *published by Sweet Maxwell in* 1991

4. Law

   *by David Barker & Colin Padfield*

# PART I

## Cases to Be Cited for Teaching English and American Contract Law

| 1 | **Agreement** |

The terms of the offer must be certain.

## (1) Scammell v. Ouston

[1941] A. C. 251; [1941] 1 All E. R. 14

*House of Lords*

The parties entered into negotiations for the supply of a <u>motorlorry</u>, giving an old lorry in <u>part exchange</u>. The parties were agreed as to the new lorry to be supplied, the price and the <u>rebate</u> <u>in respect of</u> the old lorry and further, they were agreed that the <u>balance of the purchase price</u> was to be had <u>on hire-purchase terms</u> over a period of two years. The precise terms of the <u>hire-purchase</u> agreement were not settled. The <u>prospective hirer</u> subsequently <u>repudiated</u> the transaction <u>contending</u> that there never was any concluded agreement between the parties because the terms of the prospective hire-purchase agreement had not been settled.

HELD, by VISCOUNT SIMON L. C. , VISCOUNT MAUGHAM, LORD RUSSELL and LORD WRIGHT, the expression "on hire-purchase terms" was too <u>vague</u> to be given any definite meaning.  Therefore there was no concluded agreement.

### ♣ Notes

1. motor lorry    （英）卡車；載重汽車 ＝（美）truck
2. giving old lorry in part exchange    拿舊卡車換新卡車
   part exchange ＝ transaction in which
   goods are given as part of the payment
3. rebate *n.*    付款總額的減少、折扣、回扣
4. the balance of the purchase price    購買價的餘額
5. on hire-purchase terms    按分期付款購買的條款
6. hire-purchase agreement    分期付款購置協議／契約

| | |
|---|---|
| 7. the prospective hirer | 預期中的／未來的分期付款購置者 |
| 8. to repudiate the transaction | 否認交易的有效 |
| 9. to contend *vt.* | 主張；堅決認為 |
| 10. held | 裁定 = It is held |
| 11. vague *a.* | 含糊的 |

An invitation to treat is not an offer.

# (2) Harris v. Nickerson

[1873] L. R. 8 Q. B. 286

*Court of Queen's Bench*

The defendant, an auctioneer, advertised that he would hold an auction sale of certain brewing materials, plant and office furniture on a specified date and the days following. The furniture was advertised for sale on the third day. The plaintiff, a London commission broker, obtained a commission to buy the office furniture and attended the sale. The defendant withdrew the office furniture from the sale and the plaintiff ( who had purchased lots other than the office furniture) brought this action contending that the advertisement was akin to an advertisement for reward, i. e. general in its inception, but becoming a promise to the particular person who acts upon it before it is withdrawn.

HELD, by BLACKBURN, QUAIN and ARCHIBALD, JJ., that there was no contract, the advertisement being a mere declaration of intention.

## ♣ Notes

| | |
|---|---|
| **1.** auctioneer *n.* | 拍賣商；拍賣人 |
| **2.** to advertise *vt.* | 做廣告 |
| **3.** to hold an auction sale of sth. | 對……舉行拍賣（會） |
| **4.** brewing materials | 釀造啤酒等的材料 |
| **5.** commission broker | 經紀人 |
| **6.** commission *n.* | 代理佣金 |
| **7.** to be akin to | 近似於…… |
| **8.** inception *n.* | 開始 |
| **9.** to act upon... | 按……去行為（動） |

Generally, an acceptance does not take effect unless and until it is <u>communicated</u> to the <u>offeror</u>.

# (3) Felthouse v. Bindley
[1862] 6 L. T. 157; 11 C. B. (N. S.) 869
*Court of Common Bench*

The plaintiff wished to buy a horse belonging to his nephew and, not having reached agreement as to price, wrote on 2nd January 1862 as follows:

"Dear Nephew,

Your price, I admit, was 30 <u>guineas</u>. I offered £30-never offered more: and you said the horse was mine. However, as there may be a mistake about him, I will <u>split the difference</u>-£30 15s. -I paying all expenses from Tamworth. You can send him <u>at your convenience</u>, between now and the 25th of March. If I hear no more about him, I <u>consider the horse mine</u> at £30 15s. Paul Felthouse."

The nephew did not <u>reply</u> to his letter, but having a sale of his animals shortly afterwards, he instructed the defendant, an auctioneer, to <u>keep that</u> horse <u>out of the sale</u>. The auctioneer forgot his instructions and sold the horse. The plaintiff brought his action for <u>conversion</u> of the horse.

HELD, by WILLES, BYLES and KEATING, JJ., that <u>with regard to</u> the question whether ownership had <u>vested</u> in the plaintiff, there was no contract for the sale of the horse.

## 🍀 Notes

| | | |
|---|---|---|
| **1.** | to take effect = to become effective | 生效 |
| **2.** | offeror *n.* | 要約人 |
| **3.** | to be communicated to sb. | 傳達到某人 |
| **4.** | Court of Common Bench | （英）高等民事法院 |
| **5.** | guinea *n.* | 幾尼（舊）英國金幣 = 21 先令或 1.05 英鎊 |
| **6.** | to split the difference | 平分差額 |
| **7.** | at your convenience | 在你方便的時候 |
| **8.** | to consider sth. mine | 將……看成自己的 |
| **9.** | to keep sth. out of the sale | 將……從銷售中撤出來 |
| **10.** | conversion *n.* | 侵占行為；侵占動產罪 |
| **11.** | with regard to | 關於 |
| **12.** | to vest in sb. | 歸屬某人 |

In the case of unilateral contract, acceptance need not be communicated.

# (4) Carlivll v. Carbolic Smoke Ball Co.

[1893] 1Q. B. 256; [1891-4] All E. R. Rep. 127

*Court of Appeal*

The defendants published the following advertisement in a newspaper: "£100 reward will be paid by the Carbolic Smoke Ball Co. to any person who contracts the increasing epidemic influenza, colds, or any disease caused by taking cold, after having used the ball three times daily for two weeks according to the printed directions supplied with each ball. £1, 000 is deposited with Alliance Bank, Regent Street, showing our sincerity in the matter. During the last epidemic of influenza many thousand Carbolic Smoke Balls were sold as preventives against this disease, and in no ascertained case was the disease contracted by those using the Carbolic Smoke Ball. One Carbolic Smoke Ball will last a family several months, making it the cheapest remedy in the world at the price-10s. post free. The ball can te refilled at a cost of 5s. Address: Carbolic Smoke Ball Co., 27, Princes Street, Hanover Square, London W. 1." On the faith of this advertisement, the plaintiff bought a smoke ball and used it three times daily according to the printed directions from mid November, 1891, to 17th January, 1892, when she contracted influenza. She then claimed the £100 regard and the defendants refused to pay.

HELD, by LINDLEY, BOWEN and A. L. SMITH, L. JJ., that (i) the deposit of £1,000 showed that the company intended to create legal relations-that the promise was not mere advertising puff, (ii) the advertisement was an offer made to all the world, and a contract was made with that limited portion of the public who came forward and performed the condition on the faith of the advertisement, and (iii) the offer contained an intimation that performance of the condition was sufficient acceptance and that there was no need for notification of acceptance to be given to the offeror.

## ♣ Notes

| | | |
|---|---|---|
| 1. | unilateral contract | 單邊契約（只含有一個允諾的契約）；單務契約 |
| 2. | reward *n.* | 獎賞；獎金 |
| 3. | to contract influenza | （感染上）傳染上流行性感冒 |
| 4. | epidemic *a.* | 流行性的；傳染的 |
| 5. | to take cold | 著涼 |
| 6. | to be deposited with a bank | 將……存入銀行 |

| | | |
|---|---|---|
| 7. | preventives against this disease | 預防此疾病的藥 |
| | preventives | 預防藥 = preventive medicine |
| 8. | ascertained case | 已查明的病例 |
| 9. | remedy *n.* | 藥物 |
| 10. | to refill | 重新灌滿 |
| 11. | to claim the £100 | 要求獲得這 100 英鎊 |
| 12. | advertising puff | 廣告吹捧（噓） |
| 13. | on the faith of the advertisement | 在廣告的保證下 |
| 14. | intimation *n.* | 告知；通知 |
| 15. | notification of acceptance | 承諾的通知 |

Where acceptance is duly made by post, agreement is deemed to have been concluded before the acceptance actually reaches the offeror.

# (5) Henthourn v. Fraser
[1892] 2 Ch. 27
*Court of Appeal*

An appeal from the decision of the Vice-Chancellor of the County Palatine of Lancashire who gave judgment for the defendants. The plaintiff had for some time been negotiating to buy certain house property in Flamank Street, Birkenhead from the building society whom the defendants represent. On 7th July 1891 the secretary of the society, in the Liverpool office of the society, handed to the plaintiff a letter stating: "I hereby give you the refusal of the Flamank Street property at £750 for fourteen days." On 8th July a letter, written by the plaintiff's solicitor and accepting the offer, was posted in Birkenhead at 3.50 p.m. This letter was not received at the defendants' office until after working hours on the 8th. Earlier on that day, a letter was sent to the plaintiff by the secretary of the building society saying: "Please take notice that my letter to you of the 7th inst. giving you the option of purchasing the property Flamank Street, Birkenhead, for £750, in fourteen days, is withdrawn and the offer cancelled." This was posted in Liverpool shortly after mid-day and was received by the plaintiff at 5.30 p.m. The plaintiff, contending that a contract was made on 8th July, brought this action for specific performance. The Vice-Chancellor of the County Palatine of Lancashire gave judgment for the defendants. The plaintiff appealed.

HELD by LORD HERSCHELL and LINDLEY and KAY, L. JJ., that a contract was made when the plaintiff's letter of acceptance(written by his solicitor) was posted.

### Notes

**1.** vice-chancellor：（英）副大法官

**2.** to give judgement for the defendant：作出有利被告的判決

**3.** building society: financial institution in the UK traditionally offering a variety of saving accounts to attract deposits, which are used to fund long-term mortgages for house buyers or for house improvement
建築協會（能發揮銀行功能的金融機構，它所吸收的存款主要用於向購房者發放抵押貸款）

**4.** to post a letter：郵寄一封信

**5.** the 7th inst.
本月7號（inst在商業或正式函件中為「本月」之意）

**6.** to give sb. the option of doing sth.：給予某人做某事的選擇權

**7.** to purchase sth. for £750
以750鎊的價錢購買某物

**8.** the offer cancelled
要約被取消，在offer與cancelled之間的「is」省掉了

**9.** specific performance
依約履行（一種衡平法上給予的違約救濟方式）；強制履行令

**10.** to appeal *vt.*
上訴（appeal也可當名詞用，如：court of appeal上訴法庭（院））

**11.** held by sb.：被某人裁定

Where a counter-offer is accepted, then the terms of the counter-offer become the terms of the contract.

# (6) Hyde v. Wrench
### [1840] 3 Beav. 334
*Rolls Court*

On 6th June the defendant made a written offer to sell his farm to the plaintiff for £1,000. The plaintiff's agent then called on the defendant and made a counter-offer of £950, which the defendant said he wished to have a few days to consider. On 27th June the defendant wrote to say that he <u>did not feel disposed to</u> accept the offer of £950 for his farm. On receipt of this letter the plaintiff's agent replied as follows: "I beg <u>to acknowledge the receipt of</u> your <u>letter of the 27th instant</u>, informing me that your are not disposed to accept the sum of £950 for your farm at Luddenham. This being the case, I at once agree to the terms on which you offered the farm, <u>viz.</u>, £1,000 through your tenant Mr Kent, by your letter of the 6th instant." The plaintiff claimed specific performance of the sale for £1,000.

HELD by LORD LANGDALE, M.R., that there was no contract. The counter-offer of £950 operated as <u>a rejection of the</u> offer to sell at £1, 000 which could not subsequently be accepted.

## Notes

| | |
|---|---|
| **1.** counter offer | 反要約 |
| **2.** terms of the contract | 契約條款 |
| **3.** to feel disposed to do sth. | 傾向於做某事 |
| **4.** viz | （拉）縮寫 = namely 即；也就是 |
| **5.** rejection of the offer | 對要約的否決／駁回 |

Acceptance must be made in a reasonable time otherwise there will be no contract.

# (7) Quenerduaine v. Cole
### [1883] 32W. R. 185
*Queen's Bench Division*

The defendant, a Bristol <u>merchant</u>, made an offer through B, the plaintiff's agent, to buy <u>a cargo of potatoes</u> from the plaintiff, who was resident in France. B telegraphed the offer to the plaintiff on 30th December. There being no answer from the plaintiff by 31st December, the defendant went to B's office on that date and withdrew his offer. The plaintiff had answered the telegram by letter dated 30th December, which arrived after the withdrawal of the offer on 31th December. The defendant refused to accept delivery of the cargo of potatoes and the plaintiff <u>brought this action for damages</u>.

HELD, by GROVE and MATTHEW, JJ., that the plaintiff's acceptance was not made <u>in a reasonable time</u>. No contract was made.

**Notes**

| | |
|---|---|
| **1.** Queen's Bench Division | 英國高等法院三個法庭之一的後（王）座法庭 |
| **2.** a cargo of potatoes | 一船馬鈴薯貨物 |
| **3.** to bring an action for damages | 提起要求獲得損失賠償金的訴訟 |
| **4.** in a reasonable time | 在合理時間內 |
| **5.** Bristol *n.* | 布里斯托爾（英國港口） |

# Intention to create legal relations

## (8) Rose and Frank Co. v. Crompton & Bros. Ltd.
### [1923] 2K. B. 261; [1924] All E. R. Rep. 245
*Court of Appeal*

The plaintiffs and defendants signed an agreement <u>to the effect that</u> the existing commercial arrangements between them should be continued for a specified period and that prices should be <u>quoted</u> for periods of six months. The document provided <u>in detail</u> for <u>the course of business</u> to be followed by the parties. The <u>penultimate</u> clause of the document provided that: This arrangement is not <u>entered into</u>, nor is this <u>memorandum</u> written, as a formal or legal agreement, and shall not be <u>subject to</u> legal jurisdiction in the law courts either of the United States or England, but it is only a definite expression and record of the purpose and intention of the <u>three parties concerned</u>, to which they each honourably <u>pledge themselves with the fullest confidence</u> based on past business with each other that it will be <u>carried through</u> by each of the three parties whether the document expressed the terms of a binding contract:

HELD, by BANKES, SCPUTTON and ATKIN, L. JJ., that the agreement was not a <u>binding contract</u> because the parties had expressed an intention not create legal relations.

### 🍀 Notes

| | | |
|---|---|---|
| **1.** | to the effect that... | 大意是…… |
| **2.** | to quote prices | 報價 |
| **3.** | in detail | 詳細地 |
| **4.** | the course of business | 慣常的貿易方式 |
| **5.** | penultimate *a.* | 倒數第二的 |
| **6.** | clause *n.* | 條款 |
| **7.** | to enter into this arrangement | 作出此安排 |
| **8.** | the three parties concerned | 有關的三方 |
| **9.** | to carry through | 進行到底；貫徹 |
| **10.** | a binding contract | 有拘束力的契約 |

# (9) Jones v. Padavatton

[1969] 1 W. L. R. 328; [1969] 2 All E. R. 616

*Court of Appeal*

In this action the plaintiff and defendant were mother and daughter, respectively. There was an agreement between the parties to the effect that if the daughter gave up her very satisfactory <u>pensionable job</u> in the USA and came to London to read for <u>the Bar</u> with the intention of <u>practising law</u> in <u>Trinidad</u> (where the mother lived), the mother would pay <u>an allowance</u> of 200 dollars a month to <u>maintain the daughter</u> and her small son while in England. According to this agreement, the daughter began her <u>legal studies</u> in November 1962, continuing up to the time this action was brought. At the time of the agreement, the mother meant 200 West Indian dollars a month and the daughter understood it to be 200 US dollars. But once arrived, the daughter accepted the allowance in West Indian dollars without dispute. In 1964, because the daughter was finding it difficult to <u>live on her allowance</u>, a house was found and the purchase price of £6,000 was provided by the mother, to whom the property was conveyed. The <u>varied</u> arrangement was that the daughter should live in part of the house and let <u>the rest furnished</u>, using the rent to <u>cover expenses</u> and the daughter's maintenance <u>in place of</u> the 200 dollars a month. In 1967 the parties <u>quarrelled</u> and the mother, complaining that she could not <u>get any accounts</u>, brought this action for <u>possession of</u> the house, on the grounds that the agreement between the parties was not made with the intention to create legal relations.

HELD, by DANCKWERTS, SALMON and FENTON ATKINSON, L. JJ., that the arrangement of 1964 by which the daughter had the use of the house was <u>lacking in contractual intent</u>. The mother was entitled to possession.

---

 **Notes**

| | | |
|---|---|---|
| **1.** | pensionable *a.* | 可領取養老金的 |
| **2.** | the Bar | 律師界 |
| **3.** | to practise law | 開業做律師 |
| **4.** | Trinidad *n.* | （英）千里達（地名） |
| **5.** | to pay an allowance of 200 dollars a month | 每月給付 200 美元的生活補助費 / 津貼費 |
| **6.** | to maintain sb. | 扶養；供養某人 |
| **7.** | legal studies | 本案中表示「攻讀法律」 |
| **8.** | to live on one's allowance | 靠本人補助費生活 |
| **9.** | to convey *vt.* | 轉讓 |

**10.** to let the rest furnished      將提供的其餘部分出租

**11.** to cover expenses      支付費用

**12.** in place of...      取代

**13.** to quarrel vi      吵架

**14.** to get accounts      獲得利潤

**15.** to lack in contractual intent      缺少訂約意圖

**16.** to be entitled to possession      有權占有

# 3

# Consideration

"A valuable consideration, in the sense of the law, may consist either in some right, interest, or benefit accruing to the one party, or some forbearance, detriment, loss or responsibility, given, suffered, or undertaken by the other" A promise must be supported by consideration, if a promise is given for no consideration it will not be binding even though there may have been some good moral reason for the making of the promise.

## (10) Eastwood v. Kenyon
[1840] 11 Ad. & El. 438; [1835-42] All E. R. Rep.
*133 Court of Queen's Bench*

The plaintiff was the executor of John Sutcliffe, who had died intestate as to his real property leaving as his heir-at-law his only child, Sarah, an infant at the time of his death. The plaintiff spent his own money on the improvement of the realty. To reimburse himself, the plaintiff borrowed £140 from one Blackburn, giving a promissory note. When Sarah reached full age she promised the plaintiff that she would pay the amount of the note. After Sarah's marriage, her husband promised the plaintiff that he would pay to the plaintiff the amount of the note. The plaintiff sued Sarah's husband on this promise and was met with the defence that there was no consideration given for the promise.

HELD, by LORD DENMAN, C.J., PATTESON, WILLIAMS and COLERIDGE, JJ., the benefit conferred on the defendant (through his wife) by the plaintiff was not consideration to support the defendant's subsequent promise to pay the plaintiff.

### 🍀 Notes

| | | |
|---|---|---|
| **1.** | consideration *n.* | 對價 |
| **2.** | in the sense of the law | 就法律上的意義而講 |
| **3.** | to consist in | 存在於…… |
| **4.** | to accrue to sb. | 按理給予某人（= come to sb. by right） |
| | | 如：Money kept in a savings bank will accrue to you with interest. |
| **5.** | forbearance *n.* | 克制；忍耐 |
| **6.** | detriment *n.* | 損害；傷害 |

| 7. | executor *n.* | 本案中表示「遺囑執行人」 |
|----|----|----|
| 8. | to die intestate | 不留遺囑死亡 |
| 9. | as to | 關於 |
| 10. | real property | 不動產；房地產 |
| 11. | heir-at-law | 法定繼承人 |
| 12. | infant *n.* | 未成年人（= minor） |
| 13. | realty *n.* | 不動產；房地產 |
| 14. | to reimburse | 補償；賠償 |
| 15. | promissory note | 期票；本票 |
| 16. | to reach full age | 成年 |
| 17. | defence *n.* | 抗辯 |
| 18. | to confer on sb sth. | 給予某人某物 |

# (11) Hartley v. Ponsonby

[1857] 7 El. & Bl. 872

*Queen's Bench*

The plaintiff was a seaman who had signed articles to serve on a voyage from Liverpool to Port Philip (Australia) and thence to other ports and places in the Pacific and Indian Oceans. While the ship was at Port Philip, seventeen of the complement of thirty-six refused to work and were sent to prison. The remaining nineteen men included only four or five able seamen. To induce this diminished crew to sail the vessel to Bombay, the master promised the plaintiff and eight others an additional payment. It was unreasonable or unsafe to attempt the voyage with such a depleted crew. The plaintiff brought this action against the master to recover the promised payment.

HELD, by LORD CAMPBELL, C. J., COLERIDGE, J., ERLE, J. and CROMPTON, J., that the plaintiff was not bound by his original contract to undertake an unsafe voyage with such a seriously diminished crew, His undertaking to make the voyage was, accordingly, a good consideration to support the master's promise of additional payment.

## ♣ Notes

| 1. | seaman *n.* | 海員；水手 |
|----|----|----|
| 2. | to sign articles | 簽署契約（注意此處的article必須用複數） |
| 3. | voyage *n.* | 航行 |
| 4. | thence *adv.* | 從那裡起 |

5. to be sent to prison        被送入監獄

6. diminished crew        縮小的水手隊伍（人數）

7. to sail the vessel to...        將船航行到⋯⋯

8. complement *n.*        編制人數

9. depleted crew        被減少的水手隊伍（人數）

10. to be bound by a contract        受契約的約束／拘束

11. to undertake *vt.*        進行；從事；承擔

12. master *n.*        船長

# (12) Roscorla v. Thomas
### [1842] 3 Q. B. 234
*Court of Queen's Bench*

The defendant sold a horse to the plaintiff and then promised the plaintiff that the horse was sound and free from vice. The plaintiff brought this <u>action in assumpsit</u> for the <u>breach of warranty</u> of the soundness of the horse, <u>contending</u> that an executed consideration with a request, express or implied, will support a promise. The defendant contended that the warranty, being given after the sale, was made without consideration.

HELD, by <u>LORD</u> DENMAN, C. J., PATTESON, WILLIAMS and WIGHTMAN JJ., the plaintiff gave no consideration for the defendant's warranty which was, accordingly, not binding.

 **Notes**

1. be free from vice        不受惡癖的影響＝ having no vice(s)

2. action in assumpsit        要求賠償違約所造成損失的訴訟

3. breach of warranty        違反擔保

4. to contend *vt.*        主張；堅持認為

5. without consideration        無對價

6. lord *n.*        （英）對高等法院法官的尊稱

# Express terms

The express terms of a contract comprise those statements made by the parties to one another during negotiations leading to a contract and by which they intended to be bound. To discover intention, the court will apply an objective test. The court will seek an answer to the question, "what would a reasonable man understand to be the intention of the parties, having regard to all the circumstances".

## (13) Dick Bentley Productions, Ltd v. Harold Smith (Motors), Ltd.
[1965] W. L. R. 623; [1965] 2 All E. R. 65

*Court of Appeal*

The second plaintiff, Mr. Bentley, told Mr. Smith of the defendant company that he was on the look-out for a well vetted Bentley car. Mr. Smith subsequently obtained a Bentley car and Mr. Bentley went to see it. Mr. Smith told Mr. Bentley that the car had done twenty thousand miles only since the fitting of a new engine and gear box. (The speedmeter showed twenty thousand miles.) later that day Mr. Bentley took his wife to see the car and Mr. Smith repeated his statement. Mr. Bentley took the car out for a run and then bought it for £1,850, paying by cheque. The car was a disappointment to Mr. Bentley and it soon became clear that the car had done more than twenty thousand miles since the change of engine and gear box. The action for £400 damages was brought against the defendant company in the county court, the plaintiffs alleging fraud. The defendants counterclaimed for £190 for work carried out on the car. His Honour JUDGE HERBERT held that there was a breach of warranty, awarding £400 damages to the plaintiffs and £77 to the defendants on their counterclaim. The defendants appealed, contending that their representation did not amount to a warranty.

HELD, by LORD DENNING, M.R., DANCKWERTS and SOLOMON, L. JJ., that the representation was warranty.

---

### Notes

| | | |
|---|---|---|
| 1. | to comprise | 包括（= to include） |
| 2. | leading to a contract | 導致契約的簽訂 |
| 3. | to apply an objective test | 運用客觀檢驗法 |
| 4. | on the look-out for sth. | 搜尋某物 |

5. a well vetted car　　　　　經過很好檢查的小汽車

6. subsequently *adv.*　　　　後來

7. to do twenty thousand miles　跑了 20,000 多英里

8. fitting *n.*　　　　　　　　裝備

9. gear box　　　　　　　　　齒輪箱

10. speedmeter *n.*　　　　　　里程表 / 計

11. to take the car out for a run　將車開出去試跑

12. to pay by cheque　　　　　用支票付款（to pay in cash 用現金付款）

13. county court　　　　　　　（英）郡（州）法院

14. to allege fraud　　　　　　宣稱有欺騙行為或欺詐

15. to counterclaim *vt.*　　　　反要求；反索賠

16. representation *n.*　　　　　說明

17. to amount to a warranty　　相當於擔保

# (14) J Evans & Son (Portsmouth) Ltd. v. Andrea Merzario Ltd.
[1976] 2 All E. R. 930 Court of Appeal,
*Civil Division*

The plaintiffs were importers of machines from Italy. Since 1959 they had contracted under standard form conditions with the defendants to make arrangements for the carriage of the machines to England. The defendant forwarding agents proposed in 1967 to change to container transportation. The defendants gave an oral assurance to the plaintiffs that their machines to be transported in containers would be shipped under deck. On the faith of this assurance the plaintiffs accepted the defendant's new quotations for container transportation of their machines. Owing to an oversight on the part of the defendants, a container with one of the plaintiff's machines inside was shipped on deck and the machine was lost overboard. By the standard form conditions of contract between the parties, (a) the defendants were free in respect of the means and procedures to be followed in the transportation and (b) they were exempted from liability for loss or damage to the goods in certain circumstances. The plaintiff claimed damages for loss of the machine, alleging that the carriage of the container on deck was a breach of contract. KERR, J. dismissed the action on the grounds that the oral statement made by the defendants as to carriage below deck did not constitute a binding collateral warranty and therefore did not prevail over the standard form conditions. The plaintiff appealed.

HELD, by LORD DENNING, M. R. ROSKILL and GEOFFREY LANE, L. JJ., that th oral statement made by the defendants was a binding warranty which was to be treated as overriding the printed conditions and the plaintiffs were entitled to damages for its breach. The statement was (per LORD DENNING, M. R.) binding as a collateral warranty because it induced the plaintiff to enter the contract. Alternatively (per ROSKILL and GEOFFREY LANE, L. JJ.) the oral statement constituted an express term of the contract of carriage which overrode the printed conditions because these would have made the oral assurance illusory.

## Notes

| | | |
|---|---|---|
| 1. | Ltd. = Limited | 有限（公司）它必須在英國私人有限責任公司名字裡出現 |
| 2. | forwarding agent | 運輸行；運輸商 |
| 3. | container transportation | 集裝箱運輸；貨櫃運輸 |
| 4. | to give an oral assurance | 口頭上保證 |
| 5. | to be shipped under deck | 放在甲板下運輸 |
| 6. | on the faith of this assurance | 在此保證的保證下 |
| 7. | oversight *n.* | 忽略 |
| 8. | on the part of sb. | 就……而言；就某人的一方面來說 |
| 9. | overboard *adv.* | 從船上落入水中 |
| 10. | to be exempted from... | 不承擔……；被免除…… |
| 11. | oral statement | 口頭陳述 |
| 12. | collateral warranty | 附屬的擔保 |
| 13. | to prevail over | 勝過；超過 |
| 14. | a binding warranty | 有拘束力的擔保 |
| 15. | to induce *vt.* | 勸使 |
| 16. | to enter the contract | 簽訂契約 |
| 17. | alternatively *adv.* | 兩者選一地 |
| 18. | to override *vt.* | 壓倒 |
| 19. | illusory *a.* | 迷惑人的；虛幻的 |

# 5

# Implied terms of contract

There are two kinds of implied contract terms, namely, terms implied in fact and terms implied in law.

## (15) Liverpool city council v. Irwin

[1977] A. C. 235; [1976] 2W. L. R. 562; [1976] 2 All E. R. 39

*House of Lords*

The City Council was owner of a tower block containing some 70 units. Access was provided by a common staircase and two electrically controlled lifts. Tenants were provided with an internal rubbish chute. In July 1966 the defendants (husband and wife) became tenants of a maisonette in the block. There was no formal lease or tenancy agreement. There was, however, a document described as "Conditions of Tenancy" consisting entirely of obligations on the tenants: there was no mention of any obligations on the Council. In the course of time, the condition of the block deteriorated badly, partly because of vandalism and partly because of the lack of co-operation on the part of tenants. The defects included the following (a) continual failure of the lifts, (b) lack of proper lighting on the stairs and (c) blockage of the rubbish chutes. The defendants protested by refusing to pay rent to the Council. The Council sought an order for possession of the defendants "maisonette and the defendants counterclaimed alleging a breach on the part of the Council of its implied covenant for the defendants" quiet enjoyment of the property. The trial judge granted an order for possession to the Council but awarded £10 damages against it for breach of the implied covenant to repair the common parts. The Council appealed to the Court of Appeal where it was held that there was no implied covenant on the part of the council to repair the common parts. The defendants appealed to the House of Lords, contending that there was an implied obligation on the Council to keep the staircase and corridors of the block in repair and the lights in working order, and that the Council was in breach of it.

HELD, by LORD WILBERFORCE, LORD CROSS, LORD SALMON, LORD EDMUND DAVIES and LORD FRASER, that, since it was necessary for the tenants occupying the block to use the stairs, lifts and rubbish chutes, the appropriate easements (or rights in the nature of easements) would be implied into the tenancy agreements. Further, the subject-matter of the agreement, and the nature of the relationship of landlord and tenant of necessity required the implication of a contractual obligation on the part of the Council with regard to those easements. But the obligation was not absolute, being subject to the tenants' own responsibilities, and was related to what reasonable tenants should do for themselves. The obligation to be implied was, therefore, to take reasonable care to maintain the common parts in a state of reasonable repair and efficiency. It had not been shown that the Council had not taken such reasonable care and, accordingly, the appeal should be dismissed.

## Notes

| | | |
|---|---|---|
| 1. | implied terms of contract | 契約的默示條款 |
| 2. | implied in fact | 事實默示 |
| 3. | implied in law | 法律默示 |
| 4. | City Council | 市政會；市參議會 |
| 5. | tower block | 一排高樓；高樓街區 |
| 6. | access *n.* | 進入；通道 |
| 7. | staircase *n.* | 樓梯 |
| 8. | electrically controlled lifts | 電控的電梯 |
| 9. | rubbish chute | 垃圾清運道 |
| 10. | tenant *n.* | 承租人；租戶 |
| 11. | maisonette *n.* | 小屋；二層樓的公寓房子 |
| 12. | lease *n.* | 租借契約；租約 |
| 13. | tenancy agreement | 租借契約；租賃協議 |
| 14. | to consist of | 包括 |
| 15. | vandalism *n.* | 故意破壞 |
| 16. | blockage *n.* | 阻塞 |
| 17. | to protest *v.* | 抗議 |
| 18. | covenant *n.* | 契約；契約中大家同意的條款 |
| 19. | corridor(s) *n.* | 走廊 |
| 20. | easement(s) *n.* | 地役權 |
| 21. | subject matter | （契約）標的物 |
| 22. | be subject to... | 受制於…… |
| 23. | be related to... | 與……有關 |
| 24. | to dismiss an appeal | 駁回上訴 |

# 6

# Privity of contract

One fundamental principle in contract law is that only a person who is a party to a contract can sue on it.

## (16) Dunlop Poeumatic Tyre Co., Ltd.v. Selfridge & Co., Ltd.
### [1915] A. C. 847; [1914-15] All E. R. Rep. 333
*House of Lords*

There was a contract dated 12th October 1911 by which Dew & Co., agreed to purchase a quantity of tyres and other goods from Dunlop. By this contract, Dew & Co., undertook not to sell at prices below the current list prices except to genuine trade customers, to whom they could sell at a discount. The contract provided that such discount would be substantially less than the discount that Dews themselves were to receive from Dunlop's. Where such sales took place, Dews undertook, as the agents of Dunlop, to obtain from the customer a written undertaking that he similarly would observe the terms so undertaken to be observed by themselves. On 2nd January 1912 Selfridges agreed to purchase goods made by Dunlop from Dew & Co., and gave the required undertaking to resell at the current list prices. Selfridge's broke this agreement and dunlop sued for breach of contract.

HELD, by VISCOUNT HALDANE, L.C., LORD DUNEDIN, LORD ATKINSON, LORD PARKER OF WADDINGTON, LORD SUMNER and LORD PARMOOR, that the agreement of 2nd January 1912 was between Selfridge and Dew only and that Dunlop was not a party to that contract because no consideration moved from them to Selfridges.

## ♣ Notes

| | | |
|---|---|---|
| 1. | privity of contract | 契約有關當事人之間的相互關係 |
| 2. | poeumatic *a.* | 氣體的 ～tyre 充氣輪胎 |
| 3. | House of Lords | （英）議會中的上院；上議院；元老院；貴族院 |
| 4. | Co. | =company 的縮寫 |
| 5. | the current list prices | 現行的目錄價格 |
| 6. | to sell at discount | 打折出售 |
| 7. | to observe the terms | 遵守條款 |
| 8. | to break the agreement | 違反協議 |

**9.** a party to a contract          契約當事人
**10.** No consideration moved      某人沒給另一個人對價
    from sb. to sb. else

# (17) Beswick v. Beswick
## [1968] A. C. 58; [1967] 2 All E. R. 1197
### *House of Lords*

In March 1962, a coal merchant, Peter Beswick, agreed to sell his business to his nephew John in return for the following undertakings: (i) that John should pay to Peter the weekly sum of £6 10s. during the rest of Peter's life: (ii) that, in the event of Peter's wife surviving him, John should pay her an annuity of £5 weekly. Peter died intestate in November 1963 and in 1964 his widow took out letters of administration. After Peter's death, John made one payment of £5 only to the widow, refusing to make any further payments. The widow, who brought this action as administratrix of her husband's estate and also in her personal capacity, claimed arrears of the annuity and specific performance of the contract between Peter and John. It was held by the Court of Appeal that she was entitled, as administratrix, to specific performance of the contract. And LORD DENNING and DANCKWERTS, L. J., held further that she could succeed under s.56(1) of the Law of Property Act, 1925. (Section 56(1) provides that: "A person may take an immediate or other interest in land or other property, or the benefit of any condition, right of entry, covenant or agreement over or respecting land or other property, although he may not be named as a party to the conveyance or other instrument." The Act further provides, by s.205, that: "unless the context otherwise requires, the following expressions have the meaning hereby assigned to them respectively, that is to say…'Property includes any thing in action, and any interest in real or personal property, '") John appealed to the House of Lords.

HELD, by LORD REID, LORD HODSON, LORD GUEST, LORD PEARCE and LORD UPJOHN, that the widow, as administratrix, was entitled to specific performance of the agreement to which her deceased husband was a contracting party; but that the statute gave her no right of action against John in her personal capacity.

 **Notes**

**1.** to sell one's business          出售某人的企業（此短語中的 business 表示「企業」）
**2.** nephew *n.*                      侄子；外甥
**3.** in return for...                作為對……的交換

4. in the event of...　　　　　　如果發生……
　～Peter's wife surviving　　如果發生彼得妻子比他活得長的情況
　him

5. annuity *n.*　　　　　　　　養老金；年金

6. letters of administration　　遺產管理委任書

7. widow *n.*　　　　　　　　寡婦

8. administratrix *n.*　　　　　（女）遺產管理人

9. in one's personal capacity　以個人資格

10. arrears of the annuity　　　（年金）養老金的拖欠款
　　　　　　　　　　　　　　(amount of money still outstanding or uncompleted)

11. to succeed *v.*　　　　　　繼承

12. conveyance *n.*　　　　　　財產轉讓；讓與

13. respecting *prep.*　　　　　關於；由於

14. other instrument　　　　　其他文具

15. to assign *vt.*　　　　　　讓與

16. one's deceased husband　某人已故的丈夫

17. contracting party　　　　　訂約人；契約當事人

# Misrepresentation

Misrepresentation means a false stuferent of a material fact.

## (18) Edgington v. Fitzmaurice
[1885] 29 Ch.D.459; [1881-5] All E.R. Rep. 856
*Court of Appeal*

The defendants, who were the directors of a company, issued a prospectus inviting members of the public to subscribe for debentures. The prospectus contained statements that the debentures were issued for the purpose of obtaining funds to purchase horses and vans, to complete alterations to the company's premises and to develop the company's business. In fact, the main purpose in raising money by the issue of debentures was to pay off debts. The plaintiff, who had advanced money to the company in reliance on the prospectus, brought this action for fraudulent misrepresentation.

HELD, by COTTON, BOWEN and FRY, L. JJ.; that the statements in the prospectus as to the objects of the issue were false in fact and were relied on by the plaintiff. The defendants were liable in deceit even though the plaintiff was influenced by matters other than those contained in the prospectus.

### ♣ Notes

| | | |
|---|---|---|
| 1. | misrepresentation *n.* | （對重要事實的）虛偽陳述 |
| 2. | the directors of a company | 公司的董事 |
| 3. | prospectus *n.* | 招股章程；公開說明書 |
| 4. | debenture *n.* | 一般指英國公司以其資產作抵押所發行的公司債券 |
| 5. | van *n.* | 運貨的大篷車 |
| 6. | the company's premises | 公司房屋 |
| 7. | alterations to sth. | 對……進行改進 |
| 8. | to raise money | 籌款 |
| 9. | to pay off debts | 償還債務 |
| 10. | the objects of the issue | 發行的目的 |
| 11. | to be liable in deceit | 承擔欺騙責任 |
| 12. | other than | 不是；不同於；非 |

# (19) Esso Petroleum Co. Ltd v. Mardon

[1976] Q. B. 801; [1976] 2 All E. R. 5

*Court of Appeal*

In 1961 the plaintiffs, Esso, acquired a site for a proposed petrol filling station on a busy main street. Esso had calculated that the estimated annual consumption of petrol would be 200, 000 gallons from the third year of operation. The local planning authority then required the forecourt of the station to be sited at the rear of the plot, with the result that it was not visible from the main road and was accessible only from side streets. Subsequently Esso negotiated with the defendant for the grant of a tenancy of the station. An experienced Esso representative told the defendant that the throughput would be 200, 000 gallons in the third year of operation. This statement was made in good faith. On the basis of the representation as to throughput, the defendant entered into a tenancy agreement in April 1963 and another, at reduced rent, in September 1964. Because of the planning change, the maximum annual throughput could only be in the region of 70, 000 gallons. As a result, the defendant lost all his capital and also incurred a substantial overdraft. He was unable to pay Esso for petrol supplied up to August 1966. Esso brought this action, claiming possession of the station and the money due for the petrol. The defendant counterclaimed for damages in respect of the representation made by the Esso representative that the potential throughput was 200, 000 gallons. He alleged (i) that it was a warranty, for breach of which he was entitled to damages, and (ii) that it amounted to negligent misrepresentation in breach of Esso's duty of care in advising as to potential throughput. The trial judge rejected the claim for breach of warranty, but held that Esso were liable in damages for breach of their duty of care to the defendant. The judge limited damages to the loss suffered between April 1963 and September 1964 on the ground that the misrepresentation made in 1963 had not induced the defendant to enter the agreement of September 1964. The defendant appealed.

HELD, by LORD DENNING, M.R., ORMROD and SHAW, L. JJ., (i) where a party with special knowledge and expertise concerning the subject-matter of pre-contract negotiations makes a forecast based on that knowledge and expertise with the intention of inducing the other party to enter into the contract, and in reliance on the forecast the other party did enter into the contract, the forecast could be construed as a warranty that it was reliable, i.e., that it had been made with reasonable skill and care. Since the estimate had been made negligently it was therefore unsound and Esso were liable for breach of warranty. (ii) There were no grounds for excluding liability for negligence in relation to statements made in the course of negotiations which culminated in the making of a contract. (iii) The measure of damages was the loss suffered by the defendant including that suffered after the agreement of September 1964, since that was also <u>attributable to</u> the original misrepresentation.

## Notes

| | | |
|---|---|---|
| **1.** | to acquire *vt.* | 獲得；得到 |
| **2.** | site *n.* | 場所；地點 |
| | construction | 工地 |
| **3.** | petrol filing station | 英國（汽車）加油站（= 美汽油加油站 gas station） |
| **4.** | to calculate *vt.* | 計算 |
| **5.** | the estimated annual consumption of petrol | 估計的每年汽油消費量 |
| **6.** | gallon *n.* | 加侖 |
| **7.** | the local planning authority | 地方計畫當局 |
| **8.** | forecourt *n.* | 前院 |
| **9.** | at the rear of the plot | 在一塊地的後面 |
| **10.** | to be not visible from the main road | 從主街道不能被看見 |
| **11.** | to be accessible only from side streets | 只能從輔街進入 |
| **12.** | throughput *n.* | 消費量 |
| **13.** | in good faith | 善意的；誠意地 |
| **14.** | to enter into a tenancy agreement | 簽訂了一個租賃契約 |
| **15.** | at reduced rent | 按減少的租金 |
| **16.** | in the region of 70, 000 gallons | 在 70,000 加侖左右 |
| **17.** | to incur a substantial overdraft | 引起相當大的一筆透支 |
| **18.** | in respect of... | 就……而言 |
| **19.** | negligent misrepresentation | 過失誤述；粗心大意的虛偽陳述 |
| **20.** | breach of duty of care | 未履行注意責任 |
| **21.** | to limit damages to the loss | 將損害賠償金限制在損失上 |
| **22.** | pre-contract negotiations | 訂約前的談判 |
| **23.** | to make a forecast | 進行預測 |
| **24.** | expertise *n.* | 專門技能；專長 |
| **25.** | in reliance on... | 依賴…… |
| **26.** | to be construed as... | 被解釋成…… |
| **27.** | to exclude liability for negligence | 排除疏忽（過失）**責任** |
| **28.** | to be attributable to... | 可歸因於…… |

# 8

# Mistake at Common Law

The general rule is that if the mind of one of the parties, or both parties, at the time of contracting, is affected by mistake, then, at common law, the contract remains valid and enforceable notwithstanding the mistake.

## (20) Bell v. Lever Bros. Ltd.
[1932] A. C. 161; [1931] All E. R. Rep.1
*House of Lords*

The appellant was appointed chairman of one of the subsidiaries of the respondent company. He subsequently engaged in certain private business activities in breach of his service contract for which he could have been dismissed without compensation. Neither party realising that this was the appellant's position, they entered another agreement by which the appellant agreed to resign his position prematurely in return for the sum of £30,000 by way of compensation for loss of office. Neither party was aware that it was then open to the company to dismiss the appellant without compensation: both parties believed erroneously that a fresh agreement was necessary to discharge the service contract. On discovering the mistake, the company sought to recover the £30,000 on the grounds that the compensation agreement was void for mistake. The company succeeded at first instance and before the Court of Appeal. The appellants appealed to the House of Lords.

HELD, by LORD HAILSHAM, LORD BLANESBURGH, LORD WARRINGTON, LORD ATKIN and LORD THANKERTON, that the compensation contract was valid and binding, the mistake of the parties not being sufficient to render the contract void. The agreement to terminate a broken contract is not essentially different from an agreement to terminate an unbroken contract, even where the breach gave the innocent party the right to declare the contract at an end.

### Notes

| | | |
|---|---|---|
| 1. | mistake *n.* | 錯誤 |
| 2. | at common law | 普通法上的 |
| 3. | appellant *n.* | 上訴方；上訴人 |

4. to appoint sb. Chairman　　　　任命某人為主席
   to appoint sb. to a post　　　　派某人任某職
5. to be affected by mistake　　　受錯誤的影響
6. enforceable *a.*　　　　　　　　可受強制執行的
7. notwithstanding *prep.*　　　　儘管
8. subsidiary *n.*　　　　　　　　分公司；子公司；附屬機構
9. the respondent company　　　　被告公司
10. to engage in certain private　　從事某些私人商務活動
    business activities
11. to dismiss *vt.*　　　　　　　　解僱；免……的職
12. compensation *n.*　　　　　　　補償；賠償
13. position *n.*　　　　　　　　　立場；主張；態度
14. to resign one's position　　　　辭去某人的職務
15. prematurely *adv.*　　　　　　未到期地；過早地
16. by way of...　　　　　　　　　透過……方法
17. loss of office　　　　　　　　（公）職務的損失
18. erroneously *adv.*　　　　　　錯誤地
19. to discharge a service　　　　撤銷勞務契約
    contract
20. at first instance　　　　　　　起初
21. to terminate a broken　　　　　終止一個已被破壞的契約
    contract
22. the innocent party　　　　　　清白無辜的一方當事人
23. to declare the contract at　　　宣布終止契約
    end

# 9

# Undue Influence

A contract may be set aside where it was made unden undue influence.

## (21) National Westminster Bank v. Morgan
[1985] A. C. 686 [1985] 1 All E. R. 821
*House of Lords*

A husband and wife were joint owner of their home. The husband was unsuccessful in a business venture and was unable to meet the repayments due under a mortgage secured over the home. The then mortgagee commenced proceedings to take possession. The husband tried to save the situation by entering a refinancing arrangement with a bank. The refinancing was secured by a legal charge in favour of the bank. The bank manager made a brief visit to the home so that the wife could execute the charge. The wife made it clear to the bank manager that she had little faith in her husband's business ability and that she did not want the charge to cover his business liabilities. The bank manager assured her that the charge secured only the amount advanced to refinance the mortgage. Nevertheless, it was the bank's intention to treat it as limited to the amount required to refinance the mortgage. This assurance was given in good faith but was incorrect. The terms of the charge were unlimited in extent and extended to all of the husband's liabilities to the bank.

The wife did not receive independent legal advice before signing the charge. The husband fell into arrears with payments and the bank obtained an order for possession of the home. The husband then died without owing the bank on any business advances. The wife appealed against the order for possession contending that the charge should be set aside as it had been signed as a result of undue influence from the bank. The bank argued that undue influence could be raised only when the transaction was manifestly disadvantageous to the defendant. The bank contended that the refinancing arrangement had averted the earlier possession by the previous mortgagee and that this was manifestly advantageous to the wife. The Court of Appeal found in favour of the wife on the grounds that a special relationship had been created which the bank was unable to rebut because of the failure to advise the wife to seek independent legal advice. The bank appealed to the House of Lords.

HELD, by LORD SCARMAN, LORD KEITH, LORD ROSKILL, LORD BRIDGE and LORD BRANDON, that the appeal should be allowed and possession of the house be given to the bank. A transaction could not be set aside on the grounds of undue influence unless it is shown that the transaction was to the manifest disadvantage of the person subjected to the dominating influence. The Court of Appeal erred in law in holding that the presumption of undue influence can arise from the evidence of the relationship of the parties without also evidence that the transaction itself was wrongful in that it constituted an advantage taken of the person subjected to the influence which, failing proof to the contrary, was explicable only on the basis that undue influence had been exercised to procure it. The bank manager never crossed the line. The transaction was not unfair to the wife. The bank was, therefore, under no duty to ensure that she had independent advice. It was an ordinary banking transaction whereby the wife sought to save her home; and she obtained an honest and truthful explanation of the bank's intention which, notwithstanding the terms of the mortgage deed, was correct; for the bank had not sought to make the wife liable, nor to make the home a security, for any business debt of the husband.

 **Notes**

| | | |
|---|---|---|
| 1. | undue influence | 不適當影響 |
| 2. | to set aside a contract | 撤銷／廢止契約 |
| 3. | joint owner | 共同共有人；共有人；有共同所有權的物主 |
| 4. | business venture | 商業企業 |
| 5. | unable to meet the repayments due under a mortgage secured over the home | 不能對用房屋作抵押所獲已到期貸款的付還 |
| 6. | the then mortgagee | 當時的承受抵押人 |
| | then a | 當時的 |
| 7. | to commence proceedings to take possession | 開始以占有為目的的訴訟（proceedings） |
| 8. | a refinancing arrangement | 再融資安排；重新籌措資金的安排 |
| 9. | legal charge | 合法的抵債 |
| 10. | to execute the charge | 執行此抵債 |
| 11. | to have little faith in... | 對……幾乎不信任 |
| 12. | to fall into arrears with payments | 陷入付款的拖欠；拖欠應付款項 |
| 13. | to set aside the charge | 撤銷此抵債 |
| 14. | to avert *vt.* | 防止；擋住 |
| 15. | manifestly *adv.* | 明顯地 |
| 16. | to be advantageous to sb. | 對某人有好處 |
| 17. | to find in favour of the wife. | 作出有利於妻子的判決 |
| 18. | to the manifest disadvantage of sb. | 明顯對某人不利 |

| | |
|---|---|
| **19.** to be subjected to the dominating influence | 受支配地位的影響 |
| **20.** to cover one's business liabilities | 包括或適用於商務上的債務責任 |
| **21.** to err in law | 將法律弄錯；在法律方面出錯 |
| **22.** presumption *n.* | 推斷；設想 |
| **23.** to constitute *vt.* | 構成 |
| **24.** failing proof to the contrary | 無相反的證明 |
| **25.** explicable *a.* | 可解釋的；可說明的 |
| **26.** to exercise undue influence | 運用非正當影響 |
| **27.** to procure *vt.* | （努力）取得 |
| **28.** to cross the line | 超越界限 |
| **29.** the mortgage deed | 抵押契據；質權契據 |

# 10

# Illegality

No court will lend its aid to a man who founds his cause of action upon an immoral or illegal act or goes against the public policy.

## (22) Napier v. National Business Agency, Ltd.
### [1951] 2 All E. R. 264
*Court of Appeal*

The plaintiff was employed by the defendant company as secretary and accountant. The plaintiff was remunerated by means of a salary of £13 a week together with £6 a week for expenses. It was known to both parties that the plaintiff's expenses could never be as much as £6 a week. In fact, not more than £1 a week could be treated as fairly representing his expenses. The plaintiff was paid his salary subject to income tax deduction by means of the P.A.Y.E. system and the defendant company made the appropriate deductions before paying him. The defendant company showed in its returns to the Inland Revenue Commissioners the payment of £6 a week as being a reimbursement of expenses to the plaintiff. After being summarily dismissed by the defendant company, the plaintiff claimed repayment, in lieu of notice, of £13 a week for the notice period. At first instance it was held that the contract was against public policy as being intended to defraud the revenue and that, therefore, the plaintiff was unable to enforce any part of it. The plaintiff appealed.

HELD, by SIR RAYMOND EVERSHED, M.R., DENNING and HODSON, L. JJ., that the agreement to pay £6 a week as expenses was intended to evade tax and that the agreement was therefore against public policy and, further, that the agreement relating to the salary of £13 a week was not severable from the expenses agreement, and was similarly unenforceable.

## Notes

| | | |
|---|---|---|
| **1.** | cause of action | 訴訟理由；訴因 |
| **2.** | public policy | 公共政策 |
| **3.** | to employ *vt.* | 僱用；聘用 |
| **4.** | accountant *n.* | 會計 |
| **5.** | to remunerate *vt.* | 給……補償；給……報酬 |
| **6.** | by means of a salary | 用發薪水的方法 |

| 7. income tax | 所得稅 |
|---|---|
| 8. to make the appropriate deductions | 進行合適的扣除 |
| 9. returns *n.* | 報稅單 |
| 10. the Inland Revenue Commissioners | 國內稅務局專員 |
| 11. reimbursement of expenses | 對開支的償還 |
| 12. summarily *adv.* | 速決地；即決地 |
| 13. in lieu of... | 作為對⋯⋯的替代 |
| 14. at first instance | 初審時 |
| 15. to defraud the revenue | 欺騙稅務局 |
| 16. to evade tax | 逃稅 |
| 17. relating to... | 與⋯⋯有關 |
| 18. severable *a.* | 可分開的 |
| 19. illegality *n.* | 非法性 |

20. the P.A.Y.E system：所得稅預扣制度

A means of collecting income tax by deducting it from wages and salaries at source. Because it is often difficult to collect tax at the end of the year from wage-and-salary-earners, the onus is placed on employers to collect the tax from their employees as payments are made to them.

# 11

# Minors' Contract

The general rule at common law is that a contract between a minor and a person of full age is enforceable by the minor but not against him. Such a contract could become binding on the minor only if he ratified it on or after reaching full age.

## (23) Nash v. Inman
[1908] 2 K. B. 1; [1908-10] All E. R. Rep. 317
*Court of Appeal*

The plaintiff had supplied to the defendant clothing to the value of £45 10s. 3d. at a time when te defendant was a Cambridge undergraduate. The clothes supplied by the plaintiff included eleven fancy waistcoats. The defendant raised the defence of infancy at the time the goods were supplied and that the goods were not "necessaries". The defendant's father had amply supplied the defendant with proper clothes according to his condition in life. It was held by RIDLEY, J. that there was no evidence that the goods were"necessaries" and judgment was entered for the defendant. The plaintiff appealed.

HELD, by SIR HERBERT COZENS-HARDY, M.R., FLETCHER MOULTON and BUCKLEY, L. JJ., that there was no evidence that the goods supplied were necessary to the defendant's requirements; that, on the contrary, the defendant was amply supplied with suitable and necessary clothes. The trial judge was correct in the view that he took.

## 🍀 Notes

| | | |
|---|---|---|
| 1. | minors' contract | 未成年人契約 |
| 2. | person of full age | 成年人（根據英國 Family Law Reform Act, a person will be deemed to be a person of full age when reaching the age of 18 at the commencement of the eighteenth anniversary of his birth） |
| 3. | to ratify *vt.* | 認可；追認 |
| 4. | to supply clothing to sb. | 向某人供應衣服 |
| 5. | to the value of ... | 價值為…… |
| 6. | undergraduate *n.* | 大學生 |
| 7. | fancy *a.* | 價格高的 |

8. waistcoat *n.*            背心；馬甲

9. to raise the defence of infancy      提出未成年的抗辯

10. necessaries *n.*        必需品（也可用 necessities）

11. to amply supply sb. with proper clothes      對某人提供足夠的合適衣服

12. to enter judgment for sb.      作出有利於某人的判決

13. necessary to the defendant's requirements      滿足被告需要的必需品

14. on the contrary      相反

# Discharge of Contract

(A) Discharge by performance

The general rule is that a contractual obligation is discharged by complete performance of the undertaking. Where performance falls short of the completed undertaking, there is no discharge of the obligation or of the contract.

## (24) Cutter v. Powell
[1795] 6 T. R.320
*King's Bench*

The plaintiff sued as administratrix of her deceased husband's estate. The defendant had, in Jamaica, subscribed and delivered to T Cutter, the intestate, a note as follows: "Ten days after the ship Governor Parry, myself master, arrives at Liverpool, I promise to pay to Mr.T. Cutter the sum of thirty guineas, provided he proceeds, continues and does his duty as second mate in the said ship from hence to the port of Liverpool. Kingston, July 21, 1793." The Governor Parry sailed from Kingstion on 2nd August 1793 and arrived in Liverpool on 9th October. But T. Cutter died on 20th September, until which date he did his duty as second mate. The plaintiff claimed payment on a *quantum merit*.

HELD, by LORD KENYON, C.J., ASHURST, GROSE and LAWRENCE, JJ., that, according to the express terms of the contract, the sum of thirty guineas was payable only on completion of the whole voyage. A term to the effect that proportional payment should be made in case of partial performance could not be implied. The plaintiff could not, therefore succeed in her claim on a quantum merit.

## 🍀 Notes

| | | |
|---|---|---|
| 1. | discharge of contract | 契約的消滅；契約的解除 |
| 2. | discharge by performance | 用履行使契約歸於消滅 |
| 3. | undertaking *n.* | 承擔的義務 |
| 4. | to fall short of... | 達不到…… |
| 5. | administratrix *n.* | （女）遺產管理人 |
| 6. | her deceased husband | 她已故的丈夫 |
| 7. | estate *n.* | 產業 |

| | | |
|---|---|---|
| 8. | the intestate *n.* | 未留遺囑的人 |
| 9. | to subscribe *vt.* | 簽署；簽名 |
| 10. | note *n.* | 便條 |
| 11. | as follows | 如下 |
| 12. | guinea *n.* | 幾尼（舊英國金幣） |
| 13. | provided *conj.* | 如果；假如 |
| 14. | to proceed *vi.* | 繼續做下去 |
| 15. | master *n.* | 船長 |
| 16. | second mate | （船上的）二副 |
| | the first or the chief mate | 大副 |
| 17. | from hence to the port of | 由此去……港口 |
| 18. | to sail *vi.* | 航行 |
| 19. | payment on a quantum merit | 按服務計酬付款；相當的給付 |
| 20. | express terms of the contract | 契約明示條款 |
| 21. | the whole voyage | 全航程 |
| 22. | to imply *vi.* | 默示 |
| 23. | to succeed in one's claim | 成功索賠 |

(B) Discharge by agreement

A contract may be discharged by a subsequent binding agreement to that effect. This occurs where there is a mutual waiver or accord and satisfaction. Also, contractual obligations may be discharged by release under seal.

## (25) D. & C. Builders Ltd.v.Rees

[1966] 2 QB.617; [1965] 3 All E. R. 837

*Court of Appeal*

In July 1964 the defendant owed £482 13s. 1d. to the plaintiffs for work done by them as jobbing builders. In August and again in October the plaintiffs wrote to the defendant asking for payment. In November 1964 the defendant's wife telephoned the plaintiffs and said, "My husband will offer £300 in settlement. That is all you'll get. It is to be in satisfaction, " The plaintiffs then discussed the problem between themselves. The company was a small one and it was in desperate financial straits: for this reason the plaintiffs decided to accept the £300. The plaintiffs then telephoned the defendant's wife, telling her that "£300 will not even clear our commitments on the job. We will accept £300 and give you a year to find the balance." She replied, "No, we will never have enough money to pay the balance. £300 is better than nothing." When she was told by the plaintiffs that they had no choice but to accept, she said, "Would you like the money by cash or by cheque. If it is cash, you can have it on Monday. If by cheque; you can have it tomorrow(Saturday)." The next day, the defendant's wife gave the plaintiffs a cheque for £300, asking for a receipt, and insisting on the words "in completion of account". So that the wording of the receipt was as follows: "Received the sum of £300 from Mr. Rees in completion of the account. Paid, M. Casey." In evidence, Mr. Casey explained why he gave a receipt in those terms: "If I did not have the £300 the company would have gone bankrupt. The only reason we took it was to save the company. She knew the position we were in," The plaintiffs brought this action to recover the balance of £182 13s. 1d. On a preliminary point whether there was accord and satisfaction, it was held by the county court judge that the taking of the cheque for £300 did not discharge the debt of £482 13s. 1d. The defendant appealed.

HELD, by LORD DENNING, M.R., DANCKWERTS and WINN, L. JJ., that there was no accord and satisfaction and that the plaintiff was entitled to recover the balance.

## Notes

| 1. | mutual waiver | 雙方棄權；共同棄權 |
|---|---|---|
| 2. | accord and satisfaction | 和解與清償（the substitution of another agreement for an existing claim and full execution of the new agreement） |
| 3. | release under seal | 加蓋印鑑的棄權或放棄 |
| 4. | to owe £40 to sb. | 欠某人40英鎊 |
| 5. | jobbing builders | 中間建築商 |
| 6. | to ask for. | 向⋯⋯要；請求 |
| 7. | to offer £300 in settlement | 提供 300 英鎊進行結算 |
| 8. | in desperate financial straits | 處於極端的經濟困難之中 |
| 9. | to clear one's commitments on the job. | 清算完成工作義務的所得 |
| 10. | to find the balance | 找到差額 |
| 11. | to pay the balance | 支付所差的錢 |
| 12. | receipt *n.* | 收據 |
| 13. | in completion of account | 清帳 |
| 14. | to go bankrupt | 破產 |
| 15. | on a preliminary point whether... | 就是否⋯⋯這個初步話題 |

**16.** to recover the balance　　　　獲得差額
**17.** to be entitled　　　　　　　　有權

(C) Discharge by frustration（契約無法履行）

# (26) Joseph Constantine Steamship Line Ltd. v. Imperial Smelting Corporation Ltd.
[1942] A.C.154; [1941] 2 All E. R. 165
*House of Lords*

A ship was chartered to load a cargo at Port Pirie in South Australia and to carry it to Europe. While the vessel was anchored in the roads off Pirie and before she became an "arrived ship" there was a violent explosion near her auxiliary boiler, causing damage and making it impossible to perform the charterparty. The charterers claimed damages, alleging that the owners had broken the charterparty by their failure to load the cargo. The owners contended that the contract was frustrated by the destructive consequences of the explosion. There was no evidence that the explosion was due to the fault of the owners. It was held by the Court of Appeal that the defence raised by the owners, that the charter was frustrated, must fail unless the owners could prove affirmatively that the frustration occurred without their default. The owners appealed.

HELD, by VISCOUNT SIMON, L.C., VISCOUNT MAUGHAN, LORD RUSSELL OF KILLOWEN, LORD WRIGHT and LORD PORTER, that the onus of proving default lies upon the party denying the frustration. Since there was no evidence that the explosion was attributable to the fault of the owners, the contract was frustrated.

---

### ☘ Notes

| | | |
|---|---|---|
| **1.** | frustration *n.* | 契約受挫失效、落空或不能被履行 |
| **2.** | to charter a ship | 租船 |
| **3.** | to load a cargo | 裝載一批貨物 |
| **4.** | vessel *n.* | 船 |
| **5.** | to anchor | 拋錨泊船；（船）停靠 |
| **6.** | violent explosion | 劇烈的爆炸 |
| **7.** | auxiliary boiler | 附屬的鍋爐 |

| | |
|---|---|
| **8.** to perform the charter party | 履行租船（傭船）契約 |
| **9.** the charters *n.* | 租船人 |
| **10.** allege *vt.* | 宣稱 |
| **11.** to break the charter party | 違反租船（傭船）契約 |
| **12.** to contend *vt.* | 爭論 |
| **13.** to frustrate *vt.* | 挫敗 |
| **14.** destructive consequence | 破壞性的後果 |
| **15.** to raise the defence | 提出抗辯 |
| **16.** charter | 租船契約（= charterparty） |
| **17.** affirmatively *adv.* | 肯定地 |
| **18.** without one's fault | 沒有一個人的過錯 |
| **19.** to occur *vi.* | 發生 |
| **20.** viscount *n.* | （英國的）子爵 |
| **21.** onus *n.* | 義務；責任 |
| **22.** to lie on | 落在…… |
| **23.** attributable *a.* | 可歸因的 |
| ～ to the fault of owners | 可歸因於船的所有人的過錯 |

# (27) Robinson v. Davison
[1871] L. R.6 Exch. 269; [1861-73] All E. R. Rep.699

*Court of Exchequer*

The plaintiff was a professor of music and a giver of musical entertainments, and the defendant was the husband of a celebrated pianist. The plaintiff entered into a contract with the defendant's wife (as her husband's agent) to perform at a concert he had arranged for a specified evening. A few hours before the concert was due to begin the plaintiff received a letter from the defendant's wife informing him that on account of her illness she could not perform at the concert. The plaintiff brought this action for breach of contract.

HELD, by KELLY, C.B., and CHANNEL, BRAMWELL and CLEASBY, BB., that the contract was conditional upon the defendant's wife being well enough to perform and that, consequently, the defendant was excused.

 **Notes**

| | |
|---|---|
| **1.** musical entertainments | 音樂招待 |
| **2.** a celebrated pianist | 一位著名的鋼琴演奏家 |

| | | |
|---|---|---|
| **3.** | to enter into a contract with sb. | 與某人簽訂契約 |
| **4.** | to perform a concert | 演奏音樂會 |
| **5.** | to arrange for... | 為……作安排 |
| **6.** | before the concert was due to begin | 在音樂會按規定時間開始前 |
| **7.** | to inform *vt.* | 通知；告知 |
| **8.** | on account of her illness | 因為她有病 |
| **9.** | breach of contract | 違約（此處 breach 當名詞用） |
| **10.** | conditional upon... | 以……為條件 |
| **11.** | being well enough | 身體足夠的健康 |
| **12.** | consequently *adv.* | 所以 |
| **13.** | to excuse *vt.* | 免除…… |

(D) Discharge by acceptance of breach

Where there is a fundamental breach or a breach of condition, the aggrieved party may elect either to affirm the contract by treating it as still in force, or treat it as being conclusively discharged by his acceptance of the other party's breach.

# (28) General Billposting Co. Ltd. v. Atkinson
[1909] A. C. 118; [1908-10] All E. R. Rep. 619
*House of Lords*

The defendant, a billposter, entered into a contract of employment with the plaintiff company, the contract being subject to termination by either party giving twelve months notice in writing. By the contract, the defendant undertook that he would not, within two years of leaving the plaintiff company's employment, engage as a billposter within a radius of fifty miles of the company's registered office. The company dismissed him without giving the agreed twelve months notice. He then set himself up as a billposter within fifty miles of the company's registered office. The company brought this action against him, claiming damages and an injunction to restrain him from working as a billposter within the range of fifty miles as agreed in the contract of employment. The action came before NEVILLE, J., who gave judgment for the plaintiff company. The defendant appealed and it was held by the Court of Appeal that the company, by dismissing the employee without the agreed period of notice had completely and totally repudiated the contract of employment and that, accordingly, the employee was entitled to accept the repudiation and regard himself as no longer bound by any of its terms. The company appealed to the House of Lords.

HELD, by the EARL OF HALSBURY, LORD COLLINS, LORD ROBERTSON and LORD LOREBURN, L.C., that the employers dismissed the defendant in deliberate disregard of the terms of the contract, and that he was thereupon justified in rescinding the contract and treating himself as absolved from further performance of it on his part.

## Notes

| | | |
|---|---|---|
| 1. | acceptance of breach | 接受違約 |
| 2. | the aggrieved party | 受害方（受違約損害的契約當事人） |
| 3. | to affirm the contract | 證實契約（指立契約人對可取消的契約當作有效契約來執行） |
| 4. | still in force | 仍然有效 |
| 5. | conclusively *adv.* | 確定地 |
| 6. | billposter *n.* | 張貼廣告的人 |
| 7. | billposting Co.Ltd. | 張貼廣告有限責任公司 |
| 8. | a contract of employment | 僱用契約 |
| 9. | to enter into | 簽訂 |
| 10. | termination *n.* | 終止 |
| 11. | to leave the company's employment | 離開公司所聘用的職位 |
| 12. | within a radius of fifty miles | 在50英里的為半徑的範圍內；在周圍50英里的範圍內 |
| 13. | to dismiss sb. | 解僱某人 |
| 14. | to set oneself up as a billposter | 以廣告張貼人為自居 |
| 15. | registered office | 註冊辦事處 |
| 16. | injunction *n.* | 禁止令 |
| 17. | to restrain sb. from doing sth. | 制止某人做某事 |
| 18. | to work as... | 以……身分進行工作 |
| 19. | to give judgement for sb. | 作出有利於某人的判決 |
| 20. | to repudiate a contract | 推翻契約；否認契約的有效性 |
| 21. | in deliberate disregard of the terms of the contract | 故意漠視契約的條款 |
| 22. | to be justified in rescinding the contract | 有理由撤銷契約 |
| 23. | to treat oneself as absolved from farther performance | 將自己看成可以免除進一步履行的責任 |
| 24. | on one's part | 就某人而言 |

In equity, the party who waived his rights may, if he sues, be estopped from denying that he intended the waiver to be binding.

## (29) Central London Property Trust Ltd. v. High Trees House Ltd.
### [1947] K. B.130; [1956] 1 All E. R.256
*King's Bench Division*

The plaintiff company(the landlords) let a new block of flats to the defendant company(the tenants) in 1937 for a term of ninety-nine years at a rent of £2, 500 a year. The plaintiff company held all the shares of the defendant company. The block of flats was not fully occupied when war broken out in 1939, nor was there any possibility of letting all the flats with war conditions prevailing in London. It became clear that the defendants' profits would not be sufficient to pay the agreed rent and, as a result of discussions between the directors concerned, an arrangement was made by which the plaintiffs wrote to the defendants in the following terms: "We confirm the arrangement made between us by which the ground rent should be reduced as from the commencement of the lease to £1, 250 per annum". The period during which the reduction was to operate was not specified, nor was there any consideration given by the defendant company in return for the reduction. The defendants paid the reduced rent, but by early in 1945 the flats were fully let and the rents received from them had been increased to a figure higher than that which had originally been anticipated. In 1941 the debenture-holders of the plaintiff company appointed a receiver who was still managing the affairs of the company at the time of this action. In September 1945 the receiver discovered for the first time that the rent reserved in the lease was £2, 500 a year and he, accordingly, informed the defendants that this was the annual sum due. The plaintiffs brought this action to recover £625 rent for the quarter ended 29th September 1945, and also £625 for the quarter ended 25th December 1945. The defendants contended that the reduction was to apply throughout the term of ninety-nine years and, alternatively, that the reduction was to apply up to 24th September 1945, after when the original rent of £2, 500 a year would become payable.

HELD, by DENNING, J., that the amounts claimed in the action were fully payable, the reduction arrangement not being binding after early 1945.

**Notes**

| | | |
|---|---|---|
| 1. | promissory estoppel | 允諾後不得否認的原則；不可反悔原則 |
| 2. | to waive one's rights | 放棄某人的權利 |
| 3. | to be estopped from denying... | 禁止某人否認…… |
| 4. | to intend the waiver to be binding | 有意使棄權有拘束力 |
| 5. | King's Bench Division | （英）王座法庭 |
| 6. | landlord *n.* | 地主 |
| 7. | tennant *n.* | 佃戶 |
| 8. | to let a new block of flats to sb. | 將一座公寓大廈出租給某人 |
| 9. | a term of ninety-nine years | 期限 99 年 |
| 10. | to be fully occupied | （房子）全部住人 |
| 11. | to break out | 發生 |
| 12. | to prevail *vi.* | 流行 |
| 13. | per annum | 每年（= per year） |
| 14. | to specify *vi.* | 使具體化 |
| 15. | debenture-holder | 公司債券持有人 |
| 16. | receiver *n.* | 涉訟財產管理人 |
| 17. | to anticipate *vt.* | 預期；期望 |
| 18. | to be increased to a figure higher than that | 提高到一個比那還要高的數字 |
| 19. | to reserve *vt.* | 保留 |
| 20. | in equity | 從衡平法上講 |

The usual common law remedy for breach of contract is damages, that is to say, monetary compensation. Damages are of two categories: unliquidated damages and liquidated damages. The following case shows you in what case liquidated damages will be void and disregarded.

## (30) Dunlop Pneumatic Tyre Co., Ltd. v. New Garage Co., Ltd.

[1915] A. C. 79; [1914-15] All E. R. Rep. 739

*House of Lords*

Dunlop, through an agent, entered into a contract with New Garage Co., by which they supplied them with their goods, consisting mainly of motor car tyres, covers and tubes. By this contract, New Garage Co. undertook not to do a number of things, including the following: Not to tamper with the manufacturer's marks; not to sell to any customer at prices less than the current list prices; not to supply to persons whose supplies Dunlop had decided to suspend; not to exhibit or to export without Dunlop's assent. The agreement contained the following clause: "We agree to pay to the Dunlop company the sum of £5 for each and every tyre, cover or tube sold or offered in breach of this agreement, as and by way of liquidated damages and not as a penalty." The New Garage Co.sold covers and tubes at prices below the list prices and Dunlop brought this action for liquidated damages. On the question whether the £5 stipulated in the agreement was penalty or liquidated damage:

HELD, by LORD DUNEDIN, LORD ATKINSON, LORD PARKER and LORD PARMOOR, that the stipulation was one for liquidated damages and that the New Garage Co. was liable to pay the sum specified in respect of each and every breach of the contract. LORD PARMOOR. There is no question as to the competency of parties to agree beforehand the amount of damages, uncertain in their nature, payable on the breach of a contract. There are cases, however, in which the courts have interfered with the free right of contract, although the parties have specified the definite sum agreed on by them to be in the nature of liquidated damages, and not of a penalty. If the court, after looking at the language of the contract, the character of the transaction, and the circumstances under which it was entered into, comes to the conclusion that the parties have made a mistake in calling the agreed sum liquidated damages, and that such sum is not really a pactional pre-estimate of loss within the contemplation of the parties at the time when the arrangement was made, but a penal sum inserted as a punishment on the defaulter irrespective of the amount of any loss which could at the time have been in contemplation of th parties, then such sum is a penalty, and the defaulter is only liable in respect of damages which can be proved against him.

## ♣ Notes

| | | |
|---|---|---|
| **1.** | damages *n.* | 損害賠償金 |
| **2.** | remedy *n.* | （對違約的）補救 |
| **3.** | monetary compensation | 金錢上的補償 |
| **4.** | category *n.* | 類型；種類 |
| **5.** | unliquidated damages | 等待法庭裁定的損害賠償金；未在契約中確定的損害賠償金 |
| **6.** | void *a.* | 無法律效力的；無效的 |
| **7.** | to be disregarded | 被漠視；被不予理睬 |
| **8.** | to supply sb. with goods | 向某人提供某種商品 |
| **9.** | to consist of... | 包括…… |
| **10.** | tyres *n.* | 輪胎 |
| **11.** | covers *n.* | 蓋子 |
| **12.** | tubes *n.* | 管子 |
| **13.** | to tamper with sth. | 損害某種東西 |
| **14.** | the manufactures' marks | 製造商的記號 |
| **15.** | list prices | 價目表上的價格 |
| **16.** | to suspend *vt.* | 中止；暫停 |
| **17.** | supplies *n.* | 供貨 |
| **18.** | to exhibit *vt.* | 展出 |
| **19.** | without sb's consent | 沒有某人的同意 |
| **20.** | in breach of this agreement | 違反此協議／契約 |
| **21.** | penalty *n.* | 罰款 |
| **22.** | liquidated damages | （契約中確定的）違約賠償金或預定的違約賠償金 |
| **23.** | stipulation *n.* | 規定；條款 |
| **24.** | competency *n.* | 資格；許可權 |
| **25.** | to agree beforehand | 事先同意 |
| **26.** | to interfere with... | 對……進行干預 |
| **27.** | the definite sum agreed on by them | 他們都一致同意的確切金額 |
| **28.** | to come to the conclusion | 得出結論 |
| **29.** | pactional *a.* | 契約上的 |
| **30.** | pre-estimate *n.* | 原先的估計 |

| 31. | within the contemplation of the parties | 在當事人期待中的 |
| 32. | penal *a.* | 刑罰的 |
| 33. | to insert *vt.* | 插入 |
| 34. | punishment *n.* | 懲罰 |
| | a punishment on sb. | 對某人的懲罰 |
| 35. | defaulter *n.* | 違約人 |
| 36. | irrespective of... | 不論……；不考慮…… |
| 37. | in respect of... | 就……而言 |

# (31) Hadley v. Baxendale
[1854] 9 Exch. 341; [1843-60] All E. R. Rep. 461
*Court of Exchequer*

The plaintiffs were <u>millers</u> in Gloucestershire and the defendants were common carriers of goods. The <u>crankshaft</u> of the plaintiffs' <u>steam engine</u> was broken with the result that work in the mill had <u>come to a halt</u>. They had ordered a new shaft from an engineer in Greenwich and arranged with the defendants to carry the broken shaft from Gloucester to Greenwich to be used by the engineer as a model for the new shaft. The defendants did not know that the plaintiffs had no <u>spare shaft</u> and that the mill could not operate until the new shaft was <u>installed</u>. The defendants <u>delayed delivery</u> of the <u>broken shaft</u> to the engineer for several days, with resulting delay to the plaintiffs in <u>getting their steam-mill working</u>. The plaintiffs claimed damages for breach of contract. On the question whether damages should include loss of profits:

HELD, by PAKE, ALDERSON, PLATT and MARTIN, B.B., that the loss of profits was not <u>recoverable</u> as it could not reasonably be considered a <u>consequence of the breach of contract</u> as could have been fairly and reasonably <u>contemplated</u> by both the parties when they made the contract.

## Notes

| 1. | millers *n.* | 磨坊主 |
| 2. | common carriers of good | 貨物公共承運人 |
| 3. | crankshaft *n.* | 曲軸 |
| 4. | steam engine | 蒸汽機 |
| 5. | to come to a halt | 停下 |

| | | | |
|---|---|---|---|
| 6. | spare shaft | | 多餘的（曲）軸 |
| 7. | to install *vt.* | | （設備的）安裝 |
| 8. | to delay the delivery of sth. | | 延誤了某物的交貨 |
| 9. | to get the steam-mill working | | 使蒸汽機磨坊工作 |
| 10. | loss of profits | | 利潤損失 |
| 11. | recoverable *a.* | | 可獲得的 |
| 12. | consequence of th breach of contract | | 違約的後果 |
| 13. | to contemplate *vt.* | | 期待 |

# (32) The Heron ll, Koufos v. Czarnikow Ltd.

[1967] 2 Lloyd's Rep. 457; [1967] 3 All E. R. 686

*House of Lords*

The respondents chartered the appellant's vessel, Heron II, to sail to Constanza, and there to load a cargo of sugar and to carry this to Basrah or to Jeddah, at the charterer's opinion. The option was not exercised and the vessel arrived at Basrah with a delay of nine days due to deviations made in breach of contract. The respondents had intended to sell the sugar promptly after arrival at Basrah but the appellant did not know this , although he was aware that there existed a sugar market at Basrah. Shortly before the sugar was sold at Basrah, the market price fell partly by reason of the arrival of another cargo of sugar. If the appellant's vessel had not been in delay by nine days, the sugar would have fetched £32 10s. per ton. The price realised on the market was £31 2s. 9d. per ton. The respondent charterers brought this action to recover the difference as damages for breach of contract. The appellant shipowner, while admitting liability to pay interest for nine days on the value of the sugar, denied that the fall in market value should be taken into account in assessing damages. It was held by the Court of Appeal that the loss due to the fall in market price was not too remote and could be recovered as damages. The shipowner appealed to the House of Lords.

HELD, by LORD REID, LORD MORRIS OF BORTH-Y-GEST, LORD HODSON, LORD PEARCE and LORD UPJOHN, that the case fell within the first branch of the rule in Hadley v. Baxendale and that the difference was recoverable as damages for breach of contract.

## ♣ Notes

| | |
|---|---|
| respondents *n.* | 被告（尤指上訴及離婚案件的被告） |
| to charter *vt.* | 租；包（船、飛機、車輪……） |

| | | |
|---|---|---|
| 3. | vessel *n.* | 船 |
| 4. | to sail to a place | 航行到某地 |
| 5. | to load a cargo of sugar | 裝載一船糖貨 |
| 6. | to carry sth. to a place | 將某物運到某一地方 |
| 7. | at the charterer's opinion | 按租船人的意見 |
| 8. | to exercise the option | 行使選擇權 |
| 9. | with a delay of nine days | 晚了9天 |
| 10. | due to | 由於 |
| 11. | deviation *n.* | 偏離（航線） |
| 12. | market price | 市價 |
| 13. | by reason of | 由於；因為 |
| 14. | shipowner *n.* | 船舶所有人 |
| 15. | to admit liability | 承認責任 |
| 16. | to be taken into account | 得到考慮或重視 |
| 17. | to assess *vt.* | 估計 |
| 18. | remote *a.* | 遙遠的 |

# (33) Victoria Laundry Ltd. v. Newman Industries Ltd.
[1949] 2 K. B. 528; [1949] 1 All E. R. 997

*Court of Appeal*

The plaintiffs, who were launderers and dyers, decided to extend their business, and with this end in view, purchased a large boiler from the defendants. The defendants knew at the time of the contract that the plaintiffs were laundry-men and dyers and that they required the boiler for the purposes of their business. They also were aware that the plaintiffs wanted the boiler for immediate use. But the defendants did not know at the time the contract was made exactly how the plaintiffs planned to use the boiler in their business. They did not know whether (as the fact was) it was to function as a substitute for a smaller boiler already in operation, or as a replacement of an existing boiler of equal capacity, or as an extra unit to be operated in addition to any boilers already in use. The defendants, in breach of contract delayed delivery of the boiler for five months. The plaintiffs brought this action for damages. The defendants disputed that the plaintiffs were entitled to damages for the loss of profits they would have earned if the boiler had been delivered on time. The plaintiffs contended that they could have taken on a large number of new customers in the course of their laundry business and that they could and would have accepted a number of highly lucrative dyeing contracts for the Ministry of Supply. STREATFEILD, J., awarded £110 damages under certain minor heads but no damages in respect of loss of profits on the grounds that this was too remote. The plaintiffs appealed to the Court of Appeal.

HELD, by TUCKER, ASQUITH and SINGLETON, L. JJ., that there were ample means of knowledge on the part of the defendants that business loss of some sort would be likely to result to the plaintiffs from the defendants' default in performing their contract; and that the appeal should, therefore, be allowed and the issue referred to an official referee as to what damage, if any, is recoverable in addition to the £110 awarded by the trial judge.

## Notes

| | | |
|---|---|---|
| 1. | launderers and dyers | 洗衣染色工 |
| 2. | to extend one's business | 擴大某人的生意 |
| 3. | with this end in view | 帶著這個被期待的目的（此短語中的end表示「目的」、「目標」） |
| 4. | boiler *n.* | 鍋爐；煮器 |
| 5. | at the time of contract | 在訂契約時 |
| 6. | laundry-men *n.* | 洗衣男工 |
| 7. | to require the boiler for the purposes of their business | 做生意需要這個煮器或鍋爐 |
| 8. | to function as... | 作為……發揮作用 |
| 9. | a substitute for or replacement of sth. | 作為某物的替用品 |
| 10. | an existing boiler of equal capacity | 同等容量的現有鍋爐 |
| 11. | in use | 在使用中的 |
| 12. | to dispute *vt.* | 爭論 |
| 13. | loss of profits they would have earned if the boiler had been delivered on time | 注意此句中的虛擬語態，如果鍋爐按時到達他們可能得到的利潤之損失 |
| 14. | to contend *vt.* | 堅決認為 |
| 15. | to take on a large number of new customers | 接納很多新顧客 |
| 16. | highly lucrative dyeing contracts | 非常賺錢的染色工作契約 |
| 17. | under certain minor heads | 根據某些小的專案 |
| 18. | in respect of | 就……而言 |
| 19. | ample means of knowledge | 足夠瞭解的手段 |
| 20. | to perform their contract | 履行他們的契約 |
| 21. | referee *n.* | 公斷人；仲裁人 |
| 22. | trial judge | 初審法官 |
| 23. | default in performing their contract | 在履約時的疏怠職責 |

# PART II

## Classic Cases to Be Uesed for Teaching English Law of Negotiable Instruments

### 15                                                              Cheques

## (1) North and South Wales Bank Ltd. v. Macbeth (1908), In the case we use M.to stand for Macbeth and W. North and South Wales Bank Ltd.

M. was <u>induced</u> by the fraud of W. to <u>draw a cheque in favour of</u> K. M., when he signed, intended that K. should take the money. W. <u>forged</u> K's <u>indorsement</u> and paid the cheque into his own bank, which received payment. M. sued W's bank for the amount of the cheque. Held he was <u>entitled to</u> succeed, because K.being intended by M.to receive the money, was not a <u>fictitious payee</u>, and the cheque was consequently not <u>payable to</u> bearer.

### 🍀 Notes

1. to induce sb to do sth           勸誘某人做某事
2. fraud *n.*                      詐欺；欺騙
3. in favour of...              以⋯⋯為受益人（受款人）
4. to forge sb's indorsement    偽造某人的簽名
5. fictitious payee            虛擬受款人
6. to be entitled to do sth.      有權做某事
7. to be payable to bearer      向提示人支付；付給提示人

## (2) Bank of Credit and Commerce International S.A.V. Dawson and Wright (1987)

Three cheques were written by D. in favour of S., a customer of the plaintiff bank. S. <u>presented the cheques for payment</u> but did not receive payment because D. stopped the cheques. D. stopped the cheques because S., a <u>car dealer</u>, had failed to deliver certain cars to D. The bank manager of the plaintiff bank had in the past <u>credited</u> some other cheques to S.

account which the manager knew would be <u>dishonoured</u>.Also, the bank manager had <u>delayed debiting</u> some other cheques against S's account. The reason was to <u>keep S's account in credit</u>. Held, When S.became overdrawn on the account to a value <u>in excess of</u> these cheques, the plaintiff bank had a <u>lien</u> on the cheques. However, because of the actions of the plaintiff bank's manager, the plaintiff bank did not become a <u>holder in due course</u> under section 27(3) of the Bills of Exchange Act 1882. The reason was that the plaintiff bank had not <u>acted in good faith</u> as required by section 27(3) Bills of Exchange /5ct 1882.

(In the above case D. refers to Dawson and Wright and S. stands for Commerce International S.A.)

### Notes

| | | |
|---|---|---|
| **1.** | to write a cheque | 開支票 |
| **2.** | to present the cheque for payment | 將支票提示付款（此處 present = demand for payment 要求付款） |
| **3.** | car dealer | 小汽車交易商 |
| **4.** | to credit a cheque to sb's account | 將支票金額記入某人帳戶的貸方 |
| **5.** | to dishonour a cheque | 拒付支票 |
| **6.** | to delay debiting a cheque against sb's account | 推遲將支票上的金額記入某人帳戶的借方 |
| **7.** | to keep sb's account in credit | 保持某人帳戶上有存款 |
| **8.** | in excess of | 超過…… |
| **9.** | to become overdraw on the account | 透支某一（存款）帳戶 |
| **10.** | to have a lien on the cheques | 在支票上擁有留置權 |
| **11.** | to act in good faith | 誠信地行為 |
| **12.** | a holder in due course | 正當持票人 |

# (3) Mason V. Lack (1929)

An <u>instrument</u>, which is <u>void</u> as a bill of exchange because it is not <u>addressed to</u> anyone, may nevertheless be <u>valid</u> as a <u>promissory note</u>.

A document was in the following form:

"On December 31, 1928, pay to my order the sum of £125 7s. 4d. for value received."

It was not signed, but across the face were the words "accepted payable at Lloyds Bank Ltd., Highgate Branch, J. H. Lack." Held, the instrument was a promissory note on which Lack was liable as <u>maker</u>.

**Notes**

| | |
|---|---|
| **1.** instrument *n.* | 文件；契約；票據（本文中與 document 意同） |
| **2.** void *a.* | 無效的 |
| **3.** to be addressed to sb. | 開給某人的 |
| **4.** valid *a.* | 有效的 |
| **5.** promissory note | 本票；期票 |
| **6.** £125 7s. 4d. | 125英鎊7先令4便士 |
| **7.** maker *n.* | 期票出票人 |

## (4) CLaydon V. Brandley (1987)

B. K. Ltd. was <u>loaned</u> £10, 000 by C.B., who was the principal <u>share-holder</u> in B. K. Ltd., signed a document which stated that the loan was to be paid back <u>in full</u> by July 1, 1983. The question was whether this document was a promissory note within section 83 of the Bills of Exchange Act 1882. Held, the document did not <u>satisfy the requirements</u> of section 83 since there was no unconditional promise to pay at fixed or future time. The payer could choose to pay the loan at an earlier date than July 1, 1983.

 **Notes**

| | |
|---|---|
| **1.** to loan money to sb. | 將錢借給某人 |
| **2.** share-holder *n.* | （英）股東（=（美）stockholder） |
| **3.** be paid back in full | 全額付還 |
| **4.** to satisfy the requirements | 滿足要求 |

## (5) Rae V. Yorkshire Bank Plc

If a bank wrongfully dishonours a cheque, it is liable to pay damages to its customer, but only nominal damage can be recovered by persons who are not traders.

Rae who had an agreed <u>overdraft</u> of £1,000 had the overdraft extended to £1,500. The Yorkshire bank dishonoured two cheques drawn in favour of third parties, and refused to allow Rae to <u>cash a cheque</u> at the bank, even though with in the extended overdraft limit. Held, he could not recover <u>damages for inconvenience</u> and <u>humiliation</u>. Since he did not <u>allege</u> any specific loss, and since Rae was not a trader, he could only recover nominal damages for the <u>breath of contract</u> on the part of the bank.

### Notes

| | | |
|---|---|---|
| 1. | nominal damages | 名義賠償金（小金額的） |
| 2. | plc. = public limited company | 公開上市有限責任公司 |
| 3. | overdraft *n.* | 透支 |
| 4. | to cash a cheque | 兌現支票 |
| 5. | to recover damages | 獲得損害賠償金 |
| 6. | inconvenience *n.* | 不方便 |
| 7. | humiliation *n.* | 羞辱 |
| 8. | to allege *vt.* | 宣稱；提出 |
| 9. | breach of contract | 違反契約；違約 |
| 10. | on the part of sb. | 就某人而言 |

## (6)Lumsden & Co. V. London Trustee Savings Bank
### [1971] 1 Lloyd's Rep. 114.

Lumsden & Co., plaintiff stockbrokers, employed a Mr.Blake as temporary accountant. The practice of the plaintiffs was to draw cheques in favour of their clients in an abbreviated form;thus, where the cheques were payable to Brown Mills & Co., they simply drew them in favour of Brown. Blake, who was fraudulent, opened an account with the defendant bank in the name of a fictitious J.A.G. Brown whose profession he gave as a self-employed chemist. Blake gave the fictitious J.A.G. Brown an excellent reference, describing himself as a "D. Sc. Ph. D." The branch manager of the defendant bank, who thought that he was dealing with two reputable professional men, failed, contrary to his instructions, to make inquiries with Mr. Blake's bank. Mr. Blake then transferred some of the cheques due to Brown Mills & Co. but simply made payable to Brown to the fictitious J.A.G. Brown's account with the defendant bank. Held, (1) the defendant bank had acted negligently in opening the account and was not protected by section 4(1) of the Cheques Act 1957; (2) there was contributory negligence to the extent of 10 percenton the part of the plaintiffs and the damages to which they were entitled had to be reduced accordingly.

### Notes

| | | |
|---|---|---|
| 1. | stockbroker. *n.* | 股票經紀人 |
| 2. | to employ sb.as... | 僱用某人做…… |
| 3. | temporary accountant | 臨時會計 |

4. the practice of the plaintiff　　原告的業務
5. to draw cheques in favour of their clients　　開具以他們客戶為受益人的支票
6. in an abbreviated form　　用簡略形式
7. fraudulent *a.*　　欺騙性的；欺詐的
8. to open an account with a bank　　在某銀行開立帳戶
9. in the name of...　　以……名義
10. fictitious *a.*　　虛構的；非真實的
11. reference *n.*　　證明人
12. to describe oneself as　　將自己描述成……
13. Ph. D.= Doctor of Philosophy　　哲學博士
14. D. Sc.= Doctor of Science　　理學博士
15. the branch manager　　分行行長
16. to deal with sb.　　與某人打交道
17. reputable *a.*　　聲譽好的
18. professional *a.*　　專業的
19. contrary to his instruction　　違反他的指示
20. to make inquiries with...　　向……詢問
21. to transfer some of the cheques due to sb.　　將應付給某人的支票進行轉讓
22. negligenly *adv.*　　有疏忽地；過失地
23. contributory negligence　　共同過失；與有過失
24. to the extent of　　到……程度
25. accordingly *adv.*　　相應地

# (7) Underwood Ltd. v. Bank of Liverpool and Martins Ltd.
### [1924] 1 K. B.775.

U. was the sole director and practically the sole shareholder in U. Ltd. U. had a private account with the L. bank, and the company had an account with the X. bank, but the L.bank knew nothing of this account. Cheques payable to the company were indorsed, "U. Ltd.-U., sole director," and paid into the L. bank to U.'s private account. Held. U. Ltd. were entitled to recover the amount of the cheques, because the L. bank were negligent in not inquiring whether U. Ltd had an account, and, if, so, why the cheques were not paid into it: Underwood Ltd.v. Bank of Liverpool and Martins Ltd.[1924] 1 K. B.775.

### Notes

| | |
|---|---|
| **1.** sole *a.* | 唯一的 |
| **2.** to have a private account with a bank | 在銀行有一個私人銀行帳戶 |
| **3.** to know nothing of sth. | 對某事一無所知 |
| **4.** cheques payable to sb. | 應付給某人的支票 |
| **5.** to indorse *vt.* | 背書 |
| **6.** to pay into a bank to sb's private account | 付入一銀行某人的私人帳戶 |
| **7.** to be negligent in doing sth. | 在做某事方面有過失或疏忽 |

## (8) Kreditbank Cassel v. Schenkers Ltd.
### [1927] 1. K. B.826.

S. carried on business in London, and had a branch in Machester.X., the manager of the Manchester branch, without any authority from S., drew seven bills of exchange, purporting to do so on behalf of S., and signed them "X., Manchester manager." The bills having been dishonoured, K., a holder in due course, sued S.as drawer. Held, (1) the bills being drawn by X.without authority were forgeries and (2) S.was not liable on them.

### Notes

| | |
|---|---|
| **1.** to have a branch in Manchester | 在曼徹斯特有一個分公司 |
| **2.** without my authority from sh. | 沒有某人的任何授權 |
| **3.** to draw bills of exchange | 開匯票（美國人用draft表示同樣的意思） |
| **4.** purporting to do so | 聲稱這樣做 |
| **5.** on behalf of | 代表…… |
| **6.** to dishonour the bills of exchange | 對匯票進行拒付 |
| **7.** a holder in due course | 正當持票人 |
| **8.** forgeries *n.* | 偽造的票據（文件……） |
| **9.** to be liable on sth. | 對……承擔責任 |

## (9) Glasscock V. Balls (1889)

B. gave mortgage on some property to W., and also a promissory note for the amount of the mortgage. W. transferred the mortgage to X. for the full amount due thereon, and subsequently indorsed the note to G. for value. G. had no notice of the mortgage. A considerable time later, G.sued B. Held, although after his transfer of the mortgage W. had no right to sue on the note, G.was a bona fide holder for value and not affected by the defect in W.'s title.

### Notes

| | |
|---|---|
| **1.** to give a mortgage | 對某人提供抵押貨款 |
| **2.** a mortgage on some property | 以某財產作抵押的貨款 |
| **3.** a promissory note | 期票；本票 |
| **4.** for value | 因對價 |
| **5.** to have no notice of | 對……未注意 |
| **6.** to sue on the promissory note | 就本票提起訴訟 |
| **7.** a bona fide holder for value | 付對價的善意持票人 |
| **8.** to affect *vt.* | 影響 |
| **9.** defect in W's title | 在W所有權方面的欠缺 |

# (10) Diamond v. Graham

[1968] 1 W. L. R.1061.

D. agreed to lend H. £1, 650, provided H. undertook to procure a cheque for that amount from G. by a certain date, so that D. would have G.'s cheque in his possession before his own was presented. D. gave H.the cheque but because H. was unable to get in touch with G. in time D. stopped it. Soon after, H. did obtain the required cheque from G. in favour of D., at the same time giving G. his own cheque for the same amount. D. paid in G.'s cheque and authorised payment of his cheque in favour of H. G.'s cheque in favour of D. was dishonoured, and so was H.'s in favour of G. D., sued G., but the latter contended that D. was not a holder for value as no value had passed between them. Held, (1) no requirement existed for value to be given by the holder of the cheque; (2) on the facts double value had been given: by H. giving G. his own cheque in return for G.'s cheque in favour of D.; and by D. releasing his cheque in favour of H., after having stopped it; (3) accordingly D. was holder for value of G.'s cheque and was entitled to judgment on it: Diamond v.Graham[1968] 1 W. L. R. 1061.

### Notes

| | |
|---|---|
| **1.** to lend sb.£1,650 | 借給某人1,650英鎊 |
| **2.** provided *conj.* | 假如 |
| **3.** to undertake *vt.* | 同意 |

**4.** to procure *vt.*　　　　　努力取得

**5.** by a certain date　　　　在某一天

**6.** to present a cheque　　　提示支票

**7.** to get in touch with...　　與……進行聯繫

**8.** in time　　　　　　　　　及時

# PART III

## Classic Cases to Be Cited for Teaching English Property Law

# English Property Law

## (1) Graharm V. K. D. Morris and Sons Pty Ltd. (1974)

At frequent intervals the jib of the defendants' crane projected over the plaintiff's land. Held: The invasion of the plaintiff's airspace by the projection of the crane jib was a trespass and not just a nuisance.

 **Notes**

**1.** at frequent intervals      不時地
**2.** the jib of the defendants' crane      被告的起重機機臂
**3.** to project over the plaintiff's land      伸到原告的土地上
**4.** invasion of the plaintiff's airspace      對原告領空的入侵
**5.** trespass *n.*      非法侵入；侵犯行為
**6.** nuisance *n.*      妨礙行為；滋擾罪

## (2) Tulk V. Moxhay (1848)

Tulk sold the central part of Leicester Square to Elms, who covenanted on behalf of himself, his heirs and assigns not to build on the land. The land was later sold to Moxhay who knew of this covenant, but nevertheless proceeded to build on the land. Held: that Moxhay was bound by the covenant. It would be inequitable that Elms, who gave a small price for the land because of the restrictions, should be able to sell it for a larger price free from those restrictions.

 **Notes**

**1.** to covenant *vi.*      立契約
**2.** on behalf of      代表……

| | |
|---|---|
| **3.** heirs *n.* | 繼承人；後嗣 |
| **4.** assigns *n.* | 受讓人（英文中常用複數） |
| **5.** covenant *n.* | 契約 |
| **6.** to proceed to build on the land | 在土地上蓋建築 |
| **7.** to be bound by... | 受……的拘束 |
| **8.** inequitable *a.* | 不公正的 |
| **9.** to give a small price for... | 對……出低價（買進） |
| **10.** to sell for a larger price | 高價出售 |
| **11.** to be free from restrictions | 不受限制 |

# (3) Carritt V. Bradley (1903)

B held most of the shares in a tea company. He <u>mortgaged</u> them to C. The mortgage contained a <u>term</u> that B, as a shareholder would <u>induce</u> the company <u>to employ</u> C as the company's agent to sell tea. The company paid off the mortgage, and <u>ceased to</u> employ C, <u>whereupon</u> C <u>claimed damages for breach of the agreement</u> to employ him. Held: that the <u>proviso</u> in the mortgage as to employment of C <u>ceased to</u> exist after the mortgage was paid off.

### 🍀 Notes

| | |
|---|---|
| **1.** to mortgage *vt.* | 抵押 |
| to ～ a house to sb. for ＄30,000 | 用房子向某人押借30,000美元 |
| **2.** term *n.* | 條款 |
| **3.** to induce *vt.* | 勸誘 |
| **4.** to employ *vt.* | 僱用；聘用 |
| **5.** to pay off the mortgage | 付清了抵押貨款 |
| **6.** to cease to do sth. | 停止做某事 |
| **7.** whereupon *adv.* | 因此 |
| **8.** to claim damages for breach of the agreement | 要求獲得違反協定的損害賠償金 |
| **9.** the proviso *n.* | 附帶條件 |

# (4) Noakes V. Rice (1902)

The <u>tenant</u> of a <u>"free" public house</u>, under a twenty-six-year <u>lease</u>, <u>mortgaged the premises</u>

to a brewery company <u>as security for a loan</u>, and <u>covenanted</u> that <u>during the remainder</u> of the twenty six years he would not sell any beers except those provided by the brewery company(<u>the mortgagees</u>). The tenant <u>paid off</u> the mortgage three years later, and sued for a <u>declaration</u> that he was <u>free from the covenant</u>. Held: that the covenant was <u>inconsistent with</u> the <u>express proviso</u> for <u>redemption</u>( which entitled the tenant for demand a <u>reconveyance</u> of the premises upon <u>repayment</u> of the loan with interest) and was <u>a clog upon the equity</u>. Tenant <u>became entitled</u> to trade as a free public house.

## ♣ Notes

| | | |
|---|---|---|
| 1. | tenant *n.* | 承擔人；租戶；承租人 |
| 2. | "free" public house | 空閒的小旅館 |
| 3. | lease *n.* | 租約 |
| | ～under a twenty-six-year | 根據一個租期為 26 年的租賃合約 |
| 4. | to mortgage the premises to a brewery company | 將房屋抵押給一家造啤酒公司 |
| 5. | as a security for a loan | 作為一項貨款的抵押品 |
| 6. | during the remainder of the twenty-six year | 在 26 年剩餘的時間內 |
| 7. | mortgagee *n.* | 承受抵押人；被抵押人（與 mortgagor 抵押人相對） |
| 8. | declaration *n.* | 宣布 |
| 9. | to be free from the covenant | 不受契約的拘束 |
| 10. | inconsistent with... | 與……不一致 |
| 11. | the express proviso | 明示的附加條件 |
| 12. | redemption *n.* | 贖回 |
| 13. | reconveyance *n.* | 歸還；再讓與 |
| 14. | a clog upon on the equity | 對衡平法的妨礙 |
| 15. | to become entitled to do sth. | 有權做某事 |

# (5) Kreglinger V. New Patagonia Meat and Cold storage co.(1914)

A firm of <u>woolbrokers</u> (mortgagee) lent £10,000 to a meat company <u>on mortgage</u>. The woolbrokers agreed not to demand repayment for five years, but the mortgagors (the meat company) could repay the debt earlier <u>on giving notice</u>. The parties <u>covenanted</u> also that the meat company would not sell <u>sheepskins</u> to anyone except the woolbrokers for five years from the date of the agreement, <u>as long as</u> the woolbrokers were willing to purchase the skins at the agreed price. The loan was paid off before the five years. Held: that the <u>option</u> of purchasing the sheepskins did not <u>end on repayment</u>, but continued for five years. It was a <u>collateral</u> <u>contract</u> and did not <u>affect</u> <u>the right</u> to redeem.

## Notes

| | | |
|---|---|---|
| 1. | meat and cold storage co. | 肉品冷藏公司 |
| 2. | firm *n.* | 公司；企業 |
| 3. | woolbrokers *n.* | 羊毛經紀人 |
| 4. | to lend money to sb. | 將錢借給某人 |
| 5. | on mortagage | 以抵押形式 |
| 6. | on giving notice | 在給予通知的條件下 |
| 7. | sheepskins *n.* | 羊皮 |
| 8. | as long as | 只要 |
| 9. | option *n.* | 選擇權 |
| 10. | to end on repayment | 付還時結束 |
| 11. | collateral contract | 擔保契約 |
| 12. | the right to redeem | 贖回權 |
| 13. | to affect *vt.* | 影響 |

| 17 | **American Securities Laws** |
|---|---|

## (1) S.E.C. v. LIFE PARTNERS. INC.
### 87 E3d 526 (D.C.Cir.1996)
*"Investors have no direct contractual rights against the
insurance companies that issue the policies."*

### FACTS

Life Partners, facilitates the sale of life insurance policies from AIDS victims to investors at a discount. The investors then recover the face value of the policy after the policy holder's death. Meanwhile, the terminally ill sellers secure much needed income in the final years of life when employment is unlikely and medical bills are often staggering. This process is known as "viatical settlements." For acceptance into the standard Life Partners program, an insured must meet the following criteria: (1) be diagnosed with "full Blown Aids;" (2) have a life expectancy of 24 months or less as determined by Life Partners' "independent reviewing physician"; and (3) be certified as mentally competent. Life Partners also represents that a policy qualifies for purchase only if it is issued by an insurance company rated "A-" or higher by a national rating service. In addition the policy must be in god standing. The policies are assigned to Life Partners, not to investors. After the insured's death, the benefits are also paid directly to Life Partners, which then pays the investors. Investors have no direct contractual rights against the insurance companies that issue the policies. Whether they receive a return on their investment or even recover their principal depends upon Life Partners's ability to honor its contractual obligations to them. The SEC claims that Life Partners sold unregistered securities and made untrue and misleading statements in violation of the federal securities laws. Life Partners argues that the viatical settlements are not securities within the scope of the securities laws.

## ISSUE

Are the viatical settlement contracts that qualify as securities?

## DECISION

No. Although some promoters of viatical settlements do register them as securities under the federal securities laws, Life Partners observes that registration means higher costs for investors and correspondingly owner prices for terminally ill policyholders. An investment contract is a security subject to the federal securities acts if investors purchase with (1) an expectation of profits arising from (2) a common enterprise that (3) depends upon the efforts of others. The asset acquired by a Life Partner investor is a claim on future death benefits. The buyer is obviously purchasing not for consumption-unmatured claims cannot be currently consumed-but rather for the prospect of a return on investment. That is enough to satisfy the requirement that the investment be made in the expectation of profits. The second element for a security is that there be a "common enterprise." Socall horizontal commonality-defined by the pooling of investment funds, shared profits, and shared losses-is ordinarily sufficient to satisfy the common enterprise requirement. Here, Life Partners brings together multiple investors and aggregates their funds to purchase the death benefits of an insurance policy. If the insured dies in a relatively short time, then the investors realize profits; if the insured lives a relatively long time, then the investors may lose money or at best fail to realize the return they had envisioned. Any profits or losses from a Life Partners contract accrue to all investors in that contract. In that sense, the outcomes are shared among the investors; the sum that each receives is a predetermined portion of the aggregate death benefit. The final requirement for an investment to be a security is that the profits expected by the investor be derived from the efforts of others, However, purely ministerial or clerical functions performed by others are not sufficient to meet this requirement. Nothing that Life Partners could do had any effect whatsoever upon the near-exclusive determinant of the investors' rate of return, namely how long the insured survives. In sum, the SEC has not identified any significant nonministerial service that Life Partners performs for investors once they hve purchased their fractional interests in a viatical settlement. Nor do we find that any of the ministerial functions have a material impact upon the profits of the investors. In this case, it is the length of the insured' s life that is of overwhelming importance to the value of the viatical settlements marketed by Life Partners. Because the profits from their purchase do not derive predominantly from the efforts of a party or parties other than the investors, the viatical settlements are not investment contracts subject to the federal securities laws.

## 🍀 Notes

| | | |
|---|---|---|
| 1. | life partner | 活著的合夥人；有生命的合夥人 |
| 2. | life insurance | （美）人壽保險＝（英）life assurance |
| 3. | AIDS victims | 愛滋病受害者／犧牲者 |
| 4. | to facilitate the sale of... | 促進對……的出售 |
| 5. | at a discount | 低於正常的價格；打折 |
| 6. | face value | 面值 |
| 7. | life insurance policy | 人壽保險單／契約 |
| 8. | the policy holder | 文中指人壽保單持有人 |
| 9. | terminally | 晚期地，the terminally ill seller 晚期得病的賣方 |
| 10. | to secure *vt.* | 獲得 |
| 11. | medical bill | 醫療費用的帳單 |
| 12. | staggering *a.* | 令人驚愕的 |
| 13. | viatical settlement | 人身最終旅行清算 |
| 14. | an insured | 被保險人（＝ the insured） |
| 15. | to meet the following criteria | 達到下列標準 |
| 16. | diagnose *vt.* | 診斷 |
| 17. | with full Blown Aids | 用完全吹脹的輔助物 |
| 18. | life expectancy | 估計壽命 |
| 19. | independent reviewing physician | 獨立檢查內科醫生 |
| 20. | to be certified as mentally competent | 被證明精神上正常 |
| 21. | to qualify for... | 有……資格 |
| 22. | insurance company | 保險公司 |
| 23. | to be rated "A⁻" | 評等為A⁻ |
| 24. | a national rating service | 國家評等服務（公司） |
| 25. | in good standing | 在有效期內 |
| 26. | to be assigned to sb. | 讓與給某人 |
| 27. | to have no direct contractual rights against... | 沒有針對……的直接契約權利 |
| 28. | to receive a return on one's investment | 獲得某人投資的回報 |
| 29. | principal *n.* | 本金 |
| | to recover one's principa | 收回某人的本金 |

| | |
|---|---|
| **30.** to honour one's contractual obligations to sb. | 向某人履行契約義務 |
| **31.** the SEC | （美）證券交易委員會（Securities Exchange Commission = A U.S. government agency that closely monitors the activities of stockbrokers and traders in securities.） |
| **32.** unregistered securities | 未註冊的證券 |
| **33.** in violation of... | 違反…… |
| **34.** within the scope of... | 在……範圍內 |
| **35.** to qualify as... | 作為……獲得承認 |
| **36.** promoter *n.* | 推廣人；促銷人 |
| **37.** correspondingly *adv.* | 相應地 |
| **38.** the Federal Securities Acts | （美）聯邦證券法 |
| **39.** asset *n.* | 資產 |
| **40.** a claim on future death benefits | 對未來殘廢撫恤金提出的索賠 |
| **41.** unmatured claims | 未到期的索賠權利 |
| **42.** prospect *n.* | 預期 |
| **43.** to satisfy the requirement | 滿足要求 |
| **44.** horisontal commonality | 水平式共同體；水平式共同企業 |
| **45.** in expectation of... | 期望…… |
| **46.** pooling of investment funds | 投資資金的合夥 |
| **47.** multiple *a.* | 多樣的 |
| **48.** to aggregate *vt.* | 使……聚集在一起 |
| **49.** to realize profits | 獲得利潤（to realize the return 實現回報） |
| **50.** at best | 至多；充其量 |
| **51.** to accrue *vi.* | 自然增長 |
| **52.** outcome *n.* | 後果；結果；成果 |
| **53.** predetermined *a.* | 事先決定的 |
| **54.** to derive from... | 從……取得 |
| **55.** ministerial *a.* | 行政性的 |
| **56.** clerical *a.* | 辦公室工作的 |
| **57.** to have effect on sth. | 對某事產生影響 |
| **58.** near-exclusive *a.* | 幾乎獨有的 |
| **59.** rate of return | 回報率 |
| **60.** to survive *vi.* | 活下來 |
| **61.** overwhelming *a.* | 有壓倒之勢的 |

**62.** predominantly *adv.*　　　主要地

**63.** be subject to the federal　　　受聯邦證券法支配
securities laws

**64.** nonministerial service　　　非行政性服務

**65.** fractional *a.*　　　部分的

**66.** to have a material impact　　　對……有主要或重要影響
on...

## Additional case questions

**1**. What does Life Partners, Inc. sell?

**2**. What is meant by "viatical settlements"?

**3**. What criteria must an insured meet for acceptance into the standard Life Partners Program?

**4**. Has Life Partners violated the federal securities laws as claimed by the SEC?

**5**. Are the viatical settlement contracts that qualify as securities?

**6**. On what condition will an investment contract be regarded as a security subject to the Federal Securities Acts?

**7**. What is of overwhelming importance to the value of the viatical settlements marketed by Life Partners?

**8**. What is the reason given for saying that the viatical settlements are not investment contracts subject to the federal securities laws?

# (2) GUSTAFSON V. ALLOYD COMPANY
### 115S. Ct. 1061(U.S. Sup. Ct. 1995)

**FACTS**

Gustafson, McLean, and Butler (collectively Gustafson) were in 1989 the sole shareholders of Alloyd, Inc. a manufacturer of plastic packaging and automatic heatsealing equipment. Alloyd was formed, and its stock issued, in 1961. In 1989, Gustafson decided to sell Alloyd and engaged KPMG Peat Marwick to find a buyer. In response to information distributed by KPMG, Wind Point agreed to buy substantially all of the issued and outstanding stock of the corporation. In preparation for negotiating the contract with Gustafson, Wild Point undertook an extensive analysis of the company, relying in part on a formal business review prepared by

KPMG. After the sale, <u>year-end audit</u> of Alloyd revealed that Alloyd's <u>actual earnings</u> for 1989 were lower than <u>the estimates</u> relied upon by the parties. Wind Point claimed that the contract of sale was a <u>prospectus</u>, so that any <u>misstatements contained</u> in the agreement <u>gave rise to</u> liability under Section 12(2) of the 1933 Act. Wind Point sued under Section 12(2), <u>seeking rescission</u> of the contract.

## ISSUE

Is the contract of sale a prospectus that creates Section 12(2) liability?

## DECISION

No. As this case reaches us, we must <u>assume</u> the stock purchase agreement contained material misstatements of fact made by the sellers. <u>On this assumption</u>, the buyer would have the right to obtain a rescission if those misstatements were made "by means of a prospectus or <u>oral communication</u> (<u>related</u> to a prospectus)." The 1933 Act created federal duties for the most part, registration and <u>disclosure obligations-in connection with</u> public <u>offerings of</u> securities. It does not <u>extend to</u> a private sales contract, such as this. When the 1933 Act was <u>drawn</u> and <u>adopted</u>, the term "prospectus" was well understood to refer to a document <u>soliciting the public to acquire securities from the issuer</u>. It is <u>understandable that</u> Congress would <u>provide buyers with</u> a right to rescind, without proof of fraud or reliance, as to misstatements contained in a document prepared with care, following well-established <u>procedures</u> relating to <u>investigations with due diligence</u> and <u>in the context of</u> a public offering by an issuer or its controlling shareholders. It is not <u>plausible</u> to <u>infer</u> that Congress created this extensive liability for every <u>casual communication</u> between buyer and seller in <u>the secondary market. In sum,</u> the word "prospectus" is a <u>term</u> of art <u>referring to a document</u> that describes a public offering of securities by an issuer or controlling shareholder. This contract of sle, and its <u>recitations</u>, were not <u>held out to</u> the public and were not a prospectus as the term is used in the 1993 Act.

 **Notes**

| | | |
|---|---|---|
| **1.** | share-holder *n.* | 股東（美國人常用 stockholder 表示同樣的意思） |
| **2.** | plastic packaging | 塑膠包裝 |
| **3.** | automatic heating equipment | 自動加熱設備 |
| **4.** | to issue stock | 發行股票 |
| **5.** | to engage sb. to do sth. | 聘用某人做某事 |
| **6.** | in response to | 對……回應 |

| | | |
|---|---|---|
| 7. | outstanding stock | 已公開發行但未售出的股票；庫藏股 |
| 8. | in preparation for doing sth. | 為做某事作準備 |
| 9. | to undertake an extensive analysis | 進行一項廣泛性的分析 |
| 10. | in part | 部分地（＝ partly or partially） |
| 11. | business review | 商業評論 |
| 12. | year-end audit | 年終審計；年終查核 |
| 13. | to reveal *vt.* | 揭示；展現 |
| 14. | actual earnings | 實際收入；實際利潤 |
| 15. | the estimates | 估計數字 |
| 16. | prospectus *n.* | 公開說明書；證券募集書 |
| 17. | misstatement(s) *n.* | 錯誤說明 |
| 18. | to contain *vt.* | 包含 |
| 19. | to give rise to | 引起；使發生 |
| 20. | to seek rescission of the contract | 謀求契約的撤銷 |
| 21. | to assume *vt.* | 假定；設想 |
| 22. | material *a.* | 重要的；實質性的 |
| 23. | on this assumption | 在此假設下 |
| 24. | oral communication | 口頭上的溝通；言詞上的聯繫 |
| 25. | to be related to... | 與……有關 |
| 26. | to draw an Act | 草擬一個法令 |
| 27. | to adopt *vt.* | 採用 |
| 28. | to refer to sth. | 涉及 |
| 29. | to solicit sb to do sth. | 請求某人做某事 |
| 30. | to acquire securities from the issuer | 從發行人那裡收購證券 |
| 31. | understandable *a.* | 可理解的 |
| 32. | to provide sb. with sth. | 向某人提供某物 |
| 33. | procedures *n.* | 程式 |
| 34. | with due diligence | 適當勤奮地 |
| 35. | investigation *n.* | 調查 |
| 36. | in the context of... | 在……的背景下 |
| 37. | public offering | （證券的）公開發行；公開募集 |
| 38. | plausible *a.* | 似乎有道理的 |
| 39. | to infer *vt.* | 推斷；推論 |

| | |
|---|---|
| **40.** casual communication | 隨便的溝通 |
| **41.** in the secondary market | 在次級市場上 |
| **42.** in sum | 簡言之 |
| **43.** term of art | 藝術術語 |
| **44.** recitations *n.* | 敘述 |
| **45.** to be held out to the public | 向公眾提出 |
| **46.** KPMG | 安侯建業（美國五大會計事務所之一）其餘四家為：PWC（資誠）、Arthur Andersen（安達信）、Deloitte & Touche（勤業眾信）以及 Ernst & Young（安永） |

## Additional case questions

**1.** Is the contract of sale in this case a prospectus? why not?

**2.** Why did Wind Pornt sue?

**3.** In what case can the buyer have the right to obtain a rescission of the contract of sale with Gustafson?

**4.** What is public offering?

**5.** What is the correct legal definition of the word "prospectus"?

# (3) SAN LEANDRO EMERGENCY MEDICAL GROUP V. PHILIP MORRIS

1996 U.S. App. Lexis 1083 (2d Cir. 1996)

### FACTS

In recent years, cigarette sales have been declining because of health concerns and changing demographics. The entry of discount brands into the marketplace has led to a further decline in the sales of premium brands such as Philip Morris's Marlboro line. Historically, in order to decreasing demand for Marlboro by raising Marlboro's price and at the same time narrowing the price gap between its discount and premium brands in order to make the discount brands less attractive. Philip Morris engaged in this strategy through the first quarter of 1993, and implemented price increases on discount cigarettes during that period. However, retailers foiled the company's strategy by deciding to absorb the price increases rather than pass them on to consumers, thus maintaining the large retail price gap between discount and premium brand cigarettes. At the end of the first quarter of 1993, in the face of declining sales volume and <u>decreasing market share</u> for Marlboro, Philip Morris <u>adopted</u> a new marketing strategy. Philip Morris announced that it would cut the price of Marlboro by ＄0.40 per <u>pack</u>, a <u>move</u> estimated to reduce its earnings by ＄2 billion in 1993. Following this announcement, Philip Morris <u>stock</u> dropped almost 25 percent. This <u>prompted</u> the <u>filing of numerous lawsuits</u> under Rule 10b-5, <u>alleging</u> that Philip Morris <u>misrepresented</u> or failed to disclose to the market that Marlboro sales were declining at such a rate that raising prices would not <u>compensate for</u> the loss of sales, and that the company was actively considering a new and <u>alternative</u> strategy of cutting Marlboro prices <u>at the expense of</u> short-term profits.

## ISSUE

Did Philip Morris violate Rule 10b-5 through the <u>omission</u> of a material fact?

## DECISION

No. To state <u>a cause of action</u> under Section 10(b) and Rule 10b-5, the plaintiffs must plead that Philip Morris <u>made a false statement</u> or <u>omitted a material fact</u>, with <u>scienter</u>, and that plaintiff's reliance on that action caused injury. Plaintiffs <u>contend</u> that <u>prior to</u> April 2, 1993, Philip Morris <u>misstated</u> and failed to disclose that it was <u>planning a radical change</u> in <u>pricing strategy</u> for Marlboro that would reduce the company's 1993 profits by ＄2 billion. Specifically, the plaintiffs argued that Philip Morris had made <u>numerous statements</u> that it would continue its <u>historic</u> strategy of raising the price of Marlboro in order to <u>sustain profits</u>. Further, the revised <u>marketing plan</u> in this case <u>marked a sharp break</u> from the company's historic practices and was <u>important</u> enough that a reasonable investor <u>probably</u> would want to know about it. However, we are <u>concerned about interpreting the securities laws</u> to force companies to <u>give</u> their competitors <u>advance notice</u> of <u>sensitive pricing information</u>. Thus, absent a showing that Philip Morris's earlier public statements were materially <u>misleading</u>, the company had no duty to <u>disclose</u> its new marketing plan. During the first quarter of 1993, the company <u>pursued</u> its historic marketing <u>strategy</u> and there was no reason to believe its <u>optimistic</u> assessments of that <u>course of action</u> were unreasonable given the past success of that strategy.

 **Notes**

| | | |
|---|---|---|
| 1. | health concerns | 對健康的關心 |
| 2. | demographics *n.* | 人口統計 |
| 3. | the entry of sth.into the marketplace | 商品進入市場 |
| 4. | sales have been declining | 銷售量一直在下降 |
| 5. | discount brands | 打折品牌 |

| | | |
|---|---|---|
| **6.** | to lead to | 導致 |
| **7.** | premium brands | 溢價品牌 |
| **8.** | line *n.* | 商品大類 |
| **9.** | to sustain *vt.* | 維持 |
| **10.** | profit levels | 利潤水平 |
| **11.** | to respond to | 對……作出反應 |
| **12.** | to raise price | 提價 |
| **13.** | to narrow the price gap | 縮小價差 |
| **14.** | to engage in this strategy | 採取了此戰略 |
| **15.** | to implement price increases | 進行加價 |
| **16.** | discount cigarettes | 打折香煙 |
| **17.** | retailer *n.* | 零售商（與 wholesaler「批發商」相對） |
| **18.** | to foil the company's strategy | 使公司戰略變成泡影 |
| **19.** | to absorb the price increases rather than pass them on to consumers | 承擔價格上漲的費用而不將它們轉嫁於消費者 |
| **20.** | thus maintaining the large retail price gap between discount and premium brand cigarettes | 從而保持了打折品牌煙與加價品牌煙之間大幅零售差價 |
| **21.** | in the face of | 面臨…… |
| **22.** | declining sales volume | 持續下降的銷售額 |
| **23.** | decreasing market share | 不斷下降的市場占有額 |
| **24.** | to adopt a new marketing strategy | 採用一種新的銷售戰略 |
| **25.** | to cut the price by $ 0.40 per pack | 每包煙減價40美分 |
| **26.** | a move | 一種行為 |
| **27.** | to reduce its earnings by... | 使其利潤減少…… |
| **28.** | stock *n.* | 股票 |
| **29.** | to drop *vi.* | 下降 |
| **30.** | to prompt *vt.* | 引起 |
| **31.** | the filing of numerous lawsuits | 無數的起訴 |
| **32.** | to allege *vt.* | 斷言；宣稱 |
| **33.** | to misrepresent *vt.* | 虛偽陳述；錯誤陳述 |
| **34.** | to disclose to the market | 向市場揭露 |
| **35.** | to compensate for the loss of... | 補償……的損失 |
| **36.** | alternative *a.* | 替代的 |
| **37.** | at the expense of... | 在損害……的情況下 |
| **38.** | short-term profits | 短期利潤 |

| | |
|---|---|
| **39.** omission *n.* | 遺漏 |
| **40.** cause of action | 訴因；案由 |
| **41.** to plead *vt.* | 請求 |
| **42.** to make a false statement | 進行虛偽陳述 |
| **43.** to omit a material fact | 省略了一個重要事實 |
| **44.** scienter *n.* | 故意 |
| **45.** to contend *vt.* | 主張 |
| **46.** prior to... | 在……之前 |
| **47.** a radical change | 根本徹底的改變 |
| **48.** pricing strategy | 定價戰略 |
| **49.** numerous statements | 無數的聲明／陳述 |
| **50.** historic *a.* | 具有歷史意義的 |
| **51.** to sustain profits | 維持利潤 |
| **52.** the revised marketing plan | 已修正的行銷計畫 |
| **53.** to mark a sharp break from... | 標明與……的決裂 |
| **54.** important enough | 足夠的重要（注意用 enough 來修飾形容詞時要將它放在形容詞的後面如：good enough…） |
| **55.** probably *adv.* | 很可能地 |
| **56.** to be concerned about... | 對……關心 |
| **57.** to interprete the securities laws | 解釋證券法 |
| **58.** to give advance notice | 提前通知；預先通知 |
| **59.** sensitive pricing information | 敏感性定價訊息 |
| **60.** thus, absent showing... | 因此在無……跡象的情況下 |
| **61.** misleading *a.* | 有誤導性的 |
| **62.** to discloses its new marketing plan | 揭露它的新行銷計畫 |
| **63.** to pursue *v.* | 實行；執行 |
| **64.** course of action | 行動方向 |
| **65.** given the past success of that strategy | 假如此戰略過去是成功的 |
| **66.** optimistic *a.* | 樂觀的 |
| **67.** assessments *n.* | 估計 |

 **Additional Case questions**

**1.** Why have cigarette sales been declining?

**2**. What has led to further decline in the sales of premium brands such as Philip Morris's Marlboro line?

**3**. What method or strategy was used by Philip Morris in the past to respond to decreasing demand for Marlboro?

**4**. How was this strategy foiled later?

**5**. Under what circumstances did Philip Morris adopt a new marketing strategy of cutting the price of Marlboro by ＄0.40 per pack?

**6**. What was the outcome of implementing the new marketing strategy like?

**7**. Did Philip Morris violate Rule 10b-5 through the omission of a material fact? If your answer is "no", give reasons for it.

**8**. Should a company be forced to give their competitors advance notice of sensitive pricing information?

# (4)UNITED STATES V. O'HAGAN
117S. Ct. 2199(U.S. Sup. Ct. 1997)
*"Trading on such information qualifies as a 'deceptive decice'…"*

## FACTS

James Herman O'Hagan was a partner in the law firm of Dorsey & Whitney. In July 1988, Grand Metropolitan retained Dorsey as legal counsel for a potential tender offer for the common stock of the Pillsbury Company. Both Grand Metropolitan and Dorsey & Whitney took precautions to protect the confidentiality of Grand Metropolitan's tender offer plans. While Dorsey & Whitney was still representing Grand Metropolitan, O'Hagan began purchasing call options for Pillsbury stock. Each option gave him the right to purchase 100 shares of Pillsbury stock by a specified date in 1988 at a price just under ＄39 per share. When Grand Metropolitan announced its tender offer, the price of Pillsbury stock rose to nearly ＄60 per share. O'Hagan then sold his Pillsbury call options and common stock, making a profit of more than ＄4.3 million. After the SEC investigated O'Hagan's transactions, it claimed that he defrauded his law firm and its client, Grand Metropolitan, by using for his own trading purposes material, nonpublic information regarding Grand Metropolitan's planned tender offer. O'Hagan was charged with securities fraud in violation of Section 10(b) and Rule 10b-5. He claimed that criminal liability under Section 10(b) and Rule 10b-5 could not be predicated on the misappropriation theory.

## ISSUE

Could O'Hagan's criminal liability be based on the misappropriation theory?

## DECISION

Yes. Section 10(b) prescribes (1) using any deceptive device (2) in connection with the purchase or sale of securities, in contravention of rules prescribed by the SEC. The provision, as written, does not confine its coverage to deception of a purchaser or seller of securities, rather, the statute reaches any deceptive device use "in connection with the purchase or sale of any security." Liability under Rule 10b-5 does not extend beyond conduct encompassed by Section 10(b)'s prohibition. Under the "traditional" or "classical theory" of insider trading liability, Section 10(b) and Rule 10b-5 are violated when a corporate insider trades in the securities of his corporation on the basis of material, nonpublic information. Trading on such information qualifies as a "deceptive device" under Section 10(b) because a relationship of trust and confidence exists between the shareholders of a corporation and those insiders who have obtained confidential information by reason of their position with that corporation. That relationship gives rise to a duty to disclose (or to abstain from trading) because of the necessity of preventing a corporate insider from taking unfair advantage of uninformed stockholders. The classical theory applies not only to officers, directors, and other permanent insiders of a corporation, but also to attorneys, accountants, consultants, and others who temporarily become fiduciaries of a corporation. The "misappropriation theory" holds that a person commits fraud in connection with a securities transaction, and thereby violates Section 10(b) and Rule 10b-5, when he misappropriates confidential information for securities trading purposes, in breach of a duty owed to the source of the information. Under this theory, a fiduciary's undisclosed, self-serving use of a principal's information to purchase or sell securities, in breach of duty of loyalty and confidentiality, defrauds the principal of the exclusive use of that information. The two theories are complementary, each addressing efforts to capitalize on nonpublic information through the purchase or sale of securities. The classical theory targets a corporate insider's breach of duty to shareholders with whom the insider transacts; the misappropriation theory outlaws trading on the basis of nonpublic information by a corporate outsider in breach of a duty not to a trading party but to the source of the information. The misappropriation theory is thus designed to protect the integrity of the securities markets against abuses by outsiders to a corporation who have access to confidential information that will affect the corporation's security price when revealed, but who owe no fiduciary or other duty to that corporation's shareholders. We hold that O'Hagan's misappropriation satisfies Section 10(b)'s requirement that chargeable conduct involve a "deceptive device or contrivance" used "in connection with" the purchase or sale of securities. Misappropriators <u>deal in</u> deception. A fidu-ciary who <u>pretends loyalty</u> to the principal while secretly <u>converting</u> the principal's information for <u>personal gain dupes</u> or defrauds the principal. The misappropriation theory is also <u>well-tuned</u> to an animating purpose of the SEC Act: to insure honest securities markets and thereby <u>promote investor confidence</u>. Although information <u>disparity</u> is inevitable in the securities markets, investors likely would hesitate to <u>venture their capital</u> in a market where trading based on misappropriated nonpublic information is <u>unchecked</u> by law.

## ♣ Notes

| | | |
|---|---|---|
| 1. | law firm | （英）法律事務所（美國人常用 law office 來取代） |
| 2. | legal counsel | 法律顧問 |
| 3. | to retain sb. as... | 聘某人為……（律師等） |
| 4. | potential *a.* | 潛在的 |
| 5. | tender offer | 透過公開招標出售證券，美國人常這樣做 |
| 6. | common stock | （美）普通股＝（英）ordinary share |
| 7. | to take precautions to do sth. | 採取做某事的預防措施 |
| 8. | confidentiality *n.* | 機密性 |
| 9. | a partner in the law firm | 律師事務所的合夥人 |
| 10. | to represent *vt.* | 代理 |
| 11. | call options | 買入期權（與 put option 賣出期權相對） |
| 12. | to rise to... | 漲到…… |
| 13. | to investigate *vt.* | 調查 |
| 14. | transactions *n.* | 交易 |
| 15. | to defraud *vt.* | 欺騙 |
| 16. | client *n.* | 客戶 |
| 17. | for one's own trading purpose | 為某人自己的交易目的 |
| 18. | non-public *a.* | 未公開的 |
| 19. | to be charged with securities fraud | 被指控進行證券欺騙或欺詐 |
| 20. | in violation of | 違反…… |
| 21. | to predict *vt.* | 預告；預言 |
| 22. | misappropriation *n.* | 濫用 |
| 23. | to prescribe *vt.* | 規定 |
| 24. | in contravention of... | 違反…… |
| 25. | provision *n.* | 規定 |

26. to confine its coverage to... 　　　將其包括範圍限制在……

27. deception *n.* 　　　欺騙

28. statute *n.* 　　　成文法

29. deceptive device 　　　欺騙手段

30. in connection with... 　　　與……有關的

31. conduct *n.* 　　　行為

32. to encompass *vt.* 　　　包括

33. insider trading 　　　內線交易；內幕人交易

34. corporate insider 　　　公司知情人

35. on the basis of... 　　　根據……

36. to qualify as... 　　　具備成為……的條件

37. a relationship of trust and confidence 　　　信託信賴關係

38. confidential information 　　　機密資訊

39. by reason of... 　　　由於……；因為……

40. to give rise to... 　　　引起……；使……發生

41. to take unfair advantage of sb. 　　　不公正地欺騙某人

42. uninformed *a.* 　　　不知情的

43. to apply to... 　　　適用於……

44. permanent *a.* 　　　永久性的

45. attorney *n.* 　　　（美）律師＝（英）solicitor

46. accountant *n.* 　　　會計；會計師

47. consultant *n.* 　　　顧問

48. temporarily *adv.* 　　　暫時地

49. fiduciary *n.* 　　　受信託人

50. to hold *vt.* 　　　認為

51. to commit fraud 　　　犯欺騙（詐欺）罪

52. in breach of a duty 　　　未履行義務

53. undisclosed *a.* 　　　未被揭露的；保持秘密的

54. self-serving *a.* 　　　為自己服務的

55. principal *n.* 　　　本人；委託人

56. duty of loyalty and confidentiality 　　　忠誠與保密責任／義務

57. complementary *a.* 　　　互補的

58. to capitalize on sth. 　　　利用……

59. to outlaw *vt.* 　　　宣告……非法

60. corporate outsider 　　　公司的非知情者

| | |
|---|---|
| **61.** a trading party | 買賣當事人 |
| **62.** source of information | 資訊來源 |
| **63.** to be designed to do sth. | 被事先計畫好用來做某事 |
| **64.** to protect the integrity of the securities markets against abuses of... | 保護證券市場的正直性不受……的濫用 |
| **65.** to have access to confidential information | 能獲得秘密資訊 |
| **66.** to affect the corporation's security price | 影響公司證券價格 |
| **67.** when revealed | 當被洩漏後 |
| **68.** to owe no fiduciary duty to sb. | 對某人不具有信託責任 |
| **69.** chargeable conduct | 可能被指控的行為 |
| **70.** contrivance *n.* | 設計；詭計 |
| **71.** to deal in deception | 經營欺騙 |
| **72.** to pretend loyalty to sb. | 假裝對某人忠誠 |
| **73.** to convert secretly the principal's information for personal gain | 為個人的所獲將委託人的資訊秘密進行轉換 |
| **74.** to dupe or defraud the principal | 愚弄或欺騙 |
| **75.** be well-tuned to an animating purpose | 與有生命力的目的很好地相協調 |
| **76.** to insure honest securities markets | 保證證券市場的可信任 |
| **77.** to promote investor confidence | 增加投資者的信心 |
| **78.** information disparity | 資訊的不一致性；資訊不對稱 |
| **79.** inevitable *a.* | 不可避免的 |
| **80.** to venture one's capital in a market | 將某人的資本冒風險地投資於一市場 |
| **81.** to be unchecked by law | 沒有被法律抑制 |

 **Additional case questions**

**1.** What is meant by tender offer?

**2.** What is common stock?

**3.** Can you tell the exact meaning of option? How many types of options do you know?

**4.** What was the result of the SEC'S investigation of O'Hagan's transactions?

**5.** Could O'Hagan's criminal liability be based on the misappropriation theory?

**6.** What is insider trading? Why is it illegal?

# (5) HOCKING V. DUBOIS

839 F. 2d 560(1988) United States Court of Appeals, Ninth Circuit

## FACTS

Gerald Hocking visited Hawaii and became interested in buying a condominium there as an investment. Maylee Dubois, who was a licensed real estate broker in Hawaii, agreed to help Hocking find a suitable unit. Dubois found a condominium unit owned by Tovik and Yaacov Liberman that was for sale. The unit was located in a resort complex developed by Aetna Life Insurance Company (Aetna) and managed by the Hotel Corporation of the Pacific(HCP). Aetna and HCP offered purchasers of condominium units in the project to participate in a rental pool agreement. The Libermans had not participated in the pool. Hocking purchased the unit from the Libermans and entered into a rental pool agreement with HCP. Hocking subsequently filed suit against Dubois, alleging violations of federal securities laws. The trial court granted summary judgment in favor of the defendants. Hocking appealed.

## ISSUE

Was the offer of a condominium unit with an option to participate in a rental pool agreement a "security" under federal securities laws?

## DECISION

Yes. The court of appeals held that the transaction constituted an offer of a security, and that Hocking could sue Dubois for alleged violations of federal securities laws. Reversed and remanded.

## REASON

Generally, simple transactions in real estate do not satisfy the Howey criteria. When a purchaser is motivated exclusively by a desire to occupy or develop the land personally, no security is involved. Real estate transactions may involve an offer of securities when an investor is offered both an interest in real estate and a collateral expectation of profits. The court held that under the three Howey criteria an offer of condominium with a rental pool agreement constitutes an offer of an investment contract.

1. Investment of money. Hocking invested money in the condominium.

2. Common enterprise. Each investor buys one share-a condominium-in a common venture that pools the rents from all of the units. The success of each participant's individual investment clearly depends on the entire rental pool agreement's success.

3. Expectation of profits produced by others' efforts. Where a rental pool is made available in the course of the offering, what is really being sold to the purchaser is an investment contract whereby profits are expected to be produced, if at all, through the efforts of a party other than the purchaser-owner.

The court stated that the definition of an investment contract "embodies a flexible principle capable of adaptation to meet the countless and variable schemes devised by those who seek the use of the money of others on the promise of profits."

## Notes

| | | |
|---|---|---|
| **1.** | Hawaii *n.* | 夏威夷 |
| **2.** | to become interested in... | 對……表示有興趣 |
| **3.** | to buy sth. as an investment | 作為投資購買某物 |
| **4.** | licensed *a.* | 領有執照的 |
| **5.** | real estate broker | 房地產經紀人 |
| **6.** | condominium *n.* | 由個人占用的一套公寓房間（注意勿將它與 condom 「避孕套」相混） |
| **7.** | condominium unit | 公寓房中的一個單元 |
| **8.** | for sale | 供出售 |
| **9.** | to be located in... | 位於……地方 |
| **10.** | a resort complex | 勝地建築群 |
| **11.** | to participate in... | 參與；參加…… |
| **12.** | a rental pool agreement | 租金聯營協定 |
| **13.** | to enter into a rental pool agreement with... | 和……簽訂了一個租金聯營協定 |
| **14.** | subsequently *adv.* | 後來地 |
| **15.** | to file suit against sb. | 提起針對……的訴訟 |
| **16.** | to grant summary judgement | 作了即決審判 |
| **17.** | in favor of... | 對……有利 |
| **18.** | option *n.* | 選擇權 |
| **19.** | under federal securities laws | 根據聯邦證券法 |
| **20.** | to constitute *ve.* | 構成 |
| **21.** | reversed and remanded | （判決）被撤銷和發回重審 |
| **22.** | the Howey criteria | 哈威標準（Criteria in the Howey Test: a test to determine whether an instrument or contract is a security for purpose of federal securities laws） |

| | |
|---|---|
| 23. to motivate *vt.* | 促動；以……為動力 |
| 24. an interest in real estate | 不動產中的權益 |
| 25. collateral expectation of profits | 附屬性的作為擔保的利潤期待 |
| 26. investment contract | 投資契約 |
| 27. to pool the rents from... | 從……共用租金 |
| 28. in the course of... | 在……過程中；在……期間 |
| 29. to embody *vt.* | 包含 |
| 30. flexible *a.* | 靈活的 |
| 31. to be capable of... | 有能力…… |
| 32. adaptation *n.* | 適合；適應 |
| 33. countless *a.* | 無數的 |
| 34. variable *a.* | 易變的 |
| 35. schemes *n.* | 計畫；方案 |
| 36. to devise *vt.* | 想出；計畫；設計 |
| 37. to seek the use of... | 尋求使用…… |
| 38. on the promise of profits | 憑利潤允諾 |

## Additional case questions

1. Why did Hocking decide to buy a condominium in Hawaii?

2. For what reason did Hocking file suit against Dubois?

3. On what ground did the trial court grant summary judgment in favor of the defendantsDubois?

4. What is the content of the Howey criteria?

5. Was the offer of a condominium unit with an option to participate in a rental pool agreement a "security" under federal securities laws?

# (6) ESCOTT V. BARCHRIS CONSITUCTION CORP.

283 F. S. upp.643 (1968) United Sttes District Court. Southern District of New York

### FACTS

In 1961, BarChris Construction Corp.(BarChris), a company <u>primarily</u> engaged in the construction and sale of <u>bowling alleys</u>, was <u>in need</u> of additional <u>financing</u>. To <u>raise working</u>

capital, BarChris decided to issue debentures to investors. A registration statement, including a prospectus, was filed with the SEC on March 30, 1961. After two amendments, the registration statement became effective May 16, 1961. Peat, Marwick, Mitchell & Co.(Peat, Marwick) audited the financial statements of the company that were included in the registration statement and prospectus. The debentures were sold by May 24, 1961. Investors were provided a final prospectus concerning the debentures. Unknown to the investors, however, the registration statement and prospectus contained the following material misrepresentations and omissions of material fact:

1. Current assets on the 1960 balance sheet were overstated $609, 689 (15 percent).

2. Contingent liabilities as of April 30, 1961, were understated $618,853 (42 percent).

3. Sales for the quarter ending March 31, 1961, were overstated $519,810 (32 percent.)

4. Gross profit for the quarter ending March 31, 1961, was overstated $230,755 (92 percent).

5. Backlog of orders as of March 31, 1961, was overstated $4,490,000 (186 percent).

6. Loans to officers of BarChris of $386,615 were not disclosed.

7. Customer delinquencies and BarChris' potential liability thereto of $350,000 were not disclosed.

8. The use of the proceeds of the debentures to pay old debts was not disclosed.

In 1962, BarChris was failing financially, and on October 29, 1962, it filed a petition for protection to be recognized under federal bankruptcy law. On November 1, 1962, BarChris defaulted on interest payments due to be paid on the debentures to investors. Barry Escott and other purchasers of the debentures brought this civil action against executive officers, directors, and the outside accountants of BarChris. The plaintiffs alleged that the defendants had violated Section 11 of the Securities Act of 1993 by submitting misrepresentations and omissions of material facts in the registration statement filed with the SEC.

## ISSUE

Are the defendants liable for violating Section 11?

## DECISION

Yes. The district court held that the defendants had failed to prove their due diligence defenses.

## REASON

The district court addressed the liability of the individual defendants and the accounting firm.

***Russo.*** Russo was, <u>to all intents and purposes</u>, the chief executive officer of BarChris. He was a member of <u>the executive committee</u>. He was <u>familiar with</u> all aspects of the business. He was thoroughly <u>aware of</u> BarChris' <u>stringent financial condition</u> in May 1961. <u>In short</u>, Russo knew all the relevant facts. He could not have believed that there were no <u>untrue</u> statements or material omissions in the prospectus. Russo has no due diligence defenses.

***Vitolo and Pugliese.*** They were the <u>founders of</u> the business. Vitolo was <u>president</u> and Pugliese was <u>vice president</u>. Vitolo and Pugliese each are men of limited education. It is not hard to believe that for them the prospectus was <u>difficult reading</u>, if indeed they read it at all. But whether it was or not is <u>irrelevant</u>. The liability of director who signs a registration statement does not depend upon whether or not he read it or, if he did, whether or not he understood what he was reading. And in any case, there is nothing to show that they <u>made any investigation</u> of anything that they may not have known about or understood. They have not proved their due diligence defenses.

***Trilling.*** Trilling was BarChris's <u>controller</u>. He signed the registration statement <u>in that capacity</u>, although he was not a director. He was a <u>comparatively minor figure</u> in BarChris. He was not <u>considered an executive officer</u>. Trilling may well have been <u>unaware of</u> several of the inaccuracies in the <u>prospectus</u>. But he must have known of some of them. As a <u>financial officer</u>, he was familiar with BarChris's finances and with its <u>books of account</u>. Trilling did not <u>sustain the burden of</u> proving his due diligence defenses.

***Auslander.*** Auslander was an <u>"outside" director</u>, that is, one who was not an officer, of BarChris. He was chairman of the board of Valley Stream National Bank in Valley Stream, Long Island. In February 1961 Vitolo asked him to become a director of BarChris. Vitolo <u>gave him an enthusiastic account of</u> BarChris's <u>progress</u> and prospects. As an <u>inducements</u>, Vitolo said that when BarChris received the proceeds of a <u>forthcoming</u> issue of securities, it would deposit ＄1 million in Auslander's bank. Auslander was <u>elected a director</u> on April 17, 1961. The registration statement <u>in its original form</u> had already been filed, of course, <u>without his signature</u>. On May 10, 1961, he signed a signature page for the first amendment to the registration statement that was filed with the SEC on May 11, 1961. This was a separate sheet without any document attached. Auslander did not know that it was a signature page for a registration statement. He <u>vaguely</u> understood that it was something "for the SEC." Auslander never saw a copy of the registration statement <u>in its final form</u>. Section 11 imposes liability upon a director no matter how new he is. Auslander has not established his due diligence defenses.

***Peat, Marwick.*** Peat, Marwick's work was <u>in general charge of</u> a member of the firm Cummings, and more immediately in charge of Peat, Marwick's manager, Logan. Most of the actual work was performed by a senior accountant, Berardi, who had junior assistants, one of whom was Kennedy. Berardi was then about 30 years old. He was not yet a CPA. He had had no previous experience with the bowling industry. This was his first job as a senior accountant. He could hardly have been given a more difficult assignment.

First and foremost is Berardi's failure to discover that Capital Lanes had not been sold. This error affected both the sales figure and the liability side of the balance sheet. Berrdi erred in computing the contingent liabilities. Berardi did not make a reasonable investigation in this instance. The purpose of reviewing events subsequent to the date of a certified balance sheet (referred to as an S-1 review when made with reference to a registration statement) is to ascertain whether any material change has occurred in the company's financial position that should be disclosed in order to prevent the balance sheet figures from being misleading. The scope of such a review, under generally accepted uniting standards, is limited. It does not amount to a complete audit. Berardi made the S-1 review in May 1961. He devoted a little over two days to it, a total of 20 1/2 hours. He did not discover any of the errors or omissions pertaining to the state of affairs in 1961, all of which were material. Apparently the only BarChris officer with whom Berardi communicated was Trilling. He could not recall making any inquiries of Russo, Vitolo, or Pugliese. In conducting the S-1 review, Berardi did not examine any important financial records other than the trial balance. As to minutes, he read only the board of directors' minutes of BarChris. He did not read such minutes as there were of the executive committee. He did not know that there was an executive committee. He did not read the minutes of any subsidiary. He asked questions, he got answers that he considered satisfactory, and he did nothing to verify them.

Berardi had no conception of how tight the cash position was. He did not discover that BarChris was holding up checks in substantial amounts because there was no money in the bank to cover them. He did not know of the officers' loans. Since he never read the prospectus, he was not even aware that there had ever been any problem about loans. There had been a material change for the worse in BarChris's financial position. That change was sufficiently serious so that the failure to disclose it made the 1960 figures misleading. Berardi did not discover it. As far as results were concerned, his S-1 review was useless.

Accountants should not be held to a standard higher than that recognized in their profession. Berardi's review did not come up to that standard. He did not take some of the steps that Peat, Marwick's written program prescribed. He did not spend an adequate amount of time on a task of this magnitude. Most important of all, he was too easily satisfied with glib answers to his inquiries. There were enough danger signals to require some further investigation on his part. Generally accepted accounting standards required such further investigation under these circumstances. It is not always sufficient merely to ask questions. Here, again, <u>the burden of proof in on Peat</u>, Marwick, That burden has not been satisfied. Peat, Marwick has not established its due diligence defense.

## CASE QUESTIONS

### CRITICAL LEGAL THINKING

Should defendants in a Section 11 lawsuit be permitted to prove a due diligence defense to the imposition of liability? Or should liability be strictly imposed?

### ETHICS

Who do you think committed the fraud in this case? Did any of the other defendants act unethically in this case?

### BUSINESS IMPLICATION

Who do you think bore the burden of paying the judgment in this case?

## Notes

1. primarily *adv.* 主要地
2. bowling alleys 滾球巷道
3. in need of... 需要……
4. additional financing 額外的融資
5. to raise working capital 籌措流動資金或周轉資金
6. to issue debenture to investors 向投資者發行公司債券（在英國 debenture 常指以公司資產做抵押的公司債券）
7. registration statement 註冊說明書（包括證券募集書 prospectus）In the USA, a lengthy document that has to be lodged with the SEC. It contains all the information relevant to a new securities issue that will enable an investor to make an informed decision whether or not to purchase the security.
8. to be filed with the SEC 交給證券交易委員會備案
9. amendment *n.* 改正；修正
10. to become effective （法律上）生效
11. to audit *vt.* 查帳；審計

| | |
|---|---|
| **12.** financial statements | 財務報表（包括「資產負債表」balance sheet，「損益表」income statement 和「現金流量表」statement of cash flow） |
| **13.** concerning the debenture | 關於公司債券 |
| **14.** unknown to sb. | 不被某人所知 |
| **15.** material misrepresentation | 重要錯誤陳述或說明 |
| **16.** material fact | 主要或重要事實 |
| **17.** to overstate *vt.* | 誇大 |
| **18.** current assets | 流動資產 |
| **19.** contingent liabilities | 或有負債；不確定負債 |
| **20.** to understate *vt.* | 不充分的陳述 |
| **21.** gross profit | 毛利 |
| **22.** backlog of orders | 已接受訂貨總數 |
| **23.** customer delinquencies | 顧客犯罪行為 |
| **24.** potential liability | 可能發生的債務責任 |
| **25.** proceeds *n.* | 收入；收益 |
| **26.** to fail financially | 財政上失敗；破產 |
| **27.** to file a petition for protection | 提出獲得保護的請求 |
| **28.** under federal bankruptcy law | 根據聯邦破產法 |
| **29.** civil action | 民事訴訟 |
| **30.** executive officers | 執事的高級職員 |
| **31.** to default on interest payments | 到期不付利息；拖欠利息的支付 |
| **32.** to submit *vt.* | 提交 |
| **33.** to be liable for violating section 11 | 承擔違反第11款的責任 |
| **34.** outside accountants | 外部會計師 |
| **35.** to prove one's due diligence defenses | 證明某人擁有應有的勤奮抗辯 |
| **36.** to address *vt.* | 處理 |
| **37.** to all intent and purposes | 實際上；實質上 |
| **38.** the chief executive officer (CEO) | （公司）首席執行長；首席業務領導人；企業最高業務領導人 |
| **39.** executive committee | 執行委員會 |

**40.** to be thoroughly aware of...　　　對……徹底瞭解

**41.** stringent financial condition　　　吃緊的財政狀況

**42.** in short　　　簡言之；總之

**43.** untrue *a.*　　　不真實的；假的

**44.** founders of the business　　　企業的創辦人

**45.** president *n.*　　　（美）企業的總裁

**46.** vice president　　　（美）副總裁

**47.** to be difficult reading = be
difficult to read

**48.** irrelevant *a.*　　　不相干的

**49.** to make investigation of...　　　調查某事

**50.** controller *n.*　　　總會計師

**51.** in that capacity　　　以那個資格或身分

**52.** comparatively *adv.*　　　相當地；比較地

**53.** minor figure　　　小人物

**54.** executive officer　　　（公司）執事高級職員

**55.** to be unaware of...　　　不知道……

**56.** inaccuracies *n.*　　　不準確之處

**57.** prospectus *n.*　　　招股說明書；證券募集書

**58.** financial officer　　　財務主任

**59.** to be familiar with...　　　對……熟悉

**60.** book of account　　　帳冊；帳簿

**61.** to sustain the burden of
proving one's due diligence
defences　　　承受證明某人應有勤奮抗辯的舉證責任

**62.** outside director　　　外部董事

**63.** to give sb. an account of
sth.　　　向某人解釋某事

**64.** inducement *n.*　　　引誘；勸誘

**65.** to receive the proceeds
of a forthcoming issue of
securities　　　得到即將發行證券的款項

**66.** to be elected a director　　　被選為董事

**67.** in its original form　　　以原形

**68.** a separate sheet without
any document attached　　　是單獨成頁沒有與任何文件附在一起

**69.** vaguely *adv.*　　　不明確地；含糊地

| | | |
|---|---|---|
| **70.** in general charge of... | 全面負責…… | |
| **71.** to perform the actual work | 做實際工作 | |
| **72.** senior accountant | 高級會計師；主任會計師 | |
| **73.** junior assistant | 年輕的助理 | |
| **74.** CPA = Certified Public Accountant | 註冊會計師 | |
| **75.** to have no previous experience with... | 以前沒有……方面的經驗 | |
| **76.** bowling industry | 保齡球產業 | |
| **77.** to be given a difficult assignment | 接受一項困難的任務 | |
| **78.** first and foremost | 首先 | |
| **79.** to err in doing sth. | 在做某事方面出錯 | |
| **80.** in this instance | 在此情況下 | |
| **81.** with reference to | 關於…… | |
| **82.** to ascertain *vt.* | 確定；查明 | |
| **83.** financial position | 財務狀況 | |
| **84.** misleading *a.* | 有誤導性的 | |
| **85.** to amount to... | 等於…… | |
| **86.** complete audit | 詳細審計；全面查帳 | |
| **87.** to make a review | 進行檢查 | |
| **88.** to devote a little over two days to sth. | 在某事上花費2天多的時間 | |
| **89.** pertaining to | 關於…… | |
| **90.** apparently *adv.* | 顯而易見地 | |
| **91.** to communicate with sb. | 與某人溝通 | |
| **92.** to recall doing sth. | 回憶做某事；回想做某事 | |
| **93.** to make inquiries of sb. about sth. | 向某人詢問某事 | |
| **94.** in conducting the S-1 review | 在做第1款第1條中的審查時 | |
| **95.** financial records | 財務紀錄 | |
| **96.** as to minutes | 至於會議紀錄 | |
| **97.** board of directors | 董事會 | |
| **98.** to read the minutes of a subsidiary | 閱讀一個子公司的會議紀錄 | |
| **99.** to verify *vt.* | 證實；查證 | |

| | |
|---|---|
| **100.** to have no conception of... | 對……完全不懂 |
| **101.** how tight the cash position was | 現金狀況有多麼吃緊 |
| **102.** to hold up checks in substantial amounts | 大額支票的支付被耽擱或推遲 |
| **103.** because there was no money in the bank to cover them | 因為銀行裡無錢可用來對它們進行支付 |
| **104.** a material change for the worse | 一個使情況變糟的重大變化 |
| **105.** to be held to a standard | 使……堅持一個標準 |
| **106.** to take steps | 採取步驟 |
| **107.** magnitude *n.* | 巨大；重大 a task of this ～如此重大任務 |
| **108.** glib *a.* | 隨便的；油嘴滑舌的 |

**109.** trial balance：試算表

A listing of the balances on all the accounts of an organization with debit balances in one column and credit balances in the other. If the processes of double-entry book-keeping have been accurate, the totals of each column should be the same. If they are not the same, checks must be carried out to find the discrepancy. The figures in the trial balance after some adjustments, e.g. for closing stocks, prepayments and accruals, depreciation, etc, are used to prepare the final accounts (profit and loss account and balance sheet).

## Further discussion questions on the case

**1.** What's wrong with the registration statement?

**2.** What material misrepresentations and omissions were contained in the registration statement?

**3.** Why are the defendants liable for violating section 11?

**4.** What is trial balance? Did Berardi examine it? If he didn't what liabilities he must bear?

# (7) SECURITIES AND EXCHANGE COMMISSION V. TEXAS GULF SULPHUR CO.

## 401 F. 2d 833(1968) United States Court of Appeals, Second Circuit

### FACTS

Texas Gulf Sulphur Co.(TGS) had for several years conducted aerial geophysical surveys in eastern Canada. On November 12, 1963, TGS drilled an exploratory hole-Kidd 55-near Timmins, Ontario. Assay reports showed that the ore from this drilling proved to be remarkably high in copper, zinc, and silver. Since TGS did not own the mineral rights to properties surrounding the drill site, TGS kept the discovery secret, camouflaged the drill site, and diverted drilling efforts to another site. This allowed TGS to engage in extensive land acquisition around Kidd 55.

Eventually, rumors of a rich mineral strike began circulating. On Saturday, April 11, 1964, the New York Times and the New York Herald Tribune published unauthorized reports of TGS drilling efforts in Canada and its rich mineral strike. On Sunday, April 12, officers of TGS met with a public relations consultant and drafted a press release that was issued that afternoon. The press release appeared in morning newspapers of general circulation on Monday, April 13. It read in pertinent part.

The work done to date has not been sufficient to reach definite conclusions and any statement as to size and grade of ore would be premature and possibly misleading. When we have progressed to the point where reasonable and logical conclusions can be made, TGS will issue a definite statement to its stockholders and to the public in order to clarify the Timmins project.

The rumors persisted. On April 16, 1994, at 10:00 A.M., TGS held a press conference for the financial media. At this conference, which lasted about 10 minutes, TGS disclosed the richness of the Timmins' mineral strike and that the strike would run to at least 25 million tons of ore. In early November 1963, TGS stock was trading at $ 17 3/8 per share. On April 15, 1964, the stock closed at $ 29 3/8. Several officers, directors, and other employees of TGS who had knowledge of the mineral strike at Timmins traded in the stock of TGS during the period November 12, 1963, and April 16, 1964. By May 15, 1964, he stock was selling at $ 58 1/4.

The securities and Exchange Commission(SEC) brought this action against David M. Crawford and Francis G. Coates, two TGS executives who possessed the nonpublic information about the ore strike and who traded in TGS securities. The SEC sought to rescind their stock purchases. The district court found Crawford liable for insider trading but dismissed the complaint against Coates. Appeals were taken from this judgment.

## ISSUE

Are Crawford and Coates liable for trading on material inside information in violation of Section 10(b) and Rule 10b-5?

## DECISION

Yes. The court of appeals held that both executives, Crawford and Coates, had engaged in illegal insider trading.

## REASON

The insiders here were not trading on an equal footing with the outside investors. They alone were in a position to evaluate the probability and magnitude of what seemed from the outset to be a major ore strike.

***Crawford.*** Crawford telephoned his orders to his Chicago broker about midnight on April 15 and again at 8:30 on the morning of April 16 with instructions to buy at the opening of the Midwest Stock Exchange that morning. The trial court's finding that "he sought to, and did, 'beat the news,'" is well documented by the record. Before insiders may act upon material information, such information must have been effectively disclosed in a manner sufficient to ensure its availability to the investing public. Particularly here, where a formal announcement to the entire financial news media had been promised in a prior official release known to the media, all insider activity must await dissemination of the promised official announcement.

***Coates.*** Coates was absolved by the court below because his telephone order was placed shortly before 10:20 A.M. on April 16, which was after the announcement had been made even though the news could not be considered already a mater of public information. This result seems to have been predicated upon a misinterpretation of dicta in Cady, Roberts, where the SEC instructed insiders to "keep out of the market until the established procedures for public release of the information are carried out instead of hastening to execute transactions in advance of, and in frustration of, the objectives of the release." The reading of a news release, which prompted Coates into action, is merely the first step in the process of dissemination required for compliance with the regulatory objective of providing all investors with an equal opportunity to make informed investment judgments. Assuming that the contents of the official release could instantaneously be acted upon, at the minimum Coates should have waited until the news could reasonably have been expected to appear over the media of widest circulation, the Dow Jones broad tape, rather than hastening to ensure and advantage to hisself and his broker son-in-law.

## CASE QUESTIONS

### ITICAL LEGAL THINKING

Should insider trading be illegal? Why or why not?

### ETHICS

Did Crawford and Coates act ethically in this case?

### BUSINESS IMPLICAION

How can businesses protect against their employees engaging in insider trading? Explain.

## Notes

| | | |
|---|---|---|
| 1. | to conduct aerial geophysical surveys | 進行空中地球物理的勘測 |
| 2. | to drill an exploratory hole | 鑽了一個勘探用的洞 |
| 3. | Ontario *n.* | （加）安大略 |
| 4. | drilling *n.* | 鑽探 |
| 5. | the ore from the drilling | 所鑽的礦砂或礦石 |
| 6. | to prove to be remarkably high in copper | 證明有非常高品位的銅 |
| 7. | zinc *n.* | 鋅 |
| 8. | mineral rights | 開礦權 |
| 9. | properties surrounding the drill site | 鑽孔處周圍的地產 |
| 10. | to keep sth. secret | 保持某事的秘密 |
| 11. | to camouflage *vt.* | 偽裝 |
| 12. | to divert drilling efforts to another site | 將鑽探努力轉移到另一個地點 |
| 13. | to engage in extensive land acquisition | 進行廣泛的土地探測 |
| 14. | eventually *adv.* | 最後；最終 |
| 15. | rumors *n.* | 謠傳 |
| 16. | a rich mineral strike | 豐富礦產的意外發現 |
| 17. | to circulate *vi.* | 流傳開 |
| 18. | the New York Times | 紐約時報 |
| 19. | the New York Herald Tribune | 紐約先驅論壇報 |
| 20. | to publish an authorized reports | 發表了未被授權的報導 |
| 21. | public relations consultant | 公共關係顧問 |

**22.** to draft a press release 　　　　起草一份新聞稿

**23.** to issue *vt.* 　　　　發布

**24.** general circulation 　　　　廣泛流傳

**25.** pertinent *a.* 　　　　有關的

**26.** to date 　　　　到此刻為止

**27.** to reach definite conclusions 　　　　得出肯定的結論

**28.** as to 　　　　至於；關於

**29.** grade of ore 　　　　礦的等級

**30.** premature *a.* 　　　　過早的；不成熟的

**31.** to make logical conclusion 　　　　作出有邏輯性的結論

**32.** to clarify *vt.* 　　　　澄清

**33.** to persist *vi.* 　　　　持續保留

**34.** to hold a press conference 　　　　舉行記者招待會

**35.** the financial media 　　　　負責金融消息報導的媒體

**36.** richness of the mineral strike 　　　　意外發現礦產的豐富

**37.** to run to... 　　　　達到……

**38.** per share 　　　　每股

**39.** the stock closed at $ 29 $\frac{3}{8}$ 　　　　收盤時每股價為 29 $\frac{3}{8}$ 美元

**40.** to have knowledge of... 　　　　知道……

**41.** to trade in the stock of TGS 　　　　做 TGS 這支股票的買賣交易

**42.** non-public *a.* 　　　　非公開的；非公共的

**43.** insider activity 　　　　知情人的交易活動；內幕人的交易活動；內線人的買賣活動

**44.** dissemination of the promised official announcement 　　　　發布承諾的官方公告

**45.** to be absolved by the court 　　　　被法庭寬恕

**46.** shortly before 10: 20 A.M 　　　　早晨 10 點 20 分前不久

**47.** to place one's telephone order 　　　　用電話下訂單

**48.** to predict *vt.* 　　　　預言；預告

**49.** dicta *n.* 　　　　名言；格言（其單數為 dictum）

**50.** to keep out of the market 　　　　置身於市場之外

**51.** the established procedures 　　　　規定的程式

**52.** public release of the information 　　　　資訊的公開發表

**53.** to hasten to execute transaction 　　　　匆忙完成交易

**54.** in frustration of... 　　　　使……受挫

**55.** objectives *n.*                       目標；目的

**56.** in advance of...                   在……的前面

**57.** news release                    新聞稿

**58.** to prompt sb. into action      促使某人行動

**59.** to act upon...                   按照……行動

**60.** instantaneously *adv.*         立即地

**61.** at the minimum                至少

**62.** son-in-law *n.*                女婿（複數為 sons-in-law）

**63.** to beat the news             超越此新聞

# (8) UNITED STATES V. CHESTMAN

947 F. 2d 551(1991) United States Court of Appeals. Second Circuit

## FACTS

Waldbaum, Inc., was a publicly traded company that owned a large supermarket chain. Julia Waldbaum was a member of the board of directors, shareholder, and wife of the company's founder. Her son, Ira Waldbaum, was the president and controlling shareholder of the company. Ira's sister, Shirley Waldbaum Witkin, was a shareholder. Shirley's daughter, Susan Loeb, a shareholder, was married to Keith Loeb.

On November 21, 1986, Ira Waldbaum agreed to sell his controlling interest in Waldbaum, Inc., to Great Atlantic and Pacific Tea Company(A&P), a national supermarket chain, for ＄50 per share. A&P agreed to make the same offer to other family members and then make a public tender offer for the remaining shares at ＄50 per share. Ira told Shirley, who told Susan, who in turn told Keith.

Keith telephoned his securities broker, Robert Chestman, and told Chestman of the impending sale. Chestman purchased 3,000 shares of Waldbaum, Inc., for his own account at ＄24.65 per share. He purchased 8,000 shares for clients' accounts at prices ranging from ＄25.75 to ＄26.00 per share. At the close of trading on November 26, A&P's tender offer was publicly announced. Waldbaum, Inc.'s stock then rose to ＄49 per share on the next business day.

When the U.S.government investigated the excessive trading in Waldbaum's stock prior to the tender offer, Keith Loeb agreed to cooperate with the government. A grand jury returned an indictment against Chestman, charging him with fraudulent trading in violation of Section 10(b) and Rule 10b-5. At trial, Chestman was found guilty. A panel of the court of appeals reversed Chestman's convictions. A majority of the judges of the court of appeals voted to rehear en banc the panel's decision.

## ISSUE

Is Chestman criminally guilty of violating Section 10(b) and Rule 10b-5?

## DECISION

No. The court of appeals, sitting en banc, agreed that Chestman had not violated Section 10(b) and Rule 10b-5.

## REASON

Chestman was indicted as a "tippee." A tippee is not liable for trading on nonpublic information unless (1) he or she knew or should have known that it was nonpublic information, and (2) the insider-tipper breached his or her fiduciary duty by tipping the information. The court of appeals found the second element missing in this case. The court held that family relationships and marriage do not, without more, create a fiduciary relationship: "The court stated," "It is clear that the relationships involved in this case-those between Keith and Susan Loeb and between the Waldbaum family-were not traditional fiduciary relationships." Because the tippers who tipped Keith Loeb(Ira, Shirley, and Susan) did not breach their fiduciary relationship in doing so, the second element of tippee liability is not met.

 **CASE QUESTIONS**

### CRITICAL LEGAL THINKING

Do you think Section 10(b) and Rule 10b-5 were violated in this case? Is this a confusing area of the law?

### ETHICS

Did Keith Loeb act ethically in tipping Chestman? Did Chestman act ethically in trading on the tip?

### BUSINESS IMPLICATION

Should you receive nonpublic information as a tip, what do you hope has happened prior to that time?

## ♣ Notes

| | | |
|---|---|---|
| 1. | publicly traded company | 公開發行股票的公司 |
| 2. | supermarket chain | 連鎖超市 |
| 3. | a member of the board of directors | 董事會成員 |
| 4. | the company's founder | 公司創辦人 |
| 5. | controlling share holder | 控股股東 |
| 6. | to be married to sb. | 與某人結婚 |
| 7. | controlling interest | 多數股權；控股權 |
| 8. | to make the same offer | 作同樣要約 |
| 9. | to make public tender offer | 用公開招標方式出售證券 |
| 10. | the remaining shares | 剩餘的股份 |
| 11. | securities broker | 證券經紀人 |
| 12. | the impending sale | 即將發生的銷售 |
| 13. | to tell sb. of sth. | 告訴某人某件事情 |
| 14. | for one's own account | 為某人自己的緣故 |
| 15. | ranging from...to... | 在……範圍內 |
| 16. | at the close of trading | 在交易結束時 |
| 17. | to rise to... | 漲到…… |
| 18. | on the next business day | 在第二天營業日 |
| 19. | excessive trading | 過多交易 |
| 20. | to cooperate with | 與……合作 |
| 21. | a grand jury | 大陪審團（在美國多半由 16-23 人組成） |
| 22. | to return an indictment against sb. | 正式宣布一項針對某人的公訴 |
| 23. | to charge sb. with fraudulent trading | 指控某人進行欺詐性交易 |
| 24. | to be found guilty | 被查明有罪；被裁決有罪 |
| 25. | at trial | 在審判時 |
| 26. | panel n. | 全體陪審員 |
| 27. | to reverse sb's convictions | 推翻對某人的定罪 |
| 28. | to rehear en banc the panel's decision | 全體出庭法官重新審理陪審團的裁定 |
| 29. | sitting en banc | 全體出庭法官聽審 |
| 30. | to be indicted as a "tippee" | 作為被密告者受控告 |
| 31. | the insider-tipper | 知情人；告密者 |

| | |
|---|---|
| **32.** to breach one's fiduciary duty by tipping the information | 用向別人告知秘密資訊方式違反了某人的受託人責任 |
| **33.** to find sth. missing | 發現缺少某物 |
| **34.** to create a fiduciary relationship | 建立信託關係 |
| **35.** tippee liability | 被密告者責任 |
| **36.** confusing area | 令人困惑的領域 |

## Further questions on the case

**1**. What is the meaning of tender offer?

**2**. What is meant by sitting en banc?

**3**. Under what circumstances is a tippee liable for trading on non-public information under American Securities laws?

## 18 | American Intellectual Property

# (1) MCNELL-P.C.C., INC. V. BRISTOL-MYERS QUIBB CO.

### 938 F. 2d 1544(1991) United States Court of Appeals, Second Circuit

## FACTS

McNeil-P.C.C., Inc. (McNeil), the leading manufacturer of over-the-counter analgesic pain remedies, markets Extra-Strength Tylenol (Tylenol). A two-tablet dose of Tylenol contains 1,000 milligrams of acetaminophen. In the spring of 1990, Bristol-Myers Squibb Company(Bristol-Myers) began marketing a competing analgesic pain remedy called Aspirin-Free Excedrin(Excedrin). A two tablet dose of Excedrin cotains 1,000 milligrams of acetaminophen plus 130 milligrams of caffeine. To market its new pain reliever, Bristol-Myers sent promotional literature to drug retailers and began a television advertising campaign that claimed that Excedrin "works better" than Tylenol. The claim was based on a "cross-over" study conducted by Bristol-Myers. A cross-over study has the patients take one drug in period one and another drug in period two and then evaluates the performance of both drugs. Because McNeil believed that the Bristol-Myers "works better" claim was false, it sued Bristol-Myers for violating Section 43(a) of the Lanham Act. The district court held in favor of McNeil and permanently enjoined Bristol-Myers from making such a claim. Bristol-Myers appealed.

## ISSUE

Did defendant Bristol-Myers make false adverttising claims about the superiority of its product in violation of the Lanham Act?

## DECISION

Yes. The court of appeals held that Bristol-Myers had made false advertising claims and therefore violated the Lanham Act.

## REASON

The evidence showed that the period one tests showed no <u>statistical</u> difference between the performance of Excedrin and Tylenol. The court found that although period two tests showed a slight difference, the results were <u>tainted</u> because they were <u>distorted</u> by <u>psychological</u> effects. Consequently, the court <u>determined</u> that the Bristol-Myers tests did not prove the superiority of its product. McNeil proved that the Bristol-Myers "works better" claim was false.

 **CASE QUESTIONS**

### CRITICAL LEGAL THINKING

Should false advertising constitute a tort?

### ETHICS

Did Bristol-Myers act <u>ethically</u> in making its "works better" claim?

### BUSINESS IMPLICATION

Should companies be permitted to engage in <u>comparative</u> advertising? If so, when?

 **Notes**

| | | |
|---|---|---|
| 1. | second circuit | （美）第二巡迴法庭 |
| 2. | leading manufacturer | 主要生產廠商 |
| 3. | over-the-counter | 場外；店頭 |
| 4. | analgesic pain remedies | 止痛藥 |
| 5. | two-tablet dose | 一服或一劑兩片 |
| 6. | milligram *n.* | 毫克 |
| 7. | acetaminophen *n.* | 乙醯胺酚 |
| 8. | to market *vt.* | 銷售 |
| 9. | Aspirin-Free Excedrin | 不含阿斯匹林的艾克賽丁 |
| 10. | caffeine *n.* | 咖啡因 |
| 11. | pain reliever | 止痛藥（= pain killer） |
| 12. | promotion literature | 促銷廣告或傳單 |
| 13. | drug retailer | 藥物零售商 |
| 14. | television advertising campaign | 電視廣告運動 |
| 15. | Tylenol *n.* | 泰諾（一種止痛藥名） |
| 16. | cross-over study | 交叉服用研究 |

**17.** to conduct a study 　　　　　進行一項研究

**18.** to violate *vt.* 　　　　　　　違反（法規……）

**19.** district court 　　　　　　　（美國聯邦法院的）地區法院

**20.** permanently *adv.* 　　　　　永久地

**21.** to enjoin sb.from doing sth. 　禁止某人做某事

**22.** statistical *a.* 　　　　　　　統計的

**23.** to taint *vt.* 　　　　　　　　使感染

**24.** to distort *vt.* 　　　　　　　歪曲

**25.** psychological effects 　　　　心理（上的）作用

**26.** to determine *vt.* 　　　　　　確定

**27.** ethically *adv.* 　　　　　　　倫理上；道德上

**28.** comparative advertising 　　　比較性廣告

# (2) MITCHELL V. GLOBE INTERNATIONAL PUBLISHING INC.
### 978 F.2d 1065(1992) United States Court of Appeals. Eighth Circuit

### FACTS

　Globe International, Inc.(Globe) publishes several supermarket tabloids, including the National Examiner and the Sun. In 1980, the National Examiner published an article about Nellie Mitchell, a 96-year-old Arkansas woman, a single parent who had raised her family on what she earned from delivering newspapers. A photograph of Mitchell accompanied the article. On October 2, 1990, the the Sun published a front-page headline story "Pregnancy Forces Granny to Quit Work at Age101." The story purported to be about a woman named Audrey Wiles from Stirling, Australia. Supposedly, Audrey delivered newspapers for 94 years before she became pregnant by a reclusive millionaire she met on her route. The previously published photograph of Mitchell was published on the Sun's cover as being that of Audrey Wiles. When the Sun walnt published, Mitchell, who was then 106, suffered severe humiliation and embarrassments. She sued Globe for false light invasion of privacy. The jury returned a verdict awarding her ＄650,000 in compensatory damages and ＄850,000 in punitive damages. Globe appealed.

### ISSUE

　Was Globe International, Inc., liable for the tort of false light invasion of privacy?

## DECISION

Yes. The appellate court held that Globe had committed the tort of false light invasion of privacy by publishing the photograph of Nellie Mitchell as that of a pregnant <u>centenarian</u>. The appellate court <u>upheld</u> the award of punitive damages but <u>remanded the case</u> to the trial court with instructions to reduce the award of compensatory damages.

## REASON

The appellate court held that the plaintiff proved that (1) the false light in which she was <u>placed</u> by the <u>publicity</u> would be highly <u>offensive</u> to a reasonable person, and (2) the defendant acted with actual malice in publishing the article. Globe <u>asserted</u> that the story was "<u>pure fiction</u>" and that no reasonable reader could have believed it. The court <u>rejected</u> this argument, noting that <u>the format and style of the newspaper</u> suggest that its contents are based on fact. The court held that Globe acted <u>maliciously</u>. It <u>cited evidence</u> that the editor of the pregnancy story was the same editor who had written the original story about Nellie Mitchell and that he intentionally used her picture for the second story because he thought she was dead.

## CASE QUESTIONS

### CRITICAL LEGAL THINKING

Should the courts recognize the tort of invasion of privacy? Why or why not?

### FTHICS

Did Globe act ethically in this case? Do you think many stories in supermarket tabloids are fictitious?

### BUSINESS IMPLICATION

Did the facts of this case warrant the imposition of punitive damages?

### Notes

1. supermarket *n.* — 超市
2. tabloid *n.* — （以轟動性為特點的、多圖畫的）小報
3. the Sun — 太陽報
4. to raise one's family on what one earns — 用某人掙來的錢養家
5. to deliver newspapers — 送報紙

| | |
|---|---|
| **6.** front-page headline | 頭版大標題 |
| **7.** pregnancy *n.* | 懷孕 |
| **8.** granny *n.* | 老奶奶；老婆婆 |
| **9.** to quit work | 放棄工作 |
| **10.** to purport *vt.* | 大意是…… |
| **11.** to become pregnant by sb. | 某人使其懷孕 |
| **12.** reclusive *a.* | 隱退的；幽居的 |
| **13.** millionaire *n.* | 百萬富翁 |
| **14.** on one's route | 在路上 |
| **15.** cover *n.* | 封面 |
| **16.** to suffer severe humiliation and embarrasment | 遭到嚴重羞辱和窘迫 |
| **17.** jury *n.* | 陪審團 |
| **18.** light invasion of privacy | 輕微的隱私侵犯 |
| **19.** compensatory damages | 補償金；賠償金 |
| **20.** punitive damages | 懲罰性損害賠償金 |
| **21.** tort *n.* | 侵權（罪）to commit a tort 實施侵權行為 |
| **22.** centenarian *n.* | 百歲或百歲以上的老人 |
| **23.** to uphold *vt.* | 堅持 |
| **24.** award *n.* | 判定 |
| **25.** to remand *vt.* | 發回案件讓下級法院重審 |
| **26.** the fake light | 虛假的見解或眼光 |
| **27.** offensive *a.* | 冒犯的；令人作嘔的 |
| **28.** malice *n.* | 惡意 |
| **29.** to assert *vt.* | 斷言；宣稱 |
| **30.** maliciously *adv.* | 惡意地 |
| **31.** to cite evidence | 引用證據 |
| **32.** pure fiction | 純屬虛構 |
| **33.** fictious *a.* | 虛構的 |

# (3) WHITE V. SAMSUNG ELECTRONICS MERICA, INC.

### 971 F. 2d 1395(1991) United States Court of Appeals, Ninth Circuit

## FACTS

Vanna White is the <u>hostess</u> of "The Wheel of Fortune," one of the most <u>popular game shows</u>

in television history. An estimated 40 million people watch the program daily. Capitalizing on her fame, White markets her identity to various advertisers. Samsung Electronics America, Inc. (Samsung) distributes various electronics products in the United States. Samsung and its advertising agency, David Deutsch Associates, Inc. (Deutsch), devised a series of advertisements that followed the same theme. Each depicted a current item of popular culture and a Samsung electronics product. The advertisements were set in the twenty-first century in order to convey the message that the Samsung product would still be in use at that time.

The advertisement that prompted the current dispute was for Samsung videocassette recorders (VCRs). The ad depicted a robot that was outfitted to resemble White. The set in which the robot was posed was instantly recognizable as "The Wheel of Fortune" game show set, and the robot's stance was one for which White is famous. The caption of the ad read: "Longes-trunning game show. 2012 A.D." Defendants referred to the ad as the "Vanna White" ad. White did not consent to the ads and was not paid. White sued Samsung and Deutsch to recover damages for alleged misappropriation of her right to publicity. The district court granted defendants' motions for summary judgment. White appealed.

## ISSUE

Did White properly plead the claim of misappropriation of the right to publicity?

## DECISION

Yes. The court of appeals held that the law of misappropriation of the right of publicity had been properly pleaed by White under the facts of this case. The court reversed and remanded the case. The case went to trial, and in January 1994 the jury awarded Vanna White $ 403, 000 in damages.

## REASON

The individual aspects of the advertisement in the present case say little. Viewed together, though, they leave little doubt about whom the celebrity is that the ad meant to depict. Although the female-shaped robot was dressed exactly like Vanna White dresses at times, so do many other women. The look-alike robot is in the process of turning a block letter on a gameboard, but similarly attired Scrabble-playing women may do this as well. But the robot is standing on what looks to be "The Wheel of Fortune" game show set-and Vanna White is the only one who dresses like this and turns setters on "The Wheel of Fortune" game show. Indeed, the defendants themselves referred to their ad as the "Vanna White" ad. Television exposure created Vanna White's marketable celebrity value. The court stated, "The law protects the celebrity's sole right to exploit this value whether the celebrity has achieved her fame out of rare ability, dumb luck, or a combination thereof."

## CASE QUESTIONS

### CRITICAL LEGAL THINKING

Should the right to publicity be a protected right? Why or why not?

### ETHICS

Did Samsung act ethically in using Vanna White's celebrity status without getting her permission or paying her?

### BUSINESS IMPLICATION

Sometimes the worth of a celebrity's publicity goes up in value after his or her death. Can you think of any examples?

## Notes

| | | |
|---|---|---|
| **1.** | hostess *n.* | 女服務員 |
| **2.** | popular game shows | 流行的或大眾喜愛的遊戲節目 |
| **3.** | program *n.* | 節目 |
| **4.** | to capitalize on... | 利用…… |
| **5.** | to market her identity to sb. | 將她的身分出售給某人 |
| **6.** | advertiser *n.* | 登廣告的人 |
| **7.** | to distribute various electronics products | 銷售不同的電子產品 |
| **8.** | advertising agency | 廣告代理 |
| **9.** | to devise *vt.* | 想出；設計 |
| **10.** | theme *n.* | 題目；主題 |
| **11.** | to depict *vt.* | 描繪 |
| **12.** | to convey *vt.* | 轉達 |
| **13.** | to prompt *vt.* | 引起；激起 |
| | to ～ the current dispute | 引起現在的爭論 |
| **14.** | Samsung Videocassette recorders | 三星卡式錄影機 |
| **15.** | ad. *n.* | 廣告（「advertisement」的縮寫） |
| **16.** | robot *n.* | 機器人 |

**17.** to outfit *vt.*      準備；配備

**18.** to resemble *vt.*      像；類似

**19.** to pose *vt.*      擺好姿勢

**20.** recognizable *a.*      可被認出的；可辨認的

**21.** stance *n.*      姿態

**22.** to refer to sth. as...      稱某物為……

**23.** to consent to sth.      同意某事；贊同某事

**24.** alleged *a.*      被宣稱的

**25.** misappropriation *n.*      濫用

**26.** publicity *n.*      宣傳；廣告，right to publicity 廣告權

**27.** motions *n.*      申請；請求

**28.** summary judgement      即決審判

**29.** properly *adv.*      適當地

**30.** to plead *vt.*      請求

**31.** to reverse and remand the case      撤銷並發回此案件重審

**32.** to award sb. $100 in damages      裁定給某人 100 美元的損害賠償金

**33.** celebrity *n.*      著名

**34.** female-shaped *a.*      女性形狀的

**35.** at times      有時；平時

**36.** look-like *a.*      看上去相似的

**37.** in the process of...      在……過程中

**38.** gameboard *n.*      遊戲板

**39.** attired *a.*      穿服裝的

**40.** scrabble playing *a.*      亂塗；亂畫的

**41.** to turn a block letter on sth.      在……轉動一個字塊

**42.** marketable *a.*      有銷路的

**43.** celebrity value      名人價值

**44.** fame *n.*      名聲，come to fame 成名

**45.** dumb *a.*      沉默的

**46.** worth *n.*      品質

# Classical Cases for Teaching American Product Liability Law

| 19 | American Product Liability Law |

# (1) SHOSHONE COCA-COLA BOTTLING CO. V. DOLINSKI
### 420 p.2d 855 (1967) Supreme Court of Nevada

## FACTS

Leo Dolinski purchased a bottle of "Squirt", a soft drink, from a vending machine at a Sea and Ski plant, his place of empoyment. Dolinski opened the bottle and consumed part of its contents. He immediately became ill. Upon examination, it was found that the bottle contained the decomposed body of a mouse, mouse hair, and mouse feces. Dolinski visited a doctor and was given medicine to counteract nausea. Dolinski suffered physical and mental distress from consuming the decomposed mouse and possessed an aversion to soft drinks. The Shoshone CocaCola Bottling Company (Shoshone) manufactured and distributed the Squirt bottle. Dolinski sued Shoshone, basing his lawsuit on the doctrine of strict liability. The state of Nevada had not previously recognized the doctrine of strict liability. The trial court adopted the doctrine of strict liability and the jury returned a verdict in favor of the plaintiff. Shoshone appealed.

## ISSUE

Should the state of Nevada judicially adopt the doctrine of strict liability? If so, was there a defect in the manufacture of the Squirt bottle that caused the plaintiff's injuries?

## DECISION

Yes. The Supreme Court of Nevada adopted the doctrine of strict liability and held that the evidence supported the trial court's finding that there was a defect in manufacture. Affirmed.

## REASON

In adopting the doctrine of strict liability, the court stated, "Public policy demands that one who places upon the market a bottled beverage in a condition dangerous for use must be held strictly liable to the ultimate user for injuries resulting from such use, although the seller has exercised all reasonable care."

## Case questions

**1.** Should the courts adopt the theory of strict liability? Why or why not?

**2.** Was it ethical for Shoshone to argue that it was not liable to dolinski?

**3.** Should all in the chain of distribution of a defective product-even those parties who are not responsible for the defect-be held liable under the doctrine of strict liability? Or should liability be based only on fault?

## Notes

| | | |
|---|---|---|
| **1.** | soft drink | 無酒精飲料 |
| **2.** | vending machine | 自動販賣機 |
| **3.** | plant *n.* | 工廠；車間 |
| **4.** | to consume *vt.* | 消費 |
| **5.** | the decomposed body of a mouse | 一隻老鼠的腐爛屍體 |
| **6.** | mouse feces | 老鼠排泄物 |
| **7.** | to counteract nausea | 緩解噁心 |
| **8.** | to suffer physical are mental destress | 遭受身體上和精神上的苦惱 |
| **9.** | to base one's lawsuit on the doctrine of strict liability | 以嚴格責任說作為起訴的根據 |
| **10.** | previously *adv.* | 過去地 |
| **11.** | trial court | 審判法院；初審法院 |
| **12.** | to return a verdict | 宣告裁決 |
| **13.** | judicially *adv.* | 司法上地 |
| **14.** | evidence *n.* | 證據 |
| **15.** | to affirm *vt.* | 確認 |
| **16.** | public policy | 公共政策 |
| **17.** | a bottled beverage | 瓶裝的飲料 |

# (2) STANLEY-BOSTITCH, INC. V. DRABIK

796 F. Supp. 1271(1992) United States District Court, W. D. Missouri

## FACTS

Traditionally, hammers are used to pound nails into wood. If a number of nails are needed, the process is slow. So Staley-Bostitch, Inc. (Bostitch), and other manufacturers began producing pneumatic nail guns. These guns would fire a nail when the gun came into contact with the wood and the trigger on the gun was depressed. In 1984, Bostitch developed the "contact trip nailer" to enable users to pound nails even faster. Using this device, if the trigger was depressed once, a nail would be ejected each time the equipment came into contact with the wood. This was called "bump-nailing" in the trade.

One day, Leonard Drabik was working on a two-man carpentry crew. Drabik's companion on the job was using a Bostitch contact trip nailer. He was holding the equipment with the trigger depressed so that the nailer would automatically fire on contact. Unfortunately, Drabik was bent down during a pause in the nailing operation and raised his head into the area where his companion happened to be holding the nailer. When Drabik's head came in contact with the nailer, the equipment fired a nail into Drabik's head and lodged in his brain.

The evidence showed that Drabik had brain damage. His thought process was badly and permanently affected. He becomes confused and has memory lapses and seizures. Drabik sued Bostitch for damages for strict liability, alleging that the contact trip nailer was defectively designed. The jury awarded Drabik $1.5 million in actual damages and $7.5 million in punitive damages. Bostitch appealed.

## ISSUE

Was there a design defect in the contact trip nailer manufactured by Bostitch?

## DECISION

The court of appeals held that Bostitch's contact trip nailer was a defectively designed product. Affirmed.

## REASON

The court of appeals held that the risk-utility analysis was properly applied by the jury in finding Bostitch's contact trip nailer to be defectively designed. The jury found that industrial efficiency did not outweigh the personal iniury of a grievous nature that could be caused by the nailer. The court upheld the $7.5-million award of punitive damages on the ground that it would deter Bostitch and other companies <u>from</u> manufacturing this kind of contact trip nailer in the future.

 **CASE QUESTIONS**

### CRITICAL LEGAL THINKING

Do you think the utility served by the contact trip nailer outweighed its risk of personal injury?

### ETHICS

Did Bostitch act in conscious disregard of safety factors when it designed, manufactured, and sold the contact trip nailer?

### BUSINESS IMPLICATION

Do you think the award of punitive damages was warranted in this case?

### Notes

| | | |
|---|---|---|
| 1. | hammer *n.* | 錘子；榔頭 |
| 2. | to pound nails into wood | 將釘子敲進木板 |
| 3. | pneumatic nail guns | 氣動釘槍 |
| 4. | to fire a nail | 射出一個釘子 |
| 5. | to come into contact with... | 與……相接觸 |
| 6. | the trigger on the gun | 釘槍上的扳機 |
| 7. | to depress *vt.* | 使壓低 |
| 8. | to eject *vt.* | 射出；噴射；吐出 |
| 9. | contact trip nailer | 接觸式敲釘機 |
| 10. | device *n.* | 裝置 |
| 11. | "bump-nailing" | 撞擊式敲釘子 |
| 12. | in the trade | 在此行業中 |
| 13. | companion *n.* | 同伴 |
| 14. | on contact | 一旦接觸時 |
| 15. | to be bent down | 俯身；彎身 |
| 16. | during a pause | 在停止時 |
| 17. | in the nailing operation | 在敲釘子的操作過程中 |
| 18. | to be lodged in one's brain | 殘留在某人的大腦裡 |
| 19. | brain damage | 大腦損傷 |

| | |
|---|---|
| **20.** thought process | 思維過程 |
| **21.** to become confused | 變糊塗 |
| **22.** to have memory lapses and seizures | 記錯和失憶的發作 |
| **23.** defectively designed | 有缺陷設計 |
| **24.** actual damages | 實際損失賠償金 |
| **25.** risk-utility analysis | 風險實用分析 |
| **26.** industrial efficiency | 產業上的功效 |
| **27.** outweigh *vt.* | 超過 |
| **28.** grievous *a.* | 令人悲痛的 |
| **29.** to deter sb. from doing sth. | 阻止某人做某事 |

# (3) This case is one for the court to decide whether an express warranty had been created.

Daughtery V. Ashe 413 S. E. 2d 336 (1992) Supreme Court of Virginia

## FACTS

In October 1985, W. Hayes Daughtery <u>consulted</u> Sidney Ashe, a <u>jeweler</u>, about the purchase of a <u>diamond bracelet</u> as a Christmas present for his wife. A she showed Daughtery a diamond bracelet that he had for sale for $ 15,000. When Daughtery decided to purchase the bracelet, Asbhe completed and signed an <u>appraisal form</u> that stated that the diamonds were "Hcolor and V. V. S. quality"(V. V. S. is one of the highest <u>ratings</u> in a quality classification employed by jewelers.). After Daughtery paid for the bracelet, Ashe put the bracelet and the <u>appraisal form</u> in a box. Daughtery gave the bracelet to his wife as a Christmas present. In February 1987, when an other jeweler looked at the bracelet, Daughtery discovered that the diamonds were of <u>substantially lower grade</u> than V. V. S. Daughtery <u>filed a specific performance suit</u> against Ashe to compel him to replace the bracelet with one <u>mounted</u> with V. V. S. diamonds or pay appropriate damages. The trial court denied <u>relief</u> for <u>breach of</u> warranty. Daughtery appealed.

## ISSUE

Was an express warranty made by Ashe regarding the quality of the diamonds in the bracelet?

## DECISION

Yes. The <u>appellate court</u> held that an express warranty had been created. The trial court's decision was <u>reversed</u> and the case was <u>remanded</u> for a determination of appropriate damages to be awarded to Daughtery.

## REASON

Any <u>description</u> of the goods which is made <u>a basis of the bargain</u> creates an express warranty that the goods shall <u>conform</u> to the description. The appellate court <u>found</u> that Ashe's description of the diamonds created an express warranty that became a part of the basis of the bargain between Ashe and Daughtery. The court noted that it was not necessary for Ashe to have used the word <u>warrant or guarantee</u> to create an express warranty.

### Case questions

**1**. What is the remedy when an <u>express warranty</u> has been breached? Is the remedy sufficient?

**2**. Do businesses have to make express warranties? Why do businesses make warranties about the quality of their products?

### Notes

| | | |
|---|---|---|
| **1.** | to consult sb. | 向某人請教或諮詢 |
| **2.** | supreme court | 最高法院 |
| **3.** | jeweler *n.* | 珠寶商 |
| **4.** | the highest ratings | 最高評等 |
| **5.** | to file a specific performance suit | 提起要求依約履行的訴訟（suit = lawsuit） |
| **6.** | relief *n.* | 救濟；補救 = remedy |
| **7.** | to be mounted with V. V. S diamonds | 被嵌上頂尖質量的寶石（v. v. s.=very, very supreme） |
| **8.** | appellate court | 上訴法院 = court of appeal |
| **9.** | to reverse a decision | 撤銷裁定 |
| **10.** | to be remanded for a determination | 被發回重審並作出裁決 |
| **11.** | to conform to... | 與……一致 |
| **12.** | warrant or guarantee | 擔保；保證 |

| express warranty | 明示擔保 |
| implied warranty | 默示擔保 |

# (4) DANIELL v. FORD MOTOR CO., INC.

581 F. Supp. 728 (1984) United States District Court, D. New Mexico

## FACTS

In 1980, Connie Daniell felt "overburdened" and attempted to commit suicide by climbing into the trunk of a 1973 Ford LTD automobile and closing the trunk behind her. She remained locked inside for nine days until she was rescued. Daniell then sued Ford Motor Company, Inc. (Ford), the manufacturer of the LTD automobile, for strict liability to recover for psychological and physical injuries arising from the occurrence. She contended that the automobile had a design defect because the trunk lock or latch did not have an internal release or opening mechanism. She also maintained that Ford was liable for failing to warn her of this condition. Ford filed a motion for summary judgment.

## ISSUE

Was there an abnormal misuse of the automobile trunk which would relieve Ford Motor Company of strict liability?

## DECISION

Yes. The court held that the plaintiff's use of the trunk of the Ford LTD automobile to attempt to commit suicide was an abnormal and unforeseeable misuse of the product, and that the manufacturer had no duty to design the trunk with an internal release mechanism. The court also held that climbing into a trunk and closing the trunk lid behind you in an attempt to commit suicide is a known danger and the manufacturer owes no duty to warn against this danger. The court granted defendant Ford Motor Company's motion for summary judgment.

## REASON

A risk is not foreseeable by a manufacturer where a product is used in a manner which could not reasonably be anticipated by the manufacturer and that use is the cause of the plaintiff' injury. In this case, the court held that the "plaintiff's use of the trunk compartment as a means to attempt suicide was an unforeseeable use as a matter of law." The manufacturer had no duty to warn the plaintiff of the risk inherent in crawling into an automobile trunk and closing the trunk lid because such a risk is obvious.

**Case questions**

### CRITICAL LEGAL THINKING

Should any defenses be allowed against the application of strict liability? Do you think there was a foreseeable or abnormal misuse of the product in this case?

### ETHICS

Was it ethical for the plaintiff to sue Ford Motor Company for her injuries?

### BUSINESS IMPLICATION

Do you think the doctrine of strict liability advances or harms the economic development of business in this country? Explain.

**Notes**

| | | |
|---|---|---|
| 1. | to feel overburdened | 感到負擔過重 |
| 2. | to attempt to commit suicide | 企圖自殺 |
| 3. | to climb into | 爬進（與 to crawl into 意同） |
| 4. | automobile *n.* | （美）汽車；機動車 |
| 5. | to close the trunk behind her | 隨手將箱蓋關上 |
| 6. | to remain locked inside | 一直被關在裡面 |
| 7. | to rescue *vt.* | 營救 |
| 8. | to sue sb. for strict liability | 因嚴格責任起訴某人 |
| 9. | to recover for psychological and physical injuries | 為精神與身體上的損傷獲得賠償金 |
| 10. | to arise from... | 由……引起 |
| 11. | occurrence *n.* | 發生 |
| 12. | design defect | 設計缺陷 |
| 13. | the trunk lock | 汽車行李箱的鎖 |
| 14. | latch *n.* | 閂 |
| 15. | internal release | 內部打開裝置 |
| 16. | opening mechanism | 能打開的機械裝置 |
| 17. | to warn sb. of sth. | 就某事向某人發出預先警告 |
| 18. | to file a motion for summary judgement | 提出要求獲得即決審判的申請 |
| 19. | abnormal misuse | 反常的使用 |
| 20. | to relieve sb. of strict liability | 免除某人的嚴格責任 |

| | |
|---|---|
| **21.** to owe no duty to do sth. | 沒有做某事的責任或義務 |
| **22.** to warn sb. against this danger | 事先警告某人此危險 |
| **23.** foreseeable *a.* | 可預見的（與 unforeseeable「不可預見的」相對） |
| **24.** in a manner | 依照一種方式 |
| **25.** the trunk compartment | 汽車裡的分隔空間 |
| **26.** to use sth. as a means to do sth. | 將某物作為做某事的手段 |
| **27.** a matter of law | 法律問題 |
| **28.** to attempt suicide | 企圖自殺 |
| **29.** inherent in... | 在……中固有的 |
| **30.** the trunk lid | 汽車行李箱蓋子 |

# (5) NOWAK V. FABERGE USA INC.

32 F. 3d 755 (1994) United States Court of Appeals, Third Circuit

## FACTS

Faberge USA Inc. (Faberge) manufactures Aqua Net, a hair spray that is sold in an aerosol can. In addition to the hair holding spray, Aqua Net contains a mixture of butane or propane as the aerosol propellant and alcohol as a solvent. Alcohol, butane, and propane all are extremely flammable. Aerosol cans of Aqua Net carry a warning on the back stating, "Do not puncture" and "Do not use near fire or flame."

Alison Nowak, a fourteen-year-old girl, tried to spray her hair with a newly purchased can of Aqua Net. The spray valve would not work properly, so she cut open the can with a can opener. She thought she could then pour the contents into an empty aerosol bottle and use it. Nowak was standing in the kitchen near a gas stove when she punctured the can. A cloud of hair spray gushed from the can and the stove's pilot light ignited the spray into a ball of flame. She suffered severe, permanently disfiguring burns over 20 percent of her body.

Nowak sued Faberge for damages under strict liability, alleging that Faberge failed to warn her of the dangers of the flammability of Aqua Net. The jury held against Faberge and awarded Nowak $ 1.5 million. Faberge appealed.

## ISSUE

Did Faberge adequately warn the plaintiff of the flammability of Aque Net?

## DECISION

No. The court of appeals held that Faberge's warning was not adequate. Affirmed.

## REASON

A manufacturer owes a duty to adequately warn users of the dangerous <u>propensities</u> of their products. A product is defective if it is distributed without sufficient warnings to notify the ultimate user of the dangers <u>inherent in the product</u>. The trial court properly determined to <u>send the case to the jury for this determination</u>. The jury's <u>verdict</u> that Faberge's warning was inadequate is upheld.

## CASE QUESTIONS

### CRITICAL LEGAL THINKING

Should the law <u>recognize</u> a failure to warn <u>as a basis</u> for <u>imposing strict liability</u> on manufacturers and sellers of products? Why or why not?

### ETHICS

Did Faberge violate its duty of <u>social responsibility</u> in this case? Explain.

### BUSINESS IMPLICATION

Do you think this case was <u>decided properly</u>? What else could Faberge have done to avoid liability?

## Notes

| | | |
|---|---|---|
| 1. | hair spray | 噴發定形劑；發膠 |
| 2. | aerosol can | 氣溶膠劑容器 |
| 3. | in addition to | 除……之外 |
| 4. | hair holding spray | 發膠液；頭髮定型劑 |
| 5. | butane *n.* | 丁烷 |
| 6. | propane *n.* | 丙烷 |
| 7. | aerosol propellant | 氣溶發射劑 |
| 8. | a mixture of... | ……的混合體 |
| 9. | alcohol *n.* | 乙醇；酒精 |
| 10. | solvent *n.* | 溶劑 |
| 11. | extremely *adv.* | 極度地 |
| 12. | flammable *a.* | 易燃的 |
| 13. | to puncture *vt.* | 刺破；刺孔 |
| 14. | to spray one's hair | 噴某人頭髮 |

**15.** spray valve　　　　　　　　　噴霧器的閥門

**16.** to work properly　　　　　　　合適地工作

**17.** to cut open the can　　　　　　將容器切開

**18.** can opener　　　　　　　　　　開瓶器

**19.** flame *n.*　　　　　　　　　　火焰；火舌

**20.** to pour the contents into　　　　將……注入……

**21.** gas stove　　　　　　　　　　煤氣火爐

**22.** to gush from...　　　　　　　　從……噴出

**23.** pilot light　　　　　　　　　　煤氣爐中的小火

**24.** to ignite *vt.*　　　　　　　　　使燃燒；點燃

**25.** a ball of flame　　　　　　　　火球

**26.** disfiguring burns　　　　　　　毀容的燒傷

**27.** flammability *n.*　　　　　　　易燃性

**28.** jury *n.*　　　　　　　　　　　陪審團

**29.** adequate *a.*　　　　　　　　　足夠的

**30.** propensities *n.*　　　　　　　傾向

**31.** sufficient warning　　　　　　　足夠的警告

**32.** defective *a.*　　　　　　　　　有缺陷的；有缺點的

**33.** ultimate user　　　　　　　　　最終用戶；最終使用者

**34.** dangers inherent in the product　產品中固有的危險

**35.** to send the case to the jury for this determination　將案子送交陪審團作此裁定

**36.** verdict *n.*　　　　　　　　　　正式判決

**37.** inadequate *a.*　　　　　　　　不充分的

**38.** to uphold *vt.*　　　　　　　　維持；支持

**39.** to recognize a failure to do sth.　承認沒做某事

**40.** as a basis for doing sth.　　　　作為做某事的根據

**41.** to impose strict liability on sb.　將嚴格責任強加在某人身上

**42.** social responsibility　　　　　　社會責任

**43.** to decide a case properly　　　　合適地判決某一個案子

| 20 | **English Law on Business Organizations** |
|---|---|

Churton V. Douglas (1859)

B., C. and J.D. <u>carried on</u> a business as J.D. & Co. J.D. retired and B. and C. carried on the business <u>under a new name</u> with the addition of "<u>late</u> J.D. & Co." J.D. formed a new firm carrying on the same kind of business in premises <u>adjoining</u> the old firm's premises in the name of J.D. & Co., and <u>circularised</u> the old firm's customers. Held, (1) he could carry on his new business <u>in competition with</u> the old firm and in <u>the immediate vicinity</u>, but (2) although his name was J.D., he could not carry on his new business in the name of J.D. & Co., and (3) he could be <u>restrained</u> by the old firm <u>from canvassing</u> their customers: Churton v. Douglas (1859) Johns.174.

### ♣ Notes

1. to carry on a business      繼續擁有並辦好企業
2. under a new name      按新的名字
3. a new firm      新公司／企業
4. in the name of...      以……名義；憑……名稱
5. to adjoin *vt.*      靠近；毗連
6. to circularise *vt.*      發通知給……
7. in competition with...      與……進行競爭
8. in the immediate vicinity      就在附近
9. to restrain sb. from doing sth.      制止某人做某事
10. to canvass *vt.*      對顧客進行遊說

Higgins V. Beauchamp (1914)

B. and M. carried on business in <u>partnership</u> as <u>proprietors</u> and manages of <u>picture houses</u>.

The <u>partnership</u> deed prohibited a partner from borrowing money on behalf of the firm. M. borrowed money from H. Held, the firm was <u>not liable for</u> the debt, because it was not a trading firm, and M. had therefore no <u>implied authority</u> to borrow on the firm's behalf: Higgins v.Beauchamp [1914] 3 K. B. 1192.

## 🍀 Notes

| | |
|---|---|
| **1.** in partnership | 合夥（做生意） |
| **2.** proprietor *n.* | 業主；所有人 |
| **3.** picture house | （英）電影院 |
| **4.** partnership deed | 合夥契約 |
| **5.** to prohibit sb. from doing sth. | 不准某人做某事 |
| **6.** on behalf of... | 代表…… |
| **7.** not liable for... | 對……不負責任 |
| **8.** implied authority | 默示授權 |

Mann v. D'Arcy and others (1968)

D. & Co. were a partnership consisting of D., T. and L. and carrying on the business of <u>produce dealers</u>. D. was the only <u>active partner</u>. To <u>cover the possibility of loss</u>, D. asked M., the plaintiff, whether M.was prepared to buy a consignment of potatoes ex s.s. Anna Schaar as a <u>joint venture</u>, i.e. on the basis of <u>sharing profits and loss</u>, and M. agreed. M. contended that the joint venture was itself a partnership between him and D. & Co., and sued T. and L. for half his share in the profits <u>arising from</u> that venture. Held, the contention of M. was correct and the venture was concluded by D. for the partnership and could not <u>be considered as</u> "another" business; consequently, D. bound not only himself but also T. and L.

## 🍀 Notes

| | |
|---|---|
| **1.** produce dealer | 農產品經營商 |
| **2.** active partner | 任職合夥人 |
| **3.** to cover the possibility of loss | 彌補損失的可能性 |
| **4.** consignment *n.* | 寄售的一批貨物 |
| **5.** joint venture | 合資企業 |
| **6.** to share profits and loss | 分享利潤共擔損失 |
| **7.** to arise from... | 因……而產生 |
| **8.** to be considered as... | 被看成…… |

## (1) HILL V. SOUTHEASTERN FLOOR COVERING CO., INC.

596 So.2d 874 (1992) Supreme Court of Mississippi

### FACTS

Danny Hill was an officer and the general manager of Southeastern Floor Covering Company, Inc. (Southeastern). Southeastern did jobs in floor covering and ceilings for general contractors. Southeastern did much of its own work, and it subcontracted out the work it could not do. Southeastern often subcontracted asbestos removal work to Southern Interiors (Interiors). In 1983, Southeastern bid on a job with Chata Construction Company for various work. Hill made a deal with the owner of Interiors to bid on the asbestos work on the Chata project without Southeastern being involved. Chata awarded the asbestos work to Interiors, and Hill made $90,000 on the transaction. When Southeastern discovered this fact, it sued Hill to recover his secret profits. The trial court held that Hill had breached his duty of loyalty to Southeastern by usurping a corporate opportunity, and it awarded Southeastern $90,000. Hill appealed.

### ISSUE

Did Hill violate his duty of loyalty to his corporate employer ?

### DECISION

Yes. The supreme court of Mississippi held that Hill violated his duty of loyalty by usurping a corporate opportunity. Affirmed.

### REASON

The doctrine of corporate opportunity prohibits directors and officers from appropriating to themselves business opportunities which in fairness should belong to the corporation. The supreme court held that Hill diverted an opportunity that could have been Southeastern's, and thereby violated his duty of loyalty.

 **CASE QUESTIONS**

## CRITICAL LEGAL THINKING

When can a corporate director or officer take an opportunity for him- or herself? Explain.

## ETHICS

Did Hill act ethically in this case? Do you think he usurped a corporate opportunity?

## BUSINESS IMPLICATION

Do you think the award in this case is sufficient to deter breaches of loyalty by corporate directors and officers?

## Notes

| | | |
|---|---|---|
| **1.** | general manager | 總經理 |
| **2.** | Floor Covering Company | 地板鋪設公司 |
| **3.** | Inc = incorporated | 組成公司的 |
| **4.** | jobs in floor covering and ceiling | 鋪設地板和天花板的任務 |
| **5.** | general contractors | 總承包商；建築公司 |
| **6.** | to subcontract out the work it cannot do | 將它不能做的工作分包或轉包出去（分包給他人） |
| **7.** | asbestos removal work | 除掉石棉的工作 |
| **8.** | to bid on a job with a company | 投標承包某一公司的任務 |
| **9.** | to make a deal with... | 與……訂密約 |
| **10.** | project n. | 項目 |
| **11.** | to award the asbestos work to... | 將（除掉）石棉的業務交給…… |
| **12.** | to breach one's duty of loyalty to sb. | 違反了自己對某人忠誠的責任 |
| **13.** | to usurp vt. | 侵占；盜用 |
| **14.** | to affirm vt. | 維持（原判） |
| **15.** | to prohibit sb. from doing sth. | 禁止某人做某事 |
| **16.** | to appropriate business opportunities to themselves | 將商業機會占為己用 |

| | |
|---|---|
| **17.** in fairness | 清楚地；完全地 |
| **18.** to belong to | 屬於…… |
| **19.** to divert *vt.* | 轉移 |
| **20.** an opportunity that could have been Southeastern's | 一個可能屬於東南公司的機會或機遇 |
| **21.** thereby *adv.* | 因此 |
| **22.** to violate one's duty of loyalty | 違反了某人的忠誠義務 |
| **23.** to deter *vt.* | 阻止 |

# (2) FRESH FANCY PRODUCE, INC, V. BRANTLEY
### 378 S. E. 2d 379 (1989) Court of Appeals of Georgia

## FACTS

Charies C. Collins was the president of Fresh & Fancy Produce, Inc. (Fresh & Fancy), a corporation organized under the laws of Geogia. A bylaw of the corporation stipulated that the president "shall only borrow money on behalf of the corporation pursuant to specific authority from the board of directors." Collins, without authority from the board of directors, borrowed money for the corporation from Sam Brantley. He executed two corporate promissory notes, in the amounts of $25,000 and $6,000, in favor of Brantley. When Brantley tried to enforce the notes, the corporation denied liability. Brantley sued. Fresh & Fancy appealed, alleging that the ultra vires doctrine precluded enforcement of the notes against it. The trial court entered summary judgment in favor of Brantley. Fresh & Fancy appealed.

## ISSUE

Does the ultra vires doctrine prevent enforcement of the notes?

## DECISION

No. The court of appeals held that the ultra vires doctrine did not prevent enforcement of the notes under the circumstances of this case. Affirmed.

## REASON

In order for the ultra vires doctrine to be used as a defense by a corporation, the party against whom the defense is asserted must have had knowledge of the restriction on authority. There is no evidence that Brantley knew of any such restriction or lack of authority. Therefore, the ultra vires doctrine does not prevent enforcement of the notes by Brantley against the corporation.

## CASE QUESTIONS

### CRITICAL LEGAL THINKING

Should the law recognize the doctrine of ultra vires? Why or why not?

### ETHICS

Did the board of directors of the corporation act ethically in denying liability on the notes?

### BUSINESS IMPLICATION

What should a corporation do if it really wants to enforce a restriction on an officer's contract authority?

## Notes

1. Fresh & Fancy Produce, Inc.      新鮮高級農產品公司
2. to be organized under the laws of Georgia      按照喬治亞州法律成立
3. bylaw of the corporation      內部規則（regulation made by a corporation）
4. to stipulate *vt.*      規定
5. pursuant to      按照；依據
6. specific authority      具體授權
7. without authority from the board of directors      沒有董事會的授權
8. to execute *vt.*      透過簽名蓋印使生效
9. in favor of sb.      以某人為受益人
10. to enforce the note      強制執行期票（要求開票人付款）
11. to deny liability      否認責任（本案中指付款責任或義務）
12. ultra vires doctrine      越權理論
13. to preclude *vt.*      阻止
14. to enter summary judgment in favor of sb.      作出有利於某人的即決審判／判決
15. under the circumstances of this case      在此案的情況下
16. affirmed      維持原判
17. to assert the defense against sb.      堅持針對某人的抗辯
18. the restriction on authority      授權限制
19. lack of authority      缺少授權
20. contract authority      訂契約權力
21. two corporate promissory notes：兩張公司本票（期票）
    promissory note: a note containing on unconditional promise to pay on demand or at a fixed or determined future time a particular sum of money to or to the order of a specified person or to the bearer

# (3) SMITH V. VAN GORKOM

488 A. 2d 858(1985)

*Supreme Court of Delaware*

## FACTS

Trans Union Corporation (Trans Union) was a publicly traded, diversified holding company that was incorporated in Delaware. Its principal earnings were generated by its railcar leasing. Jerome W. van Gorkom was a Trans Union officer for more than 24 years, its chief executive officer for more than 17 years, and the chairman of the board of directors for 2 years. Van Gorkom, a lawyer and certified public accountant, owned 75,000 shares of Trans Union. He was approaching 65 years of age and mandatory retirement. Trans Union's board of directors was composed of ten members-five inside directors and five outside directors.

In September 1980, Van Gorkom decided to meet with Jay A. Pritzker, a well-known corporate takeover specialist and a social acquaintance of Van Gorkom's, to discuss the possible sale of Trans Union to Pritzker. Van Gorkom met Pritzker at Pritzker's home on Saturday, September 13, 1980. He did so without consulting Trans Union's board of directors. At this meeting, Van Gorkom proposed a sale of Trans Union to Prizker at a price of $55 per share. The stock was trading at about $38 in the market. On Monday, September 15, Pritzker notified Van Gorkom that he was interested in the $55 cash-out merger proposal. Van Gorkom, along with two inside directors, privately met with Pritzker on September 16 and 17. After meeting with Van Gorkom on Thursday, September 18, Pritzker notified his attorney to begin drafting the merger documents.

On Friday, September 19, Van Gorkom called a special meeting of Trans Union's board of directors for the following day. The board members were not told the purpose of the meeting. At the meeting, Van Gorkom disclosed the Pritzker offer and described its terms in a 20-minute presentation. Neither the merger agreement nor a written summary of the terms of the agreement was furnished to the directors. No valuation study as to the value of Trans Union was prepared for the meeting. After two hours, the board voted in favor of the cash-out merger with Pritzker's company at $55 per share for Trans Union's stock. The board also voted not to solicit other offers. The merger agreement was executed by Van Gorkom during the evening of September 20 at a formal social event he hosted for the opening of the Chicago Lyric Opera's season. Neither he nor any other director read the agreement prior to its signing and delivery to Pritzker.

Trans Union's board of directors recommended the merger be approved by its shareholders and distributed proxy materials to the shareholders, stating that the $55 per share price for their stock was fair. In the meantime, Trans Union's board of directors took steps to dissuade two other possible suitors who <u>showed an interest in</u> purchasing Trans Union. On February 10, 1981, 69, 9 percent of the shares of Trans Union stock was voted in favor of the merger. The merger was consummated. Alden Smith and other Trans Union shareholders sued Van Gorkom and the other directors for damages. The plaintiffs alleged that the defendants were negligent in their conduct in selling Trans Union to Pritzker. The Delaware Court of Chancery held in favor of the defendants. The plaintiffs appealed.

## ISSUE

Did Trans Union's directors breach <u>their duty of care</u>?

## DECISION

Yes, The supreme court of Delaware held that the defendant directors had breached their duty of care. The supreme court <u>remanded the case to the court of chancery</u> to <u>conduct an evidentiary hearing</u> to determine the fair value of the shares represented by the plaintiffs' class. If that value is higher than $55 per share, the difference shall be awarded to the plaintiffs as damages. Reversed and remanded.

## REASON

The business judgment rule exists to protect and promote the full and free exercise of the managerial power granted to Delaware directors. The rule itself is a presumption that in making a business decision, the directors of a corporation acted (1) on an informed basis, (2) in good faith, and (3) in the honest belief that the action taken was <u>in the best interests of</u> the company. Thus, the party attacking a board decision as uninformed must <u>rebut</u> the <u>presumption</u> that its business judgment was an informed one. The determination of whether a business judgment is an informed one turns on whether the directors have informed themselves prior to making a business decision, of all material information available to them. Under the business judgment rule, there is no protection for directors who have made an <u>unintelligent</u> or <u>unadvised</u> judgment.

The supreme court held that the business judgment rule did not protect the directors' actions in this case. The court stated, "The directors (1) did not adequately inform themselves as to Van Gorkom's role in forcing the sale of the company and in establishing the per share purchase price; (2) they were <u>uninformed</u> as to the <u>intrinsic</u> value of the company; and (3) <u>given these circumstances</u>, <u>at a minimum</u>, they were <u>grossly negligent</u> in approving the sale of the company upon two hours' consideration, without prior notice, and without the <u>exigency</u> of a crisis or emergency."

**CASE QUESTIONS**

## CRITICAL LEGAL THINKING

What does the business judgment rule provide? Is this a good rule? Explain.

## EIHICS

Do you think that Van Gorkom and the other directors had the shareholders' best interests in mind? Were the plaintiff-shareholders being greedy?

## BUSINESS IMPLICATION

Is there any liability exposure for sitting on a board of directors?

 **Notes**

| | | |
|---|---|---|
| 1. | diversified holding company | 多樣經營的控股公司 |
| 2. | incorporated in Delaware | 公司在（美國）德拉威爾州成立 |
| 3. | principal earnings | 主要收入 |
| 4. | to be generated by... | 由……產生 |
| 5. | railcar leasing business | 單節機動有軌車的租賃生意 |
| 6. | chairman of the board of directors | 董事長 |
| 7. | lawyer *n.* | 律師 |
| 8. | certified public accountant | 註冊會計師 |
| 9. | to approach 65 years of age | 接近 65 歲 |
| 10. | mandatory retirement | 強制性退休 |
| 11. | to be composed of ten members | 由 10 名成員組成 |
| 12. | inside directors | 內部董事 |
| 13. | outside directors | 外部董事 |
| 14. | a well-known corporate takeover specialist | 一位知名的公司收購專家 |
| 15. | a social acquaintance of sb's | 某個人在社會上的相識 |
| 16. | without consulting the board of directors | 未與董事會商量 |
| 17. | to notify *vt.* | 通知 |
| 18. | cash-out merger | 透過用現金收購小股東股份進行的兼併（合併） |
| 19. | attorney *n.* | （美）律師 |
| 20. | to draft the merger documents | 起草兼併（合併）文件 |
| 21. | to call a special meeting | 召開一次特別會議 |

**22.** to disclose *vt.*　　　　　　　　披露

**23.** terms *n.*　　　　　　　　　　交易條件

**24.** a 20-minute presentation　　　20分鐘的演講

**25.** to be furnished to sb.　　　　被提供給某人

**26.** valuation study　　　　　　　價值研究

**27.** to vote in favor of sth.　　　投票贊成／支持某事

**28.** to solicit other offers　　　要求其他報盤（價）

**29.** at a formal social event　　在一次正式社交動上

**30.** its signing and delivery to sb.　它的簽署和交給某人

**31.** to recommend the merger (should) be approved by　　建議此兼併（合併）應由……批准（注意 merger 後的 should 可省略）

**32.** proxy materials　　　　　　　代理材料

**33.** to take steps to do sth.　　採取步驟做某事

**34.** to dissuade *vt.*　　　　　　勸阻；勸止

**35.** to show interest in doing sth.　對做某事表示興趣

**36.** duty of care　　　　　　　　謹慎責任；注意義務

**37.** to remand the case to the court of chancery　　將案子送回衡平法院

**38.** to conduct an evidentiary hearing　進行取證審訊

**39.** in the best interest of the company　　為了公司的最大利益

**40.** to rebut the presumption　　反駁（駁回）假定

**41.** unintelligent *a.*　　　　　缺乏才智的；愚蠢的

**42.** unadvised *a.*　　　　　　　輕率的；魯莽的

**43.** uninformed *a.*　　　　　　未被告知的

**44.** intrinsic *a.*　　　　　　　內在的；固有的

**45.** given these circumstances　假使有這些情況

**46.** at a minimum　　　　　　　至少

**47.** grossly negligent　　　　　嚴重疏忽；重大過失

**48.** exigency *n.*　　　　　　　危急

**49.** emergency *n.*　　　　　　緊急情況

**50.** to have sb's best interest in mind　想到某人的最大利益；將某人最大利益放在心中

**51.** liability exposure　　　　責任暴露

**52.** to sit on a board of directors　為董事會的成員

# (4) KAMEN V. KEMPER FINANCIAL SERVICES, INC.

## 111S. Ct.1711, 114 L.Ed. 2d 152, (1991)

### *United States Supreme Court*

## FACTS

Jill S. Kamen is a shareholder of Cash Equivalent Fund. Inc. (Fund), a mutual fund that employs Kemper Financial Services, Inc. (Kemper), as its investment adviser. Kamen brought a derivative lawsuit on behalf of the Fund against Kemper, alleging that Kemper violated fiduciary duties owed to the Fund as imposed by the Investment Company Act of 1940 (Act), a federal statute. Kamen did not make a demand on the Fud's board of directors to sue Kemper any earlier. She alleged that it would have been futile to do so because the directors were acting in a conspiracy with Kemper. The Act was silent as to the rule concerning derivative actions under the Act. The trial court granted Kemper's motion to dismiss the lawsuit. The court of appeals adopted a "universal demand rule" as part of the federal common law and affirmed. This rule requires a shareholder always to make a demand on the directors of a corporation before bringing a derivative lawsuit.

Kamen appealed to the U.S. Supreme Court.

## ISSUE

Should federal law adopt the universal demand rule for bringing derivative actions?

## DECISION

No. The U.S. Supreme Court refused to adopt the universal demand rule as federal common law, but instead held that federal law should follow the appropriate state law concerning demands in derivative lawsuits if a federal statute is silent as to this issue. Reversed.

## FEASON

The Supreme Court held that where a federal statute is silent as to the demand rule, the appropriate state law concerning demand should be followed. Therefore, the universal demand rule cannot become part of the federal common law. Thus, this exception should be applied in states that recognize a "futility" exception to the demand rule. This exception provides that a shareholder is excused from making a demand on the directors of a corporation to sue a third party if the directors are involved in the alleged wrongdoing or are otherwise not disinterested parties.

## CASE QUESTIONS

### CRITICAL LEGAL THINKING

Which do you think is the better rule: (1) the universal demand rule or (2) the futility exception rule?

### ETHICS

Should Kamen have given the directors of the Fund the opportunity to have used Kemper before she did?

### BUSINESS IMPLICATION

Do derivative lawsuits serve any legitimate purposes? Explain.

## Notes

| | |
|---|---|
| **1.** fund *n.* | 基金（a separate pool of monetary or other resources used to support designated activities） |
| **2.** a mutual fund | 互助基金；共同基金（一種資本結構靈活的投資公司） |
| **3.** investment adviser | 投資顧問 |
| **4.** to bring a derivative lawsuit (action) | 提起股東訴訟 |
| **5.** to violate fiduciary duties | 違反受託人責任 |
| **6.** duties owed to sb. | 對某人的責任 |
| **7.** imposed by | 由……強加的 |
| **8.** a federal statute | （美）聯邦成文法 |
| **9.** to make a demand on sb. | 要求某人 |
| **10.** to sue sb. | 起訴某人 |
| **11.** futile *a.* | 無效的；無益的 |
| **12.** to act in conspiracy with sb. | 與某人密謀做某事 |
| **13.** the Act was silent as to sth. | 此法案對某事表示沉默 |
| **14.** to grant sb's motion to dismiss the lawsuit | 准許某人不予受理此訴訟的申請 |
| **15.** to adopt a "universal demand rule" | 採用了通用的要求規則 |
| **16.** to follow the state law | 按州法辦 |
| **17.** to be excused from doing sth. | 同意某人不做某事 |
| **18.** wrongdoing *n.* | 惡行；犯罪 |
| **19.** disinterested party | 無利害關係當事人 |

| | |
|---|---|
| **20.** futility exception rule | 無益例外規則 |
| **21.** legitimate *a.* | 合法的；合理的 |
| **22.** to serve a purpose | 為某一目的服務 |

## 1

# 好的法律寫作
# Good Legal Writing

George Orwell once wrote that "[g] ood prose is like a window pane." What I take Orwell to have meant by that remark is that when people read good prose, it makes them feel as if they've "seen" something (whatever the author was trying to convey) more clearly. Put another way, if a writer can induce his or her reader to feel that the reader would have come to the same conclusion that the author reached had the reader done his or her own investigation of the subject matter, the writer has achieved a kind of "window pane" effect on the reader.

There are certainly many styles of successful writing. Some charm by exotic imagery, others by suspense, some even by subtle obfuscations. However, the style of writing I have found to be most successful for legal analyses is the sort which Orwell's comment conjures up: flawlessly clear, lucid, and enlightening. As I have worked with law students on supervised writing projects, I have noticed that lucidity does not come naturally to most law students, perhaps because they have been forced in their legal studies to read so much bad writing that they mistake what they've read for the true and proper model. I have also noticed that simply directing someone to be lucid doesn't often help him or her to become so. Over time I have developed a set of ideas about how one can make one's legal prose become like a window pane. In this Essay, I will share those ideas with you.

You will soon notice that this Essay is addressed chiefly to an audience of inexperienced legal writers, most specifically to those law students whom I teach. More experienced writers may find the Essay mildly entertaining, perhaps even picking up a tip or two for improving their own writing technique. I hope that at least some of my readers who are experienced writers, especially those who try, as I do, to teach others to write, will find a fellow traveller's exposition helpful to further their own thinking about the mysterious process of learning to write well.

Despite what you may infer from the detailed comments within, I do not believe in a formulaic approach to legal writing. There is no one "right" way to organize, analyze, or write about any legal issue. There are thousands, if not millions, of "right" ways. My aim in reviewing other people's writing is to help them find the analytic approach, organization, and style that will work for the ideas they want to convey. To put it another way, I try to help each of them find his or her "voice" as a writer. No one can learn to write well by aping another person's style. I tell my students: The first thing you must do when you write is be yourself; the second thing you must do is learn to appreciate and enhance your natural strengths as a writer (yes, you have them); and the third thing you must do is understand and work on removing whatever weaknesses are undermining your strengths. I see my role as facilitating this process of self-discovery.

Now for the framework of this Essay: In Section I, I set forth what are for me the six paramount rules of good legal writing. These have general applicability to the whole of one's writing. This is followed in Section II by a set of fourteen additional rules, which pertain, for the most part, to specific aspects of a legal analysis. Sections III and IV briefly advise inexperienced writers on how much research to do for a legal analysis and on strategies for overcoming writer's block. The final section suggests an approach to editing other people's work and communicating with the writers about their work. This approach, in my view, is the one most likely to be successful in yielding the intended result of improving the quality of the writer's next draft. As you'll see, I view an editor's job as well done when he or she has rendered himself or herself obsolete. (Now that I have given you this structure, I feel free to be a bit jaunty and jocular, hoping to lead you further into my web.)

## The Six Paramount Rules of Good Legal Writing

### 1. Have a point

In order to write a good legal analysis, you've got to have a point (that is, a thesis) you want to make. In reviewing student papers, I have noticed two sorts of problems students have with the seemingly simple point of having a point. One is not to have a point at all. There are two main subcategories of this problem: one is being very descriptive about one's topic, that is, surveying rather than analyzing it; the other is demonstrating the author's ambivalence about the issue. Not having a thesis is unacceptable. So is being ambivalent about what your thesis is. Go ahead. Take a risk. Bite the bullet. Choose your thesis and see where it takes you.

The other sort of problem — one to which enthusiasts, in particular, are prone — is to have twelve or thirteen points. It is very easy, as one begins to get familiar with a subject, to get captivated by the myriad issues which any reasonably interesting subject will raise. One may find it difficult to resist the temptation to put all of the interesting issues in at least the first draft without tying them together in a single thematic structure.

I tell my students: Very few people can write in any depth about more than one major issue at a time, and you probably aren't one of them. From my perspective, the aim of this exercise is to explore one thing (your thesis) in depth. While it may very well be possible to weave some of the more closely related tantalizing issues into the fabric of your paper (or, better, into the footnotes), you must make them work in service of your thesis. However sharp your insight, if it doesn't advance your argument, drop it.

### 2. Get to the point

Quite as important as having a point is getting to it with reasonable dispatch. This means that you should tell your reader what the point is in your first paragraph, if possible, or at the most by the end of the second page. It means that you should start your analysis of the thesis on page two or three, not on page twenty or thirty. It means that you should remind your reader of your thesis as you go along by such means as section titles and transitional sentences. Think of your thesis as the spice of your paper. Just as you wouldn't put all the spice for your dinner into your dessert, don't put all of your analysis in the latter third or quarter of your paper.

### 3. Adopt a structure for your analysis that will allow you to integrate the facts, court analysis, and policies into the body of your argument

The reason many law students seem to take so long to get to the point is that they have adopted what I deem to be an artificial structure, often a structure which could be used for any paper, no matter what its thesis. If this has been your habit, think about breaking it. It's time to try a more unified, more integrated, and more analytical structure. It is time to learn to get to the point on page two. It is time to learn to develop a structure which can be the structure only for that paper because it's based on the particular analysis you've developed to support your thesis.

What do I mean when I say law students tend to adopt an "artificial structure?" Here's an example:

(1) Introduction

Often this is an introduction to the general subject matter of the paper. If it mentions the paper's thesis, it often does it in a sentence tucked away at the bottom of page three or five in an inconspicuous place.

(2) Background

This is often an overview of some of the historical context of the problem and/or of legal concepts which are to be discussed in the analytic section fifteen pages later. It often reads like an encyclopedia or a dispassionate general treatise on the subject.

(3) Facts

Often this is a recitation of "the facts" of a particular case which will be under the analytic microscope in Section (5). It often meanders through the odds and ends of the case, often giving many more facts than is necessary to make the analytic point.

(4) Court Decision (s)

This is usually a report on the trial and any appellate court's holdings — usually all of the issues, not just the ones pertinent to the discussion — and sometimes also of arguments rejected or accepted and any titillating dicta, pertinent or not.

(5) Analysis

Finally. The author now attacks court A for this and court B for that, repeating in the process all the arguments or holdings discussed in the previous section, the facts of the next previous section, and the concepts of the background section, and inadequately developing all of them in terms of their relationships to one another.

(6) Policy

If law students mention the policy implications of their thesis at all, the policy issues are trotted out in a page or so near the end, usually held up for display as if they were the recently severed head of John the Baptist. Horrors!

(7) Conclusion

This is often a rather mechanical repetition of the kernel of the analysis from Section (5). It rarely contains anything new or interesting.

What's so bad about this structure, you may ask. Lots of things, I will answer. The worst thing about it is that it's the sort of structure that doesn't start getting to the point until page twenty.

A concomitant bad effect is that along the route to your analytic section, your reader is very likely to get distracted by the unfocused discussion of history, concepts, facts, and the like. Your reader isn't your mother who might be willing to read everything you write with fascinated attention. Even if you've told your reader what your thesis is in the first page or so, your reader will have forgotten it by the fifth page of your meandering history. And by the time you get to the analysis itself, your reader will have forgotten the background stuff mentioned in your earlier sections. Unless you repeat in Section (5) what you said in Section (2) a diligent reader may have to turn back to Section (2) and reread it, which again is a distraction from the smooth development of your argument.

This brings me to a third bad thing about the kind of structure I've been discussing. It requires a lot of repetition as glue. Repetition is all right if it's necessary, but if you organize an analysis well, there is little or no need to repeat yourself.

A fourth ill effect of this structure is that the potential power of your argument is dissipated by having been so severely chopped up into bits and sprinkled throughout the paper. If the historical context of argument A is discussed on pages four and five, the facts on seven, the courts' holdings briefly on eleven and thirteen, your analysis of them on sixteen, and the policy implications on twenty two, the forcefulness of the argument will be less than if all are integrated into one section of seven pages. A highly diligent reader will feel forced to do the work for you, but most readers will say, "Ho, hum, I'm glad I got through that mess, but what was it about?"

Remember that the whole point of legal writing is to persuade your reader of your thesis, so you shouldn't structure your paper to impede your ability to persuade. Integrate, and your prose will be like a window pane.

### 4. Break your analysis up into its component parts and develop them separately, but in an organized way

One can only analyze an issue in an organized way. There are a great many ways to organize the analysis of any thesis, but all good ways have this in common: One's analysis must be broken down into component parts, and each element must be examined and developed in an orderly and integrated way. The structure of your paper should reflect the basic components of the argument which has to be made to support your thesis. It's hard to be more specific than this about how to break down the analysis into its component parts because not only does each thesis demand a different set of components, but each writer on the same thesis might use different components or might order his or her components differently.

Do make an outline before you begin to write. It needn't be a formal outline with I, A, l, a, iii's in it, but it should break the argument up into the basic components and it should reflect the order in which the strongest case for your position can be made. Play around with the ordering of the elements. Ask yourself why what you put first needs to be there.

Try not to have more than three basic elements in your argument. Why, you ask. Simple. Human beings are limited creatures. They get bored or confused if you make six, twelve, or twenty arguments at once. People are pretty good at holding onto two or three basic arguments or components or arguments at the same time. So pander to them; pick what's most important to say in the text and put everything else in footnotes (or in a folder for your next book).

Allow yourself to revise your structure as you go along if, as you write, you find yourself dissatisfied with your initial organization. Reread the paper after you've written it to see if the organization you tried has been successful. If not, try to rework it in outline form before rewriting the whole paper.

### 5. Adopt a measured tone

The importance of tone is often overlooked by neophyte writers.

To decide what kind of tone your paper should have, think about whom you want to persuade of the point you're making in the paper. When you know to whom the piece is addressed, you will (hopefully) be able to figure out what tone would be most likely to facilitate your goal of convincing that person. If you keep this audience in mind throughout your paper, you will be able to keep the tone constant.

In legal papers, it is generally a good idea to adopt a tone of measured rationality, as if you were saying "let us reason together on this issue." Target the paper as if the audience were a reasonably intelligent and diligent judge who until now has had little or no exposure to the issue on which you write but who is about to make an important decision on it. Assume this judge has some serious reservations about the position you take, but has not yet made up his or her mind on the subject. Your job is to anticipate and meet all of his or her objections and other concerns. It is more effective to do this not in a defensive way but by incorporating those considerations that seem to cut against your position within the framework of your affirmative analysis of the issue.

Too forceful or strident a tone will make the reader feel bludgeoned. This will not only make the reader angry, but it will also distract him or her from perceiving the merit of your argument. Even your supporters, who may look to your piece for intellectual support, may be offended by too harsh a tone.

Too colloquial or journalistic a tone will make the reader think you are not really taking the issue seriously, or are not capable of taking the issue seriously, except perhaps in an emotional way. Too wishy-washy, vague, or ambivalent a tone will cause the reader to doubt whether he or she can gain anything by reading what you have to say about the matter.

The tone of a paper is one of the primary things which will make a reader decide whether to trust or distrust the writer. If the tone is wrong, most readers will stop reading the paper.

### 6. Be concrete and simplify whenever possible

Concreteness is related to tone, but it is worth emphasizing as a separate concern. My advice is this: Whenever there is a choice between saying something in an abstract way or saying it in a concrete way, opt for the concrete expression. Or, if you feel you must speak abstractly, at least give a concrete example to illustrate the abstract point. Abstraction and reification seem to be occupational hazards of the legal profession, but one can fight one's impulses to be abstract. Generally, it is wise to do so.

A friend once told me that Albert Einstein said: "Make things as simple as possible — but no simpler." That is a basic rule of science; it should be a basic rule of writing as well. It should apply to everything about your writing from your theories, to the thread of your argumentation, to your descriptions, and to the language you use to express your ideas.

Almost any subject can be made to seem to be unremittingly complex. The world is, in fact, a complicated place. However, we can understand the world (or one of its facets) only by simplifying it. The more complicated your argument is, the harder it will be for your reader to follow it. That's why if there's a simpler way to develop your argument, use it.

Don't try to impress your reader with fancy words and long, complex sentences structures. (An occasional fancy word is okay.) When you finish writing, go back over your text and prune the sentence structure and wording. We all tend to be a bit prolix (is this a well-placed fancy word?), especially in our early drafts. At least five to ten percent of your text can usually be trimmed without loss of meaning. Often, the excision of that excess five to ten percent will, in fact, enhance the effectiveness of your communication.

# Other Rules of Good Legal Writing

### 1. Write a strong introduction to the paper

The introduction to a legal analysis is like the overture to an opera. It should introduce the audience to and prepare it for the major themes that will recur throughout the work.

Switching metaphors, an introduction should be a kind of roadmap of the terrain you are planning to visit on the journey you have set for your reader. Suspense works in detective fiction, but it's a lousy technique in legal writing. Readers want to know where you're headed. They want to know your destination (your thesis) and your intended route to it (the component elements of your analysis in the order you'll develop them). Your readers will be more inclined to trust you if you pay minimal attention to this need they have. A good introduction prevents anxious readers from being distracted by the question, "Will the author discuss this or that issue?"

The introduction is also your best chance to make the reader excited about the topic and your thesis about it, so don't blow it. Don't just tell the reader that the subject is important or interesting, demonstrate that it is. Your reader should finish the introduction with the thought "hey, what a snappy idea; I can't wait to read about it." A good introduction gets your reader prepared to work along with you. He or she anticipates what you will say as the paper unfolds its argument.

### 2. Use meaningful titles to introduce each section of your paper

First of all, use section titles. It keeps the reader awake and helps the reader get oriented about what to expect. Apart from the introduction and conclusion, section titles should make reference to the aspect of your argument addressed in the section. (Titles such as "facts", "background," and "analysis" are not meaningful titles.)

You need not make section titles into full sentences about what you intend to "prove" in the section, but use section titles to remind your reader of the purpose of the section and where it fits into your overall argument. On the other hand, don't assume that the reader has read the title or that the reader has treated the title as the first sentence of a new paragraph. Section titles are section titles, not part of the text.

Two other things: Be affirmative in your statement of the purpose of a section. "No" or "not" should not appear therein if you can think of a way to say it well without the negation. And avoid like the plague cute or journalistic titles to sections or subsections. Only the most subtle of puns is acceptable.

### 3. Make your case discussions as thorough and yet brief as possible

Disembodied rules extracted from cases are virtually worthless. To understand why a rule makes sense, one must understand the particular circumstances in which the rule was applied and the considerations which attended that application. Therefore, my rule is: Never mention a case in the text of your paper unless you describe at least briefly the context from which the principle you are interested in emerged. If it is an important case, more of the circumstances should be discussed. If the context is not worth discussing, the case is not worth mentioning in the text, although it may be worth a footnote.

### 4. Have a strong opening line into case discussions

There are few things more boring than a twenty or thirty page paper consisting of page after page of case discussion in which each paragraph begins: "In A v. B..."; "In C v. D..."; "In E v. F..." By the third one, the reader feels like saying "who cares?"

Add a little zip to these paragraphs by a strong lead-in sentence. Use the opening line to give the reader some clue about what's interesting (or whatever) about the case. In other words, what's the point of discussing the case? Tell your reader as you open your discussion of it. Then he or she will work along with you to make the point.

### 5. Make transitions smoothly

One often writes paragraphs in chunks. The first rough draft may be an assemblage of these chunks. One's main concern when writing a rough draft is to get the chunks into some semblance of order. One way to tell whether the chunks are in proper order is by trying to write transitional sentences to tie one chunk to the next. If you can't find some way to connect the ideas developed in one paragraph to those being developed in the one that follows, it is likely that you have left out some component of the argument.

As you begin to polish the piece, continue to work on your transitions from paragraph to paragraph and from point to point. The paper should flow, not start and stop abruptly like a train on a milk run.

### 6. Resolve issues as you go along and at the end of the paper

Another transition problem, but one worth emphasizing separately, occurs when a writer goes back and forth about pros and cons of an issue and then goes on to another issue. Your reader needs a sense of closure on one issue before you go on to the next or a sense that closure is coming. In concluding your discussion of an issue, pull all the strands of your argument together and give that part of the piece a resolution. The same thing should be done at the end of the whole paper. It is not pedantic to tell your reader from time to time what you have already shown and what you are about to show.

**7. Foresee and address respectfully the arguments that might be made in opposition to your thesis**

Although I urge my students to take a position on the issue about which they are writing, I do not want them to act as though they are advocates writing a brief. A brief is written to argue the strongest case for one side of an issue. In a brief, the writer, consciously or unconsciously, undertakes to minimize the difficulties with his or her own position and to ignore or minimize the strengths of his or her opponent's arguments. The brief writer typically feels that it is his or her opponent's job to develop these positions. If the opponent fails to do so, the brief writer feels no sense of loss.

I tell my students: I want you to be as fair to the strengths of your imaginary antagonist's arguments about the matter as you are to your own position's strengths. You should also be prepared to show the weaknesses of your position, as well as the weaknesses in arguments that would be made against you. Your paper can and should incorporate all of these things. You may be surprised to discover that your paper will be the stronger for its inclusion of these differing perspectives and its frank admission of its limitations.

Anticipate what critics of your thesis would say about your position (if they haven't already made their criticisms known) and incorporate consideration of their concerns into your paper in an affirmative way. That is, don't pose your critic's concerns in his or her terms and then argue the negative. Rather, restructure the critic's points in such a way that any weaknesses in them are apparent. Your reader should gain insights about the problems with your critic's position from your reformulation of the criticisms. Also, guard against setting up straw men. That is, don't oversimplify the position of your opponent and attack only the oversimplified version. It weakens your position in your reader's eyes.

**8. Make use of footnotes for a variety of purposes**

Footnotes can be useful for a wide range of purposes. Experience has taught me that most people are aware of only a few of them. Although some functions of footnotes will be familiar to you, it seems worthwhile to iterate some additional functions of footnotes which many of my students in the past have not known:

(1) to give the reader an instance illustrating a generalization you make in the text (that's what the "See, e. g., X v. Y..." is about);

(2) to send the reader to source materials about a particular subject;

(3) to demonstrate additional depth in your research and to give credit to those whose thinking has influenced you;

(4) to demonstrate the depth of your understanding of the complexities of a subject;

(5) to raise issues which are related to the main thesis of your paper but which would seem digressions if developed in the text; and

(6) to raise and address some potential objections your reader may have about your thesis that you judge do not need to be developed at length in the paper, but can not be ignored.

Footnotes allow you to keep your text trim, while still being attentive to your reader's need to be assured of the depth of your understanding of the complexity of an issue.

You should never assume that your reader will read your footnotes so don't put any truly important points in the footnotes. Use footnotes to elaborate, not to make your argument.

### 9. Never end a paragraph or a section with a quotation

A quotation at the end of a paragraph or a section looks lazy, as if you couldn't summon the energy to finish saying what you intended to say. You must tie any quotation into your argument and emphasize the point for which the quotation has been included in the text. Remember that the quotation arose in a different context than your paper; it must be worked into your context.

### 10. Keep your quotations short and to the point

Long quotations look like a lazy way to make a paper long. A good general rule is that you should have no more than ten continuous lines of indented single-spaced quotation in your text at any one time. Apart from suggesting author laziness, the problem with long quotations is that they invite readers to skim. Remember that it's hard to read single-spaced text. In a long quotation, the average reader is likely to read the first four and last four lines. If the point is buried in the middle of a twenty-line indented quotation, the reader is likely to miss it altogether.

### 11. Don't track the language of an article or case you are discussing any more closely than is necessary to convey the ideas with precision

Occasionally, it is tempting to track closely the language of a case or an article. The more technical the subject matter, the more beautiful the prose, the stronger is the temptation. Resist the temptation. It's plagiarism. Frequent footnotes acknowledging the source does not make it something other than plagiarism. You won't have truly analyzed an issue until you incorporate it into your own terms of expression.

### 12. Be attentive to proper form

One of the things you have to adjust to if you want to be a lawyer is that form counts. In legal writing, form is part of the substance. If you are sloppy about your form, your reader will assume you may well be sloppy as to the substance as well. (In my experience, this is usually a good inference.)

A few particular form rules: (1) Always cite cases and statutes in proper "bluebook" form. It is your responsibility to teach yourself the form rules. (2) Never (well, almost never) split infinitives. (3) Spell all the words in your piece correctly. (4) Don't get cute about personal pronouns. ("He" or "he/she" or "he or she" is ok; "she" is too cute.) (5) Don't construct run-on sentences.

Your seventh-grade English teacher may have been a bore, but he or she was right to insist that you pay attention to spelling, grammar, diction, and the like. You can't afford to take the chance of your argument being dismissed because of your sloppiness about the little things.

### 13. Have a healthy balance to your paper

How much introduction, background, case discussion, analysis, etc. is needed in any paper depends on its subject. A good rule of thumb is to keep your introduction to about five percent of your text (3/4 of a page for a fifteen page paper; one page for twenty pages); your conclusion to five to ten percent of the paper (five percent if you're only summing up; ten percent if you're suggesting a new approach); and equal quanta per internal argument (twenty-five to thirty percent per issue if you have three arguments sections; forty to forty-five percent per issue if you use tow). Watch for imbalance in your paper. After you write your first draft, read it over and ask yourself whether you need to do more development of one part or need to cut another. If you can't tell if it's imbalanced, ask a friend to read it.

### 14. Consider the policy implications of your thesis

Questions you should address include the following: What effect would the rule you propose have on the way the world works? What effect would a contrary rule have? Is the intended effect achievable? Is the effect you seek to bring about worth the cost? What consequences besides the ones you intend are likely to result from the rule you espouse?

The reason your legal analysis should consider the policy implications of your proposal should be obvious. Words have power. They often serve as a basis for action, and, when carried out, they have an effect on the society of which you are a part. You are about to cease being a student (whose words rarely have much effect on anything but their grades) and about to become a professional whose words and actions have effects on real people-not only on your clients and their opponents but on other people in society. I think you have a responsibility to use your words to do good and to persuade others you are doing good. Also, people don't adopt rules just because they are clear or consistent; they adopt rules because they make sense in ordering human affairs.

## Doing Research Adequate to the Task

A question almost all inexperienced writers have that they almost never have the temerity to ask is: How much research should I do? I know you'd like to ask me this question, and surprise, I'll even answer it. The answer is simple: Do research adequate to the task you've undertaken.

You will no doubt protest, "but that tells me nothing at all!" Don't be so hasty. It does tell you something. It tells you that different topics require different amounts of research. Usually, although not always, it's possible to have a pretty good sense at the start as to how much or how little research a particular topic will require.

If you decide to tackle a very difficult topic, you will have taken on a commitment to do the research adequate to the task. That may mean you'll have to do more work than one of your colleagues, but remember, you chose the topic. Choosing a topic about which there is little in the traditionally recognized literature doesn't necessarily mean you'll have it easy. In that case, you will be expected to find everything there is on the topic, make the most of what there is, and be more creative in your analysis than your less adventurous colleagues.

At a minimum, you must read all the pertinent cases, treatises, law review articles, other commentaries, legislative history, and whatever else you can get your hands on. What if there is an unmanageably large volume of material to read? One response is to abandon your thesis and look for a new one. Another response is to refine your thesis in such a way that you can pare down the volume of pertinent material. A third — the one you read — is to go ahead and get started. Ambition is a great thing if you've got the energy to satisfy it. (I advise you to try the second strategy before consigning yourself to a new search or six years in the library.)

What to read first is another important question, and I have advice about this as well. The temptation is often to go to secondary or tertiary sources first (that is, annotations describing cases or treatises) and read them to find out what's going on. While I urge my students to comb through these sources to find cases and references to other source materials, I believe quite firmly that the best and most original papers are written when the writer reads the primary sources first and reads them very thoroughly before getting into the secondary sources. For most legal analyses, this means reading the cases first, and the law review articles, treatises, etc., second. If you read the cases first, your mind will be fresh and unencumbered by the analytic constructs of other authors. You'll have a chance to form your own opinion about the cases, to be attentive to certain details or arguments other writers may have overlooked, and to formulate an analytic framework form your fresh impressions. If you read the treatises or law review articles first, they are likely to color your vision. They may well give you a handle on what the issues are. But the cost you're likely to pay is that you'll use the other writer's analytic perspective as a selection mechanism when you read the cases and may lose the chance to come up with a more original approach.

When to stop researching is also an important concern of yours. The truth is that just as it is impossible to overknead bread, it is impossible to do too much research for a paper. As with kneading, at some point you've done enough to make the bread have the proper texture. It is at that point you begin to fashion the loaf.

To know when to stop researching, you really have to be honest with yourself about what kind of person you are. Are you the sort of person who tries to scrape through life with the most minimal exertion? If so, push yourself a little harder to do research for your paper. Or are you the sort of person who tends to take out his or her anxiety about committing words to paper by setting off on an unfruitful search for the "perfect" case, or worse, for the tenth source to support a minor point? If you are this sort of person, then work on holding your impulses somewhat in check. Find the important cases and deal with them. Put your anxiety to work on writing.

I have two main criticisms about my students' research: It lacks depth, or it lacks breadth. When I talk of lack of depth, I generally mean one of two things: either that you have discussed or referred to too few of the pertinent cases about the issue or that you have unduly restricted the scope of the question, and thereby missed cases relatively close to the point.

When I speak of a need for greater breadth, what I am likely to mean is this: To make a convincing argument about a point it may be necessary to refer to sources other than cases or law review articles. If you have restricted your discussion to these sources, your paper lacks breadth. I will urge you to hunt out other types of sources.

# Overcoming Writer's Block

We have all had the experience of facing a blank pad of yellow paper with an equally blank mind. If this happens to you as you try to write the introduction (or whatever) to your analytic paper and it lasts long enough to make you fear you've caught the dread disease "writer's block," don't panic. It's not terminal. The best way to overcome it is often to try getting started a different way from the one you initially chose.

Everyone has a different set of techniques for making a breakthrough on a writing project. A technique that may work for you may not work for me and vice versa. Still, you may be interested to know about a few things I do when I get stuck in the muck when I'm writing.

If I've made an outline (and that's the first thing to do if you're stuck), I go back over it to see if there is something in there about which I feel I can write at least a paragraph. If so, I do it. I continue to write in chunks until I've found a narrative line to tie a set of chunks together. When I've done this, I usually find I've broken the ice and can begin writing the earlier parts of the paper.

Or if there is a case that is of particular importance to my paper, I start writing about that. I start with a description of the facts. Then I write about the court's analysis and finally about my view of the implications of the case. Again, this usually breaks the ice and gets me going.

At other times I find it helpful to jot down a set of ideas about one part of my argument (in somewhat greater detail than my outline would show). Then I monkey around with ordering the jotted ideas; then I try to write a paragraph or more using this order.

If none of this works, I try to find someone who will let me explain what I am trying to say in my paper. I try to remember what I said or I ask my friend to take notes. (It can also help to tape it if one can talk without feeling self-conscious because of the machine.) Then I write up what I've just said. Of course it won't be perfect, but it's a start. Most people find it easier to work from a rough draft than from nothing.

Sometimes talking to a friend can also help you detect if there's some missing link in your argument. Often what's blocking your writing is that you unconsciously know there's some unsolved problem with your analysis. Once you find it, you may be able to solve it, and that may break the block.

# The Roles of Editor and Editee

Everyone feels a little naked when another person reads some thing he or she has written. This is particularly true if the reason for allowing the other person to read it is to find its imperfections. Every writer knows there are the prose equivalents of warts, scaly skin, or a roll of fat around the waistline of the body of his or her writing. If you are asked to edit someone's work, think of your role as similar to the job of a plastic surgeon who has been asked to remove a wart or the nurse at a weight reduction clinic who has been consulted to help a fat person lose weight. You will not be doing your job properly if by your silence you communicate to your clients that they really haven't got the problems they came to you to have fixed, whether those be warts, rolls of fat, or lumpy muddy prose.

On the other hand, if your enthusiasm for your job impels you to a fevered description of the multiplicity of defects you see, the listener may be so devastated by the criticism that he or she will be paralyzed and unable to summon the motivation or confidence to remedy the situation. The hard thing, then, is to find a way to communicate enough of a positive response to make the person feel as though there is something about his or her writing to be salvaged and enough of a negative response to make the person feel that much work remains to be done. Here is what I tell my students about my role as editor and how they should take my comments.

It is unlikely that anyone will ever have read your papers with as much care as I do. Whatever else you may feel after getting my comments, you are unlikely to feel neglected. However good your paper is, you are likely to get extensive comments from me. It is important that even the best students know how much further they could develop their analyses. The extensiveness of my comments should be taken not as a sign of my displeasure, but as a sign of how engaged I've become in your work and as an indicator of how rich are the opportunities for further exploration. It will only be the outstandingly good or bad papers that will leave me speechless.

My comments will range from scoldings about split infinitives to questions about your interpretation of a case or statute or to disquisitions about issues you raise which I think deserve fuller treatment. If you take my comments in the way I wish you to take them, you will do two things: (1) Respond to each of them not by automatically making changes as I have directed (or as you think I have directed), but by making a judgment whether some change I have suggested makes sense to you. Don't make the change unless you are persuaded that there is an ambiguity which needs to be corrected or that the question I raise needs to be addressed. Just be prepared to defend your decision if I challenge you about the issue a second time. (2) Treat my remarks as an invitation to go back over your own writing with a critical eye. Use my remarks as an aid to your reexamination of your writing; look for things I missed or things I only hinted at. Use the insights you gain from this process to rebuild your paper. A friend once told me that his dissertation adviser would heavily edit two or three paragraphs of his dissertation draft and then simply direct my friend to "continue on in this fashion". You should do the same.

Understand that the point of my remarks is to help you develop your own self-critical capacities, to make you your own best editor. When you have gotten to the point that you can read a page or two of your own prose and anticipate what I will say about it (or better still, think of things I should have said about it but didn't), you don't need me any more.

Well, that will do for preliminaries. Now get to work and have fun. Yes, at the same time.

## ♣ New Words

| | | |
|---|---|---|
| **1.** | prose *n.* | 散文 |
| **2.** | window pane | 窗玻璃 |
| **3.** | charm *v.* | 迷住；使人陶醉 |
| **4.** | exotic *a.* | 異乎尋常的 |
| **5.** | imagery *n.* | 形象化的描述 |
| **6.** | suspense *n.* | 懸而不決；未定 |
| **7.** | subtle *a.* | 微妙的；細微的 |
| **8.** | obfuscation *n.* | 困惑 |
| **9.** | flawlessly *adv.* | 完美無瑕地 |
| **10.** | lucid *a.* | 易懂的 |
| **11.** | enlightening *a.* | 富有啟發性的 |
| **12.** | lucidity *n.* | 易懂 |
| **13.** | essay *n.* | 文章；短文 |
| **14.** | exposition *n.* | 評注；講解 |
| **15.** | formulaic *a.* | 刻板的；公式化的 |
| **16.** | analytic *a.* | 分析的 |
| **17.** | ape *v.* | 模仿 |

| | |
|---|---|
| **18.** paramount *a.* | 首要的；最高的 |
| **19.** applicability *n.* | 應用性；適用性 |
| **20.** block *n.* | 障礙物 |
| **21.** jaunty *a.* | 活潑的；時髦的 |
| **22.** jocular *a.* | 詼諧的 |
| **23.** thesis *n.* | 論文；畢業（或學位）論文 |
| **24.** subcategory *n.* | 亞類；子種類 |
| **25.** descriptive *a.* | 描述的；敘述的 |
| **26.** ambivalence *n.* | 矛盾情緒；舉棋不定 |
| **27.** enthusiast *n.* | 熱心人；熱情者；熱衷者 |
| **28.** myriad *a.* | 無數的 |
| **29.** temptation *n.* | 誘惑 |
| **30.** thematic *a.* | 題目的；主題的 |
| **31.** tantalize *v.* | 逗弄 |
| **32.** fabric *n.* | 結構；構造 |
| **33.** footnote *n.* | 註腳 |
| **34.** insight *n.* | 洞察（力）；見識 |
| **35.** section titles | 段落標題 |
| **36.** transitional sentences | 過渡句子 |
| **37.** spice *n.* | 香料；調味品 |
| **38.** dessert *n.* | 甜食 |
| **39.** deem *v.* | 認為 |
| **40.** integrated *a.* | 使成為一體的 |
| **41.** analytical *a.* | 分析的 |
| **42.** inconspicuous *a.* | 不顯著的；不引人注意的 |
| **43.** recitation *n.* | 敘述；詳述 |
| **44.** encyclopedia *n.* | 百科全書 |
| **45.** dispassionate *a.* | 不動情感的；不帶偏見的 |
| **46.** treatise *n.* | 專題論文 |
| **47.** odds and ends | 殘餘的東西；瑣碎事 |
| **48.** titillating dicta | 令人興奮的名言 |
| **49.** the Baptist *n.* | （基督教新教）浸禮會 |
| **50.** kernel *n.* | 核心 |
| **51.** concomitant *a.* | 相伴的；伴隨的 |
| **52.** distracted *a.* | 被弄得糊裡糊塗 |

| | | |
|---|---|---|
| **53.** unfocused *a.* | 不集中的 |
| **54.** meandering *a.* | 曲折的 |
| **55.** glue *n.* | 膠水 |
| **56.** ill effect | 壞效果 |
| **57.** dissipate *v.* | 浪費 |
| **58.** forcefulness *n.* | 有說服力 |
| **59.** folder *n.* | 文件夾 |
| **60.** rework *v.* | 重新做；再做 |
| **61.** neophyte *n.* | 初學者；新手 |
| **62.** rationality *n.* | 合理性 |
| **63.** reservation *n.* | 保留 |
| **64.** strident *a.* | 刺耳的 |
| **65.** bludgeoned *a.* | 被人猛烈攻擊的 |
| **66.** distract *v.* | 分散（注意力）；使人糊塗 |
| **67.** journalistic *a.* | 新聞工作者的 |
| **68.** emotional *a.* | 感情上的；易動情感的 |
| **69.** concreteness *n.* | 具體 |
| **70.** abstractly *adv.* | 抽象地 |
| **71.** abstract *a.* | 抽象的 |
| **72.** thread of argumentation | 論證的思路 |
| **73.** unremittingly *adv.* | 不停地；持續地 |
| **74.** excision *n.* | 刪除 |
| **75.** overture *n.* | 前奏曲 |
| **76.** metaphor *n.* | 比喻 |
| **77.** detective fiction | 偵探小說 |
| **78.** snappy *a.* | 時髦的；直截了當的 |
| **79.** plague cute | 令人煩惱的裝腔作勢 |
| **80.** pun *n.* | 雙關語 |
| **81.** disembodied rules | 脫離現實的規則 |
| **82.** assemblage *n.* | 集合 |
| **83.** semblance *n.* | 偽裝 |
| **84.** pros and cons | 贊成和反對 |
| **85.** strand *n.* | （論據的）一個組成部分 |
| **86.** brief *n.* | 訴訟要點摘錄；律師的書狀 |
| **87.** antagonist *n.* | 對手；敵手 |

| | | |
|---|---|---|
| **88.** | iterate *v.* | 重述；再說 |
| **89.** | digression *n.* | 離題 |
| **90.** | skim *v.* | 略讀；浮光掠影地看 |
| **91.** | track *v.* | 跟蹤 |
| **92.** | plagiarism *n.* | 剽竊；抄襲 |
| **93.** | "bluebook" form | 「藍皮書」形式 |
| **94.** | run-on sentences | 亂加從句的冗長句子 |
| **95.** | diction. *n.* | 措辭；用詞風格 |
| **96.** | quanta *n.* | 份額 |
| **97.** | espouse *v.* | 採納 |
| **98.** | commentary *n.* | 評論 |
| **99.** | refine *v.* | 使精練優美 |
| **100.** | annotation *n.* | 注釋 |
| **101.** | exertion *n.* | 盡力 |
| **102.** | law review | 法律期刊 |
| **103.** | blank pad | 空白本子 |
| **104.** | editee *n.* | 被修改者 |
| **105.** | warts *n.* | 疣 |
| **106.** | scaly *a.* | 有鱗片的 |
| **107.** | plastic surgeon | 整形外科醫生 |
| **108.** | lumpy *a.* | 不平的 |
| **109.** | muddy *a.* | 糊塗的 |
| **110.** | impel *v.* | 推動；激勵 |
| **111.** | paralyze *v.* | 使氣餒 |
| **112.** | scoldings *n.* | 責罵；申斥 |
| **113.** | disquisition *n.* | 專題論文 |
| **114.** | dissertation *n.* | 學位論文 |
| **115.** | preliminaries *n.* | 開端 |
| **116.** | wishy-washy *a.* | 淡而無味的 |

## ♣ New Phrases and Idiomatic Expressions

| | | |
|---|---|---|
| 1. | to come to a conclusion or reach a conclusion | 得到結論 |
| 2. | over time | 過去一段時間裡 |
| 3. | to pick up a tip or two for | 獲得一些關於……的忠告 |
| 4. | to ape another person's style | 模仿另一個人的風格 |
| 5. | to bite the bullet | 勇敢地行動 |
| 6. | to get captivated by sth. | 被……所吸引 |
| 7. | to trot out | 提出……供參考 |
| 8. | to be dissipated by | 被……所分離 |
| 9. | to get through | 挨過 |
| 10. | to pander to | 迎合…… |
| 11. | to have little or no exposure to sth. | 很少或沒有暴露在…… |
| 12. | to distract sb. from doing sth. | 使某人不能專心做某事 |
| 13. | to feel like doing sth. | 想要做某事 |
| 14. | to add a little zip to | 增加一些活力 |
| 15. | in chunks | 大量地 |
| 16. | on a milk run | 執行例行任務 |
| 17. | to set up straw men | 提出脆弱的假想論點 |
| 18. | at length | 詳細地 |
| 19. | to be sloppy about sth. | 對……馬虎 |
| 20. | to get one's hands on sth. | 把……弄到手 |
| 21. | to pare down | 削減;縮減 |
| 22. | to comb through | 尋找;搜尋 |
| 23. | to form one's opinion about sth. | 形成某人對某事的意見 |
| 24. | to give sb. a handle on sth. | 使某人能對某事進行控制 |
| 25. | to scrape through | 艱難地度過 |
| 26. | to hold one's impulses in check | 控制住某人的衝動 |
| 27. | to get stuck in the muck | 被卡在淤泥之中 |
| 28. | to fell a little naked | 被暴露 |
| 29. | to monkey around | 胡鬧 |

| **30.** to be devastated by sth. | 被某事搞混亂；被某事壓垮 |
| **31.** to leave sb. speechless | 使某人一時不知道講什麼 |
| **32.** to overcome sb's block | 克服某人的障礙 |
| **33.** to hunt out | 找出；找到 |
| **34.** to conjure up | 提出；想起 |

## ♣ Notes

**1.** metaphor：隱喻；比喻。

英語中的一種修辭手段，如...prose is like a window pane 中的 window pane。

**2.** pun：雙關語。

常用同音異義詞或多義詞構成，如：He laid down his arms.

在此句中的 arms 就是一個雙關語。

**3.** the primary sources：第一淵源。

the secondary sources：第二淵源。

the tertiary sources：第三淵源。

在以上表達法中不能用first, second and third來取代，這是英國人的習慣用語。

類似的例子還有第一產業，第二產業，第三產業，英文必須用primary industry, secondary industry and tertiary industry；同樣的道理，當談論證券市場中的一級市場，二級市場，三級市場時應分別用primary market, secondary market and tertiary market，而不能寫成first market, second market和third market。

**4.** to overknead bread

直譯是「做麵包的麵團不能揉得過分」，在課文中指在寫法律文章時不能查閱太多的資料。

**5.** to fashion the loaf

直譯是「使麵包成形」，在課文中表示查閱資料到適當程度就應動筆寫文章並使其成形。

**6.** ...who may be offended by too harsh a tone這裡要注意，不能將too harsh a tone寫成a too harsh tone，因為這不符合英語習慣用法。

**7.** If the context is not worth discussing...此句子worth（值得）後面經常跟動名詞表示值得做某事。例如，This book is worth reading（此書值得一讀）；This case is not worth mentioning（此案不值一提）。在這裡要特別注意避免和worthwhile相混淆。worthwhile也是形容詞，也有「值得」的意思，但在用法上有區別。其一，它後面不跟動名詞而是跟動詞不定式，如，It seems worthwhile to do so；其二，它可作謂語，例如：These results were not worthwhile（這些結果並不合算），而worth後必須跟動名詞，否則意思不完整。

**Exercises**

## I. Answer the following questions:

**1**. What sort of writing style do you prefer?

**2**. How can one make one's legal prose become like a window pane?

**3**. What are the six paramount rules of good legal writing?

  Do you agree to the six rules?

**4**. Is an introduction to a legal analysis necessary?

  What should it be like?

**5**. Is it a must to use meaningful titles to introduce each section of your paper?

**6**. What purposes can footnotes serve?

**7**. What is the correct way of treating quotations in your legal writing?

**8**. What should you do when you get stuck in the muck when you are writing?

## II. Translate the following Chinese passages into English:

**1**. 要將一篇法律文章寫好，必須記住以下幾點：(1)有論點；(2)要切題；(3)要將蒐集的事實、法院的分析融在你的論點之中；(4)要將你的分析分成不同部分加以發揮；(5)要有一個適當的基調；(6)在可能情況下要具體簡明。

**2**. 在法律文章中可以引用他人的話或文章，但要短並扣住主題。如果引文太長，讀者就會不高興，或者最多浮光掠影地看一下。這樣一來就失去了引文的意義。

**3**. 在寫法律文章時，在開頭部分、背景部分、問題討論和分析以及結論之間要保持一個良好的平衡。開頭部分一般占5%，結論占5%-10%，其餘為文章的正文。

**4**. 使寫作成功的風格很多，但許多人認為最成功的風格是：完美無暇地清楚、易懂和富有啟發性。

## III. Find out all the metaphors used in the text.

This glossary contains brief definitions of more than 350 legal terms. Some are concise restatements of more detailed definitions given elsewhere in the text. Some are new terms that are not defined in the text, but terms that may be encountered in your future personal business relationships. Approximately 500 other specialized terms defined in the text are not included in this glossary because of limited space. For a thorough review of the vocabulary of business law, review each of the 48 separate parts as well as this glossary.

**Abandonment**, the relinquishment or surrender of a right or property with the intent not to reclaim.

**Abet**, to encourage and aid another in an act of a criminal nature.

**Abrogate**, to annul or repeal; to abolish a law.

**Abscond**, to flee secretly; to hide or absent oneself with intent to avoid legal process.

**Abstract of title**, a summary of the history of the title to land, including all conveyances, mortgages, liens, and other changes affecting a parcel of land.

**Acceptance**, the act of the drawee of a bill of exchange which signifies he agrees to pay it; also, the bill itself after acceptance.

**Acceptor**, the drawee of a bill of exchange after he has agreed to pay it.

**Accessory** (ak-″ses-′ŏ-re), one who, though not present, aids or abets a crime.

**Accommodation paper**, a check, note, or draft drawn or endorsed by one person for another without consideration.

**Accord and satisfaction**, the substitution of another agreement for an existing claim and the full execution of the new agreement.

**Accounting**, the science of accounts; statement of receipts and payments in trust or contract relationships.

**Accretion** (ah-kre-′shun), growth by natural enlargement, as an addition to land by a gradual deposit of soil along its borders.

**Acknowledgment**, the act by which a party who has executed an instrument goes before a competent officer and swears that he did execute the instrument and that it is genuine.

**Acquittal**, a verdict of not guilty; the discharge by a court of a party charged with a crime.

**Act of bankruptcy**, any act, as defined by the laws of bankruptcy, that will cause a person to be adjudged a bankrupt.

**Act of God**, an accident due to a force beyond human control, such as an earthquake or tornado.

**Action**, a lawsuit; proceeding in a court for enforcement of a right.

**Adjective law**, the part of our law that deals with the supplying of remedies to reimburse the injured party when his rights have been interfered with.

**Adjourn** (ah-jern′), to postpone action of a court or a body until a specified time.

**Adjudication** (ah-ju-″dĭ-ka-′shun), the act of a court in giving judgment in a lawsuit.

**Administrator**, the person appointed by the court to settle the estate of one who died intestate, that is, without making a will.

**Affidavit** (af-″ĭ-da-′vit), a signed, written statement sworn to before one who is authorized to take oaths.

**Agent**, one who acts for another in dealings with third parties.

**Alias** (a-′le-us), an assumed name; otherwise; different; another.

**Alibi**, a defense based upon the statement that the defendant was not present when the tort or crime was committed.

**Alien** (āl-′yen), a person who lives in one country but owes allegiance to another country.

**Alienate** (āl′yen-āt), to convey the title to property.

**Allegation** (al-″ĭ-ga-′shun), a statement of fact made during a legal proceeding.

**Allonge** (a-lunj′), a strip of paper attached to a negotiable instrument for the writing of additional endorsements.

**Alteration**, a change in the terms of a written contract or instrument.

**Amalgamation**, the union of two incorporated companies or societies by the merging of one in the other.

**Annuity**, an amount of money payable annually until the death of recipient.

**Annul**, to make void, to cancel, or to destroy.

**Answer**, a formal written statement containing the defense to an action; a reply to a charge.

**Antedated**, dated at a time earlier than the actual date.

**Appeal**, the referring, or attempting to refer, a case to a higher court for reexamination and review.

**Appraise**, to set a price or value upon something.

**Appurtenance** (ah-′pert′-nans), any right with reference to land that goes with the land in a deed or lease.

**Arbitration**, a method of settling disputes between parties by referring to third parties for settlement.

**Arraignment** (ah-rān-′ment), calling a prisoner to the bar of a court to answer an indictment.

**Arrears**, any money due and unpaid.

**Arson**, the deliberate and malicious burning of any structure.

**Assault**, a threat or attempt to injure a person by physical violence.

**Assign**, to transfer to another.

**Assignment**, the transfer of any property right from one person to another; usually used in connection with the transfer of intangible rights, such as the right to collect money.

**Attachment**, legal seizure, usually of goods.

**Attest**, to certify as to the genuineness of a document; to bear witness to.

**Attorney in fact** (ah-ter-'ne), a person appointed by another to act for him.

**Award**, the decision reached by arbitrators or referees.

**Bail**, security given for the release from legal custody of a defendant with assurance that he shall appear when summoned by court.

**Bailment**, the delivery of goods to another for a certain purpose, the goods to be returned later.

**Bankrupt**, one who has been adjudged a bankrupt under the Federal bankruptcy laws.

**Barter**, the exchange of goods for other goods.

**Battery**, the unlawful striking or touching of another person.

**Beneficiary** (ben-"ĭ-fish-'ē-er-"ē), (1) one who is entitled to the proceeds of a life insurance policy; (2) one who is entitled to the benefit of property held by another as trustee; (3) one who receives a gift under a will.

**Bequeath** (bĭ-kwēth'), to give personal property by will to another.

**Bequest**, that which is left by a will; a legacy.

**Bilateral**, a term used to indicate two promises or two obligations. Thus, in a bilateral contract there is a mutual obligation, consisting of a promise by each party that is binding on both parties.

**Bill of lading**, a combination contract and receipt given by the common carrier to the person shipping certain goods.

**Bill of sale**, a written contract transferring personal property from one person to another.

**Binder**, memorandum given insured when it is agreed that contract of insurance is to be effective before the written contract is executed.

**Blue-sky laws**, statutes for the protection of investing public from the sale of worthless securities.

**Bona fide** (bo-'nā fi-d"), in good faith; honestly; without fraud or unfair dealing.

**Boycott**, a combination between persons to discontinue dealings with other persons who refuse to comply with their requests.

**Breach**, a violation of an agreement or obligation.

**Brief**, the written or printed arguments and legal authorities furnished the court by lawyers.

**Bulk sale**, the sale of an entire business, made secretly and with the intent to defraud the seller's creditors.

**Bylaws**, the rules which a private corporation adopts for its internal regulation.

**Capital stock**, the total designated value of shares issued by a corporation.

**Cause of action**, the grounds for a lawsuit.

**Caveat emptor** (ka-′ve-at″ emp′tor), Latin phrase meaning, "Let the buyer beware."

**Caveat venditor** (ka-′ve-at″ ven-′dĭ-tor), a Latin phrase meaning, "Let the seller beware."

**Certificate of deposit**, a bank certificate stating that the person named has deposited a stated amount of money payable to his order.

**Certificate of stock**, a certificate issued by a corporation showing that a certain party has a specified number of shares of the corporation's stock.

**Chattel**, a piece of personal property.

**Chattel mortgage**, a mortgage on personal property.

**Civil law**, a system of codified law, common on the continent of Europe, based on Roman law. Or, used in a different context, that division of laws that deals with the rights and duties of private parties, as contrasted with criminal law.

**Client**, one who employs an attorney; one who seeks professional advice or assistance.

**Code**, an organized collection of laws.

**Codicil** (kod-′ĭ-sil″), a formal supplement to a will.

**Collateral security**, additional obligations, usually stocks or bonds, pledged as security for a personal performance of an agreement.

**Collusion**, a secret agreement designed to attain an unlawful objective or advantage.

**Common law**, the part of our law that comes from custom or precedent; usually refers to the long-established law of England that was based on the recorded decisions of the early law courts.

**Complaint**, the plaintiff's statement of his cause of action.

**Composition**, an agreement among creditors and with the debtor that the creditors will accept part of the debts in full settlement.

**Compromise**, a settlement reached by mutual agreement and concessions.

**Concurrent**, happening at the same time; acting together.

**Conditional sale**, a contract in which it is agreed that title to goods shall not pass from the seller to the buyer until the happening of a certain condition, usually the payment of the purchase price.

**Confiscation**, the appropriation by the state of private property for public use.

**Consanguinity** (kŏn-"san-"gwin-"ĭ-te), blood relationship.

**Consideration**, in contracts, the impelling influence that causes a contracting party to enter the contract; a benefit received by the promisor or a detriment suffered by the promisee.

**Consignment**, goods directed by one person to another to be sold for the first person and credited to him by the second person.

**Consignor**, one who directs goods to a consignee for sale.

**Contract to sell goods**, a contract whereby the seller agrees to transfer the ownership of goods to the buyer for a consideration called the price.

**Conversion**, the unlawful assumption of ownership or destruction of property of another.

**Conveyance**, the transfer of title to real property; the instrument used to transfer title to real property.

**Copyright**, a right granted to an author, photographer, artist, or the agent of any one of these by the Government to publish and sell exclusively an artistic or literary work for twenty-eight years.

**Costs**, an allowance granted by the court to a successful party to a suit to reimburse him for his expenses in conducting the suit.

**Counterclaim**, a claim set up to offset another claim.

**Covenant** (kuv-'ē-nant), an agreement under seal; a promise in a sealed contract.

**Cover**, after a breach of contract by seller, a purchase by the buyer, in good faith, of goods as substitute for those not delivered by the seller.

**Crime**, a wrong which the government recognizes as injurious to the public; a violation of a public law.

**Curtesy** (ker-"tĕ-se), the life estate given by law in some states to the husband in all real property owned by his wife at the time of her death.


**Damages**, the money recovered by court action for injury or loss caused by another.

**Days of grace**, additional days in which to complete a contract after maturity.

**De facto** (de fak-'to), as a matter of fact; from the fact.

**Decedent** (dĭ-se-'dent), a deceased person.

**Deceit**, a fraudulent misrepresentation or contrivance, by which a person is misled to his injury.

**Declaration**, the statement by the plaintiff setting forth his cause of action.

**Decree**, an order made by the court in a suit in equity.

**Deed**, a formal written document granting the right to real property.

**Default** (dĭ-fawlt'), a neglect or failure to act.

**Defendant**, the person sued in a civil action; the person charged with a crime in a criminal action.

**Defense**, the answer to a cause of action or indictment.

**Del credere** (del krād′-er-ē), used to describe an agent who guarantees payment for goods which he sells in his principal's name.

**Delegation**, the transfer of an obligation from one person to another, usually the substitution of one debtor for another.

**Demand**, a request for payment of a claim.

**Demurrer** (dǐ-mur-′er), the formal mode of disputing the sufficiency in law of the pleading of the other side.

**Deponent**, one who makes a sworn statement.

**Deposition**, the testimony of a witness, given under oath, for use in the trial of a case.

**Descent**, the passing of an estate by inheritance and not by will.

**Devise** (dǐ-vīz′), a gift of real property contained in a will.

**Dictum**, an opinion expressed by a court which is not necessary in deciding the question that is currently before the court.

**Disaffirm**, to repudiate a voidable contract.

**Discharge**, the act by which a person is freed from performing a legal obligation.

**Dishonor**, to refuse to pay a negotiable instrument when due.

**Domicile**, that place where a man has his permanent home.

**Dower** (dow-′er), the right given by law to a widow in her late husband's real property.

**Due process of law**, the right to the protections and privileges afforded by constitutions, statutes, and courts.

**Duress** (du-res′), restraint or compulsion, usually by threat or fear of injury.

**Duties**, obligations that are the correlative of rights; also taxes, such as customs duties.


**Earnest**, the payment of part of the purchase price to bind a sale.

**Easement**, the right of an owner of land to use the land of another in a limited way.

**Embezzlement**, the fraudulent appropriation of goods or money by one to whom they were entrusted.

**Emblements** (em-′ble-mentz), products of the earth produced annually by labor and industry.

**Eminent domain** (do-mān′), the right of the government to appropriate private property for public use.

**Enact**, to make or establish a law.

**Encumbrance**, a lien or claim attached to property.

**Endorsement**, a name, with or without other words, written on the back of a negotiable paper.

**Enemy aliens**, aliens who are subjects of a hostile country.

**Equity**, a branch of law granting relief when there is no adequate relief otherwise available.

**Equity of redemption**, the right of the mortgagor to reclaim his property after the time of payment has expired.

**Escheat** (es-'chēt), the reversion of property to the state if the property holder dies without legal heirs.

**Escrow** (es-'kro), a written document held by a third person until a prescribed condition comes about.

**Estate**, an interest in property.

**Estoppel**, a rule of law that precludes the denying of certain facts by a man or conditions arising from his previous conduct, allegations, or admissions.

**Eviction**, dispossession by process of law.

**Evidence**, proof, either written or unwritten, of the allegations in issue between parties; that which is used to induce belief in the minds of the jury or of the court.

**Ex post facto law**, a law that renders criminal an act that was not criminal at the time it was committed; these laws are prohibited by the Constitution.

**Executed**, that which has been fully performed.

**Execution**, the performance of an act, or the completion of an instrument; a writ directing an officer to enforce a judgment.

**Executor** (ig-zek-'ū-ter), the party named in a will to carry out the terms of the will.

**Executory**, that which is yet to be performed.

**Express warranty**, any statement of fact or any promise by the seller that would have the natural tendency to induce the buyer to buy the goods.

**Extradition**, the surrender by one government to another of a person charged with a crime.

**Facsimile** (fak-sim-'ĭ-le), an exact reproduction or copy.

**Fact**, a thing done, or existing. Whether a thing was done or does exist is a question of fact for the jury. If the facts are proved, the matter of the rights and liabilities of the parties is a matter of law for the court.

**Factor**, an agent appointed to sell goods sent to him on a commission basis.

**Fee simple**, the full ownership in lands.

**Felony**, a crime punishable by death or by imprisonment in a state prison.

**Fiduciary** (fĭ-doo-'she-er″-ē), a person who possesses rights and powers to be exercised for the benefit of another person; a trustee.

**Firm**, all members of a partnership taken collectively; the name or title under which a partnership transacts business.

**Fixture**, usually considered as an article of personal property physically attached to realty in such a manner that it becomes a part thereof.

**Foreclosure**, a legal proceeding to apply mortgaged property to the payment of a mortgage.

**Forfeiture**, the loss of some privilege or right, usually as a penalty for some illegal act or some negligence or breach of contract.

**Forgery**, the act of falsely making or materially altering a document with intent to defraud.

**Franchise**, a special privilege conferred by law.

**Fraud**, the gain of an advantage to another's detriment by deceitful or unfair means.

**Freight**, goods which one party entrusts to another for transportation.

**Friendly fire**, a fire which stays within its natural boundaries.

**Fungible goods** (fun-ˈjĭ-bl), movable goods composed of like units which can be estimated and replaced by like units according to weight, measure, and number.

**Garnishment**, a court order authorizing the attachment of property, usually wages, in order to satisfy an unpaid claim.

**Gift**, a voluntary transfer of property without consideration.

**Good faith**, an honest intention not to take advantage of another.

**Goods**, tangible personal property; articles of merchandise; chattels.

**Goodwill**, the advantage or benefit that is acquired by a business, beyond the capital or stock used therein, resulting from having a body of regular customers and a good reputation.

**Grand jury**, a jury that hears evidence prior to an actual trial for the purpose of determining whether a criminal charge should be brought against an individual.

**Grant**, the transfer of title to real property by means of a deed.

**Gratuitous**, without value or legal consideration.

**Guaranty** (gar-ˈan-te), a contract whereby one party agrees to answer for the debt or default of another.

**Guardian**, one having legal custody of the property or the person of a minor or incompetent.

**Habeas corpus** (ha-ˈbe-as kor-ˈpus), a writ issued by a court ordering a person who detains another in custody to bring the person held before the court to determine if the detention is legal.

**Heir**, one who inherits by right of relationship.

**Holding over**, the act of retaining possession, without the landlord's consent, of leased property after the term of the lease has expired.

**Holographic will**, a will written in the testator's handwriting.

**Honor**, to accept and pay a bill of exchange, note, or check.

**Idiot**, one who never had reasoning power.

**Immaterial**, unimportant; without weight or significance.

**Implied warranty**, a warranty that is proved by the acts of the seller or by surrounding circumstances rather than by words spoken or written.

**Incidental beneficiary**, one who indirectly benefits from the performance of a contract without the specific intention of the contracting parties.

**Incumbrance**, a mortgage, lien, or claim on real property.

**Indemnity**, an agreement that one party will secure another party against loss or damage due to the happening of a specified event.

**Indenture** (in-den-'cher), a sealed agreement between two or more parties.

**Indictment**, a formal charge of a crime of a public nature handed up by a grand jury.

**Injunction**, a court order forbidding the doing of a specified act.

**Inland bill**, a bill of exchange drawn and payable in the same state.

**Insolvency**, a state wherein one does not have sufficient property for the full payment of his debts or is unable to pay his debts as they become due.

**Interstate commerce**, traffic, intercourse, commercial trading, or the transportation of persons or property between different states.

**Intestate**, one who dies without leaving a will.

**Intrastate commerce**, commerce that is begun, carried on, and completed wholly within the limits of a single state.

**Invalid**, of no legal force; void.

**Ipso facto** (ip-'so fak-'to), of itself; by the fact or act itself.

**Irrevocable** (ir-rev-'ah-kǎ-bl), that which can not be revoked, or rescinded legally.

**Issue**, direct descendants; children.

**Jettison** (jet-'ĭ-sun), the act of throwing overboard part of the cargo of a ship in time of peril.

**Joint tenants**, two or more tenants holding land under conditions whereby the survivor takes the whole interest.

**Judgment**, the official decision of a court.

**Judgment by default**, a judgment rendered in favor of a plaintiff on his evidence alone because of the failure of the defendant to answer the summons or appear.

**Jurisdiction** (joor-"is-dik-'shun), the legal authority of a court to try a case.

**Larceny**, the wrongful taking and carrying away of personal property of another.

**Lease**, a contract granting the use of certain real property to another for a specified period, in consideration for the payment of rent.

**Legacy**, a gift of personal property as designated by will.

**Legal tender**, money, according to law, which must be accepted in payment of a debt.

**Levy**, the legal seizure of property in order to raise money to satisfy an unpaid judgment, fine, or tax.

**Libel**, a slanderous or untruthful written or printed statement that reflects upon another person's reputation or character.

**Lien** (lēn), a right to retain certain property as security for a claim or debt.

**Life estate**, the right of a person to use or receive the income from property for life.

**Liquidated damages**, an amount agreed upon that is to be paid in case of a breach of contract.

**Litigants**, the parties involved in a lawsuit.

**Litigation**, a contest in a court of justice for the purpose of enforcing a right.

**L.S.**, locus sigilli (lo-′kus sij-ĭ-li), the place of the seal; a seal.

**Lunatic**, one who has lost his reason, usually confined in an asylum.

**Majority**, of legal age, usually twenty-one years.

**Malfeasance** (mal-fe-′zans), the commission of an unlawful act.

**Mandamus** (man-da-′mus), a court order demanding the performance of an act or certain acts, as required by law. The writ may be directed to an individual, government official, or corporation.

**Martial law**, a system of law which governs the army and navy and in war or serious emergency may be declared in any place to govern the civilian population.

**Maturity**, the time when a bill becomes due.

**Mediation**, where a third party acts to settle the dispute of two contending parties.

**Memorandum**, a note or instrument stating something that the parties desire to fix in memory by the aid of written evidence.

**Merchantable quality**, goods of a quality that can be resold under the same description at ordinary market prices.

**Minor**, also called infant, one under the age of legal maturity, which is usually twenty one years of age.

**Misdemeanor** (mis-″dĕ-mēn-′er), a minor criminal offense of less serious nature than a felony.

**Misrepresentation**, a false statement of fact, innocently made, without any intent to deceive.

**Mistrial**, an erroneous trial.

**Mortgage**, a lien given on property as security for a loan.

**Necessaries**, things indispensable or things proper and useful for the sustenance of human life. This is a relative term, and its meaning will contract or expand according to the situation and social condition of the person referred to.

**Negligence**, the failure to exercise the degree of care required by law.

**Nominal damages**, a small award given to one whose legal right has been violated but who sustained no actual loss.

**Nominal partner**, a person who is not a partner but who holds himself out as a partner or permits others to do so.

**Non compos mentis** (non kom-'pōs men-'tis), not of sound mind; insane.

**Notary public**, a public official who certifies under his seal various documents such as deeds and affidavits; he has the power to present and formally protest notes and bills of exchange.

**Notice of protest**, a formal notice that a bill of exchange or note has been dishonored.

**Novation**, the substitution of a new debt or obligation for an old one, which cancels the latter.

**Nuncupative will**, an oral will made and declared in the presence of witnesses by the testator during his last illness.


**Oath**, a solemn affirmation that statements made or to be made are true; testimony in court is given under oath.

**Option**, the right, usually obtained for a consideration, to purchase anything within a specified time at a stated price.

**Order bill of lading**, a receipt for goods shipped, issued by a carrier and containing a promise by the carrier not to redeliver the goods to anyone unless the original order bill, properly endorsed, is returned to the carrier.

**Ordinance**, the legislative act of a municipal corporation; a law, statute, or decree.

**Outlawed**, a claim barred by the Statute of Limitations; something that is outside the protection of the law.


**Panel**, a list of persons summoned to act as jurors at a particular sitting.

**Parol**, by word of mouth; oral; verbal.

**Parole**, the conditional release of a prisoner before the full expiration of his regular sentence.

**Patent**, a right granted by the Government to an inventor or his agent to manufacture and sell a patented article for a period of seventeen years.

**Pawnbroker**, a person licensed to lend money on goods pledged to him.

**Per se**, in, through, or by itself.

**Perjury**, a false statement made while testifying under oath in court, made willfully concerning some material point.

**Personalty** (pers-'nal-te), personal property as distinguished from real property.

**Petit jury**, the trial jury that has the duty of determining the facts at issue after hearing the evidence presented in open court by each party; called a petit jury because the number of jurors is usually smaller than in a grand jury.

**Picketing**, in labor law, the stationing of union members, usually with placards and signs, in such a way as to convey the union's grievances to the public or to management.

**Plaintiff**, the party who brings an action in court against another party.

**Pleadings**, the written statement of claims and defenses of the parties involved in a court action.

**Police power**, the power to govern; the power to enact laws for the protection of the public health, welfare, morals, and safety.

**Polling the jury**, asking each juror individually in open court if the verdict of the jury as announced by the foreman was agreed to by him.

**Post mortem**, after death.

**Postdated**, to date an instrument as of a later date than the one on which it was made.

**Power of attorney**, a written instrument which empowers one person to act for or represent another in specified matters.

**Premium**, the price paid for insurance.

**Prima facie** (pri-'mǎ fa-'shǐ-ē), evidence that is sufficient for proof unless it is rebutted or contradicted.

**Principle**, as of law; a fundamental truth or doctrine that is almost universally accepted.

**Pro rata** (pro ra-'tah), proportionately; to divide into shares according to the interest of each.

**Probate** (pro-'bāt), the legal procedure of proving or establishing a will.

**Probate court**, sometimes called a surrogate court or a widows' and orphans' court. A specialized court that has the responsibility for the administration of the estates of deceased persons or persons who are under the jurisdiction of the court by reason of some incapacity.

**Proof**, the establishment of a fact by evidence.

**Prosecute**, to proceed against a person by legal means.

**Protest** (pro-'test), a statement by a notary public that an instrument has been refused payment at maturity.

**Proxy**, a document by which one person authorizes another to act for him.

**Public policy**, that principle of law which holds that no person may lawfully do an act that has a tendency to be injurious to the public.

**Quasi** (kwa-'zi), almost; bearing some resemblance to but not having all the requisites.

**Quiet possession**, undisturbed possession; as used in the law of sales, the right to hold goods free and clear of the claims of all other persons.

**Quitclaim**, a deed granting any interest that the grantor may have in the property, without covenants.

**Quorum** (kwōr-'um), the minimum number of persons that must be present in order to transact business.

**Ratification**, the subsequent approval of an act that previously had not been binding.

**Realty** (re-'al-te), real property, as distinguished from personal property; land and anything permanently attached thereto.

**Rebate**, a discount or reduction; a return of part of a debt after full payment has been made.

**Receiver**, a person legally appointed to receive and hold in trust property that is or may be subject to litigation.

**Redress**, to correct; to make right.

**Referee**, a person appointed by a court to hear and decide a disputed matter.

**Reimburse**, to pay back; to make return or restoration of an equivalent for something paid, expended, or lost.

**Release**, the giving up, or surrender, of a claim or right of action; an instrument evidencing such a surrender.

**Remedy**, the legal means to recover a right or to redress a wrong.

**Replevin** (rĭ-plev-'ĭn), a court action for the purpose of recovering possession of personal property wrongfully taken or held.

**Reprieve**, to suspend the execution of a sentence for a time.

**Repudiate**, to reject; to renounce a right or obligation.

**Rescind** (re-sind'), to cancel; to annul; to avoid.

**Rescission**, the annulling of a contract by mutual consent by one of the parties or by a court.

**Restraint of trade**, actions designed to eliminate or stifle competition, effect a monopoly, or artificially maintain prices.

**Revert**, to fall back into the possession of the former proprietor.

**Revocation** (rev-"ŭ-ka-'shun), the act of recalling a power conferred previously.

**Rider**, in insurance, an attached writing which modifies or supplements the printed policy.

**Right to work law**, a law in force in some states that prohibits compulsory union membership. It bans, in effect, the union shop as well as the closed shop.

**Roman Code**, a comprehensive system of laws, established by Emperor Justinian and the emperors who followed him for the better administration of the vast Roman Empire.

**Sale**, a contract whereby property is transferred from one person, called the seller, to another person, called the buyer, for a consideration, called the price.

**Satisfaction piece**, a written acknowledgment that a claim between plaintiff and defendant has been satisfied.

**Seal**, a seal is a particular sign adopted and used by an individual to attest in the most formal manner the execution of an instrument.

**Security interest**, an interest in personal property which secures payment or performance of an obligation.

**Setoff**, a counterclaim or cross action that a defendant sets up against the claim of the plaintiff.

**Sine die** (si-″ne di-′e″), literally, without a day; indefinitely.

**Sinking fund**, an amount set aside for the payment of the interest and principal of a loan.

**Social legislation**, laws passed to improve the welfare of the masses, especially working people and those with small incomes.

**Solvency**, the state of being able to pay one's debts as they become due.

**Sovereign**, a person, body, or state in which independent and supreme authority is vested.

**Specialty** (spesh-′al-te), a contract under seal.

**Specific performance**, the performance of an agreement according to the exact terms originally agreed upon.

**Squatter**, one who settles upon the land of another without permission.

**SS**, abbreviation for Latin word scilicet, meaning that is to say, to wit, namely.

**Station in life**, an expression used to aid in the determination of what constitutes necessaries for particular individuals whose social or economic position may vary from the average.

**Status quo**, the existing state of things.

**Statute**, a law enacted by a legislature.

**Statute of frauds**, a law requiring written evidence to support certain contracts if they are to be enforced in court.

**Statute of limitations**, a law that prevents bringing an action if not begun within a specified time.

**Stipulation**, an article or material condition in a contract.

**Stoppage in transite**, the right of an unpaid seller to stop goods in transit and order the carrier to hold the goods for the benefit of the unpaid seller, in cases where the buyer becomes insolvent after the goods have been shipped.

**Straight bill of lading**, a receipt for goods shipped, issued by a carrier to a shipper and containing the contractual terms under which the goods are received for shipment.

**Subpoena**, an order or writ commanding a person to appear and testify in a legal action or proceeding.

**Subrogation**, the substitution of one person in place of another.

**Substantial performance**, a principle of law that allows the collection of the full contract price, less damages for any breach, when a contract has been essentially fully performed and in good faith, even though there has been some slight defect in the performance.

**Substantive law**, that part of our laws that deals with the determining of rights and duties.

**Summons**, a notice issued from a court requiring a person to appear therein to answer the complaint of a plaintiff within a specified time.

**Surety**, one who promises to answer for a debt on behalf of a second person to a third person.

**Surrogate**, the name given in some states to the judge who has the administration of probate matters.

**Syndicate**, an association of individuals formed to conduct a specific business transaction.

**Talesman**, a person who is ordered to report for jury duty.

**Tangible**, something that occupies space; something that you can touch or put your hands on.

**Tender**, an unconditional offer to deliver money or other personal property in pursuance of a contract.

**Testator** (tes-'ta-"ter), a person who makes a will.

**Tort**, a private or civil wrong arising from something other than a breach of contract.

**Trademark**, a mark or symbol a manufacturer places on goods he produces.

**Transcript**, an official copy of certain proceedings in a court.

**Treasury stock**, stock of a corporation issued by it and later reacquired.

**Trespass**, an injury done to the person, property, or right of another individual, with force or violence, either actual or implied in law.

**Trust**, a property interest held by one person for the benefit of another.

**Trust receipt**, a document issued by a borrower of money, stating that the borrower holds title to certain named goods as a trustee for the benefit of the lender.

**Trustee**, a person who holds property in trust.

**Ultra vires act** (ul-"tră vi-'rez), an act by a corporation that is beyond its express or implied powers.

**Umpire**, one who decides a question in dispute.

**Underwriter**, one who insures another against some risk, usually an insurance company.

**Unilateral** (u-"nĭ-lat-'er-al), a term used to indicate only one promise, action, or obligation.

**Unpaid seller's lien**, the right of an unpaid seller, who is still in possession of the goods, to hold the goods until the purchase price has been paid, when the sale is for cash; or when the sale is on credit, but the credit terms have expired; or when the buyer has become insolvent.

**Unwritten law**, the portion of the law not found in constitutions, statutes, or ordinances. Most of the unwritten law is found in reports of cases.

**Usury** (ūzh-'ĕ-re), a charge for the use of money beyond the rate of interest set by law.

**Valid**, having legal force; lawful or binding.

**Validity**, the quality of being good in law.

**Vendee**, a buyer or purchaser.

**Vendor**, a seller.

**Venire** (vĕ-ni-'re), a judge's writ or order summoning a jury for court trial.

**Venue** (ven-'ū), the geographical area over which the court has jurisdiction.

**Verbal**, oral, or by word of mouth.

**Verbatim** (ver-"ba-'tim), word for word.

**Verdict**, the official finding of fact by the jury.

**Verify**, to determine, fix, or establish a fact. In court the fact is determined under oath.

**Versus**, against; abbreviated as vs. or v.

**Vested**, established; fixed; settled; something that should be maintained.

**Void**, of no legal effect or force.

**Voidable**, capable of being voided or nullified, usually at the election of one party to a contract.

**Voucher**, a document that evidences a transaction; a receipt.

**Wager**, a bet; an agreement that one will gain or lose in accordance with the determination or happening of an event.

**Wages**, the agreed compensation paid by an employer to an employee for work done.

**Waiver**, the surrender of some right, claim, or privilege granted by law.

**Warehouseman**, a person whose business is to store goods for other persons.

**Warranty**, an agreement to be responsible if a thing is not as represented; the covenant of the grantor of real property and of his heirs that the grantee will have title to the property.

**Watered stock**, stock issued for insufficient values, or for no value at all.

**Will**, a document drawn in conformity with the laws of a state indicating how property is to be disposed of after the death of the testator.

**Willful**, intentional; deliberate.

**Writ**, anything written; a judicial process by which a person is summoned to appear; a legal instrument to enforce obedience to the orders and sentences of the court.

**Wrong**, the infringement of a right.

**Zoning law**, an ordinance restricting or permitting certain uses of land in specified areas.

The Parties to this Agreement,

*Recognizing* that their relations in the field of trade and economic endeavor should be conducted with a view to raising standards of living, ensuring full employment and a large and steadily growing volume of real income and effective demand, and expanding the production of and trade in goods and services, while allowing for the optimal use of the world's resources in accordance with the objective of sustainable development, seeking both to protect and preserve the environment and to enhance the means for doing so in a manner consistent with their respective needs and concerns at different levels of economic development,

*Recognizing* further that there is need for positive efforts designed to ensure that developing countries, and especially the least developed among them, secure a share in the growth in international trade commensurate with the needs of their economic development,

*Being desirous* of contributing to these objectives by entering into reciprocal and mutually advantageous arrangements directed to the substantial reduction of tariffs and other barriers to trade and to the elimination of discriminatory treatment in international trade relations,

*Resolved*, therefore, to develop an integrated, more viable and durable multilateral trading system encompassing the General Agreement on Tariffs and Trade, the results of past trade liberalization efforts, and all of the results of the Uruguay Round of Multilateral Trade Negotiations,

*Determined* to preserve the basic principles and to further the objectives underlying this multilateral trading system.

*Agree* as follows:


## *Article I*
## **Establishment of the Organization**

The World Trade Organization (hereinafter referred to as "the WTO") is hereby established.

## *Article II*
## Scope of the WTO

1. The WTO shall provide the common institutional framework for the conduct of trade relations among its Members in matters related to the agreements and associated legal instruments included in the Annexes to this Agreement.

2. The agreements and associated legal instruments included in Annexes 1, 2 and 3 (hereinafter referred to as "Multilateral Trade Agreements") are integral parts of this Agreement, binding on all Members.

3. The agreements and associated legal instruments included in Annex 4 (hereinafter referred to as "Plurilateral Trade Agreements") are also part of this Agreement for those Members that have accepted them, and are binding on those Members. The Plurilateral Trade Agreements do not create either obligations or rights for Members that have not accepted them.

4. The General Agreement on Tariffs and Trade 1994 as specified in Annex 1A (hereinafter referred to as "GATT 1994") is legally distinct from the General Agreement on Tariffs and Trade, dated 30 October 1947, annexed to the Final Act adopted at the conclusion of the Second Session of the Preparatory Committee of the United Nations Conference on Trade and Employment, as subsequently rectified, amended or modified (hereinafter referred to as "GATT 1947").

## *Article III*
## Functions of the WTO

1. The WTO shall facilitate the implementation, administration and operation, and further the objectives, of this Agreement and of the Multilateral Trade Agreements, and shall also provide the framework for the implementation, administration and operation of the Plurilateral Trade Agreements.

2. The WTO shall provide the forum for negotiations among its Members concerning their multilateral trade relations in matters dealt with under the agreements in the Annexes to this Agreement. The WTO may also provide a forum for further negotiations among its Members concerning their multilateral trade relations, and a framework for the implementation of the results of such negotiations, as may be decided by the Ministerial Conference.

3. The WTO shall administer the Understanding on Rules and Procedures Governing the Settlement of Disputes (hereinafter referred to as the "Dispute Settlement Understanding" or "DSU") in Annex 2 to this Agreement.

4. The WTO shall administer the Trade Policy Review Mechanism (hereinafter referred to as the

"TPRM") provided for in Annex 3 to this Agreement.

5. With a view to achieving greater coherence in global economic policy-making, the WTO shall cooperate, as appropriate, with the International Monetary Fund and with the International Bank for Reconstruction and Development and its affiliated agencies.

# *Article IV*
# **Structure of the WTO**

1. There shall be a Ministerial Conference composed of representatives of all the Members, which shall meet at least once every two years. The Ministerial Conference shall carry out the functions of the WTO and take actions necessary to this effect. The Ministerial Conference shall have the authority to take decisions on all matters under any of the Multilateral Trade Agreements, if so requested by a Member, in accordance with the specific requirements for decision-making in this Agreement and in the relevant Multilateral Trade Agreement.

2. There shall be a General Council composed of representatives of all the Members, which shall meet as appropriate. In the intervals between meetings of the Ministerial Conference, its functions shall be conducted by the General Council. The General Council shall also carry out the functions assigned to it by this Agreement. The General Council shall establish its rules of procedure and approve the rules of procedure for the Committees provided for in paragraph 7.

3. The General Council shall convene as appropriate to discharge the responsibilities of the Dispute Settlement Body provided for in the Dispute Settlement Understanding. The Dispute Settlement Body may have its own chairman and shall establish such rules of procedure as it deems necessary for the fulfillment of those responsibilities.

4. The General Council shall convene as appropriate to discharge the responsibilities of the Trade Policy Review Body provided for in the TPRM. The Trade Policy Review Body may have its own chairman and shall establish such rules of procedure as it deems necessary for the fulfillment of those responsibilities.

5. There shall be a Council for Trade in Goods, a Council for Trade in Services and a Council for Trade-Related Aspects of Intellectual Property Rights (hereinafter referred to as the "Council for TRIPS"), which shall operate under the general guidance of the General Council. The Council for Trade in Goods shall oversee the functioning of the Multilateral Trade Agreements in Annex 1A. The Council for Trade in Services shall oversee the functioning of the General Agreement on Trade in Services(hereinafter referred to as "GATS").The Council for TRIPS shall oversee the functioning of the Agreement on Trade-Related Aspects of Intellectual Property Rights (hereinafter referred to as the "Agreement on TRIPS"). These Councils shall carry out the functions assigned

to them by their respective agreements and by the General Council. They shall establish their respective rules of procedure subject to the approval of the General Council. Membership in these Councils shall be open to representatives of all Members. These Councils shall meet as necessary to carry out their functions.

6. The Council for Trade in Goods, the Council for Trade in Services and the Council for TRIPS shall establish subsidiary bodies as required. These subsidiary bodies shall establish their respective rules of procedure subject to the approval of their respective Councils.

7. The Ministerial Conference shall establish a Committee on Trade and Development, a Committee on Balance-of-Payments Restrictions and a Committee on Budget, Finance and Administration, which shall carry out the functions assigned to them by this Agreement and by the Multilateral Trade Agreements, and any additional functions assigned to them by the General Council, and may establish such additional Committees with such functions as it may deem appropriate. As part of its functions, the Committee on Trade and Development shall periodically review the special provisions in the Multilateral Trade Agreements in favour of the least-developed country Members and report to the General Council for appropriate action. Membership in these Committees shall be open to representatives of all Members.

8. The bodies provided for under the Plurilateral Trade Agreements shall carry out the functions assigned to them under those Agreements and shall operate within the institutional framework of the WTO. These bodies shall keep the General Council informed of their activities on a regular basis.

## *Article V*
## **Relations with Other Organizations**

1. The General Council shall make appropriate arrangements for effective cooperation with other intergovernmental organizations that have responsibilities related to those of the WTO.

2. The General Council may make appropriate arrangements for consultation and cooperation with non-governmental organizations concerned with matters related to those of the WTO.

## *Article VI*
## **The Secretariat**

1. There shall be a Secretariat of the WTO (hereinafter referred to as "the Secretariat") headed by a Director-General.

2. The Ministerial Conference shall appoint the Director-General and adopt regulations setting

out the powers, duties, conditions of service and term of office of the Director-General.

3. The Director-General shall appoint the members of the staff of the Secretariat and determine their duties and conditions of service in accordance with regulations adopted by the Ministerial Conference.

4. The responsibilities of the Director-General and of the staff of the Secretariat shall be exclusively international in character. In the discharge of their duties, the Director-General and the staff of the Secretariat shall not seek or accept instructions from any government or any other authority external to the WTO. They shall refrain from any action which might adversely reflect on their position as international officials. The Members of the WTO shall respect the international character of the responsibilities of the Director-General and of the staff of the Secretariat and shall not seek to influence them in the discharge of their duties.

## Article VII
## Budget and Contributions

1. The Director-General shall present to the Committee on Budget, Finance and Administration the annual budget estimate and financial statement of the WTO. The Committee on Budget, Finance and Administration shall review the annual budget estimate and the financial statement presented by the Director-General and make recommendations thereon to the General Council. The annual budget estimate shall be subject to approval by the General Council.

2. The Committee on Budget, Finance and Administration shall propose to the General Council financial regulations which shall include provisions setting out:

(a) the scale of contributions apportioning the expenses of the WTO among its Members; and

(b) the measures to be taken in respect of Members in arrears.

The financial regulations shall be based, as far as practicable, on the regulations and practices of GATT 1947.

3. The General Council shall adopt the financial regulations and the annual budget estimate by a two-thirds majority comprising more than half of the Members of the WTO.

4. Each Member shall promptly contribute to the WTO its share in the expenses of the WTO in accordance with the financial regulations adopted by the General Council.

## Article VIII
## Status of the WTO

1. The WTO shall have legal personality, and shall be accorded by each of its Members such

legal capacity as may be necessary for the exercise of its functions.

2. The WTO shall be accorded by each of its Members such privileges and immunities as are necessary for the exercise of its functions.

3. The officials of the WTO and the representatives of the Members shall similarly be accorded by each of its Members such privileges and immunities as are necessary for the independent exercise of their functions in connection with the WTO.

4. The privileges and immunities to be accorded by a Member to the WTO, its officials, and the representatives of its Members shall be similar to the privileges and immunities stipulated in the Convention on the Privileges and Immunities of the Specialized Agencies, approved by the General Assembly of the United Nations on 21 November 1947.

5. The WTO may conclude a headquarters agreement.

# *Article IX*
# **Decision-Making**

1. The WTO shall continue the practice of decision-making by consensus followed under GATT 1947. [1]Except as otherwise provided, where a decision cannot be arrived at by consensus, the matter at issue shall be decided by voting. At meetings of the Ministerial Conference and the General Council, each Member of the WTO shall have one vote. Where the European Communities exercise their right to vote, they shall have a number of votes equal to the number of their member States[2] which are Members of the WTO. Decisions of the Ministerial Conference and the General Council shall be taken by a majority of the votes cast, unless otherwise provided in this Agreement or in the relevant Multilateral Trade Agreement.[3]

2. The Ministerial Conference and the General Council shall have the exclusive authority to adopt interpretations of this Agreement and of the Multilateral Trade Agreements. In the case of an interpretation of a Multilateral Trade Agreement in Annex 1, they shall exercise their authority on the basis of a recommendation by the Council overseeing the functioning of that Agreement. The decision to adopt an interpretation shall be taken by a three-fourths majority of the Members. This paragraph shall not be used in a manner that would undermine the amendment provisions in Article X.

---

[1] The body concerned shall be deemed to have decided by consensus on a matter submitted for its consideration, if no Member, present at the meeting when the decision is taken, formally objects to the proposed decision.

[2] The number of votes of the European Communities and their member States shall in no case exceed the number of the member States of the European Communities.

[3] Decisions by the General Council when convened as the Dispute Settlement Body shall be taken only in accordance with the provisions of paragraph 4 of Article 2 of the Dispute Settlement Understanding.

3. In exceptional circumstances, the Ministerial Conference may decide to waive an obligation imposed on a Member by this Agreement or any of the Multilateral Trade Agreements, provided that any such decision shall be taken by three fourths[4] of the Members unless otherwise provided for in this paragraph.

(a) A request for a waiver concerning this Agreement shall be submitted to the Ministerial Conference for consideration pursuant to the practice of decision-making by consensus. The Ministerial Conference shall establish a time period, which shall not exceed 90 days, to consider the request. If consensus is not reached during the time period, any decision to grant a waiver shall be taken by three fourths of the Members.

(b) A request for a waiver concerning the Multilateral Trade Agreements in Annexes 1A or 1B or 1C and their annexes shall be submitted initially to the Council for Trade in Goods, the Council for Trade in Services or the Council for TRIPS, respectively, for consideration during a time period which shall not exceed 90 days. At the end of the time period, the relevant Council shall submit a report to the Ministerial Conference.

4. A decision by the Ministerial Conference granting a waiver shall state the exceptional circumstances justifying the decision, the terms and conditions governing the application of the waiver, and the date on which the waiver shall terminate. Any waiver granted for a period of more than one year shall be reviewed by the Ministerial Conference not later than one year after it is granted, and thereafter annually until the waiver terminates. In each review, the Ministerial Conference shall examine whether the exceptional circumstances justifying the waiver still exist and whether the terms and conditions attached to the waiver have been met. The Ministerial Conference, on the basis of the annual review, may extend, modify or terminate the waiver.

5. Decisions under a Plurilateral Trade Agreement, including any decisions on interpretations and waivers, shall be governed by the provisions of that Agreement.

## *Article X*
## Amendments

1. Any Member of the WTO may initiate a proposal to amend the provisions of this Agreement or the Multilateral Trade Agreements in Annex 1 by submitting such proposal to the Ministerial Conference. The Councils listed in paragraph 5 of Article IV may also submit to the Ministerial Conference proposals to amend the provisions of the corresponding Multilateral Trade

---

4　A decision to grant a waiver in respect of any obligation subject to a transition period or a period for staged implementation that the requesting Member has not performed by the end of the relevant period shall be taken only by consensus.

Agreements in Annex 1 the functioning of which they oversee. Unless the Ministerial Conference decides on a longer period, for a period of 90 days after the proposal has been tabled formally at the Ministerial Conference any decision by the Ministerial Conference to submit the proposed amendment to the Members for acceptance shall be taken by consensus. Unless the provisions of paragraphs 2, 5 or 6 apply, that decision shall specify whether the provisions of paragraphs 3 or 4 shall apply. If consensus is reached, the Ministerial Conference shall forthwith submit the proposed amendment to the Members for acceptance. If consensus is not reached at a meeting of the Ministerial Conference within the established period, the Ministerial Conference shall decide by a two-thirds majority of the Members whether to submit the proposed amendment to the Members for acceptance. Except as provided in paragraphs 2, 5 and 6, the provisions of paragraph 3 shall apply to the proposed amendment, unless the Ministerial Conference decides by a three-fourths majority of the Members that the provisions of paragraph 4 shall apply.

2. Amendments to the provisions of this Article and to the provisions of the following Articles shall take effect only upon acceptance by all Members:

Article IX of this Agreement;

Articles I and II of GATT 1994;

Article II:1 of GATS;

Article 4 of the Agreement on TRIPS.

3. Amendments to provisions of this Agreement, or of the Multilateral Trade Agreements in Annexes 1A and 1C,other than those listed in paragraphs 2 and 6, of a nature that would alter the rights and obligations of the Members, shall take effect for the Members that have accepted them upon acceptance by two thirds of the Members and thereafter for each other Member upon acceptance by it. The Ministerial Conference may decide by a three-fourths majority of the Members that any amendment made effective under this paragraph is of such a nature that any Member which has not accepted it within a period specified by the Ministerial Conference in each case shall be free to withdraw from the WTO or to remain a Member with the consent of the Ministerial Conference.

4. Amendments to provisions of this Agreement or of the Multilateral Trade Agreements in Annexes 1A and 1C, other than those listed in paragraphs 2 and 6, of a nature that would not alter the rights and obligations of the Members, shall take effect for all Members upon acceptance by two thirds of the Members.

5. Except as provided in paragraph 2 above, amendments to Parts I, II and III of GATS and the respective annexes shall take effect for the Members that have accepted them upon acceptance by two thirds of the Members and thereafter for each Member upon acceptance by it. The Ministerial Conference may decide by a three-fourths majority of the Members that any amendment made

effective under the preceding provision is of such a nature that any Member which has not accepted it within a period specified by the Ministerial Conference in each case shall be free to withdraw from the WTO or to remain a Member with the consent of the Ministerial Conference. Amendments to Parts IV, V and VI of GATS and the respective annexes shall take effect for all Members upon acceptance by two thirds of the Members.

6. Notwithstanding the other provisions of this Article, amendments to the Agreement on TRIPS meeting the requirements of paragraph 2 of Article 71 thereof may be adopted by the Ministerial Conference without further formal acceptance process.

7. Any Member accepting an amendment to this Agreement or to a Multilateral Trade Agreement in Annex 1 shall deposit an instrument of acceptance with the Director-General of the WTO within the period of acceptance specified by the Ministerial Conference.

8. Any Member of the WTO may initiate a proposal to amend the provisions of the Multilateral Trade Agreements in Annexes 2 and 3 by submitting such proposal to the Ministerial Conference. The decision to approve amendments to the Multilateral Trade Agreement in Annex 2 shall be made by consensus and these amendments shall take effect for all Members upon approval by the Ministerial Conference. Decisions to approve amendments to the Multilateral Trade Agreement in Annex 3 shall take effect for all Members upon approval by the Ministerial Conference.

9. The Ministerial Conference, upon the request of the Members parties to a trade agreement, may decide exclusively by consensus to add that agreement to Annex 4. The Ministerial Conference, upon the request of the Members parties to a Plurilateral Trade Agreement, may decide to delete that Agreement from Annex 4.

10. Amendments to a Plurilateral Trade Agreement shall be governed by the provisions of that Agreement.

## Article XI
## Original Membership

1. The contracting parties to GATT 1947 as of the date of entry into force of this Agreement, and the European Communities, which accept this Agreement and the Multilateral Trade Agreements and for which Schedules of Concessions and Commitments are annexed to GATT 1944 and for which Schedules of Specific Commitments are annexed to GATS shall become original Members of the WTO.

2. The least-developed countries recognized as such by the United Nations will only be required to undertake commitments and concessions to the extent consistent with their individual development, financial and trade needs or their administrative and institutional capabilities.

## *Article XII*
# Accession

1. Any State or separate customs territory possessing full autonomy in the conduct of its external commercial relations and of the other matters provided for in this Agreement and the Multilateral Trade Agreements may accede to this Agreement, on terms to be agreed between it and the WTO. Such accession shall apply to this Agreement and the Multilateral Trade Agreements annexed thereto.

2. Decisions on accession shall be taken by the Ministerial Conference. The Ministerial Conference shall approve the agreement on the terms of accession by a two-thirds majority of the Members of the WTO.

3. Accession to a Plurilateral Trade Agreement shall be governed by the provisions of that Agreement.

## *Article XIII*
# Non-Application of Multilateral Trade Agreements between Particular Members

1. This Agreement and the Multilateral Trade Agreements in Annexes 1 and 2 shall not apply as between any Member and any other Member if either of the Members, at the time either becomes a Member, does not consent to such application.

2. Paragraph 1 may be invoked between original Members of the WTO which were contracting parties to GATT 1947 only where Article XXXV of that Agreement had been invoked earlier and was effective as between those contracting parties at the time of entry into force for them of this Agreement.

3. Paragraph 1 shall apply between a Member and another Member which has acceded under Article XII only if the Member not consenting to the application has so notified the Ministerial Conference before the approval of the agreement on the terms of accession by the Ministerial Conference.

4. The Ministerial Conference may review the operation of this Article in particular cases at the request of any Member and make appropriate recommendations.

5. Non-application of a Plurilateral Trade Agreement between parties to that Agreement shall be governed by the provisions of that Agreement.

## *Article XIV*
## Acceptance, Entry into Force and Deposit

1. This Agreement shall be open for acceptance, by signature or otherwise, by contracting parties to GATT 1947, and the European Communities, which are eligible to become original Members of the WTO in accordance with Article XI of this Agreement. Such acceptance shall apply to this Agreement and the Multilateral Trade Agreements annexed hereto. This Agreement and the Multilateral Trade Agreements annexed hereto shall enter into force on the date determined by Ministers in accordance with paragraph 3 of the Final Act Embodying the Results of the Uruguay Round of Multilateral Trade Negotiations and shall remain open for acceptance for a period of two years following that date unless the Ministers decide otherwise. An acceptance following the entry into force of this Agreement shall enter into force on the 30th day following the date of such acceptance.

2. A Member which accepts this Agreement after its entry into force shall implement those concessions and obligations in the Multilateral Trade Agreements that are to be implemented over a period of time starting with the entry into force of this Agreement as if it had accepted this Agreement on the date of its entry into force.

3. Until the entry into force of this Agreement, the text of this Agreement and the Multilateral Trade Agreements shall be deposited with the Director-General to the CONTRACTING PARTIES to GATT 1947.The Director-General shall promptly furnish a certified true copy of this Agreement and the Multilateral Trade Agreements, and a notification of each acceptance thereof, to each government and the European Communities having accepted this Agreement. This Agreement and the Multilateral Trade Agreements, and any amendments thereto, shall, upon the entry into force of this Agreement, be deposited with the Director-General of the WTO.

4. The acceptance and entry into force of a Plurilateral Trade Agreement shall be governed by the provisions of that Agreement. Such Agreements shall be deposited with the Director-General to the CONTRACTING PARTIES to GATT 1947. Upon the entry into force of this Agreement, such Agreements shall be deposited with the Director-General of the WTO.

## *Article XV*
## Withdrawal

1. Any Member may withdraw from this Agreement. Such withdrawal shall apply both to this Agreement and the Multilateral Trade Agreements and shall take effect upon the expiration of six months from the date on which written notice of withdrawal is received by the Director-General of the WTO.

2. Withdrawal from a Plurilateral Trade Agreement shall be governed by the provisions of that Agreement.

# *Article XVI*
# **Miscellaneous Provisions**

1. Except as otherwise provided under this Agreement or the Multilateral Trade Agreements, the WTO shall be guided by the decisions, procedures and customary practices followed by the CONTRACTING PARTIES to GATT 1947 and the bodies established in the framework of GATT 1947.

2. To the extent practicable, the Secretariat of GATT 1947 shall become the Secretariat of the WTO, and the Director-General to the CONTRACTING PARTIES to GATT 1947, until such time as the Ministerial Conference has appointed a Director-General in accordance with paragraph 2 of Article VI of this Agreement, shall serve as Director-General of the WTO.

3. In the event of a conflict between a provision of this Agreement and a provision of any of the Multilateral Trade Agreements, the provision of this Agreement shall prevail to the extent of the conflict.

4. Each Member shall ensure the conformity of its laws, regulations and administrative procedures with its obligations as provided in the annexed Agreements.

5. No reservations may be made in respect of any provision of this Agreement. Reservations in respect of any of the provisions of the Multilateral Trade Agreements may only be made to the extent provided for in those Agreements. Reservations in respect of a provision of a Plurilateral Trade Agreement shall be governed by the provisions of that Agreement.

6. This Agreement shall be registered in accordance with the provisions of Article 102 of the Charter of the United Nations.

DONE at Marrakesh this fifteenth day of April one thousand nine hundred and ninety-four, in a single copy, in the English, French and Spanish languages, each text being authentic.

*Explanatory Notes*

The terms "country" or "countries" as used in this Agreement and the Multilateral Trade Agreements are to be understood to include any separate customs territory Member of the WTO.

In the case of a separate customs territory Member of the WTO, where an expression in this Agreement and the Multilateral Trade Agreements is qualified by the term "national", such expression shall be read as pertaining to that customs territory, unless otherwise specified.

# WTO關於爭端解決的規則與程序諒解書

## Understanding on Rules and Procedures Goverring the Settlenent of Disputes

Members hereby agree as follows:

## *Article 1*
## Coverage and Application

1. The rules and procedures of this Understanding shall apply to disputes brought pursuant to the consultation and dispute settlement provisions of the agreements listed in Appendix 1 to this Understanding (referred to in this Understanding as the "covered agreements"). The rules and procedures of this Understanding shall also apply to consultations and the settlement of disputes between Members concerning their rights and obligations under the provisions of the Agreement Establishing the World Trade Organization (referred to in this Understanding as the "WTO Agreement") and of this Understanding taken in isolation or in combination with any other covered agreement.

2. The rules and procedures of this Understanding shall apply subject to such special or additional rules and procedures on dispute settlement contained in the covered agreements as are identified in Appendix 2 to this Understanding. To the extent that there is a difference between the rules and procedures of this Understanding and the special or additional rules and procedures set forth in Appendix 2, the special or additional rules and procedures in Appendix 2 shall prevail. In disputes involving rules and procedures under more than one covered agreement, if there is a conflict between special or additional rules and procedures of such agreements under review, and where the parties to the dispute cannot agree on rules and procedures within 20 days of the establishment of the panel, the Chairman of the Dispute Settlement Body provided for in paragraph 1 of Article 2(referred to in this Understanding as the "DSB"), in consultation with the parties to the dispute, shall determine the rules and procedures to be followed within 10 days after a request by either Member. The Chairman shall be guided by the principle that special or additional rules and procedures should be used where possible, and the rules and procedures set out in this Understanding should be used to the extent necessary to avoid conflict.

# *Article 2*
# **Administration**

1. The Dispute Settlement Body is hereby established to administer these rules and procedures and, except as otherwise provided in a covered agreement, the consultation and dispute settlement provisions of the covered agreements. Accordingly, the DSB shall have the authority to establish panels, adopt panel and Appellate Body reports, maintain surveillance of implementation of rulings and recommendations, and authorize suspension of concessions and other obligations under the covered agreements. With respect to disputes arising under a covered agreement which is a Plurilateral Trade Agreement, the term "Member" as used herein shall refer only to those Members that are parties to the relevant Plurilateral Trade Agreement. Where the DSB administers the dispute settlement provisions of a Plurilateral Trade Agreement, only those Members that are parties to that Agreement may participate in decisions or actions taken by the DSB with respect to that dispute.

2. The DSB shall inform the relevant WTO Councils and Committees of any developments in disputes related to provisions of the respective covered agreements.

3. The DSB shall meet as often as necessary to carry out its functions within the time-frames provided in this Understanding.

4. Where the rules and procedures of this Understanding provide for the DSB to take a decision, it shall do so by consensus.[1]

# *Article 3*
# **General Provisions**

1. Members affirm their adherence to the principles for the management of disputes heretofore applied under Articles XXII and XXIII of GATT 1947, and the rules and procedures as further elaborated and modified herein.

2. The dispute settlement system of the WTO is a central element in providing security and predictability to the multilateral trading system. The Members recognize that it serves to preserve the rights and obligations of Members under the covered agreements, and to clarify the existing provisions of those agreements in accordance with customary rules of interpretation of public international law. Recommendations and rulings of the DSB cannot add to or diminish the rights

---

1 The DSB shall be deemed to have decided by consensus on a matter submitted for its consideration, if no Member present at the meeting of the DSB when the decision is taken, formally objects to the proposed decision.

and obligations provided in the covered agreements.

3. The prompt settlement of situations in which a Member considers that any benefits accruing to it directly or indirectly under the covered agreements are being impaired by measures taken by another Member is essential to the effective functioning of the WTO and the maintenance of a proper balance between the rights and obligations of Members.

4. Recommendations or rulings made by the DSB shall be aimed at achieving a satisfactory settlement of the matter in accordance with the rights and obligations under this Understanding and under the covered agreements.

5. All solutions to matters formally raised under the consultation and dispute settlement provisions of the covered agreements, including arbitration awards, shall be consistent with those agreements and shall not nullify or impair benefits accruing to any Member under those agreements, nor impede the attainment of any objective of those agreements.

6. Mutually agreed solutions to matters formally raised under the consultation and dispute settlement provisions of the covered agreements shall be notified to the DSB and the relevant Councils and Committees, where any Member may raise any point relating thereto.

7. Before bringing a case, a Member shall exercise its judgment as to whether action under these procedures would be fruitful. The aim of the dispute settlement mechanism is to secure a positive solution to a dispute. A solution mutually acceptable to the parties to a dispute and consistent with the covered agreements is clearly to be preferred. In the absence of a mutually agreed solution, the first objective of the dispute settlement mechanism is usually to secure the withdrawal of the measures concerned if these are found to be inconsistent with the provisions of any of the covered agreements. The provision of compensation should be resorted to only if the immediate withdrawal of the measure is impracticable and as a temporary measure pending the withdrawal of the measure which is inconsistent with a covered agreement. The last resort which this Understanding provides to the Member invoking the dispute settlement procedures is the possibility of suspending the application of concessions or other obligations under the covered agreements on a discriminatory basis vis-a-vis the other Member, subject to authorization by the DSB of such measures.

8. In cases where there is an infringement of the obligations assumed under a covered agreement, the action is considered prima facie to constitute a case of nullification or impairment. This means that there is normally a presumption that a breach of the rules has an adverse impact on other Members parties to that covered agreement, and in such cases, it shall be up to the Member against whom the complaint has been brought to rebut the charge.

9. The provisions of this Understanding are without prejudice to the rights of Members to seek authoritative interpretation of provisions of a covered agreement through decision-making under

the WTO Agreement or a covered agreement which is a Plurilateral Trade Agreement.

10. It is understood that requests for conciliation and the use of the dispute settlement procedures should not be intended or considered as contentious acts and that, if a dispute arises, all Members will engage in these procedures in good faith in an effort to resolve the dispute. It is also understood that complaints and counter-complaints in regard to distinct matters should not be linked.

11. This Understanding shall be applied only with respect to new requests for consultations under the consultation provisions of the covered agreements made on or after the date of entry into force of the WTO Agreement. With respect to disputes for which the request for consultations was made under GATT 1947 or under any other predecessor agreement to the covered agreements before the date of entry into force of the WTO Agreement, the relevant dispute settlement rules and procedures in effect immediately prior to the date of entry into force of the WTO Agreement shall continue to apply.[2]

12. Notwithstanding paragraph 11, if a complaint based on any of the covered agreements is brought by a developing country Member against a developed country Member, the complaining party shall have the right to invoke, as an alternative of the provisions contained in Articles 4, 5, 6 and 12 of this Understanding, the corresponding provisions of the Decision of 5 April 1966 (BISD 14S/18), except that where the Panel considers that the time-frame provided for in paragraph 7 of that Decision is insufficient to provide its report and with the agreement of the complaining party, that time-frame may be extended. To the extent that there is a difference between the rules and procedures of Articles 4, 5, 6 and 12 and the corresponding rules and procedures of the Decision, the latter shall prevail.

# *Article 4*
# **Consultations**

1. Members affirm their resolve to strengthen and improve the effectiveness of the consultation procedures employed by Members.

2. Each Member undertakes to accord sympathetic consideration to and afford adequate opportunity for consultation regarding any representations made by another Member concerning measures affecting the operation of any covered agreement taken within the territory of the former.[3]

---

[2] This paragraph shall also be applied to disputes on which panel reports have not been adopted or fully implemented.

[3] Where the provisions of any other covered agreement concerning measures taken by regional or local governments

3. If a request for consultations is made pursuant to a covered agreement, the Member to which the request is made shall, unless otherwise mutually agreed, reply to the request within 10 days after the date of its receipt and shall enter into consultations in good faith within a period of no more than 30 days after the date of receipt of the request, with a view to reaching a mutually satisfactory solution. If the Member does not respond within 10 days after the date of receipt of the request, or does not enter into consultations within a period of no more than 30 days, or a period otherwise mutually agreed, after the date of receipt of the request, then the Member that requested the holding of consultations may proceed directly to request the establishment of a panel.

4. All such requests for consultations shall be notified to the DSB and the relevant Councils and Committees by the Member which requests consultations. Any request for consultations shall be submitted in writing and shall give the reasons for the request, including identification of the measures at issue and an indication of the legal basis for the complaint.

5. In the course of consultations in accordance with the provisions of a covered agreement, before resorting to further action under this Understanding, Members should attempt to obtain satisfactory adjustment of the matter.

6. Consultations shall be confidential, and without prejudice to the rights of any Member in any further proceedings.

7. If the consultations fail to settle a dispute within 60 days after the date of receipt of the request for consultations, the complaining party may request the establishment of a panel. The complaining party may request a panel during the 60-day period if the consulting parties jointly consider that consultations have failed to settle the dispute.

8. In cases of urgency, including those which concern perishable goods, Members shall enter into consultations within a period of no more than 10 days after the date of receipt of the request. If the consultations have failed to settle the dispute within a period of 20 days after the date of receipt of the request, the complaining party may request the establishment of a panel.

9. In cases of urgency, including those which concern perishable goods, the parties to the dispute, panels and the Appellate Body shall make every effort to accelerate the proceedings to the greatest extent possible.

10. During consultations Members should give special attention to the particular problems and interests of developing country Members.

11. Whenever a Member other than the consulting Members considers that it has a substantial

---

or authorities within the territory of a Member contain provisions different from the provisions of this paragraph, the provisions of such other covered agreement shall prevail.

trade interest in consultations being held pursuant to paragraph 1 of Article XXII of GATT 1994, paragraph 1 of Article XXII of GATS, or the corresponding provisions in other covered agreements, [4] such Member may notify the consulting Members and the DSB, within 10 days after the date of the circulation of the request for consultations under said Article, of its desire to be joined in the consultations. Such Member shall be joined in the consultations, provided that the Member to which the request for consultations was addressed agrees that the claim of substantial interest is well-founded. In that event they shall so inform the DSB. If the request to be joined in the consultations is not accepted, the applicant Member shall be free to request consultations under paragraph 1 of Article XXII or paragraph 1 of Article XXIII of GATT 1994, paragraph 1 of Article XXII or paragraph 1 of Article XXIII of GATS, or the corresponding provisions in other covered agreements.

## *Article 5*
## Good Offices, Conciliation and Mediation

1. Good offices, conciliation and mediation are procedures that are undertaken voluntarily if the parties to the dispute so agree.

2. Proceedings involving good offices, conciliation and mediation, and in particular positions taken by the parties to the dispute during these proceedings, shall be confidential, and without prejudice to the rights of either party in any further proceedings under these procedures.

3. Good offices, conciliation or mediation may be requested at any time by any party to a dispute. They may begin at any time and be terminated at any time. Once procedures for good offices, conciliation or mediation are terminated, a complaining party may then proceed with a request for the establishment of a panel.

4. When good offices, conciliation or mediation are entered into within 60 days after the date of receipt of a request for consultations, the complaining party must allow a period of 60 days after the date of receipt of the request for consultations before requesting the establishment of a panel.

---

[4] The corresponding consultation provisions in the covered agreements are listed hereunder: Agreement on Agriculture, Article 19: Agreement on the Application of Sanitary and Phytosanitary Measures, paragraph 1 of Article 11: Agreement on Textiles and Clothing, paragraph 4 of Article 8: Agreement on Technical Barriers to Trade, paragraph 1 of Article 14: Agreement on Trade-Related Investment Measures, Article 8: Agreement on Implementation of Article VI of GATT 1994,paragraph 2 of Article 17: Agreement on Implementation of Article VII of GATT 1994,paragraph 2 of Article 19: Agreement on Preshipment Inspection, Article 7: Agreement on Rules of Origin, Article 7: Agreement on Import Licensing Procedures, Article 6: Agreement on Subsidies and Countervailing Measures, Article 30: Agreement on Safeguards, Article 14: Agreement on Trade-Related Aspects of Intellectual Property Rights, Article 64.1; and any corresponding consultation provisions in Plurilateral Trade Agreements as determined by the competent bodies of each Agreement and as notified to the DSB.

The complaining party may request the establishment of a panel during the 60-day period if the parties to the dispute jointly consider that the good offices, conciliation or mediation process has failed to settle the dispute.

5. If the parties to a dispute agree, procedures for good offices, conciliation or mediation may continue while the panel process proceeds.

6. The Director-General may, acting in an ex officio capacity, offer good offices, conciliation or mediation with the view to assisting Members to settle a dispute.

# *Article 6*
# **Establishment of Panels**

1. If the complaining party so requests, a panel shall be established at the latest at the DSB meeting following that at which the request first appears as an item on the DSB's agenda, unless at that meeting the DSB decides by consensus not to establish a panel.[5]

2. The request for the establishment of a panel shall be made in writing. It shall indicate whether consultations were held, identify the specific measures at issue and provide a brief summary of the legal basis of the complaint sufficient to present the problem clearly. In case the applicant requests the establishment of a panel with other than standard terms of reference, the written request shall include the proposed text of special terms of reference.

# *Article 7*
# **Terms of Reference of Panels**

1. Panels shall have the following terms of reference unless the parties to the dispute agree otherwise within 20 days from the establishment of the panel:

"To examine, in the light of the relevant provisions in (name of the covered agreement(s) cited by the parties to the dispute), the matter referred to the DSB by (name of party) in document and to make such findings as will assist the DSB in making the recommendations or in giving the rulings provided for in that/those agreement(s)."

2. Panels shall address the relevant provisions in any covered agreement or agreements cited by the parties to the dispute.

3. In establishing a panel, the DSB may authorize its Chairman to draw up the terms o

---

5   If the complaining party so requests, a meeting of the DSB shall be convened for this purpose within 15 days of the request, provided that at least 10 days' advance notice of the meeting is given.

reference of the panel in consultation with the parties to the dispute, subject to the provisions of paragraph 1. The terms of reference thus drawn up shall be circulated to all Members. If other than standard terms of reference are agreed upon, any Member may raise any point relating thereto in the DSB.

# *Article 8*
# **Composition of Panels**

1. Panels shall be composed of well-qualified governmental and/or non-governmental individuals, including persons who have served on or presented a case to a panel, served as a representative of a Member or of a contracting party to GATT 1947 or as a representative to the Council or Committee of any covered agreement or its predecessor agreement, or in the Secretariat, taught or published on international trade law or policy, or served as a senior trade policy official of a Member.

2. Panel members should be selected with a view to ensuring the independence of the members,a sufficiently diverse background and a wide spectrum of experience.

3. Citizens of Members whose governments[6] are parties to the dispute or third parties as defined in paragraph 2 of Article 10 shall not serve on a panel concerned with that dispute, unless the parties to the dispute agree otherwise.

4. To assist in the selection of panelists, the Secretariat shall maintain an indicative list of governmental and non-governmental individuals possessing the qualifications outlined in paragraph 1, from which panelists may be drawn as appropriate. That list shall include the roster of non-governmental panelists established on 30 November 1984(BISD31S/9), and other rosters and indicative lists established under any of the covered agreements, and shall retain the names of persons on those rosters and indicative lists at the time of entry into force of the WTO Agreement. Members may periodically suggest names of governmental and non-governmental individuals for inclusion on the indicative list, providing relevant information on their knowledge of international trade and of the sectors or subject matter of the covered agreements, and those names shall be added to the list upon approval by the DSB. For each of the individuals on the list, the list shall indicate specific areas of experience or expertise of the individuals in the sectors or subject matter of the covered agreements.

5. Panels shall be composed of three panelists unless the parties to the dispute agree,within 10

---

6 In the case where customs unions or common markets are parties to a dispute, this provision applies to citizens of all member countries of the customs unions or common markets.

days from the establishment of the panel, to a panel composed of five panelists. Members shall be informed promptly of the composition of the panel.

6. The Secretariat shall propose nominations for the panel to the parties to the dispute. The parties to the dispute shall not oppose nominations except for compelling reasons.

7. If there is no agreement on the panelists within 20 days after the date of the establishment of a panel, at the request of either party, the Director-General, in consultation with the Chairman of the DSB and the Chairman of the relevant Council or Committee, shall determine the composition of the panel by appointing the panelists whom the Director-General considers most appropriate in accordance with any relevant special or additional rules or procedures of the covered agreement or covered agreements which are at issue in the dispute, after consulting with the parties to the dispute. The Chairman of the DSB shall inform the Members of the composition of the panel thus formed no later than 10 days after the date the Chairman receives such a request.

8. Members shall undertake, as a general rule, to permit their officials to serve as panelists.

9. Panelists shall serve in their individual capacities and not as government representatives, nor as representatives of any organization. Members shall therefore not give them instructions nor seek to influence them as individuals with regard to matters before a panel.

10. When a dispute is between a developing country Member and a developed country Member the panel shall, if the developing country Member so requests, include at least one panelist from a developing country Member.

11. Panelists' expenses, including travel and subsistence allowance, shall be met from the WTO budget in accordance with criteria to be adopted by the General Council, based on recommendations of the Committee on Budget, Finance and Administration.

# Article 9
## Procedures for Multiple Complainants

1. Where more than one Member requests the establishment of a panel related to the same matter, a single panel may be established to examine these complaints taking into account the rights of all Members concerned. A single panel should be established to examine such complaints whenever feasible.

2. The single panel shall organize its examination and present its findings to the DSB in such a manner that the rights which the parties to the dispute would have enjoyed had separate panels examined the complaints are in no way impaired. If one of the parties to the dispute so requests, the panel shall submit separate reports on the dispute concerned. The written submissions by each

of the complainants shall be made available to the other complainants, and each complainant shall have the right to be present when any one of the other complainants presents its views to the panel.

3. If more than one panel is established to examine the complaints related to the same matter, to the greatest extent possible the same persons shall serve as panelists on each of the separate panels and the timetable for the panel process in such disputes shall be harmonized.

### *Article 10*
### **Third Parties**

1. The interests of the parties to a dispute and those of other Members under a covered agreement at issue in the dispute shall be fully taken into account during the panel process.

2. Any Member having a substantial interest in a matter before a panel and having notified its interest to the DSB (referred to in this Understanding as a "third party") shall have an opportunity to be heard by the panel and to make written submissions to the panel. These submissions shall also be given to the parties to the dispute and shall be reflected in the panel report.

3. Third parties shall receive the submissions of the parties to the dispute to the first meeting of the panel.

4. If a third party considers that a measure already the subject of a panel proceeding nullifies or impairs benefits accruing to it under any covered agreement, that Member may have recourse to normal dispute settlement procedures under this Understanding. Such a dispute shall be referred to the original panel wherever possible.

### *Article 11*
### **Function of Panels**

The function of panels is to assist the DSB in discharging its responsibilities under this Understanding and the covered agreements. Accordingly, a panel should make an objective assessment of the matter before it, including an objective assessment of the facts of the case and the applicability of and conformity with the relevant covered agreements, and make such other findings as will assist the DSB in making the recommendations or in giving the rulings provided for in the covered agreements. Panels should consult regularly with the parties to the dispute and give them adequate opportunity to develop a mutually satisfactory solution.

## *Article 12*
## Panel Procedures

1. Panels shall follow the Working Procedures in Appendix 3 unless the panel decides otherwise after consulting the parties to the dispute.

2. Panel procedures should provide sufficient flexibility so as to ensure high-quality panel reports, while not unduly delaying the panel process.

3. After consulting the parties to the dispute, the panelists shall,as soon as practicable and whenever possible within one week after the composition and terms of reference of the panel have been agreed upon, fix the timetable for the panel process, taking into account the provisions of paragraph 9 of Article 4, if relevant.

4. In determining the timetable for the panel process, the panel shall provide sufficient time for the parties to the dispute to prepare their submissions.

5. Panels should set precise deadlines for written submissions by the parties and the parties should respect those deadlines.

6. Each party to the dispute shall deposit its written submissions with the Secretariat for immediate transmission to the panel and to the other party or parties to the dispute. The complaining party shall submit its first submission in advance of the responding party's first submission unless the panel decides, in fixing the timetable referred to in paragraph 3 and after consultations with the parties to the dispute, that the parties should submit their first submissions simultaneously. When there are sequential arrangements for the deposit of first submissions, the panel shall establish a firm time period for receipt of the responding party's submission. Any subsequent written submissions shall be submitted simultaneously.

7. Where the parties to the dispute have failed to develop a mutually satisfactory solution, the panel shall submit its findings in the form of a written report to the DSB. In such cases, the report of a panel shall set out the findings of fact, the applicability of relevant provisions and the basic rationale behind any findings and recommendations that it makes. Where a settlement of the matter among the parties to the dispute has been found, the report of the panel shall be confined to a brief description of the case and to reporting that a solution has been reached.

8. In order to make the procedures more efficient, the period in which the panel shall conduct its examination, from the date that the composition and terms of reference of the panel have been agreed upon until the date the final report is issued to the parties to the dispute, shall, as a general rule, not exceed six months. In cases of urgency, including those relating to perishable goods, the panel shall aim to issue its report to the parties to the dispute within three months.

9. When the panel considers that it cannot issue its report within six months, or within three

months in cases of urgency, it shall inform the DSB in writing of the reasons for the delay together with an estimate of the period within which it will issue its report. In no case should the period from the establishment of the panel to the circulation of the report to the Members exceed nine months.

10. In the context of consultations involving a measure taken by a developing country Member, the parties may agree to extend the periods established in paragraphs 7 and 8 of Article 4. If, after the relevant period has elapsed, the consulting parties cannot agree that the consultations have concluded, the Chairman of the DSB shall decide, after consultation with the parties, whether to extend the relevant period and, if so, for how long. In addition, in examining a complaint against a developing country Member, the panel shall accord sufficient time for the developing country Member to prepare and present its argumentation. The provisions of paragraph 1 of Article 20 and paragraph 4 of Article 21 are not affected by any action pursuant to this paragraph.

11. Where one or more of the parties is a developing country Member, the panel's report shall explicitly indicate the form in which account has been taken of relevant provisions on differential and more-favourable treatment for developing country Members that form part of the covered agreements which have been raised by the developing country Member in the course of the dispute settlement procedures.

12. The panel may suspend its work at any time at the request of the complaining party for a period not to exceed 12 months. In the event of such a suspension, the time-frames set out in paragraphs 8 and 9 of this Article, paragraph 1 of Article 20,and paragraph 4 of Article 21 shall be extended by the amount of time that the work was suspended. If the work of the panel has been suspended for more than 12 months, the authority for establishment of the panel shall lapse.

# *Article 13*
# **Right to Seek Information**

1. Each panel shall have the right to seek information and technical advice from any individual or body which it deems appropriate. However, before a panel seeks such information or advice from any individual or body within the jurisdiction of a Member it shall inform the authorities of that Member. A Member should respond promptly and fully to any request by a panel for such information as the panel considers necessary and appropriate. Confidential information which is provided shall not be revealed without formal authorization from the individual, body, or authorities of the Member providing the information.

2. Panels may seek information from any relevant source and may consult experts to obtain their opinion on certain aspects of the matter. With respect to a factual issue concerning a

scientific or other technical matter raised by a party to a dispute, a panel may request an advisory report in writing from an expert review group. Rules for the establishment of such a group and its procedures are set forth in Appendix 4.

# Article 14
## Confidentiality

1. Panel deliberations shall be confidential.

2. The reports of panels shall be drafted without the presence of the parties to the dispute in the light of the information provided and the statements made.

3. Opinions expressed in the panel report by individual panelists shall be anonymous.

# Article 15
## Interim Review Stage

1. Following the consideration of rebuttal submissions and oral arguments, the panel shall issue the descriptive (factual and argument) sections of its draft report to the parties to the dispute. Within a period of time set by the panel, the parties shall submit their comments in writing.

2. Following the expiration of the set period of time for receipt of comments from the parties to the dispute, the panel shall issue an interim report to the parties, including both the descriptive sections and the panel's findings and conclusions. Within a period of time set by the panel, a party may submit a written request for the panel to review precise aspects of the interim report prior to circulation of the final report to the Members. At the request of a party, the panel shall hold a further meeting with the parties on the issues identified in the written comments. If no comments are received from any party within the comment period, the interim report shall be considered the final panel report and circulated promptly to the Members.

3. The findings of the final panel report shall include a discussion of the arguments made at the interim review stage. The interim review stage shall be conducted within the time period set out in paragraph 8 of Article 12.

# Article 16
## Adoption of Panel Reports

1. In order to provide sufficient time for the Members to consider panel reports, the reports shall not be considered for adoption by the DSB until 20 days after the date they have been

circulated to the Members.

2. Members having objections to a panel report shall give written reasons to explain their objections for circulation at least 10 days prior to the DSB meeting at which the panel report will be considered.

3. The parties to a dispute shall have the right to participate fully in the consideration of the panel report by the DSB, and their views shall be fully recorded.

4. Within 60 days after the date of circulation of a panel report to the Members, the report shall be adopted at a DSB meeting[7] unless a party to the dispute formally notifies the DSB of its decision to appeal or the DSB decides by consensus not to adopt the report. If a party has notified its decision to appeal, the report by the panel shall not be considered for adoption by the DSB until after completion of the appeal. This adoption procedure is without prejudice to the right of Members to express their views on a panel report.

## *Article 17*
## Appellate Review Standing Appellate Body

1. A standing Appellate Body shall be established by the DSB. The Appellate Body shall hear appeals from panel cases. It shall be composed of seven persons, three of whom shall serve on any one case. Persons serving on the Appellate Body shall serve in rotation. Such rotation shall be determined in the working procedures of the Appellate Body.

2. The DSB shall appoint persons to serve on the Appellate Body for a four-year term, and each person may be reappointed once. However, the terms of three of the seven persons appointed immediately after the entry into force of the WTO Agreement shall expire at the end of two years, to be determined by lot. Vacancies shall be filled as they arise. A person appointed to replace a person whose term of office has not expired shall hold office for the remainder of the predecessor's term.

3. The Appellate Body shall comprise persons of recognized authority, with demonstrated expertise in law, international trade and the subject matter of the covered agreements generally. They shall be unaffiliated with any government. The Appellate Body membership shall be broadly representative of membership in the WTO. All persons serving on the Appellate Body shall be available at all times and on short notice, and shall stay abreast of dispute settlement activities and other relevant activities of the WTO. They shall not participate in the consideration of any

---

7  If a meeting of the DSB is not scheduled within this period at a time that enables the requirements of paragraphs 1 and 4 of Article 16 to be met, a meeting of the DSB shall be held for this purpose.

disputes that would create a direct or indirect conflict of interest.

4. Only parties to the dispute, not third parties, may appeal a panel report. Third parties which have notified the DSB of a substantial interest in the matter pursuant to paragraph 2 of Article 10 may make written submissions to, and be given an opportunity to be heard by, the Appellate Body.

5. As a general rule, the proceedings shall not exceed 60 days from the date a party to the dispute formally notifies its decision to appeal to the date the Appellate Body circulates its report. In fixing its timetable the Appellate Body shall take into account the provisions of paragraph 9 of Article 4, if relevant. When the Appellate Body considers that it cannot provide its report within 60 days, it shall inform the DSB in writing of the reasons for the delay together with an estimate of the period within which it will submit its report. In no case shall the proceedings exceed 90 days.

6. An appeal shall be limited to issues of law covered in the panel report and legal interpretations developed by the panel.

7. The Appellate Body shall be provided with appropriate administrative and legal support as it requires.

8. The expenses of persons serving on the Appellate Body, including travel and subsistence allowance, shall be met from the WTO budget in accordance with criteria to be adopted by the General Council, based on recommendations of the Committee on Budget, Finance and Administration.

### Procedures for Appellate Review

9. Working procedures shall be drawn up by the Appellate Body in consultation with the Chairman of the DSB and the Director-General, and communicated to the Members for their information.

10. The proceedings of the Appellate Body shall be confidential. The reports of the Appellate Body shall be drafted without the presence of the parties to the dispute and in the light of the information provided and the statements made.

11. Opinions expressed in the Appellate Body report by individuals serving on the Appellate Body shall be anonymous.

12. The Appellate Body shall address each of the issues raised in accordance with paragraph 6 during the appellate proceeding.

13. The Appellate Body may uphold, modify or reverse the legal findings and conclusions of the panel.

### Adoption of Appellate Body Reports

14. An Appellate Body report shall be adopted by the DSB and unconditionally accepted by the

parties to the dispute unless the DSB decides by consensus not to adopt the Appellate Body report within 30 days following its circulation to the Members. [8]This adoption procedure is without prejudice to the right of Members to express their views on an Appellate Body report.

# Article 18
## Communications with the Panel or Appellate Body

1. There shall be no ex parte communications with the panel or Appellate Body concerning matters under consideration by the panel or Appellate Body.

2. Written submissions to the panel or the Appellate Body shall be treated as confidential, but shall be made available to the parties to the dispute. Nothing in this Understanding shall preclude a party to a dispute from disclosing statements of its own positions to the public. Members shall treat as confidential information submitted by another Member to the panel or the Appellate Body which that Member has designated as confidential. A party to a dispute shall also, upon request of a Member, provide a non-confidential summary of the information contained in its written submissions that could be disclosed to the public.

# Article 19
## Panel and Appellate Body Recommendations

1. Where a panel or the Appellate Body concludes that a measure is inconsistent with a covered agreement, it shall recommend that the Member concerned[9] bring the measure into conformity with that agreement.[10]In addition to its recommendations, the panel or Appellate Body may suggest ways in which the Member concerned could implement the recommendations.

2. In accordance with paragraph 2 of Article 3, in their findings and recommendations, the panel and Appellate Body cannot add to or diminish the rights and obligations provided in the covered agreements.

---

8  If a meeting of the DSB is not scheduled during this period, such a meeting of the DSB shall be held for this purpose.

9  The "Member concerned" is the party to the dispute to which the panel or Appellate Body recommendations are directed.

10 With respect to recommendations in cases not involving a violation of GATT 1994 or any other covered agreement, see Article 26.

## *Article 20*
# Time-frame for DSB Decisions

Unless otherwise agreed to by the parties to the dispute, the period from the date of establishment of the panel by the DSB until the date the DSB considers the panel or appellate report for adoption shall as a general rule not exceed nine months where the panel report is not appealed or 12 months where the report is appealed. Where either the panel or the Appellate Body has acted, pursuant to paragraph 9 of Article 12 or paragraph 5 of Article 17, to extend the time for providing its report, the additional time taken shall be added to the above periods.

## *Article 21*
# Surveillance of Implementation
# of Recommendations and Rulings

1. Prompt compliance with recommendations or rulings of the DSB is essential in order to ensure effective resolution of disputes to the benefit of all Members.

2. Particular attention should be paid to matters affecting the interests of developing country Members with respect to measures which have been subject to dispute settlement.

3. At a DSB meeting held within 30 days[11] after the date of adoption of the panel or Appellate Body report, the Member concerned shall inform the DSB of its intentions in respect of implementation of the recommendations and rulings of the DSB. If it is impracticable to comply immediately with the recommendations and rulings, the Member concerned shall have a reasonable period of time in which to do so. The reasonable period of time shall be:

(a) the period of time proposed by the Member concerned, provided that such period is approved by the DSB: or, in the absence of such approval,

(b) a period of time mutually agreed by the parties to the dispute within 45 days after the date of adoption of the recommendations and rulings; or, in the absence of such agreement,

(c) a period of time determined through binding arbitration within 90 days after the date of adoption of the recommendations and rulings.[12] In such arbitration, a guideline for the arbitrator[13] should be that the reasonable period of time to implement panel or Appellate Body

---

[11] If a meeting of the DSB is not scheduled during this period, such a meeting of the DSB shall be held for this purpose.

[12] If the parties cannot agree on an arbitrator within 10 days after referring the matter to arbitration, the arbitrator shall be appointed by the Director-General within 10 days, after consulting the parties.

[13] The expression "arbitrator" shall be interpreted as referring either to an individual or a group.

recommendations should not exceed 15 months from the date of adoption of a panel or Appellate Body report. However, that time may be shorter or longer, depending upon the particular circumstances.

4. Except where the panel or the Appellate Body has extended, pursuant to paragraph 9 of Article 12 or paragraph 5 of Article 17, the time of providing its report, the period from the date of establishment of the panel by the DSB until the date of determination of the reasonable period of time shall not exceed 15 months unless the parties to the dispute agree otherwise. Where either the panel or the Appellate Body has acted to extend the time of providing its report, the additional time taken shall be added to the 15-month period; provided that unless the parties to the dispute agree that there are exceptional circumstances, the total time shall not exceed 18 months.

5. Where there is disagreement as to the existence or consistency with a covered agreement of measures taken to comply with the recommendations and rulings such dispute shall be decided through recourse to these dispute settlement procedures, including wherever possible resort to the original panel. The panel shall circulate its report within 90 days after the date of referral of the matter to it. When the panel considers that it cannot provide its report within this time frame, it shall inform the DSB in writing of the reasons for the delay together with an estimate of the period within which it will submit its report.

6. The DSB shall keep under surveillance the implementation of adopted recommendations or rulings. The issue of implementation of the recommendations or rulings may be raised at the DSB by any Member at any time following their adoption. Unless the DSB decides otherwise, the issue of implementation of the recommendations or rulings shall be placed on the agenda of the DSB meeting after six months following the date of establishment of the reasonable period of time pursuant to paragraph 3 and shall remain on the DSB's agenda until the issue is resolved. At least 10 days prior to each such DSB meeting, the Member concerned shall provide the DSB with a status report in writing of its progress in the implementation of the recommendations or rulings.

7. If the matter is one which has been raised by a developing country Member, the DSB shall consider what further action it might take which would be appropriate to the circumstances.

8. If the case is one brought by a developing country Member, in considering what appropriate action might be taken, the DSB shall take into account not only the trade coverage of measures complained of, but also their impact on the economy of developing country Members concerned.

## *Article 22*
# Compensation and the Suspension of Concessions

1. Compensation and the suspension of concessions or other obligations are temporary measures available in the event that the recommendations and rulings are not implemented within a reasonable period of time. However, neither compensation nor the suspension of concessions or other obligations is preferred to full implementation of a recommendation to bring a measure into conformity with the covered agreements. Compensation is voluntary and, if granted, shall be consistent with the covered agreements.

2. If the Member concerned fails to bring the measure found to be inconsistent with a covered agreement into compliance therewith or otherwise comply with the recommendations and rulings within the reasonable period of time determined pursuant to paragraph 3 of Article 21, such Member shall, if so requested, and no later than the expiry of the reasonable period of time, enter into negotiations with any party having invoked the dispute settlement procedures, with a view to developing mutually acceptable compensation. If no satisfactory compensation has been agreed within 20 days after the date of expiry of the reasonable period of time, any party having invoked the dispute settlement procedures may request authorization from the DSB to suspend the application to the Member concerned of concessions or other obligations under the covered agreements.

3. In considering what concessions or other obligations to suspend, the complaining party shall apply the following principles and procedures:

(a) the general principle is that the complaining party should first seek to suspend concessions or other obligations with respect to the same sector(s) as that in which the panel or Appellate Body has found a violation or other nullification or impairment;

(b) if that party considers that it is not practicable or effective to suspend concessions or other obligations with respect to the same sector(s), it may seek to suspend concessions or other obligations in other sectors under the same agreement;

(c) if that party considers that it is not practicable or effective to suspend concessions or other obligations with respect to other sectors under the same agreement, and that the circumstances are serious enough, it may seek to suspend concessions or other obligations under another covered agreement;

(d) in applying the above principles, that party shall take into account:

(i) the trade in the sector or under the agreement under which the panel or Appellate Body has found a violation or other nullification or impairment, and the importance of such trade to that party;

(ii) the broader economic elements related to the nullification or impairment and the broader economic consequences of the suspension of concessions or other obligations;

(e) if that party decides to request authorization to suspend concessions or other obligations pursuant to subparagraphs (b) or (c), it shall state the reasons therefor in its request. At the same time as the request is forwarded to the DSB, it also shall be forwarded to the relevant Councils and also, in the case of a request pursuant to subparagraph (b), the relevant sectoral bodies;

(f) for purposes of this paragraph, "sector" means:

(i) with respect to goods, all goods;

(ii) with respect to services, a principal sector as identified in the current "Services Sectoral Classification List" which identifies such sectors;[14]

(iii) with respect to trade-related intellectual property rights, each of the categories of intellectual property rights covered in Section 1, or Section 2, or Section 3, or Section 4, or Section 5,or Section 6, or Section 7 of Part II, or the obligations under Part III, or Part IV of the Agreement on TRIPS;

(g) for purposes of this paragraph, "agreement" means:

(i) with respect to goods, the agreements listed in Annex 1A of the WTO Agreement, taken as a whole as well as the Plurilateral Trade Agreements in so far as the relevant parties to the dispute are parties to these agreements;

(ii) with respect to services, the GATS;

(iii) with respect to intellectual property rights, the Agreement on TRIPS.

4. The level of the suspension of concessions or other obligations authorized by the DSB shall be equivalent to the level of the nullification or impairment.

5. The DSB shall not authorize suspension of concessions or other obligations if a covered agreement prohibits such suspension.

6. When the situation described in paragraph 2 occurs, the DSB, upon request, shall grant authorization to suspend concessions or other obligations within 30 days of the expiry of the reasonable period of time unless the DSB decides by consensus to reject the request. However, if the Member concerned objects to the level of suspension proposed, or claims that the principles and procedures set forth in paragraph 3 have not been followed where a complaining party has requested authorization to suspend concessions or other obligations pursuant to paragraph 3(b) or (c), the matter shall be referred to arbitration. Such arbitration shall be carried out by the original panel, if members are available, or by an arbitrator[15] appointed by the Director-General

---

14 The list in document MTN. GNS/W/120 identifies 11 sectors.

15 The expression "arbitrator" shall be interpreted as referring either to an individual or a group.

and shall be completed within 60 days after the date of expiry of the reasonable period of time. Concessions or other obligations shall not be suspended during the course of the arbitration.

7. The arbitrator[16] acting pursuant to paragraph 6 shall not examine the nature of the concessions or other obligations to be suspended but shall determine whether the level of such suspension is equivalent to the level of nullification or impairment. The arbitrator may also determine if the proposed suspension of concessions or other obligations is allowed under the covered agreement. However, if the matter referred to arbitration includes a claim that the principles and procedures set forth in paragraph 3 have not been followed, the arbitrator shall examine that claim. In the event the arbitrator determines that those principles and procedures have not been followed, the complaining party shall apply them consistent with paragraph 3. The parties shall accept the arbitrator's decision as final and the parties concerned shall not seek a second arbitration. The DSB shall be informed promptly of the decision of the arbitrator and shall upon request, grant authorization to suspend concessions or other obligations where the request is consistent with the decision of the arbitrator, unless the DSB decides by consensus to reject the request.

8. The suspension of concessions or other obligations shall be temporary and shall only be applied until such time as the measure found to be inconsistent with a covered agreement has been removed, or the Member that must implement recommendations or rulings provides a solution to the nullification or impairment of benefits, or a mutually satisfactory solution is reached. In accordance with paragraph 6 of Article 21, the DSB shall continue to keep under surveillance the implementation of adopted recommendations or rulings, including those cases where compensation has been provided or concessions or other obligations have been suspended but the recommendations to bring a measure into conformity with the covered agreements have not been implemented.

9. The dispute settlement provisions of the covered agreements may be invoked in respect of measures affecting their observance taken by regional or local governments or authorities within the territory of a Member. When the DSB has ruled that a provision of a covered agreement has not been observed, the responsible Member shall take such reasonable measures as may be available to it to ensure its observance. The provisions of the covered agreements and this Understanding relating to compensation and suspension of concessions or other obligations apply in cases where it has not been possible to secure such observance.[17]

---

16 The expression "arbitrator" shall be interpreted as referring either to an individual or a group or to the members of the original panel when serving in the capacity of arbitrator.

17 Where the provisions of any covered agreement concerning measures taken by regional or local governments or authorities within the territory of a Member contain provisions different from the provisions of this paragraph, the

## *Article 23*
## **Strengthening of the Multilateral System**

1. When Members seek the redress of a violation of obligations or other nullification or impairment of benefits under the covered agreements or an impediment to the attainment of any objective of the covered agreements, they shall have recourse to, and abide by, the rules and procedures of this Understanding.

2. In such cases, Members shall:

(a) not make a determination to the effect that a violation has occurred, that benefits have been nullified or impaired or that the attainment of any objective of the covered agreements has been impeded, except through recourse to dispute settlement in accordance with the rules and procedures of this Understanding, and shall make any such determination consistent with the findings contained in the panel or Appellate Body report adopted by the DSB or an arbitration award rendered under this Understanding;

(b) follow the procedures set forth in Article 21 to determine the reasonable period of time for the Member concerned to implement the recommendations and rulings; and

(c) follow the procedures set forth in Article 22 to determine the level of suspension of concessions or other obligations and obtain DSB authorization in accordance with those procedures before suspending concessions or other obligations under the covered agreements in response to the failure of the Member concerned to implement the recommendations and rulings within that reasonable period of time.

## *Article 24*
## **Special Procedures Involving**
## **Least-Developed Country Members**

1. At all stages of the determination of the causes of a dispute and of dispute settlement procedures involving a least-developed country Member, particular consideration shall be given to the special situation of least-developed country Members. In this regard, Members shall exercise due restraint in raising matters under these procedures involving a least-developed country Member. If nullification or impairment is found to result from a measure taken by a least-developed country Member, complaining parties shall exercise due restraint in asking for compensation or seeking authorization to suspend the application of concessions or other

provisions of such covered agreement shall prevail.

obligations pursuant to these procedures.

2. In dispute settlement cases involving a least-developed country Member, where a satisfactory solution has not been found in the course of consultations the Director-General or the Chairman of the DSB shall, upon request by a least-developed country Member offer their good offices, conciliation and mediation with a view to assisting the parties to settle the dispute, before a request for a panel is made. The Director-General or the Chairman of the DSB, in providing the above assistance, may consult any source which either deems appropriate.

# Article 25
# Arbitration

1. Expeditious arbitration within the WTO as an alternative means of dispute settlement can facilitate the solution of certain disputes that concern issues that are clearly defined by both parties.

2. Except as otherwise provided in this Understanding, resort to arbitration shall be subject to mutual agreement of the parties which shall agree on the procedures to be followed. Agreements to resort to arbitration shall be notified to all Members sufficiently in advance of the actual commencement of the arbitration process.

3. Other Members may become party to an arbitration proceeding only upon the agreement of the parties which have agreed to have recourse to arbitration. The parties to the proceeding shall agree to abide by the arbitration award. Arbitration awards shall be notified to the DSB and the Council or Committee of any relevant agreement where any Member may raise any point relating thereto.

4. Articles 21 and 22 of this Understanding shall apply mutatis mutandis to arbitration awards.

# Article 26

1. *Non-Violation Complaints of the Type Described in Paragraph 1(b) of Article XXIII of GATT 1994*

Where the provisions of paragraph 1(b) of Article XXIII of GATT 1994 are applicable to a covered agreement, a panel or the Appellate Body may only make rulings and recommendations where a party to the dispute considers that any benefit accruing to it directly or indirectly under the relevant covered agreement is being nullified or impaired or the attainment of any objective of that Agreement is being impeded as a result of the application by a Member of any measure, whether or not it conflicts with the provisions of that Agreement. Where and to the extent that such party considers and a panel or the Appellate Body determines that a case concerns a measure that does not conflict with the provisions of a covered agreement to which the provisions of paragraph 1(b) of Article XXIII of GATT 1994 are applicable, the procedures in this Understanding shall apply, subject to the following:

(a) the complaining party shall present a detailed justification in support of any complaint relating to a measure which does not conflict with the relevant covered agreement;

(b) where a measure has been found to nullify or impair benefits under, or impede the attainment of objectives, of the relevant covered agreement without violation thereof, there is no obligation to withdraw the measure. However, in such cases, the panel or the Appellate Body shall recommend that the Member concerned make a mutually satisfactory adjustment;

(c) notwithstanding the provisions of Article 21, the arbitration provided for in paragraph 3 of Article 21, upon request of either party, may include a determination of the level of benefits which have been nullified or impaired, and may also suggest ways and means of reaching a mutually satisfactory adjustment: such suggestions shall not be binding upon the parties to the dispute;

(d) notwithstanding the provisions of paragraph 1 of Article 22, compensation may be part of a mutually satisfactory adjustment as final settlement of the dispute.

2. *Complaints of the Type Described in Paragraph 1(c) of Article XXIII of GATT 1994*

Where the provisions of paragraph 1(c) of Article XXIII of GATT 1994 are applicable to a covered agreement, a panel may only make rulings and recommendations where a party considers that any benefit accruing to it directly or indirectly under the relevant covered agreement is being nullified or impaired or the attainment of any objective of that Agreement is being impeded as a result of the existence of any situation other than those to which the provisions of paragraphs 1(a) and 1(b) of Article XXIII of GATT 1994 are applicable. Where and to the extent that such party considers and a panel determines that the matter is covered by this paragraph, the procedures of this Understanding shall apply only up to and including the point in the proceedings where the panel report has been circulated to the Members. The dispute settlement rules and procedures contained in the Decision of 12 April 1989 (BISD 36S/61-67) shall apply to consideration for adoption, and surveillance and implementation of recommendations and rulings. The following shall also apply:

(a) the complaining party shall present a detailed justification in support of any argument made with respect to issues covered under this paragraph;

(b) in cases involving matters covered by this paragraph, if a panel finds that cases also involve dispute settlement matters other than those covered by this paragraph, the panel shall circulate a report to the DSB addressing any such matters and a separate report on matters falling under this paragraph.

## *Article 27*
## Responsibilities of the Secretariat

1. The Secretariat shall have the responsibility of assisting panels, especially on the legal, historical and procedural aspects of the matters dealt with, and of providing secretarial and technical support.

2. While the Secretariat assists Members in respect of dispute settlement at their request, there may also be a need to provide additional legal advice and assistance in respect of dispute settlement to developing country Members. To this end, the Secretariat shall make available a qualified legal expert from the WTO technical cooperation services to any developing country Member which so requests. This expert shall assist the developing country Member in a manner ensuring the continued impartiality of the Secretariat.

3. The Secretariat shall conduct special training courses for interested Members concerning these dispute settlement procedures and practices so as to enable Members' experts to be better informed in this regard.

# APPENDICES

(Omitted)

# 略論法律英語的特點

## 法律英語的英文說法

這在美國學術界是一個頗有爭議的問題。有人主張用「legal English」，但許多人不同意。加州大學洛杉磯分院著名法學教授大衛·梅林可夫就撰文公開反對過。理由是「Legal」這個字常含有「合法」（Lawful）的意思。這樣一來，「legal English」就很可能被人誤解成「合法英語」（Lawful English）。由於同樣的原因，用帶有「legal」的其他說法，如：「Legal Parlance」、「Legal Lingo」或「Legal Jargon」也都是不適當的。本人表示同意梅林可夫教授的見解。

因此，為了避免不必要的混亂，將來說「法律英語」時最好用梅林可夫教授所建議的「the English Language of law」或簡稱為「the language of law」。

## 法律英語的範圍

什麼是法律英語？有人講，凡是涉及法律的英語（辭彙、表達方法、句子結構……）都是法律英語。

這樣一來，法律英語的範圍被不適當地擴大了。根據我個人的調查研究，英美法學界所公認的法律英語主要是指普通法國家（Common Law Countries）的律師、法官、法學工作者所用的習慣語言（Customary Language），它包括某些辭彙、短語，或具有特色的一些表達方法（mode of expressions）。

## 法律英語的特點

就英語語言而言，它包括文學語言、科技語言、日常會話用語等各有千秋，各有自身的特色。作為英語滄海中一粟（a single grain of sand at the bottom of a great sea）的法律英語同樣也具有自己的特徵。歸納起來有以下幾點：

**1. 準確（precise or exact）**

在正常情況下，起草法律文件時，用詞造句必須十分準確（with great exactness），因為一旦筆者的思想、觀點、企圖落實成文字，它就成了法庭判斷是非的重要依據（在法學界盛行很久的「嚴格解釋原則」（Principle of strict construction）或「唯名論原則」

（Principle of nominalism）未遭目前崛起的「推測意圖原則」（Principle of presumed intent）所全面否定前，書面文字仍然是法官解釋法律文件的唯一依據。由於這方面的理論與本文所闡述的內容關係不大，就無需在此細述了）。

根據有關文章的報導，由於對法律文件中文字的理解不一，所造成的糾紛案是屢見不鮮的。爲說明問題，在此我僅舉兩例：

一例發生在路易斯安那州。爭論主要是圍繞公司章程一句話中的「on」字而展開的。原話是這樣的：The Charter required that directors "shall be elected on a vote of the stockholders representing not less than two-thirds of outstanding capital stock of the corporation."

甲方的理解是：被選上董事的人需三分之二的股東投票贊成（a Candidate needs the votes of two-thirds of the stockholders to be elected）；乙方則認爲：選董事時必須有三分之二的股東出席（two-thirds of the stockholders must be present at the meeting at which the election is held）。

由於雙方爭執不下，公說公有理，婆說婆有理，只好讓法庭進行判決。法官認定甲方的理解不當。若按甲方的解釋，句子中「on」必須改爲「by」。句子中用了「on」，就只能是乙方的理解。「on a vote...」與後頭的「三分之二」應解釋成參加選舉的法定人數（quorum）；

第二例發生在阿肯色州：

一個美國人臨終前寫了一個遺囑，遺囑是這樣寫的：The remainder of the testator's property should be "divided equally between all of our nephews and nieces on my wife's side and my niece."

這次問題出在對「between」這個字的理解上。立遺囑人妻子的外甥和外甥女加在一起，一共有22個。這句話是指立遺囑人遺產的一半歸其妻子方的22個外甥和外甥女，另一半歸其本人一方的外甥女？還是指將遺產在雙方的外甥和外甥女中平均分配呢？

最後，阿肯色州最高法庭的裁定是前者 —— 即遺產的一半歸立遺囑人的外甥女，另一半歸立遺囑人妻子方的22個外甥和外甥女。其理由是，按字典的解釋只有表示在兩者之間，兩方之間才用「between」。如果是後種解釋 —— 即在23個人中平均分攤，就必須用「among」。

在英國法庭有時也有類似爭議發生。因受篇幅限制，恕不贅述。

**2. 拘謹（formal）**

造成法律英語的拘謹不大衆化，其原因是多方面的，而其中最明顯、最主要的一條就是，許多律師、法官、法學工作者爲了顯示自己與衆不同的才華，常常用些與衆不同的詞或表達方法。如：通常情況下我們說「Come here!」而律師往往就用「approach the bench!」；通常我們說他當上法官了，用「He has become a judge.」而法律界常用「He is the bench」；通常我們用「trust each other」（互相信任），法學工作者常用「repose in one another」。爲了進一步說明問題，請看下面的對照表：

| 通常人們用 | 法學界常用 |
|---|---|
| law teacher | law don |
| refer | advert |
| tell | advise |
| inform | apprise |
| begin or start | commence |
| show | demonstrate |
| building | edifice |
| bring about | effectuate |
| use | employ |
| unfriendly | inimical |
| work | employment |
| follow | ensue |
| for the same reason | by the same token |

　　律師的這種做法已經受到來自各個方面的批評。美國許多有關學者著書批評或在報刊上撰文，要求法律界進行文字改革，呼籲他們「能用小字時不用大字」，「能用短字時不用長字」。只有這樣，才能讓大多數人看懂法律文字或聽懂法律語言。

　　**3. 費解（tough）**

　　造成法律英語難學、難懂的原因除上述的原因外還有以下幾方面的因素：

　　(1) 常用平常的字表示不平常的意思

　　法律書文中不少字和短語看上去並不陌生，似乎很容易，但看不懂法律英語，你就捕捉不了它們所表示的準確意思，不信，請看下列一些詞或短語：

| 平常的詞或短語 | 不平常的意思 |
|---|---|
| ①action（行動） | lawsuit（訴訟） |
| ②avoid（避免） | cancel（撤銷） |
| ③consideration（考慮） | the price you pay for one's promise（對價） |
| ④instrument（儀器；器械） | legal document（法律文件） |
| ⑤party（黨） | person contracting or litigation（訂約人或訴訟方） |

⑥save（救）　　　　　　　　　except（除……外）

⑦sentence（句子）　　　　　　decision of a court（法庭判決）

⑧without prejudice（無偏見）　without loss of any rights（不使權利喪失）

⑨case（箱子；盒子）　　　　　lawsuit（案例）

⑩minor and major（次要學科與主科）　a person under the legal age（未成年）

　　　　　　　　　　　　　　and a person come of age（已成年）

(2) 經常使用古英語和中古英語

古英語（old English）指西元450-1100年所流行的英語；中古英語（middle English），指西元1100-1500年之間常用的英語。

在現代英語（modern English）中還常常發現古英語和中古英語的痕跡，在法律英語中尤爲如此。

如西元1500年前十分常用的一些字：wherefore（爲什麼）、herewith（與此一道）、thereto（此外；又）、thence（從那裡起；從那時起）或thenceforth, thenceforwards，在現代英語中，尤其是在（現代）口語中已經過時，但在法律文件中還常常出現。律師們對這些詞還戀戀不捨。

(3) 對其他語言的大量借用

在英國，人們把拉丁文看成是一個人深造的基礎（the basis for advanced learning）。對學法律的學生來說，學拉丁文就更有必要。

隨便翻開一本法律教科書，閱讀一個案例或學習一篇有關法學研究的論文，拉丁文比比皆是。例如：

alibi [ælibai] —— 不在犯罪現場

alias [eiliæs] —— 別名

bona fide [bounə faidi] —— 眞正的；眞誠的

caveat emptor —— 貨物一經售出，賣主概不負責

inter alia —— 特別

proviso —— 附文；限制性條款

quasi —— 好像；准

quorum —— 法定人數

ex parte —— 單方面地（的）

還有許許多多的例子可舉，一一列出可出一本字典，實際上，美國和英國都已出版了這樣的字典。

據有關語言學家考證，法律英語中的外來語（foreign terms）除有不少拉丁文外，從法語中借用來的也爲數可觀。如：action（訴訟）、appeal（上訴）、contract（契約）、damage(s)（賠償金）、defendant（被告）、heir（繼承人）、lien（扣押權）、larceny（偷竊罪）、parties（當事人）、plaintiff（原告）、reprieve（緩期執行）、sentence（判刑）、tort（侵權）、treason（叛國罪）、trespass（未經許可侵入他人土地）、verdict（裁決）等。

(4) 對法律專門術語（terms of art）的使用

如在契約中當表示「仍然由賣方負責時」，不說「the responsibility still remains with the seller」，而常寫成或說成「the onus still remains with the seller」；法院常把協助它解釋某種法律問題的人稱爲「amicus curiue」[aˈmaikəs ˈkjuerii:] 而不用「those who help the court to construe a certain legal matter」。英國常用「take silk」表示「當上了王室的法律顧問」。

律師們、法官們、法學工作者們常常認爲準確的用詞、拘謹的文體加上對外來語和法律專門術語的恰當運用可以使自己起草的法律文件或使自己的言詞變得莊重（solemn）、神祕（mystical）和高貴（dignified）。

**4. 對模糊語言的有意使用（intentional use of ambiguous language）**

在下述三種情況下法律界人士常用模糊語言：

(1) 不願肯定地表示自己立場與觀點時

請看這句話：「Unless this account is paid within next ten days,it will be necessary to take appropriate action.」（除非在十天內把帳付清，否則就有必要採取適當的行動）。這句話中的「take appropriate action」就是一種模糊語言，它完全可被「start legal proceedings」或「bring suit」（進行訴訟）等字眼所取代，但律師並沒這樣做，因爲他認爲在講話時就把它說得如此肯定，還爲時過早。

(2) 爲表示禮貌和對他人的尊重

這在外交照會中常常會出現這樣的情況。如出於禮節（out of courtesy），當發照會的政府認爲公開點名還不到火候時，他常用被動式來進行措辭「The city was raided.」

(3) 爲不把自己的手腳捆住

美國聯邦貿易委員會（FTC）所制定的有關反非公平競爭法中，故意用了「unfair methods of competition」（非公平競爭方法），但究竟什麼方法才屬非公正競爭就沒有下確切的定義。這樣做可以爭取更多的主動。

類似的例子在著名的美國統一商法典（UCC）中也能找到。該法中常常用reasonable time（合理時間）到底多長？也沒有十分肯定的答案。

1. Business Law

   Third Edition by James Barnes

   Learning System Company

   Printed in 1978 in the United States

2. Business Law

   Fifteenth Edition

   Sweet & Maxwell

   Printed in 1991 in the U.K.

3. Schmitthoff's Export Trade

   —The Law and Practice of International Trade

   Seventh Edition

   London Stevens & Sons

   Printed in 1980

4. Japanese Securities Regulations

   —Comparative Study of Both U.S. and Japanese securities

   Laws by Louis Loss

   Printed in Japan 1989

5. 比較民事訴訟法初論

   沈達明著

   中信出版社1990年版

6. 美國商業訴訟

   格裡芬律師著

   陳慶柏　嚴啓明譯

   1981年三藩市中國編譯印務公司出版

國家圖書館出版品預行編目資料

涉外經濟法律英語／陳慶柏編著. -- 二版.
-- 臺北市：五南圖書出版股份有限公司,
2022.04
　面；　公分
ISBN 978-626-317-681-2（平裝）

1.CST：法學英語　2.CST：讀本

805.18　　　　　　　　111002672

1QJ3

# 涉外經濟法律英語

編 著 者 ― 陳慶柏

校 訂 者 ― 方元沂

發 行 人 ― 楊榮川

總 經 理 ― 楊士清

總 編 輯 ― 楊秀麗

副總編輯 ― 劉靜芬

責任編輯 ― 林佳瑩

封面設計 ― 姚孝慈

出 版 者 ― 五南圖書出版股份有限公司

地　　　址：106台北市大安區和平東路二段339號4樓

電　　　話：(02)2705-5066　　傳　　真：(02)2706-6100

網　　　址：https://www.wunan.com.tw

電子郵件：wunan@wunan.com.tw

劃撥帳號：01068953

戶　　名：五南圖書出版股份有限公司

法律顧問　林勝安律師事務所　林勝安律師

出版日期　2009年 4 月初版一刷
　　　　　2020年10月初版二刷
　　　　　2022年 4 月二版一刷

定　　價　新臺幣680元

◎ 本書之繁體中文版由法律出版社授權五南圖書出版股份有
限公司出版發行

# 經典永恆・名著常在

## 五十週年的獻禮 —— 經典名著文庫

五南，五十年了，半個世紀，人生旅程的一大半，走過來了。

思索著，邁向百年的未來歷程，能為知識界、文化學術界作些什麼？

在速食文化的生態下，有什麼值得讓人雋永品味的？

歷代經典・當今名著，經過時間的洗禮，千錘百鍊，流傳至今，光芒耀人；

不僅使我們能領悟前人的智慧，同時也增深加廣我們思考的深度與視野。

我們決心投入巨資，有計畫的系統梳選，成立「經典名著文庫」，

希望收入古今中外思想性的、充滿睿智與獨見的經典、名著。

這是一項理想性的、永續性的巨大出版工程。

不在意讀者的眾寡，只考慮它的學術價值，力求完整展現先哲思想的軌跡；

為知識界開啟一片智慧之窗，營造一座百花綻放的世界文明公園，

任君遨遊、取菁吸蜜、嘉惠學子！